BATTLE FOR MANALAR

SISTER SEEKERS BOOK 8

BY
A.S. ETASKI

Published by Corpus Nexus Press
ISBN: 978-1-949552-15-7

etaski.com
www.patreon.com/etaski
miurag.etaski.com
smarturl.it/readsisterseekers
www.goodreads.com/etaski
www.bookbub.com/authors/a-s-etaski
www.facebook.com/asetaski
www.twitter.com/asetaski

Cover Design by Eris Adderly
Book layout by DocKangey

Dedicated to all who have wondered why Bilbo was knocked out for the Battle of the Five Armies.

CHAPTER 1

WE STEPPED OFF THE FERRY ONTO AN EMPTY DOCK. THE SUN HAD SET OVER Augran hours ago, and the moons had gone some time before it. What would have been the darkest of nights out in the mountains blurred around the edges as street lanterns, hearths, window candles, and the occasional glowing stone competed with the stars offering their light above.

I squinted up from beneath the hem of my hood, noting clusters of night-fuzz insects beating themselves against a tall lamp post whose live, stretching flame was encased in thick glass. The flyers spiraled with such determination that I listened to the quiet thwap of numerous tiny heads. This held a morbid fascination for me.

The ferryman yawned as he accepted payment for dropping us off across the Big Ker River from Yong-wen onto the bank of Bor. I inhaled the vastness of the Great Lake effortlessly at night, but the onshore breezes also brought the varied scents of Alran in the Northeast quadrant of Augran, mixing with those of Bor surrounding me.

I smell ale. And piss.

Mourn was wearing his pale-skinned, dark-haired man's form and touched the middle of my back, motioning me farther from the dock. He noticed me glancing at the lantern until we rounded the corner.

"Moths," he said.

Moths? I might have glimpsed some here or there, but I wasn't sure. Grasping details of flitting specks among the shadows was difficult even with Dark Sight, but the moons and fires on the Surface always kicked me back into my color vision which blurred the edges more.

"Moths are drawn to the fire?" I asked.

"They are sensitive to light. Out in the wild, they orient their flight by the moons."

I frowned. "Can they not differentiate between moonlight and fire?"

He smiled a little. "Apparently not. On a night like this and if there's fire nearby, they may think it's a sister moon by which they tell up from down or East from West."

"A bit slow adapting to sentients wielding light on purpose."

"Heh. Even the best of us become confused by the world's signals and may remain so for a long time."

A wry smile tugged into place on my lips. "True. I suppose we best hope to survive and learn before it's too late."

We hadn't passed four cross streets when Mourn signed to take the next alley. I slowed my step to avoid the days-old dung and muddled puddles, wrinkling my nose as I listened for anyone awake in the buildings on either side of us.

Storage, Mourn signed, shifting his appearance back to his natural one, his tongue flicking out the first chance it had, as if unable to resist double-tasting the pungent air.

I didn't envy his senses then.

He pointed a claw toward the roof. *Climb up or hold my back?* *Climb...?*

One glance at the scalable wall and mild slope of several rooftops brought back our exchange a few days ago, about traveling Augran's streets less openly once we were outside of Yong-wen.

"Running rooftops? I can't jump these streets, I haven't the equipment."

I looked over what I could see of his harness. *Hmph. And he does?*

I'll climb this first one, I replied with a growing smirk, *and

6

reevaluate the next.★

His first response was to smile, which seemed to have grown easier for him. ★Very well.★

I had the training for climbing rocks, cliff faces, and the sides of Noble Houses in Sivaraus, and this rustic storage place built by Humans in Bor was much easier. However, I did *not* have the bursts of speed or boosted jumps which extended the Dragonchild's reach between handholds, allowing him to skim over whole segments of my climb and reach the top in half the time.

Flaunter.

I'd expected this outcome, however, and had no difficulty imagining Lead Jaunda or Corpora Kiren doing the same if they'd possessed those muscles.

They would have a lot of fun bouncing around above Matrons' heads.

I would experience this first, if vicariously.

Atop that first roof which was mostly flat, my limbs burned pleasantly from the effort, the air was fresher as I breathed in, and I could see a great distance around us.

The lack of long-term planning struck me first, from the winding way of the streets with baffling dead-ends to the patchwork of structures built together in rushes, the style and design changing what appeared to be every decade.

Sivaraus was almost uniform by comparison. While rebuilding occurred as needed, it was slow, and the strong structures hardly changed from the completion of one to the start of another. What worked to build up in the Deepearth with stone and fiberstalk, devoid of rain, daylight, or extreme winds, had worked for centuries.

Augran's stone and wood use seemed either a work in progress or simply the effect of building on the Surface and living with the weather. This made me wonder what Taiding's Dwarven halls were like. Were there similarities to home by virtue of their location and the expected building materials?

Mourn walked across the roof, barefoot and silent as always, heading to the north side. He let me learn my footing on the unfamiliar construction. My first steps caused unwelcome scratches and creaks, but I would get better. This wasn't the time to copy Mourn's methods, anyway; I had neither the hard calluses nor the Draconic scales.

Perhaps I could grow the former in time but never the latter.

Standing near the roof's edge, I looked down. Like in Yong-wen, the streets were much wider compared to alleys. In Sivaraus, there wasn't much difference between the two in the markets, especially those close to the Palace-Sanctuary. How we described them had more to do with the lighting than the width. This also meant there wasn't such disparity in the direction one chose to creep above street level.

I definitely don't have the equipment for the streets.

Reevaluating? Mourn signed, his tail waving with calm and patience.

I sighed, scanning farther out. *If we kept to the alleys only, I could possibly jump. I'll not deny each time would be a greater risk as I tire and not worth the cost if I miss.*

Agreed. My bodyguard gazed out, scanning the skyline. *I navigate these buildings regularly by jumping the alleys. I cross the streets only if I need to lose someone. My path is jagged as a lightning bolt with the roads as they are, weaving like rivers, but it would carry us across Bor into Alran well before dawn without touching the cobbles below. This is recommended in Bor at night.*

My heart had picked up to imagine, but at least we'd avoid the horse and Human dung. *How much of your navigation included a rider?*

his gut. More laughter bubbled up at the thought. ★What do we wager you shall have a *significant* distraction prodding between us within three rooftops?★

Mourn narrowed his eyes without threat, just a mild pricking of his pride. ★Ten rooftops.★

I hummed. At least he didn't deny he'd get hard sooner or later. ★Ten rooftops, not counting this one?★

★Yes.★

★Before we give it proper attention, or before I first feel it *quicken*?★

He had to think about that but then smirked. ★Before you feel it quicken. Take it for granted we pay 'proper' attention.★

★I say within five rooftops, and I may give my best effort to *encourage* it.★

He chuckled with a tiny but rueful shake of his head. ★I presume the part of our Bargain holds, about you not doing stupid things for sex?★

★Of course,★ I signed with mock indignation. ★I'd rather *not* plummet to the city streets on account of vigorous cock rubbing, mercenary.★

His tail suggested he was *very* amused, even if he kept his silence and his smaller smirk. ★Alright. If five or less when we feel it quicken, you choose your orifice that I rut. If five to ten, I choose for you. If more than ten, we'll eat the hand pies in your satchel *and* I'll find a sweet pie to follow it.★

My mouth sagged as my *other* appetite stirred. ★What?! At this time of night?★

He looked smug. ★At this time of night.★

I squinted. ★You have some place in mind, don't you?★

★I do. Eleven rooftops away.★

Fucking cock-weight.

★Wait. Is it no sweet pie at all if you get to choose?★

★Correct.★

★*Not* a balanced tease, Dragon son.★

★I disagree, Baenar. It's perfectly balanced.★

His face had broken into a grin as bright as a moon while we negotiated, and the sounds rising from my throat had fallen somewhere between a snicker and a growl.

To tempt me with a sweet pie meant I must avoid all intents to give him an erection from our first leap. To seize my own choice before then, I must grind hard against him and do what I'd claimed I could do without hesitation. However, then I would never know which he wanted more: to feed me some special pie or surprise me with the hole he most wanted to fill.

It would be our first time since the Shi family dinner.

First time alone.

Whatever I chose would tell him more about me regardless, though I could be left with an amusing unknown if I simply must win.

I sighed. At least he knew how to make our grander Bargain imaginative and unpredictable.

Food or sex?

Both would be continuous needs between us for the foreseeable future, but which did I desire more in this moment? And how?

I was undecided as I shifted my traveling spider pouch and weapons with care before hopping up into place on Mourn's front. His hands caught hold of my ass for support as my legs clasped his middle and my hands slipped beneath his cloak to take hold of his harness.

Settling close together, Mourn secured me in his hold then tested his gait with my body clinging beneath his chin. Suddenly, I couldn't smell the Human city or the Great Lake at all. All scents which surrounded me were him: a musky and baffling blend of an Elven reptile, whose patchwork skin exuded scant amounts of sweat yet often poured out excessive heat.

Mm. No complaints.

As Mourn paced the roof, gauging his first leap, he breathed in slowly through his nose without peeling back his lips or flicking his tongue. He might have been trying to avoid immediate disqualification on our wager.

I smiled and murmured, "Ready when you are."

"Hold tight, no sudden moves."

My heart picked up its pace against his chest. "Right."

Like the swift scaling up the building by hand, he tested and claimed his gait an instant before he surged into a sprint. I clung to him hard, counting seven long strides before we hit the edge where his muscles coiled and erupted in a fluent flash of motion. The following careen into empty space seemed like the blur of a dream until we landed with that waking jolt, then he kept on without slowing.

Uh-oh. He wasn't resting between rooftops.

Anticipating the next long leap, I held tight and forgot to slide my crotch down along his abdomen, taking a breath only as we landed a second time. Abruptly, he turned to the right as he adjusted his pacing, setting us up for his third rooftop. Seducing him this way was harder than I expected, but I took the slight slow-down as he turned to sniff a soft line on his throat before giving it a lick.

"Mm, *again,*" I said suggestively.

A rumble vibrated in his chest as he pushed his focus to what was around us, his sprint speeding up to take that third roof. Then he was lucky and had a straight shot for the next two; he sped up even more.

Grinding, licking, talking? Not possible now.

Not luck. He knew.

When we reached that fifth ledge, I accepted the pathetic showing for my boast. Maybe next time.

At least I'll find out if we're sharing long meat or eating pie, first.

I relaxed and enjoyed the ride and the high, even as I kept counting his strides and rooftops. As I'd learned from Tanzi in Yong-wen to jump fences with a horse, I "listened" to the Dragonchild's body, anticipating, moving cooperatively through every launch and landing.

We could use this practice regardless, wager or not.

Especially before Manalar.

"*Arrgh,*" Mourn groaned, huffing heavily after arriving on the ninth rooftop which was the flattest one so far. "Fuck…"

He was slowing down to stop, and I grinned as I adjusted my grip.

Hello, stiff one, welcome back.

"Two roofs short of the pie?" I teased, squeezing him suggestively with my thighs even though they were getting tired. "Planned?"

"No," he admitted. "You relaxed into me."

"Relaxed 'into?'"

"Your aura," he panted, lifting me by my bottom as he straightened up, "and your trust… when I jumped each… time."

I blinked as he settled the prominent log between us, grunting with satisfaction as he held me tight enough that any movement at all massaged his length beneath his loose, Yungian pants.

So…

A contest of wills between us didn't cause his prick to spike beyond his control, but my "trusting him" as we tried dangerous things together caused him to fall short of pie?

You're so strange, bua.

But I knew that.

"Hmm," I hummed with a firm grind of my leathers along his length. "In that case, which hole do you want to use in easing this ache?"

Mourn's eyelids were at half-mast, even as he checked around us, smelling the air fully. His last exhale sounded like a sigh, and a wry smile took over half his mouth.

"I regret needing to stop you abruptly," he said, "when you took me into your mouth to prepare me for Dandan. But I was too close."

My eyebrows lifted, as did my mood. "Oh? You want me to open my mouth and roll out my tongue so you can slide it back in?"

His cock pulsed, and his vertical pupils expanded as he stared at me. He nodded without speaking, and I unlocked my ankles with an eager grin. Easing myself down his front with his assistance, I made sure to tease his tented trousers everywhere possible.

"Well," I said. "I can wait for pie if I'm swallowing a snack regardless."

His tail grew lively around his feet, his skin and scale patches becoming quite hot. He showed teeth as his shoulders shook with silent laughter. "Swallow? You are sure?"

I tilted my head, cocked one brow, and started to kneel and take hold of his waistline.

"Wait, wait," he whispered, pulling me back up to guide me behind what looked like a small shed with a door. No doubt it led into the box-shaped building from here.

There were also a few crates and Mourn urged me to sit on one which placed my head at the level of his straining groin. We had some shelter from most views and breezes, and it would save my knees from aching.

Perfect.

He didn't stop me a second time from pulling on his pants with one hand and tugging his heavy genitals out with the other. The hole in the back of his pants designed for his tail caught and prevented his bottoms from going far down his partially scaled thighs. It was enough, though, and the tough fabric wouldn't drop around his ankles no matter what.

Clear fluid glossed his glans, and the foreskin was pulled back enough. *No sense delaying.*

I tucked his spear-shaped cock into my mouth the same way I had in Dandan's bridal suite, swirling my tongue around the head, and fully tasting his flavor where the swollen ridge arose from its receding protection.

"*Ohhh,*" Mourn breathed out above my head, tilting his chin up and resting one hand on my shoulder. "Yes. Start soft. Do not bite yet."

I filled my mouth to its fullest, testing how much I could fit, when his words made sense. *Yet?*

He liked bites on his cock? *Where?*

"*Mmm-hmmm,*" I hummed as loudly as I dared, both as acknowledgment and to send gentle vibrations along his most sensitive skin.

He growled appreciatively with the effort, reaching for one of my hands to wrap it around his curved, bottom-heavy shaft. He placed my fingers above the bulge at the base, which was still small compared to how it had swelled inside me to lock us together the previous night.

"No squeezing the knot," he murmured, "if you please."

I signed an affirmative, sucking harder on his tip while caressing and tugging his shaft. His tail jerked and his hips moved in a rut thrust.

Then he quivered, and his tail slithered to wrap snugly around my entire left calf, flexing in a wave to massage my leg.

Mm. He likes.

I stroked firmly with my hand, used my suckling mouth in tandem, and tested a few reasonable paces for a shape so uneven compared to what I'd been trained on. He seemed to like the slower, harder sucks best, but only if my touch periodically became feather-light in contrast.

"*Rrrrgh, guh,*" he grunted, braced against the wall above me. He sucked in some saliva before he drooled on me. "*Sssirana…*"

He coasted in bliss, and I kept going, hoping his balls were tingling. With the thought, I experimented, reaching my second hand to cradle his hairless scrotum. When he didn't protest, I massaged and tugged on this as well, but softly.

The sac drew up tight, and its owner pushed his cock deeper in my throat in response. I was ready; I didn't gag. My Sisters had trained me well, and it would be a while before I was tired of this. The real limitation seemed to be how wide my jaw could open.

Mourn's tail had been climbing up my leg but so gradually that I didn't notice until the curling end stroked affectionately along my inner thigh. My eyes opened when it settled against my crotch, though I didn't remember closing them.

I wish I'd thought to pull my pants down.

All the same, his control of that most distal end of him was impressive; writhing side to side like that was as least as good as the flats of a Davrin's fingers stroking and fondling me through my leathers, and no claws to be concerned about ripping them.

Very welcome.

I sucked and licked his stout pole harder with added pleasure, using both hands with a solid hold on his shaft. He growled low as his member flexed and pulsed, and his arousal grew between my palms.

Recalling what he'd said, I paused and tested a slow bite, gradually closing my jaws until my teeth held him without breaking skin.

He stiffened, hissed, and a sustained tremor passed through him as he waited until I released him as slowly as I'd clamped down. The blood rushed through his erection again, and my tongue slapped and battered the tip as his prick was freed. He groaned, his tail starting to slap and batter at my crotch in return.

"Again," he said through his teeth.

Mm. Gladly.

"Yes...!" he choked as my mouth tightened down on him and held on, and another shiver passed through him.

This time, when I released him and the blood rushed in, he wrapped his hand around both of mine, speeding up our pace as he pushed his prick deeper between my lips. The tip swelled yet more as the claws on his toes dug into the rooftop, as his tail constricted around my thigh in clear warning of imminent release.

I was ready when he spurted full in my mouth; I swallowed quickly, several times, feeling it slide down my throat, thick and voluminous, scorching hot and salty. The rumble in his chest was so low it nearly missed my hearing; I wondered if Humans could detect the half-blood's groan of climax at all.

Clever.

Sore and tired as my jaw was, I waited patiently for Mourn to pull himself out, noting his knot had grown some as he finished. I wasn't sure if that was the size I'd felt in my cunt.

It seemed bigger.

I also hadn't felt the overwhelming surge of magic that tested my will to stay awake. *Hm.*

Was it because we hadn't made eye contact? Or because I hadn't been close to climaxing myself? Not that I regretted holding back; with potential to harm from using my teeth on him and my hands clutching his eggs, I'd *wanted* to remain aware of what I was doing.

As soon as my bodyguard stepped back, I needed a cloth to wipe my hands and my lower face. I studied him while I cleaned up; he looked dizzy.

"You alright, Mourn?"

"Hm? Oh," he breathed, managing a nod. "Yes. ...Wow."

I grinned. "Wow?"

"Mm-hm." He sat on the crate next to me, careful not to land too heavily and crack it. "I... Mm. As... skilled as you hinted it might be."

"Mm, thank you," I chuckled, wiping between my fingers now that my chin was dry. "I enjoyed that."

"As did I."

"I could tell. And you have a fun shape."

He sat quietly while I finished up and tucked away my cloth, then he placed one hot hand on my thigh. I blinked at him.

"I won't understate, Red Sister," he added with modest chagrin. "That was the best of...that service I have received. Especially for a first time. All sensation, much nuance. Thank you."

My grin was locked on my face to hear such praise from my efforts; I was without doubt flattered, yet I wasn't sure how to respond. Was it only as he said, it was a top-tier mouth fuck for him?

Makes me wonder how the experienced races up here do it.

Or was he trying to say that, per our To'vah Bargain, such pleasure had changed some unseen and mystical thing in his Hoard, and he was pleased about this, too? What else could it be, if not one or both?

I shrugged. "I'll do it again for certain. There are some things I haven't tried yet."

The slight widening of his eyes was worth my scrabbling for a response.

He could ponder for a while what I meant.

CHAPTER 2

AFTER A GRATIFYING RELEASE, MOURN TUCKED ME AGAINST HIS FRONT, AND I clung to him to continue along the rooftops. We'd skipped the roof where he might have obtained pie before sating our mutual appetite, but my bodyguard promised he knew of better pies in Alran.

"Bor is a greater mix of Humans but less Dwarves, you said?"

"Yes," he panted, catching his breath as he paced before turning sharply in another direction. "And Alran is home to more generations of Dwarves. As such… greater stability, wealth… and better ingredients for sweet pies."

Plus enough with the status to buy them. I grinned and shook my head. "You *cannot* let me leave without eating one."

"You will. I promise. Hold tight."

Here we go again.

This manner of travel took far more energy and effort than walking or riding the streets, so our exchanges were brief when he needed to pause. I could readily accept the quiet; he cautioned us against walking the streets of Bor at night and expressed desire to train for Manalar.

Good enough to me.

I heard several dogs barking below when we passed over and Mourn disturbed a handful of startled birds sleeping in their nests. A candle was lit now and then, accompanied by an occasional silhouette or tentative call out of a window from someone awake, but no one obstructed us in any way. If the Dragonchild woke anyone, they were far too slow getting out of bed to catch sight of his real form.

Meanwhile, my brunette woman illusion had faded a distance back, when Mourn had stopped with an erection pushing into my gut. Whether he intended it or not, he looked upon my true appearance as I'd sucked him. I'd also noticed he didn't set it back yet, and I didn't ask him to. I expected that would happen when he shifted back into the Noiri man, Roewn.

We have interesting tasks to complete with the Guildsmen, after all.

"Enough," he announced after a rougher landing where his balance wavered. "That is all I can do while carrying you."

"That is 'all?'" I repeated, incredulous. "You leaped thirty-two alleys and crossed thirty-three rooftops. I would have started stumbling before ten."

He huffed, both amused and pleased that I'd counted. "Alone, I can surpass fifty, but it is good to know my limits here."

"Hmph. I'm that heavy?"

"You and your passengers."

"*Pfeh!*"

I slid stiffly off him and stood on my feet before checking on my spiders. They were vastly annoyed with the constant jostling.

~Best grow accustomed to this if we must cling and climb with him to get out of a siege, little guardians.~

They chimed in unison, forgetting their grievances when I let them climb out of their pouch into my hand. I placed them on my nape where they settled into their usual place in my hair.

"We'll climb down here," Mourn said, "and walk the rest of the way. We've passed the common hour for their second sleep, made it through the contested streets, and bypassed the current vice dens entirely. If we walk quietly and quickly, avoid dead-ends, and do not stop, we should pass without trouble. If we are approached, let me negotiate. Follow my instructions, they are to keep you safe. Drawing any weapon should be a last resort."

"Check."

He made me look Human before shifting his own form, and I bore his detailed instructions in mind. If we aren't left alone, however, some fool was going to get bitten before they got stabbed.

WE PASSED THE STREETS IN SILENCE, HEADS COVERED, APPEARING HUMAN enough at first glance. I listened to the oddly familiar sounds of whatever creatures or sentients were awake this late. They were all hungry or in pain.

The first poorer neighborhood seemed to become better in a quick transition, as we passed through the haphazard mix of brick, stone, wood, and mud among dwellings. Unlike Yong-wen, there were fewer plants kept in hanging pots and the decorations seemed random and highly individual without the same collective unity.

I had to think that, even if this was no longer a slum, it was not as prosperous as other parts of Augran simply must be with all the ships I'd seen floating in and out of the mouth of the Big Ker River or on the Great Lake itself.

Through powerful scents of clustered bodies and waste, I also saw remnants of Dwarven architecture and useful drainage for the streets. The materials weren't so recent or of the same quality as had been built in Yong-wen but the form managed to serve its function alongside other Human designs and half-measures.

Hmm.

If this drainage stopped short of the river itself, and some obstacle prevented the construction necessary to help it along, that would explain an abrupt cliff where two-story buildings ceased to the South. I would wager why Bor's river docks were the least desired among the four quadrants of the city.

There's a shit swamp somewhere in between the river commerce and the inland residents.

That would explain both the smell when the wind shifted North and Mourn spending such effort to jump buildings as he gave me his tour.

Meanwhile, here in the northern half of Bor, we rarely had to step in slurries or mud. We were followed a few times but maintained our confident gaits and never drifted too close to the walls or corners. By whatever unspoken warnings had swayed their thinking, none chose to confront us in the middle of this moonless way.

"We will reach Alran within a mark," Mourn murmured in Davrin. "The Dwarves maintain a passage into their merchant streets close to the border. We'll enter there."

I repeated his instructions in my head as we drew close to seeking out others.

Avoid using hand sign.

It would be mistaken for Guild sign and draws the wrong kind of attention here. A real Guildsman would not be so obvious.

Speak the Davrin language when I must, but not loudly.

There were many languages in this city, so most sentients wouldn't take a second glance. If I shouted, however, I may sound too foreign to those seeking a target without roots.

Bring Soul Drinker but draw it only if we are separated.

Mourn promised to do everything possible to prevent that.

I'd been told there were mages in Augran who may be able to sense the relic, but was I likely to encounter them?

"Not by chance," Krithannia had said. "Augran has reached the age and development where their best-trained mages aren't wandering in public alone. Not only would you see them coming as part of a larger group, but Mourn's illusion can also mask the blade's aura from most eyes that may have the ability to see it."

"Why bring it at all?" Gavin had asked in Mourn's library, lacing his fingers. "We know it is undetectable here."

The Guild Mistress had looked to Talov to respond, and the elder, grey-bearded Dwarf smiled.

"Because when things like that show up in this city," he rumbled after taking a sip of his drink, "we like to see who it tempts or persuades."

"We'd also like to know if it *can* be ignored," Mourn added, long tail coiling. "Better to test that here in my city before we enter Manalar."

'*My city.*'

No one had questioned that or thought it odd, perhaps because it lacked that recognizable tone of possession. Augran was the city he knew best, and he'd chosen to stash his Hoard here somewhere.

The Deathwalker's grunt and final remark echoed in my head as I walked.

"I suppose risk is always unavoidable. May the rune blade among the populace not sever too many interconnected accords."

Indeed. More mutual stories, desires, and goals entwined on the Surface than I might ever see plainly, even after many converged on that other city to the South. It was an odd sort of blessing coming from the death mage.

Following the roads, Mourn and I finally left the homes and governing spaces of Bor only to come upon a wide sash of trees, grasses, ponds, and pathways cutting up the endless roads.

"What—?" I asked, looking both ways, unable to make out much of the buildings on the other side.

"The Greenway," Mourn said, something he obviously could have mentioned sooner. "Alran and Bor share a 'transition field' owned by neither but maintained by both for their publics." He chuckled. "The Dwarves' idea, long ago, when the two cities were separate. You may imagine what lies beneath our feet."

I arched my eyebrow. "I can guess. Secured escape tunnels, with ways of watching who comes and goes from Alran?"

"Correct."

"Does that mean when 'Roewn' arrives and vouches for his ladyfriend, the Dwarves will let us in?"

He smiled as we entered the tall grass. "Also correct."

"And I wager 'Retaliation' will find us shortly thereafter."

"The word is '*Reprisal*,' and we may need to come to them, though do not be surprised if they're expecting us."

I made a face. "*Reprisal*? I take it that word has no translation. Was I close?"

"Yes, very close." Mourn thought this over. "But there is an extra facet in the concept among Humans."

Something small and dark sprinted into the grass on my left. I glanced that way but carried on. "Another facet. Which is?"

He exhaled, glancing up at the patches of stars seen through the clouds. "The 'retaliation' you are familiar with is a response in kind for some loss or suffering done to you, correct?"

I nodded.

"And it can be anyone. Individuals, servants, commoners, Matrons. There are no formal rules guiding it in public. It's all unspoken, correct? Whatever is within one's resources and capability to revisit that harm."

"I suppose."

"*Reprisal* is similar, except they use it to describe groups acting against each other, short of war."

"Hm," I grunted, scanning between the tree trunks. " 'Short' of war? That makes little sense."

"Not if there's formality to the fighting. And there *are* spoken rules guiding their actions within each group, though that is not to say the groups always agree on the rules."

I couldn't help myself; I laughed. "Sounds delusional."

Mourn smirked. "If conflict with your own kind is merely a contest of dominance, but conflict with any other race is war, I can see why you'd think so. But imagine there are enough Davrin to have many, many conflicts every decade, amid vast stretches of land and shore, and total extermination through war is not always necessary to guard one's territory because of greater abundance and space on the Surface than the Deepearth."

"What? Are you saying 'reprisal' is a contest of dominance among their own kind, but with rules governing what one can do in groups?"

"That's right. It is a distinctly Human challenge to engage those among them causing the most harm and obtain redress for grievances, yet also do it without destroying themselves, their loved ones, or the innocent around the harm-bringers." Mourn shrugged. "After all, those living near the harm-bringers might be able to change the side they work for."

"What? You mean as captures?"

"No, not captures. Voluntary." He smiled. "Innocents able to change their mind and choose another life for themselves than where they were born, if only the fear of the harm-bringers can be thrown aside."

My frown of thought had turned into a scowl as I considered our topic of conversation the first time that I'd heard this word that was a name for a group.

We were talking about Witch Hunters. He said I might like them.

Perhaps Reprisal confronted the harm-bringers deserving retaliation but must speak rules to follow to avoid destroying themselves. If I squinted inward, *perhaps* that was more like my Sisterhood than not; we had a few limits no Sister crossed if they wanted to live.

"Could Reprisal be…" I paused. "*Hunters* of Witch Hunters?"

Mourn's blue, Human eyes gleamed in the scant light. "Very good. That would be a fine description for what guides them. And why."

Why…

The name of Mourn's first lover sounded in my head.

Halete. The woman executed as "the first witch" at Manalar almost four centuries ago.

"Did you 'encourage' Humans to create this group?" I asked. "If not outright form them yourself?"

He chuckled, quite satisfied. "It took little encouragement and a bit more help."

"Perfect sense, then, to choose the 'teams' to help my Sister among them."

"Agreed," he said. "Perfectly balanced."

Even though it had taken some centuries after Halete to get there.

MOURN SET THE CORRECT EXPECTATION FOR THE GATE ENTERING THE SOUTH of Alran from Bor. There were several horse-drawn merchant's carts waiting for daylight before entering; some of them were brewing a warm drink.

We waited outside with them, eating what we had on us as dawn approached quickly, giving me the opportunity to study the curious construction between the two quadrants.

The more I looked, the more confused I felt.

The wall was old but solid, and clearly of Dwarven design. It was about two stories high and extended East and West beyond where I could see. Its function, however, wasn't to keep anyone out or in. There were far too many open walkways without a gate, door, or a guard, not to mention numerous stairs leading to a path atop the wall.

How far could one walk that high road?

Perhaps it depended on how long one stayed undistracted.

Bridges branched off the top at somewhat regular intervals, allowing access to the upper stories of the buildings without using the streets below. All these square, stout structures of South Alran possessed open walkways with shelter from the weather around the perimeter of every floor, whether the second, third, or fourth. All had decorations and tools visible, plus a few windows and stalls, strongly implying these were both sleeping and working quarters.

This openness at the border was unexpected, given what I'd seen behind me at night.

"Why are we going through the market street again?" I asked, motioning at the quiet, uncrowded passageways connecting no less than ten separate buildings. "We don't have a cart or a horse."

"Fastest way to be seen," he answered.

Sigh.

"Why have a 'Greenway' separating the cities and a market gate with guards if they also have all these *unguarded* bridges giving direct access to homes in Alran?"

Mourn seemed pleased with my observations. "Some do sleep here, but these aren't the homes you are imagining. This is the center of commerce for both Alran *and* Bor and extends as far belowground as you can see above."

Really? I looked again.

"This is the Turthend Center," he continued, "and draws many visitors due to its size, variety of wares, and convenience moving from merchant to merchant."

Some of those merchants were opening the doors and windows, bringing out statues and colorful banners to signal their buyers. I smelled fresh food on the breeze and, like in Yong-wen, street cleaners tended areas both high and low which saw the most traffic.

My guide motioned to the West. "It's possible to transport goods this far inland using the wall-street itself or the large road on the far side." He indicated the other direction. "It also continues quite some distance. If your destination isn't accessible from the lakeshore, the Greenway and Turthend Road are the fastest from the Big Ker docks to the heart of both cities on this side of the river."

"Huh," I responded, gauging the distance and many nooks to pass through. "So, even though the market is in Alran, this is where Bor trades as well?"

"Correct. The Dwarves manage the upkeep and provide the space if the Humans are willing to travel here from either city, join their guild, and abide by their practices to do business."

"Guild?" I repeated in a whisper.

"Different guild," he replied with a grin on Roewn's face. "There are a lot of them, covering most professions or labors."

"Oh? Do the prostitutes have a guild?"

"In a sense. It isn't a balanced one." He jerked his chin toward the Turthend Center. "Here, it is. The Dwarven customs for truth and pride in their wares and services are enforced for all in their guild. It is not enough to simply pay the dues and benefit from the clientele. This center has a reputation for quality and reliability they must protect. The Lurishen Clan conducts investigations into dangerous or deceitful merchants and their wares. Those with ill intentions are hunted down quickly once discovered and forced to pay reparations."

I smirked. "I presume the *Guild* helps with that."

Mourn smiled and winked at me, stepping forward as the cart in front of us moved up.

"If these are indeed not where all the beds are," I said as we walked forward, "believe I see why there's no need for locking gates between Alran and Bor."

"Indeed. Bor has their challenges caring for all their people, but the Lurishen don't get involved. They merely provide a fairer place for those from their neighboring city to practice a craft and earn their living. This benefits everyone, as the Clan sees it."

We stopped talking as the redbeard inspecting the cart slapped the side twice and stepped away when the driver moved through the wall. The younger Dwarf looked at us with dark blue eyes, and I was starkly reminded of Rithal.

Where might he be if he escaped from the warp rot forest? What about Osgrid? Did they meet up as he implied they might?

"Any animals, weapons, wares ye want tah declare?" the guard asked, appearing like he expected the answer to be negative. He was modestly armed but armored light enough to retain flexibility and speed. He also had a headband with a red gem facing us that gave me a sense we were being watched by more than just him.

Hmm. Animals, weapons, wares...

My spiders counted, of course, as did Soul Drinker, but I doubted Mourn wanted me to be that honest.

I watched Mourn—Roewn—declare a sword and dagger at his belt as part of his illusion.

"Ah! Peace-knotted, good," said the guard, who then looked at me and my waist.

Interesting that he didn't assume a Human woman was weaponless.

Soul Drinker appeared as a standard dagger as part of my illusion. Slowing my breath and smiling without showing my teeth, I drew back my cloak to show him. "Just this."

"An' peace-knot. Thank ye." The Dwarf looked between us, settling on me. "We recognize him. Mind givin' yer name, lady?"

Mourn waited while I considered how we could have walked in *not* speaking to the guards.

I answered, "Jan."

"Jan? And family name?"

Jan Shi? No... Hm.

"Thall," I replied. "Jan of Thall."

The Dwarf nodded. "I'll be a moment. Wait here."

I squinted at Mourn once he had gone, but he shrugged.

"Checking their banned list. Do not worry."

I twisted my lips. "You could have warned me. Are there any 'banned' families that sound like Thall in Augran?"

"Not that I've heard. Fortunately."

The half-blood was smirking. For certain, he remembered my Matron's name.

"What about Rithal or Osgrid?" I whispered. "Do you think they could be here?"

"If they were, it would be hard to find them. We can ask around if you wish, but what do you want from this? Should they know that you live and where you can be found?"

Hm. I had to think about that.

"Alright!" the redbeard called, putting his thumb in the air. "Yer good! Fortuity, Roewn."

"Gratitude and health, Chestir," Mourn replied, motioning for me to walk into Alran proper, beginning with their massive, well-regulated market.

Eye-catching colors, sculptures, and signage rivalled Yong-wen once the day grew light, though instead of favoring red, orange, and gold, I saw many more shades of green, blue, and purple.

The crowd seemed to appear one body at a time, coalescing before my eyes as Dwarves came up from underneath the street and out of ground floors at the same time those in the upper balconies stirred with their baskets. The doorways, bars, tables, benches, and chairs I could see varied more to accommodate the wide range of height and weight of those who used them.

Above, bird calls swiftly filled the air and grew as dense as some of the forests. Only with the noise did I notice the inordinate number of suitable places for their nests. Some of them were Dwarven constructions for that purpose.

"Do Surface Dwarves like birds?" I asked curiously. "They are giving them plenty of places to huddle."

"More specific," he answered. "Clan Lurishen likes the birds of the Greenway and provides them sanctuary." He motioned around. "You may also notice more dogs as guards."

That was true. They were constantly sniffing the air and several looked toward us. *Worrisome.*

"Why?"

"Cats," Mourn answered.

"Cats?"

"They mostly hide from me, so you didn't see many, but cats overrun Bor hunting for rodents. While they are valued for controlling vermin, the southeast is not consistent keeping their population in balance. As such, cats spill into the Greenway and the Turthend Center and are a nuisance, killing too many birds. So, this Clan is known for building safe bird nests and keeping dogs who run and work the Greenway, discouraging cats who would hunt there."

Interesting. "I remember Gavin saying he had expected to see more cats in the barn in Yong-wen, but he only saw owls."

"Similar issue. The patriarchs in Yong-wen breed and train owls and hawks to help keep both cats and rodents under control. They would rather deal with the bird droppings as signs of good luck."

Astonishing. I grinned. "Rodents to cats to birds to dogs back to cats to hawks to owls and back to rodents?"

He shared my smile while scanning the streets. "Most cycles which sustain themselves begin as a circle like this. They always overlap with other circles to create complex and intricate webs. How about breakfast pie before we search for teams?"

My neck suffered the whiplash of that change in subject, but my stomach seized on it. "Is that what I've been smelling the last block?"

"I believe so."

"Oh, yes!"

The vendor he selected was a black-haired Dwarven family, all of whom were extremely busy as we waited in their queue. At this rate, they would be out of pies before midmorning, but I was glad we got some.

"Just one each?" I asked.

Mourn laughed, handing me the warm bundle wrapped in a stiff parchment. My mouth dropped to feel the sheer density, and my fingers could tell it was not delicate like the Yungian hand pies. The crust was dense and hard.

"It's a brick!"

"A tasty brick that will last your average Dwarf until noon," he countered. "So, you should be fine until then with 'just one.'"

We claimed a stone bench on the street, watching the wide Turthend Road filling up with carts and groups of travelers. At first, my back itched with the need to look over my shoulder with so much movement. I resisted since Roewn wasn't drawing that kind of attention to us.

My first bite into the pie was all bread, albeit flavorful, and alluring in its way. My belly demanded more even as I'd need swallows of water to choke down more than three.

Fortunately, my second bite encountered moist, steaming vittles: finely chopped meat and earth roots mixed in a thick, herb-filled sauce. The mix held some flavors I recognized from food Gavin had prepared at the Ley Tower and at Brom's Inn but with striking influence from elsewhere. It lacked any hint of sweet heat as in the Yungian style, but it was not without enhanced flavors of its own.

Like aged meat, mushroom, and a hint of a bark with some bite. Curious.

Mourn watched me expectantly as I chomped into my fifth bite. Distractedly, I looked at him. *"Mm?"*

"Acceptable?"

I finished chewing and took a sixth bite, nodding as my stomach felt soothed that I could have stopped there, saved the rest, and been ready to run more rooftops. I didn't.

"You're right," I said between bites. "This will keep me for hours."

"Good. I'm glad to hear it."

The way he said it had me looking around at the bustling activity. "Is something about to happen?"

"Nothing dangerous. Can you spot them?"

Them?

I nibbled my breakfast rather than blatantly swivel my neck. The rising brightness summoned the usual early-day ache behind my eyes, but we'd at least selected a bench in the shade. Mourn and I were over half finished with our large meals when I admitted no one seemed like they didn't belong except me.

"I am at a disadvantage, of course," I added. "I do not know what every day looks like."

"More or less like this, unless there's a festival."

I sighed. "And what do I look like?"

"A first-time visitor who looks tired after a long trip," he said as an observation without insult. "I would assume she arrived for a purpose rather than for leisure."

"Hm." I smiled. "And what do you look like, sitting beside me?"

"Probably hired help for said purpose. Not a husband or relative."

I huffed a quiet laugh. "Accurate."

He shrugged. "We never planned to hide what we were doing here."

"Little point, isn't there? I'm told I'm not the best liar among my group."

Mourn chuckled. "Who told you that?"

"My elders. Both of them."

"Hm. I imagine they would know. They knew you before the relic."

My mouth twisted but I said nothing.

"Continue being honest about your limits," he said. "I am forming plans on how best to find what we seek, once we get there."

"You wouldn't put me out front to lie my way into that place, would you?"

"Not on purpose."

Before I could reply, a long-legged man loped up to us, breathing heavily and smelling of wood and smoke. I leaned up and away, watching Roewn slowly uncross his leg and stand up, offering a hand for the other man to clutch.

"Ah, you made it," he said in the Trade tongue.

"Whew! Sorry I'm late!" said the new arrival. "One last chore before Gram could do without me ferra bit!"

"No worry, Tak. We just finished breakfast."

He just finished. I just stuffed the last two bites in my mouth, looking over the likely Guildsman. Drab brown, somewhat shabby coat, reasonably clean shirt, pants, well-used but strong boots, no cloak. His hair naturally grouped itself into wavy locks of a shade I decided looked like sand, his eyes were a darker brown, and his skin on the pale side between Brom and Kurn. He worked hard with his hands and had dirt under short fingernails, but after watching the streets even for a brief time, I admitted there was more which was memorable about me than him.

Tak, huh?

I stood up, washing down the last bready bite with water from my skin, which drew both Tak's eyes and his smile to me.

"Well to your morning, nym," he said, bowing slightly with hands loose at his sides. "I'm Tak Jerone. An' you?"

"Jan Thall," I answered, better prepared this time, and mimicked his bow of greeting. I saw no insult, but his smile got wider as I realized it probably looked too Yungian. "And why are you here?"

"He didn't tell you?" Tak glanced at Roewn with a glare and a sigh.

My bodyguard shrugged, his manner of speech sounding less formal in Trade. "Well, I didn't hear back before I had to leave. Figured we'd give it time here before moving on."

"You'd give me false offers?"

"No, just one misaimed." Roewn grinned. "But everyone wants what you offer, Tak."

I waited, looking between them getting the sense this interaction was only a fraction genuine. I detected a whiff of a Court performance as the Human cleared his throat.

"To answer, Nym Thall," said Tak, "I live here in the Center an' give tours sometimes. Roewn sent that note and I *did* reply." Another glare. "But I guess he missed it. I'm glad you waited."

I arched one brow. "A tour? Do we have time?"

"We do!" Tak bowed again. "I'll try to end it closest to where you need to be, milady, so you may enjoy the journey."

Court diversions in the middle of the street. If that was deemed necessary, there must be other eyes watching. Why wouldn't Mourn tell me what to expect?

And he did say 'them.'

"Very well," I said. "Show me what you believe most that I should see."

"My pleasure, Nym Thall! Follow me."

CHAPTER 3

TAK SPOKE TOO QUICKLY AND CONSTANTLY THROUGH THE SURFACE STREETS of Turthend, sweeping his arms in alternating patterns without seeming to say a lot about how the place operated or where the inevitable pitfalls had to be. The man pointed out harmless oddities, seemingly unlinked bits of their history, and spoke names with glowing praise as if I should have some special appreciation for the ones who noted our passing and raised their hands in a wave.

The enthusiastic tone of persuasion and pushing favor was so different from Mourn's instructive conversations with me that I took it as performance. Perhaps Tak had previous agreements with these shopkeepers to recommend those places to the many "visitors" to spend their coin.

I noticed plenty of loose, white bird droppings about and similar street "sweepers" like I'd seen in Yong-wen. Now that I knew about the animal balance here, however, I thought there wasn't enough avian waste beneath my boots as there should have been if the Dwarves didn't have plans in effect to either clean it regularly or encourage the birds to relieve themselves elsewhere.

That was when I saw my first permanent city trench.

"What's that?" I asked, interrupting Tak, and pointing at a long row of stout stalls which had the scent of a latrine and were covered in white and green avian leavings at each end. The droppings were being collected into a trough filled with soil. "And how did the Dwarves train the birds to use it?"

"Ah! That's… ah…" Tak started laughing. "Are you…? *Ahem*, do you need to use it yourself? We keep the smell down using powdered chalk, just scoop a bit in after you're finished. They're quite roomy and the doors have a slide latch inside when occupied. And you see the fountain to wash your hands afterward, yes?"

That was far beyond what we had in the Cloister. Taking advantage sounded like a good idea. I accepted, smiling as my curiosity piqued, and for some reason, that made Tak blush red in the face.

"I'll go, too," said Roewn, who'd said almost nothing until then.

Tak sighed, adjusting his waist belt as if he considered the same. "Alright. Let's take a potter break, then."

Potter?

Probably came from the waste pots they normally had indoors.

The public latrine was connected to a narrow, underground system that seemed capable of flushing the waste elsewhere periodically. Until then, my stall indeed had a bucket and scoop with chalk dust. I narrowly avoided sneezing—a bad event in this smaller space—but the experience of relieving myself was one of the most secure while also hearing so many individuals nearby.

The Surface Dwarves love to build useful things in ways that make you want to use them.

If only the Tragar below could be as innovative. Would there be some living in Sivaraus like there were the Clans in Augran? How different Sivaraus would look, then.

Once all three of us were out and washing our hands, I dried mine using my own cloth while I cautiously approached the bird waste catcher. Looking up, I saw a complex arrangement of perches and numerous glass bottles holding clear liquid.

Hmm.

"Clean water," Roewn said, stepping beside me, "plus a diluted potion that encourages the urge if it is there. Turthend sells the waste mixed with soil to the local farmers who grow the food. It doesn't catch everything but does reduce the amount of cleaning needed and has value of its own."

"Astonishing," I said, meaning it.

"Indeed!" Tak agreed, laughing. "I speak with utter truth, I have never had a lady from Manalar want to talk about how the Center's shit management works. Er, pardon my tongue."

Oh yes, that.

I arched one brow but didn't know what to admit so only shrugged. Mourn had been providing me minimal guidance since leaving the rooftops in Bor, and I didn't know why. At most, I understood there was no imminent danger, nor was he feeling the urgency to gather those "teams" Talov had requested.

I sighed. In contrast, a hot trickle of concern and impatience welled up inside me. "Where are we going, Roewn? Why did we come here?"

He looked at me. "Are you bored, milady?"

"Yes," I said honestly. "I haven't any coin to spend at a market. Even if I had, I lack interest from having other matters on my head. The chatter of the tour has gone over it. The most valuable thing I've learned is where to go when the urge strikes, but I need to learn more."

Standing nearer to Roewn than to me, Tak's practiced smile sobered. "Ah. Other matters, nym? Would that be concerns about home?"

If you mean the siege at Manalar.

"I have...family there. She's not safe."

The sandy-haired man's mood shifted, grounded to let the social buoyancy deflate as he looked at Roewn and back to me. "Oh. I'm sorry, I didn't realize. Are you looking for someone to talk to about it?"

Looking for someone...?

I *finally* saw the way he turned a silver ring on his middle finger with his thumb and sensed the shivering response of my spiders at my nape. I had to trust my gut. *A mage.* He'd cast something near us.

"Well, we're not far from the end of the tour," Tak offered, "if you'd like to get out of the sun early?"

I smirked. "Yes, please. The high sun always makes my eyes ache, I'll only grow more irritable."

"Oh! Well," he grinned, "we will take a shortcut down, then."

I anticipated entering the "other half" of the Turthend Center by going beneath the streets, though we passed through several large buildings, inside then out again, before Tak touched his silver-ringed hand to a subtle combination of runes scored into the stone and opened the hidden door. At least he didn't speak or dither on the way.

Once we were encased by stone, I stepped in front to slow Roewn as Tak moved ahead to pick up a heatless torch like we had in the Deepearth. He looked at me expectantly.

Why not ask him to bring us here directly if it was always the plan?

It wasn't always the plan, he replied. *That was up to him. Even my recommendation isn't a total vetting of strangers to be brought here.*

So he needed to be further convinced without a word from you?
Basically.

The mage had turned around, lifting the light above his eye level. "Roewn? Nym Thall? Is all well?"

"We're sorting something out," the half-blood said.

I rubbed my temple and sighed, grateful to be in dim light as I spoke aloud. "It seems to me I was being evaluated without knowing, as if Roewn could not inform me of anything in advance."

"Ah, you would be correct, nym. The rules we hold when our informants ask to bring a situation to our door rather than tell us where we need to go."

The rules, hm.

"And what 'situation' am I that he brought to you?" I asked. "And why?"

Tak sounded amused. "I'm not sure yet. You are not acting like a Manalari woman, Jan, and do not think like one, though you look and sound much like them. I'm curious why that is."

"I learned Trade from a Manalari monk."

"Ah! That would explain it. Where do you come from?"

"What group would I share that with?"

"He didn't tell you?"

His manner of speech had changed from the last time he said that, relinquishing his tour-giving jaunt for a speaker confident from experience, ready to engage in his own den. I glanced up at Mourn as I considered both questions, but Roewn shrugged, unwilling to take the lead even now.

Damn this tactic. You'll let me stumble around more Humans without knowing the customs or going over the backstory with me? Is this not part of your Guild?

My spiders shifted as I breathed in to clear my mind.

Very well.

If he wasn't overly concerned with what I said or did around this man the way he'd been in his tended garden across the river...

"Roewn found me in the company of two Ma'ab scouts on their way to Manalar," I said, quite truthfully. "After I escaped them with his help, I asked for a way to get my sister out of Manalar before the Ma'ab lay siege. He recommended Reprisal in Augran. I have been traveling for weeks now, and I am running out of time. Tell me now. Have I met the first of Reprisal, or was I the fool to trust him? Have I stumbled into yet *another* gang of men who will hold me for their own use?"

The mage's eyes brightened, his expression both intrigued and incensed. "You *have* met the first of Reprisal, Jan." His mouth twisted in the dim blue light. "And we'd be the last 'gang' of men alive who would carry on that tradition."

His confidence sounded clear, but I scoffed. "What 'tradition?' "

"That women are property," Tak replied with a wrinkle of his nose that belied rising anger. "Born to be trained and traded as chattel by their fathers, brothers, and husbands." The man paused, his expression dimming. "Sometimes to be burned in retaliation for the unknown making wrong in the world."

Oh, shit.

I glanced at Mourn; he *was* smirking but subtly. My irritation evaporated as I lost the desire or traction to debate my own security. "Ah, I see. That is... good to hear. So, am I safe here?"

Tak Jerone bowed. "You are safe, Jan of Thall. I promise. And if you came all this way for help, Reprisal would hear your concerns."

I squinted. *Jan of...?* "I only said *that* to the guard at the gate."

He smiled at me. "I know."

"The red gem on the Dwarf's forehead?" I guessed.

Tak pursed his lips and exhaled. "You have far more education and awareness around you than any woman at Manalar." He repeated it like a challenge and a compliment. "I ache to learn why your sister is there and needs retrieving."

Hm. Does this mean he can't see through my illusion, mage or not?

Tak's eyes had never strayed to the dagger at my belt as if he saw an aura, nor had he seemed to glimpse little black legs in my hair.

So, perhaps not.

"Very well," I said. "Do we speak about it all here in a Dwarven closet or is there some place with refreshment, a place to sit, and another latrine?"

Tak laughed softly, beckoning with his hand. "There is. Plenty of each. Nym Jan, Roewn, please, follow me."

THE SIMPLICITY OF THIS SECRET UNDERHALL APPEALED TO ME. ALTHOUGH similar to the Cloister, it lacked the disorienting ramps and curves in between precise measures of torchlight designed to keep a Davrin's senses on edge.

The halls were largely straight and wide enough for two to walk abreast. The stairs led directly to the next level, sometimes curving but not unless necessary for some architectural reason I didn't grasp. No decorations, signage, or carvings identified where we were or how to get where we headed. Not out in plain view, anyway.

No doors, either.

At first, the passageway only had one way we could go until we reached a third platform down. Here, and at the same time I finally heard some noise of the living, the walkways branched into six possible entrances depending if we would immediately climb stairs or stay on this level.

The wooden doors were visible now, and there were many of them. Several of them opened, and a chill slipped down my spine.

Deadly choke point if not invited.

Quietly, eight men stepped out into the open circle with us from every passage, and I felt a rush of cold fear.

"Wolf!" Tak greeted another man with his tour guide's smile. "I brought a damozel on a mission."

Damo-what?

"Tak. So you have." This new Human had darker brown hair, his eyes a striking blue in a somewhat pale face. He didn't seem angry but lacked a returning smile as he turned to Mourn in disguise. "Roewn. Been a while."

The black-haired Noiri bowed his head. "There's been a flood of information on Ma'ab movement outside of Augran. One task after another led me to those needing to know. I only just returned."

"Hope you've brought some information for us as well?"

Roewn casually gestured to me as the men slowly spread out behind Wolf. "The most relevant one I came across. She was traveling with Ma'ab scouts, not entirely willing, but I'll let her explain."

I studied the first eight standing in the circle with us. Paxian and Noiri breeds, with no women or Dwarves. Every one of them moved like a fighter even if some were dressed down. Most were taller than the Yungian men I'd sparred with in Yong-wen.

My gaze shifted to meet Wolf's as he focused on me.

"Jan of Thall," he began.

"Jan is preferred," I interjected.

"Jan, then. I'm Brian."

"I thought Tak said 'wolf?'"

His lips lifted into a small smile. "Brian Wolf."

"Oh."

"And I'm sure you've heard this before, but you have a convincing Manalari accent yet none of their mannerisms."

"And as I told Tak, I learned to speak Trade from a Manalari monk."

"Oh? What's his name?"

"Gavin."

"Gavin who?"

"I have no idea." I shrugged. "He never gave me any other."

"And where is he now?"

I pursed my lips. "Killed by *Dyos Guerrimos* while we were traveling."

The men reacted tellingly to that.

"The Witch Hunters," Brian sneered, his eyes becoming intense. "You've encountered them?"

"I have."

"Where?"

I shifted my weight, wondering how long I would be questioned before I could explain anything. Mourn certainly wasn't helping. When I glanced at him, he said, "You're doing well being truthful, Jan."

Thanks.

I exhaled. "In Troshin Bend."

"Oh, shit," said a different man, "you were there when it burned?"

This can't be good.

"What have you heard?" I asked.

Brian Wolf smiled at my unease. "That the town turned on the Witch Hunters when they tried to conscript their governor on a 'holy mission,' failed, and set the town on fire. We heard that they're all dead and buried. Townsfolk decided to leave before the church sent a response, and people have been showing up here talking about it."

Uh-oh.

"Has the name Amelda come up?" I asked.

Brian looked interested. "No. Why?"

"She's the governor's daughter. Be wary of her. She's half-Ma'ab and loyal to the Empire."

"Ah. Good to know."

I licked my lips. "Any gossip about the governor himself?"

"Brom Troshin?" Brian shook his head. "Vanished. Why a lot of folk there decided to run."

Fuck.

"Sounds like you caught his and his daughter's attention while learning Trade from an unlucky monk."

"True," I admitted. "The governor is a dangerous mage with a controlling impulse."

"We know. Are you a mage, then?"

Mind mage, maybe.

"I use magic, yes," I evaded.

"What kind of magic?"

Groan.

"I have strange dreams," I said, "and sometimes uncover the secrets of others in sleep. Brom found this out, and Amelda wanted to sell me to the Ma'ab."

Brian looked at the men around him, appraising something between them, and the mood shifted before I could catch its direction.

"In that case," the lead man said, "we're glad you made it here. We won't try to possess you, and we'll help if we can."

A small weight lifted. *If they can.*

"Not against Brom," I said to be clear. "I need help with what drove me into his den in the first place."

"Understood. Tak sent a message ahead. Something about a sister at Manalar?"

"Yes! But first, what do you usually ask for payment?"

Several chuckled and Brian smiled wider. "Just the task itself, if accepted, and whatever we loot from the Witch Hunters or the Bishops' toads."

That was a relief.

He added, "Would you like to sit and eat while we talk more on this?"

Although I wasn't yet hungry after that Dwarven pie, I couldn't pass up the opportunity. "I accept."

We reconvened to a long mess hall with benches and the scent of hot, simple food. From the first step into this new male den to when Mourn silently sat next to me, I ached to demand an explanation or even ask how much I should share about my travels and goals.

Yet how would I communicate with any privacy? In Trade? Davrin? By hand sign? Any of those would only raise more questions from Reprisal while my bodyguard may choose not to respond at all.

If only I could mindlink other times than in sleep or duress or using a conduit with a sorceress. How useful it would be in a situation like this.

Although, my bodyguard *could* stop testing my poise for two instants.

There were other groups of men in the mess besides us. They glanced our way and seemed interested but also like they were on their way somewhere. Meanwhile, I was served a wooden plate filled with dark red beans, pale yellow grains, red meat which had been shredded and dried, and round, bite-sized orange fruits that resembled giant berries.

The man serving placed a tankard of ale beside this. I stiffened, staring at the pale-yellow liquid. The scent made me queasy, recalling the watered-down wine from the ship.

"Um..."

Brian lifted his head. "No ale?"

I shook mine. "Or wine. I... don't like the taste. Do you have clean water?"

More than one man grimaced. Not a good sign.

"Might have to boil some," said one next to Brian.

"I'll drink it hot."

"Might still taste strange."

"I *am* thirsty, and I can't stomach the ale."

"Alright then, I'll let Jeri know."

He got up to head to the kitchen while the rest dug into the meal with wooden spoons, including Mourn. I joined them, sampling the simple fare and glad to have the patience to consume it slowly.

"So," Brian started, pointing at Roewn with his spoon. "When were you thinking of heading out?"

"As soon as I know if you will take her case," Mourn replied, appearing quite the mundane Human eating beans. "If not, I agreed to escort her somewhere else safe."

What?

"Do you think we'd refuse now that we've taken her in like this?"

"I haven't heard an agreement," he countered. "I'm her bodyguard until then."

What?! I coaxed the chewy grains off my spoon with my lips, narrowing my eyes with thought. *Don't panic, this is not remotely our To'vah Bargain...*

"Alright. So then, Roewn. Who is she, really? What's the true nature of what we are dealing with here?"

"She didn't lie to you," Roewn countered.

"I know. She passed with honor sashes, but as Tak knew from the start, she's smart," Brian bowed his head to me, "observant, and experienced enough to recognize a lot that's unseen around her and lift the panel to see how it works."

Tak found this description amusing for some reason.

"Well," Roewn replied, "I think you should keep talking to her. Her nature reveals itself as you do. That's what happened with me."

Very funny, Dragonchild.

Brian huffed a laugh, shrugged, and sighed. "Fine. Jan. Where is the 'Thall' family from? It sounds like it could be from the Dragon Coast, but you aren't Noiri."

Still thinks I'm Human.

"Actually, it's...*Thalluen*," I answered.

Several pairs of eyes blinked to hear its Elven pronunciation.

"Uh-oh," one man said, nudging Brian's elbow. "Noble runaway?"

Brian's eyebrows bounced once as he finished chewing with a noncommittal shake of his head. He scooped another bite. "And where is... *Thall*-oo-een from?"

Ouch.

"Farther down," I said.

"You mean south?"

I blinked in surprise, smiling with reluctance. "I...well, have you ever met Sal-zayr? Someone from Ahj-Zayr?"

"I have. Not many. Usually traveling entertainers or medicine men. Is that where we're talking? The southern ocean city?"

"Well, closer to the Desert, but..." I paused as he began to look suspicious. *Too far from the truth.*

I had little enough guidance, I'd been tempted to tell a story based on ancient dreams. Giving myself pause, I scooped up some beans and grains together, deciding they tasted better mixed. "I would like to go there one day. But no, my family is not from there."

The man's shoulders relaxed as he recognized the truth. About then I decided he was either a mage or one of his plain rings had been extremely well crafted. I doubted my options included being on their generous side *without* telling them the true nature of who I sought, so I changed the focus of our conversation to where it should be.

"You heard about the burning of Troshin Bend," I stated. "Have you also heard of a witch-assassin captured at Manalar?"

"What?" blurted one in surprise.

"When?" asked Brian, leaning forward with interest.

Damn.

"I don't know," I said with a shrug. "I am asking if it's happened that you know of. Otherwise there is a witch-assassin still roaming the hills."

"Witch-assassin," their lead man repeated, skeptical despite his truth magic. "And this is your 'sister?'"

I smiled. "Yes. She was sent by my queen to perform a task. I do not know what, but it is deadly. I must find her and make sure she gets out before the Ma'ab siege our queen has predicted. I need the help of capable Humans who are adversaries to the Manalari and the Ma'ab. I need those who know about assassinations, infiltrating, brokering information. You know, *Guildsmen.*"

Brian stared in naked shock. This seemed to have rung true to him.

Wordlessly, he looked at Roewn, who grinned.

"I told you her nature reveals itself the more you talk."

Chapter 4

"I haven't heard of a 'queen' involving herself in this war," Brian said cautiously.

"Nor would you." I shrugged. "I think the last time a group of us was on the Surface was before you were born. You're how old? Three decades?" I saw several of them swallow. "No? Four?"

Brian smirked, unblinking, before answering. "I'm twenty-seven."

"In your prime," I motioned to him in compliment. "Then I can say we haven't been involved since before your *father* was born."

"Holy shit," a third man with dark blond hair muttered, prodding his grains without eating, while his leader maintained the focus.

"And who is 'we?' "

"We're the blood sisters."

Brian narrowed his eyes, trying to reformulate his next question when Tak leaned forward, his elbow perilously close to tipping his mostly empty plate.

"Ah, excuse me. The... 'surface?' What does that mean in context? The surface of what?"

"Good question," added the blond through the corner of his mouth.

"The surface land you live on," I explained, drawing my gaze up along the ceiling. "The Dwarves live beneath the Surface, don't they?

The Halls of Taiding are largely underground, I've heard. I would enjoy seeing them."

"Ah!" Tak exclaimed. "That's why high sun gives you headaches."

My smile was more of a grimace. "Indeed. We live underground like the Dwarves, just… farther down. We don't come up much. Years pass."

"So far down," Brian asked, "not even the Halls of Taiding are aware you're here?"

I smiled. "Well, we don't live *directly* beneath them. There are other deep tunnel systems."

Several of the eight men present started to chuckle. My remark hadn't been *that* funny, so I supposed they were hiding or releasing tension. I noted several looks at Roewn, who kept his satisfied expression to suggest he knew the secret but let them wade in at their own pace.

This seemed to reassure a few to gather their courage. Tak was one of those.

"Are we about to see a 'real' witch?" my tour guide asked with a smile. "One that would make the Bishops shit their robes?"

"Probably," I answered. "Are you ready to see?"

Tak looked at Brian Wolf, who drew in a measured breath as he met eyes with each of the other six men. I saw the agreement before their lead spoke.

"We are." Brian nodded once to Roewn. "And understand we're in this mission one way or another."

"Very well."

Fortunately for me, Mourn was willing to play along. I felt his foot gradually press down on mine beneath the table, and I closed my eyes as if to concentrate on releasing a spell of my own. The sudden shuffling and wave of fear-laced sweat bid that I open them.

None of them shouted in alarm or launched to their feet to threaten me the way Kurn and Castis had. However, my eyes met many stunned, astonished, or disbelieving expressions not only from the eight men sharing my table but from everyone in the mess hall. About fifteen of them, plus the cook smelling of onions, who'd been approaching with

47

a spouted pot.

"Uh," said the dark-haired man, holding up the steaming pot and wooden cup. "Did you... want this?"

"Is that the water?" Roewn asked.

"Y-yeah."

"Yes, please!" I smiled. "Thank you."

"N-no trouble."

The cook passed the pot and cup to the nearest man, who passed them down until Brian set the items before me. I poured out a measure of steaming liquid immediately so it could start cooling, helping it along by blowing the surface before taking a sip. Not the best water, but it was clean.

"Alright," their lead man began slowly while the cook lingered for a closer look. "What... race do we see now?"

"Davrin."

"And this is your true form."

"It is."

"Uh-huh." Brian tapped the knuckle of his thumb on the wooden table. "And there's another 'blood sister' Davrin somewhere around Manalar, and she's on a mission."

"Correct."

"And you were sent for... extraction?"

I hesitated. "That is what I seek to do."

"I must think," their lead man continued, "that you weren't *missed* by the Guild until this moment. Were you?"

"I was not. Thanks to Roewn, I was granted an audience with Talov Baradum."

Several genuine if nervous smiles broke out, and the tension eased despite drinking in my appearance while I sipped my hot water. Clearly, that name carried a lot of weight.

"When?" Brian asked.

"Two days ago. Talov said he would find me help," I added, using his first name. "He suggested you. Reprisal."

Roewn nodded in agreement and finally spoke. "Listening to

Grandfather Baradum as he talked with her, he *does* remember stories about Davrin Elves, albeit not ones who live underground. They were said to live deep in the Red Desert."

Brian's dark brown eyebrows lifted, recognizing my earlier line of questioning and its near falsehood.

"The Baradum Clan does *not* want an Elf in the hands of the Bishops or the Ascended," Roewn further explained. "Talov said Elves live longer than Dwarves and are typically the stronger mages between them."

"*Pfft*, of course," Tak said. "They would have the time to practice." I smiled at him. He was more accurate than he knew.

Roewn bowed his head. "We all know that either side, Ma'ab Ascended or Manalari Bishop, would abuse such a capture for their own gain."

A shadow of dark thought passed over Brian Wolf's face. "Aye. One prisoner like this would be like burning a hundred innocent women at the stake."

Please, no. I sat quietly with my hands wrapped around my cup.

"So, what was she sent to do?" Brian asked. "And when?"

I shook my head. "She couldn't talk about it. I know she had to make it there by now or it would be too late. She would fail."

"And if she fails? Or gives up?"

"She's under a spell that will force her to continue. She can't give up. I think if she fails, she dies."

Brian frowned at this first dark hint of our queendom. "Then how were you supposed to find her?"

I wasn't.

"Not part of the plan," I said, though it was a struggle to keep a placid face as my stomach tightened. I lifted my cup for another sip. "But I need her help to complete my own mission which lies elsewhere, far away from this Human conflict. If she completes her mission, she can go home. If I find her, she can come with me. *We* can go home."

I paused, not knowing what to make of their careful expressions and calm faces.

"No one left behind?" Tak asked quietly, giving me the first hint.

A lopsided smile formed on my lips. "No demons but us, my blood sisters and me."

The underground mess hall seemed to brighten with their eyes, and two of them mouthed the phrase, as if trying it out: *No demons but us.*

The members of Reprisal understood this motto to a man. Mourn had said I might like them, and perhaps I understood better why.

"We'll go in with you," said Brian Wolf, shifting focus to Roewn, "but it sounds like we need solid intelligence, first."

"Agreed. The Grandfather has others working on that part."

"So, we need to be packed and ready."

"As I understand. I need to leave soon."

What?

"Understood. Will we be solely responsible for her well-being?"

Roewn shook his head. "No. The Baradum Clan is trying to reach someone who knows her culture better and can assist Reprisal in this endeavor."

Oh.

"*Heh!*" Tak leaned forward. "Not another man like us, I presume?"

My Noiri escort smiled. "That's how I interpreted it."

"Should be fun." Tak looked to Brian. "Until then?"

"Well," he began with a sigh, "honestly, you both look tired."

"We were traveling all night and morning," Roewn confirmed.

"You want a couple of rooms to rest while I check in with a few things?"

"One room," I said, reaching out and taking hold of his forearm. "He's made it unnecessary for me to kill more Humans since Troshin Bend. I sleep better when he is near."

Mourn's Human face warmed with surprise, while I thought it curious how I couldn't feel his weapons bracer beneath his cloth-mimic shirt.

An Abyss of a shifting spell.

Meanwhile, most of the men at the table stared at me until some cautiously nodded. A couple smirked like the contact was suggestive, but Brian Wolf seemed to take it at surface value.

"Makes sense," he said. "Um, if I may ask, what 'Humans' *have* you killed?"

"The Ma'ab scouts working with Amelda. And some of the Witch Hunters when they attacked Troshin Bend." I paused. "No children. I do not attack children."

The subtle tension dissipated, and more smiles appeared. Apparently, my last addition was unexpected but welcome.

"Sounds like a code we can work with," Brian said. "Honestly, I'd love to hear more of what happened to the Witch Hunters there."

Rowen smiled. "Sure. If we have time. I think you'll enjoy it."

Brian Wolf smirked. "Right. Let's get you two set up in a room."

I RELEASED MY SPIDERS TO SEEK THEIR FOOD IN THE CREVICES WHILE MOURN set the wards which would allow us to relax. He kept Roewn's shape.

"A good time for you to sleep while most of the Reprisal is awake. I'll watch over you and the relic in case there is trouble either way."

Dryly, I replied, "You mean I shall wait longer to *witness* you sleep since we met?"

Roewn's sudden, broad grin was rather handsome. "Correct. And given your current vulnerability in a resting state, that's a good quality for your bodyguard to have."

"Oh, I'm not arguing that."

"You may trust the wards dampen sound, hide magical auras, including your relic, and block scrying."

Hearing this, the weight of my limbs seemed to drag at my head and eyelids. For the first time in months, the placement of the Sun outside didn't matter in how or when I should rest.

"Are they likely to scry on us?" I asked with a yawn.

"No, but it would be foolish to leave that window open."

"Hm. How many of Reprisal are mages?"

"Currently? About one in ten."

I frowned. "Is that common for groups of Humans?"

He shook his head, removing his cloak, which was the only genuine article of clothing on Roewn. "No, that's quite concentrated. More like Baenar births, as I recall."

I sighed, beginning my dress-down using the generous number of hooks and shelving available. "If you say."

Mourn paused. "You genuinely can't see unguarded mage auras, even if you concentrate?"

I shrugged. "I can't imagine mages unguarded up here regardless."

He chuckled. "Fair."

"I can *sense* them," I added, "especially if I'm touching them."

"That's normal for Baenar. I suppose I'm curious if you could learn to see more like I do."

"Oh? Could your former 'squad' learn?"

"Not all of them," he admitted. "But some managed to 'shift their gaze' that way. And you have a unique resource that might help in unexpected ways."

Heh. Understatement.

"Well, Gavin taught me to *suppress* my aura," I said, "like he does, because it seems any Elf looks like 'magic' to Human mages."

"I've noticed, and he's correct. I'm glad he taught you, and you made the habit. This will be especially important at Manalar."

"Agreed."

By this point, I was barefoot and without gloves, cloak, tools, stolen dagger, or armor. I sighed, stretching my back, and flapping my shirt to cool my abdomen. My pendant stuck briefly to my skin.

Glancing over, I caught Roewn sticking out his short, pink tongue as he scented the air, which was funny on a man's face. He returned the amusement on my face with a smirk before initiating that skin-burning, bone-popping transition from Human to the lavender-tongued, Draconic Elf hybrid.

Eyes changed first from blue to metallic gold, his round pupils compressing, stretching top-to-bottom, and becoming sharp. Black and purple enshrouded his pale skin until he blended in with the unlit corners of the room, and his shorn hair grew and curled into a bound queue before my eyes.

The missing tail returned, dropping down long and lively, while his horns and claws erupted to return his natural weapons. The magical bracers fixed permanently on his arms appeared like a veil had been pulled back, as did his harness and the patchy spreads of hard, glossy scales. The largest of those patches covered his shoulders, most of his back, and his thighs. His long feet with the heel spur plus the angle of his lower legs vaguely reminded me of a massive bird of prey.

When he seemed finished, Mourn released the clasps of his harness the fastest I'd ever seen him do and, the moment it was off, stepped backward to the wall. The Dragonblood started scraping each of his shoulder blades hard against the stone, like when I'd been spying on him near the river. He'd scratched his back against a tree trunk just like this after taking his nap.

"Are you alright?" I asked.

"Yeh," he grunted, focusing on one particularly stubborn itch. "Sometimes shifting sets my birth form itching to induce madness."

I chuckled. "Not shifting into other forms?"

"*Nngh*. Not as often."

"That's good, Human skin being so vulnerable to fingernails by comparison."

He made a face. "I don't think Elves can speak much against soft, tender skin."

"But we scar less frequently, right?"

"Mm. True."

I pulled off my shirt as my breasts had begun to ache in earnest, testing the weight of them using both hands. They were hot and swollen, and seemed *heavy*, but I hadn't realized how much so until the support was gone.

"Point for you on the tenderness," I said with chagrin. "Do these look *bigger* to your eye?"

He was quiet at first, so I looked up and over. His gaze appraised my breasts for certain, yet he seemed caught between serious contemplation and an odd uncertainty.

"A little larger, yes," he answered. "But temporary."

His eyes flicked between my nipples in a reflex, and I pictured his tongue doing the same, coating them with tingling spit like he'd done Dandan.

Orrrr... not so odd for a half-blood who recently admitted wanting more sex.

I smiled, releasing my breasts to let them drop gently, and tugged the leather ties loose at each of my hips in deliberate play. He was watching when I hooked my thumbs in to wiggle my pants down three finger-widths, hiding my white fur but showing him my waist to the crack of my ass. The burrower in his trousers responded, as did the strangler behind him.

"I often sleep better after cumming," I suggested, pushing my leathers down my legs to pull them off my feet without delay. I shook my ass so my netherlips wouldn't stick, and my slit joined my breasts as a warm, visibly swollen invitation for the mercenary.

Mourn exhaled but did not reply.

Is he bothered somehow?

"Surely you agree this is a good opport—"

When I looked up, he was nude and within two steps of me. A familiar, reassuring scent rolled in.

"—oh."

"Come here," he breathed, his arms seizing to lift me against him, front-to-front, as when he'd carried me on the rooftops.

His prick was erect, bare, and much hotter without the clothing. I emitted an encouraging noise when he pressed it firmly to my mound and belly, rubbing his under-ridge against my pubic bone. Clutching his shoulders for leverage, I tilted my pelvis against him and guided that fire poker where its teasing would be most effective.

"Ohh, yes!" I groaned as I stroked my nub along his length.

He grunted as his tip nestled briefly in my curly muff. His hands cupped my bottom, but I felt his grip shift to spread the cheeks until cool air touched my pucker. I waited for something solid, possibly his tail, welcoming that extra limb either to test my slit's wetness or taunt my netherhole.

The mercenary held still, his swollen weapon throbbing as I encouraged him further, sliding my mound up and down once more. His hands massaged my ass appreciatively as he hummed, but neither cock nor tail sought to penetrate either of my holes.

Hmm? What...?

Bewildered, I lifted my cheek from his shoulder to look at him. This was what he was waiting for; his eyes warmed when they met mine.

"I would like to sit on the bed and do this facing each other," he said. "Are you willing?"

I recalled our mutual rejection at the Shi manor of being pressed upon our backs to fuck. When he'd asked how I preferred it, I'd turned my ass up in the air, presenting it to him. I'd known this position would send me soaring, and he had indulged me after rimming my pucker with that tongue, almost breaking my mind.

No facing each other, no eye contact. Even last night, while pleasuring him with my mouth on the roof, I hadn't opened my eyes long enough to look at him, but he'd seemed to enjoy it regardless.

"You want to... hold gazes?" I guessed, unable to hide my grimace.

"No, I'm not asking that." Mourn rubbed his pole gently against me to stay aroused, looking down and nodding to my pendant. "I'm glad you're wearing the saphgar, but eye contact is a common psionic trigger. There's no need to risk something unwanted."

My stomach clenched. *Yes, unwanted.*

I remembered the others who'd been unwanted in my head. With neither the confidence nor desire did I try mindlinking when I wasn't in danger or under pressure. I was nervous about what I'd learn about my bodyguard before I was ready.

I am enjoying this pace of sorting each other out.

Mourn said, "I'd just like more... presence from you."

I blinked. *Presence?*

What was I doing wrong?

"Um, I don't understand," I admitted.

Mourn chuckled and gathered me closer, supporting me with one hand and reaching with the other across my back. He dipped his head to nuzzle my neck, lightly licking the thin sweat from my skin, and breathing in my scent.

"For me," he murmured, "being present is actively sensing the aura while exploring the body. I am quite impressed and pleased with your fucking skills, Red Sister, do not doubt that. But I have no need for you to perform when you are tired and soon to rest."

He dragged his unusual mouth to my jaw with care, catching my ear lobe with his lips before running the tip of his tongue along the edge of my ear. I shivered as the spit began to tingle.

Ohhh…

"Alright," I breathed, adjusting my hold on his shoulders. "Sit facing each other. You in my cunt and… exploring? Do I have this right?"

"You do." He chuckled, stepping backward before turning to the sturdy bed.

"Don't forget to slather my tits. I think it might help the soreness."

"Mmm." His long tongue flicked out, just missing them. "I won't."

"Tease."

This might be a pleasant change.

Mourn reached back and took hold of my crossed ankles, hiking my legs higher on his back before pressing on them. "Hold tight here."

I did, and he sat down on the edge first. Then, using fists, heels, and tail, the hybrid brought his legs up from the floor and turned to settle in the center, facing the head of the bed. His cock hadn't softened much and had ducked underneath me, nestled between my buttocks as we shifted my position on his lap.

"Now I'm aching," I told him, leaning forward with my tits and pendant pressed to him while arching my back. "Get up in me, please."

His rumble held a hint of surprise as he caressed my body at leisure. "And the slathering of your tits I shouldn't forget?"

"With your rod in place, you'll enjoy that *with* me. Promise."

He was convinced.

Broad hands spread me wide as I helped him find the right spot. My sex was wet and spongey, lubricating part of his shaft, so once the head nestled into the warm cleft, that first, eager push felt like a Feldeu getting planted to the hilt.

"Oh, goddess, Mourn!" I blurted, clinging to him.

"Sorry," he gasped. "Too sore?"

He meant from getting locked with him two days ago.

"Um, yes," I breathed, calm enough to laugh. "Unfortunately."

"You take the rest... What you will, as you wish it."

Nodding, I moved my hips, testing our fit. He was about halfway in; I felt the under-ridge stubborn trying to wedge its way in next. His heart was pounding, as was mine. My arms wrapped around him, my cheek brushing his ear, and his hands gently massaged my back. I imagined I heard the modest hum of his powerful aura all keyed up.

Presence.

"Hold still, bodyguard," I whispered, nipping his earlobe with my teeth, pumping my sheath along his unique ride. About every other thrust down, I took a little more, gradually wetting him up. And *stretching.*

Ohh, yesss.

When I had his cock stuffed in as much as I could handle then, I wasn't sure how close I was to courting that final bulge. If I took it, I would need one of Shyntre's pellets afterward.

If I did that to myself... *Why?* I didn't know.

Performance?

The Dragonblood had asked for presence, this time.

Forgetting the challenge of that knot for the moment, I moved slowly without seizing control or pushing the pace. Mourn stroked my back, squeezed my ass, and his tail soon joined us, slithering once around my waist, and dipping to tease the crack of my ass. I squeaked.

"Lean back," he panted.

Lean...?

"Do not worry. I have you."

He certainly did. Between his hands and his tail, I had only to release his shoulders so he could ease me backward. Our eyes met as the angle of his erection changed inside me, each of us briefly amused when we simultaneously looked down to study our connection. My netherlips stretched widely around him, flushed a purplish-red, our junction hinting at the rest deep inside. His base knot remained outside, nestled against me.

"My nub is buzzing," I whispered as we stared at our crotches.

"Is it?"

"Yeah." I clenched the muscles of my pelvis, rewarded to see his eyes widen. "Because of the *pressure* inside."

His tail returned the squeeze around my torso, I chuckled, holding his forearms near the elbows as the half-blood took the first few thrusts not just using his hips but moving mine with the firm hold of his hands. I relaxed into it, felt as if I was being fucked in suspension, until Mourn licked my left nipple, coating it with his thick, slippery saliva.

Ohhhh, shiiit...

I'd thought the tingling would overtake the soreness; I was right, for what *that* was worth. The reality of the problem was the swell of my breasts ached while the nipples were hypersensitive.

The Dragonblood's spit only enhanced that further. In one spot.

My one nipple felt like someone had placed an ember on it!

"Oh, *fuck*," I cursed, bucking in his lap.

"What's wrong?"

"Lick the rest," I grunted. "My tits... all over! The nipple alone is too much!"

He obeyed swiftly, lavishly running a flatter width of his gooey tongue around the undersides before darting up between them, knocking my pendant to one side. Then he painted each from the top down, back and forth, until he returned where he started.

"Ohhh, better!" I said, rutting harder on him, my body clamping down at random intervals. From the way his breath was catching, he enjoyed that.

He tucked the saphgar behind me and kept licking, as the broad swath of wet warmth indeed eased the ache. Familiar tension and rushes of sensation began to concentrate farther down as well.

My release was rising fast.

"*Almost...*" I gasped, my eyes closed tight as we kept going, shifting, and leaning where it felt good.

Goddess, *quite* good!

Coming close, I relaxed at the right moment, taking his cock deep while gripping his arms, and he moved my hips to suit him. He withdrew again, dragging that lovely ridge along my slick flesh, creating that sought-after spark within me which caught and spread like mage's fire the next time he pushed in.

"Yes!" I cried.

All I *could* say to what was about to happen.

He sucked breath in through his teeth as my body began to ripple around him. The hum I'd felt before turned far lower in pitch. He grunted, hissing in a slow build before finally crying out himself.

"*Sssah—augh! Yes!*"

Caught in my throes, I gasped when his constricting tail whipped free, and he pulled me upright against him, withdrawing slightly to hold me off his swelling knot. With his jaw draped over my shoulder, drops of drool landed on my ass, and I stared in a stupor as his white spines lifted from his back to stick straight out.

Mourn growled with long release as I was coasting down from mine. The brief, hot splash as he spurted deep in my gut forced a gasp of surprise, and my legs began to quiver. My head felt dizzy, and my hands gripping the scales on his back was like holding two stones submerged in a hot spring.

Oh, Goddess...

I lost a bit of time as I stared into nothing yet felt all of it, floating in a quiet moment. The first thing to ground me was the sticky skin, sweltering heat, and the heavy panting.

"Mourn...?"

He rumbled in response, helping me peel away from his fevered skin as if he knew what I would say. His cock had shrunk enough to slip out from that movement alone, so I certainly wasn't sure how long we'd drifted in wordless afterglow. We'd made a mess on the bed and were far too late to catch it.

Oops.

He didn't seem to care. He tugged my pendant back to my front between my tacky breasts, where we both confirmed it was warm to the touch and faintly glowing blue.

"Hm," he grunted, the afterglow too heavy of a blanket for him to toss off. "I…felt no link."

Blearily, I shook my head. "And no knot."

"*Heh.*" Molten gold shimmered with amusement as he lightly combed damp hair back from my temple. "Good."

My legs were stiff and Mourn helped me stretch out slowly onto my back near the cool wall before lying on his side facing me. His Draconic eyes scanned me carefully, like he was checking for new injuries.

"I'm well," I said.

I think.

I hoped.

He didn't respond. He was watching my abdomen.

"What?" I asked, suddenly afraid.

Mourn looked at me hearing the tone. He seemed baffled or concerned. "How long have you carried?"

That didn't help my nerves. I had to stop and count.

"I'm… through half of the first turn. Um, six months?"

A year and a half to go. If I made it.

Mourn lifted his hand but paused with it hovering over me. "Hm. May I?"

"May you what?"

He drew a breath. "Touch your womb?"

I got on my elbows; I would have sat up if I hadn't felt so woozy. "Why? What's wrong? D-did I hurt—?"

"No, I don't think so," he said. "It is… *uhm*… I can see a mage's aura and very…new. The newest I have ever seen."

I stared at him as his eyes drifted back to my abdomen. "Is that… unusual? Can mages *tell* if a mata is carrying another mage this early?"

"I do not know, Sirana," Mourn admitted. "I left the Deepearth too early to have learned what is typical for mage births."

"Then why do you want to touch it?"

He exhaled as he looked at the far wall, his tail flicking upward as he thought it over. "If we are to keep our Bargain, I need to learn this new aura the same as I have learned yours, as you are the same and different. Doing this may give me an earlier warning if something is wrong or out of balance."

I fiddled some with the stained, rumpled blanket, then realized I was too tired to want to get up and be further worried about *this*, too.

I just want to lie down and rest.

While he wanted to put a hand on my stomach to recognize an unborn mage. *One he agreed to protect as well.*

"Very well," I said as I settled back again, reaching to take his wrist and guide his hand in place. "Do what you must. If… if there's anything I would do better to know, please tell me. And be truthful."

"I shall."

Mourn slid his palm over my sticky skin, his hand nearly spanning my hips as he focused on that "new" aura within. Stiffly, I waited for some time while the Dragonblood's gaze became unfocused, his pointed ears moving slightly like he listened to the subtlest of stirs, while his high body heat gradually drew back down to normal.

The saphgar did not start glowing again, and I had time to reflect on my crotch feeling sore in the good way, realizing that I'd come without rubbing my clit. Mourn hadn't shoved the knot in, either, despite being dragged over that cliff with me; he'd taken specific action to protect my slit from another lock so soon after the first. Lastly, we had avoided that uncontrolled surge of his aura that made me see stars.

Curious. Perhaps regular sex might lessen the frequency of those occurrences?

He claimed he is young for his Sire's race, if mature for mine.

Finally, Mourn blinked and returned from his trance, slowly withdrawing his hand with a nod of thanks.

"Well?" I asked. "Anything I should know?"

"Nothing of concern. Your child seems healthy to me." His shimmering eyes lifted to mine. "You likely carry a mage of potent lineage."

My throat closed as I tightened my lips a moment. Potent enough to purge Abyssal taint when he healed another. Something not even most Priestesses could do, even if they wanted to. "Do you know if it's the same magic as the sire? Healing and dream walking?"

Mourn shrugged. "That *is* too early to tell. This is not always determined before birth, but rather what life they are born into."

Unfortunately, that was something even I couldn't guess.

"Do you still want your Reverie?" Mourn asked.

"*Whoof*, yes," I admitted, aware as my body grew heavy against the mattress. I didn't even care to wipe myself. It could wait.

I yawned as if prompted, and he smiled. "Close your eyes. I will watch over you." He touched my wrist. "And thank you for holding to our Bargain."

"*Heh*, of course," I said. "It's a fun way to pay for causing trouble."

He chuckled in agreement.

Not long after, I fell asleep.

CHAPTER 5

A SUN-FILLED ROOM, LUSH WITH TAPESTRIES WHOSE THREADS FAVORED BLUE and gold. The walls had been painted white and contained some of the finest furniture I'd ever seen.

In one corner, a luxurious bed of dark, polished wood stood on a platform, layered with silk and the comfort of stuffed feathers. Nearby, a massive writing desk and multiple shelves of books dwarfed the collection in Cris-ri-phon's private quarters while enough room remained for a large sitting table and plenty of chairs with stitched cushions.

When I turned around, I saw another table near an open window. A pure white cloth had been draped over it, and several clean clothes and finely crafted items had been laid out precisely in a neat, orderly row. A trickle of dread touched the back of my neck as I approached it.

First, I looked out the window.

The courtyard was far below, and it had a fountain.

I've never been here.

Yet I recognized the sunburst symbol carved at the top of the fountain and heard male voices, shouting or chanting, on the edges of my senses.

Dyos Guerrimos.

I considered the items on the table beside me—ornate, expensive versions of what the Chief Warrant Bictrius had been carrying at Troshin Bend. There was a polished wooden box containing incense on one end, powdered mushrooms within a jeweled, metal box on the other. A heavy, golden goblet had been filled with clear water, and two glass vials lay on either side of it.

One blue and one yellow.

The last two items were a dagger made of silver and a pair of shining, metal manacles. Each item had an aura around it, the feeling of real magic, even a ward around them. They promised pain if one touched any of the items.

Wait. Since when can I see auras?

"Ah, a proper maiden bride has been chosen at last."

I spun at the voice, seeing an older Paxian man with penetrating grey-blue eyes, his hair a mixture of red, brown, and silver. He wore his wealth in plain sight, dressed in fine robes of dark blue accented with real gold trim and rings on his scarred fingers. The golden sunburst pendant hung from his neck had been encrusted with diamonds.

He came toward me, closing the distance with a predator's smile, and I was unable to move.

Where are my guardians?

His skin was puffier, looser, and more mottled than younger men I'd met, especially beneath the eyes, under the jaw, and at the neck. He was not handsome and young anymore, but he gave me the impression of a Davrin entering their prime age of magical power.

He knew people feared him, and I would have run under any circumstances but could not spot a door leading from this room. How was it possible there was only the window?

With a long fall to the ground.

With the warning I saw in his aura, I considered the option.

"Musanlo bless you, Lurili Derfoli."

His hands closed around my curved waist, and we both looked down at the low-cut, white dress and its tight, crisscross laces which compressed my ribs and pushed my breasts up and together. They were *pale* breasts, and large, with more cleavage than I'd ever seen.

His left hand slid up from my waist to gently squeeze and caress one, and I studied the scars on his fingers. Not caused by any blade that I could tell, but by burns or a caustic liquid.

He reached for my head, pulling a lock of red hair forward and touching it to his lips.

Pale skin. Red hair.

"Are you ready to be purified and anointed before God, Lurili?"

Oh, shit.

"I-I am, Archbishop Keros," I heard myself say, though my lips did not move. "Bless me."

"I shall. Obey, and you will be rewarded with the finest match to be made."

Keros lit the incense first, offering a pinch of the mushroom to place beneath my tongue. Then he guided me to lie back on a cushioned bench, also covered in a white sheet, with my legs parted on their side.

Without hesitation, the mage tugged at the laces of my bodice, loosening them until I could take a full breath, and heavy breasts spilled out into view. The nipples were the lightest pink of spring blossoms, much like Tamuril's.

"Most precious to think these have never been seen beneath Musanlo's Eye," the priest chuckled, then frowned as his face darkened from blood rushing to his head.

He squeezed one breast painfully, and I squeaked. "These are for feeding newborn sons, Lurili. Say it, my dear."

He was playing with the nipple, making it harden, and I felt a trickle of magic through his fingers which made it pleasurable.

"Only for feeding sons," he repeated.

I stared up at him, any reply caught sideways as the sensation increased and spread through my chest.

"Hm. Let us see what we have this day."

I had no voice when he left my breasts exposed and turned away, reaching for the hem of my white gown. The priest dragged it slowly up my legs, his hands following each curve until the fabric was bunched up. There was so much material I could not see anything below my tits:

not his hands, not my legs, or my crotch.

I could feel his fingers parting my netherlips, however, and see his eyes drinking in the sight of my sex.

"The Hells' flames surround our moment of birth," he murmured, tugging on the curls of hair hard enough to cause more pain. "And isn't *this* the cursed reminder for any righteous man?"

His fingers knew where to press next, two of them squeezing my clit between them and making my body jerk. Again, there was that trickle of magic from him.

"Your sin is looking flushed, my dear. Are you not pure in thought right now? Have we found your secret to offer up for purification?"

Trembling and gasping, I was not sure if this was agony or if I wanted more. I'd heard something like this before. I'd *felt* it.

Have we found your secret to offer up to Braqth's Threshold...?

I couldn't move or speak, but I saw her.

Lelinahdara. The Confessor.

"Open wider," said Keros. "Show me your purity, even as you leak the devil's spit."

Purity?

What in the Abyss was he talking about?

"Open *wider!*"

His bellow hurt my ears, and his arms surged to clutch me, using unnecessary excess force to spread my lax, unresisting legs as far as they could go. His finger nudged and dug around my hole some more, searching for something.

"Ah, there. You are *not* spoiled, Musanlo be praised. You will be made worthy yet, Lurili."

He retrieved the blue and yellow glass vials, set the blue one down, and unstoppered the yellow one, using his fingers to hold my netherlips apart. He dripped something viscous directly on my clit, chilly at first but then began to tingle and warm. I wanted to touch myself.

"Is it pleasant, my dear?" He gently inserted his first finger into my hole, rubbing softly at the front side. "Well, is it? *Speak.*"

My jaw unlocked, and my tongue worked.

"Y-yes, h-holy Archbishop…"

He immediately opened the blue vial and added a second compound to the substance sticking to my nub like honey. The heat flared to become much, *much* worse. Not in the way of longing like the moment before, but in the way of irreversible damage to tender flesh.

Torture.

I smelled something, and I screamed. He still had his finger inside me, grimacing as the substances burned him, too.

That explained the scars.

"You will return in a fortnight, Lurili," he commanded over my wailing. "Another blessed anointment or two, and you will remain free of temptation for the whole of your life, and untouched by the unworthy. You will be a *pure* and loyal wife, true to your husband when God finds him for you."

His erection pressed against my leg, and cruel eyes followed mine to the last objects on the altar he hadn't touched: the silver dagger and the manacles. His lips drew back with amusement.

"Have faith, Lurili," he said. "Trust in God, and we shall not need to use those tools for the possessed. Musanlo's light shall protect you and keep the shadows away."

"Sirana? Sirana."

One hand on my shoulder, shaking me gently. Another pressed between my breasts, above my heart, cupping a small, hard stone.

My head hurt.

"Sirana, wake up."

Mourn's voice.

Or rather, how he sounded as Roewn.

I opened my eyes belowground, drawing in a deep, cool breath and grateful for the dark. My bodyguard was in his Noiri form and released the saphgar pendant he'd been holding. My breasts were out but not white or gigantic, and my spiders crawled protectively over them. My crotch was modestly sore but, thankfully, not *burning*. Not scarring away all ability to feel pleasure.

"A d-dream?" I asked.

"Yes. You seemed in pain."

"*Ungh*... Thanks for waking me."

"You're welcome." He looked at our door to the halls of Reprisal and back. "I also sense some tension and activity out there, beginning about the time you grew distressed. I want to check it out. Is that alright?"

I frowned. "I could come with you."

"First, wash up and dress." He indicated the bucket of water and supplies. "Get started. If I am not back by then, feel free to come out."

Somehow, I felt better when he released the wards and opened the door. The last sense of being trapped somewhere with no doors had been broken with that motion. Still, as Roewn stepped out and closed the door behind him, I thought I heard another man in distress.

Angry. *In pain.*

Ignoring the wash bucket, I headed to the door tugging on the handle to crack it open. I listened. Their voices carried well. Some were leaving as Roewn approached.

"Is there a breach?"

"No, Roewn, everything's secure. Sorry to disturb."

"Is Derfoli alright?"

My stomach iced over. *Derfoli?*

A slight hesitation.

Then, "He dreamed of his sister. Said it was so real, but twisted, like a sorcerer had cursed his memories to make them worse. Um, but he's gone to talk about it. He'll be alright."

Shit.

"Ah-ha. I'm sorry to hear it. Is there anything I can do?"

The man chuffed a laugh. "Sounds like you have plenty to do, messenger. But Wolf's calling a huddle in half an hour if you want to be there. Shouldn't take too long."

"With or without my charge?"

"First one's without, but once we've all been briefed, she'll be called in."

My fingertips had gone grey gripping the edge of the door. They ached when I let go.

"Hm. I've promised to stay with her, and honestly, I think she'd spy on us. She's quieter than any man when she wants to be."

The other man chuckled. "Alright. We'll come get you, then."

"Thanks. We'll be ready."

I left the door open a crack as I walked away to begin washing. Mourn noted when he walked in that I had just begun. He closed the door and reset the sound ward before speaking.

"Heard it all, I presume?"

"Yeah. You don't have to repeat it." I scrubbed my skin meticulously as my spiders climbed into my hair to escape. I felt the vile, clinging filth of the man in the dream. "That was me. The 'sorcerer' who cursed his memories about his sister. Lurili Derfoli, right?"

This struck him to pause. "Hm. I should have asked if anyone was sleeping nearby."

"And tip our hand of my weakness?" I said with irony.

"This does not sound weak to me but rather growing stronger. What I recall of Derfoli's sister was that she met Archbishop Keros before he used her as a political bride against her father's wishes."

"She met him more than once, from what I saw," I murmured. "And he deformed her so she would never feel pleasure between her legs."

"Hm. That is correct." Mourn tilted his head. "Would you be willing to describe what you can while this is fresh in your mind? I would like to know what you saw. All the details, large and small."

A glum thought, but I shrugged. "That is our agreement, is it not? Once I do, is there anything you could teach me in exchange, so I'll not rip out painful secrets like this and feel ill doing it? I want them to help Jael, not burn me as a demon-witch tormenting them in their sleep."

Mourn thought this over. "I have some ideas from watching and learning your aura, especially now. Soon, you will have to practice forming a mindlink on purpose, when you're calm and awake, so you may learn how to close such a connection while you sleep. But we can work together toward that."

Together.

I sighed, running over my skin a second time to make sure I was clean, and began to dress. I wished to be fully covered before I described the dream, and whenever Brian Wolf sent for us, I wanted to be ready to leave for Manalar when necessary.

If Keros finds Jael and lays a hand on her...

"Alright," I said after a long exhale to quell the fire in my gut. "I'm ready."

Roewn listened quietly through most of the dream, occasionally lifting a finger where I'd pause as he asked for a clarification or expansion on some detail. His face remained placid and gave me few tells of his own thoughts. If he'd had his tail, I'd have at least been able to tell when he was agitated by the description.

We sat in silence after I'd finished, and I'd grown quite thirsty. Brian Wolf had had the foresight to bring the boiled water to the room to cool the rest of the way, but I'd finished it all. I would need more soon.

"That is..." Mourn began at last, "impressively accurate for the Archbishop's living quarters."

I smirked. "You've seen them."

"Of course. It's useful to see what each man in the position has changed and what he's kept the same."

"Along with the satisfaction of knowing you can still get inside."

He bared his teeth in a feral smile. "That, too. Though I have never brought another with me before, let alone a team."

"What about the fact I saw no door?"

"There are two. One to the hall, another to a passage behind the walls which is harder to see. They're made to look like wall panels on purpose."

"Ah." I touched my lower lip in thought. "A question, then. If this was the *brother* Derfoli's 'memories,' how was the dream of the sister and Archbishop?"

He took in a long draw of air, expanding his chest before letting it out on a sigh. "Lurili Derfoli… poisoned herself a few years into her marriage. She wrote of her experience with the Archbishop. She was one of the few women whose father allowed her to learn. She sent it to her closest brother in secret, knowing he would believe her. Fortunately, she chose her messenger well. It was not intercepted."

"I see. And her brother is the one I just…" I waved my hand. "Whose dreams I invaded, and made worse?"

Mourn nodded without judgment. "Gergel Derfoli. He received her letter but, by then, she was already dead. He is the second-born son rather than the heir and left his family's lands to come to Augran, where Reprisal found him. He privately renounced the church but simply vanished rather than put his parents and brother in danger of interrogation if he caused the stir that he wanted.

"His is the most common type of origin for the men here, unfortunately. Most have family, community, or land they wish to protect with their own anonymity, which means the stories aren't shared widely and only further insulates the mage-priests from retribution or consequence of their actions."

"Hm. Her letter must have been detailed for him to dream it clear enough that you recognized it."

"For Gergel, it is excruciating detail. I'm not sure if he's destroyed the letter, yet. While it's valuable evidence of the theocracy's hypocrisy and brutality, it has no bearing on Manalar's civil affairs while the Bishops remain in power.

"It's been a persuasive piece for recruitment of other members of Reprisal in the last few years, but it would also help Gergel's heart if he were able to destroy it and stop rereading it. No one will burn it but him, however. It is kept here in trust until that day."

I forced a grim smile. "And if Gavin's task is successful, perhaps that day will be sooner."

Mourn's Human smile was less grim and quite genuine. "A day many more like him have been waiting for."

"Will Reprisal know about that part of the goal?"

"Some, I'm sure. That depends on that 'huddle' coming up."

"Will we have to return to Yong-wen to retrieve him?"

"Krithannia will take care of that. We will meet them at a Guild safehouse closer to the shore in Alran. She will bring another team with her."

"Meanwhile," I said dryly, "you're stuck guarding, feeding, and fucking me."

"Heh. I might have sent and received some messages while you slept."

I lifted my eyebrows. "Oh? Nothing about Jael."

"No, I would have told you first."

"Something to do with seeing Roewn 'leaving' before his replacement can show up?"

Mourn grinned with amusement. "A bit."

"How long will I be alone when you make that change?"

"Per our Bargain, not long, and in a secure place."

I looked around. "Not here?"

He shook his head. "Roewn will stay with you until we meet up with the Deathwalker."

"And who is it the 'Grandfather' Guild Dwarf is trying to reach who understands my 'culture' better?"

"The Dragon Spirit of Yong-wen."

I blinked. "Your birth form?"

"I've been glimpsed in the city for centuries. Some rumors are more accurate than others." He shrugged. "There's not been a compelling reason to step out of the shadow beyond Yong-wen. That is the only part of the city I helped to build. The rest precedes me and has its own history which I can influence only so much."

Interesting view.

"Hm. No compelling reason until now?"

"Correct."

"What reason?"

"Your sister is likely to be seen in *her* birth form when discovered."

I twisted my mouth. "When."

"When," he repeated without apology or satisfaction. "You've not given me any reason to think she was properly prepared or given the tools necessary to infiltrate without leaving a trace. Better to show her allies that there are more like her. Nothing explains our motivation better."

I narrowed my eyes. "How many would see your Davrin half when compared to me or her?"

"More than you think if you and I act like companions where others can observe."

An odd warmth entered my cheeks. "You mean like at Yong-wen? No one seemed to consider us related races."

He smiled. "Three centuries of embracing a living spirit will blind a people to the obvious details. The same can't be said for those who never received a clear look to begin with."

I smirked. "If Krithannia brings a team with her, I can hear the Yungians arguing with the Paxians and Noiri at once."

Mourn chuckled but then his expression sobered. "Before we move forward from the dream, I wanted to ask about the details which were new and somewhat twisted for Gergel."

A twinge of illness. *Just blurt it out.*

"I've been bound to altars so often before," I said tightly, "I have trouble explaining why I am alive. My... *familiarity* being in that position cut Gergel's mind even deeper, I am sure, and I regret that. I did not know where I was or what was happening."

Mourn nodded patiently. "You recognized what the incense and mushrooms were for, if not what the two vials contained."

"Yes. There is unsettling overlap with that church's clerics and the Sivaraus Priestesses."

"And the other three items which were not used but reminded you of Chief Warrant Bictrius. The golden goblet, the silver dagger, and the shining manacles."

I frowned. "Keros said they were only for the 'possessed,' not those with 'faith.'"

"But all of them, each item, had an aura you could see."

"I don't understand that part," I said. "I assumed it leaked in from our conversation."

Mourn's expression disagreed, but gently. "Lurili was mageborn but untrained. It was why she was chosen to be given to the Temple. She could see auras of magical items but kept it secret for years for fear of being named 'witch.' Those details, and her fears, *were* in the letter. I have read it."

"Oh," I replied. "Then what about those items?"

"Well. What would a goblet be used for, pertaining to an altar?"

"To catch fluid," I replied confidently. "Most often blood. The silver dagger would be used to draw that blood, and the manacles to keep the sacrifice from escaping."

"Hm. You *are* familiar. I'm sorry."

I shrugged and said with a sneer, "Blessed by Braqth, as my sister used to say."

Mourn tilted his head at the tone. "Sister?"

Tension swept through my back.

"Not the Red Sisters," I clarified. "My Matron's firstborn daughter. She wanted to join the Priesthood and practiced early upon her siblings."

He frowned. "And your Matron did not stop that?"

I flinched when the shout filled my head.

No, she didn't! She could have stopped it but did nothing!

But I bit the inside of my cheek, holding that snarl of resentment inside. Those last times I'd seen my mother made me wonder, for the first time, *why*.

What had been going on when I was too young to understand?

First, my Mother had been pregnant at the Worship Ball with her new heir. She'd said in an odd way to be glad the Sisterhood had accepted me. Later, after I'd executed Kaltra for poisoning her, my former Matron had concern enough for that over-drugged serving bua to stay with him, and for a new cait she'd adopted.

Natia.

Gaelan's daughter, as I learned later.

Why?!

The last time had been when Wilsira had arrived with me, unannounced, and I'd witnessed that whispered, Court-level cunning in my Matron at last while she'd been nursing her newest Daughter from her own breast, and rudely in front of the Conceiver. That child was not Consort-bred like Jilrina or Kaltra but born like me.

What was her name? Vekika?

"I apologize, Sirana." Mourn's voice had softened. "That was ill-spoken of me. I know well how nothing is simple when family does you harm while you are young. You survived them and are still capable of change. That speaks much of strength, not weakness. I do understand."

I looked down with discomfort. "The would-be Priestess manipulated the whole House in every way to her advantage. She... must have exploited some vulnerability in my Matron, possibly before I was born, for it not to have ended before I..."

I hesitated. Mourn leaned forward.

"Before what?" he asked. "What action did you take to save yourself?"

One corner of my mouth lifted then tightened. "Would you tell me the same? Trade like-for-like?"

The Dragonblood exhaled, his Human fingers interlaced with his elbows on his knees. "How about I tell you first, and you match the level of detail. So it's balanced."

Setting the border by volunteering was an interesting way to protect himself.

I should remember that.

"Agreed, To'vah-krav. We have a bargain."

He smiled and shifted to sit next to me on the bed. He did not take long to decide what to say.

"For more than a century, the bracers placed on my arms prevented me from harming any Noble of House Dar'Prohn, through action or inaction, and especially the Matron Miz'ri and her Sathoet son."

The Matron and...? Oh, yes.

Vuthra'tern had Matrons who were also the Priestesses. They had no Sisterhood, and Houses engaged each other without a Valsharess.

It must be chaos.

"I was forced to endure much for Miz'ri's amusement and ambition against the other Matrons. The bracers delivered crippling pain if I so much as thought of attacking her or attempted to ignore a clear danger to her. Sometimes only acting to keep her safe eased the pain. I took to training as much as I could, staying with my squad and my blade master in the barracks, to be away from her and her children at the manor."

"Children?" I asked.

"Yes. She'd had three heirs before delivering her Sathoet, after which she was too scarred and could have no more."

"Ah. So this is the same in gaining the power of the Abyss."

"*Hmph.* Sometimes I could not tell the difference between the three not demonic on the outside and the one who was."

"You *do* understand," I murmured.

Gold eyes were tinged with distant sadness. "She summoned me regularly enough to dread it and be reminded she was my mistress. She would command me to hunt and kill on her behalf, enemies or innocents were the same to her. Or I would be called to perform some task or entertainment, and I could take no action to defend myself."

Oh, Goddess, you understand this, too.

My vision had gone blurry when I asked, "So what changed?"

He exhaled. "I had no tail when the bracers were fixed on me."

"No tail?"

"It remained short through the decades, stout and hard to bend, growing slowly. Only after I'd begun Dreaming like my Sire and experienced growth spurts did my tail become longer." He smirked. "*Much* longer. Oft times, it moved without conscious thought."

That made me chuckle. "Oh, yes. I've noticed."

His smirk softened to a smile then.

"So, what happened?"

"I began thinking of myself less as a tainted or 'impure' Elf like my cousin, and more as my Sire's son. I heard the Word for it in my sleep. *To'vah-krav*." He huffed a voiceless laugh. "It sounds ridiculous to me now, but the action I took to save myself was to *not* think of harming Miz'ri."

My eyes narrowed, and one brow arched. "What do you mean?"

"I mean there was a workaround to the spell holding me prisoner. My Dragon's tail was an… instinctive advantage I gained over time. As I did not have to think for it to respond to a threat, it was not beholden to the original enchantment."

Both my eyebrows lifted as Mourn turned his head and met my eyes with Roewn's blue ones.

"After this epiphany, I still needed to wait for the right time. When that came, I *didn't* think. We were alone when my tail strangled my Matron, snapping her neck like a chicken and breaking the compulsion against harming her blood."

I could see their terror in my mind.

The Dragon Son was loose.

"That was when House Dar'Prohn fell," he finished. "Completely."

That was when he was free.

Mourn watched me for a while, letting me imagine the rest before I swallowed.

"Wow," I responded finally. "My… um, my House was still standing when I tricked my sister into falling to her death."

Mourn smiled warmly at me. "That is alright. I would like to hear the story of how you found the workaround."

Oh. He knows.

So, I told him what I'd done to find my way out, and why. I described it in the same level of detail he'd told me.

To keep our balance.

Chapter 6

Brian Wolf's "huddle" went on for some time before we were "called in," but at least I got more boiled water from the mess hall before we needed to leave.

The strategy room was quite far from there and the sleeping quarters, and the occasional man with whom we crossed paths openly stared at me. I started giving each a wink and a lewd air-kiss like Jaunda's, and none dared to respond. They all looked away and minded their business.

I wasn't sure how many levels we crossed as they led us. Many half-levels had been constructed for reasons I didn't grasp unless they created hidden pockets and made the navigation intentionally difficult. If so, had the Davrin possibly learned that from the Dwarves or the other way around?

Seems like building underground would be quite difficult and unnecessary in sand dunes.

Perhaps we developed those advantages alone in the Deepearth.

No guards stood out front, but the door had a strong ward and needed our guide's permission to get through. Inside, the room was large enough to hold fifty men sitting, more if standing, though I counted only half that at present. I was admittedly relieved to see Gergel Derfoli was one of them.

"All mages," Mourn whispered in my ear in our native tongue.

I blinked. *All?*

This meant Reprisal's network must be at minimum two hundred-fifty men, but only if they'd summoned every mage they had in their compound for my concerns, which was doubtful. I was thankful Mourn had reminded me about suppressing my aura before we left the room. According to him, the aura of my unborn had been brightest immediately after my climax but had become less obvious as we rested.

"I doubt another mage currently in this compound is gifted enough to sense a new, non-Human aura passively or recognize it for what it is."

Currently? Passively?

These considerations put me on edge, for it implied there could be Human mages "gifted" enough to see it, whether Manalari Bishop or Ma'ab witch.

This is why I need a bodyguard.

"Welcome, Roewn, Jan," said Brian at the far side of the largest round table.

Mourn and I bowed, and I exhaled. "Sirana, actually."

Several men shook their heads like they tried to clear their ears.

"Call me Sirana," I repeated. "They called me *Janshi* in Yong-wen, where I first arrived. I was being cautious with the Dwarf at Alran's gate."

Several men nodded with understanding.

"*Janshi.*" Tak grinned a few chairs down from Brian, looking at his brothers. "That means 'fighting woman,' right?"

"Close," said a larger, Noiri man with dark eyes and a deep voice. "It means 'warrior' but implies one feminine or woman-like. There's a difference."

"How so, Kil?" Tak asked with a squint. "Sounds too similar to split horse hairs to me."

Kil shook his head firmly. "*Janshi.* Warrior of feminine essence. The difference is they do not assume a mortal. They know better."

"Huh. Well, they hit the duck's eye on that."

Good to confirm Reprisal made the effort to learn Yungian.

"They did, indeed," Brian said with a smile. "So, is it... Sirana *Thalluen?*"

Better. Maybe he'd practiced.

"It is." My heart pounded harder when I answered, though none of them seemed able to hear it. "This name would only mean anything to my sister. If a name I give you might spread among the Guild and our tasks, I would prefer it to be this one. If she overhears it somehow, she will come looking for me."

All men present agreed, including Mourn.

"Duly noted, Sirana." Brian kept his calm smile. "Bear in mind, given the trouble we tend to seek and the importance of what we have to protect, we don't shout and spread each other's names unless they're code."

"Certainly. Understood." I peered around the table. "So, what have you all been discussing and where do we begin?"

"Maps," he replied. "We'll study maps of Manalar and the sur-rounding area together."

My face brightened.

"We're also covering the basic factions, what we know about them and their leaders. The Templars, the Witch Hunters, the various temple ranks leading up to the Bishops. A lot of them are mages, too, but we've got ways of countering their tools and skills."

Brian waved me and Roewn closer as the men made space for us on his left. "Then we'll weigh possible points of entry. We don't know enough to decide now, but you should know our best options at the start."

I approached, scanning the four, large scrolls unrolled on the round table. There were little piles of colorful markers waiting to be moved.

Welcomingly familiar.

"Then we're going over our skills, including magic. After that, we're packing our bags. I see you have one, but if there's anything we can replenish, speak up."

Wonderful.

"I will, and do begin," I said. "My ears are ready."

The room broke out in laughter.

Not long ago, I'd spent an entire afternoon and into the evening sparring with one Yungian man after another. They had tested my limits on Mourn's behalf while he had observed me. Today, I wasn't sure what time of the day or night it was, but I had stepped into an intense assessment of those men Mourn had chosen to help us retrieve Jael.

At the same time, I received concentrated tutoring on Manalar's lands, people, and politics. With the breathers, meals, and naps in between, it may have been an entire day and night together. It felt like I was back in the Cloister with Shyntre, learning about the Surface and trying to speak the commerce tongue before being shoved into the unknown.

Not far from the truth.

As it had been then, I drank in every bit of knowledge I could hold. Fortunately, my capacity had increased. I could understand and find the questions which I needed to ask for much longer segments at a time before feeling overwhelmed.

In addition to embracing my key motivation, I gave mental credit to Gavin for the endurance. Keeping up with his thirst for study was impossible once he'd been granted a place to sit undisturbed near shelves of script, but when there was nothing else to do on a long horse ride, it had been fun to try.

Later, Reprisal and I had packed our bags. I received new supplies and training to use my favored distraction and stealth tools such as a choke powder or a lethargy inducer. When the discussion on magical abilities had been revisited, I had to admit I could not disguise myself at will.

"Roewn was helping with that."

"Ah, very well."

"And my dream magic is a newer talent for me with less knowledge known about it. I cannot use it on demand. I was trained as a warrior and enforcer. Best think of me as *Janshi* first, and a new mage second."

Brian Wolf, who had asked to simply be called Wolf, nodded as he listened. "Good to know."

The way he frowned in thought afterward prepared me for the inevitable as, at the next break, he motioned me and Roewn to the side out of earshot of the others.

"Was that you?" he whispered. "Gergel was resting at the same time. Were you asleep at the time he woke screaming?"

I quelled the urge to evade. "I am sorry, Wolf. I did not mean to harm him. I think… I think my magic recognized the details about the Archbishop. I knew someone similar in my life, and this was…relevant to my mission. But I wished I had not caused such distress for the knowledge I gained."

The lead man stared at me with wider eyes. "How well can you control it amid a group of resting mages? And how close must we be to risk something like this?"

Shit. I could not deny those were important questions.

Roewn spoke up. "This is why Grandfather Baradum is calling in that extra help you need. He determined this talent is not 'magic' exactly, but a 'second sight' which is much rarer yet seems to mimic magic."

"Second sight?" Wolf repeated with concern. "How rare are we speaking?"

"Rare enough that Grandfather Baradum has only seen two others in four hundred years," Mourn replied, though I wasn't sure how truthful that was. "That's why she can't cast spells or place wards, but she can break wards and use magical tools with ease. He assured me there are ways to shield sleeping minds, and that this other bodyguard knows how."

"Huh." Wolf's mouth tightened. "And if we don't get that extra help, we might be able to improvise with thought-blocking spells, but that would be more draining than we can really afford."

"You will get the extra help," the other man insisted.

"Alright. I'll hope for the best." Next, Wolf indicated my belt. "What about your dagger? It seems to have an aura when it's in my periphery. Is it magical?"

If Wolf could see its true form, he wouldn't have asked like that.

I maintained my calm. "Impressive. We've been trying to mask it."

He bowed his head once at the compliment.

"Um, it *is* magical," I confirmed. "It enhances my aim and can puncture certain kinds of armor. It also drains the will to fight."

"Sounds nice. What kinds of armor does it puncture?"

All of them.

I smiled. "The Ma'ab scout was wearing a metal chest plate when I stabbed him. It went through his heart. I haven't tried something tougher."

Dark brown eyebrows shot up.

"It's best if no one touches this dagger but her," Roewn said seriously with his arms crossed. "It is attuned to her, to her race especially. There will be a backlash if someone tries to take it from her."

"Noted." Wolf met my eyes. "You don't have to worry about anyone in Reprisal trying to take your equipment, Sirana. But if a hostile tries, and something weird happens, it's good to have that idea prepared among my men. May I tell them what you just told me? We're good at keeping our mouths shut about special tools."

A trickle of dread passed through me at the idea of *intentionally* spreading the word about Soul Drinker to more Humans. I had insisted I bring it on this mission, but how much worse could it be if one of my allies grabbed hold of it, thinking only to help me?

"Reprisal must do better than that, Wolf," I said. "This dagger is ancient and has a will of its own which tests its handler. I passed its trial, but it is one of the most difficult challenges I have ever endured. Had I failed, I would be dead."

Or worse.

Roewn and Wolf appeared similarly surprised but paying attention.

"To be safe from harm," I said, "no one must so much as graze the handle or the sheath. If I were to drop it and any of you were to pick it up, even with the honest intent to return it to me, that man would die or kill others. You *must* avoid the impulse to touch it at all costs, *and* you all must keep that secret. Allow an enemy to pick it up if it comes to that."

Wolf took his time absorbing that as Roewn watched him. "I am glad you have some care for even the shortest lives of my brothers, Davrin. I will be sure to make this aspect of the mission clear."

We stepped out of our private corner then, though I felt little relief with my confessions this time. The Prime would have said that was the worst exchange I could have made.

"How many flayers can rip secrets out of these commoners' heads if you tell them too many? You lose control of the situation, and the backlash gets traced back to you!"

Quite possible. Perhaps likely.

Cris-ri-phon would have no qualms about reading some "short-lived" minds to find me and the relic preserving his ancient Queen. Enough general awareness of the dagger, having spread, would get traced back to me. I could not control that yet would face the consequences.

Later, however, Elder Rausery had contradicted her.

"No matter how many Sisters we lose to our secrecy, and no matter if we would lose many more to protect our advantages, we will never have control of the entire situation, only our part in it. Imagining otherwise will stop you from acting. Think first, then act. Minimize the risk. Go from there."

I'd obtained a bodyguard to help me either avoid or confront the Zauyrian General as need be, and I had warned a similarly secretive group of men that "assisting" with the dagger was as bad as trying to steal it. That was my part in it, where I had control.

It was best the Humans knew how to prevent making a bad situation worse, but it was up to them to help to keep Soul Drinker in the shadows a little longer.

At least they have some practice.

MOURN, REPRISAL, AND I REMAINED UNDERGROUND FOR A THOROUGH, NEAR-exhaustive two days, with a break coming before we would receive the word from Talov.

We'd learned Gergel had been sleeping just one room down and across the hall from me, so I volunteered to rest farther and on a different floor from the men with whom I'd be infiltrating Manalar. They needed more and better rest before the mission than I did.

Mourn and I had been guessing the distance that might better protect others, but at least it worked. No dream incidents disrupted my next Reverie, which I'd chosen to take while most of the others were awake anyhow.

Sleeping nude after another wipe down, I awoke with randy thoughts, relaxed but with renewed desire between my legs. I wasn't sure whether any part of this occurred from psionic wandering or if it was me embracing my old habits from the Cloister.

Regardless, when I opened my eyes, Mourn had shifted to his birth form, leisurely nuzzling the line between my mound fuzz and closed thighs. He'd set rough hands lightly upon each hip, and his eyes were closed, enjoying the texture and scents while refraining from having a taste. No thick, tingling glaze had been smeared along my netherlips.

Not yet, but they tingled plenty on their own.

"*Fuck*," I whispered with hoarse surprise, spreading my legs to give him access. "*Yes*... Lick me."

His hands, wide and hot, skimmed down my outer thighs then ran up the inside before pushing them wide enough to make room for him. His nose fixated on the scent of my skin as his tongue flicked out to sample the soft spots on my inner thighs. His mouth moved between my thighs without crossing their junction, making me gasp and squirm.

I waited anxiously for him to reach my center, for longer than I was used to. My sex throbbed so much, with no assistance from Dragon spit, that I undulated my hips, aiming my cunt to collide with his flexible tongue.

He seized my hips to hold me still.

"Careful," he murmured. "I could nip you by accident."

Damn tease.

His nose and tongue kept roaming around and around my slit without hitting it. The closest he came to my true want was gliding his tongue along the crease between my thigh and puffy, outer lips. Then he'd whiffle at my furry patch, blowing hot air on my aching bead.

"Oh, Goddess, do *not* tease me longer! Lick me!"

He chortled at my sounding less the commanding Red Sister and more like a frustrated and horny young Noble.

"So impatient," he chided before slapping my clit three times with the tip of his tongue, making me shriek.

"Oh, fuck, yes!"

Then his tongue slid down to my sex, where he pushed it inside just enough to run it around the rim like a soft, dexterous finger, but better.

I cried out in delight. "Oh! More of that, yes! My ass, too, it's clean."

"In time, Baenar."

"This century, To'vah-krav."

He snickered.

Mourn paid lavish, marvelous attention to my whole slit, until every nerve and bit of skin was warm, and my sensitivity had risen to a level I'd rarely hit. I was heaving, trembling, and writhing; my gut tightened up as I grew achingly close to climax.

"Close," I panted. "Gonna…*ai!*"

He stiffened the arched base of his tongue against my mound and the nub peeking out lower down, his sharp teeth hovering above my soft belly. Then, *finally*, I felt the tip squirm its way down my oozing cleft and burrow between my ass cheeks.

"Hahhh, *yeh!*"

He must have seen my toes curling because he pushed the tip into my netherhole, rimming it gloriously while the rest of his tongue pressed flush against my sex. I squealed happily and peaked with an enveloping release, both holes rippling and clutching at that lavender tongue as I rode my clit against that spongey ridge.

"Fucking goddess!"

I blew out in harsh breaths, staring at the ceiling without recognizing any sight of stone, and eventually came back down to the bed.

"Good?"

"Hah! You jest."

"Mm. Perhaps."

I didn't know how he managed to sound so innocent when he shifted back enough for me to see his hand gripped on his raging cock. My response, however, was quick and wordless. I rolled over and onto all fours with knees wide set, arching my back to present his own source of relief.

Mourn had no quip then, only a soft groan before I felt him squeeze one buttock and cave to his need.

Shifting close behind me, his knees inside mine, Mourn leaned over my back with his thick, scorching spear rubbing between my thighs. It became slick wallowing in my well-prepared cleft, and my sex and pucker clenched with anticipation. For an instant, I didn't care which hole he chose.

The Dragonblood planted his left fist on the mattress next to me while using his right hand to aim, seeking my naturally slippery hole. The pointed tip soon squeezed between my netherlips and into my cunt.

We groaned in relief.

He pushed firmly with his hips, sinking in deep without resistance and spreading me wide. As his prick got fully seated, that delightful undercurve wedged in behind the rest to fill me, scraping against the swollen spot behind my bladder.

Ohhhh!

I climaxed again, abrupt and with little warning. My wet cunt squeezed and milked him, and he growled. Suddenly, his tail wrapped around our left thighs, tying them together, with the end trailing up my inner thigh. I flinched in surprise when his teeth champed the braid at my nape, as if assuring top-to-bottom that I couldn't break away as I came down from orgasm.

As if I might try?

His first thrusts were deep and hard, hungry. I grunted, bracing to keep from collapsing as something far more base took over my bodyguard. The hybrid lunged into me full-length, his phallus slick and gooey enough to let me feel the unique blend of ridges and curves.

Oh, goddess…!

He rutted me without reservation, and I could even feel his rod swelling at the base. The bulge pressed at my entrance, spreading me wider each time, eager to be invited inside a female proven capable of embracing it. Swept up in the intoxication of his open lust, I did not to *want* to protest yet my heart tripped slightly. I couldn't decide what to think.

Mourn seemed to sense this and held himself in check, his strokes becoming shallower and less satisfying as the widest part got farther away from my cunt.

"N-no, don't draw back," I complained, clutching the sheets. His simply taking it away was enough to realize I wasn't afraid. "Push it…all in."

"Sirana—?"

"Yes!" I looked over my shoulder. "I can take it. Lock with me, Mourn."

The half-blood growled, shuddering as his reluctance quickly gave way. He snugged the budding knot against me, holding it there.

Fuck the web, it's hot!

"Certain?" he asked, barely holding himself back.

"You want it, too!" I hissed, pressing my ass back against him to feel myself stretch near to the limit, prepared to engulf him. "Give it to me. We're ready."

His next thrust forward added that extra power to nudge the bulb past the point of no return. We cried out at the intensity of it, but then Mourn roared as if to test the strength of his own sound muting ward. His aura pulsed then surged as the knot expanded further inside me, his cock pumping that sizzling cum where it couldn't leak out.

I squealed and bucked while Mourn held me tight around my waist with one arm, his tail constricting around my left thigh as he peaked. His other arm braced us up on the mattress though his claws tore the blanket.

Ahhh, yesss…!

My vision blurred, yet I glimpsed my pendant swinging below me, glowing brightly blue and casting its own light upon the dark walls. My body quivered uncontrollably in Mourn's hold, my mouth hanging open as my cunt strained to contain him and all the spunk he would give me.

Z'ar Kiabil…!

I blinked, seeing only blue light and shadows.

Persvek Kiabil…z'ar Kiabil…

Two voices speaking a language I didn't know. Neither of them was mine, though I snatched at the vaguest understanding which soared between them.

Unknown before. With us now.

New companion. Not consuming.

Sustaining.

I clutched the bed with my hands, desperate to stay grounded when a third voice rumbled through our minds. Its presence was massive but had a greater sense of distance like a memory.

"Don't dismiss your mother's race. Their blood still calls to you. Their magic can help you grow."

The Dragon's son had finished spurting inside me. Even with the hybrid's hold unchanged and his knot hard and locked in tight, he was trying to catch his breath. I felt a hum all around us and heard a murmur of thought while my necklace shined.

I tried to answer.

I *needed* to be present.

~M…Morixxyleth?~

His heartbeat had been slowing but arose again, pounding stronger against my back. He'd *heard* me. I was sure.

Carefully, Mourn reached to touch the glowing blue stone to his palm then closed his hand around it, forming a fist. The hum became less voluble while the murmuring grew clearer.

Sirana. We accept your mindlink.

~We?~

Did you intend it? he asked.

~N-no.~

True. We think you...opened to us. You were listening.

~Who is 'us?'~

Me, my magic, my Hoard...my Dreams, and those who saw them before me.

A bizarre image came to me, one that each of those concepts had been responsible for filling my cunt so full it ached. Stuffed in, one after another, I must brace myself and focus on them all at once. I needed to stay "open" and experience every moment lest I become afraid and tear myself free, damaging us both in the process.

I heard a soft, rueful laugh in response, something which sounded like Morixxyleth but may have been his Hoard.

Good instincts, Baenar.

I dared not blink as I listened. ~Do we still have a Bargain?~

Of course. Why wouldn't we?

~You called me 'companion.' Kiabil?~

The Dragonchild's body shifted his weight to his knees. Holding on to my saphgar pendant, he reached with the other hand to gently caress my breasts and belly in long, soothing strokes. He was doing something to my aura, I was certain, but it felt good to relax. The hum grew quieter along with all but one murmur in my head. I sighed.

Yes. You are my Kiabil, even if for a short time.

~And what is a Kiabil to a To'vah blood?~

They are the chosen companion helping our focus and self-discovery. I told you of this benefit to me before you agreed to our Bargain, which itself protects you. It makes certain we can walk away when this bond is no longer needed.

A tiny surge of panic brought to memory the Ley Tower and my agreement with Gavin. Morixxyleth seemed to "see" this and continued soothing my breasts and caressing my skin.

Or perhaps we will renegotiate? he suggested, surprised but curiously interested. *This is not out of the question.*

My heart pounded to hear it. ~A-Alright. That's... good, I guess.~

I wasn't certain how long we'd been coupled together, but his bulge was shrinking. My sore cunt might soon be able to release him without much discomfort for either of us. As for the rest of this successful link, I dared not bite off more than I could chew.

I stopped thinking of the future.

I will pull out slowly, he thought. *As I do, create an image of something closing as intended to afford privacy. A door or a curtain. I will let it close.*

That wasn't too hard, as I discovered, feeling his presence recede along with his sensitive prick. We grunted aloud, spilling fluids down my thighs and onto the bed, and reached for the rags.

I cleaned up in a daze.

A sustained mental conversation while *conscious* was a trick I'd not done willingly since my time with Elder D'Shea and Reishel, yet I recognized when the mindlink had been released without harm. I was alone in my head.

Just me and a headache.

"Nap, if you can," Mourn suggested aloud, his voice a little hoarse. He seemed thoroughly drained. "We should receive word from Talov within four hours if not earlier." He paused. "And thank you."

"My pleasure." I smiled. "If we can figure out how to talk like that at Manalar without having to drop our bottoms first, that would be quite an advantage."

He chuckled. "Agreed, if you are willing. We shall have more time traveling to sort it out. Rest while you can."

I took his advice and closed my eyes.

Chapter 7

"Keep in touch," Talov had said in Yong-wen, "an' we'll meet in Alran three days hence, 'less ya hear somethin' sooner."

I did not regret the time spent out of the Sun or the valuable information I'd been given about Manalar's lands and people. However, I didn't see how Mourn and I *could* have heard anything about Jael sooner unless Reprisal had already when we'd arrived.

Evidently Krithannia hadn't received urgent word, either, because at last Reprisal received a follow-up on their missives with Talov. Exactly three days from my last in Yong-wen, the Dwarf invited us to join him at Violdam Hall, an established Dwarven compound built closer to the Great Lake shore.

Wolf announced this personally outside our door. "Time to go. Grab your packs. We're gathering in the sub-level."

Our lead contact did not yet walk away but looked pointedly at Roewn, whose dark brows raised inquisitively. I found amusement in our similar eye color yet also some awe, for I'd never imagined meeting so many sentients who shared my shade of blue.

"The Grandfather confirmed they found who they were looking for," Wolf added. "You were right. So, are you heading out?"

"Will you be moving streetside or staying under?" my bodyguard asked as if he didn't know.

"Mostly staying under."

Roewn glanced at me. "I'll stay as added escort until you get to Violdam."

The man excused himself with a slight twinkle in his eye noting my smile. It made me wonder whether Reprisal had heard any of the sex in our warded room, or whether Mourn was right about our acting like companions in public?

Eh, of little concern regardless.

My Dragonblood mercenary needed to create opportunities to receive his payment, for me to receive *him*.

Better that he does this before events inevitably turn to survival.

He'd also suggested there would be other moments on the way there, both for sexual release and psionic practice. The knowledge affected both my head and my crotch when I thought about it.

For now, we'd reached the point where Mourn had collected the "teams" Krithannia and Talov had requested, and we were bringing them North with us. I admitted they were impressive, and I was pleased with his choice and grateful for the Guild's resources.

Our segment of Reprisal consisted of twenty-four mageborn Humans split into three squads, each with a leader, and Brian Wolf overseeing all three. I'd observed all the proof I needed that each had multiple years of training in espionage, combat, and practical magic like we used in Sivaraus both at Court for stealth and for battlefield offense and defense.

They also had Guild ranks I could wrap my hands around, though they were not at all formal about it in the time I'd spent with them. These men knew each other's names or code names but were not required to use rank when addressing each other. Even a superior like Brian Wolf had gone more than a day and two instructive sessions before telling me his Guild rank was a "Hand."

"On this mission, the Hand wields the Foci, the Flame, and the Aether."

I learned that each squad was made up of one leader, their "Focus," and a balance of a second rank called the Flame—those men who had mastered certain spells making them less reliant on magical tools—and the first rank, the Aether. These newest mages were more like me, learning their spells but well-trained in every tool at their disposal.

I had the sense these Guild ranks mattered more to those planning and providing the training and the missions than between the men themselves at this level. Although, they were no doubt useful as a shorthand to denote their relative years of experience.

Some of them, I realized, were quite young at less than two decades old, but they were intensely motivated to learn and gain their skill as quickly as possible to survive in this organization. I could relate to them well but also bonded to the experience and advanced tutelage in the squad leaders and to something more within the Hand Brian Wolf who directed them. Yet their Hand was not yet three decades old, and the Foci were close to Wolf in age.

Ten years or less separate an Aether from a Hand.

The speed at which Humans could learn and change as they aged made my head spin.

Meanwhile, moving a group of twenty-seven armed men all carrying travel packs through and out of the Turthend Center was an endeavor neither silent nor unseen, though my appearing similar to them removed the largest concerns.

To continue the surprising likeness to the Sisterhood, I learned the Guild had secure, dedicated tunnels they used to bypass the largest gathering spaces of Alran's underground markets and neighborhoods. In those passages, every set of eyes we met were proven friendly with Guild sign.

I'd been informed we wouldn't be walking the entire Northeast quadrant of Augran to the lakeshore.

"It'll take us less than an hour to walk to the Underrails unobserved," Wolf had said. "Then only another one and a half to reach Violdam Hall."

"The Underrails," I repeated.

"You'll love it!" Tak assured me with an enormous grin. "The Dwarves made pathways for the rolling carts used in the ancient mines.

An easy five hundred years ago, they started remaking them to move passengers instead. We can ride to the shore faster than a horse could gallop through the streets above."

Admittedly impressive.

What would the people of Augran have become without this grounded and industrious race building things which benefited so many without interference? Add to that, no doubt, the subtle encouragement of a city-loving Dragonchild.

More like Manalar, perhaps? Closed off, controlled by mages, hostile to strangers and exploiting their trade, accusing all others of doing the same… Hm.

Or more like Sivaraus.

I was willing to ride the rails for the time we'd keep for Jael, but I could tell *long* before we reached the platform that this would be torture on my ears. Suggesting I would "love" this mode of travel was an overstatement.

I grimaced and swiftly grew discomforted by the loud clunks, clanging, and squealing of metal wheels on axles as the huge contraption arrived. We watched it rumble by, turning around slowly upon a tight circle to face the opposite direction from which it had appeared.

After an awkward wait, about thirty people and Dwarves brought from the North of the city opened half-doors and emptied from the linked carts. Counting five carts total, each had a wide, flat platform atop four rolling wheels, and iron bars formed a cage with hanging handholds aplenty to keep bodies inside.

Wolf headed to the front of the cart chain, where a larger, fully enclosed compartment leaked glowing lights of yellow, green, and blue. Through a small window made into the door, I spotted two Dwarves inside even before one poked her head out to do business with the Guild Hand.

"Are they the controllers?" I asked Roewn, motioning toward them.

"They are."

"How do they make it move?"

My bodyguard smiled at me, warm and amused. "Magic."

"Of course."

"That is not to make it sound easy or inexpensive," he added. "It has taken three centuries to make it this smooth and reliable. There are times the Underrails are not rolling due to lack of components or the right gems. The maintenance is hard work, too. This day, fortunately, we may take advantage of their ingenuity."

"All aboard," Wolf commanded after turning from the controllers.

Huh bua…

I exhaled from nerves and Mourn noticed.

"You will not be the only one to cover your ears while riding," he murmured. "I will catch you if you lose your balance."

"Thanks."

I covered my ears for over an hour, stumbling only once on a jolting curve as the rails split their direction. Soon, we reached the place we next needed to be.

Talov opened his arms wide as he met us on the exit platform. "There ye are, lasschen! Ye made it!"

"Uh…"

I came forward with Roewn but hadn't worked out what gesture the Dwarf sought before he hugged me around my shoulders, the crisp rub of his grey beard and his laugh near my ear causing my spider guardians to skitter as high up in my cloak's hood as they could get.

"Welcome tah Violdam Hall!"

Most of Reprisal either chuckled or smiled at the display.

Talov blinked his pale green eyes at them like he just noticed before winking. "Oh aye, an' our boys hand-picked! Ready fer tumble an' rumble?"

"Anytime, anywhere, Grandfather," Wolf said, extending his black-gloved hand to shake with the Dwarf. It vanished within the broad, gnarled grip, and Talov gave their hold an extra clap with his other hand.

"Welcome, welcome. Glad ye all are here. We need some real doers tah step up right now."

"Why each of us joined, Grand Da," Tak said as he clasped hands with Talov and bowed his head.

Surrounded by agreeable grunts and nods, the Dwarf clasped hands with each man. This took time but everyone did their part to keep Talov moving around the platform without his having to take more than a step to touch each man. I had time to scan our arrival deck, noting it empty of other passengers waiting to leave. Perhaps it was a private one.

"An' good work, Roewn," Talov finished up, "guidin' an' keepin' her safe in the city. I got a bonus waitin' fer yer trouble."

"My pleasure, Grandfather Baradum, and thank you." Mourn gave him a handshake like the other men and winked at me. "She's of a fascinating race. It was time well spent."

The light murmur behind him explained why he said it that way as Roewn turned to me with an expression a bit like Bohai's admiration the morning after at the Shi manor. He held out his Human hands for me to take, though I wasn't sure why.

When I accepted the dual grip, however, he bowed his forehead over them and removed my illusion to reveal my true form.

"The time has come I must bid farewell," Roewn said more seriously. "I'm late to my next rendezvous. Guild's Fortune to you, Sirana, and I hold every hope that you and Reprisal will find your sister and get her to safety."

This felt so weird. I almost believed he was really leaving before the mission started.

On impulse, I stood on my tiptoes and planted a kiss on his mouth, which was quite soft in this Human form. His eyes flew wide though he didn't pull away as Reprisal hooted and laughed. When I broke our contact, a smirk on my face, his pale cheeks were flushed pink.

"My Queen's gratitude for your service, Roewn," I said with a straight face. "I'm glad we met. Guild's Fortune on your next long trek."

Mourn opted not to speak further but kissed the back of my hand, bowing to Talov before stepping toward the rear exit.

I turned around to watch him leave but gasped softly when I spotted Gavin standing with four Yungian men. Roewn bowed his head to them, and they returned the gesture. Three were agemates to Reprisal and grinning much the same after witnessing that kiss.

I recognized one Yungian for certain. *Deshi.*

Had he and Gavin spoken much of death magic yet?

Wait, will he go to Manalar? The bua stands out among Paxians as much as I do.

The Yungians noticed my attention. All four of them straightened their shoulders and spines, bowing with hands at their sides in that familiar way.

"*Lantiu-janshi*," said the eldest of them before switching to accented Trade. "We are here to serve your mission beside the Dragon Spirit and Walking Death."

"Deathwalker," Gavin muttered.

A smile spread over my face as I began to see the makings of a fourth squad to aid my Sister.

To reach the final planning room, we climbed a somewhat convo-luted sequence of stairs and levels which even I might have needed a second trip to memorize. The distance was not far, however, as we had begun in the subbasements of Violdam Hall and needed only to reach the surface.

Among the first to step in, I beheld a finer space than I'd seen yet, smelling of new parchment and well-aged furnishings surrounded by recently dusted wood and cloth. Polished metal trays and vessels had been spread on a long table, offering us a meal first.

Next to me, Talov chuckled where my eyes had fixed as hunger took all my attention. "There's water, too, lasschen. Dig in."

Thank Goddess.

"Everyone, serve yerself," the greybeard invited. "We'll eat as we talk."

Reprisal and I did so generously, for there were plenty of salty, cased meats, hard cheese, dense bread, and raw vegetables to go around. Heavy drapes had been closed before two windows but, judging from the light leaking through the bottom, we seemed to have arrived at the end-of-day.

While the Humans I'd traveled with seemed to know where to sit, Gavin and I had to be coaxed to Talov's left side where he sat at the end of the table. His chair had been placed on a slight platform to meet the table meant largely for Human height.

Without similar coaxing, the Yungians took those seats closest to the Grandfather's right side, ordered eldest to youngest the same as in Yong-wen. Apparently, the youngest was Deshi.

I couldn't help sniffing the air around my ally as he sat next to me. Gavin *smelled* like he'd been sitting in a Yungian library for a week.

"Did you sleep at all?" I whispered.

He gave me a look which conveyed his reluctance to answer at first. "Yes."

"How long?" I took a big bite of my roll of meat. "More than once?"

His gaunt shoulders shrugged his annoyance as he glanced at the Yungians listening intently for his answer. This time, he chose not to.

At the same time, quite a few of Reprisal were staring at *me* while I made casual chat with the grotesquely pale man who possibly hadn't brushed his hair until recently.

Krithannia's doing, I bet.

"I can tell yer surprised by th' Deathwalker, so I'm assumin' Sirana didn't explain," Talov said bluntly as the men reluctantly began to eat. His voice carried well in this room. "Have no worries, ye'll be briefed. We're waitin' on one more tah join us."

A round of nods.

"Plus, after hearin' this one's story," Talov tilted his head toward Gavin with a grin, "I figure we finish our meal before introductions."

I chuckled as many more blinked at the table, and started eating, my appetite as healthy as ever. Soon, I noticed Gavin was the only one with his hands in his lap.

"Want any?" I asked, nudging my plate toward him.

He narrowed eerie, ice blue-on-black eyes at my offering, though I couldn't tell if it was in revulsion or contemplation until he reached for a bite-sized cut of a purple sugar root. He placed it between dry lips, careful not to reveal his black teeth, and chewed with slow deliberation.

Reprisal watched the Deathwalker take that bite from my plate, but several, including Deshi, didn't look away until they were sure he'd swallowed the root. This coupled with my obvious ease around the "death spirit" helped more of them relax and finish their own meal. All the while, Talov's eyes were twinkling with humor as he sipped ale from his tankard. In the end, Wolf spoke first.

"Um, I need to ask, Grandfather. Do we have a necrotic mage of the Ma'ab in our midst?"

"*Visri cin metad sangue,*" Gavin replied.

Several men jerked back, either scraping their chair legs on the floor or causing them to tilt and clunk back down.

"What the fuck?" Tak blurted.

"A half-blood?" said Kil, low-voiced, as he frowned deeper at the death mage. "What do you mean you've 'lived' with both?"

"Ah." Gavin looked at the large man. "You understand Manalari. Good."

"This is the Manalari monk who taught me to speak Trade with this accent," I clarified. "This is Gavin."

"Gavin No Name?" Wolf repeated, trying to focus past his disbelief. "The one killed by Witch Hunters in Troshin Bend?"

The Deathwalker deigned to show surprise. "Correct."

"What do you mean 'correct?!'" Tak asked.

"She is correct," Gavin repeated. "I was killed at Troshin Bend. With my Ma'ab blood, I had prepared, and my body stood back up. But

I'm not a 'necrotic' mage of theirs. I am a Deathwalker."

The men became quite pale before my eyes.

"What in Hells is a Deathwalker?" asked another Guildsman, Seri, with his own mild Manalari accent.

When blue-on-black eyes turned his way, Seri shuddered.

"I am not of the Church or the Empire," Gavin said. "I am an outsider rejected by both."

The Yungians whispered amongst themselves, but they seemed pleased as if knowing the difference. He was their *Sho'shien*, after all.

"And how long ago were ye killed?" Talov asked as a prompt, wiping ale from his beard. He looked amused.

Surprisingly, Gavin turned to me for that answer.

"Uhm." I counted back quickly. "About a month ago."

My ally grunted, accepting. "A month. That life seems so long ago."

"Well, you were in the 'spirit world' for a while before you recovered your body."

Yungian eyes grew huge with reverent excitement, but several of Reprisal were rubbing their bearded faces and temples.

"How is one like this going to help with our mission?" Wolf asked harshly.

"I'm not," Gavin replied, quite ready to speak for himself right now, and Talov's eyes crinkled with his satisfied smile. "I have a different task to complete."

Each Yungian nodded as if they agreed. Interesting. Had they been informed of those details earlier?

"That he does, one which the Guild is gonna help him achieve," Talov added, pointing his finger. "An' you all are part of it, even if there's a bit o' sorting to be done."

I heard groans.

"Should have known the Davrin Elf and her plight was bait to nab more men than she needed," one brother said to another, who sighed and lifted his tankard.

"Aye." The Guild brothers tapped the cups together. "Bet me

which face we'll be selected to look at for weeks."

"Either one is an honor!" Deshi said, annoyed. His Trade was not too bad.

The brothers looked at him with cocked eyebrows. "Are you volunteering for the Deathwalker, *ging*?" one said.

"I will, Pax," Deshi pulled his shirt off one shoulder, showing them his winter rose and skull tattoo. "My calling. Same as you have, to help women find better. I seek the good death."

They chose not to argue. "Nice art, there."

"I agree," Talov said, drawing their eyes, "that both tasks are of critical importance tah the Guild. We need all who go tah help, but if a one o' you don't want to look at Gavin's face, which ain't *that* bad when ye've been around a few centuries, heh! Well, we might not be able to use ye."

"We're just changing the tracks, GrandDa," Tak said apologetically. "We'll adjust, but you must also agree this aspect to our mission could have been mentioned sooner."

"I might, but fer some reason," Talov looked at me, "Sirana didn't tell ye when she could."

"It would have broken your stride," I said, looking mostly at Wolf. "Your preparation was the smoothest I could have hoped for, and I knew this would be explained in time. I learned so much from you in the meantime by *not* tripping you up with a tale of someone you would not yet meet for days. I was in *your* den, I wanted to learn *your* ways."

The Hand thought this over then smirked as he pointed at me. "So you did not lie to me, but nor did you speak too much to tilt our favor."

I smiled. "Red Sisters are good at this. I understand Guild elites are similarly skilled."

Wolf's smirk turned to a smile. "Good joust."

"What's a joust?"

He chuckled. "An old, irrelevant game. Have no concern." Then he motioned toward Gavin. "Do you know what his 'task' is?"

"Of course. I was there when he arose to tell me what he needed to do."

"Her actions assured I *would* rise," Gavin corrected.

I grimaced playfully. "My actions were more good fortune than conscious decision."

"I do not care. That is what happened."

I looked at Wolf and blinked with a smile. "We have been allies for months."

"Yeah, you seem… familiar." Wolf glanced at Gavin and exhaled as his focus shifted to the greybeard. "Do we wait for the new bodyguard to show before we learn the other half of this mission?"

"Afraid so," Talov answered, interlacing his fingers with elbows on the table. "Need tah see some honest faces before we get into it."

"I see."

"In the meantime," I offered, "would you like to hear what happened at Troshin Bend with the Witch Hunters?" I winked at Gavin. "Now that the Deathwalker is here to correct me on the finer details, I can't escape with half-truths."

To my relief, most of the tension dissipated and more of them chuckled or leaned forward.

"Yes," said several, including Wolf, Tak, and Kil, with even more nodding. "We want to hear what really happened."

"Alright. So, we were traveling with mercenaries, two of them bent on sabotaging Manalar's defenses before the Ma'ab arrived."

"The Ma'ab scouts," Tak said.

"Correct. We were crossing the Midway and encountered this green-cloud storm…"

DESPITE MY JESTING, GAVIN DID NOT FORCE ME INTO ANY UNCOMFORTABLE truths concerning what I chose to share about the innkeeper Brom and his daughter with Mathias and Jacob. While I admitted stealing the soul dagger from the sorcerer because it once belonged to my people, I also mentioned he had admitted stealing it from somewhere else while allied with the Ma'ab. Nobody questioned that.

As for detailing the encounter with the Witch Hunters, Reprisal was enraptured with anything I would share to the point where they did not notice when I left something out, such as the night's violence being triggered by my sucking on Mathias's cock.

What had I been thinking, really?

I'd begun where the tale was familiar, when Bictrius and the rest rode into town and attempted to conscript the sorcerer. I explained they'd caught a glimpse of me that night which foiled Gavin's attempt to escape out the window.

"He tried to run, but they pursued him and would not let him escape," I said, looking to the Deathwalker next. "Do you care to describe what action you took to defend yourself?"

Gavin frowned at me but looked over his shoulder at his equipment. His pack and tools were set aside from the rest of ours, placed before we'd arrived. It included his spade.

"I used the only weapon I had," he said, pointing at it leaning against the wall. "My first blow was a lucky one. That stain on the left edge is from opening the throat of the closest Witch Hunter."

"What?" Tak said. "You cut his throat with that?"

"If he'd been a little closer," Gavin reflected seriously, "I might have decapitated him."

"Wow." Tak's laughter was joined by several others.

"It gets better," I snickered. "Tell them about the heart, Gavin."

"The heart?" Wolf repeated.

The Deathwalker exhaled. "A fresh heart from a warm body contains enough Vitas for a death-focus mage to use in a spell, a necessary component much like those you use as mages. In my case, the only option I had at the time was to cut it out and take a bite to consume it quickly."

"You 'ate' the Vitas?" someone asked like he'd heard the word before.

"Correct," my ally answered. "This is common among the Ma'ab and other death mages, although there are many ways to consume it for different uses."

"He chose the messiest and most terrifying," I sniggered, unable to stop for several moments recalling the awful memory. "He had the Hunters shouting in panic."

Several of Reprisal joined me as they imagined the scene, especially when Gavin confirmed without the tiniest smirk. "The Vitas gave me the power to use the corpse in my defense."

"Wait. You...you made a Witch Hunter corpse walk to attack other Witch Hunters?" Tak was warming to the Deathwalker in the fates of their mutual enemies.

And he isn't the only one.

"Correct."

Reprisal loved hearing about every moment of that fight.

"Now we get to the part where I am truly dead and have no recollection of what happened to my body," Gavin said, motioning to me. "But she does."

All eyes turned to me, and I continued the story to make Gavin the largest figure in it. I described collecting his body with the silver dagger plunged into it alongside Brom's reluctance to remove it.

"Given his and Amelda's... *whispering*," I said, choosing my angle with care, "I felt I needed another opinion, and had heard of a Dwarven witch nearby in the woods."

Several of Reprisal looked at Talov, who was unperturbed.

"A Dwarven witch?" Wolf prompted.

"By her own words," I said. "She was wise in the way of death while not being a death mage herself."

"Who was she?"

I was committed.

"Osgrid," I said, glancing at Talov. "Though I never learned her Clan name."

The greybeard smiled with immense warmth, hiding any other insight I might have had. "Aye. We know her. Brave lass stayin' tah keep an eye on the sorcerer all that time. Glad tah know she got out in time."

That was all he would give me. None of the men seemed to recognize the name though they made note.

"She did," I countered. "And I believe she also convinced the one Dwarf mercenary with us to give up his ill-fated alliance with the Ma'ab to hurt the Manalari. He broke away from us all by the end and vanished."

With a hint of caution, Talov tilted his head. "Did she now?"

"Wait, who was that?" Wolf interjected.

"Rithal Hobgaer?" I answered in a questioning tone and saw recognition. *Finally.*

"Oh, him." Wolf nodded. "Yeah, what happened to his Clan..." He swallowed. "Our unit includes it in our lessons to remind us that it's not just Paxian women getting the shaft under Witch Hunters."

Fascinating.

"Have you met Rithal?" I asked.

"Not personally, no, but he's caused enough noise in his years as the sole survivor to spread some stories through Augran." Wolf gazed at me. "But *you* met him recently?"

I glanced at Gavin. "We did. He was a good peacemaker between us and the Ma'ab."

That made several of the men laugh, and I couldn't blame them.

I smiled and continued, "Rithal withdrew from the conflict in our group after Gavin's death in Troshin Bend. He stayed with Osgrid, who advised me not to trust the sorcerer in matters concerning Gavin's body. When the greater conflict erupted when I'd removed the Witch Hunter's dagger and Gavin reclaimed his body, Rithal did not truly take sides. I'm not sure how far he made it after he left or if he is still alive."

"Huh." Wolf and the others looked at Talov, who shrugged.

"Been noted," said the elder Dwarf. "We're keepin' ears tah the stone."

With a nod of agreement, the Hand asked, "So, what happened once you removed the dagger from Gavin's heart?"

I continued the tale of my death mage's changes and of my impression of his gained wisdom and freedom from the chains of his old religion, which made him shift uncomfortably in his chair. The description of his revisiting where each Witch Hunter had been buried by the townspeople after that fiery night held Reprisal on the edge of horror and joy to learn more.

"You visited their graves," Tak urged. "Why?"

"Sometimes," Gavin admitted, "a new death in transition will see more clearly than they did when anchored deep in their life. I sought to guide them where I had gone if they would listen. If I did not try, their Vis would stay and degrade. If not consumed by something else, it would *become* something else."

"Haunting!" one Yungian cried.

"Hungry ghost," Deshi agreed.

"Possible," Gavin confirmed.

Many of Reprisal scoffed, and Tak spoke for them. "I bet they wouldn't listen to you, right? Given how they killed you first."

"On the contrary," said the Deathwalker. "All but the three mages listened. The mundane ones accepted my guidance and completed their transition. They shall be no further harm to the living."

I felt the ruffle of resentment and skepticism.

"And what about the mage bastards?" asked Seri.

Gavin's expression changed to an unsettling half-smile. "They proved an interesting challenge."

Once again, none of the Humans seemed to pick up on missing details which neither Gavin nor I chose to share. By the time we had finished the story with the dagger theft and the crows gathering outside the shed, after Gavin admitted sacrificing the Thetri Jacob for a "higher purpose," most of Reprisal were on the edge of their seats.

They *wanted* to know what Gavin's task was and how he needed their help.

"We'll get tah that once the last one arrives," Talov reminded us.

"Holy shit, what a story," Kil said.

"No fucking kidding," Tak agreed. "Nothing like we heard from the refugees."

"Goddamn."

Listening to them process this new information, I quelled an annoying twinge of worry that I wouldn't have enough interest remaining for Jael. I sat back, letting the fighter-mages bond how they needed to in such a short time.

Gavin seemed cautious about their acceptance of him and the growing enthusiasm to hear his purpose, but I wasn't. I could see the genuine kernel of fascination the young held for strength proven through trials, much as I'd seen in the *dorji-ka* in Yong-wen.

Alright, Mourn, they're warmed up. Whenever you want to show.

General chatter and conversation were flowing along with the water and ale when a bell sounded, and Talov touched a gem on a metal band wrapped around his wrist.

"Aye, excellent! He made it."

No jesting.

"C'mon in, Shadow."

Shadow? And what the fuck were you doing, Dragonchild?

When Mourn walked in with his hood down, he looked the same as when I'd first met him: those large-size Yungian pants, no shirt, a fully decked harness, metal bracers, and a dark cloak of notably different cut than Roewn's.

The Guild's response was like Gavin's introduction but with a sharper spike in action as the Yungians launched to their feet to bow, exclaiming "*Wen-yung!*" in unison. Reprisal got about halfway out of their chairs before bumping into each other and causing a wave of noise.

"This is Sirana's new bodyguard?" Wolf asked for them, one of several on his feet.

"I am," Mourn answered in his deeper, natural voice with an unplaceable accent. "I know her. I agreed to this some time ago." He bowed to me. "I apologize for holding us up."

"Oh, we were talking about Gavin's transition," I said, "though we haven't gotten to his mission."

"We will," the greybeard reassured us.

Mourn scanned the room and settled on his favored people across the river and bowed in greeting. "Groa, Peng-lok, Nianzu, and Deshi.

Thank you for joining this effort."

"Of course, *Wen-yung*," said Groa with a knowing crease to his eyes.

"You call, we answer," said the next eldest, Peng-lok, glancing at the younger two and confirming which man was Nianzu.

Mourn had named them in their seating order.

"Wait," Kil said with a frown. "You're that 'Dragon Spirit' I keep hearing about?"

The half-blood showed a hint of his teeth in a smile. "I am, among other titles or descriptions. I have been in Augran for a while."

"Augran," Wolf asked. "Not Yong-wen?"

"There, too."

Reprisal exchanged so many glances, it was difficult to read them.

"The…whole city?" one dared to ask. "You've always been here?"

Mourn's tail came back to life, as I saw something I could call affection in being asked that question in that way.

"Not always," he said honestly. "But I have worked with the Guild for a long time."

Tak shared more looks with his squad and tapped his fingers. "We've heard… rumors."

"I might be able to confirm or deny a few." Mourn indicated Gavin and me. "If you are ready to help keep Elves out of the hands of the Bishops and Ascended, and possibly force both aggressors to lose this war at once, before it truly gets started."

All eyes in the room brightened with interest. Several whispered, excited like the Yungians had been when first seeing Gavin.

"*Both* of them lose the war," Wolf said, his intense blue eyes unblinking as he gazed at the half-blood. "You have a way, Shadow?"

"No, I do not." Mourn tilted his horns toward Gavin. "But the Deathwalker does."

I heard a large handful of men swallow at once, and Wolf motioned for everyone to sit down while he did the same.

"We're ready to help," said the Hand of Reprisal. "In all ways necessary."

CHAPTER 8

ONCE MORE, GAVIN PULLED OUT THE BLACK SHARD CONTAINING JACOB THE Witch Hunter and placed it on the table for others to see. Their reaction was quite unlike Krithannia's calm, further convincing me of the many pairs of mage's eyes we had gathered together.

"What *is* that?" whispered a man named Hawk while Deshi next to him seemed frozen in his chair.

"Retribution from all who have suffered under the Church," Gavin said, keeping the tips of his long, pale fingers touching the obsidian soul trap. "I formed this from the Vis and Vitas of the captive Witch Hunter after I returned to my body. My simplest explanation for its intended purpose is to use it as a flint knife to sever the magical leash between Manalar's sacred pool, *Pisc'sagrad,* and the mages of their Temple, the Immersed of the Mount."

"You can do that?" Tak asked, his voice hushed.

Mourn chuckled, his tail swishing over the carpet behind me. "At great cost and instant destabilization of the entire region, yes. He can."

"But the Ma'ab destabilize the region already," Wolf said.

"Which is why now is the time to help the Deathwalker."

"So how do we help?"

"The pneuma flint must be thrown into the Temple waters."

"We're going to infiltrate and throw it in?"

"*No*," Gavin interjected. "I must do it."

"Are you kidding?" Wolf countered.

"I leave that frivolity to the rest of you."

The Hand huffed a dry laugh when Deshi spoke up. "Did you not receive this quest while in the spirit world, Sho'shien?"

Icy pupils turned to him. "Essentially."

"A vision?"

"Fairly described," the death mage granted. "Though it had to be earned. I asked how to redress the corruption of the dead and dying within both peoples of my blood. I was granted an answer and instruction on how to construct a catalyst."

"Granted by who?" Wolf asked, nearly a demand.

Gavin drew in a deep breath for the air to continue speaking. If anyone had been paying attention, it was his first in over five minutes.

"A grey maiden once worshipped in these lands," my Deathwalker began, and not only I could hear the habitual reverence begin to soften his tone, but the word "maiden" had ensnared Reprisal's attention.

"When was this, Sho'shien?" Deshi prompted, his eyes more boldly watching him than he ever had me.

Gavin shook his head. "A few thousands of years? Before the Church and the Ascended, for certain. In that time, she was honored for her care in guiding the dead, and for her neutrality among the living. Her Deathwalkers spoke of the fallacy of questing for power over the living through the avoidance or transition of death. There must be a balance with the living, always."

Mourn's tail flicked hearing one of his favorite words. "Like Musanlo or *Hia-Yo*, the Grey Maiden is an indirect presence of our world which some mortals can sense in however small a way."

Each Human looked at the Dragonblood. For an instant, they each looked so *young* to my eyes. I blinked and studied my empty plate before refilling my water cup.

"Gavin has become a Deathwalker only recently," Mourn continued, "but he has sensed the presence of the Grey Maiden since he was a child in a Paxian monastery."

"*Whoof*," Wolf breathed with a slight shake of his head. "Heresy."

"Precisely," Gavin replied dryly.

"Did the monks find out?"

"There were signs I could not hide."

Glancing at Gavin's coldly intense gaze, I thought it wise none of them asked more details of his childhood. There was, however, still Tak.

"Um," my first Human guide began. "You've said twice you are both Ma'ab and Manalari, which the... irony of your mission tastes really sweet to me, you know." Tak glanced at Jacob's shard with a smile. "May we know which side your mother came from?"

Gavin narrowed his eyes. "Why my mother?"

The Guildsman shrugged. "Because she had you. We all have mothers who spent a lot more time carrying us than our fathers, right?"

Interesting.

"Hm." My ally seemed oddly mollified by the approach. "My mother came from the Ma'ab people. It was through her I gained my magic."

Down the table, I heard some rustling and a few whispers mentioning, "*bet*" and "*you lose.*"

"Truly?" Tak's brown eyes opened farther. "Wait, that must mean …"

"That a Manalari man bedded a Ma'ab witch and had a child," Gavin completed for him, folding his hands over Jacob's shard.

"No way!"

"Hypocrites."

"Fuck, we knew *that.*"

During the chatter, I noticed Talov turn his head stiffly toward the wall with a baffled look on his face. Then he and Mourn shared a glance that was subtle enough, but I could hardly miss it from my vantage point.

I poked Mourn's thigh under the table, and signed, ★What is it?★ when he glanced down.

He didn't reply but took a deeper breath before nodding to the elder Dwarf as if in confirmation. Talov's lips moved within his beard as if he might be mouthing a curse, then he planted both hands on his chair and stood up. His height while standing on the platform was enough to top the heads of the men sitting down, and he effortlessly gathered everyone's attention.

Talov cleared his throat. "Well. Ah. It appears we are expecting one more. Apologies, I did not know if she would come."

She?

"Enter, please," the greybeard invited.

Mourn signed in his lap right before the door opened. ★Stand up,★

What?

Through a different wall panel, Krithannia walked in carrying a pack, and I was on my feet before I realized it. Gavin blocked my view as he got to his feet, and I leaned out farther.

Behind me, the room had gone silent.

"Hello, everyone," said the Naulor simply, bowing to the Dwarf. "Thank you for seeing me, Talov. I have some new information which will shake up our plans a bit."

I stared incredulously because the Guild Mistress wore no disguise. Krithannia presented herself to Reprisal and the Yungians as a tall, dark-haired, and pale-skinned Elf. The men were stunned. I believed they'd never seen this form before.

Talov, however, welcomed the hug she offered in greeting, and Mourn stepped forward to claim the next one from her. The unspoken signal of protection could not be stronger. Next, Krithannia smiled with brilliant charm to Gavin and bowed her head without touching him.

"A pleasure once again, from one scholar to another."

"Krithannia," Gavin replied, keeping his hands at his sides, and echoing her. "A pleasure."

That was interesting.

Then she looked at me, her smile turning warm. "Sirana. Wonderful to meet again, even under the circumstances."

What circumstances?!

Fortunately, my back was to most of the Guild. At a loss, I bowed. "Ah…"

When she embraced me, something about that prompted the other twenty-nine men to stand up. No doubt they read my surprise, but I accepted the hug to strengthen the implied history between the long-lived beings in this room.

But why was she here? There had never been any mention of Krithannia going to Manalar, yet she was wearing a *pack*. I had to assume something critical had changed. Still, I couldn't fathom why she wouldn't have taken one of her many aliases. She was the Elf staying in Augran with the Humans, after all.

Mourn was the only one of us who didn't look surprised at this turn. As usual.

I wager that's what took you so long.

So what was wrong? What changed?

Don't panic.

"Please, sit, everyone," she invited us, moving to stand next to Talov at the head of the table.

Behind me, the Guildsmen quietly sank back down as Gavin, Mourn, and I took our seats.

"So many surprises for you all," the Naulor said with an odd grace and chagrin. "Again, I apologize for barging in like this. My name is Krithannia, and I have assisted the Clans and rare travelers like Shadow, Gavin, and Sirana for many years. As you can see, I am also a rare traveler."

Tak opened his mouth then bit his lip on what he was going to say.

"Yes, Tak?" she asked.

He blinked that she knew his name and swallowed. "Well… are there brown Elves, too? Since there are clearly…um, pale and dark."

Krithannia laughed. "If there are, I have not glimpsed any in all these years."

"Tak," Wolf groaned, rubbing his eyes.

"It's alright, Wolf," the Naulor reassured him. "I did break in on your briefing. I have new information on part of your mission. It is frankly necessary that I join your teams at this point."

"We're listenin', luv," Talov said soberly.

The Naulor bowed to him, brought her hands together with easy elegance before her, and looked at me.

Oh, no.

I didn't want to hear it, yet no chance I wouldn't stay.

"I received word of Sirana's sister a few hours ago, though I took the time to confirm. The Templars captured a sentient matching Jael's description six days ago, and she had been secured in the dungeon below the Temple."

"Six days?" Wolf repeated with concern. "It'll take another six to get there if nothing goes wrong."

"Easy, Wolf," Talov urged, holding his hand forward. "Let 'er finish."

"Of course. My apologies."

Krithannia exhaled with light nerves, nodding in thanks to the greybeard. She acted more like an experienced messenger than *the* Guild Mistress.

They don't know.

"As of now, Jael is alive," Krithannia continued, "because the Wall Captain Willven Isboern has refused to hand her over to the Witch Hunters."

There was a mass exhalation at the table, including mine.

"Knew that guy had a soul," someone whispered to his brother.

"With Inquisitor Kegyek's blessing," Krithannia continued, at which I heard a few snorts of derision, "they have kept her under Templar watch since then. Of course, the Inquisitor can rescind this protection or Archbishop Keros can override his decision, but as of now, Red Sister Jael's fate is in limbo while the city prioritizes its preparations for siege."

The Naulor paused to let us take all that in. My eyes ached while I scrambled for all the emotions which had scattered and needed to be gathered up. Terror. Relief. Rage. Need... The need to act. To run.

I need to talk to her. Or see her.

She was *alive*. I wasn't too late yet but, like with Gaelan, I still could be.

Six more days of travel without obstacles…

I feared to hope. Even with all these men at my back, it was too far. I'd spent too much time in the city.

"With this confirmed intelligence," Krithannia continued, her voice strengthening, "there is only one way Reprisal can get there in time, and that is why I'm here. That's why I've shown myself as I have. You will need a great amount of magic to both cover the distance and infiltrate one of the hardest-to-reach locations on Mount Sonai, *without* exhausting yourselves by the time the Ma'ab arrive, and Gavin fulfills his task."

Mourn lifted his chin and asked, "When are the Ma'ab arriving?"

Krithannia grimaced. "Estimates put their scouts there already, and the first of the main body visible in less than three days."

Three days. While we'd been pondering six.

We'd miss the start of the war, and if things went bad enough, the Ascended could have the sacred spring in their possession when we arrived.

"I see. How did they move past Augran that fast?"

"They've given us a wide berth this time," she explained, "and our eyes didn't reach far enough. The Ma'ab risked the ire of the Kurgan instead and have been using magic to obscure the point of their army more than they have in the past."

"Shit," Mourn cursed.

"Well said."

"So, what is the plan to trim down the travel?" Wolf asked.

Talov exhaled, drumming his fingers on the arms of his seat. "Guessin' a quick boat ride, a run, an' a gateway."

The Naulor turned to him. "Correct, elder."

The Dwarf smirked at that one but rubbed his beard as he thought this over, pursing his lips tightly. "When was the last time we checked the other end of the redoubt gate?"

"Twelve years," Mourn answered. He did not sound happy about it.

"Hm. Not ideal." The Dwarf shared a dry laugh. "Ah, shit."

"Can you be clearer, Grandfather?" Wolf asked with impressive patience. "I've used the gate between Augran and Taiding, but are you saying there's another that will get us closer to Manalar?"

"Aye, there is. But its location is far outside Augran, an' we weren't gonna use the resources on short notice. We didn't have time tah clear the other end, and doing so would clip three jumps from here tah Taiding, easy."

"But we don't have many options otherwise," Krithannia said, "with the Ma'ab much closer than we thought and Jael known to be in prison."

"Agreed. We're gonna hafta make it work."

"We can," Mourn stated, gold glinting as he glanced my way. "We will."

Talov rumbled in his chest, nodding. "Alright, then. Let's throw together a plan fer penetration an' get yer boots on a boat."

THE CHATTER AND IMPROMPTU COMMENTARY FROM THE HUMANS CEASED while Talov, Krithannia, and Mourn directed the meeting and went over the maps. The men plus Gavin and I only spoke to answer a question asked or when our thoughts were solicited on a particular specialty.

These prompts happened frequently enough to keep the eyes bouncing around the table and the timbre and tone of our voices changing. I observed how this helped keep all involved and engaged as practically none of Reprisal were taken aback being called on by these unusual and significant elders.

"We sail about twenty hours off the Great Lake and down the Big Ker River," Mourn said, tracing one claw above the delicate art without touching the parchment. "Then we disembark six hours prior to the Big and Little Ker split and head into the Kerut River Mounds."

I spotted a few young men who seemed not to recognize the name despite their familiarity with the map. The older ones did, however, and glanced at me for some reason.

Odd.

Gavin leaned forward with a frown. "You point to a place marked 'Iron Will' written in Manalari."

Wolf cleared his throat and lifted his hand; Mourn motioned to him to explain.

"The Iron Will is what the Witch Hunters named their new garrison after they massacred the Kerut Clan," Wolf glanced at me. "They took over their bridges across the Ker about sixty years ago?"

"Sixty-six," Mourn answered. "Kerut is the most used name for these hills even with mostly Humans living there now."

"What is the significance of that name?" I asked plainly.

Many reacted, but Talov was the one who answered. "The Dwarven mercenary ye traveled with, Rithal Hobgaer? He was from these hills. 'Twas where his family were murdered, an' all Dwarves lost access tah the bridges built by his kin."

"Oh."

Rithal's grief and tears at Jacob's sacrifice came vividly to mind.

"The Manalari are also letting those magnificent bridges rot," Mourn added with an annoyed swipe of his tail where he stood. "They use them to cross by horse and expand Manalar's influence among villages and towns on the other side. They use them to delay and extort the traders floating between Manalar and Augran. But they do not know how to maintain them, nor will they work with the Tundar to learn."

"If any o' us would work with *them* after what they did?" Talov harrumphed. "Filthy sow-squirts."

"No plans ever since for retaliation?" Gavin asked, motioning to the map. "This seems a significant strategic loss."

The greybeard grinned. "Funny ye should mention that!"

Krithannia smiled at Talov while Gavin frowned, and the Naulor reached to place a marker on the map.

"After the murders and loss of our allies," she explained, "this was far too close to Augran for comfort. Many at the time believed Manalar might be setting up to march upon our city, though the Guild uncovered no such plans. The City of the Sun has merely kept the river advantage since then. Regardless, the Clans of Taiding and Alran cooperated to begin building an underground redoubt and a new jump gate within the Kerut Mounds, in case we must move resources or defenders quickly."

Such as now.

Wolf was leaning as far forward as the Yungians, his expression intense. "Perfect for extraction, too."

Talov nodded. "If we can get enough o' the right gems, yeh."

"And that gate goes to Manalar?"

"To the valley behind it," Mourn said as Krithannia placed another marker. "One far older than the one in Kerut, but they have been linked."

Several of Reprisal blinked in surprise while the men from Yongwen squinted closer at the area indicated.

"That's the side with the sheer cliff face and the watchtower," Wolf said with a grimace.

Indeed, it was.

"But Shadow knows ways in that go *under* the cliff," Talov said. "Yer not scalin' anythin' and all o' ya know how to mask yer movement."

Tak raised his hand. "Ways? More than one?"

"Yup. Which ye'll take depends on whether the Bishops have found any in the last twelve years and are botherin' tah guard it."

"Meaning we may use up to three if they are all open," Mourn continued, "or one if we must burrow through resistance."

"Will you describe all you remember, Shadow?" Wolf asked. "And which you'd choose, if only one?"

"Of course."

"That is the next step of the plan," Krithannia said, turning to dig something out of her pack on the floor. "And to practice a better way for our leads to communicate in silence, beyond Guild sign."

I perked up. *Better way?*

The Naulor straightened and placed six strange stones on the table. They were of high gloss yet composed of dark, muddled colors difficult to make out. Each had pointed tips offering the impression of a falling raindrop, unique from each other, but all were from the same place or maker.

"We call these Dragon pearls," Krithannia explained while I bit my cheek and tried not to look at Mourn. "The keeper of each can, with training, send and receive messages like the spell, but these have far greater range."

She paused as if waiting for someone to ask how great, but they just stared at her.

"Chances are good, with no magical interference," she continued, "the keepers can communicate anywhere inside Manalar's walls and half a league outside them."

"What?" Wolf blurted in shock in front of a few other exhalations. *Not bad.*

This was similar range for our message pellets in the Great Cavern, but now I knew such reach wasn't common among Humans, making it an advantage.

"Yes. I intend one for myself, one for Groa, for Wolf, and the Focus of each squad: Hawk, Bear, and Crow."

Kil chuckled. "And 'Groa' means 'firelight,' right?"

As the eldest Yungian bowed forward in his chair, the Naulor smiled to confirm. "Yes, firelight, or sometimes 'torch.' "

"Ah-ha. Nice." Kil looked at the eldest brother. "May we call you Torch, in a pinch?"

The Yungian smirked but bowed his head. "I will respond to Torch."

"Very good," Talov chimed in. "We thank ye fer that."

"We'll be using the time sailing to train with these pearls," Krithannia said before anyone could ask, "and I will confirm that our fourth 'squad' is comprised of those who do not blend in at Manalar: Shadow, myself, Sirana, Gavin, and the Yungian brothers. We will be using illusion to help with that, but it's best if none of us compromise any of Reprisal should we be unmasked or must spread out."

"I understand the squads are numbered simply?" Mourn interjected, pointing at Hawk first. "One, two, three?"

The Hand and Foci confirmed, looking at the rest of us. "And four."

"Four," agreed Mourn, Krithannia, and Torch.

"Check." Wolf scanned everyone at the table. "I imagine we'll have to split up to accomplish both objectives."

"Quite likely," Mourn replied. "At least once we are inside. The entry points available and whether the Red Sister is in their jail or not will determine that."

"Agreed. And what about getting out? You mentioned more gems needed?"

"Aye," Talov said. "They're comin' through on the next jump from Taiding, but it'll be after ye need tah leave. Separate team o' my kin is gonna follow ye, takin' the same path, an' get the gate ready for extraction, as ye said."

"Or evacuation," Krithannia said, placing her fingertips lightly upon the table. "If we are to use these heavy resources, then if it is feasible to move refugees out of Manalar, we may take some back with us to Kerut Mounds."

Many of the men sat up in their chairs to hear this.

"Evacuating refugees of Manalar is *not* your mission," Krithannia restated, unblinking.

"Tis mine," Talov said. "My decision. If the Clans are gonna be down there an' usin' the gate in this siege, there's a good chance we're gonna hafta disable or destroy it as we leave. So, fer one last trip, send those fleeing our way, especially women an' kids willing tah leave. If they make it, the Dwarves will take 'em with."

Krithannia said, "Further taskers are in motion to create a refuge in the Mounds with extra supplies. We're prepared to move those able from there into housing south of Bor, as well."

Reprisal listened soberly, each man reacting with a nod or facial expression as they absorbed this.

"That's good to hear, Grandfather, Krithannia," said Wolf after a pause. He bowed his head to each. "It's good when we can show mercy."

There was a moment of silence, and then, unexpectedly, Gavin spoke. His drab monotone was a harsh contrast to Krithannia's and Talov's compassionate tones.

"As for the mission itself," he said, "I have another tool we *must* use."

The Naulor, the Dwarf, and the half-blood all motioned for Gavin to continue, and the Deathwalker responded by scooting out his chair to stand and walk to his pack. We waited on what he meant to retrieve, but I had an idea when I heard bones clack together. It reminded me of the talisman I had in a pouch.

I poked Mourn's thigh, and signed when he looked down, ★What of Night-mare?★

★Nearby and waiting,★ he replied.

She was? If she was in a stable, I hoped she'd been fed well back in Yong-wen to pass as living in Alran.

"I did not know how many would be here," Gavin began, carefully tilting two new cloth bags to show us a spread of small, white bones bearing ink-black carvings crafted with familiar precision. I counted twenty and doubted these were from the animals we'd eaten.

"I shall have to work more on the boat," he stated.

Among the Humans, only Deshi smiled and eagerly waited for more.

"Are those bones?" Tak asked.

"The base component, yes." Gavin picked up three and gave each another inspection. "I don't know who will be near *Pisc'sagrad* when the pneuma flint is tossed in, but know that if you are, you will suffer to some degree."

The room stilled as Talov tried not to chuckle at their expressions.

"Could you be more specific?" Wolf finally asked.

Gavin sighed, tapping his chin with creepy eyes narrowing.

This'll be fun.

"All mages in the area will be affected by this one action," he began. "No matter their alliances. The Bishops and their apprentices presently leashing *Pisc'sagrad* shall suffer the most with this surge ripping through their aura. If they aren't killed outright by this, then their ability to channel magic at all might be completely burned away."

While most men's faces hardened against sympathy, a few grimaced like they could imagine this devastation to a mage. For myself, I'd seen something like it in Wilsira after Kerse had been killed. Her "leash" to power had been ravaged and depleted upon her Sathoet son's death, and the Priestess had appeared shrunken, aged, and grotesque when we'd all been called before the Valsharess.

"So, if they live," said Bear, an overall brown man possibly named for his beard, "they'll be toothless?"

I withheld a guffaw when Gavin first tilted then shook his head in the negative. "I would not describe it that way. Survivors with auras damaged like this are either consumed by madness or wander as open wounds that others can exploit. Equally a mercy and a precaution to kill them."

"Well said." Mourn's voice recaptured Reprisal's attention. "And I agree. Mages with scorched auras can harm many innocents in their descent to madness, and there are other creatures who feed on such pain to become stronger themselves. A quick death is the best outcome."

When none argued this fate for the mages of Manalar, Wolf prompted, "And those of us not 'leashing' the pool?"

"Will suffer," Gavin repeated without much inflection, "unless you properly shield yourselves in that exact moment, but the timing and the power brought to bear would be critical. Whether you are shielded or not, the damage will not be permanent without that direct link to *Pisc'sagrad*, even as all mages will be disoriented following the surge regardless."

"Even the Ma'ab," Wolf checked.

"Yes, though distance will blunt the experience, compared to those who are inside the Temple."

"Wait," Tak said, "what about the Templars and Witch Hunters? Are they leashed, too?"

Mourn shook his head and answered, "No, they are not. Their experience will mirror yours."

"Unless you carry one of these," Gavin added, plucking up a carved bone from his palm. "This will absorb the magic surge and blunt its effects, offering you a chance to recover before the Manalari get to their feet."

Most of the table bared teeth as they smiled.

"There will also be lasting consequences in destabilizing *Pisc'sagrad*," Krithannia interjected, "of which you *must* be aware in the conflict which follows." She bid the Deathwalker to continue. "Please, describe what you said to me."

Gavin's thin lips pursed to recall. "Even protected by the charm, do not expect your first spells afterward to be cast with ease or the expected results. I would avoid using a powerful or wide effect spell first, as this only adds to the strain on your aura after a significant jolt. Act with the caution of a student first learning, and you should be fine."

"Makes sense," Wolf acknowledged, sharing nods around. "Also sounds like we need to gain distance from the Manalari as they recover."

"That would be wise," the Deathwalker replied. "After a few spells kept under control, each mage can center their focus to deal with the changes."

Torch pulled out the Dragon pearl he'd been given. "What of this, elders? You mentioned 'magical interference' could stop us hearing through it? Could this surge shatter or disable them?"

Mourn shook his head in the negative while Krithannia turned and bowed to the elder Yungian. "A good question, Groa. The interference I mentioned would be either deliberate counter magic from another mage, like a silence ward, or a temporary effect, as in the surge itself. These pearls and other magical devices with which you've been equipped should remain unaffected assuming they aren't in active use during the surge."

Torch bowed his head.

Gavin pushed the mass forward in general offering when Krithannia and Mourn reached forward to distribute them. The Guild Mistress began with the Hand, the three Foci, and her four chosen Yungians, while my bodyguard handed one to me first and gave the rest to eleven other men by rank.

"We need ten more, minimum," Krithannia said. "We will obtain the supplies for you, Gavin."

"I should have time on the boat if I am left in peace. I could make extras if you think them useful."

"Quite possibly. There could be others who will help us."

I caught a note of concern in the Naulor's voice which made me straighten up and speak for the first time. "Like who? You have someone in mind?"

Krithannia blinked her silvery-grey eyes at me, pursing her mouth briefly. "As you bring it up, Sirana, yes. I have urged my own sister to leave the city before the siege, but I will not know if she has until we arrive."

Tamuril? I frowned but kept myself from saying her name as the Guild Mistress continued.

"If we find her, yes, I want her to carry one of these charms."

If she will even touch it, knowing who made it.

"Your own sister, elder." Wolf leaned forward. "What is her name, and what does she look like?"

Krithannia exhaled. "My general shape with blonde hair and green eyes. I do not know the name she's using and would prefer not to endanger her with her true one. She *will* respond to it if she hears it."

"What do you mean?"

"She is wearing a disguise, acting as a page boy for the Templars."

"The Templars. Why?" Most of the men frowned skeptically along with Wolf. "And why can't they tell she's not Human?"

"That's dangerous," Tak added.

"Oh, she is aware," Krithannia assured them, lifting her chin. "She comes from the same mountains as Captain Isboern. He is shielding her as an ally."

I wasn't the only one to put it together.

"Wait, is that why Isboern refused to hand Red Sister Jael over to the Witch Hunters?" Wolf continued. "He *knows* what race she is!"

Krithannia smiled with pride. "Indeed, he does. And my sister helped him to find Jael before anyone else could. The message I received was carried out of the city by a falcon, given to eyes we have outside of it. But my sister isn't literate in Trade, so someone scribed it for her."

"*Fuck*," Tak exhaled, "hope it wasn't the Captain himself. That's treason."

Krithannia shrugged. "We know someone else within the walls knows what my sister shared about the prisoner. I do not know who scribed the message, but it could be him."

"Hmph," Gavin grunted. "I will make at least five extra. Yourself, and the Shadow. Your sister, Captain Isboern, and another ally."

"Thank you," the Naulor replied, sounding sincere and a bit nervous.

"If anyone must go without a charm," Mourn said, "I can bear surges better than most."

Tak lifted his hand, looking around the table. "Anyone surprised?"

A round of quiet chuckles and a lot of swiveling heads as Peng-lok bowed his head at the table, adding, "We are lucky to have our spirit guardian's strength with us!"

"No arguing that," Wolf agreed. "So, I suggest we revisit all this on the boat, save some time and head out while there's more activity in the streets before the second rest."

Those in the room decided that was a good idea. We had a workable plan understood by all, and it wasn't yet midnight.

Not bad.

CHAPTER 9

WE BEGAN BELOW THE STREETS TO REACH THE DOCKS OF THE GREAT LAKE, intending to stay under for as long as we could. Talov had remained above in Violdam Hall, but Krithannia was with us, covered in a cloak and carrying a pack like the rest of us.

At the base of a subterranean hall, Gavin retrieved Nightmare from a nearby storage room, bringing her out with surprisingly little noise or scents clinging to her.

"What will we do with a single horse?" Wolf asked, betraying irritation with yet another surprise after we'd thought all was settled.

"Probably bury her," Gavin replied. "But that's not possible here."

"*What?* Bury...?"

Mourn cleared his throat. "The mare comes with us as far as the Kerut Mounds. We will leave her there, but until then she could carry some weight when we run across land from Big Ker. Lighten some loads."

"That is one calm horse," Kil remarked, squinting like he tried to see through an illusion.

A good idea, but she wasn't disguised this way. It hadn't occurred to him or most others yet that she lacked the right scent for a living beast of burden, as well as the breath and heartbeat. I leaned and glanced into the storage room. Not even dung on the floor.

Once again, the Yungians were ahead in awareness and acceptance.

"Sho'shien has a spirit steed, the Nightmare," Deshi said, bowing to Gavin. "She eats meat and does not move if Deathwalker does not command it. She makes no noise but her hooves."

"No noise…?" the Focus Crow dared to get closer. He was a blond man with near-black eyes. "Wait. Is she breathing?"

About then, Reprisal caught on, and I put my glove over my lips to see their faces.

"Fuck, she's dead."

"Walking dead, you mean."

"Like the Far North."

"Or the Witch Hunter at Troshin Bend."

I spoke up, then. "This is the mare who grew lame in that storm on the Midway. She wasn't well. Gavin helped her transition with him so we could escape the sorcerer."

"Ohh, this is her?"

The hall filled with coos of understanding as they took a closer look, and Kil turned to Gavin then. "She eats meat, you said?"

My death mage made a hand motion toward Nightmare, who lifted her head high and opened her mouth to display the sharp teeth capable of rending flesh and crushing bone. No one shouted in alarm, but I heard a few sharp intakes of breath.

"If you catch rats aboard the ship," Gavin said, "she will gladly dispose of the bodies for us."

Several men laughed, if nervously.

"Are we ready to go?" Mourn asked, and the space buzzed in the affirmative. "On to the docks. When we go topside, we'll break up in groups of five or six and each make our way to the Rasker Dock."

Reprisal nodded.

"We're ready, Shadow."

REPRISAL CLIMBED THE LAST STAIRS AND EXITED THROUGH A GUILD-RUN building in five groups of men. Meanwhile, Krithannia gave each of us in Squad Four a temporary illusion which would hold up for enough time and a few elbow bumps without draining her concentration. She even included Mourn so he would not have to expend the energy to shift; he was once again a Noiri man but not Roewn.

We all had quite ordinary coloring for the diverse city, though I noted the Naulor hadn't chosen any Dwarven shapes. This might be because the Tundar around here knew each other's Clans, if not each face, and that was a test we would all fail if a genuine Dwarf approached.

"Split in four, but keep close," she said.

Interestingly, Krithannia went with Torch, Peng-lok, and Nianzu while Deshi stayed with me, Mourn, Gavin, and Nightmare. This seemed to have been decided when I wasn't looking, and Gavin managed a grunt of acknowledgment when the young Guild mage took his position opposite of Nightmare, watching the Deathwalker's flank like a guard.

Once, Deshi and I met eyes, but he looked away when I smiled knowingly at him. I enjoyed how Krithannia's disguises remained responsive to blushes.

Looking around the streets, Wolf had been correct that there were a few more shops open and other groups walking with us. The air was warm and moist despite the Sun having set hours ago, and I detected the remnants of many animals despite none of them being in view.

As we drew closer to the water, I heard...

Music.

Energetic and syncopated, with trembling breath notes and percussive rhythms. Hands clapped and boots stamped; my heart picked up just listening. Jubilant voices added foreign words, and for an instant, I thought I knew which language it was. Then I lost it and blinked, glancing at the stars above the rooftops.

Mourn noticed me stretching my neck up and chin out, tilting one ear forward to better determine, and he chuckled. "Do you want to go closer?"

"Hm? Uh, well—"

"It's on the way. I think you'll like it."

"Closer to where?" Gavin asked.

I looked at him. "You don't hear it?"

His oddly normal face barely moved. "Not *yet*, it seems."

Deshi looked blank, too.

"Let us go this way," Mourn offered. "I have a few coins if you like their performance."

Street performers. Yes.

One of many entertaining activities Mourn said he enjoyed in Augran. Humans playing instruments, singing, dancing, sometimes "acting."

Telling stories as if they are happening on a stage.

"Um, alright," I said, and my bodyguard passed me a few silver coins to hold. "As long as it's on the way?"

"It is. We won't keep the ship waiting."

Or Jael.

Still, I looked forward to what I might see when we rounded the final obstacle. Deshi exclaimed softly when he could hear the music, and Gavin frowned; neither of them seemed to recognize it. I would have recognized the Yungian instruments or language if it had been them. I also didn't know if Manalar even offered much in the way of music or dancing, but Gavin certainly hadn't enjoyed any growing up.

So, what else? Some other Paxian or Noiri subset in this city?

We arrived on the main street running parallel to the docks, drawing closer to a stretch well-lit with torches and multi-colored lanterns. Along with us, more and more people exited the shadowed alleys and quieter streets to join the midnight activity. I smelled fresh food being made, more ale, flowers, perfume, and sweat.

"Small festival," Mourn told us. "There are many of them through the summer in various parts of Augran."

"So many you don't know its name?" Gavin suggested.

"Heh. Correct. The similarity through the centuries have left me behind in their continuous name changes. The basic purpose remains the same."

"How imprecise of you, *Wen-yung!*" I jested. "I'm shocked."

Deshi laughed with nervous surprise as Mourn reached to squeeze my ass in response and I jumped.

"We are almost there," said our guide, motioning ahead. "Look. On that platform."

"Easy for you to say," I said, standing on tiptoe to see over tall men's hats. The music was clear for all to hear by now, though the stomping feet and clapping hands confused some of the nuance for me.

"Do you wish to sit on my shoulders?"

I blinked. "Huh? Well, er—"

"If we get closer," Gavin groused to Mourn while motioning to his packed mare, "we will be crowded."

"You may stay back, if you wish."

"I do."

"I will stay here, too," Deshi announced, nodding once.

"Thank you." Mourn motioned me to a public bench yet unoccupied. "Here. Step here and climb on my shoulders. I will get closer."

I couldn't waste more time with indecision, so I stepped up on the stone as Mourn faced away from it and took to one knee, squaring his shoulders for me to get on. I dangled one leg over his shoulder to his front before swinging my other and settling my crotch against his dropped hood and the nape of his neck.

After the practice on the rooftops, I found it easy to trust his balance, working with him as he stood up to give me a marvelous view of the stage, even before he began weaving closer through the crowd.

"We will be quick," he said over his shoulder.

Deshi offered an affirmative while Gavin mumbled something and, looking forward, I could say nothing at all.

The stage was circular with a curtain blocking off one part while the rest glowed with warm yellow and orange light. Eight young Humans danced around their five music makers playing in the middle, and the street's illumination seemed to set the bright reds, golds, and blues of their costumes ablaze with a shine of their own.

Even more stunning was the darker shades of their skin, from the deep brown color of Tak's eyes to skin almost as dark as mine. None had white or blond hair or pointed ears. The enhanced muscles and shining sweat of the male dancers was as foreign to the buas I knew as the language in which they sang. Yet, still, I saw the first Humans who looked most like me upon that stage.

"Sal-Zayr?!" I hissed in Mourn's ear. "Are they—?"

"They are." He sounded pleased. "Their troupe has traveled a long way from the South Ocean."

"And the language?"

"The same."

"Do you know what they're saying?"

I saw his smile beneath me as he turned his head. "A song about being most alive within a storm. Quite simple but I think that is why others like us listen."

Despite the lanterns and sheltered candles, I hardly blinked as Mourn drew quite close for me to study them better. Both men and women danced, each wearing attractive sandals like I'd seen on our Royal Consorts in Sivaraus. They'd each donned jewelry that glittered, exaggerating every movement while showing off their shoulders and bellies. Their waists were wrapped in loose, flowing fabric, and female breasts were covered with glimmering scarves.

We said nothing as I watched the performers complete one song, receive their applause and coins tossed in and around three baskets set around the stage. They consolidated their earnings then began another song. Meanwhile, I clutched the silver Mourn had given me.

"Oh, damn," I muttered, peeling my tight fingers back open and loosening the clinking coins from my glove. "We need to get to the boat!"

"You could throw it in the basket before they are done. Others do."

I frowned as the crowd started clapping with the song and crowding closer to the stage. A few coins were tossed in as some turned to go on their way, but I saw several onlookers who were interested in the ill-aimed coins which didn't land in the baskets.

"How do I know someone won't steal their basket after I do?" I asked.

My bodyguard paused. "An interesting worry. I suppose you do not, though someone who tried would be hard-pressed to escape."

I watched the second performance, admiring their quick and light feet for their height, and wondered why it was always only the buas who danced for us back home. These women had practiced dancing just as much, and they looked wonderful next to their men, their faces expressing something like... *Elation*.

I wanted to stay longer, to watch and ask them questions when they rested.

But I couldn't.

"If I get closer," Mourn said, "would you like to hand the coins to one of them?"

"Um—"

The second song was ending, and he'd known it.

Choose. Quickly.

"Yes! I would."

The Dragon's son must have been doing something with his aura to keep others from brushing against him, because despite his large size and illusion, he squeezed in between bodies right up to the stage without getting jostled. I wasn't the only woman in the crowd being held aloft by a larger man, but I was the closest and had to wonder what my expression must have looked like to the Sal-Zayr performers as they turned to notice me.

Perhaps it was a little intense.

The women giggled but kept their distance or engaged some of the men calling them closer while holding a coin up. However, one young man smiled widely and grabbed a shiny bag as he approached me. Everything about him was dark, from his long, braided hair to black eyes to familiar, black skin, yet much reminded me of warm earth. The palms of his hands and bottoms of his feet were lighter shades, unlike mine.

"Greetings, pretty *miyi!*" he said in Trade with an entirely new accent to me. "You enjoy our show?"

Both his natural scent and an added fragrance wafted over me as he lowered gracefully on one knee. He was groomed and appealing.

Then he held out his bag, a few coins clinking together, and I looked at it.

Say something. Do something.

"Oh, much!" I managed, reaching my arm out to drop the silver coins in the bag with care. "Beautiful dance!"

Beneath me, Mourn reached up and added one more coin to the bag. I saw a flash of gold, and the young dancer's eyes widened briefly.

"Share with your musicians," the Dragonchild said.

"Of course, *syri!*" The dancer pulled his bag to his chest as he bowed his head, the many, neat braids falling forward and waving before us with gold beads shining. "We are family! Your generosity warms us all! Ah, would you care to join us later for a bath?"

Yes, please.

I mean…

Damn it.

"Perhaps if our paths cross again," Mourn replied for us as I chewed on my regret. He was, for certain, amused by my gaping silence. "We are passing through but thank you for brightening the festivals this year."

"Indeed, *syri,*" the Sal-Zayr man said with a chuckle as he rose to his feet. "We may be here for some time if the telling upon the street are true. Oh! But we are the Firebirds." He bowed. "Our music lights up the night."

Firebird?

"Well met," Mourn replied with a straight face.

Huh, bua.

"Rifi!" called one of the women, beckoning to our dancer as the players prepared for another set.

"I must go," he said with a coyness that had fully awakened the Court Noble in me, despite being taller than me. My face flushed hot when he winked. "A pleasure to be so appreciated, *miyi*. Shade and clean water."

The dancer returned to center stage while Mourn moved us out and back toward Gavin, Deshi, and Nightmare. Before we got there, I whispered in Mourn's ear.

"What did he mean, join them for a 'bath' later?"

"Exactly what you thought it meant," he replied. "Rifi offered us an opportunity for private pleasure later. You made it obvious by staring at him like that, and we paid him ten times what most of the audience offer for a song."

"What? We did?"

Mourn laughed at my flustered tone.

"But... *you* counted the coins! And he wasn't wearing a shirt!"

My bodyguard's low, rolling humor continued beneath me, and I closed my mouth while I was behind in the exchange. My thoughts felt scrambled meeting my first dark Human, anyway.

Even with this illusion, he offered sex.

And I would have taken it.

Deshi was grinning when we returned. "You are blushing, Janshi."

I blinked. *What?*

"She enjoyed the show," Mourn said.

"Ah-ha. I *do* see why, elder."

Now Deshi was being coy, and Krithannia's magic worked both ways. I wasn't used to that. I sighed in annoyance, and Gavin took that moment to interject with a similar tone.

"Shall we join the others on the dock now?"

"We shall," Mourn said, helping me down off his shoulders. "We can run if you want."

Gavin mounted up on Nightmare for the first time I'd seen since we got on the ship in Port Fortnight.

"Let us go," he said by way of agreement.

Fair enough.

I needed to work off my fluster before I met up with Reprisal anyway.

OUR TEAM WAS THE LAST ABOARD THE *Sky Skimmer* BUT NOT LONG AFTER the previous one. No one questioned what had kept us, not even Krithannia.

This boat was smaller than the one Gavin and I had ridden through the Archipelago and seemed to rest higher in the water. This gave us an edge when the sailors quietly pushed away from the dock in the middle of the night.

Soon after, everyone was assigned to one tiny, windowless cabin, two bodies per, though Gavin and Nightmare went down in the hold to work on his charms. That was when I learned this boat had been built to carry passengers rather than cargo.

"Are we staying in here the whole twenty hours?" I asked, able to walk forward and in between the two bunks while Mourn had to turn sideways to step in.

"Until sunrise, at least," he said, closing the door to ward it. "Give the time for the men to rest more deeply while they can and provide Gavin the peace to work on his charms."

The Dragonblood's horns made a few indents in the ceiling when he straightened too quickly and bumped his head. He grunted as he glanced up in annoyance.

I chuckled. "This is too small for us to get much rest."

"Oh? Are you tired?"

"Not yet."

"Good. I had wanted to begin mutual exercises which might encourage at-will mindlinking between us—"

"That sounds good."

"—but then I caught your change of scent watching the Firebirds." The half-blood smiled at me, his tail coiling with a sense of play. "Especially when you could hardly speak to the youth charming you."

"Uhhh…" I swallowed, glancing down to see the rising ridge in his pants. "Um. That aroused you?"

Mourn hummed with a nod, removing his cloak, and rolling it up to tuck in a corner. "I would have accepted his offer if we had the time."

"You would?" I frowned, coaxing my spiders onto the ceiling above my head before rolling my cloak as well. "I thought you said you have no taste for other males."

"True, but it seems I have one for watching *you* enjoy them, and I might have coaxed one of the female Firebirds to join us."

My frown transformed to a broad smile, and I removed my bracers and belt with a tight blow of air through my lips. "You're *almost* making me regret that we had a boat to catch."

"Almost." Mourn removed his harness, his deep, rumbling laugh filling the small space. "But, instead, we have this final stretch of downtime, a warded room, small as it is, and… I can smell you."

"Still?" I teased, starting to loosen my leather armor. "What did you think about when I sat on your shoulders with your head between my thighs?"

That dry smirk could have given Gavin competition. "Grant me your best guess, Baenar."

That was nice and open.

"Perhaps," I suggested, "you thought about tossing me forward onto the stage so I might kiss the bua from his lips to his cock. Meanwhile, you would pull down my leathers, doing what you will with tongue and tail, before climbing upon the stage behind me, working your fat beast between my netherlips as I suck the dancer's pole."

He showed a predatory smile as his prick pressed against the restraint of his pants. "And you claim not to be a mind reader."

I laughed. "Bold bua! Let me get my boots off."

The swaying boat tilted strongly to one side the moment I stood on one leg, sending me toppling over onto one bunk with an aggravated laugh.

"I should have sat down first," I groaned.

"I got it."

Mourn reached for my partly extracted ankle and lifted my leg up straight, tugging off my boot and stocking for me. He set them aside on the bunk behind him before reaching for the other.

While he worked, I tugged loose the leather knots at my hips and started pushing my pants toward the ceiling. I watched for the moment Mourn glanced down to see what I was doing. He sniffed, his lavender tongue flashing out and vertical pupils expanding with interest.

His cock twitched within his trousers as he reached for mine, deftly stripping them off to bare my legs.

"Sit up," he said. "Lift your arms."

Goddess, yes.

Once I had, rough palms ran up my ribs to my shoulders, bunching my shirt before dragging it up my arms and over my head. Mourn added it to the pile, and I sat nude but for my pendant between my breasts.

"So, uh," I began, reaching for his waistband to pull out his full erection. "Position?" I sucked the musky glans firmly before tonguing the underside; he groaned as my lips came off. "And hole?"

Once my lips wrapped around his pole again, he grabbed my braid, making me pause with my mouth full. My tongue writhed continuously, as far as it could reach.

"You make it—" He grunted. "*Ah...* hard to choose."

I hummed and signed with one hand, ★Both? Or all three?★

His brief laugh came out alongside another strained grunt his tail coiled slowly up my left calf. The boat swayed side-to-side, forward and back, but Mourn's balance was solid as he could brace himself against any surface of the cabin. He pulled the tie out of my hair and began combing my braid loose, working his way up. It felt nice.

"Not a good time to try your third hole," he said with a touch of chagrin. "Especially on a boat."

With his fingers loose in my hair, I sucked with more enthusiasm. ★Maybe later? Off the boat?★

He grunted again, sounding doubtful even as my memories served him well.

★Some of my Sisters wear larger poles. I learned to take them in any hole they desired.★

He paused. "Were any as large as me?"

★No. But I *learned*.★

"Ah." Mourn enjoyed me mouthing him in the tilting vessel, exhaling with a hiss and massaging my shoulders with his hands. "And you truly… feel pleasure in it."

It wasn't a question, but I opened my eyes and looked up at him, my smile stretched around his cock. He was surprised but watched me, and we held gazes for a while.

"Mmm," he hummed at last. "I will consider."

Good enough.

I closed my eyes and continued to service my bodyguard with my full effort, knowing this might be our last opportunity for quite some time.

"Oh…alright, slowly," he breathed. "Pull off. I've made my choice."

Delightful.

My lips drew off his tip, flushed and drenched with saliva. Mourn took half a step to sit down on the bunk across from me, drawing me forward with my wrist.

"Stand and turn around. Show me your backside."

I grinned; this took half an instant, and in the other half, I felt his thumbs carefully spread my buttocks apart.

"Oh!"

His gooey tongue swiped over my netherhole, and thick Dragon spit brought my little ring alive and aching in an instant.

"Ohhh, tease!" I cried. "Unless you've reconsidered fucking it now?"

"I have not."

My bare toes gripped the smooth floorboards as we tilted again, and I put my hands to the ceiling. "You're a cruel beast."

"Shall I *not* penetrate you here with my tail?"

My gut flared with heat. "What?"

"Then bring you onto my lap and fill your slit next?"

"Oh…"

He chuckled in the lull. "Well?"

If he couldn't hear my heart pounding over the water, his Davrin ears were stone deaf.

"Do it," I panted. "Sounds good."

Better than good, as it turned out. Mourn kept strong hands on my ass, his thumbs holding me open as the tip of his tongue rimmed me until he could work it in and out easily. Then, a stiff appendage with smooth scales joined it, dipping into the center of my pucker.

My fingernails dug into the wood of the ceiling as I squeaked and whimpered, but neither paused as they worked together: tongue and tail penetrating, stretching me, loosening me up.

"*Oh, yes…!*"

Slowly, his tail became the dominant presence, exploring my glazed, tingling netherhole with curves and twists unlike I'd ever felt before. Mourn took his time, to the point my legs began to quiver, and I felt fluid drip down my inner thighs.

"Goddess," I moaned when his tail paused inside me and his tongue withdrew, giving me a chance to truly feel what he'd done. The prehensile tail had gone deep, its girth stretching me as wide as a Feldeu preparing to fuck me.

"Mourn, ah, fu—!"

"Sit!" he gasped, tugging gently on my hips. "My lap. Your weight won't hurt me."

I learned what he meant as I moved between his thighs to sit facing away. His tail angled itself along the bottom curve of my right buttock and rested against his thigh where my ass would compress it between us.

Meanwhile, every time my asshole squeezed around this inextricable presence in my effort to impale myself on the larger, rigid pole, I gasped or grunted at the sizzling flash of sensation. Any doubt that my bodyguard could penetrate two holes at once dissipated in delighted anticipation.

The ship swayed, and his thick arms braced on either side to keep us upright. When the heat of a wet and engorged prick pressed between my thighs like a branding iron, I bent over, reaching between my legs to ease him into the right spot.

"Ah, yes, Sirana…"

Trying to squeeze him in, I fumbled my hold, prompting Mourn to join in the task. He reached around to aim with one hand, took my shoulder with the other, and drew me down, easing in until I groaned and could take over.

So full!

I lowered myself to sit, swiveling my hips to take more of him. I filled my slit with cock, aware of every vanishing finger-width while his other lengthy part plugged my backside. Soon, I had all inside me but for the knot.

"Good," he breathed near my ear. "Now, feet up. On my knees."

Fun.

My holes flexed around him as I lifted my legs to brace my heels just above his knees. Encouraged further by the movement of the water, I leaned back against his rising chest, earning a flick from his tongue along the ridge of my ear. I shuddered.

His arms came around me, one crossed at an angle between my swollen breasts, pressing down on the saphgar pendant. The other took hold behind my right thigh and pulled it wider, so that when his hips next thrust up, his cock sank deeper still. Such a small move, yet the sustained pressure from his shaft's undercurve met… no, *smashed* that thrilling spot inside my cunt.

My body went rigid as the urge welled up like a natural spring.

Oh, Goddess…!

I would peak regardless, but then his tail jerked suddenly, drawing out a few finger-widths before writhing in to regain lost ground. My mouth opened as the irrepressible release swept through me, overtaking my senses, my cries and grunts nonsensical as I squirmed and gasped in his lap.

"Oohhh, ah! Ah-*ah*-ah, *ai!!*"

Mourn sucked in a huge breath and grunted. The first two shots of his cum sluiced my insides to add yet more heat as his cock flexed. His tail trembled, caught within the clenching, rippling muscle of my pucker as he growled over my shoulder, holding me tight.

"*Rrrr, yesss…!*"

My vision swam with the continuing sense of movement of the boat. My heart slammed against my pendant caught beneath his arm as I caught my breath, and the waves receded.

"Um…" I licked my lips, wetting my mouth. "Too soon?"

My cunt had become a lot slicker with what he'd added.

"Not at all," he gasped, cycling another thrust to coat his length with the abundant lubricant. "I could continue… if you wish?"

He could?

Bracing my feet on his thighs and my shoulders against him, I lifted my ass up to give him another stroke or two. His prick plumped up, growing turgid in response.

Oh, yes. Still awake.

Well, if he was ready and willing, I *did* wish.

Legs wide, I began fucking him, my cunt comfortably stretched and lubricated to take him in long strokes. Mourn's broad, dry palms cupped and squeezed my rump as he held me up and let me down again. His added support eased the strain on my legs.

"S'Good," I grunted, tilting my head back.

He responded with a voiceless, airy rattle in his throat, his hot breath puffing at the back of my neck, and every so often a soft lick as we eagerly rutted each other. Tiny bumps spread over my thighs and ass as his tail coiled slowly within my asshole, the churning muscle teasing me toward a fine and familiar ache.

If only Jael were here to suck my pleading nub at the same time.

Sucking web.

Impulsively, I reached for his wrist, tugging one hand off my ass to place the pads of two fingers on my hot netherlips stretched around his shaft. The half-blood inhaled slowly at my neck, seeming to wait on me to instruct him, and I slowed.

Maybe he doesn't have a lot of practice with his claws out?

142

Gradually, I covered his fingers with mine and pressed on them to move them around, squeezing my hard clit in between my folds and his firm touch. As I repeated this, he hummed in understanding and maintained this pressure, gently fondling me.

However, he also stopped thrusting with his cock and tail, and I accepted that unspoken signal to set the rhythm as he held his hands in place. The slick sounds between us grew louder, and I looked down to see that vibrantly wet rod pumping in and out of view between splayed legs.

"Ohhh, shhhit…"

"Yeah?" he breathed.

"Mm-hm! Looking…down there."

He hummed. "I see it. Can you hear it?"

I could hear plenty within the tiny cabin: our hearts thudding, breath rushing, skin slapping, our sexes mingling…

Practically sloshing.

"Oh, yeah! A fine mess!"

My bodyguard risked a little claw, pressing down with his fingers so my movement intensified the sensations behind my mound. A rush of heat skidded along my skin as I began to sweat.

"Avoid the knot," he whispered, even as my netherlips caressed and polished that nearby bulge with every thrust down.

"Oh? Reason?"

"Keep listening. Tell me when you hear it."

As if to make that harder, Mourn's tail became lively in my ass again, and I turned my head to nip him on the scaled tip of his nose. He returned the favor by biting the hair at my nape, and we fucked harder for a few strokes, coming close to slipping that knot in where it wouldn't come out for a while.

Mourn hissed through his teeth and pulled my body up off it. "Very well… so you need to come, first?"

I laughed in confusion, breathless. "What else… are we going for here?"

He replied by running the slippery pads of his fingers directly across the folds protecting my nub while pulling his tail halfway out. I yelped, clenching, and pushed my cunt down over the erection which nearly escaped.

"Yes! More!"

Mourn tail-fucked me as my cunt drooled and rippled around him. A minor sting along my thigh from a talon enhanced the next circle of fingers around the flushed junction of my legs. The rise to my peak at last became unavoidable, hurtling to overtake me.

Just the way I liked it.

The half-blood growled when my cunt clenched him in rhythmic spasms. Lights seemed to flash behind my eyes as I embraced my freefall, ready to wring every bit of pleasure bearing down on us. My body snared a renewed and powerful orgasm when Mourn tugged his tail out of my ass without warning.

He'd chosen the right moment.

"*Ai,* goddess of *fuck!*" I cried, taken in my throes while, inside me, Mourn erupted a second time.

"Kiabil!" he groaned.

For a brief time, all I heard was song. Different from the music I'd heard in the streets, more like the subtle signal which had drawn me closer to Tamuril's hovel and then the Ley Tower...

Z'ar Kiabil...

I began to come down, feeling heat bleeding off around me as I breathed in a familiar and welcome scent. Water splashed and slapped against the outside of our cabin, and I felt a distinguished buzz which *wasn't* between my legs.

It seemed alive between my ears.

I opened my mouth with caution, hesitant in case it faded.

It did not.

"Um. ...I hear it, I think."

But I was afraid to hear what it was.

Exhaling slowly, Mourn nuzzled the back of my neck; I thought he might have kissed it. His arms recrossed lightly around my ribs while his cock pulsed softly within my sheath and began to shrink. He said nothing and seemed in no hurry now, so we waited until he'd slipped out of me before I eased my stiff legs to drape down from his broad thighs.

I'd expended every mote of effort into this coupling, for his benefit and mine, and I had nothing left for the moment. I was not even sure I could stand on my feet yet, but I could hear the song.

The pattern within it, I recognized. Something... *whole* which needed no thought or word to define it as a damp, Draconic hand hovered above my chest, drawing my drifting focus to a shimmering, blue pool of light.

No. Not a pool.

A stone.

There.

The still point.

My mind quieted, and a pressure I'd not noticed before eased. I was awake and aware. I was on a sailing craft, headed toward Manalar. I felt almost normal, but the song remained.

Frowning in thought, I turned my head from my warm, dimly glowing pendant to look at the rumpled bunk. "Is that you?"

"Is what me?" he rumbled.

He sounded tired, but also relaxed.

"That... The, um..."

I had no words.

He huffed a soft laugh. "Would you meet my eyes to find out?"

I stiffened. "Is that a request?"

"No. It is just a question."

Just a question.

A loaded and important one, and I was running out of time to find the answer.

I swallowed, glancing up when my spiders chimed at me in greeting. Then I looked over at my belt resting upon my clothing and gear in the bunk corner. The silent Soul Drinker waited there along with the Elsewhere.

Would I leave *all* my answers unexplored until the moment my life depended upon knowing where I stood? Or beyond knowing, I must *understand* my limits.

The song hadn't diminished by the time I had taken a deep breath and grabbed hold of my courage the way Rifi had grabbed his coin purse to cross the stage.

Go ahead. Ask.

Swinging one leg over from Mourn's, I scooted my bottom off his lap and gained my knees, turning around to face him. At the same time, the Dragon's son climbed to meet me halfway and face me. He reached to draw me close.

"We're filthy wet," I said, looking down at our crotches and all the smears of sweat. The room had become hot and stuffy.

He chuckled and said nothing, though the song continued.

Inviting me.

All I had to do was look up to meet his gaze.

And I did.

CHAPTER 10

The song we hear is… Us.

Mourn heard it, too, and he knew what it was. The Dragon's son recognized the song with neither fear nor consternation, for he had confronted and embraced these moments when his Hoard must experience the next change.

Morixxyleth gave me the Words.

Sentients touching the raw flow of magic, our auras mingling as one. We exist within Miurag's Dreams as a unique pattern, a shared presence.

~Presence.~

I understood some but let the rest filter through me like water through sand.

~Miurag?~ I thought.

Yes. Miurag. Our world in its entirety. The whole of it. My Sire calls her Miurag.

~And she dreams?~

For as long as we Dream, so shall our world.

For this sightless instant, I could not feel the weight of a body, yet I did not feel lost. The essence of me felt anchored and safe even as my flesh drifted without control upon the surface of the Great Lake.

~Why… did you want me to listen to mingling auras?~

Because most mages never learn. They do not need to when they can see it. And feel it.

~I'm not a mage.~

Your child is, and your thoughts detect the pattern which includes us. I was never sure if psions could hear this, but now I know one of them can.

~Heh. And what will you do knowing this?~

An unfamiliar part of the Deepearth began fading into view from nothing.

I may be able to mindlink with you in a way I recognize during a threat. I have done this, even as I block psionic influence from habit.

Mourn as I recognized him appeared as he explained, and although much of the labyrinthine depths looked so similar as to be impossible to determine from sight alone where one stood, I would also recognize this place if I ever found it again.

Clean water spilled down near the top of a narrow canyon, filling it with mist. We stood farther down in the stream, chilled water swirling around our calves. Scaling the slick, moss-covered walls would be impossible without the right tools; even then falling was a risk. I couldn't easily see a ledge above that would make the effort worth it.

I looked to my right, a stoic-faced Davrin whom I did not know hand-signed to me.

This way. In silence.

Her body language spoke as a leader, and the other five followed her without question to a gap in the stone hollowed out by once-flowing water. They entered one at a time and began climbing, no scrapes, skids, or curses rising over the sound of rushing water. Mourn motioned for me to go next.

I will cover your rear.

~Uh-huh. Funny.~

He smirked.

I didn't recognize the worn uniforms and equipment of the six Davrin, but I knew they were fighters and had been for decades or possibly centuries. They were some of the best and could be trusted with their given task.

Among the rarest in Vuthra'tern, Mourn thought. *From House Dar'Prohn.*

Before it fell.

~Ah-ha.~

The passage leveled off and inclined by turns as we crawled through the guts of the canyon, though at no point were we able to stand upright. We tackled the climbs one at a time with rests to prevent audible panting, and by the time we entered a long cavern with a high ceiling and more air, I bore the strong sense of having bypassed some obstacle both dangerous and impassable.

I watched the Davrin leader remove a pouch from her belt and open it, meticulously removing seven padded objects and unwrapping each to reveal a gold coin. She replaced the coins in the pouch without the padding, giving them a shake to let them clink together. Most of us flinched at the noise. We couldn't help it, even knowing it was necessary.

Tucking the coin purse in a rock crevice, the leader signed that we would continue. She looked sternly at Mourn. I could not see the exact shade of her eyes traveling in the dark.

Do not take the gold this time, Tihgra. We cannot afford the delay.

I won't, Commander, the young half-blood replied. *I apologize for doing so before.*

The others smirked, though this reprimand seemed to have some true humor behind it. None seemed truly resentful.

Are you sure, Commander? signed a bua younger than her. *Not the highest cost we've ever paid.*

The flirt in his hands was impossible to miss. She seemed to smile despite herself and reached to tweak the tip of his ear through his hood.

Keep your cock leashed, Eallo. We don't want him raising that cost.

Yes, Vian, he replied, boldly using her given name.

It struck me like a fist how comfortable he was doing it, that he knew she wouldn't be angry, nor would he suffer for insolence. I *finally* noticed that the squad was made up of three caits and three buas, plus

Mourn. Not unheard of in the Queen's Army, but the free-gliding ease between them implied something much more.

They were lovers, Mourn said.

I swallowed. ~All of them?~

Yes. All of them.

Though we kept walking, my thoughts seemed drawn through a muck which took more effort to pass through. ~The...buas...?~

Mourn gave me his attention and waited patiently.

~They... were allowed to touch? Or did they only do it to entertain the caits?~

He smiled sadly. *As I witnessed, Eallo, Jahn, and Kerym touched but were never coerced to do this by Vian, Ilse, or Saida. They did not need to be.*

~Ah. Are these the... males you mentioned who would look out for each other's offspring?~

Mm, no. Vian's squad had no children when I last saw them. He hesitated in a way that made me strain to listen. *They already had me...*

I did not reply until I'd considered what I knew about the trials from our youth. ~Do you mean... were you a child when you fought as part of their squad?~

Cautiously, Mourn nodded. *I didn't look like a child by the time I was assigned to the Guard, and no one treated me as such, so I didn't truly know at first. I knew they were wrong somehow, but I didn't know where I stood compared to the other Davrin. I was fighting beside children I once knew, and they were grown. They kept talking about how I was the tallest and most deadly fighter among them, even back then. How could I argue?*

~Did this lead to the, um, unpleasant associations you told me about?~

Inevitably, but I could run from everyone except my aunt. Vian and Eallo even invited me to join them in their play, a generous attempt to put me at ease with the rapid changes of my body and position with the Matron. But... I didn't want to join them... for reasons I could not explain until later.

~And Vian didn't force you.~

She didn't force any male under her command if the Matron wasn't involved. She said she would give me time.

~And you trusted her.~

He motioned behind us. *The first time we came this way, she figured it out. Vian realized the Dragonchild under her command was still a child, despite my size. She advocated for me, trying to buy me patience with our Matron. It was a secret my aunt wanted kept for the sake of the hard-earned reputation of her best killer.*

~Oh, shit.~

Mourn chuckled ruefully. *For what it's worth, Vian's squad provided a second place to feel safe, and it made a difference.*

~A second. What was the first?~

Up ahead, Jahn shouted.

"Thralls!"

The To'vah-krav's hunched back straightened until he could see above all the squad's heads. The young half-blood brought his arms forward, summoning his sliding blades from his manacle-bracers and into his grip. The metal looked newly forged.

"In formation!" Vian bellowed. "Stand your ground!"

The first was learning to fight with Grandmaster Y'shir, he answered and launched forward to defend his Commander as the tunnels filled with noise.

I backed up out of the way, to a place where I felt less grounded; none seemed to see me much less try to attack. Cautiously, I looked around me, half-expecting to see Kain spying with me as we had when Elder D'Shea had been trying to save Reishel from the Prime in the tunnels.

For the moment, I was the lone observer.

The ambushing thralls outnumbered seven fighters, but the puppets were too hungry and the squad's positions too deliberate for the first charge to work. These creatures were used to hit and run tactics from the Davrin of Vuthra'tern, anticipating the need to chase and cut off their escape, yet Vian had commanded something else.

Stand your ground.

Even for so small a group, this had worked before.

They relied on Jahn and Saida to deflect the area attacks, on Kerym and Ilse to return fire at range. Vian, Eallo, and Mourn cut down the closers. The seven Davrin worked together as a tight ball of flashing magic and stabbing metal in constant motion. Attempts by thralls to enter a gap in their defense proved too narrow to penetrate before they lost a limb.

By now, I saw how this would end.

With Mourn in their formation, drawing the most ire as the largest threat, it was only a matter of time as long as their line didn't break. The thralls would fall one by one, and their masters would have to show themselves or abandon their prey.

We had the answer when the three mind flayers appeared. They had decided not to run.

"Gems!" Vian shouted, reaching for her emerald around her neck.

It wasn't a command; it was a warning.

Hoods had fallen in the fight, and Mourn's memory drew my attention to the matching studded emeralds pierced through the edge of each left ear. She had based her idea on the Dragon pearls but made it her own.

They've been speaking to each other this entire time.

No wonder they fought as one.

Now Vian and her team must try something new against the Ornilleth for her squad's survival.

Mourn braced himself as her magic tapped his fears, stirring the confusion and pain inside him much like a psion would. He allowed it because he needed to protect his found family, and they *had* practiced this together before the fight. These six Baenar had no desire to breed him and had never lifted a hand to hurt him outside of training.

They knew what it felt like, and he believed them.

So he let it out.

If the Ornilleth want our minds, they are welcome to them. We will force Us, all at once, down their beaked throats.

No secrets, no plans, no further threats. What followed was the rage and pain of the city's most powerful slave backed by the focus and deep reserves of strength from the others surrounding him.

We are Rin'oveaus.

They were a singular force of will in their drive to survive, entwined as individuals in their passions for each other. The Elder Mind did not yet know how to counter this, and the battle of wills with its children ended as fast and sudden as it had begun.

I witnessed the burst of color Mourn remembered, the unique pattern of their merged auras shattering clear crystal, scorching quivering thought. The Elder Mind blinked, temporarily blind within the blank eyes of the flayers when Vian and Eallo sprinted forward with their Dragonchild, severing their tentacled heads from their thin frames with a roar of victory.

They shouted with release, crying with relief.

We won!

We live!

Each of us...

We shall remain.

Now, let go.

Don't be afraid.

The deep, chilling quiet after Vian dispelled the magical link frightened me, as did the dazed expressions of the Davrin as they looked around, each alone and separate.

The colors had gone, but shards of crystal remained scattered where I stared at the Ornilleths' heads. They stared back.

~No...~

I knew.

The knowledge of those minds had returned to the Great Work, and the Elder Mind would remember the Rin'oveaus.

The prisoner I'd released had existed within these flayers, when Mourn was a youth. It existed when I was born *and* when it was captured.

Ullipmious.

That sudden blackness was not a final death.

~Death never has been for us. Death shall never be. We do not fear this.~

These flayers and the prisoner were one and the same.

Mourn turned around, his sliders bloodied, each appearing older.

His pupils expanded from the sharp slits they'd been, and he focused on me.

He could *see* me.

Sirana?

I couldn't move.

The To'vah-krav sent his weapons away before he approached me.
Sirana. Look at me.

~I-I can't.~

I knew this nest. This conclave.

They escaped, and she returned with it.

Reishel returned to *this* conclave.

~What have I done?~

What do you mean? What happened?

He was holding me. Anchoring me.

Look at me, Sirana. Talk to me. We must protect each other when we are like this. And we will. Tell me what happened.

The moment I lifted my chin and saw his golden eyes, the tunnel began to change around us.

It became familiar.

Horribly familiar.

Silent tears drained down from unblinking eyes.

~I can't move...!~

I am here. You are protected.

I was afraid to believe him. I wanted to.

Listen, he insisted. *When you feel lost, listen to our pattern. The three of us.*

Three.

I listened, followed the song, and finally managed to blink. It was a relief, and the Deepearth was not void-silent anymore.

Mourn looked around the cave which had concealed the prisoner for the Priestesses. *Can you tell me what happened here?*

My breath quickened, my pulse throbbed in my ears, and I buried my nose against him, imagining his scent.

~Listen. Listen to the pattern.~

My bodyguard waited patiently, wrapping his tail lightly around my waist while rubbing my back. Nothing came to grab me. Nothing hurt me.

~What do you see?~ I asked, shivering.

Mourn exhaled slowly and turned us in a slow circle, waiting for each of my steps to match his.

I see a cursed Davrin. Contorted Elven essence.

~Drider.~

A dead Drider, he continued. *Killed by something with claws and teeth, about my size. I see a boulder recently rolled to one side. It had been covering a hole in the rock. The...hole is filled with filth.*

~A prison cell... The Drider was guarding it.~

Whatever was inside escaped.

~B-because of me...~

If I'd had my body, I would have vomited. Mourn held me tighter, both arms and his tail, as if trying to hold me together.

What was being kept there?

My throat hurt. ~A mind flayer. Ullipmious. Or...part of Ullipmious. It told me...after I broke the ward... that it had been cut off from the whole for more than two turns. I even remember the battle where we must have captured it alive, though I don't know who did it.~

Mourn exhaled. *Did it puppet you to release it?*

~No. It couldn't. Too weak. But it got my Sister when she was vulnerable, and she left to... carry its body home. Before that could happen, it made a bargain with a Priestess's Sathoet to bring me to help make that happen.~

The Dragonblood's arms never loosened while he listened, and the song never faded though he was quiet.

Then, *It bargained with a demon?*

I nodded.

I did not know Ornilleth knew how to bargain. Or that a half-blood tainted by the Abyss could fulfill one.

~They were both desperate, I suppose.~

Is this what changed you?

~No. I was compromised several turns earlier. These two exploited it before I *learned control. They... were going to kill me, b–but my Sisters and my...my wizard...found me in time. They killed the Sathoet, but the Ornilleth escaped with Reishel...~*

Even my mental voice cracked on her name, and I wept.

Mourn paused, considering it all. *You can tell me about this.*

I forced a laugh. ~For now. We go much deeper, I don't know what'll happen.*

Understood. But this was recent. I can taste how fresh, less than a year.

~About six months.~

The silence that followed was as pregnant as I was.

The wizard, Mourn deduced slowly, *took you to the only Davrin he trusted, the healer, and you conceived during that time.*

I huffed and sniffled. ~I was all torn up from...the...demon. I shouldn't have been able to catch from him, but... When I awakened, I–I wanted to thank him, and he was so...unguarded. And willing. I–I've wanted him ever since I found him. I thought I was dead...!~

Mourn adjusted his arms and tail, squeezing me again, and keeping me close so I didn't have to look at the old Drider den and its tiny prison. I felt him press his muzzle to my hair and inhale before breathing out. The heat of his breath seemed real.

Let us leave the Deepearth for now, he suggested, *and return to the boat on the river. We are close to the surface.*

~Close to the Surface...~

A thin ray of golden light cut into the cave, disturbing the dust, and causing some of the den to crumble. A passage behind me opened wider, letting in more light.

Yes, he said with a surprised laugh. *Like that. We shall leave together.*

~Alright, but...~

But?

~When we leave, what happens if I... let go?~

A good question. I only have half the answer.

~Which is?~

That I shall be well and able to hear you when I wish.

I clutched him by reflex, baring my teeth in a grimace. ~*So confident, Dragonchild.*~

Well, you saw that Vian and Eallo and each of us were alright when we let go. We were all well. That was what I wanted to show you. It can be done, and it need not hurt even if letting go is frightening at first. Your feet will catch you, and if they do not, your hands can push you back up.

I took a deep breath then let it out. I knew this. My elders had all said the same thing, and they'd all done it.

With a step back, I released him first, his palms lightly caressing down my arms. His tail uncurled from around my waist, and there was space to take a full breath.

I held tight his one large hand when I said, ~*Let's get out of here.*~

WHEN MY EYES OPENED, MY VISION WAS BLURRY BUT DETECTED MOVEMENT. Blinking rapidly, I met the glassy eyes of my spider guardians as they crept carefully over the uneven textures of Mourn's shoulder.

Wha—?

He and I were crammed into the same bunk lying on our sides with so little spare space that we needed to take turns breathing.

"Your watchers would not let me escape if you did not wake up soon," said my bodyguard, amused. "I think we made them nervous."

Thank goddess he was keeping his voice low.

"My head's pounding," I muttered.

"And you need food and water."

"Do I need to dress?"

"Not for the first serving. I will get it for you. They need not be shouting in your ears."

I moaned in relief as he got up to don his pants, my spiders hopping quickly from his shoulders to mine.

As he dispelled the ward and reached for the door handle, I got up on my elbow and asked, "Was I having a nightmare? Or do you remember all that, too? In the Deepearth, with the flayers."

Mourn smiled at me, his tail relaxed. "I remember every moment, and I have never been more impressed by you. I do not doubt you can recoup the ground you lost after your injuries and go even farther when you need to."

With that, he let himself out and closed the door behind him, leaving me naked and sticky on the bed to ponder an unsettling sense of exposure and vulnerability which had nothing to do with my lack of clothing. Though I knew exactly what it was and why it was there, it didn't hurt. Not even a sting.

Not yet, anyway.

The song, however, had finally receded to the back of my mind and I could relax, feeling secure with my guardians.

CHAPTER 11

I WAITED UNTIL THE FOUR GUILD SQUADS HAD AWAKENED TO THE SUN BEFORE I felt safe to drop back into Reverie. By then, I had a full stomach, empty bladder, cleaner skin, and three well-pleasured holes. I fell asleep smiling after Mourn left to walk about the boat, and I stayed in Reverie longer on the *Sky Skimmer* than I ever had on the *Trickster of Isles*, according to him.

Mourn checked on me regularly and kept watch for any of Reprisal heading to rest in a cabin near ours. Nothing awful happened this time.

I learned later, after refreshing and joining more teams aboveboard, that Krithannia and her bodyguards from Yong-wen had taken the cabins closest to Mourn and me, while Wolf had chosen the men whose nightmares weren't as fresh to rest closest to the Yungians. Most of them had stayed awake anyway.

Sigh. Word travels fast.

I could not blame them; I'd *told* Wolf enough of the truth to protect themselves after the dream about Keros. For the moment, this was better than the revulsion or paranoid hostility I could have expected back home if my own people had known. If those sleeping on this boat spoke only caution and concern for my presence on account of my psionics, then I was grateful how few knew I was pregnant.

Especially where we were going.

"Why can't they tell she's not Human?"

"It's dangerous."

"Oh, she is aware."

Indeed. How could we not be?

Tamuril knew I carried, too. If she was here and should we find her, I must preclude her blurting it out.

I stood at the railing breathing some fresh air while the *Sky Skimmer* sailed down the Big Ker River. I faced East so the setting Sun was at my back, my hood providing me shade. Still, rippling water occasionally reflected light into my eyes. I had to pull the hood down farther until I only watched the splashes and froth where the boat cut through the water. It helped the occasional rise of nausea.

Light footsteps sounded behind me.

"Janshi? Are you well?"

I smiled, wondering at once what had motivated him enough to join me at the side. I had a guess.

"Hello, Deshi. I'm well enough." I tilted my head until I could see him with one eye. "Have you checked on Sho'shien recently?"

The young man nodded. "He is near finished with charms to protect our brothers."

"Good. Have you spoken with him much?"

Deshi looked embarrassed. "No, not yet. Yunze summoned us then my brothers and I waited while she retrieved Sho'shien from where he was. We left for Alran at once."

"Uh-huh. Hm, wait. Yunze?"

Deshi blinked. "Ah. The cloud keeper. Krithannia?"

Krithannia the cloud keeper?

"Ah, of course," I said, nodding sagely. "Do you understand what this means, then?"

"I do, Janshi! Fascinating." He smiled widely. "She keeps the stories of her elders and walks among us to offer young mortals her wisdom. She is not a warrior like yourself but a scholar with knowledge to weave the clouds from which the sky warriors rise."

Hm. Clever.

"Yunze," I repeated. "That is shorter to say in battle than Krithannia. I wonder why she did not tell Reprisal at the meeting?"

Deshi bowed his head. "This was sorted later, Janshi. Reprisal will use Cloud."

Torch and Cloud. They liked their single syllable translations.

"And myself?" I asked. "Or Gavin?"

"Sho'shien has said he prefers Gavin, Janshi, and Reprisal seems accustomed to 'Sirana.' "

"Oh. Of course. Yes, I did tell them that."

Three syllables. They're being generous.

The young man smiled shyly, adding, "Should it matter, I am Deshi, and my brothers, Peng-lok and Nianzu. Reprisal wanted object names for leaders and their methods using hand sign and the Dragon pearls. Shadow, Cloud, and Torch. They do not insist for us as we will follow our leaders."

I smirked at that. *I'm not a leader even to kids under twenty, huh?*

Probably wise. With my Queen's compulsion lurking beneath my thoughts and no one able to imagine the circumstances in which I may next lay eyes on Jael, I could not promise any Human that I could be relied upon to lead him to the objective and survive it.

They should not look to me in a crisis.

"I have a question, Deshi."

"Yes, Janshi?"

"Do you feel drawn to Gavin's magic at all? Or is it spirit duty?"

Deshi frowned as he considered that. "Both?"

"Mm-hm." I turned toward him, resting on my elbow, smiling to make him blush. "You know, Gavin was a death mage as a Manalari monk, even before he became Sho'shien. I have heard Human death mages aren't known for teaching each other much, but I believe that's the loss of the Grey Maiden's influence, not because there is essential harm in it. That is one reason he returned."

The young man's cat-like eyes glimmered in the fading light.

"Gavin does not have much practice but *is* a good enough tutor once you learn how to ask him questions. Though you must not be intimidated by impatient sighs and an abrupt end to a spontaneous lesson."

The Yungian started to smile but caught himself. "That is not the type of teacher we honor in Yong-wen. Such a one is rather difficult."

I chuckled, breathing in the humid air when a breeze picked up. "I agree, he is not a 'teacher' like Master Shi in the *dorji-ka*. By far, he prefers to study alone and would recoil from the task of managing boys like those we sparred with. Like Yunze, he is a scholar, but only one who can tutor another who challenges him in small bursts. The goal must be to make each other better."

Deshi squinted. "I have…heard something like this before. But it is for learners persistent in seeking the best craftsmen or performers."

That brought a genuine laugh. "After what you heard about Troshin Bend, what is a death mage of the Grey Maiden, if not a bit of both?"

His young face split into a grin as he bowed; he understood. I allowed the natural sounds of the river passage to fill the silence as he watched over the side with me as dusk unobtrusively arrived.

The boat would be anchoring another four hours past sundown, and we'd disembark at night to avoid the Manalari garrison and reach the redoubt in the Kerut Mounds before dawn. Then…

The gate to take us to the canyon at the bottom of a cliff.

Mourn had described this in more detail in our bunk. At first the description sounded much like the jump circles I was familiar with, but it had a few important differences.

"The Dwarven gates are much less flexible in where they can take you than jump circles," he said. *"Usually, only two gates are connected to each other at a time, and each takes time and the proper materials to build. But the advantages are the longevity, the sheer distance which is dizzying and never matched by any circle I've seen, the time they can remain open, and the volume of people or materials which can be moved through them at once. If they're staged properly and well-planned, the magic expenditure is more than worth the cost."*

I pondered that. "Talov and Krithannia gave me the impression it took a lot of gems to open them in the first place."

"Not just the gems, but properly enchanted first. It takes even more to keep them open for a longer period, with enough mages who know how to work the runes to reduce the risk of magic going awry."

"Huh. That's why a 'team' of Tundar is following behind us?"

"Correct."

"And why this wasn't part of the original plan with Reprisal, even with Gavin's crucial soul shard."

Mourn shrugged. "We thought we had time. We do not, so we adapt."

"Even knowing they will have to destroy such an old piece of magical equipment."

"Correct. As you said, Gavin's role is crucial."

"Still a pity to lose that secret under the Bishops' noses."

"Agreed, but no secret is kept forever. Ofttimes choosing the time to use it is the best option."

"Quite true." After a pause, I said, "You mentioned risk. Have... pregnant Dwarves or Humans gone through before, that you know?"

"Yes." He squeezed my arm, reassuring me. "We did not overlook that detail. With proper training and procedure by those who keep it open, the gate feels like jumping out of a first-floor window. There's a brief sense of freefall, an increase in speed, and a jolt at the end where you could stumble and fall if your landing is off. But you will not be fundamentally changed or harmed for having jumped. At worst, you will be scraped."

That had been a relief to hear.

"Ah, there you are."

Deshi and I turned, and I smiled. "Gavin."

My ally had climbed out of the hold at a time his white skin wouldn't turn void-black in front of Deshi while standing on the deck, though I wasn't sure if it was intended. I didn't see the Deathwalker planning around the comfort of others with regards to the unexpected; he was frequently in too deep a thought to see those moments coming.

"Have you finished the charms?" I asked.

"I have." He reached into a pouch. "I would prefer if you carried three."

"Three?"

"To gift at your discretion."

"Gift. You mean if I find Jael and the druid?"

Gavin paused awkwardly, dimly glowing irises flicking to Deshi. "Correct. Although, think carefully about who you would protect while keeping one for yourself."

His remark being more oblique than subtle, it took me a moment. *Oh*.

I accepted an additional two marked knucklebones, briefly inspecting them before adding it to the first. "Is the protection of two... like stacking armor and shield?"

"To some extent, yes, though there is a threshold where hoarding the charms would not shield an individual mage further and only mean fewer have protection."

"Understood. I won't hoard."

But the Deathwalker wanted me to keep two; one for me, one for my baby, with the third spare should I meet someone who needed it more.

Why? I wondered. After defeating the warp rot, Gavin had claimed expedience in warning Mourn about my pregnancy when I was sick and starved. What was the word he used?

Relevant.

Was my child relevant to him?

With Deshi here, it wasn't the time to ask. Perhaps this did not matter since this was equally relevant to my Bargain with the Dragon-child. Accepting Gavin's advice was also staying vigilant in favoring the outcome Mourn and I had negotiated for.

"Thank you, Gavin."

The Deathwalker looked around the deck though little seemed to interest him. By the way he placed his feet, I wagered he was about to return to the hold; he would have if Deshi hadn't spoken.

"Sho'shien? A moment?"

Gavin sighed, turning to replant his feet on the tilting deck. "Yes?"

Obviously, Deshi hadn't expected him to give his full attention like that. Belatedly, the Yungian removed his long dagger with sheath from his belt. Laying it across both open palms, he lifted it up for Gavin to see.

"I may have to kill with this weapon," he said. "Is there some way to honor the Grey Maiden in these acts of war? Perhaps she may guide their transition as you did the Witch Hunters in Troshin Bend."

I had never seen Gavin look so stunned by a question before. He brought a knuckle to his mouth, eyes unfocused and brow beetled as he gave this serious thought. I almost chuckled aloud.

"Interesting question," said the Deathwalker. "I will contemplate an answer for you."

Deshi brought his blade closer to his chest and bowed at the waist. "I am honored, Sho'shien."

Although I watched to signal Deshi to leave his progress there for now, I found no need when he excused himself. The Yungian understood patience.

Good work, bua.

I WAS GENERALLY AWARE OF MOURN'S PRESENCE AND POSITION MOST PLACES aboard the *Sky Skimmer*. Neither of us avoided the other; we made eye contact and signed acknowledgment, confirming wellness whenever we encountered each other.

However, following what was to be our last, intense coupling before we tried to free Jael, combined with a deep and prolonged mindlink inside our cabin, each of us had taken the last opportunity for some time apart.

I had many threads of thought to sort through.

It also helped separate Roewn from Shadow better in the Humans' minds. Reprisal wasn't aware that the Noiri Guildsman they knew and the mysterious legend, Shadow, were the same. It might seem odd if we were always together as we'd been in the barracks beneath the Turthend Center.

We're still having sex in small rooms, though.

I wasn't sure if anyone had heard us or caught the scents clinging afterward. If they had, the men were subtle; perhaps they thought that I mounted *all* my bodyguards. If Deshi had mentioned my gawking at the Firebird dancer, they could assume—correctly—that I frequently flirted with new cock.

For now, though, I was grateful for some breathing space in the dark with only the stars above.

"Sirana? Are you well?"

Heh.

I glanced over my shoulder at the Guild Mistress. "Yes. I've kept my meals better since the last time I was on a ship."

Meanwhile, Krithannia effortlessly maintained her balance on the deck. "Well, the Big Ker is much calmer than the Great Lake."

"I'm grateful for that. Truly."

She sat upon a crate strapped down nearby, leaning one shoulder against the railing. As we watched the waves trailing behind the boat, the lingering silence from the Naulor wrecked my relaxation.

"You have further information about Jael?" I guessed.

"Not really. I'd have told you."

"Hm."

"But I wanted to ask about Mathias Briar, if I may?"

I turned my head from the water and stars, squinting. "Do you know him? Like Talov knows Rithal and Osgrid, even if he isn't saying?"

Krithannia smiled. "No, not personally. I know *of* him. I know the Guild has hired him from time to time, though he was never my first choice for tasks I oversaw."

I glanced around us and lowered my voice further. "Are you not the pinnacle leader of the Guild?"

The Naulor chuckled. "I am not. Think of me more like the eldest councilor in a collective government. There are many lieutenants and enforcers in the organization who must make decisions on how to address certain problems or respond to crises. Most importantly, I am not a queen over Humans. I do not decide their fate but try to guide them. That is all."

"Hmph. Very well." I cleaned under a fingernail. "What did you want to ask about the skin hunter?"

"Well. After hearing the men talk about the story you and Gavin told before I arrived, I was reminded of a detail you shared with Mourn. That Mathias acted like a bodyguard for Amelda. Did this seem in any way like a bargain with Brom which happened after you escaped?"

"Why do you ask?"

"I know Mathias has worked with Brom before but being leashed to his daughter is a new development. Can you offer any insight?"

I had to think back. That encounter had confused me.

"And you, Mathias?" I asked. "I thought you ran from the town's mob. These Ma'ab were in no shape to stop you."

The skin hunter offered a lax smile and a shrug. "Turns out I forgot something."

Although I'd waited for him to add something, anything else to explain that, he didn't. He "forgot" something.

This was also after Mathias had remained in the shed with Gavin during Jacob's sacrifice, but I hadn't known that at the time. I'd only seen that in Gavin's dreams, while we were both unconscious from the surge of the unraveling warp rot.

Hm. Seems relevant.

I shared these details with the Guild Mistress, about Mathias's last known involvement with Jacob before the town mob arrived and Amelda attempted to turn them against Gavin.

"I saw him run from the shed," I said, "and nothing in that moment or anything before suggested Mathias gave a lizard's fart of concern for her. He also didn't seem enthused chasing after us with Amelda and the Ma'ab. He said he 'forgot' something, which I thought was strange."

"Hm." Krithannia considered. "Perhaps Brom caught and coerced him to help, either through mundane or magical means."

"Magical coercion, hm?" I muttered.

We have a word for that.

Then I blinked. "Uh-oh. If Brom comes after me and the dagger…"

"Mathias could be sent as a scout or spy, yes," Krithannia finished. "Mourn and I discussed this possibility and I wanted to raise your awareness. He speaks Manalari and would blend in better than Amelda. If you think you see him, report it immediately."

"Well, of course, I would."

"Very well."

The Naulor glanced down at my waist, and I waited for either Soul Drinker or my unborn as the next topic, suppressing the urge to distract her by mentioning Tamuril. There was no need; the pale elder was on Mourn's team and always would be.

And for now, so am I.

Krithannia seemed to be weighing her approach when, finally, her expression softened. "I would like to thank you for being fair and unreserved in your bargain, Sirana. The balance has done some good for you both. I can see it."

I frowned. "What do you mean? What can you see?"

She shrugged. "Well, there's the ease with which you and he are around each other, and I can also tell your auras merged recently."

I shifted my weight, holding the rail. "Hm. And?"

The Naulor smiled. "Doing so did not hurt either of you, for which I'm grateful. The aura in your belly—"

There we go.

"—I can see when I focus, even without touching like before."

I grimaced. "Not good if I'm trying to keep it secret."

"Agreed. For what it's worth, your bond with Mourn has helped to camouflage your aura and your pregnancy. Even now, when you are not suppressing it, your aura is difficult to read. I would propose even the Archbishop or a Commander in the Ma'ab army wouldn't know what sort of mage you are if they saw you nor would they understand your condition."

My expression didn't change much. "But Cris-ri-phon would. If he can tell like you can, that might make it worse. He was incredibly jealous of his Davrin Queen."

And he'd smashed the only vial I had to safely end this "condition" if necessary. He wanted to force the birth into his hands under the guise of "protecting" me when I'd never asked him to.

Unlike Mourn.

Krithannia pursed her lips at my sudden tension, her eyebrows bouncing once in thought. "That is a fair point and good to keep in mind. But I understand, that *is* why you sought to hire him. To stand between you and the Deathless while you search for Jael."

"Piss in that sorcerer's mouth for making it necessary," I muttered, and a smile tugged at my lips when she laughed unexpectedly.

"Well said. But you've chosen well, and I hope you continue to be fair with him. He can and will do what he says."

Her confidence was reassuring though, inwardly, I sighed. I'd hired him for this and so much more I could hardly describe. Could I possibly coax enough cream from the hybrid, using every hole and trick in my sexual armory, to satisfy the difficulty of the task and invite a "renegotiation" afterward?

I'm going to try. That's the Bargain.

And the compulsion.

At least our play thus far was having a desired effect, according to the half-blood and his former lover. Though, it seemed like more than play the last time. That song. Its pattern.

The three of us.

"Um, question, if I may?"

Krithannia's elegant eyebrows lifted. Her skin almost glowed as the first rising moon touched it. "Of course you may. What is it?"

I cleared my throat. I was getting thirsty and took a sip from my skin. "Once, when I communed with the... Elsewhere, the ancient queen asked me if I'd seen the face of my daughter yet. I have not. I also think she assumed a *cait*, though I have no way to know."

The Naulor held her eyes on me, waiting for me to finish.

"Do, um, do you know if Naulor mothers have such dreams of their unborn? If they see a face or know, son or daughter?"

Her silver eyes warmed and turned limpid; it appeared like I'd given her a gift by asking. "Yes, we do. That dream is important, a bond made to aid the birth itself. It occurs usually after the first year or even up until the month before the birth."

"So... Do you also wait two years?"

Krithannia nodded with more enthusiasm. "We do! It seemed to me you were at a familiar stage, although you have an earlier and more ravenous appetite than I recall."

"Heh. That could be circumstance."

"It could be, yes. The *edain* back home aren't warriors like you."

That was so odd to imagine.

"*Edain*," I repeated, tilting my head toward her.

"Yes. *Cait. Edain.* Woman. Lass. Female."

"Ah-ha." I smirked. "What do you call a *bua*?"

Krithannia smiled. "*Adan.*"

Hmm.

"And *guded*?" I tried.

The Guild Mistress chuckled. "*Edain* with shamanistic magic, or a feminine druid. I am a little surprised Tamuril told you."

I shrugged. "She was weakened and trying to placate me at the time. So there are male druids?"

"There are."

Oddly, she hesitated to say what it was at first. Perhaps she had recalled something particular about that; it didn't seem pleasant.

"*Odad*," she finally said. "The father druids are *odad*."

Guded and odad. Hm.

"And what about you being a 'cloud keeper?' " I asked, putting my chin in my palm, though that didn't last the next time the ship rolled. "Or so Deshi says."

Krithannia chuckled. "Well. There was a similar story back home. It's fairly old, referencing a Stormseeker. A grandfather of mine was such a one. He traveled far from home, searching for new learning, or 'seeking storms,' as they used to call it. When he would return and share this knowledge, it was described as weaving clouds together to show a tale." She shrugged. "I suppose I have done the same thing with my life, but for returning home."

"You are a 'Stormseeker.' "

"And a cloud keeper to the Yungian Guild, like you are a sky warrior."

"Oh! Are they Guild? I was curious why you chose those four."

"Indeed. An old family who has seen my true form before and is good at keeping secrets. They are blessed with many sons, and three of them came with Groa to help defend me and Gavin, so neither Reprisal nor Mourn need to split their focus."

I thought so.

"What about the Dragon pearls? Did Mourn have anything to do with them?"

Krithannia's straight, white teeth catch bluish moonlight. "Yes. He made them. He can also sense where they are and hear anything which is said through them, so he will be well-informed of our positions and missives while he guards you."

I smirked. *Sneaky lizard.* "That's why he was so certain a surge from the sacred pool wouldn't neutralize the pearls."

"Correct. They've been tested over decades. We can be sure they will function under most magical pressures we expect."

"And Gavin's charms? You have one?"

"I do, and one for Tamuril."

I felt oddly relieved. "I have an extra Gavin gave to me."

"Oh, he did! Perhaps you should keep two?"

"I am. I have one extra."

"Ah. Now I understand."

"Was that your suggestion to Gavin?"

"What suggestion?"

"That I carry two charms."

Krithannia shook her head. "No. I'm sorry to say I did not think of it until now."

Huh. So it was all his idea.

The Naulor and I could have chatted in this cautious exchange for longer, but the activity on the ship increased shortly before Mourn joined us at the back of the boat.

"Do I interrupt?" he asked.

"No, my friend," Krithannia said. "I was asking Sirana about Mathias and how she was feeling lately. Worth noting Mathias may have a geas placed on him, so he will be unpredictable from what we know of him."

"Understood, and not surprised. We'll be dropping anchor soon and disembarking for the shore."

Krithannia stood up. "I shall get ready. Thank you for the talk, Sirana. Until soon."

Mourn waited until she'd left before saying anything.

I crossed my arms. "What?"

"I have two things I'd like to ask you."

"Alright. First?"

"Are you willing to scout ahead with me to the redoubt and leave Gavin with Krithannia and Reprisal for that time?"

I exhaled. "You mean we are running much faster than those who are jogging the whole way?"

"You are not. Just me. You must hold tight."

"I'm riding you?"

He smiled. "One way to say it."

I smirked. "Well, I can see the need. Say that I am willing. What is the second question?"

He sobered a little. "Do you remember the emerald earrings worn by Vian's squad?"

"Yes. You could all communicate in battle wearing them."

"And we could track one another if separated or captured," he added.

"Ah. Krithannia was saying the Dragon pearls did something similar, except only you can sense them and hear through them all."

"That is correct. It would be like that."

"What would be 'like that?'"

He touched his jaw, massaging it like it was sore. "I am making another, smaller pearl for you. If we are separated, I can track you. If we practice on our scouting trek, you may be able to use it at Manalar as a psionic focus to speak to me at range, but not necessarily where all the others can hear."

Those words made sense and even communicated a plan, except...

"Wait, you're 'making' another?"

He touched his jaw again. "Well. Growing one. It is irritating."

I blinked thrice before I had a response. "Um. How would you attach it?"

"That is the easy part. A fixative will attach it to your ear lobe since we don't have time to make a piercing."

I touched my ear reflexively. "That, and I've never punctured my ear before."

"There is no need to. So, response?"

"Ah. Yes, to both. I'm willing to aid the team where I can."

"Excellent. Let us wait until we are on shore and have checked the surroundings. Once we gain some distance, we will see how this works."

CHAPTER 12

THE *Sky Skimmer* REMAINED IN THE CENTER OF THE BIG KER WHILE WE reached the dockless eastern bank by rowboat. The sailors were suitably unsettled by Nightmare's silent cooperation being lowered into the water. Even Reprisal stared when she began swimming behind the shore boat carrying her Deathwalker without a lead on her halter.

Getting into the second land boat, I heard a sailor whisper to another, "Glad we got one on our side."

A grunt. "Still twisted, though."

Once we stood on land, tall, wild grasses and gently rolling fields well-lit by moonlight surrounded us, the soil soft beneath our boots. I was thankful the sky was clear with no sign of rain, even if it increased our chance of being spotted at a distance by a village or the garrison.

We spent enough time redistributing the weight to be carried on foot or by Gavin's mare that we also observed the *Skimmer* pull up anchor and continue its way downriver.

"They'll turn around before the Big-Little split, drop their supplies, and float back upriver," Wolf murmured to me in response to my quizzical expression. "Much beyond that, they'll risk Manalari search at the Iron Will bridge."

"An' they don't have a current trade sigil," added Tak. "Just extra tribute to the Bishops before they even sell anything near Manalar. We were lucky to catch them headed this way."

"No one's going down south anyway," Hawk said. "Word's traveling fast. Will make the bridge tolls even worse."

Mourn and Krithannia signaled when they were ready for him and me to scout ahead, making me realize we hadn't said enough on the boat to visualize how I'd be "riding" him quickly over such distance.

Will he carry me on his back instead of his front? Seems arduous.

"Sirana and I will stay in range of the pearls and give the squads what intelligence we find," said the half-blood as we watched him first remove his cloak, then detach and shrug out of part of his loaded harness. "If all is clear, make every effort to reach the rendezvous point before dawn. Every measure of darkness we can save before the gate gives me time to check the entrances beneath Manalar after we jump."

I saw hand motions or head nodding, and heard no murmurs, which boded well for the Humans' experience. By this point, however, we also stared at Mourn's harness which now fit his torso all wrong.

"Um," Tak began, but Wolf signed him to wait in a way I could almost read.

Then, the Dragon son began to shift right before our eyes.

Mourn grunted and exhaled softly with the effort, and I detected his familiar scent of physical stress as his body magically adjusted itself. He kept his Elven ears, horns, hair, and night-purple face, but developed more of a snout and longer muscles in his neck at the same time the curve of his spine and his hind legs elongated.

"What the gods…" someone gasped under his breath.

The half-blood arched as if he was about to double over and fall. Hands and feet contacted the ground while they morphed into massive paws in the grass beneath him, his long tail lifting above the ground to extend out and up as an even better counterbalance.

Oh, my…

Krithannia alone was smiling while the rest of us gradually absorbed that "Shadow" had a quadruped form, vaguely reptilian, feline, and something else. Not only did his harness fit him properly now, but I understood better why he wore his pants notably loose like the Yungians. He'd be constantly stripping nude or ripping the cloth to shift like this if they were any tighter.

"Hm," Gavin grunted. "Impressive."

I think most agreed, but none opened his mouth to say so.

"My new mount, I presume?" I asked aloud, playful and confident enough to bring a couple chuckles from the men.

My bodyguard swung a powerful neck my way and hissed a laugh, his lavender tongue long as ever, flicking out to taste the air as he padded over to me. His shoulder blades nearly reached my chest, and he looked twice as long as I was tall even if I didn't include his tail. Although the same color, mass, and scale coverage as before, he'd redistributed all that bone and muscle with precision to create a new animal predator.

Not just a distance runner, but a jumper, climber, and swimmer as well.

"Might your spines come up as you run?" I asked, seeing I was to lie flush along his spinal column right on top of them.

"Harness keeps them down," he said, sounding gruff and words less distinct. "Bundle our cloaks. Lie upon them."

Extra padding for my sore chest and belly? *Perfect.*

I secured the thick fold of cloth as directed, readjusted the pack on my back, and saw no reason to linger. I mounted him as easily as I had any Deepearth lizard. Leaning forward I hooked my bracers through his harness, holding on and squeezing my thighs to him.

"We will meet you at the rendezvous," Krithannia confirmed as Mourn rumbled acknowledgement, dipping his feral head to her.

Gavin took that as the signal to mount up on Nightmare, and I waved to him and Deshi before saying to the rest, "See you before sunrise."

"We'll be there," Wolf replied.

MOURN TOOK US AT AN EASY LOPE OVER A FEW CRESTS TO WARM UP, BUT AS soon as we were away from the party, he murmured a few To'vah words and gradually lengthened his stride.

Soon, he was ripping up turf behind him as he galloped full out, boosted by his magic. Without any real turns or obstacles, the wind whistled in my ears, and I had to close my eyes more often as the air dried them out horribly.

Wild scents filled the night and were pushed into my nose even on an exhale, concentrated and lush when I breathed in. I wondered at the many new layers of growth, decay, and living animals I could not identify. We moved too fast for me to explore them, and this created a collective scent which could be the equivalent of a single, detailed image woven into a tapestry.

These were the Kerut Mounds. Upon one breath, I would know it instantly even if I was blind.

The broad rise in the landscape was more subtle than the immediate hills going up and down, and perhaps only detectable at this speed. I possessed old habits from the Deepearth of being ever aware when the ground rose under my feet, but without a ceiling above me, this wasn't as easy to use. I might not have noticed the cumulative effect except for how quickly Mourn propelled us forward.

He slowed to a stop periodically, turning around to focus behind us, no doubt connecting with Krithannia's pearl to offer information. I had these chances to determine he must be weaving a path between small settlements. Although we caught the scents of dung and livestock, they remained out of sight, which meant we did, too.

Krithannia and our many Human mages should be able to track us and follow the same, clear path.

Once we finally stopped to tend to bodily needs, I recalled the last point he'd made on the boat.

"So, what about that 'smaller' pearl you're making?" I asked. "You said we might practice with it away from the others."

Mourn dipped his head like a stallion and moved his jaw around with a growl. "Been worrrking it loose."

"Where? In your mouth?"

"Beneath my... tongue."

It was harder for him to speak, either due to the new shape of his mouth or from messing with the stubborn pearl where I couldn't see.

"Do you want some help?"

The feral-looking half-blood squinted at me. "Not had one offerrr to put fingerrrs in mah mouth."

I caught myself watching his teeth when he said that. His bite was even larger now, the strength of his jaw formidable.

"Well, I am interested in that pearl," I said, "and we don't have much time to practice before dawn."

He grunted in agreement. A moment later, he settled down, belly in the grass and forelimbs stretched in front of him. His tail betrayed tension as it curled around, extending past his elbow.

"Left ssside," he instructed. "Deep back. Fffeel a hard ssswell, massage it to loossen."

Mourn opened his mouth wide as a yawning cat.

That's a lot of teeth.

I settled next to him in the grass, removing my right glove as his tongue curled back and to the side. The flesh beneath appeared mottled, lavender with dark shades of purple and black. I reached in.

Only as my finger extended between the rows of molars did this strike me as odd. I wouldn't have needed to do this with Roewn or the half-blood's birth form. Those had genuine, useful fingers.

What other shapes can he take to fulfill our Bargain?

The first touch was similar to touching the inside of my mouth, nothing unusual. As soon as I found the "hard swell" far back on the left side and started massaging, he started salivating in excess. Clear, stringy drips just missed my leathers.

"Hey."

"Thawry."

After more exploring, Mourn grunted with discomfort.

"Did that hurt?"

"Yeh. Again."

"Again?"

"Yeh."

I sighed, gradually increasing the pressure as I rubbed the side he said had hurt. Then I felt something dislodge, and he grunted again, a brief groan vibrating his chest.

"Was that it?"

"Yeh."

Then I caught the scent. "You're bleeding."

He shrugged. "Geh ih."

"What?"

His tongue coiled to click against the roof of his mouth as air puffed across the back of my hand. "Geh-*tuh*. Ih-*tuh*."

"Oh. 'Get it.' Right."

I felt like I was pulling an ingrown tooth out from beneath the hot, swollen spot in his mouth, and that was accurate enough. When I finally massaged the pearl out from the slippery fold of flesh where it had been hiding, I pinched it between my thumb and forefinger and withdrew my spit-covered hand with care.

"Got it." I held it up. "See?"

Metallic eyes inspected it before he spit the excess blood and drool into the dirt, scraping the dirt with a paw to cover it up. "Thank you. Tha'sss better."

It sounded like it.

I pulled out a cloth to wipe the pearl and my hand dry before inspecting it myself. "It is smaller."

"Hasn't been growing long. Range will be shorter."

I huffed with fair amazement. "How did you figure out you could do this? Making these muddy, glossy 'pearls' in your mouth which allow you to talk to others."

Mourn didn't seem eager to tell me the full story. "Insssight in my firssst Dream."

"First dream?"

"To'vah Dream. Less Elf, more Dragon."

"Ah." I decided not to push. "So how do I use it?"

"Touch with ssskin. Try psssionic thought. Like your ssspiders. I will lisssten for you."

Then he lifted his head toward the sky and closed his eyes. He looked like one of the many guardian statues in Yong-wen.

Smiling with the thought, I closed my fingers around the pearl which was barely larger than my canine. Then I shut my eyes and found that familiar quiet space where my guardians could hear me.

They chimed in questioning unison.

~No, not you. Sorry. We're safe.~

My mind drifted as I squeezed the pearl against my palm using the pad of my middle finger. I reached out where I couldn't see.

~Mourn? Can you hear me? Are you near?~

There you are.

My eyes flew open, my empty hand clapping to my ear as if he'd shouted in it. "Oww!"

Mourn opened his eyes. "Oops."

"What, 'oops?!' "

"Apologiesss. I forgot word enhance thought in reverse."

"Whaaat?" I groaned without a lick of understanding. The last thing I needed was a headache.

"It can wait." His long runner's body shifted in the grass. "Try again?"

I sighed, closed my eyes, and managed not to alert my spiders this time. ~Mourn? Me, again.~

Yes. I can hear you. Is this better?

I smiled, nodding my head as my thoughts focused forward. ~Much better.~

And astonishing. I didn't need to meet his eyes or have his cock buried between my legs.

My bodyguard stood up on four legs. *Will you climb on and try to maintain this link while I run?*

My eyes remained closed. ~And if I lose it?~

I shall slow down until we can reconnect, and we'll try once more.

Keep trying. About all we could ever do when running short on time.

I took a moment to wrap my eyes in a blindfold and tuck the pearl against my palm within my glove. Then I stood up and mounted on his back again.

~Let's fly, Dragon son.~

He chuckled, muscles bunching up before he sprang forward, speeding again through Rithal's former Dwarven hills.

WE ENTERED THE THICKETS AND TREES ON THE NORTHERN FRINGE OF KERUT when the smaller sister moon had barely risen. She lagged far behind her elder sister this night, while Mourn had been changing direction constantly for the last quarter hour to avoid the trees.

I'd taken my blindfold off earlier when our mindlink had become effortless, so I could practice our mental communication under distraction by swift movement, fast-closing objects, and near misses.

~Gahh, watch out!~

Roll with me. Not so stiff. Remember your horse riding lessons.

~No horse moves like you! Aaa! Wait—!~

Duck.

~Shit—! Oof!~

You're doing well, psion. Once we've entered the redoubt and I've shifted back, we'll attach the pearl to your ear and practice until the others arrive. How's your head?

~It's—Fuck! …What was that?~

Territorial owl. No magic.

~Oh, good, so we won't run into a Druid's hovel before we find the Dwarven fortress this time?~

Heh! You'll have to tell me about that.

~If ever you're in a confined space with Pilla, wear ear mufflers. She goes berserk if someone drops a berry near Tamuril.~

Probably for good reason.

~If none of the Templars have a scratch from the page boy's pet, I think the

181

Witch Hunters have been looking the wrong way.~

Mourn rumbled a laugh which scared a few night flyers away. He wasn't worried about unsettling noise in this part of the forest. The Iron Will garrison lay to the Southwest, far behind us, for the Manalari wanted to be as close to the river and to Manalar as they could be.

The hidden Dwarven redoubt was situated on the North end, created as an underground base from which the Clans could observe any movement toward Augran between the Big Ker River to the West and the Raguruos Mountains to the East. Both landmarks would lead directly to Manalar, but instead of following either of them South for days, we stopped here to use a gate which would send us to the far side of the Temple City before the next dawn.

The way had been cleared for those coming behind us, and they wouldn't take too long. Like Mourn, the Guild was using magic to boost their speed and endurance before this last leg of the journey. Gavin kept up with them on his mare.

Mourn chose his moment to stop, and I discovered standing still for the first time in hours to be strikingly disorienting. Out of my periphery, the trees tilted and leaned until I looked at them to confirm they were natural and not warp rot. My skin tingled from the abrupt ceasing of the wind blasting my face, and the base of my braid had a tangled nest forming which concealed my spiders all the better.

We're here. Dismount, please.

~Nice.~

Now I just had to convince my hands to release their grip.

Eventually, our bodies and thoughts separated with only lingering aches, and I stretched my legs with boots resting atop orange pine needles beneath a higher canopy. Holding our wrapped cloaks in one arm, I reached down with the other, plucking at leathers wedged into my crotch.

While I readjusted a few things, the hybrid gradually morphed back into his birth form, and I listened as my bodyguard's deep, rowing breaths finally slowed down. Mourn's body had given off so much heat I might have thought him fevered or randy if not for the scent of pure exertion filling my nose.

"*Rrrrr*, shit," he hissed, scratching his back against a tree even before he had righted the fit of his harness.

"Itching again?" I whispered.

He exhaled when he brought the source of irritation under control and adjusted his harness into its original shape. "Yes. Good now."

"Want me to look?" I asked, offering his wrinkled cloak, which he accepted.

"There is nothing to see."

He turned around to show me, and I peered closer in the moonlight. He was right. Other than some of the old scars from the Deepearth threaded between patches of scales, I could see nothing which might explain why an intense itch might arise with a shapeshift.

"Hm. Alright." I peered around us but only saw more forest. "Which way now?"

"First, will you redon your blindfold?"

I squinted. "What? In case I'm captured and interrogated?"

He gave me a dry smile. "A reasonable precaution that will ease the minds of those posted here. They are aware of us."

"Very well." I got out my blindfold again, looked up at him with a smile before putting it on. "It's not like I've never wandered the underground totally blind before."

Mourn's smile warmed and he dipped his chin to that, waiting until I was indeed blind before taking my arm. Probably for appearance's sake.

"This way," he said.

THE DWARF GREETED US FROM A HOLE IN THE GROUND AFTER AN IMPRESSIVELY quiet sequence of confirmation signals and the revelation of a well-maintained door underneath natural camouflage. I only knew it was open when I smelled cool earth.

Mourn leaned close and tugged me to stop. "Ladder. Squat down here, I have you."

I didn't need the half-blood to hold my hand to find the ladder with my feet but, given that the Dwarf hovered as if to catch me should I slip, I figured Mourn was being expedient. No reason to insist we were reckless and noisy visitors in addition to being strange.

I stood patiently with my blindfold, comfortable at once in the underground space, while Mourn and the Dwarf secured the opening and joined me.

"Ye may remove th' blind, lass," said a new voice with a thicker accent than Talov.

A younger, short-bearded blond Tundar filled my view beneath the gentle glow of yellow and orange stones above our heads. Mourn couldn't straighten up without bumping his head, though the Dwarf and I stood quite comfortably.

The blond thrust out his fuzzy, broad hand to me. "Hallo. I'm Geir. Word is 'tween Clan an' Guild. I honor both."

I glanced at his hand. At least I'd seen this greeting before.

"Sirana," I said, clasping his hand in mine. "Searching for my sister."

His hand pump seemed cautious as he looked me up and down, inspecting. "Aye. Ye fit the word."

My mouth twisted. "Word from Augran or from Manalar?"

"Both." Geir shifted on wide feet. "We knew ye were comin' but we also relayed th' falcon message back tah Alran. Somethin' weird is gonna happen this time, eh?"

Mourn's tail swished behind him. "You could say that."

"Well, don' worry, we're preparin' fer a lot o' company."

"The first squads are only an hour behind us."

"Got it. Food or drink while yer waitin?'"

My bodyguard looked at me to answer, and as was frequent, I felt both hungry and a little ill.

"Yes, please," I said. "Bread, cheese, or vegetables. Water, if you have any?"

Geir grinned while seeming confused. "Aye, course! Water's not somethin' tah go without. Plenny o' that grub, too." He motioned as he turned to lead us down the hall. "Come with."

We did, though a morose weight laid upon me as I realized I would have to sit and do little for that hour when I was so close to jumping to my sister's aid.

We're coming, Jael. Please stay alive and sane in that place.

THERE WEREN'T MANY DWARVES HERE YET, THOUGH THAT WAS SOON TO change drastically. After getting us cold food and water in a near-empty mess, Geir returned to his post to keep watch for Reprisal, while a few others poked their heads in and muttered to each other in Dwarvish but opted not to speak to us before leaving.

★Did we do something wrong?★ I signed close to my chest.

★No,★ he replied. ★They're nervous waiting for confirmation that others are coming. They were never posted here to entertain.★

So some Dwarves could be as reticent as others were jovial. Not a surprise but it felt awkward. For the first time, none gawked at me or cared to ask any questions.

Well. Mourn's not worried.

After we'd eaten something relatively small and Mourn especially had drunk his fill of fresh water, sex crossed my mind as another way to pass the time. We stood up to quickly wash our cups and plates, preparing to leave the mess hall. I thought he might have read my shift in mood when he lifted his hand to sign.

★Let's attach the pearl and be sure we can communicate.★

Or that.

With a wry grimace, I tugged off my glove and held the pearl as he selected a small, leather-wrapped cylinder from his harness. I'd met some who were impressed that I could keep the location of everything straight on my belt, but Mourn's harness looked to contain twice as many items in distinct containers. He seemed to have little trouble finding what he needed.

"The fixative?" I asked as he lifted it up.

"Quick drying," he confirmed, "very strong. Do not touch until I'm satisfied, or you may have to clip a hole in your glove."

"Noted."

I coaxed my spiders back into their pouch for the time being.

"Good idea. Now, hold still."

The Dragonblood tucked his claw behind my ear to lift my earlobe with the pad of his finger. With the other hand, he touched my skin with one end of his cylinder before setting it aside on the table. Pinching the smoky, magical bead between his talons, Mourn lifted it from my palm, his pupils slimming to tiny lines as he focused on exactly where to drop it.

I barely felt anything when he muttered, "Good."

"Is it there?"

"A moment."

He touched something with the point of his claw, *then* I could feel a hard nodule nudged securely against my skin.

"There," he said. "Do not touch it yet. Let it dry. Come this way."

Mourn knew his way around, that much was clear. Even if it had been twelve years since he'd last used the jump gate, there were too many stout and well-constructed halls, doors, stairs, and gathering places for him *not* to be familiar with the place.

"This place would survive an earthquake," I murmured.

"Mostly, yes. They have a lot of practice and learned from cave-ins over millennia."

"They built this in the last sixty years since the Kerut Clan was purged?"

"Yes. The Taiding and Augran Clans were motivated."

"How could the Manalari *not* notice all the construction?"

Mourn glanced at me with a smirk. "Hubris? Plus the more subtle uses of magic which the Bishops don't value enough to teach in their construction. The Tundar are experts. They hollowed out enough space and built the gate first to move bodies and supplies in and out. It was once connected to Taiding before they altered it."

I arched my brow skeptically. "And *none* of the Tundar ever decided to split and cause trouble for Witch Hunters close by who brutally killed their kin?"

"Those who would have been tempted were not invited to help. The Clan leadership are strict about not starting revenge wars with Humans, and they have plenty of volunteers to get this done. The Tundar have the luxury of collective patience with Yungar; most Dwarves can wait longer than their adversaries for resolution."

"Why?"

"Imagine a young crafter helping to build a stronghold out of sight in the time it takes a Human soldier to cause some noise, retreat from injury, perhaps have children, and then be too old to do anything when that still-young crafter has matured toward the next solution. It's why no one in recent memory has been successful forcing Dwarves out of a belowground clan hall, though we have seen it happen with above-ground settlements."

Build a stronghold out of sight...

"Do you know the Dwarves who built the fortress which is now the Ley Tower?" I asked. "Where Sarilis is holed up? I mean, there, the Dwarves are just *gone*. I don't know if they were forced out, but it looked abandoned, not much left behind. Yet the final stairs leading to the top room of the watchtower are blocked by a strange ward, to which neither Gavin nor I could place an origin."

Mourn fell suspiciously quiet. I stared at him even when we finally came up to a door which he seemed willing to open.

"I do not know the Clan that built that fortress in the mountains," he finally said, retrieving two thin tools which he used to unlock the door without the Dwarves' assistance. "Talov has not found anyone he credits with the task, and it was abandoned by the time I escaped the Deepearth."

I perked up. "You found it that early?"

"In my wanderings, yes. Graul and I used it as temporary shelter our first winter. That ward you describe was not there at the time, nor was Tamuril yet wandering around."

My attention stayed keen as he opened the door and motioned me inside. Hoping we could continue this subject, I stepped in and made space for him without trouble. In the dark my senses measured this room as one of the largest, longer than it was wide. At one end, most of the wall had been constructed with a series of interconnected circles of stones rather than those laid in horizontal blocks to retain the wall.

"Uh... the gate room?" I asked.

"Correct. And your pearl should be fixed firm."

I refrained from touching it.

"We can practice more—"

"Wait, don't change the subject." I grimaced as my stomach tensed. "You were there when you stopped me from 'chasing' Tamuril. You saw me and Gavin leave, and you followed. You said you *asked* Talov about which Clan built that place, and you don't know yet. What else do you know? How many times have you been there, and why?"

We stood in the dark, and I watched him frown with thought.

"Are you just curious?" he asked.

"No—"

My throat squeezed down threateningly, clipping off the word. He noticed. As we stared at each other's eyes, my mind settled into a recent, familiar place. I stopped thinking about pushing through the block.

He smiled slightly, signing, ★Try touching your pearl.★

Sigh.

Glancing down to tug off my glove, I squeezed my earlobe cautiously at first, tracing the shape of the new, functional decoration. It absolutely was not coming off unless it took some skin with it.

The moment I looked up again—

We connected.

★*I have been to the Ley Tower seven times since I found it,*★ he thought with his usual precision. ★*At first, the Ley Lines intersecting caused stress within my aura. Graul and I had endured worse, however, and we did not have much choice with the depth of the snow in the mountains. It was a hungry winter. We left as soon as we could and did not return for some time. I imagine the* dissonance caused within magical auras is why it stood empty for decades. Few races can endure it for long.*

I dared not blink. ~Why go back at all?~

To test if the dissonance had lessened. The tower being relatively close to a Deepearth cave held my interest, not to mention the allure of Ley Lines intersecting. By measures, the Ley became calmer over the years, and the song began drawing the interest of others.

My heartrate picked up. ~Drawing whose interests?~

The Naulor Queen. The Ascended. Mourn watched me. *The Davrin Queen?*

Panic pressed up within me. I breathed, slowing my heart before simply *not* considering a struggle of wills my tongue couldn't win.

~Yes.~

Mourn's eyes shone in the dark. *Hm. Interesting. And someone set that ward on the top of the tower which Sarilis and Gavin seemed to avoid. Another unknown.*

~Correct. And Gavin said he was drawn across the Midway with the help of Nyx.~

The Dragonblood considered. *Unavoidable, then, that the Ley Tower will grow evermore contested until someone learns how to hold that intersection.*

As my Queen foretold. The machinations of the Hells fouling the Crossroads. Gavin had to go back, and I had to help him.

~Uhm. S-so you said the Ma'ab were drawn there but did not take the tower then, for whatever reason. How long ago was this?~

He studied my expression. *You already know.*

~I do *not*. I know what my elders suggested, and I know what Kurn claimed while drugged, boasting as a quarter-century child.~

Mourn smirked. *Very well. The Ma'ab were near the Ley Tower one hundred and one years ago.*

Queasiness surged but I kept thinking without pushing my body. ~Were you present as witness?~

Yes, with Krithannia, Talov, and Graul. Tamuril showed up for the first time as well, sent by Queen Yivon. She nearly ran into the Ma'ab. If we had known she was coming, we would have headed her off.

Oh, my Goddess.

~*Did you see our Priestess, too?*~ I blurted, clutching the saphgar pendant. ~*At the same time? A Davrin was s-sent, too! Kurn said he never saw an Elf before, and I can only say the Sathoet was alive in Ennikar about five years ago because Kurn trained with him when he failed the Hellhound trials!*~

Our mindlink helped me interpret Mourn's expression as it changed. Dread.

The Ma'ab have a Sathoet which they have kept alive and secret for a century? he asked as if he was hoping he was wrong.

I finally blinked. ~*You mean the Guild doesn't know?*~

He curled his lip. *Few who go into Ennikar make it back out to tell of it. In addition, no one has successfully interrogated a Hellhound until you found this failed exile sired by the first one.*

The first one...

~*The first Hellhound? Divigna?*~

Kreshel Divigna. Correct.

~*He has... he has existed about as long as the Priestess has been missing, yes? Much longer than a Human should live and sire children. The timing seems...odd, but perhaps I'm wrong? Paranoid?*~

Possible.

Yet the dread in Mourn's mood remained, and he didn't look away from me. His pupils constricted while I watched, to become so thin the sight made my skin prickle.

Damn.

~*What?*~ I pressed. ~*What do you remember?*~

Something which suggests my misjudgment of leaving you too soon in Troshin Bend was not the first time I made that mistake. For almost the same reason.

~*What?! What reason? What do you mean?*~

Krithannia's voice broke his focus on me.

"Shadow? Sirana? Are you alright?"

Damnit!

I blinked, pressing my hand to my brow as if to keep the sharp ache from burrowing out through my skull. Mourn's recovery was much smoother; he'd probably heard warning through the pearls.

"Yes," he said. "We were waiting for all of you."

All?

The edges of my vision were blurred as the Guildsmen lit a few heatless torches in the gate room so they could see. Everyone had arrived, however, Krithannia, Gavin, the Yungian Guild and Reprisal, smelling like they had just scrubbed down without soap.

"Practicing?" Gavin asked me, tilting his head to peer at the dark irregularity attached to my ear.

"Um. Yeah. We've been slowly improving my silent tongue."

The Deathwalker nodded with lessening interest.

"Where's Nightmare?" I asked.

Most of the men had been doing last moment checks on their equipment, but quite a few chortled and glanced either at Gavin or Deshi.

"Literally buried her to wait outside," Tak volunteered. "The damnedest thing I've seen with a corpse yet."

"Think the Ma'ab can do that?" asked Kil.

"Do what?" I asked both of them, glancing impatiently at Gavin.

"I withdrew most of the Vitas from her body," he said, pulling his spade from his backpack. "This being the fastest way to dry her flesh and skeleton and preserve her beneath the earth."

"Sho'shien touched her brow, and she fell over," Deshi described in more detail, for certain with more energy. He used his forearm to pantomime something once upright toppling sideways to the ground. "Then dark dirt flowed around her like water, covering her skin and bones! Grass went under but toadstool and dead leaves came up!"

Several of Reprisal confirmed.

"Yeah, that's basically what happened," Hawk said, sounding disconcerted where Deshi was excited.

I looked back at Gavin, blinking in surprise. "You really did that?"

He shrugged. "We've each been improving ourselves since landing in Augran."

"The Guild's good for that," Wolf quipped with a satisfied smirk as Krithannia and Mourn smiled with subtle satisfaction.

About then, five of the Dwarves posted at Kerut entered behind the thirty men going to Manalar.

"Still got 'bout an hour tah sunrise," said the first with a short black beard with Geir behind him. "Yah ready?"

Jael.

"We are," Krithannia answered with a bow. "I can also help with the gate if you like."

The blackbeard's bushy eyebrows sprang up, better showing a pair of quite beautiful, dark green eyes. "Ye know how?"

"I've assisted the Guild many times between Alran and Taiding."

"Ah! Excellent. Aye, some help tah keep it stable be appreciated."

Gavin and I studied them carefully, as Krithannia and three Dwarves from the post brought out a box of six gems and used a step ladder to place each in the center of a rune carved deep into the wall. I hadn't realized how stark the relief was for each foreign shape, though once the different colored gems were set, I could tell the center had been dug even deeper than the rest.

No falling out from magical vibration...

I heard muttering and brief instructions between Dwarves but wasn't sure if words were a crucial part of this magic. Like with the underground trolley, the Tundar mages seemed to concentrate much more on where they placed their fingers and how they traced patterns or slid small pieces of metal. Even Krithannia focused on her fingers and said nothing.

Then, suddenly, the circular stones began to hum.

Expectantly, I looked for light but saw none. Not even the gems. I glanced at Mourn. He signed, ★Normal.★

The humming increased in frequency though not in volume, every moment passing without a sparkle of light. The Guild's mages seemed on edge, for they must have felt the same, intangible pressure, as if innumerable bowstrings had been drawn back, surrounding us. We wouldn't have space to move until all that tension was released.

I prodded Mourn and signed against my middle, ★Can you work a Dwarven gate?★

To my relief, he confirmed, ★Krithannia and I can do it alone.★

That's good.

★What about just you?★

★More difficult, and for only few bodies, but possible.★

I frowned. ★How many is 'few bodies?'★

★Three. Maybe four.★

So, not all four squads. Mourn working alone would leave a lot of them behind.

★Is Krithannia that powerful? That adding her gets everyone out?★

Mourn's smile arrived slowly. ★I told you she was greater than me.★

I pursed my lips. ★So we can't let the Ma'ab get her, too, can we?★

He looked surprised. ★We?★

★Seems bad for everyone,★ I added. ★Eventually. Like most things with the Ascended.★

He smirked. ★Truer signs were never motioned.★

The hum had risen in pitch before, finally, it stopped.

Just...ceased.

I wasn't alone when I gasped to watch the stone lose its solid form without either draining away like mud or blowing up in a puff of dust. The designs within the arch of gems had seemed to vanish until I realized the wall had become transparent. On the other side was another underground room without light.

"I'll go first," Mourn said aloud, startling everyone. "And set a light for you to follow if it's clear."

"Go, then," said the blackbeard, his eyes narrowed to slits in his concentration. "Nothin' seems off here."

Squeezing my shoulder and signing for me to wait, Mourn took two long steps before springing forward on his third, passing through the stone as if it were made of something a touch firmer than water. The wall seemed to wobble for an instant, then it was simply dark with hints of a body moving around in the void.

Then, finally, a light.

I saw more stone, a wall visibly worn compared to the newly constructed redoubt. Though it appeared to be situated only the next room over, the raw mix of yellowish-brown sediment and quartz-riddled rock could not be more different from the dark soil and measured, grey stone here in Kerut.

So, that's Manalar? Right there?

Mourn stood in the center of a barren room, turning to us with a pale glowing stone in his palm. He signaled the way was clear.

"One hour tah go," the lead Dwarf reminded us.

Gavin stepped forward first, entering while neither speeding nor slowing his pace. I waited to see if a leap like Mourn's was required to catch one's feet at the end, or if he displayed prowess.

The Deathwalker *did* stumble as he entered the other room so far away; Mourn caught him by the shoulder but released him quickly enough not to see Gavin shake him off.

Wolf and Torch looked at me, motioned at the same moment that I should go next.

Right.

I took a few steps to build momentum, holding to Mourn's description about it feeling like jumping out of a window onto the ground below. I prepared for that scenario, imagining it as clearly as I could. I felt that brief experience of weightlessness followed by acceleration as the downward pull caught me—

Until my boots landed on a dusty, gritty floor, scuffing my heel, as I slowed myself. Mourn stepped up to guide me to the side as Torch and his brothers entered next, followed by all of Reprisal, one squad at a time. Finally, Krithannia stepped into view and jumped. Mourn rushed forward to catch her, too. The moment she was through, the stone returned to its opaque and solid state.

The new gate of Kerut had closed, and we were alone in hostile territory.

CHAPTER 13

THE WAY OUT HAD THREE STONES BLOCKING THE ROUTE TO A NATURAL PATH-way that bent back on itself twice, all of which helped prevent the gate's accidental discovery over long periods of time.

I noted how easy it was to breathe, even with so many mouths in a tight space, and observed as Mourn and Krithannia inspected each obstacle before shifting it. They used either magic or brute strength, not both, and I dared consider that the method on each mattered.

A few of Reprisal whispered to each other, nervous in the tight passage and wondering why the air seemed "fresh." At the same time, I found the sources of air exchange which either appeared natural or were expertly hidden to the average Human eye.

Brilliant.

The gate was extremely difficult to reach, but it wasn't sealed completely from the outside. When the final wall parted at an invisible seal and both halves retreated and became part of the tunnel, we could hear the chirps of insects and ribbits of frogs.

We held still to listen. No horses, bridles, or bootsteps. No scent of camp, dung, or fire smoke. Most importantly, no distant sounds of an army camp on the far side of the ridge.

"Everyone stay behind the ward," Mourn whispered as Krithannia prepared to cast one between herself and him. "I need this hour of darkness to choose our best way inside."

"Wouldn't it be better for us to creep closer under darkness, too?" Wolf asked. "We don't need more than moonlight."

"I know, and yes, it would. But we have not the time." The half-blood's metallic eyes remained steady on the Hand of Reprisal without being threatening. "There is no safe place to hide this many of us with the certainty I require to bring you with me. With Krithannia here, retreat through the gate is an option if I discover certain death for you all."

Gavin and I shook our heads in silent refusal and Mourn smiled wryly at us.

"Give me time," he repeated. "Stay hidden. Remain uncaptured."

Simple.

"*Ithilidrinithica,*" Krithannia murmured, the trilling accent rolling like a fine liquid off her tongue. She placed the ward at the open crevice after Mourn slipped through and disappeared into the last hour of night, ending all debate.

Afterward, the Naulor leaned against the wall, crossed her arms, and looked outside at the starlight while the rest of us peered at each other. With a silent sigh, Wolf exchanged Guild sign with Torch, Hawk, Bear, and Crow before the messages were passed along. I saw several men sneak back up the passage, listening as they chose a place to sit or lie down.

Not foolish taking the moment to rest while they could, though the pre-mission quivers would pass through each of us at one point or another.

Moving across from Krithannia, I could sense the line I shouldn't cross even if I couldn't see it. The stars were visible outside, the sky as clear as it had been up North, and the small moon trailed behind the large one setting. I marveled that the arrangement of the stars appeared the same regardless. To my eye, they'd never changed from the western mountains to the Midway, all the way to the Great Lake, to Augran and Kerut.

And now here. Manalar.

The sky was the same when Jael was captured.

How much distance must we be seeing above the Surface for this to be true? Was the Nexus out there somewhere alone with the Abyss? Were each represented by one of the points of light or were they something else unseen?

Gavin stepped into my periphery, I thought, also to look out at the sky. Then he ducked down and scraped some dirt from the passage floor and straightened up to contemplate the dry dust and pebbles in his palm, rubbing it briefly with his thumb.

I frowned, glancing at Krithannia, who shrugged.

"Back to my native ground," he murmured.

I didn't point out the obvious, that we weren't where his Ma'ab mother had birthed him. Instead I asked, "Same type of rock as the monastery?"

"Drier weather, less water, tougher scrub on this side of the Temple City."

Most of the men heard us talking and a few eased forward to listen. They were curious and, somehow, this reminded me of Wolf's question about Gavin's name.

"Did all the monks have only one name?" I asked.

The Deathwalker turned his head and frowned. In the night shadows, he looked quite gruesome. "What?"

"You only gave me one name, and I've since learned that was odd. Did you ever have a house name?"

"House name," he repeated, scoffing. "Not one I would claim or wish to speak again."

"What about your mother's name?" I asked. "Did you ever learn this?"

Gavin glanced at Krithannia but didn't seem to think he had much more of an audience besides her. Meanwhile, I knew several of the Guildsmen were listening quite intently; Deshi and Tak were two of them.

His frown deepening, his hand cradling the dry soil with no sign of sweat, several quiet moments passed as he reflected on my question.

"Ada," he said at last. "That was what my father called her when speaking of the dead. I do not know if that was her own name from Ennikar."

"Ada," I repeated. "Well then, this is what we have to work with, Gavin, son of Ada."

He harrumphed before looking back outside, although he didn't seem displeased.

I glanced behind me, and several Guildsmen were smiling, including Wolf, without risking the shine of their teeth. Meanwhile, Gavin contemplated the dirt in his hand once more.

Then, suddenly, he turned around. His motion startled those closest as eyes widened and spines leaned back, but he focused on one.

"Deshi," he began.

The latent death mage straightened. "Sho'shien?"

"Do you still want to honor the Grey Maiden in the deaths you cause?"

"Y-yes, Sho'shien."

"Use Deathwalker, please."

Deshi bowed. "Deathwalker."

"Will you hand me your blade?"

Without hesitation, the youth slid his long dagger from its sheath, offering it laid flat in both hands like before. The blade had been blackened to reflect no light.

"*Mordanta shenti ro'geth*," Gavin murmured as he reached for it with dirt in his palm. His icy, blue irises vanished even under the paltry shine of stars and the smaller sister moon, and the air close to him grew chilled.

Several Guildsmen drew back unobtrusively, though Deshi remained at attention where he stood, watching with open fascination as Nyx's messenger closed both hands around the naked blade and allowed it to bite into his flesh, his black blood welling up along the metal's edge.

"*Fuck!*" Tak whispered.

I took a step back myself, watching one streak of viscous fluid overflow and drip off the back of his pale hand. Gavin caught it in the palm of his other hand, letting it mix with the dirt from his "native" ground.

"Ursuren palniti unvushhh."

The Deathwalker's hushed words continued, escaping through black teeth as he smeared dark, muddy blood along Deshi's matte dagger. His voice held a similar tone of speaking with the dead, as when he visited the Witch Hunters' shallow graves, and I felt a subtle pressure to turn Soul Drinker away from him.

Just to be safe.

The passage became a little colder, and Deshi's eyes remained fixed on his weapon stained with the inhuman blood of Sho'shien. Even if Reprisal saw Gavin as something else—a half-Ma'ab using the Far North's magic to step around his death—the Yungian's expression confirmed a far more spiritual experience.

Suddenly, Gavin's ghostly whisper turned to Trade.

"Add to this the red blood of the living soul," he rasped, *"should that soul wish to be known to the Steward of the old pact, the Grey Maiden of the Nexus."*

The young man considered this request seriously, and understandably so. How many in Yong-wen sought to draw the attention of powerful spirits?

Only those with ambition.

"Deathwalker," Krithannia said, noting Deshi wasn't the only one looking wary. "Is Deshi making *any* promise of any kind in doing so?"

"No promises to be kept yet." His voice was hoarse, its tenor becoming odd and less familiar. *"Only what has been said. Deshi will be known to the Grey Maiden. In sending those killed by his blade to meet her halfway, he grants her a soul's worth of worship upon this world by his own will. Nothing more."*

A soul's worth?

"To meet her halfway," Deshi considered. "And then what, Deathwalker?"

"She provides safe passage through the Nexus to the next transition," Gavin answered, his eyes black as the space between the stars. *"Know that*

Existence shall continue underneath her guiding hand, in whatever form this may take."

Quietly, more of the Guild encircled this impromptu ritual. In his favor, Deshi did not take too long to decide.

The young Guildsman withdrew a second, smaller dagger before removing his dark glove. "How much red to add, Deathwalker?"

"A drop or two. Do not touch your wound to the weapon."

With a nod, Deshi created a shallow cut on the back of his hand and turned it to coax those one or two drops to land in the mess. As soon as they had, Gavin began firmly rubbing the flat of the blade with his thumbs as if trying to clean it. Astonishingly, it seemed to be working.

"Whoa," one of Reprisal breathed.

We witnessed the drying mix of blood and soil seeming to vanish before our eyes, either into the blade or into thin air. Krithannia observed intensely, one gloved hand covering her mouth while her silvery eyes never blinked. When Gavin offered the blade across open palms, his wounds swiftly vanishing, Deshi glanced at the Guild Mistress, who nodded once.

"An enchantment, of sorts," she said quietly. "Aligned to your aura, Deshi."

"Of course, it is," Gavin replied, sounding more like himself; even Wolf didn't seem to think he was lying.

The combination of this broke the last thread of hesitation within the Yungian, and Deshi gratefully reached out to accept his curiously clean weapon back from my ally.

"*Shi'sheh,* Deathwalker," he said with reverence. "May I be known to your maiden and serve well those who must die by my hand."

Gavin grunted, flexing his long fingers as he watched the last of the cuts close.

"I don't suppose," said Kil, "there is a way to do that same on another weapon *without* pledging to be under the Maiden's eye?"

I watched my death mage glower. "No. Although, without the red blood, it would simply aid in transition to the Nexus without any devotion or invitation."

"Hm." Kil looked to Wolf. "But we have time?"

"Until Shadow returns," the Hand agreed. "Are you willing to bless a few more blades in the name of your lady, Gavin Ada-son, without the red blood from those of us who may worship in other ways?"

The Deathwalker's ice blue irises had only partly returned at the time he heard that. "Better for those who would be lost or consumed otherwise, I suppose."

Several men didn't enjoy hearing that, but Kil stepped forward nonetheless to offer his favorite dagger to the Deathwalker. Gavin accepted before he stooped, reaching for more dirt.

The grave-speak continued until dawn.

KRITHANNIA KNEW FIRST WHEN SOMEONE APPROACHED THE WARD. WE ALL waited with hope it was Mourn, but I didn't exhale until I saw his familiar outline. He was smirking but seemed in deep thought, and the flick of his tail told me it was something interesting.

Not necessarily good.

The Naulor let him into the passage before resetting what seemed a less robust ward, either dampening sound or warning of approach, requiring less effort to unravel it. Once the squad leaders were in front and everybody had crowded forward, Mourn used hand-sign to speak. It wasn't Davrin sign; I could only make out one in five motions.

Shit.

I glanced at him in annoyance, but he didn't look back. His tail, however, reached to tap my boot. Belatedly, I remembered the pearl on my earlobe. *Right.*

I touched it.

There you are.

I smirked as I focused, finally picking up on the briefing that many were getting through Guild sign.

The passage through the southern quarry is open, he thought at the same time his hands moved, *and I detected few sentries. The southern wall seems unusually light while they reinforce the north and east. The Guild has used the quarry most frequently to enter the city's streets and alleys, and this is the best option for Reprisal's teams to enter in stages.*

Just Reprisal?

Wolf, Bear, Hawk, and Crow all smiled like they expected this. I frowned slightly. Had I missed something at the beginning?

Gavin had the same bewildered expression as he looked at Krithannia, who glanced back in silence. He nodded to acknowledge something, and I blinked in realization.

My Deathwalker must have practiced missive spells with the Guild Mistress back in the library, for he would recognize even less of the Guild sign than I did. Several small holes in our plan had been filled while I'd focused on filling my own.

I smirked as Mourn continued.

To our benefit, the city has emptied the quarry of workers to prepare for the siege. However, there are two significant threats on your way in. He paused, signaling enough significance to heighten our attention, then looked at Krithannia. *First, there are Ma'ab scouts in the area.*

Fuck.

Bodies shifted in the cave as most of Reprisal visibly shared my concern. Krithannia signed to Mourn, and he shook his head.

*No, I did not lay eyes on them. I caught a light scent on the wind coming from the north side, but it was too far away to stalk and deal with them before returning here on time. Be extremely cautious while moving to the quarry on the south side in case you cross paths or sense anyone following you. They could be looking for these same entrances.

If you find sign or spot them too close, alert everyone. We can try to take them out before they find anything useful. Hopefully it will take time for the main body to realize their scouts are overdue. At the same time, the second threat will be traps and alarms intended for these same Ma'ab, so be on high alert at every step.

The teams acknowledged and agreed, and Mourn bowed his head, continuing.

*Once you're inside, we also have the added difficulty of men and mages being conscripted for the walls' defenses. Obviously, Teams One, Two, and Three can't move around as able-bodied mercenaries. *

I saw dry smiles and more signs of agreement.

Appear as a non-combatant, either much older than you are or shrouded as one lame or ill, Mourn instructed. *As you position yourselves to enter the Temple when called, try to mimic the middle clergy, not the lowest but not anyone of importance. I recommend against appearing as a woman, young or old, for we know Witch Hunters search for sport under times of perceived threat. *

A few jaw muscles flexed at this part. Understanding remained clear as the ever-lightening sky.

*You'll have to split up and avoid the city watch and the Templars until then. Give regular reports of all movements you observe. No engaging Witch Hunters in open conflict. If you can quietly kill and hide a body, so be it, but evaluate your risk, and do nothing if you could be caught. Otherwise, you risk this entire mission. *

Mourn waited for confirmation from every man before he continued. *Spare the Templars, street guards, and soldiers, but don't allow yourself to be detained by them. The pearls will keep us in contact and apprised of what trouble we encounter. We'll coordinate distractions and assistance as needed. *

Reprisal nodded as a wave of heads; every expression was solemn while they listened in silence. Their hands stayed down; no questions from them yet. I had one so interrupted Mourn's thoughts.

~Are there other ways to enter besides the quarry? You didn't mention Team Four, unless I missed it at the beginning.~

Mourn glanced at me, his hands seeming to repeat my question to the others. Wolf and the Foci signed agreement, waiting expectantly.

*There are two other entrances. One lies in this eastern canyon and the other on the north face. Both were sealed when Archbishop Iarmod came to power, on multiple levels. Over time, the Guild reopened part of each but hid the mechanisms. I checked them both, and they remained undiscovered like in the quarry, but the north wall is where the city expects to see the Ma'ab approaching and also where I scented the scouts. *

~Hm. I assume we take the eastern canyon entrance?~

*Correct. *

203

~Where does it lead?~

Mourn translated our mental conversation with his hands. *First, it's worth noting that the north-face entrance is the closest access to the Temple itself through the cisterns. As such, there are far too many eyes on both sides, with the city's water being at extreme risk of fouling attempts from the enemy. None of us should attempt this route, in or out.*

We nodded and waited for the rest.

The canyon entrance connects to the water system eventually but is a long climb up to city-level on the surface of Mount Sonai. Over the centuries, it has become something of a labyrinth, built in segments over many regimes, some by Dwarves, some not. It is the oldest part of this city, also easy to get lost. There are many hallways which are gated or bricked up, if they have not caved in and never repaired.

Delightful. It sounded like home.

Torch signed something and Mourn acknowledged him. *Yes, I know the way to reach the lower levels of the Temple from this entrance at the mountain's base. In theory, there exists a path by which we could reach the dungeons first, free Sirana's sister, and head up to the sacred spring. We will follow this path, but, if events go that smoothly, I will wonder if the entire Temple has been poisoned in their beds.*

Some audible chuckles escaped the mouths of these men, though they were subtle as a few looked out where the daylight grew stronger. The brightness was starting to make me squint.

Tak lifted his hand and waited for a sign before asking his question.

Hm. Correct, Tak. There is no easy way for refugees to escape and reach this jump gate. Our methods of entry were never intended to move large groups of untrained citizens quickly.

Krithannia signed something, and the men bowed their heads to her, returning affirmatives.

She reminds them that their mission is not to guide people out, Mourn told me.

~Understood. So, how long before we leave?~

Now, if there are no other questions.

There were a few more clarifying or confirming details, but Reprisal seemed to understand there were many unknowns we had yet to work out and continual threats to be ready for. All those answers would appear only as events occurred.

Are we ready?

We were.

It's time.

REPRISAL HAD THE LONGER JOG THAT EARLY MORNING, SO THEY LEFT FIRST, second, and third in their squads, camouflaging themselves to reach the quarry. Mourn, Krithannia, and Torch would know about their movement at every step, even within the belly of the mountain. Amusingly, Mourn estimated that they would reach the streets before we found our way up through the maze.

He'd even wager on it.

~Well, if we fall behind, at least I'll be out of the Sun.~

They'll also be listening to gossip on the streets and gathering intelligence, Mourn reassured me. *Our goal isn't to hurry. It's to not be seen until Gavin throws the shard.*

My heart jumped to imagine that happening.

On our way to the base of the mountain, we each suppressed our auras although none wore individual illusions or altered forms. For the moment, Mourn and Krithannia provided a collective one which blurred our lines and muted our colors to better mimic the land around us.

The Dragonblood slinked around and between trees slightly ahead and apart from us, his tongue frequently tasting the air as he scouted ahead, though we were all on alert for any sign of the Ma'ab doing the same. The four Yungians flanked Krithannia, me, and Gavin.

The Deathwalker's determination showed in how he could keep up with us even without his horse. Even burdened with a muffled pack, he proved somehow stronger than he had been before his death. Though not light on his feet, his subdued heat and scent mimicked various stealth spells.

As the elevation grew steeper and the boulders larger, I noted his breathing, his sipping water twice, while taking great care not to stumble and scrape his skin on the rocks. Good to be especially mindful of leaving black blood to be found with the Ma'ab in the area.

We followed a frothing stream, thin and almost hidden within the rest of the canyon. I never saw the source before Mourn led us farther to the north. The morning grew warmer as the Sun extended rays stubbornly through the evergreens and brightened the mix of yellow and pale grey stones.

We followed and trusted our guide, but he needed to point out more than once the narrow crease of stone we aimed for. The high, slim gap in the stone lay hidden from every angle until we climbed closer and spotted the ledge. This deeper recess eased my headache instantly as we entered the solid, welcome shade of stone.

The relief didn't last when, ahead, Mourn stopped in his tracks. Even his tail froze as he signed for us to do the same. A second later, my eyes fixed where the white spines lay on his back, as they tried to rise beneath his cloak but were stopped by his harness.

I'd never seen *that* response outside of orgasm.

Shit.

He signed, *Human sign. Watch the rear.*

The Yungians turned so they could watch the crevice in both directions while Mourn moved forward slowly and carefully enough to barely shift a pebble on the gritty floor. Krithannia stayed as she was, controlling her breathing, while Gavin took hold of a dagger handle at his belt without drawing it.

Keeping my palm from Soul Drinker for the moment, I released my spiders from their pouch, and they skittered up into my hair.

With the daylight's glare behind us, the Dragonchild vanished in deep shadow as he approached what I assumed was the entrance he'd checked over two hours ago. Agitated that I couldn't see what might be happening, I touched my earlobe and took the complete silence as a sign that nothing had gotten worse.

Come forward. No noise. No light source.

I noted a slight delay between my first step and those of Gavin, Peng-lok, Nianzu, and Deshi receiving the same signal through Krithannia and Torch. Slim enough that any observer unaware of our communication methods might say we had moved together.

We joined Mourn near the back of the crevice and immediately saw the problem: the door was open.

Ma'ab, he confirmed, going over the sign and flicking out his tongue, his tail tip whipping back and forth. *A team of at least four. One female, three to four male.*

My pulse surged. *Already? Shit!*

How had they found this place at *exactly* this time? Had one of them detected Mourn moving about the mountain and followed him? Had they simply paid enough to get this intelligence about their enemy?

They broke the mechanism and left a trip-trap, he continued. *I removed it without setting off the alarm, but we can't close the door without repairing it. I don't have the means on me.*

More ill tidings.

~But they wouldn't have a map to follow, would they?~ I asked.

Metallic eyes glanced at me. *No. We never made one.*

~So they could get lost. Or we could trap them, make sure they don't leave to tell their host how to reach the Temple.~

Bear in mind, one-time distance communication isn't beyond Ma'ab mage ability, but it depends who just entered.

~Yes, but first we must know *who* entered.~

True.

Mourn looked troubled as he communicated with Krithannia and Torch along with the Hand and Foci. A quick plan came back.

Dark sight and silence spell. We stalk them and take them out in the underhalls.

Thank goddess.

One at a time, I watched the mages cast their spells, even Gavin. Had he practiced this before now?

Reprisal had magic which allowed them to see Radiants in the absence of light, and Krithannia had centuries to learn its uses. Was I surprised my studious ally would have set aside his scrolls in Yong-wen long enough to learn how to remove this disadvantage when moving in dark spaces?

This could save our chances to reach our goals for the Bishops, but the first real test would be the Ma'ab standing between me and Jael.

CHAPTER 14

MOURN REMAINED IN FRONT FOR THE FIRST HALF HOUR, TRACKING IN THE pitch black, and catching what hasty pitfalls the Ma'ab had left for us. He and Krithannia disabled them all without alerting those who set them as far as I could tell. From the exchanges through the pearls, they held the opinion that the Ma'ab hadn't taken the time to do better.

They were probably right. Even I could see without trying the signs of recent passage in the disturbed dust and scuffed stone from large pairs of boots.

We didn't know yet how far they were in front of us, but our attention stayed keen for such signs. Having to climb to the recess then find and break the Guild's mechanism on the old entrance, they could not have gone deeply into an unmapped maze in the time it took for Mourn to check on it and bring us back.

Unnerving to think the scouting party had spotted or found traces of Mourn in the night, however. I didn't know if that happened or was ill timing, but Mourn wouldn't have been careless.

The rough, natural passage changed into a worn but deliberately hewn stone hallway with ancient, crumbling steps. The air within the cave of the Dwarven gate moved, changing over regularly. In these early passages, hallways, and staircases, the air was stale and without flow.

We passed empty rooms where nothing remained, but they were barely more than old storage rooms or guard's quarters. The ceilings were relatively high, enough for Human men not to worry about bumping their heads when they jumped, but the space remained too tight for Mourn to use his sliders for quite some time.

Eventually, we no longer had to pause and wait on the traps and wards to be released; the Ma'ab had stopped placing such obstacles. Mourn's lips were always drawn back, inhaling the air slowly through his teeth and across his sensitive tongue as he turned his head whenever the path split.

Krithannia asked a question and Mourn slowed, choosing to sign and think his response simultaneously.

They follow the path we would have taken so far.

His neutrality belied the frustration of that statement.

I watched the Dragonblood's tail for early warnings when he did not speak through the pearl for the second half of that hour. Krithannia remained in front and Gavin measured his gait behind me, with the four Yungians protecting our rear. My eyes detected carvings every so often, either wayfinding signs or shapes which had once been significant to whomever had built these underhalls.

I wasn't convinced it was entirely Dwarven, but also not wholly Human, either, having seen many recent examples. Although many principles for building a lasting structure underground were universal, subtle aspects reminded me of rock-shaping magic we used in Sivaraus.

Could Elves have once settled on this mountain like we had in the Desert? Or another race? How had the Orcs constructed their dwellings in a time when they were known?

I blinked, cursing myself for drifting in distraction when Mourn stopped before an intersection. He had cleared several such corridors of surprises before but waited longer this time.

Sirana...?

He kept his back to me, his focus on what lay in front of him. Though I wore gloves, I clasped my earlobe because it helped the link feel tangible.

...can you hear me?

~Yes! Yes, sorry, I hear you.~

His tail waved slowly to one side then the other. *I must tell you something. I was not certain before but am now.*

I swallowed, glancing around; the others didn't seem to be listening yet. ~Certain of what?~

A demonblood is with them.

The others noticed me flinch. ~What?! You mean the Sathoet they stole? The scouts are sneaking in with him?~

Mourn hesitated. *I smell Abyssal blood for certain, not Human. Yes, possibly Elven. If Kurn was right in what he saw, likely one and the same.*

~But... what about his mother?~

I smell no Baenar but you.

Krithannia glanced at me with serious concern, as if she could hear my heart beating harder in the dark. She wasn't overreacting; I did feel ill, and I wasn't sure what I could do about it except grasp tight control of my breath as it grew wilder, the pain escalating.

"Listen to all rumors of half-bloods of Elven origin."

~No.~

All rumors.

"If you find any, bring them to Us."

All.

~No, no!~

Sirana?

My mind seized with indecision. My eyes couldn't see what lay directly in front of me, and my limbs felt oddly hollow. I leaned one shoulder against the wall, pressing myself to it to stay upright when the passageway seemed to warp.

All rumors. All half-bloods. Not just the ones I picked!

This was the worst I could imagine would happen. After everything I'd done to work within my restraints, all the choices I'd made, the bargaining, the patience, the learning...!

This might tear it all up into shreds. I would watch it happen, and I wouldn't be able to stop myself.

~Help... Morixxyleth... our Bargain...~

Mourn turned around, slow, and cautious. *Our Bargain is not in danger, Sirana. I promise.*

~I-I'm sorry...I-I must find him... but I don't know what I'll do... I'm not in... I c-can't—!~

Alright. Breathe. What does our Bargain need now, Sirana? Should the Sathoet be killed to save you?

I gasped loudly as if to scream.

~NO!~

Mourn blinked in surprise, watching me stiffen, beginning to quiver against the stone.

~Don't kill... he's of Elven origin...don't kill him. Please.~

I sounded so confused. Lost. *Afraid.* Why would I *want* a Sathoet to live after what the last one did to me?!

~I don't want it! I don't... Don't! No, stop, please—!~

Mourn stepped close and drew me to him as he had the last time I froze up in our memory. Tightening his arms and trapping my hands up and away from my belt, he held me while I shook. My spiders crept out onto my chest, over the burning saphgar above my panicked heart, before they hid back in my hair, chiming constantly with perplexed agitation.

Bite, or don't bite? Where?

~Nothing. Not yet.~

The rest of my team were concerned, of course. They must be, to be seeing this weakness at a time and place they were most at risk.

Oh, goddess... so foolish.

So weak!

After everything, I hadn't even made it to the dungeon.

We have a Bargain still, you and I, he said. * We must see it through. We will not stop here. If the Sathoet does not seek to harm us, I will not harm him. But I must protect you, and I cannot allow Krithannia to be captured.*

How likely was that for a half-blood traveling with the Ma'ab for a century?

What do I do now?

I tried to muffle an aching sob, wincing at the noise and pain in my throat. Whatever Mourn was saying to Krithannia and Torch, he wasn't sharing with me.

~Oh, Jael...~

Yes. Our Bargain, Red Sister. We must find her.

~B-but I must find the Sathoet...I can't walk away, I must...discover if it's true, what Kurn claimed...~

Yes, we will discover this, one way or another. We will help you.

My Dark Sight had gradually cleared as we talked, though I must have seemed feverish because Krithannia offered me water from her own skin. Mourn encouraged me to accept.

She says it will soothe your body beyond thirst, though you won't be tired, Mourn promised. *Drink.*

I accepted with minor reluctance, tasting only water, albeit some of the most refreshing I'd had recently. To the Naulor's side, Gavin looked down at me, frowning. Inside I grimaced at how, just a few weeks ago, he needed me to watch his back and help find enough to eat. *Not anymore.*

Gavin looked to Krithannia, who looked to Mourn and him to me.

The Deathwalker wants to know if he may touch your brow. He says this will not harm you or your unborn.

What? The pale man *wanted* to touch me? My face?

That had *never* happened.

My eyes flicked to and fro. ~Uh...alright?~

Mourn motioned to Gavin, who did what he said, laying his cool, dry hand on my sweaty brow. Then, even seeing only Radiants, his pupils vanished from my sight, and something happened within our auras, I was sure.

Not merging, but...

Calming.

Or maybe that was Krithannia's water?

Whatever combination of things, my saphgar no longer seared my skin, my spiders' chimes had quieted at the back of my head, and the panic in my body receded. I could breathe normally.

~Ohh…what did you do, Gavin?~

The Deathwalker blinked thrice at hearing my voice; it was then his icy pupils returned within his black eyes. He leaned back to remove his hand but stopped himself, watching me without blinking. I heard one clear voice in a sea of whispers, though I wasn't sure if it was him.

You bear a far-reaching anchor but not by choice.

The whispers seemed to muffle everything else in that moment, and all was calm around me. I attempted to answer.

~…This is…true.~

Rather than see it, I felt the nod in the affirmative.

And we approach one of the elicitors of this anchor, correct?

~Yes. I–If it's him, he and his mother disappeared near the Ley Tower. I–I've been searching for stories…of what might have happened.~

And you found one. You heard that the Ma'ab may hold one of your blood.

~Not… my blood but… Yes. Ours.~

And what if this is found true, River child? What must you do then?

I shuddered. *~Bring him back home. To his Queen.~*

The Deathwalker's face was corpse-still yet the voice continued.

We see no reason you cannot do this and keep your agreements. There is less conflict than you assume. Unraveling this will free your mind. Look where the threads intersect, for home can be reached by any direction.

I barely withheld a laugh of disbelief, swallowing it down as Gavin lifted his palm from my forehead. He wiped it off on his long grey robe, looked to Krithannia and Mourn for some silent discussion about what to do next.

My stomach felt hollow for more than one reason. I sneaked a precious handful of my travel mix into my mouth, chewing hungrily. Mourn seemed to take that as a good sign. He smiled.

We're in agreement, Sirana, he said through his pearl. *Should we encounter the Sathoet, we will not seek to destroy him first, but neutralize him if we can. We will kill the Ma'ab first.*

The cramping knot of anxiety in my chest had eased. I finished my mouthful of food before daring to look at each of them: Gavin, the

Guild Mistress, and the Yungian brothers. Deshi bowed first when we met eyes, and the other three followed his lead a moment later. They signed something I couldn't read.

They will honor the Sky Warrior's capture mission as best they can, but not at undue cost to the rest of our objectives.

I made certain my feet were steady before bowing to them in return.

A capture mission, huh? This was the most I could beg of any of them on behalf of my Queen, despite myself.

Despite everything I'd suffered at the hands of Wilsira's son.

Goddess damn Her.

I watched and listened to what communication followed as we made our way up through the labyrinth. Mourn relayed much of it to me, whether he signed critical portions to the Yungians or let Torch convey the meaning a moment later. I could only assume Krithannia maintained her contact with Gavin.

They must have intelligence from somewhere, the Dragonchild said. *I expected them to take more wrong turns and we would catch them doubling back by now.*

But we dare not grow reckless, Krithannia replied. *We cannot hurry and give ourselves away.*

Agreed. But if they reach the dungeon levels before we make gains, I don't know what will happen then.

We must see what options we have. If they are disruptive enough, Gavin could make it up to the sanctum with our team while we look for Jael.

Perhaps.

Krithannia had glanced at me at one point. I was both glad and writhing inside that Mourn told me what she was saying. It was like listening in on a conversation from a spyway.

I am glad you said something once you knew for certain. I fear what would have happened if she'd been caught unaware.

You and me both.

She is ashamed. She need not be. No one with less than a connection like Gavin's could have asked her and heard so much.

We shall talk about that afterward. Metallic eyes held mine a second. *We will make time.*

My face and ears burned hot. I didn't want to talk about this but might not have a choice. Especially if outcomes went *really* bad for the Guild. And what did she mean, no one with less than a connection like his? With who? Me, or…?

There is less conflict than you assume.

For the moment, I was afraid to consider further.

Huh-bua.

My urge to keep going was relentless, but at least I was in control of myself to infiltrate an underground space as a Red Sister should. However, I couldn't have slowed down or left Mourn's side if hot magma had been hurtling toward us.

Keep going.

We were close. So close.

Finally, my bodyguard paused, his tail flicking in surprise as he stared up a short stairway to his right which, at first glance, led to a brick wall. He lifted his chin and tasted the air.

Odd. That door has been shifted.

Door?

Mourn cleared the stairs of dangers before the rest of us followed behind him. Sure enough, an alarm had been set in place, and new dust had fallen onto the top step. The ward was no match for the Guild Mistress, who dispelled it and reset one for silence, followed by the Dragonchild quickly locating how to open it. He nudged us backward so he could first pull and then slide the heavy stone to one side, creating a gap in the wall.

This led to a hallway with many curving decorations carved into the stone with segments of cobwebs swept aside. Mourn stepped in first, looking both directions but pausing to his left, cursing through our link.

Serpent's dead tongue.

~What?~

This passage had been sealed but was recently reopened with an explosion collapsing the bricks.

~Explosion? We would have heard something like that, wouldn't we?~

Not if it happened yesterday. He sniffed the air. *Yes, I'm certain this passage was opened within the last day. A group of armored Manalari came through.*

I looked down and around as I came through next, stepping aside for the others to follow. The footprints disturbing the dust seemed to match his estimation. Then I studied the piles of bricks pushed against the walls.

~Which way does that exit go?~

Mourn's tail coiled closer to his heel spurs. *The dungeon. Two levels up.*

I flushed in excitement. ~We're here?~

Almost. Mourn motioned toward Gavin, who had put his back to the wall and stared intently toward the vanishing point of the hallway. *But the Ma'ab went that way.*

~Of course they did.~

And now we know why the Ma'ab did not get lost in the labyrinth.

~We do?~

My bodyguard looked to Krithannia and Gavin again; the latter hadn't shifted his gaze. *The Deathwalker says a spirit beckons him.*

The hall was becoming crowded. I stood in front of Krithannia, with Torch and Peng-lok slipping in behind her, nearest to the fallen bricks. In front of me were Deshi, Nianzu, and Mourn, with Gavin presumably between us and his ghost.

The Deathwalker held up his palm, urging all of us to stay back. In response, Deshi had drawn his death-blessed blade. Within an instant, the Yungian gasped out loud, staring ahead as he signed one-handed. The Guild Mistress responded by taking her own Dragon pearl and pressing it into the palm of that flailing hand, closing both of her hands over his.

Mourn let me in on this one.

What do you see, Deshi? Krithannia asked. *Describe it to us.*

An elder Paxian, he answered. *Bald, wearing simple robes. His eyes are sightless yet stare into me.*

We could observe Gavin's actions, but like at Troshin Bend, he interacted with something I could not see. He whispered quietly, the ethereal rasp sending a shiver up my spine as he held up his arm with his fingers curled.

Sho'shien repels the ancient lost one from coming too close, Deshi said. *Its mouth opens in a scream I cannot hear... H-he still speaks to it.*

If there had been a death scream, it seemed to affect my ally as his back stiffened and his other hand clenched into a fist. Then, I watched with amazement as Gavin reached into a pocket of his robe and brought out a brass sunburst medallion on an old rope. Although the Deathwalker did not don it, he did hold it up high in front of him.

I'd never seen it before, but it was not newly crafted. Had it belonged to Bictrius? Or Jacob?

The spirit recognizes the symbol, Deshi whispered through the pearl.

Next time Gavin whispered in Manalari instead of the dead tongue.

It listens to him.

Cautiously, Nyx's messenger stepped closer.

The spirit waits...

With long, pale fingers curling further, Gavin appeared to grip either a rope or a cover made of air; he pulled it toward him, away from the spirit.

Then his shoulders relaxed.

Deshi swallowed. *A shackle... a leash? Uh...*

We waited.

It leads down the hall. To the crypt. The Yungian gripped his blade harder than he realized as it quivered. *The...ancient one beckons, leading the Deathwalker farther where the Ma'ab have gone...*

Gavin turned around, his eyes solid black in his white face. Krithannia gathered his silent message, taking her pearl from Deshi.

You were correct, Shadow. The Ma'ab have a sorceress with tattooed body-

guards, and she is capable of summoning and compelling a native spirit to lead them where they wished to go. The monk was left out here as a final obstacle and barred from entering the crypt after them. Gavin has removed the anchor holding him in this passage. ★

★*What do they seek?*★ Mourn asked.

The Guild Mistress glanced at Gavin as if he said something. ★*Nothing specific. They aim to loot the crypt and disturb the burials before returning undiscovered to their host. They'll have new information and traps set beneath the temple.*★

The same expression touched Mourn and Torch, who signed to his brothers.

★*Sounds like they need to be discovered.*★

★*Agreed,*★ Krithannia replied. ★*Lead us, Shadow.*★

My bodyguard accepted, taking me forward to be near Gavin as we reportedly followed the spirit to the entrance of the crypt. While I placed one foot in front of the other, a wave of nausea tried to rise as I thought about the non-Human demonblood with them.

Time to discover the truth of this rumor.

Whether I wanted to or not.

Chapter 15

We heard the murmurs and scuffles before we found the opening into a cavernous space. Long, distorted shadows thrown upon the ceiling pinpointed the Ma'ab with dim lanterns, standing far below the under-earth balcony. Gavin held back with his ghost while Mourn checked the passage for further warnings or traps. His next thought sounded surprised.

Huh. They can't see in the dark.

The Ma'ab weren't using fire, either; we would have smelled it. By now, I assumed all races with capable mages had developed smokeless glowstones or torches to use when open flames were too dangerous. This, however, suggested that the Guild using Dark Sight was not common, even in clandestine moments like this.

Mourn sneaked forward, creeping low on four points of contact to peer over the balcony. His tail hovered above the ground, waving with controlled grace, an easy measure for us how far to keep back.

Four Hellhounds, male. One death mage, female. The males are smashing open burial vaults on the wall and pushing lids off the sarcophagi onto the floor. The death mage is sorting through the remains and leaving something behind.

They did so without care for the damage, from the sound of it.

I forced one thought to be clear. ~And the half-blood?~

Not visible but present. Probably keeping guard.

Shit.

We cannot cover these stairs without being detected, Mourn continued. *We can ambush with a thunder-flash spell or we can attempt to intimidate and out-maneuver them.*

The Guildsmen offered brief, brusque hand motions, Gavin scowled, and Krithannia nodded. Mourn looked at me.

They vote thunder-flash, he said. *This means I jump from the balcony and engage the Hellhounds as fast as possible with the Guildsmen backing me up.*

~Yes, ambush,~ I agreed.

You three and the monk spirit stay up here. Krithannia will help muffle the noise. Keep your cover and distance with spiders and the relic at the ready to defend yourself and them. They have means to do the same for you.

My stomach tremored. ~Understood.~

Through pearls and signs, it took mere moments passed for each of us to be on the same plan. At the final signal, we covered our ears and eyes. I pulled my hood farther down. An instant later, a concussive blast of light landed at the bottom of the crypt.

Then Mourn went over the stone wall, and a huge male voice bellowed, *"Edu'un kafir!"*

Shouts filled the cavern, masking the next four sets of Yungian feet sprinting away from me and down the stairs. I parsed out the sound of a chain dropped to the floor, being dragged along the stone, then whipped around to smash a piece out of a nearby crypt.

"Kiljab! Vesram!" called the woman. *"Iyhimina!"*

Her tone sounded remarkably like Amelda but older. Older often meant more dangerous.

I heard a sword clash with the chain and bind up; a brief struggle ensued, ending with a wet, meaty sound and a grunt. The male bodyguards roared at the same time I opened my eyes in the dark.

"Shotan! Shotan!"

"Edu'un shotaaaaan!"

There were only three male voices now, and the high-pitched tenor of the mage lifted her orders over them as she brought back their light by which to see. She sounded less certain than before, especially when Mourn growled something, his sliders rushing through the air. An orange light flared, with more cursing following another thunderstone.

This time from the Ma'ab.

I flinched back. *Ow.*

I waited for my ears to stop ringing, but Krithannia seemed unaffected, concentrating on her sound-dampening spell which must be under constant stress to prevent this skirmish from alerting the Manalari above. Mourn's blades blocked and scraped with chains twice more, male grunting following several attempts to pull each other off balance.

The Dragon son was holding up well for three against one.

Meanwhile, Gavin stood stiff as iron, his eyes gone black once again, his hands flexing at his sides.

Did the last flash blind him?

I waved my hand, and he tilted his head. He *could* see me, and he watched as I pointed at myself, at my eyes, and toward the balcony. His chin dipped in a nod.

Here we go.

I kept low while crawling into the crypt, scanning the ceiling when I crossed the threshold. There was nothing I could see. Once I reached the wall forming the balcony's border, thanks to the glowstone strapped to her head, I easily spotted the tiny Ma'ab mage casting behind three giant males. The Hellhounds were as Mourn had described.

What Kurn desired most.

Tattoos covered her bodyguards' naked chests, and they used the spiked chains anchored around their right arms with impeccable accuracy. Lengths of metal thorns protected most of the width of the crypt, lashing out and snapping at the Dragonchild like serpents. This prevented the mercenary from getting closer to their mage while she did—

Something.

Between our bodyguards—mine and the mage's—lay a pale, headless body spilling blood enough to outline the nearest sarcophagus. Mourn and four Guildsmen were ready to intercept any attempt for the stairs, but leading from the blood to in between them, a strange, thick dust started rising.

Uh-oh.

Bones moved, piling up, splitting our forces as skeletal hands reached atop the stone coffins to drag themselves up. I saw skulls without jaws, but the necks twisted as if to look at the Yungians.

My mouth opened. "Uh, Gavin?"

He didn't hear me.

Abruptly, more skeletons crawled out of the damaged crypts, and my blood chilled to count twenty and more. Shifting movements continued up and toward the Ma'ab in the lines of broken burial holes.

"Gavin!" I called over my shoulder. "She's raising the dead!"

"I feel it," he replied.

"Can you contest it like you did Castis?"

Gavin kneeled next to me, looking down with a frown. "Not from up here."

While we spoke, Mourn dismissed his sliders in an eyeblink, replacing them with a whip in one hand and a wooden staff in the other. The Yungians followed his lead, swapping their drawn short swords for fighting sticks as they backed up from the nearest skeletons. They would soon be surrounded, and the brothers turned outward, keeping their backs to each other.

"What do you need?" I asked.

"Ideally, a drop of my blood on each one to even have a chance to break her control."

I should have known he'd have to cut himself.

The Yungians moved fluidly, cracking ribs, knocking off skulls, and disabling limbs as a cohesive unit. Mourn swung his staff, aiming well and shattering the knees of the nearest two skeletons before lashing the whip above his head to meet the incoming chain of the next Hellhound challenger. When the two weapons entangled, the Hellhound yanked back, trying to make the hybrid stumble.

The attempt didn't go well.

"Mitneh Ekess Iejir!" Mourn rumbled, drawing his arm up and

pulling the whip taut.

A blinding streak of light darted from his fist, along the tough line, and into the chain, where the shock struck the Hellhound. The large, tattooed body jerked and shuddered as if he were having a seizure on his feet, though he didn't fall.

At the same time, the other two side-stepped their brother and each tossed something small and dark at the Dragon's son. In the dim light and wildly contorting shadows, I wasn't sure what exactly happened. Mourn had dropped his whip and swung his staff with both hands. He hit something I couldn't make out before throwing himself backward into the skeletons, toppling several over and into the Yungians' reach.

"Blast!" he called, and the Yungians braced themselves.

I ducked behind the wall and covered my ears.

Twin thunderstones exploded: one among the Guild and their swarm of bones, and the other among the Ma'ab. By the time I could hear anything at all, my ears picked out the woman shouting in distress and anger. She had backed up even more from her guardians, taking the light with her while Mourn and our team got back on their feet among twitching remains.

Some of the dead prepared to get up again; others climbed or fell down the burial wall to the stone floor.

~Mourn?!~

We are well! We are not finished.

That was an understatement.

~The mage is backing away from the Hellhounds! Is there a way out behind her?~

I do not know. I cannot see the end. Keep her in sight if you can.

I needed to stand up and lean over the balcony to do that. Once I'd found her again, I watched the sorceress leap and climb onto something hidden from my eyes. At first, she seemed to be floating in the air, but then I squinted and saw the wavering outline of a light-masked body.

Fuck.

The illusion of invisibility faded away and a Sathoet appeared before my eyes. Everything he should be: tall and strong but deformed, like a hairless wolf standing on his hind legs; black skinned and white-maned with tufts of white hair at his chin, elbows, groin, and knees. He bared white teeth as the pale woman scrambled into place, flexing sharp claws mirrored on his feet.

~*It's him*—!~ I blurted.

★What?★

~*The demonblood! He's a Sathoet!*~

The Priestess Son sprinted away from Mourn and the Hellhounds, carrying the tiny Ma'ab woman on his back. Sickness swept over me as I gripped the railing, watching him leap onto a sarcophagus and run to the end before launching onto the wall opposite of where Guildsmen fought for space. The mage gripped his white mane with both small hands while the demonblood scaled the wall with extraordinary speed.

~*He's coming this way! For the balcony!*~

★Do not let them escape!★

~*Sucking web, how?!*~

Krithannia and Gavin apparently had heard something of this as they prepared to act. I had no idea what they'd do but I shouted before I could stop myself.

"Sathoet!" I screamed in Davrin, as loud as I was able, amid the scabbling of claws and heavy breaths. ★"Sathoet, listen! I've been searching! I've found you! In the name of the Valsharess,★ stop, now!"

He paused like a fly on the wall, astonished to be staring up at me. I saw his red, pupilless eyes in a monstrous face with an upturned nose. He was younger than Kerse, and that was not the color his eyes should be.

What did they do to him?

I forced myself to blink but could not stop the shaking, nor could I draw my dagger; I couldn't even hear the chiming of my spiders.

Meanwhile, with their mage out of harm's reach for now, the Hellhounds finally charged as one with raucous roars. Mourn swapped out his weapons again, drawing the bow and black arrow, striking one enemy before sending the bow away to charge forward. He met them with two *new* blades, not his sliders. One Hellhound bled from the dissolving arrow; like the lightning strike earlier, he had staggered but didn't fall.

Fucking tough bastards.

Thus, the Yungians were left to handle the amassing skeletons alone for a little longer.

"*Vesram!*" The pale sorceress kicked the stiffened Sathoet, hissing at him and pointing back down toward the fighters. Then she looked up at me, squinted, and gasped. "Davrin...?"

I blinked. She knew what I was. *Not good.*

The Sathoet snarled as he took her kick, sounding like he couldn't remember how to speak, if he ever could.

"*Where is your mother?*" I demanded, my stomach heaving.

A whine threaded its way through his teeth, followed by a hiss, and Gavin came up beside me, his shovel at the ready. The sorceress's headlight turned from me and finally shone on him. As the former monk stared back, I watched an ugly, ferocious look overtake the Ma'ab's face.

She reminded me of the Prime whenever mind flayers came up.

"*Maknuut!*" she cried, pointing. "*Vesram, hiljum!*"

The Sathoet spat something which might have been a curse, abruptly gathering strength and surging up the wall toward us.

He wouldn't stop this time.

Quickly, Gavin and I backed up from the railing.

"Don't kill him!" I squeaked.

"Inevitable if he bites me," Gavin replied.

Bite.

I reached to snatch one of my spiders, forming a loose cage with my fingers, and tossed the arachnid at the Ma'ab witch who clung to the Sathoet's back. I aimed at the white mane, easiest to see, as he came over the ledge and landed on the balcony.

~*Bite **her**! Not him!*~

"*Kaiyithri!*" Krithannia shouted, surprising us all from the doorway.

I watched in horror as the Guild Mistress summoned a wind blast, pushing the fleeing demonblood backward and away from the hallway. He and his rider slammed against the stone railing and toppled over the side.

"No!" I cried.

The Sathoet flailed for purchase, catching himself first before hooking the woman around her waist. The Ma'ab had lost her hold on the demonblood and would have fallen down into the crypt without his reflex. Then my spider chimed to me. She hadn't blown off.

~*Bite her!*~

The sorceress flinched with a yelp, slapping at her neck, and a last chime cut off inside my mind. I clutched my head as if a stone had fallen on it.

~*AAA!*~

Sirana, are you hurt?!

~*Mourn...I——*~

Shaken, feeling the skittering stress of my two living small ones, I backed up toward the stairs as the Sathoet hauled his sorceress back over the railing. The Ma'ab shrieked at us, struggling ferociously in his grip. He had no choice but to toss her onto the floor of the balcony before pulling himself safe at last. The demonblood then covered her with his body, snarling at us.

"Do not move," Krithannia said to them, blocking the hallway as Gavin brandished his shovel nearby.

The Sathoet blinked at her then looked at me.

Our eyes met, and I froze.

The Valsharess sent you...?

A new voice.

I gulped, and answered. ~*Yes.*~

"Sho'shien!" Deshi called desperately. "Sho'shien Ada-son! Please! The dead must rest!"

The Sathoet glanced toward the shout, and in the valley of silence between us, I heard his next thought.

Ada... son?

"A moment!" Gavin called back.

The demonblood turned his neck back from the crypt, peering at the Deathwalker.

227

Ada...son.

I witnessed the spark of recognition in the demonblood's memory as the thoughts of Gavin's mistress echoed in mine.

There is less conflict than you believe.

"Th-the demon knew Ada among the Ma'ab!" I croaked, beginning to shake as I backed up to help the other two block the exit. "A woman named Ada."

"That cannot be her," Gavin denied.

"*Maknuut!*" the sorceress spat from behind her living shield, attempting to cast but was interrupted when Krithannia used a slingshot to strike her face with a pebble.

"Only a matter of time before your Hellhounds go down," said the Guild Mistress. "We have means to overtake your other servants. Surrender, Commander."

Sweat had sprung up on the Ma'ab witch's pale face, and she sneered at the Naulor, even as she flinched at the honorific. I wondered how the Naulor could tell.

"A...matter of time..." the Ma'ab hissed, "and my gods will *flay* your essence through eternity."

So. She could speak Trade.

Commander...

I'd heard that before, questioning Kurn in the canyon.

"*Commander Vo'traj brought him to arena.*"

"*Does he have a name?*"

"*Only... his mistress knows the demon's name.*"

I saw my dead spider's bite mark swelling at her neck, but the small woman wasn't losing body control as quickly as Tamuril had after six bites. The Ma'ab struck the hesitant Sathoet with her fist, her tone belittling and frightened.

"Vo'traj!" I barked.

She jerked, looked at me as she worked to breathe.

I smirked. "Kurn Divigna sold your secrets for blocking his training. He told me everything."

The pale commander looked like she'd been slapped. "T-treason!"

"I know."

The Ma'ab growled something incredibly complex.

"Vesram'czitrig'shantufricet!"

At first, I didn't understand, but then the Sathoet's spine contorted as he bent backward, throwing his head back with an agonized howl.

"Hiljum gefah!" Vo'traj screeched, pointing at us.

The demonblood's red eyes blazed, froth forming at the corners of his mouth as his white mane stood up on end. The violence about to be unleashed was palpable.

Gavin readied his spade for a high chop; Krithannia stepped behind him, bringing up her hands as her aura started to sing. Meanwhile, my spiders hid in my hair, and I couldn't make myself reach for the relic at the small of my back.

Shit.

Tears blurred my vision, so I didn't have to watch what I did next.

As during my trials, I placed myself in direct danger with a Sathoet, throwing myself into the demonblood's charge.

"Sirana, no!" Krithannia cried as I darted forward.

Our collision hit me harder than before, and the demonblood continued forward at a slowing stagger as I threw my arms around him, wrapping my legs around his waist and locking my ankles together. I forced a contested stare with those frightening eyes, inhaling his strange and sour scent, so far away from home.

Yet somehow, red was easier to swallow than the sickly yellow.

~*Vesram!*~ I demanded, grasping that I'd heard his common name. ~*Vesram, stop!*~

Nnnnooooo! he howled. **Paaain!**

Pain. And grief.

Within his mind, I saw the chains bonding him to the one who held his true name. Not by choice.

Like a needle capable of a thousand pricks at once.

And the manacled beast couldn't make her stop.

She ssstole it…

~*From your mother?*~

Yesss…

~Is the Priestess alive?~

He hesitated and Mourn broke into the link.

Hellhounds are down! We are coming but we need Gavin!

~Hurry… ~

The half-blood would not flee from us. I couldn't let him.

"Vesram!" Vo'traj cried, a different, fearful pain joining the link through her thrall.

The spider bite started to hurt. I cried as I told my living guardians to stay in hiding.

"Vesram! *Astarjae! Hana!*"

~No. Do not help her, Priestess son. Let her die.~

His body burned, trembled. *Feel venom…hurts.*

~The Queen wills her death. The pain is not yours, it's a ghost passing through. Let her die. You will be free.~

He flinched. *No! Never freee…*

True. From before his birth in the Sanctuary, he'd never known this feeling.

He was terrified.

Never, never!

~Vesram! Stop!~

I shuddered. Such fear of the unseen Void.

What are you? he hissed. *You do not have my name! I… must…obey sssoul naaame!*

My eyes were closed when Vesram lunged; I didn't know who his target had been, but he was strong enough to ignore my weight. In response, someone swept the two of us free from contact with the ground.

Vesram landed hard on his back with a grunt, the blunt pain in my ankles forcing my legs to let go at once. Then, a familiar, fleshy coil wrapped around our knees, mine and the Sathoet's, and squeezed as a heavier weight flattened our bodies. I was squished between two half-bloods in a secure hold neither of us could break. The Sathoet began to shriek in mind, body, and soul.

"*Noooo!*" he screamed in Davrin. "*Mihstresss! Sssave meee!*"

Vo'traj didn't answer him.

Krithannia is covering the Ma'ab, Mourn said. *Gavin aids the Guildsmen as the commander's control of the dead slips. Keep going, Sirana. Whatever you are doing, you do not harm him. His aura is intact.*

My consciousness hovered on the edge of my body. ~*But——*~

The Sathoet bucked beneath me, snapping sharp teeth at the Dragonchild with a longer muzzle. Mourn leaned his head up out of range, growling in reply but keeping his mouth closed. I kept my forehead pressed to the hollow of the demonblood's throat so he couldn't try the same with me. He'd begun to stink from his sweat.

Keep going, he said.

~*What happens when the last soul clutching your name dies?*~

Vesram and Mourn both heard my question.

Not the lassst. The Sathoet's thoughts were laced with pain, some new and others quite old. *Ascended. They will find me… they summon demons, they will summon me!*

Damn. I pursed my lips. ~*But that can't be all? You are Elfblood, true? Priestesses can banish your sires, but they can't banish you. Not even your Mother could do that. You could only be compelled or killed, like me. You have a will, an anchor, a claim to this world the demons do not.*~

Something shifted in his mind when he heard that. The agonizing pitch of his fear seemed on the cusp of breaking, if not the pain lingering from Vo'traj as Krithannia attempted to question her.

Like you, his thoughts murmured. *What are you?*

He'd asked that before.

"*Vloszia Dalna,*" I said aloud.

His chin bonked my head when he nodded. "…Red Sssister."

Something inside shifted farther, even as neither of us looked at each other, and I saw vague, dimly recalled faces from Sivaraus, heard several voices overlapping each other, above which rose three distinct pitches of laughter.

Jaunda.

Wilsira.

Lelinahdara.

I recognized each of them.

~*You know Jaunda, Vesram?*~

I wasn't prepared for the touch of warmth at the back of his mind. It seemed so long ago.

Ssstrong Sister, he murmured.

I chuckled inside. He admired my Lead, even a bit? What would she think about *that?*

~*That she is. And... Wilsira is dead. As is her son.*~

His heartbeat surged beneath me, and he began to pant.

Kerssse? he asked. *Dead?*

Fear. He'd been afraid of that older Sathoet. Him and me, both.

~*Yes. Kerse is dead.*~

Fear remained, but now mixed with caution and hope.

I knew *this* feeling.

~*He is dead. The Sisterhood killed him. Jaunda helped kill him.*~

Joy. He felt joy. *And...you were sssent to find me?*

~*I was. Yes. Do you want to go home?*~

I tasted his cautious longing for that path. He'd seen another take it. *Ada.*

Ada had escaped even though she hadn't known where "home" was. She had been alone.

And so was he.

I cannot go home.

A harsh, lancing pain scored through my chest. ~*What?*~

In Sivarausss, he said, *Sathoet do not exist without a mother holding his name. Per the Valsharesss. Without Mother, I see immediate death. Like Kersse...*

This Sathoet wasn't a mindless animal. He hadn't been even back then.

*Unless... **you** will hold my name now, Red Sister?* he asked me, an impulsive chortle escaping him. *Will the Sisterhood claim me against the Sanctuary? It may please Varessa D'Shea to use me for revenge.*

Goddess, he knew her, too? I felt sick. ~*Have you told the Ma'ab this?~*

The demonblood's head flopped back like he was exhausted. *No. I forgot. Until you. Too much…pain.*

But now, that pain was fading, along with the source of it.

Vo'traj was fading.

I arose back into my body, bleary, my head pounding. I tried to speak but needed to wet my lips first. "Mourn?"

"Do not relax yet," he warned, his mouth aimed toward the balcony where he watched something.

Vesram growled at him but lay limp in our clutches for the moment. Unable to shift free, I turned my head where I'd last seen the Ma'ab witch screaming. Gavin kneeled in front of her, his long back blocking most of my view. Her feet twitched, and I noted the dagger in the Deathwalker's left hand plus the large eyes on Krithannia's face.

Nonetheless, the Guild Mistress did not object when Gavin cut deep into the Ma'ab Commander's chest and reached forward with his other hand. The wet, squishy sounds were familiar; I'd heard them last at Jacob's sacrifice in the shed.

Vesram's body jolted beneath us and Mourn held him down as he thrashed and shrieked to the top of the crypt.

"Sssave me, mistresss, ssave meeee!"

I shook my head, recoiling from his plea.

"Take my name, take my naaaame!" the Sathoet pleaded in our native tongue as the last threads of his bond with Vo'traj dissolved.

"I c-can't!"

With everything I wanted, with everything I *didn't* want, I couldn't handle *this*, too!

*"You were sssent to **find** me, Sssister!"* he snarled. *"You now let me fall?"*

"You won't fall," I said, clutching my sore head as if that would protect it from learning his name.

*"I will! I will if you fail to catch! Claim it, claim **me!**"*

"Stop," Mourn ordered. *"She said no. The Red Sister is right. You do not want to die, so gather the courage that has kept you alive, and you will survive this transition."*

233

Vesram hissed at the Dragonchild and his foreign accent, and then Gavin pulled Vo'traj's heart out of her ribcage.

The last thread of life snapped.

Followed by a terrifying silence.

Vesram sucked in breath, wailing with horror as Mourn finally lifted his weight.

"Stairs!" he ordered.

My head felt close to splitting as I rolled off the demonblood, scrambling for the stairs as Vesram swiped at my boot. Mourn blocked his arm, threw him off balance, and prepared to go hand and claw with the Sathoet to keep him back.

"Don't kil—aaa!" I cried, twisting my ankle as I stumbled.

"Have you, Janshi!"

Deshi and Peng-lok had run forward to catch me. I hadn't realized they'd gotten this close.

Mourn shoved the Sathoet toward the hallway. *"Go! Run, before the Ascended clamp the chains back on your wrists!"*

"Will happen again!" Vesram spat at us. *"With **more** pain, thanksss to you! Nowhere! She will not have me, so I have **nowhere**, mother-killersss!"*

Behind them, Gavin stood up from the small, female corpse, holding her heart in his fist. He turned around to look at the scuffle with void-black eyes, his face stoic and largely ignoring the fevered intensity of the shouting on the balcony.

"The Elf-blood speaks true," Gavin said with understated calm. "He and Vo'traj both knew Ada, my mother. Vesram helped her escape into the Raguruos Mountains."

Mourn moved back to give the Sathoet space, guarding against a sprint toward the stairs. Wary, weak, and more afraid than I dared show, I watched the quivering slave lacking his mistress, still in shock from his abrupt release. Slowly, Vesram turned toward my black-blooded ally, staring at the dripping heart clutched in his hand. Though I held my breath for him to charge in a rage, Gavin merely tilted his head.

"Isn't that so, Vesram?" the Deathwalker asked. "You knew a Ma'ab woman named Ada. Low caste, a *maknuut*, yet somehow a death mage of extraordinary potency, captured in a raid of the slums."

Vesram shook his mane as if trying to clear water from his tapered ears. "Uh…yesss. Are you Ada ssson?"

"As I have become. Because Ada escaped Vo'traj, for which you suffered in her place."

"Better that way," the Sathoet growled.

"Oh? May I ask why, Davrin son?"

Vesram paused.

"Why?" he repeated, his shoulders and back slumping with oncoming exhaustion. "Ada heard a voice. She followed the voice. I wanted her to ssstay… but the Hellhound ssspared her for a reassson."

"The Hellhound?"

"The Eternal. Ssspared her. Ada said she must get *out*, or *he* would return for her."

We listened, enraptured as the Deathwalker calmed and distracted the demonblood with his frank curiosity in a connection strangely stronger than mine. I watched something unbelievable happen to Vesram's eyes. The crimson color faded, bled out to give way to a cool, flowing grey which I'd never seen before.

Not a flicker of that sickly yellow remained.

How? From living a century among death mages?

"But later," Gavin said, "Ada found my father at a Manalari monastery, and she conceived a child."

"Worships the God of the Sun, yes?"

The Deathwalker blinked. "Did she *seek* them out with intent? Do you know?"

The Sathoet showed all his teeth at that. He said nothing, for the first time enjoying his new freedom to choose whether to answer.

Mourn frowned at him, glanced at me, then spoke. "Do you remember the direction of the Ley Tower where you were captured?"

Vesram snapped his head, his grey eyes opening wide and fixing on the Dragon son. "What?"

"The Ley Tower," the mercenary repeated. "Do you remember how to get there?"

I could hear the demonblood's heart speed up and took a step back in the hopes I wouldn't pick up uninvited details of that encounter.

Vesram's foot claws tapped the stone. "Where the Sun sets. Follow the Ley, here to the tallest mountains."

"Exactly. Now is the time for you to escape, as Ada did. Hide *within* the Ley. With distance, the Ascended's visions and reach will be baffled. They cannot summon you."

The Sathoet looked surprised and wary. "Can they not?"

"The Ascended are not gods," he replied flatly.

"Indeed," Gavin agreed. "Much as they claim to be."

Vesram must have witnessed this claim closer than either of them. He growled, "Why go at all?"

"We shall meet you there," Mourn said, shocking me. "We have tasks here to complete first. If you stay, they will drag you back north."

The Sathoet narrowed his grey eyes at the To'vah-krav before seeming to remember I was there. When Vesram refocused on me, I swallowed and worked hard to speak my concurrence.

It was…not as difficult as I feared.

"There's an old death mage at the Ley Tower," I said, nodding toward the Deathwalker. "Gavin and I must return to kill him. Then I go back home to my Sisters." My vision swam briefly, and I took a deep breath. "If you return to the Western mountains, be wary of him. He's greedy as Vo'traj, but without an empire behind him."

The crypt fell quiet as we waited on the response from a new half-blood without his leash. Vesram remained on his feet, alert and expecting coercion. He heard nothing more, only breathing, and me massaging my ankle through my boot.

I could meet him at the tower. Maybe I could even bring him back.

I just couldn't take his name.

Finally, the Priestess's son responded, accusing. "You lie about the tower. I will travel far, and you will *not* follow. It'sss a trap."

Of course, that *was* the obvious concern.

"If I do not follow," Gavin stated, "Ada's service and her escape was for nothing. I *will* follow my service back to that tower."

"And I must," I said. "The Queen demands it."

The last person I'd been able to say that to was Cris-ri-phon, with Gavin and Tamuril before him. Yet I'd only ever *implied* who'd given me the mission. Curious. Was the geas getting lighter, somehow?

"…less conflict than you believe…"

Vesram swiveled his head, sniffing in our direction. *"Hrm. Valsha-resss…"*

"What's more," the Deathwalker continued, "with you knowing this, you may spoil the nest if you truly want revenge for your freedom. No one can stop you but yourself. My Lady would recommend you think on it."

Blank, unfamiliar eyes narrowed. "Lady… Your mistress?"

"Ada's mistress is my Lady. The voice she once heard, I hear the same. My Lady is the Grave Mother."

"Mother…" Vesram repeated.

Mourn stepped in then. "If you kept the secret of Ada's escape because of that voice, then keep Gavin's return to that tower a secret for the same cause. In exchange, you may witness a chance for which you suffered. You and Ada."

To my surprise, Vesram's harden expression softened. I had never seen a Priestess's son look so… Elvish. Despite the contortions of his face and his body, I could think we reasoned with another Davrin where it counted.

He is allowing himself to be persuaded. He wants to live.

"Escape while you can, Vesram," I added. "Meet us out West. You might be the first Sathoet with that choice. I don't need your name to force you."

He looked at me, tilting his head. "You do not…*need* it."

"No. I do not." I smiled at him. "I can't control any Davrin by their name alone. Neither can Jaunda, she uses other methods. Why should we start with you?"

The corner of his mouth twitched. Was that amusement? Then Vesram grunted, glancing at the silent Naulor and then to Gavin and Mourn again, and back to me. His shifting suggested he was nervous.

"What is…the Red Sister name?" he asked. "Who are you?"

I swallowed a guffaw. *Aw, fuck, we missed that.* "Heh. Um. I am Sirana."

"Sssirana."

"Yeah." I shrugged uncomfortably. "Lead Jaunda and Elder D'Shea are my tutors. I know Lelinahdara, but I would rather spit poison in her eyes than stand in the same room."

Vesram hissed as he chuckled, nodding. "Tarra inspires this."

Oh shit, he knows her given name.

"Tarra turned on Mother," he finished, his breath quickening as he admitted this. "She is why we were sent… up here."

"Ah. I'd…I'd wondered." I managed another shrug. "Wilsira is why I'm here. Because the Red Sisters killed Kerse. Then D'Shea killed her. Finally."

Vesram sucked in breath with delight then tossed his head back and laughed. The sound was part howl and part unknown screaming in the night. Shivers coursed down the spines of the Yungians as they made signs and clutched talismans as if to shield themselves from the tainted Elf.

I truly regretted speaking so freely when the Sathoet stepped back from us and into the hall. Krithannia made a motion to dispel the ward she'd placed and, from body language alone, Vesram knew he was free to go. He paused first, pointing toward the crypt's floor.

"There is magic in the far coffin. Mistr—*ahm.* Vo'traj did not open it before you attacked."

The half-blood turned and sprinted down the hall with hardly a sound.

None of us had any control over what he did next.

CHAPTER 16

"HE TOOK THE SECRET PASSAGE LEADING DOWN," KRITHANNIA MURMURED, resetting her ward. "Back the way we came."

Several of us had been holding our breaths.

"Better than fleeing up toward the Temple," Gavin muttered.

Regardless, we waited for any sound of others coming, and I took the opportunity to eat something, as my empty stomach punished my thoughtlessness with severe pangs. Peering down into the crypt, I chewed on one of the Guild's ration bars, hoping my headache would ease alongside my middle.

Ugh. What a mess of bones.

Along the wall of mass burials lay a carpet of splintered fragments, scattered atop and around the sarcophagi. Leading away from the wall and toward the stairs, the bone fragments became skeletal bodies held together by some strange method. Although many seemed to have fallen where they stood in contorted positions, the pile of shattered bones growing at the base of the stairs informed me what the Yungians had been doing while I grappled with Vesram.

"Did you need Gavin's help against the risen dead?" I asked curiously of anyone who would answer. "I don't see black blood on the bones."

Krithannia answered. "We needed his help, yes, but once we realized you'd poisoned her and the control would fail with time, the Deathwalker oversaw her transition as a more direct way of exerting pressure on the dead to lie back down."

The Yungians' heads confirmed this with enthusiasm, and a morbid humor touched my lips.

"Oversaw?" I teased. "You mean quickened her transition?"

"No," Gavin grunted, slipping the bruised heart into a stained pouch, tying it shut and placing it on the balcony railing before wiping his hands on a rough cloth tucked at his waist. "I had questions for her Vis."

I tipped my head toward the pouch. "But you cut out her heart."

Our ghastly monk pursed thin lips. "She was being drawn back to her 'gods,' whether she wished it or not. Choosing the moment to sever that connection meant we could talk, and she has a chance to cross over rather than remain here. I believe she will take it."

Deshi gasped softly as Mourn squared his shoulders.

"Wait," he said, "what do you mean 'drawn back to her gods?' "

Gavin scowled but I sensed no anger aimed at my bodyguard. Instead, he motioned toward Deshi. "The same as his weapon marks the Vis to be found quickly by the Grey Maiden in the Nexus, the Ma'ab noble was marked to return to Ennikar and the Ascended."

"And you intercepted that," Mourn stated.

"Correct."

"How? Why would she listen to a *'maknuut'* and buck against her traditions?"

Gavin shrugged. "Self-preservation. Her success could have seen her given an honored place by the Ascended, but this failure would only prove her as worthy to be a meal. Her resistance to that fate allowed me to interfere with the pull for now. Eventually, she will make a choice, but until then a new opportunity may present itself."

"Interesting. Will the Ascended notice that missing Vis?"

Gavin exhaled, his hands filthy but no longer wet with gore as he placed the cloth and pouch containing Vo'traj's heart into his pack. "Perhaps? Not quickly, however. We are some distance from Ennikar, and souls tend to drift, even when they know where to go."

"Hm. If you say so, Deathwalker."

Deshi and I chuckled at Mourn's bemused tone, although mine didn't last when the initiator of that "transition" came back to me like a splash of cold in my face.

~*My little ones… Will you come out? It's over.*~

My two remaining spider guardians crawled out onto my left shoulder, and I gathered them into my hands to be sure they were whole. Krithannia seemed to be watching for this, as she reached into a pouch, withdrawing something small and dark in a delicate pinch.

"Oh…" I breathed, the dismay clear on my face.

"Do you want her back?" The Guild Mistress wisely handled the crushed spider with gloved hands, placing the body into her open palm where I could see it.

"I…uh…"

I hadn't even thought about what I'd do if I lost one of them. D'Shea would say it was just a spider. An obedient, protective, enchanted spider who had tilted the conflict in our favor…

Sigh.

"I don't know," I said, hugging myself.

"How do you handle the dead in your city?" Gavin asked.

"Um, well," I considered. "Burning the body. Or…sometimes feeding something else."

"I recommend fire," Mourn suggested quietly. "It will be small and quick, and the venom might be lethal to anything that eats it."

"Good point."

Then the surrealness of this struck me like a falling stalactite. I looked around in disbelief, witnessing a modest sadness and regret on even the Yungian faces. "Wait. You…suggest a death ritual for my spider?"

"Why not?" Gavin asked. "She served well. Krithannia retrieved the body. It is an option."

The Prime would be having seizures, caught between laughing and railing at a bunch of "soft spines."

"Do you want to set the flame?" Mourn asked me, studying my dazed expression. "I will do the honors if you wish. I remember her on my arm in the warp forest."

Yeah. I did, too.

"Um. Yes," I said. "You do it, please. Jael is waiting, maybe close by."

"Of course."

Krithannia and Mourn worked together, her placing the spider on the railing and stepping back so the Dragonchild could hover his claw over my deceased guardian.

"Ekess relgas," he rumbled. *"Ekess bilaes."*

The arachnid's body erupted in a tiny, orange flame, burning and smoking only briefly as the legs curled. The body dissolved to black ash before being swept up in a light gust of air and floating over the crypt, spreading out to vanish from sight. When Gavin nodded slowly, that seemed the end of the impromptu ritual.

"Do we have time to investigate the last sarcophagus?" he asked.

I pressed my lips shut. *We have all the time we want to waste.*

Mourn smiled at him. "Go with Krithannia and the Guildsmen. Sirana and I will scout ahead toward the dungeon and meet you where they unsealed the passage. Do not take long."

"We won't," Krithannia assured him.

Mourn met my eyes and tossed his chin toward the hall.

Thank goddess.

WHATEVER MOURN MIGHT HAVE BEEN HEARING THROUGH THE PEARLS ABOUT what they might have found, he kept us moving upward. Clearing the path, tasting the air, his tail keeping tabs on my position, Mourn maintained Deepearth silence and I followed suit.

With our bodies, if not our minds.

The Sathoet didn't come this way.

~*Glad to confirm.*~

How do you feel after that encounter?

I hesitated. ~*I don't know.*~

Very well. If anything seems important, speak it anytime.

~*I'm more afraid of what I'm soon to learn.*~

Understandable. Try not to dwell on it. Listen for adversaries who will sound the alarm.

Right.

Many footprints recently disturbed the dust, and the stairway grew narrower as we climbed.

~*Hey.*~

**Hm?*~

~*Did you kill the three remaining Hellhounds in melee without gaining a scratch?*~

The tip of his tail nearly tapped me on the nose.

Fortunately, yes. No surprises we hadn't seen before, and no serious mis-judgments on my part to keep the chains away from me and the Guildsmen. If even one of Torch's team had broken from fear of the skeletons, that would have overwhelmed them and forced my hand. But they didn't because that's what Vo'traj wanted.

~*Oh.*~

Why do you ask?

~*Well... Did Vo'traj not bring their best Hellhounds?*~

Hm. No, she didn't. Those were younger ones. I think she relied on the Sathoet's abilities for this and only needed guards capable of covering her escape if they were discovered.

Which would have worked if the Deathwalker, the Guild Mistress, and I hadn't been on the balcony.

~*But she's a 'commander?'*~

Yes.

~*Isn't that higher up? Not low on the ground like this?*~

Mourn's tail flicked. **It is unusual, yes. In finding a pathway for others, the fewer, the better, if they're meant to return and share that information. But it shouldn't have been a commander with a pet demon.**

I frowned. ~*A pet, perhaps, but he is half-Elf. Bound as you were.*~

Mourn looked over his shoulder with a cocked brow ridge. *Our sires make all the difference between us.*

~*Both of which were chosen by your mothers, correct?*~

The mindlink quieted noticeably, and I sensed a depth I shouldn't explore yet. I brought us back to the present.

~*Why do you think they felt compelled to smash a Manalari crypt instead and risk being caught as they were?*~

I'm not sure. We'll ask Krithannia or Gavin if they discovered anything about this before the sorceress died.

Mourn didn't have to ask for focus when we reached a gate which had been closed and locked, the blackened metal relatively clean.

No wards, he noted, sounding surprised.

I watched him withdraw two thin pieces of metal from his harness and crouch in front of a keyhole. I leaned over his shoulder to watch, hoping to gain insight on this different mechanism.

Listen for approaching thoughts, would you?

I blinked. ~*Can I do that?*~

You certainly heard something from Vesram to tell us that he knew Gavin's mother.

~*Oh. You heard that in the middle of your fight?*~

I heard it through the pearls.

~*Oh.*~

Mourn prodded the hole with metal sticks like he searched a bowl of broth for that last noodle before pulling out a third stick. *I also wanted to ask you how you felt about the offer.*

~*What offer?*~

To Vesram. Us meeting him at the Ley Tower. You seemed much calmer, your aura and your thoughts.

~*Ah. Yes, I was.*~

Come to think of it, I hadn't felt so much as a squeeze of nausea since, and the headache was from something else with which I was growing more familiar.

Do you need help with Sarilis?

I swallowed. ~*Probably.*~

Consider the Guild interested in extending our contract, then.

I smirked. ~*And the payment?*~

That depends on our success here.

~*True…*~

He made some final motion, and something sounded as though it turned inside the metal contraption. *There we go.*

Mourn stood up, put away his tools, and flicked out his tongue, murmuring in Draconic before opening the gate. It was unnaturally silent. He left it open, turned to me, and waved his hand, mouth moving in a subtle hiss as he closed his eyes.

My skin prickled. ~*Uh… what if someone comes down this hall?*~

His eyes opened. *We're cloaked for now, same trick as the Sathoet. Even with a torch, we're difficult to see. They'd have to run into us or have a dog sniffing around.*

~*But… I can still see you.*~

Stay within your body's length of me, and you will.

My belly trembled with excitement. ~*So we're going forward? Or waiting for the others?*~

Forward, if you're willing to let me handle the guards until I say otherwise.

~*Very well. How far to where they keep the prisoners?*~

He lifted his nose, sniffing the air. *The hall to the dungeon is around the corner.*

So close.

I turned my ear and listened, leaving my aura as relaxed as I could make it in case I might pick up some of those "incoming thoughts."

~*It's quiet, for now.*~

Agreed. Let us go.

WE ENCOUNTERED FEW MAGICAL BLOCKS ON OUR WAY TO THE STAIRS LEADING down to the dungeon. Quite baffling after the constant trail while following the Ma'ab.

~*Part of the hubris of the Temple?*~ I wondered. ~*They think no one can get in from above but didn't consider below?*~

Partly. I also think some were in place recently but not reset for some reason.

Not exactly what I wanted to hear but all the better for Jael if Mourn's mage sense was keen enough to detect lingering and spent spells. Although he'd smelled the jail cells farther away, my nose soon caught up and wrinkled at the inevitable thickness of odors from multiple bodies trapped in small spaces.

It was not as bad as when the frail body of Ullipmious slipped out of its tomb, however, and I had yet to see a scattering swarm of scavengers left to run amok. There existed some process of cleanliness and waste disposal, even for prisoners.

We started down the stairs, placing our feet with care so as not to scrape a single pebble against the stone.

~*Can you smell another Davrin yet?*~ I asked.

I will say when I am certain, as I did the Sathoet.

He'd done well by me there. I must trust him with this, too. I also had my ears and heightened underground senses on my side, and my psionic eavesdropping if I dared. I had only to gather my courage to use them.

Starting with my most basic sense, it seemed quieter than I'd have guessed. Bodies shifted, sighed, or grunted. Two wore boots and paced around or sat in a chair. I looked down at my feet and noted the fresher scrapes of many feet having used these stairs compared to those we'd climbed from the base of the mountain.

At the bottom of the stone stairs was a platform followed by a few more steps before the area grew more spacious with two halls leading right and left. Three closed doors faced the stairs as we sneaked in, and torches with living flame burned at intervals much more frequent than the Palace in Sivaraus.

We listened. We scented. Then Mourn signed to me, *Left hall.*

He smelled something.

I followed him in silence, aware of the prisoners behind solid doors with only a slot to pass food and waste along the ground. No doubt these rooms tormented day creatures further, but our dungeons were little different back home.

Finally, we encountered a guard in front of another locked door. He was a brown-bearded man in modest leather armor who seemed about to nod off in his chair and he had a key ring looped on his belt.

I felt my stomach sink as I shook my head. ~*She can't be here. It lacks all the enforcers for a black witch.*~

Agreed. But she was here, Sirana, and not long ago. His tail grew more lively. *Best search for leads while we can.*

I bit my lip on my protest, observing Mourn gently help the guard to sleep in the same way as the stable boys in Yong-wen. He undid the man's belt to take the keys, using them to unlock the door. Then, as back at the gate, he opened it in silence.

The dark, torchless room contained three open doors and no live prisoners. Mourn was correct that Jael had been here, though. I could smell her. The Humans had kept her here away from the others.

A heavy cloak of dread tried to overtake me.

~*Oh, goddess, am I too late again...?*~

Calm, Sirana. Krithannia says the other teams have made it in the streets. They will find the latest word for us.

For now, we were undetected and free to look around. I peered into the cell which had once held my Sister. I could admit I was looking for red smears.

~*Clean stones,*~ I remarked. ~*And a woven pallet intact. Unstained.*~

Good, Mourn answered, sounding to mean it. *I smell no blood. Remember, the psion Captain Isboern was the one who captured her. It appears he held her safe from the Witch Hunters, as reported.*

~*In here, yes. So, where is she? Where are the Templars?*~

They were here, too, I think. Mourn inspected the cell and the broad space outside of it, though I didn't know what he found important. *Long enough for the scent of their magic and equipment to linger. I think I even scent the Druid.*

~*Tamuril was here?*~

Look around for bird droppings.

~Good idea.~

It didn't take long to find some. The falcon had been here for certain. So where *was* she?

I hated thinking it, but I did. ~*Krithannia said the Archbishop could overrule Captain Isboern at any time. Something changed quickly.*~

Mourn didn't reply at first, but he looked back at the sleeping guard. He signed for me to come with him. *I will ask him something while he sleeps. Try to listen for his thoughts.*

~I will try.~

For Jael, I had to.

We both crouched near the guard, getting comfortable but keeping alert for activity elsewhere in the prison. Mourn touched the man's brow, rumbling something soft and low in his Sire's tongue. The guard's face scrunched up, either annoyed or concerned with the interruption, with whatever Mourn had said to him.

I heard nothing, audible or otherwise, but the man was making more noise in his sleep, so I tried removing my glove. Reaching first for my pearl then my saphgar to focus on my "hum," I watched the man's face intently before touching his oily brow with bare fingers.

~Show me what you remember.~

The flash of stark, colorful imagery startled me, and I jerked my hand back like it stung. Mourn's tail flicked curiously as he watched me.

What happened?

~Uh... I saw...something.~

Details?

~What?~

Details. Tell me one detail you saw.

~Uh. A white-haired man wearing black robes, casting blue lightning. And...a blond man with blue eyes, wearing clean, metal armor. Talking, face-to-face.~

Good. Will you touch again?

I glanced down the oddly quiet hall then returned my fingers to my spot on the man's forehead. I didn't pull away this time, but nothing happened until Mourn tried his quiet rumbling trick again. I witnessed enough through the man's eyes, though the murmuring of his thoughts was vague and distant.

...Coming at last. His grace...down here... remove her, please, Captain...

Frowning with thoughts not mine, I communicated what I was seeing.

~Um. The Archbishop and his man in black...?~

The Inquisitor Kegyek.

~They arrived yesterday and ordered the Captain and his Templars to carry her away. It was quiet for a while, but then he heard a... great commotion above.~

Great commotion?

~Shouting. The...Archbishop was angry, in pain, and the demoness was fighting, trying to get away while the others tried to keep order. There were...lights flashing, magic spells... The guard didn't know where they'd come from or where the Templars were headed. He hid until he confirmed they were not bringing her back to the cell.~

They didn't?

I swallowed, taking back my hand. ~No. They went upstairs.~

Into the Temple.

~Yes.~

I heard Mourn's internal sigh as he lifted his hand next.

Well, this just became more difficult. Let us head back. Gavin and Kri-thannia are waiting at the open gate.

CHAPTER 17

MOURN AND I SLIPPED BACK DOWN THE LONG HALL, TAKING THE RIGHT TURN back to the stairs to the crypt. Torch was on lookout. We spotted each other before I knew Gavin and Krithannia were close-by. The Yungian smiled at us and made a respectful hand sign, bowing his head with grace.

The squad leader looked over his shoulder and motioned us to follow him around the corner to the open gate.

The Naulor proved astute in reading our faces, as she was immediately concerned, reaching out to touch Mourn's arm.

What news?

I was less surprised hearing her voice in my head this time, knowing the maker of the pearls could let the messages pass through him when he wanted to. One day, may I have such precise control of which voices passed through my mind.

~She's not in the dungeon anymore,~ I replied, as my throat began to ache. ~The Archbishop took her up into the Temple last evening. We're half a day too late.~

The Guild Mistress acknowledged me without looking at Mourn to confirm first. That made me feel better, but my overall state was not good.

An odd pause followed before Krithannia spoke. *And now Wolf and his Focus know what to listen for. They are searching, Sirana.*

~But she's in here, not out there! How could they——~

Gently, Mourn touched my shoulder. *Trust us. Reprisal is well-trained in finding missing women. They know what to listen for and how to ask.*

I scowled. ~Jael isn't missing, we know who took her. And if the Archbishop was the only one in pain, then I wager she did whatever had him bellowing for the guard to hear. He's probably hurt her for that. I don't see a mage like him being bold enough to face a female who can fight back on a level field. And if he has? I will flay his skin with Soul Drinker.~

Mourn, Krithannia, and Torch each looked grim, proving they listened. I tried to calm down before the Dragonchild felt he had to touch me again.

~So what's next?~

If Tamuril hasn't fled, as I begged her, Krithannia answered with a somber sigh, *find her instead. Learn through her what you can of the Templars. If you see Captain Willven Isboern himself, try to signal his attention. Psionically, if you can. You can trust him to listen and help if he can.*

After seeing the unmarked jail cell my Sister left behind, I dared to believe that.

Meanwhile, she continued, *myself and the Guildsmen must aid Gavin, to position ourselves to break the Bishops' hold on Pisc'sagrad.*

Oh yes, I remembered, that was the priority mission.

I looked at Gavin, an unbidden sting pricking my chest. Were we about to go our own ways, parting company to seek our own goals as we'd borne since Troshin Bend? Would I see him again? Would we meet up to return to the Ley Tower?

~Um, wait, I have a question for Gavin.~

The Naulor's black eyebrows lifted; she was ready to listen.

~We wondered if Vo'traj told you what she wanted? Why did they smash the Manalari crypt rather than continue to the Temple or return to their host? I mean, she was a commander with a unique slave. A noble of higher rank doing reconnaissance seems strange.~

Krithannia exchanged a look with Gavin, who made a motion to remove his pack from his back. Mourn held up a claw, set a better sound ward, and waited a few moments for any worrisome activity. After he was satisfied, he motioned for the Deathwalker to continue.

Gavin set his pack down and removed something he'd wrapped up in a strip of cloth taken from Vo'traj's cloak. The death mage was cautious unwrapping it. A bright chain and an onyx handle dropped into my view, connected to what appeared to be a bowl-shaped lantern made of silvery metal hammered thin. Uneven holes punctured only the top half, making me wonder if enough light could escape to illuminate a small room.

"We found a thurible in that last sarcophagus," Gavin murmured, holding the vessel up, swinging by its chain. "Made of white gold instead of silver. It does feel enchanted, though we do not yet know its purpose."

"A th…a what?" I stuttered.

"A thurible. Intended to burn incense during rituals or ceremonial parades."

My face showed my disgust. "Oh. I suppose ours look… different."

Despite his face hardly changing, Gavin looked interested. "How so?"

"Um. Like thin sticks placed in a…" I measured my palms vertically to a height less than my forearm. "Vessel. Like this. Metal or glass, open at the top as the sticks burn downward."

"Like a vase," Mourn offered, and that seemed to translate.

I shifted uncomfortably. "So, what does a thurible have to do with a commander looting tombs?"

"I am not certain it does," Gavin replied.

I watched as he inspected the shining relic with care. As his pale fingers traced one of the odd holes in the burner, I realized it had been crafted into the shape of a crow's head.

"Or perhaps not by itself," the Deathwalker added. "There was another tomb disturbed when she arrived. A warrior's resting place rather than the cleric who was buried with this piece." He held up the thurible. "Whatever was there had been taken."

Mourn grunted, looking at me. "The passage was newly unsealed when we arrived. If the Ma'ab didn't take it, then the Archbishop did."

"Correct," Gavin said, looking over his shoulder and in the space behind the Yungians who followed his gaze. "The native spirit whom Vo'traj leashed to guide her also bore witness to the Manalari searching the crypt. He seems to believe they awoke a powerful presence when they fought over the sun shield."

Mourn's tail stilled. "They what?"

"This nearly matched Vo'traj's mission," Gavin continued as I watched the suddenly nervous Guildsmen press their backs to the wall. "She claimed her gods sent her and the Elven demon to find something beyond value underneath Manalar. Supposedly powerful enough to wake sleeping guardians when needed."

"Sleeping guardians," the Dragonchild repeated, vertical pupils thinning in his eyes.

Krithannia and the Yungians all turned their heads. The mercenary neither looked nor sounded pleased in the least, but Gavin seemed not to notice as he began rewrapping the thurible.

"Have you heard of a 'sun shield,' Shadow?" Krithannia asked gently.

After a subtly rattling exhale through his nostrils as if to calm himself, Mourn shook his head. "Not until now. And you're saying they fought over it, Gavin?"

The Deathwalker carefully replaced his find in his pack, and cinching it closed before replacing it on his back. "Sirana's sister was part of the fight. She appeared to demand the 'city's defender' have the shield, as per tradition, but the clerics fought her and took it instead."

"She 'demanded?'" Mourn repeated, sounding skeptical.

"Per tradition?" Krithannia asked.

Gavin just shrugged, and I didn't blame their incredulity. Why *would* a Red Sister care which Human took the relic unless something compelled her to care?

Something like a geas. Is that it?

Had I been half right with my intent to frighten Tamuril that Jael had been sent after Captain Isboern. I got the target but not the intent.

The Defender of the Wall, who protected her from Witch Hunters for days...

Had my Sister *not* been sent to kill him, as Gaelan and I had been sent to deal with corrupt things? Or she *was* meant to deal with a corrupting influence, but not in the same way.

Why?

What could the Valsharess want with all these Surface events which do not impact Sivaraus?

"What sort of 'presence' did they awaken, Deathwalker?" Deshi asked worriedly, and his brothers all seemed to want that answer.

Gavin shook his head. "The native only spoke of a presence. It could be connected to the shield being disturbed, or it could be Sirana's sister, for she nearly died in the attempt but recovered."

"What?" I demanded. "*What* did that ghost say about my sister?"

He blinked at me. "She nearly died. The spirit says the 'defender' healed her. When the shield was lost to them both, yet she was revived. Only then could the presence be felt in the tomb."

I hadn't begun to imagine what to make of *that* information collected from a ghost, then Mourn stepped in to help us focus.

"Perhaps the presence will make itself known, perhaps it will not," the Dragonchild said, "but if this sun shield could aid the Ascended in waking something they have no right to awaken, then we must be sure the Ma'ab do not claim this thurible, either."

"Agreed," Krithannia said, seeming worried. "But there's only so much we can do to mitigate this conflict. You *know* this."

He frowned at her. "There are more perilous pieces than we knew about which need to be taken out of Human hands of power. *You* know this, too."

She sighed, then paused like she heard something at the back of her mind. Mourn listened, too, and Torch's eyes went wide a moment later.

Oh, shit.

Wolf and his teams must have found something.

"The courtyard," the Naulor whispered, her grey eyes wide as she looked upward.

"What's happening?" I hissed, my back aching with tension.

"The Witch Hunters are preventing a crowd from entering the Temple," Mourn said. "The Templars have arrived, and the situation becomes volatile."

"Ssso," I began slowly, "what does that mean? Is now a good time to search the Temple? Or to get near the pool?"

Krithannia shook her head in the negative, appearing genuinely frightened. "No…"

"Why not?"

"Because Captain Isboern and Tamuril are both in the courtyard trying to help," Mourn answered with a frustrated whip of his tail. "The crowd is talking about a relic meant for the Godblood to defend their city, of it being 'stolen from the people' to keep in the Bishops' vault."

"What? We only just found out about this from a ghost!" I said in exasperation. "And the city is already gossiping and protesting for the Godblood to get the shield?"

"You knew about the deep split in the factions," the mercenary replied. "This is why Manalar will fall, even if we did nothing."

"If the factions fight and something happens to the Captain," Krithannia said, "we won't be able to stop the Ma'ab from taking *Pisc'sagrad*. We don't have the ability. It will happen."

"Hm." Gavin's look of concentration had intensified, and his pale, leathery neck twisted as if contemplating his backpack.

Or whatever it contains.

Mourn said, "We must get out there and protect Tamuril and Isboern first."

I grimaced. *That* wasn't searching for Jael.

My bodyguard noticed. "We needed to find them anyway, Sirana. Reprisal did the work for us, and they tell us the Captain and Druid are in imminent danger which could trigger something beyond anyone's control."

"Understood," I replied. "But I *don't* understand how I could help you unless it's to stab some Witch Hunters."

He smirked. "Hold that thought. Under the distraction, Wolf and the others will be infiltrating the Temple. They will find where she is, Sirana, and through the pearls, help us see from all angles so we do not run into a space with no way out."

"Got it." I looked at Krithannia. "I assume you're staying with Gavin?"

The Guild Mistress seemed as conflicted as I was. "Yes. I must make sure he is not discovered until it is time."

"Then while I'm gone, ask him to explain the idea he had when you said you couldn't hold back the Ma'ab if the Manalari start fighting each other."

She blinked and looked at the Deathwalker, who made a face at me and shrugged.

"A theory only," he admitted. "I need time and quiet to harmonize with the aura of the thurible."

"Aha," Krithannia breathed, nodding. "Very well. We'll stay down here."

"Come on," Mourn said, tapping my shoulder. "I know a way out from here without using the Temple."

"Coming."

Although I still thought the damned Druid should have run when her sister told her to.

If we save that psion's skin, he'd better help us find Jael.

KEROS HANDED HIM ANOTHER TONIC.

"Drink, Inquisitor," he ordered, sounding haggard. "Do *not* close your eyes. Not until she breaks. Not until we can show them, *we* are in control."

Vene accepted the tiny, gold cup, tossing back the familiar, bitter fluid without hesitation. As he swallowed, his mouth pursed with stern distaste, but hopefully it would ease the headache.

He hadn't slept all night after helping to contain and guard the demoness. Neither had the Archbishop because, thus far, that mad witch refused to close her devil's red eyes.

The "daeva," as Keros called her, wore the manacles which Vene had designed to interfere with a mage's concentration when summoning magic. Slivers of sharp pain scored the wearer's flesh when the aura drew upon the Vitas, for a mage *always* had both, thus spoiling most manifestations while draining their vital strength each time they tried.

"Musanlo's Splinters," the Bishops called them.

I had to run and get them. We were fortunate to get them on her before she killed one of us.

Despite Emil's fury over his injured knee when the demoness landed a lucky kick, the Capitan and his Templars had done their duty extraordinarily well, protecting their Most Holy until the Inquisitor returned with the manacles.

Once secured to her wrists, they seemed to work as intended. For all too brief a time, the black witch was coerced by pain to cooperate.

Unfortunately, yesterday's noise and struggle to subdue her in the lower levels had alerted numerous chaplains and pages. The rising alarm and details of the story had only grown worse after Emil insisted on drawing her to the one room he felt they could "work on her."

The Archbishop had been limping by then, at least able to walk after using more than one of his enchantments on himself. Emil had foolishly dismissed the Capitan and his men, and Vene and he alone had dragged both the desecrating creature and the shining relic through sacred halls where others could see.

"We must break her first," Keros had insisted in the holy tongue unknown to the demoness. "We must present her to the others, docile and harmless, before I lead the purge."

"Yes, Holiness."

Keros had expected it to take only a few hours. Now, they hadn't slept and had barely eaten for more than a day.

It isn't going well. She deceived us.

For days the captive had sat in the dungeon with no man, not the

Inquisitor or even the Godblood, either witnessing or sensing her capabilities. Now, after revealing her true form in the crypt, she used magic.

Powerful magic.

Through the evening and night and well past the dawn of the next day, the evil creature was *still* not drained by the manacles despite her body's clear exhaustion. Her aura surged with little discretion or predictability other than when she was under threat.

This was a core flaw in his design, Vene soon realized, the workaround she had discovered. She wasn't concentrating on spells. She had no precision, showing neither intent nor training. He doubted she focused on any affinity, be it life or death, divine inspirations or earthly patterns.

No. She was *chaos.*

The only sure protection they had was the golden shield she had been insisting they find.

Fortunately, her magic cannot distort its blessed countenance.

Keros slapped his shoulder with one hand, hefting his hold on the heavy relic with the other. "Come. As our bodies rest, so does hers."

Vene grunted, drank more water, and stood up to leave the warded, candlelit room where Emil could mix his potions without interference or distraction. When they opened the door to reenter the interrogation room, true sunlight filled the room, welcomed through a tall window facing east for the entire morning thus far.

Well. Not welcomed by everyone.

After all her time seemingly unbothered by a stone cell beneath the ground, the demoness revealed her true nature in her responses to the light of the sun. In this, Keros was right. Once the dawn arrived, this brightest of his inquisition rooms had been the first they witnessed any lessened confidence in her demeanor.

She fears the sun, he'd thought, clasping his sunburst pendant. *She cannot endure Musanlo's Eye of the Just. We need only outlast her through the night.*

Unfortunately, that prediction had not come to pass. Her eyes leaked tears of wrath, and she could no longer pierce them with that evil and contemptuous glare, but the demoness had continued to resist them until late into the morning.

Pure chaos.

He doubted she had a proper soul capable of transitioning. If they killed her, the world would be best served if she simply ceased to be.

"Daeva," Keros said as he strode up to her. "Are we ready to try again? Have you seen yet that you cannot win? You cannot escape."

She quivered in her well-defended corner, her aura flaring dangerously as she growled like a winter wolf. The manacles kept her wrists fixed, the hand-width between them unchanging thanks to the rod hooked to each metal ring.

They had not yet been able to chain her to the floor, but the sunburst of protection inscribed with inlays of topaz upon the floor provided the two men chances to recuperate without her darting for the door, locked though it was.

"Why did you risk everything for that irksome Capitan?" he sneered. "To give him *this*?"

Keros used the shield to reflect the light upon her snow-white head as he'd been doing since dawn. He took pleasure in watching her flinch, and Vene had noticed he'd been stepping closer to the topaz border with each confrontation since dawn.

She could answer none of his questions, for Keros had refused to speak to her in Trade. Vene believed that was a mistake once she'd proven resilient and unlikely to break quickly. It left them entrenched in an unshifting war of attrition when another, much larger one marched on their doorstep.

But then, he never enjoyed his women talking back.

With the daylight behind him, Keros postured but only provoked her as if he believed brute force would cow a creature inured to the trials of the world. She feared nothing which made the Manalari women weep.

"If I can press the shield upon her and hold her down," Keros murmured quietly to Vene, "can you drain her beyond what your manacles can do? Make her feel the chill of death itself through your touch?"

Vene pursed his lips, a chill of his own passing down his spine. "You see her aura as I do, your excellency."

"So what?"

"We've seen warriors with these patterns. They feel no pain. They are distanced from their body's thirst and tiredness. They do not fear death."

"So break through it." Keros casually waved his hand. "I know you can. She has been in this state all night and morning. It cannot last much longer before she burns out."

Vene shook his head once. "Forgive me, but we cannot risk your life if we underestimate her unearthly volatility *again*."

The Archbishop ground his teeth, knowing well what the Inquisitor reminded him of.

In the middle of the night, the fool had lunged at her, violently tearing her shirt, believing to lay bare her blackened skin would make her scream in fear of him. She hadn't made a peep but struck his nose with her forehead before engulfing them both in a flare of magic which left them both smoldering. Keros had been the one screaming. Not her.

Since then, Keros had grown more reckless with each passing hour and every interruption. The questioning from the Bishops, their every appeal to him to accept help only grated on his pride.

He waited too long to claim the idea as his own, and he cannot admit he was mistaken.

"You know this to be a test of endurance," Keros said during another break. "Of our faith in overcoming our enemies. Even of turning them to our cause."

What?

"To our cause?" Vene asked. "I...don't understand."

Keros chuckled. "Oh? But you see her aura as I do, yes? Or so you just explained, my High Inquisitor."

A pause filled the room.

"What... sight do you keep now, Most High?"

"This daeva is unclaimed," began the Archbishop eagerly, leaning in, his voice hushed with secrecy.

"Unclaimed?"

"Her aura is unanchored. Unchosen by god, devil, or earth! It is some of the most…*elemental* we have seen outside *Pisc'sagrad* herself. That is how she slips around your restraints! I have realized this! I have seen the vision!"

No.

"She is chaos, your excellency!" Vene replied, knowing true fear for his superior to be walking down this path. "A storm meant to collapse upon itself, rending apart that which Musanlo has made out of pure, unreasoned spite! You cannot claim this, you can only unravel it! Make her toothless! Most High, please listen, a battle for our very existence lies outside of this room!"

The Archbishop rounded on him, slate blue eyes wild. "*It is here, too!* This is the heart of our city! Can you not see the purity of it, ripe to be claimed? We *cannot* leave this room without her groveling, do you understand! I will not lose this opportunity!"

"But she is not some noble's deflowered daughter quaking in a corner!" Vene retorted.

Emil blinked, his mouth curling in disgust. "What did you say, Inquisitor?"

He clenched his jaw before he swallowed. "Forgive me, but you *must* see what she is. She is a devil sent to weaken and divide us. The more time and strength we give to her attempting to wield that which exists to tear God's Kingdom apart, the less of *all* we have remaining for the Ma'ab. This has taken too long and begun rumors spinning out of control. What if the Ma'ab themselves sent her for this purpose? If we cannot assure our own people of Musanlo's favor—"

"And *what*," Emil sneered, "do you recommend will bring victory sooner, Catechist of *Truth*?"

The Inquisitor was too exhausted to wrap those thoughts in lacey ribbon. "Bring all the Bishops together at *Pisc'sagrad*. Keep the shield with you. All of you working together can break her. You can claim her with the blessing of the Temple pool. *Then* you may do with her as you wish. The Capitan has no claim if you want to toss her to the Witch Hunters to prove to the people that we've cleansed the taint from the Temple."

Emil stared at him with deep blue eyes. The jealousy at the thought of sharing her with so many was clear.

"And what do *you* know of what is possible with the blessing of *Pisc'sagrad*?" Keros remarked. "*You* have never known Holy Immersion."

"Your excellency," Vene tried again, quelling that string. "Listen to me. Meet Musanlo halfway. This is the most powerful devil we've ever encountered. If you are right about your vision, bring the full power you wield to bear upon her. Instruct the other Bishops to obey you."

The Archbishop quieted, looking back at the captive in the corner, tears from the light trailing down her ashen cheeks.

"But then she will simply *become Pisc'sagrad*," he murmured. "Her potency...diluted to nothing. I want her as she is, Vene. I want to show the 'Godblood' the true power I have over all within my walls that he will never claim. Even the devils he captures will bow to me and defend our Jewel on the Mount from the death lords."

Vene felt the will to continue this travesty leave him.

Her rebellion has seduced him. Subverted our holy mission. I should never have found the shield for him. I should never have listened to the spirit in the library.

For once, the High Inquisitor could not muster the faith that they would overcome this lure away from the path to victory.

The final temptation has come, and he cannot see this horror so plain on her face.

Several fists pounded on the door then, their holy allies breaking decorum by forcing their voices through the privacy ward.

⋆Your Holiness! Catechist! You must come! Conscripts and peasants fill the courtyard!⋆

CHAPTER 18

I DISCOVERED THAT MOURN'S "WAY OUT" TO THE COURTYARD WASN'T LIKE our way in. The mercenary revealed no further secret passages which every guard for generations had lacked the opportunity to know about. We simply used the same pathways available to the Humans and did so as quickly and quietly as we could.

With the same camouflage as when we'd explored Jael's former cell, he led us up another level from the dungeon to an odd mix of a too-small barracks, cramped storage alcoves, and stuffy cooking or laundry rooms meant for the benefit of those upstairs.

We gave ground for every Human who approached us, quietly placing our backs to the stone walls and letting them pass by. They all appeared male as far as I could tell, but most of them seemed either too young or too old to breed. All of them either smelled or acted fearful and, according to Mourn, none of them were mages.

Our advantage while we remain in the lower levels, my bodyguard explained. *You saw how few guards remained in the dungeon, which had few prisoners?*

~I did.~

The conscripts will be every non-mage male in Manalar who appears healthy enough to fight. They've emptied out the prison and reduced their mundane Temple guard and staff to what you see.

I smirked. ~*So the mageborn males in the upper floors need to do a few more things for themselves?*~

I heard a mental chuckle. *The youngest novitiates are taking on the servants' work, which they would do and be glad they aren't being sent to the wall.*

Finally, Mourn chose a door to test, checking that the hall was empty of eyes before opening it and beckoning me inside. He seemed to know what to expect, giving the musty storeroom a tongue-lashing sniff before moving directly to a shuttered window. Hints of a strong sun leaked through the imperfect cover, and I could hear voices outside.

Prepare yourself, he warned.

I closed my eyes. ~*Ready.*~

Daylight struck me through my eyelids and felt the same as always, drawing out tears, yet my motivation pushed me through the discomfort sooner than usual. I joined him at the window to take that first breath of fresh air, recognizing angry shouts rising from the lower buzz of a crowd, and squinted out.

No Humans yet. Only a shaggy, slanting garden presently shaded by the Temple and leading to the South wall on one side. To the West, a steep slope led to a retaining wall which pointed us toward the front of the Temple where the courtyard lay. It was about two levels up if we'd been underground.

I glanced down. ~*Long drop to the ground.*~

A climb, not a drop. I'll go out first. You climb on my back and stay there until we reach the courtyard.

~*Got it.*~ I stayed close so I could watch him creeping out onto the rough stone, searching for handholds. ~*Do we have time?*~

For now. I'm hearing the updates from Reprisal. Come on out.

I climbed onto the sill and reached for the harness crossing his broad shoulders. ~*And what'll we do when we get there?*~

Identify those inciting to riot and make them irresistibly sleepy.

Something I could help with since Reprisal had provided me with one of their drowsy inhalants. *When something is simply a good idea, many others make it.*

I chuckled as I settled onto his back but did not distract him as he started whispering Draconic and scaling down the wall as surefooted as a mountain goat. When he touched ground at the walled garden, he hefted my weight higher and rebalanced himself before turning for the slope.

Although I could have run on the ground with him in between the climbs, I did not protest, for he picked up speed toward the end, and I sensed another incoming feat I could not match. His muscles bunched and his Words boosted their power, guiding his aim.

I held my breath, clenching the harness as Mourn sprinted all-out before taking a long leap onto the slope. He landed heavily enough to dislodge a clod of dirt, but we were halfway up the yellowish slope to the greyer retaining wall. From there, it would be a similar climb up to the next ledge as it had been from the window to the garden, then one final, short climb.

Once around the corner, we'd be there.

Focused on my ears and my breath, I held tight, moving with my "mount" as Mourn surged to get us where we must be without delay. The buzz of people grew louder, and I kept waiting to hear a crack or a blast, maybe the clash of swords confirming we were too late to keep the pot from boiling over.

Mourn didn't slow, and before a sliver of an hour passed, we had reached the courtyard level. The Dragonblood crouched in the shaded landscaping to let me slide off and stay low beside him. Our angle wasn't clear to see everything. I counted a score of men in the age range of who should be defending the wall but estimated three or more times that many voices.

Most wore basic armor of varying quality and were armed with short swords, butcher's blades, and gardening tools. One of them even waved a spade like Gavin's in the air. Then I glimpsed the shining armor of one of the Templars striding along the line of people, holding up his hand for them to stay back. He brandished no weapon.

~*One against twenty,*~ I commented, ~*yet none of those commoners are* prepared to handle a mage warrior trained to defend the Temple.~

Why we don't want a fight to break out. It will only result in the needless loss of men.

I listened to an oddly familiar tenor of one man's rant rising above the rest, supported by a handful of roars behind him. ~Are the Witch Hunters here?~

They are. The Witch Hunters haven't been allowed inside the Temple since the Inquisitor banned them, but they'd take this opportunity to surge inside to look for their black witch.

Mourn seemed unable to keep his tail from waving, but he did well to avoid rustling the longer and taller branches. I frowned as another chant began from the common people, arms and weapons up in the air. Two weaponless Templars came into view, pacing the line. Although I did not know what the people said, I could tell the men in shining armor tried but ultimately would *not* persuade the common people to leave.

~Hey, if the Captain's men are here, and the people want the Bishops to give him the shield, why aren't they listening to their Godblood to stand down against his own elite?~

Good question. I think someone makes it worse, but they also say they will not leave the Captain unless the Witch Hunters leave first. The Captain is calling on them all for patience and peace while he finds out more from the Bishops for them, but the Witch Hunters are threatening to follow him to find the black witch if he does. They are in a stalemate.

~Hm. If Isboern is the most powerful psion you've witnessed, could he 'persuade' them all to calm down and leave?~

If he does that, then he's as frightened as Keros must be letting the rumors rage unhindered.

~What? What are you talking about?~

Slowly, Mourn drew air in through his teeth, his pupils expanding as he tasted the air. *A lot of witnesses saw Jael and the shield yesterday. Reprisal has heard numerous stories overlapping, but most seem to contain the idea that the Archbishop and Inquisitor are locked up with both her and the shield and won't come out. That's why this crowd is here.*

My middle flared with anger, and I felt sick. *~They'd better not be——~*

They could, but don't dwell on it. Remember, she's a Red Sister like you. She is a survivor. Also, know that Team One has made it inside the Temple. They listen for more and are prepared should those new Witch Hunters enter the Temple.

I breathed out, willing myself to calm down, aware how the nerves of the crowd affected me. *~Do we have targets to make sleepy?~*

All, if necessary. The wind is cooperating for now, but I can also change it. Let's get closer.

Feeling at once better yet further on edge, I crept with my body-guard along the Temple wall until we could see almost all the courtyard. The largest landmark was a three-tiered stone fountain on the far side, burbling and splashing in circular waterfalls. Around it lay carefully tended flower beds and manicured trees. The plants snaked around the fountain and the courtyard itself, generally following the walls and lining the Temple itself.

Yellow cobbled pathways wound between the soil beds, wide and flat, clean swept, and lined with hedges which were easy to jump over. The widest of these pathways could easily fit a four-horse cart and led directly from the iron gated wall to the massive stairs leading to the sealed front door of the Temple.

I admired how the main, metal door and windows on the first floor were shaded from the afternoon Sun by a sloping roof which matched the red tile of the high towers. Its weight was supported at ground level by white marble pillars and ran from end-to-end on the West side, creating a spacious, open-air walkway and speaking platform facing the courtyard.

Unfortunately, that courtyard had plenty of room for a skirmish.

Roughly sixty common men had passed through the double iron gate and confronted the Witch Hunters and Templars, whose forces were about equal at fifteen apiece. The Witch Hunters stood apart from the commoners, snarling together, while the city defenders were spread out performing crowd control. The Templars had reinforcements waiting, though I wasn't sure if the same held true for the Hunters.

Beyond the courtyard itself, more people clustered at the gate, holding it open with a clog of bodies as more Humans, including plenty of children, climbed atop the wall to watch the building conflict. My concerns rose higher to estimate more than two hundred Humans clustered here; they would draw more the longer this stand-off lasted. This *could* lead to a massive fight at exactly the time when the city could least afford it.

Shit.

Between this crowd and the Temple, Captain Isboern was hard to miss. He sat on the back of a dappled grey stallion, speaking to all of them but engaging more with those closest and brave enough to step forward and speak. Even not knowing what they said, I could guess this Captain of the Templars was the only reason violence had not happened yet.

~*He's an easy target, isn't he?*~

Mourn chuckled. *Maybe to aim at. Getting through his protections is another matter. Reports suggest he's hard to injure, let alone kill.*

I made a face. ~*Well, that's good. So, where's Tamuril?*~

Look for a male youth with brown hair and skin who seems out of place. A green tunic, no armor. Although, reports say she hid once the crowd started to swell.

~*Wise of her. She's probably in the trees.*~

Probably.

~*Where the fuck are the Bishops?*~

Staying in their Temple.

~*Pfeh! If I was them, I'd be strutting out here as one in all our finery and at least bluff about nobody wanting any **real** trouble!*~

~*They aren't battlemages.*~

You mean they won't even help Isboern protect the wall?~

Oh, they will. Their tactics tend to be collective, sent at great range. The Holy Immersed have always remained shut away, far from the weapons and close to Pisc'sagrad to perform their greatest magic.

~*Hmph. Like Priestesses, then.*~

Pretty similar. Mourn pulled a pouch from the front of his harness.

Prepare your first handful. Don't make it too large to give away a visible signal.

I sighed and retrieved my less familiar pouch, double-checking its contents. ~We can't blow sleeping powder on everyone.~

I can enhance what we have, and it will help. We do not need to put the entire crowd down on the stones. We only need to sap some of the verve from the leaders. The rest should fall back if they haven't yet entered the Temple grounds.

~Check.~

Meanwhile, the Sun was rising high above the mountain crest. Midday was approaching, and soon our hiding spot would be baked in warm light. It was hot out here; hotter and drier than Augran for sure. Oddly, that did seem to work in our favor to carry the powder high and far when we got down to it.

Mourn and I took turns, aiming and blowing subtle puffs of sleep powder skyward, where both the natural wind and Mourn's magic helped to dissipate it far from us and down among the bickering, posturing Humans.

At first, I saw no change.

Keep at it. Next on three. One, two...

I was tempted to doubt my own ears when the buzz of voices seemed to lessen, but then I spotted someone yawn.

Good. Three more, at least.

I stayed in careful tandem with my bodyguard, and we proceeded to empty our bags over a hundred heartbeats. Finally, I was confident the Dragonchild was correct. The high tension gradually lessened, both within the crowd inside the gate and more outside of it. Even the Templars noticed the Witch Hunters' bellows had drawn down to irritable *uroans* lowing.

The only one who seemed unaffected was Isboern, and a moment later, I read a heightened concern in his body language and among the Templars. For certain, they had begun subtly looking over the courtyard for another threat.

~Uh-oh.~

Shhh.

The quiet implication that I had to cease thinking to hide from a psion was concerning. However, Isboern didn't give up on his primary concern to go hunting for whomever had altered the energy in front of him. He kept speaking to them, conveying utter confidence being an orator.

Most importantly, the common folk listened to him, and the Witch Hunters interrupted him less frequently.

They were losing their "verve."

Reason is returning, Mourn said. *Well done.*

~For what?~ I thought wryly. ~Your idea.~

And your help. You could always make this Bargain harder if you wished, Red Sister. Never forget that.

I smiled, for in truth, I was glad to see it worked. Perhaps I had doubted it would. We never used such hidden and harmless tactics in Sivaraus.

A harmless tactic, reducing further harm. Hm.

Abruptly, the delicate negotiations of the courtyard were broken with the sound of shattering glass.

Far above us, in one of the highest-rising towers, a man was screaming.

THE MORNING SUN WAS LEAVING THE INTERROGATION ROOM, SHRINKING BACK from the corner where the demoness suffered its touch. As the shadows returned, she seemed to rally, alert and wild eyes fixed on them as the news of the crowd in the courtyard forced Keros to respond.

"Have Isboern deal with them!" he bellowed, spinning toward the locked door with fists clenched. "That's his duty!"

The moment His Holiness took his focus from her, she leaned forward. Vene lifted his hand, pointing at her.

Stay. As God watches, I'm not afraid.

Her dry lips curved in a tiny smirk. She sat unnervingly still. Unblinking.

270

"The Captain is there already," explained Cognate Horus through the dense wood. He seemed to be taking the lead. "But the Hunters rile up a crowd which outnumbers us all!"

Keros sounded disbelieving. "They can't break our holy defenses even if the Templars failed. What do you even fear from that rabble?"

"They demand we give the golden shield to the city's wall defender."

"What?" the Archbishop huffed incredulously. "Is that what Is-boern told them? To turn them against us? He's breaking his sacred oath!"

"He's holding them back, your excellency—"

"I'm sure he is!"

"—but they heard this was how we won past sieges. They believe we will lose the war if we do not, that it is a sign from God."

Keros pulled the shield tighter to his own defense. "Pure offal! A *devil* came to him! She pushed him to search for it in the first place! *His* are the *wrong* hands to claim this relic!"

"But we may be wrong, Archbishop! They're saying the warrior defender had the shield and the divine cleric had a sacred thurible—"

"WHAT?!"

Vene winced at the volume.

"—which should have been buried with the shield, your Holiness!"

"Where in the Nine Hells did they hear about that?!"

"We don't know, your Holiness, but did you find such a thing?"

"There was no such thing in the crypt!"

"Of course, your excellency, but we fear they will not disperse from continued denial!"

"It's not denial! It's the truth!"

"Please, your grace, we need you to come out and bring them to heel!"

Keros looked shaken, his face once flushed but now pale and sweaty. "I... I'll be out. Soon. Grant me...a few moments to clean up, Cognate."

Horus sounded relieved. "Yes, your excellency."

When Emil looked at him, however, Vene could tell he had only bought time.

"Did we miss something, Inquisitor?" he whispered.

The Inquisitor pursed his lips. "Neither she nor the Captain ever mentioned a thurible, your excellency. That is all I know."

"Should we...look...?"

"We haven't the time or the men." Vene bowed his head. "I will come with you to face them, if you wish."

The Archbishop's breath had quickened, his eyes flicking to all corners of the room as he struggled to think. "Where is... the dagger, Inquisitor."

Vene swallowed. "The dagger?"

Emil rounded on him, stepping nose-to-nose. "Don't play innocent now, deathmaker. You know which dagger I mean. The silver one."

"There must be another way—"

"*Now!!*" Emil snarled, baring his teeth. The fact that he had moved it around recently so as not to recall its most secure location was troubling.

He was never meant to use it. It began as a method for **me** *to study... But my hands are tied.*

"In the northwest tower," he spoke softly. "In the ceremonial chambers, where you last left it with the manacles and chalice."

"Good. Are you prepared to use it?"

Vene looked at the demoness, who was gathering strength in the dark.

The Archbishop raised a sandy red eyebrow at his silence. "Well? Go get the dagger, Kegyek. Break her for me quickly, and I'll see you become one of the Immersed as your reward."

You bastard.

"The ritual won't work without the chalice," he replied, "for which there must be sunlight from the closing half of the day."

Keros looked at the demoness and smiled. He'd stopped shaking and sweating. "Then we'll take her to the ceremonial chamber. We'll use the secret hall from one end of the Temple to the other."

"That's too dangerous, Holiness," Vene said sternly, "and we don't have *time*."

"The northwest tower faces the courtyard," came the smug reply. "We can address the rabble from on high, with our new prize under clear control and far away from Isboern. *Then* we can return to the crypt for the thurible."

God help us.

"Come, Inquisitor. Keep to your own oath if the Captain will so disdainfully throw away his at the cruelest and most gainful opportunity."

If she were honest with herself, Jael didn't know how much longer she could last. She also dared not to be so honest. She would rather chew wiping leaves for her morning meal than let her captors get a glimpse of that approaching limit.

The tension and constant cajoling between the two men could not be clearer, even for one like her, who'd never been to Court. It seemed pretty simple to her.

The man in blue, gold, and white wanted to fuck her. What was more, he wanted to watch her face and willpower crumble once he got his prick inside. If his Human worm didn't match even the girth of Elder Rausery, it would be underwhelming for both of them.

Meanwhile, the man in black wouldn't touch her except to cause physical harm to her when he was allowed. He resented her for the impossible challenge his leader could not let go and remained as damage control to the Archbishop's precious reputation.

He's worse than the Prime ranting about healing potions in battle if they're relying on him to lead them against the Ma'ab.

Still, it seemed the Captain Isboern hadn't been lying in the crypt.

~I cannot help you directly now, but I'll try to reach someone who can. Stay alive for them.~

Jael had received no hints of any form of aid. As the hours dragged on, the Red Sister had to assume she was on her own.

As from the start.

She watched the men reach an agreement at last, surprised when the Archbishop knelt before the Inquisitor. Had she not thought some illicit act was about to happen in front of her, she'd have been prepared when Keros touched the topaz border which had kept her from launching at them.

The man in black—Vene—crossed it first and seized the solid bar holding her wrists together. The chill which seeped into her through the polished metal was new and frightful, making her gasp. Her vision swam, her arms felt weak, and she had to pee.

What are you doing?! Let me go!

The two men struck her in the gut and face to reassure themselves she still reacted to pain before dragging her upright by her pits. They hauled her with them into the small room where they'd been taking their rests away from her. Within that room, she should have known, was a secret door leading to a tight, black hall.

They left as another man pounded on the door.

What now? Where are we going...?

Ever since her geas was released, Jael hadn't the space in her mind to even try to understand what had happened to her. The golden eyes in the crypt, floating in front of her, *talking* to her...

Who are you?

★A long-time dreamer of this world...★

And now, instead of these Human mages using all their ruthless tricks on her, she had power to keep them back. To make them *hurt* for trying. Once. Twice, and again.

Keep going. Keep them back.

She didn't know why it worked. She couldn't think about it without it hurting. She had felt too tired some time ago, before the Sun came up, and then it got worse.

Now she didn't know *where* she was.

I've never been here before.

They left the dark hall to enter a white room blazing with the Sun, and Jael screamed. The Archbishop laughed, dragging her stumbling to something which could only be an altar standing within a column of blinding light.

Her heart seized with fear. This was how Sirana had almost died.

No! No, no, let me go! No!

The men cried out as she *hurt* them again, struggling to break free of their grip. For once, they dared not release her to hide behind that shield; they suffered with her to get her on her back upon that silk-covered slab. Once there, the Archbishop pulled her wrists above her head and leaned down, biting hard on her ear, making it bleed.

Her back arched, and the sharp, searing pain with the loud laughter through his teeth meant she couldn't feel the Inquisitor seize her ankles until it was too late. He had them secured to the altar; she could not kick or close her legs.

They'd practiced this before.

Blind as she was made to face direct Sun, Jael cursed furious nonsense she barely recognized as Davrin in her own ears. Her body and mind ran recklessly along that terrifying edge of awareness, yet she continued, defiant, just to convince herself she was awake.

Behind her eyes, in her delirium, cool blues and greys seemed to form the shape of the Inquisitor when he held her leg with one hand. Directly above and mocking her were the blood red and yellow hues of the Archbishop, kneeling on the manacle's rod so he could caress and pinch her tits beneath her shirt.

The Inquisitor held a silver dagger and golden vessel, and Jael knew what those were for.

Sirana… Sirana… how did you keep your head like this?

Her blues were a much better memory to die with than those right above her.

"GO ON, VENE," EMIL SAID, LICKING HIS LIPS IN A WAY THAT MADE VENE'S skin crawl. "Go on. Dissect her aura. Find out how she works."

Finally got what you wanted, didn't you, excellency?

The only reason the Inquisitor could parse was the Archbishop was ready for more than blood. He'd never killed any of those young women with his own hand. They more often did it themselves some years later.

If I do this...if he bears witness...

He will demand to hold the dagger next time.

Vene held the golden chalice where it could be filled with the Sun's deepest rays; he also held the silver dagger which helped to separate the soul from the body in a more controlled way as a prisoner was dying.

She wasn't dying, however. Far from it. Her aura was one of the most vibrant he'd ever seen.

"Vene! Stop staring at her. We have a public to meet at the window."

The Inquisitor tested the sharpness of the blade, cutting a slit in her black leather pants until he could see dark flesh. Gingerly, balancing the cup of sunlight, he touched her skin, surprisingly soft, with his two littlest fingers while using the tip of the enchanted blade to prick her, drawing a little blood.

She wailed and snarled as he'd expect of any demon, certainly aware of something more burrowing into her essence even if she couldn't articulate what was happening.

Her vibrancy, however, neither collected upon death's edge nor recoiled before turning to blackened ash. It started to unravel, fraying at the edges. Like a small hole in a delicate veil worried by tiny, persistent fingers.

I... do not know what this is.

But it was beautiful.

Was she...? *Could* she be something more than a demon?

"Vene," Emil barked as he stopped, hovering hands trembling. "Break her *now*."

"I...cannot," he croaked. "I fear what we unleash if I do."

Or what he might destroy, understanding neither why the ghosts spoke to him nor who the shrouded woman was in the crypt.

"Fool! Don't you dare stop now!"

Emil lunged for the dagger, but Vene anticipated that and tossed the chalice far to the side as he threw himself from the platform. His superior pulled the golden shield from his back and charged, ramming into him to knock him over. The Noiri staggered but caught himself, moving farther away with the momentum.

"You will not defy me now!"

"Excellency—"

"If you break your oath, I will break *you!* I will hand you partly flayed as a gift to the Ma'ab!"

Vene flinched, gripping the silver dagger. He had nowhere to back away, only toward the tall window. What would he do, stab His Holiness with his own heirloom? Without the chalice, it wouldn't cause him more than physical pain.

Are you mad?

Keros did not ask himself the same question before he bulled into his Inquisitor. This time, Vene tripped over a fold of carpet and fell into the windowsill with the shield on top of him and his superior's weight behind it. His back struck the glass, pressing as hard as a novitiate pushing the doors of the Temple open with both hands.

"Sir, no!" he shouted, grabbing the lip of the shield for purchase. "Listen to m—"

His ear heard the slightest, most terrifying snap before the glass shattered.

His last view was of Emil's snarling face, shoulders and arms flexing to give him one last shove through the window.

Then all which remained to hold him up was air.

Chapter 19

The crowd pointed upward at the man struggling at a window long after the Captain and his Templars had spun around and sprinted toward the base of the tower.

~*What the fuck is he going to do?!*~

Watch the crowd, not him! Mourn ordered.

I did, and three concerning events happened at once.

First, the Witch Hunters ran toward the front doors with too few Templars following or able to stop them.

Then someone broke from the crowd at a full sprint, heading for the side of the courtyard where Mourn and I had arrived.

I recognized the runner.

~*Is that Mathias?!*~

I'll alert the others.

~*Should we go after—?*~

The Inquisitor.

~*Huh?*~

Look.

Truthfully, I hadn't wanted to watch the screaming man land upon the ground. I expected to hear that scream cut off with a sickening splat, but I looked, and my mouth dropped open with everyone else.

Captain Isboern's horse closed the tower when the man in black started falling. He lifted both hands above him as if he intended to catch the thrashing body hurtling toward the bricks. In response to the gesture, the Inquisitor's fall began to slow. He didn't realize it.

His shriek filled the courtyard until the shield falling with him banged loudly on the ground, striking several shards of bricks loose and spraying them near Isboern's prancing horse. There, the shining plane of metal bounced twice and then rolled on its edge in ever-tightening circles, until the Inquisitor's body joined it nearby. The Human psion had slowed Kegyek's fall enough that he survived the landing with a startled grunt.

The crowd murmured and buzzed, some pointing up at the man peering out the broken window. The Witch Hunters were confronting the Templars at the front doors, beginning to shout again, but Mourn kept his focus on the man in black who slowly realized he had not died. The Inquisitor focused on the Captain, who dismounted from his horse to offer him a hand up.

The Dragonchild placed his hand on my shoulder. *Wait. When I say, jump on my back.*

~Check.~

Inquisitor Kegyek could barely speak as Isboern helped him to his feet, saying something to him. The young man's face held only concern, while the white-bearded man drew back first, muttering, offering a befuddled bow of gratitude.

However, it didn't take long for the Inquisitor to look up at the window from which he'd fallen. There stood another man who, after being caught staring at the golden shield several strides away from the man who should be dead, swiftly drew back out of sight.

Kegyek turned toward that shield, his body shaking from the surge of terror from falling, and he hurried to pick it up as if he expected another to try for it. The Templars stood guard between the people and their Captain; they only offered a salute. Finally, the elder mage wearing black and grey robes held the shining metal up over his head as the crowd cautiously drew closer to see. It didn't even have a dent.

Mourn translated his words through our link.

People of Manalar, do you believe this man can lead us in our time of need?

The crowd shouted and called, shaking their hands and weapons as more poured into the courtyard.

Should the Defender of the Wall carry into battle the ancient artifact of our forefathers? Does not a shield belong to a warrior, not a Bishop? Is not such a craft best used to stand between home and invader?

The noise swelled to a manic level, and Mourn's hand squeezed harder on my shoulder as we stood up to make sure we witnessed what we hoped would happen.

The High Inquisitor offered the shield to Captain Isboern with a formal bow of his head and a blessing for wisdom and strength.

Then, with a formal salute over his heart, the city's defender accepted, and the chant began. Someone started it in Trade. Mourn took the moment to adjust his harness and shift into his quadruped form.

"God-blood! God-blood! God-blood!"

I saw the psion's smile as he lifted the shield where all could see and, based on his gestures, seemed to make a promise to them. They cheered in a way I'd never heard before.

Look. The window.

I didn't have to ask which one as my four-legged bodyguard sorted himself out. The red-haired man in ragged blue and gold vestments had returned to the jagged opening in the tower. His arms braced stiff, shoulders hunched with tension, he stared down at the courtyard.

~The Archbishop?~

We're paying him a visit.

Mourn didn't have to tell me to jump on.

~Can anyone see us?~

If they look hard enough, they might notice the air bending.

We took the chance. Mourn sprinted out into the open and slipped deftly between commoner and Templars alike, giving Isboern a wide berth before bounding onto the tower wall. The Dragonchild started climbing like a cat on a tree. If anyone felt or saw something odd, no one screamed about it.

By the time Mourn reached the window with the jagged, broken-out pane, the Archbishop had withdrawn into the white room. We caught him kneeling over something...

Kneeling over *someone*.

He threatened her with a vial as if he'd force her to drink it.

~*JAEL!*~

I assumed Mourn dropped the camouflage, because he rumbled like a massive Hell-beast with me on his back. The mage threw himself back, regaining his feet despite the shock, though his aged hands fumbled, revealing two vials when they dropped harmlessly to the carpet.

They were blue and yellow, like in Derfoli's dream.

The Archbishop's mouth fell open as he stared at us, stuttering, "*Daevoni...*"

Free Jael, Mourn told me, his thoughts perfectly clear. **I'll knock him out.**

He wouldn't kill him *yet*.

I rolled off the instant before Mourn coiled tight and launched himself at the Temple's head cleric, ramming him so hard, the man lost his wind even before he lost consciousness. He wasn't my concern, however.

"Jael? Jael, can you hear me?"

She stared at me but couldn't focus. Her clothes were torn and damp, and what skin showed was bruised and scraped. She wore the manacles from my dream, and her ankles were buckled down to hold her in place. Even though the room was the brightest I'd ever seen, this was an altar of sacrifice.

So what had they taken from her?

I cupped her face, her cheeks wet with tears from the light yet her eyes stayed open. "Jael?"

She was going to blind herself looking at the midday Sun. I attempted to thumb her lids closed, but she resisted. I was scared.

Okay. Free her first. Get her out of the Sun.

I unbuckled her ankles, hooked her by the pits, and dragged her over to a shaded side of the room. She attempted to struggle, to fight me blindly, but her body was incredibly weak, as if she'd sustained intense torment since they'd dragged her out of the cell the previous day.

"Jael? Please. Speak. Can you hear me?"

Despite my rising dread, part of me was aware of Mourn tying up the unconscious Archbishop then quickly securing and searching the room. He picked up the blue and yellow vials first, recognized them as I did, and searched for the golden goblet and silver dagger. He even found the jeweled box of incense, taking everything Archbishop Keros had used against Lurili Derfoli which had caused her to kill herself.

The Dragonblood's tongue flashed out over each object, seeming to taste the air as he peered beyond its physical form. Then, one by one, he made them disappear, using his bracers to push them into the "elsewhere" where he hoarded his weapons.

"How much time do we have?" I asked.

"Unknown." He searched the walls' panels, confirming those with the exits quickly. "Nonetheless, we should leave."

"He's done something to her," I said, choking on my anger. "She won't respond. I-I don't even know if she's had water since ... I mean ... *shit!*"

I pulled out my near-empty water skin and carefully fed her what was left. At least she could swallow, and I could breathe. While I was at it, I bound her eyes with my blindfold.

Mourn watched me then studied her a moment. "We must get her to Krithannia. She can help."

I squinted in the overbright room. "And there are *how many* floors of zealot-riddled Temple beneath us?"

He smiled, though not *too* much. "Trust me. I will bring Keros, just in case."

"Good."

Because if we didn't need him for anything, and Jael died in my arms despite everything, he was going to provide some excellent flaying practice with a certain red-rune dagger.

THE VALUE OF THE DRAGON PEARLS AND THOSE WHO USED THEM AS A COHE-sive group truly could not be overstated.

The mercenary not only proved he was familiar with the layout of a Temple which hadn't changed much in centuries, but also that he used the constant updates from his fellow infiltrators in Reprisal. Even though I tried to help by listening for voices, footsteps, or even breathing, these were not the earliest warnings Mourn could act upon.

Sometimes it seemed he could see through the walls, like when he knew to wait for the Bishops as they hurried toward the tower from which the Inquisitor had fallen. By then, Mourn and I had reached a few floors down, using the secret passages intended for the Bishops. Fortunately, we received plenty of warning to avoid each of them, even when these panicking mages used this same hidden space.

We stopped when necessary for me to put my Sister down and rest. I always checked her pulse, breathing, joints, and bones to make sure I didn't miss something. Once, we had to stop and wait for someone working in a room to leave before we could slip out and take a different passage, all led down at a reasonable pace.

Once we'd reached the ground floor, Mourn found an unoccupied "pantry" which contained a cistern barrel to refill our skins. He also took a few simple "cakes" intended for Jael, and I grabbed one to eat right now, though he warned against getting greedy and giving away the presence of looters.

★*It's obvious there was a struggle between the two men in that room,*★ Mourn said. ★*I'd rather it appears that Keros gathered up his ritual items and disappeared with the black witch after pushing Kegyek out of the tower window.*★

~Understood.~

I lifted Jael back up, adjusting her weight to balance across my shoulders. Often turning to the side to navigate corners or stairs, I relied on my spiders to respond to a threat before I could.

Meanwhile, Mourn carried the Archbishop over one shoulder, oc-casionally nudging him up as the older man slid down but taking far less care with his comfort otherwise. Keros groaned now and then, his breath hitching as his face turned bright red.

~*How do you know the one pushed the other?*~ I asked.

It couldn't have been Jael after seeing how we found her. I also saw Keros trying to pull the golden shield back, but it slipped his grip and fell outside with Kegyek.

~*Hm. Why do you suppose they fought?*~

They both live to tell us. We shall find out.

I smirked. ~*Keros looks to be struggling to breathe.*~

Mourn shrugged. *I broke some ribs knocking him down. He will not get far even if we let him run.*

~*I'm glad, but you'd rather he not suffocate on the way, correct?*~

Correct. I'm monitoring his vitals. He can suffer for a while, like Kurn did.

~*Agreed. But… how will we take the manacles off of Jael?*~

*I found the key on him. We should be able to remove them anytime. However, they're enchanted to interact with a mage's aura, and you've seen it's affecting her. I want Krithannia to see it in place first before we remove them and be ready in case it causes an uncontrolled surge like the prison guard was describing."

My jaw clenched as I tried to reconcile that. ~*But she's not a mage.*~

Mourn didn't reply at first. *It appears to me that she is.*

~*No, listen! She's never used magic. Ever! She's always disdained and mistrusted mages because she's from the lowest House. The one infamous for never producing any mageborn Davrin at all!*~

Again, my bodyguard weighed his response with care.

Then something happened recently to change her. Like what happened to you. I see a mage's aura, Sirana, and potentially a strong one. But she's hurt and needs help from a mage I know can help.

I fell silent as we continued through the secret passages of the Manalari Temple, his thoughts returning within my mind.

She's hurt after something happened to change her.

Like what happened to you.

Tears filled my eyes and more than once, I blinked them away. At least she lived, and she was here with me. We were two Red Sisters on the Surface who weren't so far apart anymore.

In more than one way.

I still hoped.

MOURN AND I MET UP WITH WOLF ON OUR WAY DOWN TO THE UNDERHALLS, after we'd sneaked down the final stairway leading to the dungeon. My bodyguard let me listen in on the pearl talk this time, and the Hand went straight into his report, although he certainly kept one eye on me balancing Jael down the stairs.

★Hawk's squad is inside watching for any Witch Hunters who enter,★ said Wolf. *★Teams Crow and Bear are staying outside while the crowd figures out what they're doing next. We're keeping an eye out for Mathias Briar, now we know he's here.★*

★He could change appearance easily if the sorcerer is behind him,★ Mourn warned.

★Understood.★

Brian Wolf looked at me and my Sister again, his eyes brightening as the corners creased, which made him look pleased as word of this success had spread among his brothers. He evaluated my stance and apparent comfort in carrying her myself more than once. He probably wanted to offer to take her burden from me but held back.

★As for the front doors,★ he continued, *★the Inquisitor stands there with Isboern, both insistent the Witch Hunters stay out while the Templars clear the Temple and look for Keros and the 'devil.'★*

My bodyguard nodded. *★Yes, we heard them. We had a good head start, and the longer it takes that crowd to disperse and for them to decide what to do without Keros, the better for us to regroup.★*

Wolf smirked. *★I don't know why Isboern bothered saving Kegyek. He's a dead man after all his years torturing people for confessions.★*

★Perhaps. But we should not make that decision while he's under Captain Isboern's protection.★

So you're saying no preventative action?

Exactly what I am saying, Guildsman, and Cloud agrees. You will under-mine the incredible boost in morale the Manalari people just received from watching their Godblood perform a miracle blessed by the sun.

Hmph. And if Kegyek betrays Isboern and stabs him in the back?

Mourn's tail waved with complete calm. *I've watched the Inquisitor for decades. I believe he has more self-interest than pride, as you witnessed when he turned the shield over in an impromptu ceremony. This is largely what separated him from Keros.*

Also bear in mind the Captain has handled himself well in a snake's pit for more than five years without abandoning his own sense of honor. He's turned the Templars into loyal city defenders in action and in name. Not long ago, the Templars used more coercive tactics like the Witch Hunters because their training had lapsed.

Wolf twisted his mouth, turning his ireful look on the unconscious Archbishop slung like a sack of onions over the half-blood's shoulder. *So I understand, how long ago is 'not long ago?'*

Mourn smiled, showing teeth. *In this case, ten years.*

So, I was born. I'm surprised.

Heh heh. Isboern found them at the right time, when enough of them wanted something better. We need to let them try with what little time they have left before the inevitable change.

Understood. I just hope that 'honor' doesn't get the Captain killed right now, that's all. It'd be bad for everyone.

Agreed. But they'll do what they do best while we focus on our best.

The next time I had to stop on the underground stairs to rest, Wolf offered to take Jael.

"Let me help," he whispered.

My back, neck, and shoulders ached after having covered the entire length and height of the Temple. I was also becoming hungry; that small cake had been a teaser awakening my appetite after it had gone to sleep in the excitement.

With reluctance, I passed her over rather than risk dropping her, hoping she didn't become aware in the Guildsman's arms. She wouldn't know he was an ally.

Then again, after seeing that empty stare, her coming aware under any circumstance might be welcome.

Mourn scouted ahead to the unsealed passage leading to the crypt, encountered Torch there keeping watch for Krithannia, and confirmed all was clear. The Yungian explained that, during the tension of the near-riot and its resolution, they had remained secure behind the secret door through which we'd entered and Vesram had escaped.

Eventually, however, Gavin had insisted they return to the crypt.

At least there'll be plenty of room.

Krithannia, Gavin, and their guards met us halfway up the stairs from the crypt floor. The Guild Mistress's focus was fixed on Jael in Wolf's arms, and she hurried forward with clear intent to help.

"Quickly," she whispered, beckoning. "Let's make what nest we can for her."

While Mourn unceremoniously dropped Keros next to the short side of a sarcophagus, Jael's "nest" consisted of my backpack beside Krithannia's tucked between the long sides of two. Deshi and Nianzu each volunteered their blankets to fold and lay over them, cushioning her from neck to buttocks.

Krithannia removed the blindfold first but requested my help to give Jael more water from my skin. My Sister stared and swallowed. Nothing had changed from how we'd found her, and I didn't know how to feel about that. Swallowing with nauseated worry, I finally looked up at Gavin, who studied us from where he sat on the sarcophagus across from us.

"What wrong with her?" I asked him. "Is she dying?"

Though I couldn't see the icy blue color of his pupils in the dark, I could tell when they shifted to look at Krithannia and then Mourn. When neither of them chose to direct him, Gavin shrugged.

"No," he said. "Not in any way I recognize."

"Odd way to put it," I replied grimly.

"I am beginning to understand Elves have a completely different death cycle from Humans. Why you have said you never knew a death mage before me."

That didn't help.

"What *do* you see, Deathwalker?" Krithannia asked, managing an impressive balance between concern and curiosity, though I frowned at her pretending like she didn't know more than him.

"Hmm." Gavin considered carefully. "Well, her life aura seems bright enough to sustain her life, but her mage's aura reminds me of how the warp rot infected Kurn in the corrupted forest."

I closed my eyes against the flare of fear and rage. *Goddess damnit, she was never a mage before! What did they do to her?!*

"That's what I see, too," Mourn finally said. "Although it's not spreading the same way."

"Agreed," Krithannia said, dampening a cloth with her own water skin and carefully dabbing it on my Sister's face to cool her skin. "It's not warp rot, but the patterns seem…unfixed. Strained, certainly, but also deliberately damaged by another."

Whatever all *that* meant.

"So *what* can we do about it?" I asked with deliberate control. "Is there anything?"

"Her aura needs mending," Krithannia said, moving the damp cloth to Jael's neck next. "Which should revive the pattern, close the tear, and anchor it, for it is not the worst such injury I've seen. How this is done… well…"

The pale Elf pursed her lips, thinking while I waited in befuddled annoyance.

"There are several ways," she began vaguely but lifted her eyes to Mourn. "But for our circumstances, I think you and Sirana should be enough."

I took it as a bad sign that Mourn looked wary.

"Enough for what?" I asked.

Krithannia straightened her back and didn't answer me at first. "Sirana can't do it alone. She needs guidance."

"But Sirana tells me the cait wasn't born this way," he said, sounding like a protest. "She's never realized an affinity."

Helplessly, Krithannia shrugged. "Would you rather it be me?"

Would rather what *be you?*

"That's… a worse idea," he admitted.

I gritted my jaw. What *idea?*

"I know." The Naulor smiled, amused and a little cool. "I can't think of another solution where we stand."

Arrrgh!

"What do I need to do?" I demanded, glaring at the Naulor and then my bodyguard. "And why don't *you* want to help?"

Mourn looked at me and exhaled. "I, um…want to help, Sirana. But we'll be making a decision for your Sister. I can't see any way around it if you would have her live."

"But she *is* alive! Gavin says…"

"I think I understand," my death mage interjected. "Recall what I said of *Pisc'sagrad's* disruption 'burning out' a mage's ability to summon magic?"

I blinked at him, struck dumb, and he took it as sign to continue.

"That is 'cauterizing' a mage aura, for lack of a better description," he explained. "But what I see here looks like a tear in a cloth or a tapestry. It could be rewoven and mended, but if left to fester, it could also degrade the Vitas and slowly unravel. That way leads to madness and earlier death. We already know this."

Unravel? Jael?

Tears escaped onto my cheeks before I could prevent it, and Wolf, appointing himself guard over Keros, gazed at me with an unnerving sympathy.

"S-so, what decision?" I stuttered.

"Her affinity," said the half-blood. "If she has not realized it for herself, then we must choose an essence to set the anchor. Our realistic options are a bond to the To'vah or to the Naulor Queen."

"W-what?!"

"This type of injury requires Elves to help Elves," Krithannia explained, twisting the damp cloth in her hands. "Ordinarily, an affinity has already been realized, and we must only reset the pattern. In my experience, it is incredibly rare that she does not have one. To heal her, we must choose it for her."

Oh…

Shit.

"Shadow has enough Elf blood to assist you," the Naulor assured us, "but his *only* affinity is the To'vah. There aren't any others. I have others, but…" She hesitated. "I wouldn't wish them on a Baenar who is innocent of the history that would come with it."

I shook my head incredulously, peering between them. "Then… so, if we do this, could you… teach her something? If we go to the tower after Vesram, you'd have time, right? You said you might extend the contract."

The half-blood looked sober. "I could, and much sooner than that if she is willing. Our Bargain would obligate me to assure her lack of training didn't endanger your escape from Manalar, Sirana. The best way to accomplish that is to provide some training starting *today*. Assuming we're successful."

Too true. We must always assume success, first.

I gazed at Jael's face as Krithannia continued to tend her body. Her unfocused gaze frightened me. She wasn't dead, her eyes didn't reflect an empty vessel. She was just… unanchored. *Unraveling*. In time, she would go mad like me, maybe sooner, unless I made the decision for her.

Unless Mourn started training her on the eve of a battle.

Why did it seem like such pressure would only make her fight harder? The more I thought about it, the easier it was to consider how she and I wouldn't be so far apart in confronting these changes.

Neither of us was born this way. Maybe we could explore together.

"I understand," I said to the Dragonblood, holding Jael's limp hand. "Please help me bring her back and, per our Bargain, help us survive long enough to escape. If she's angry over this decision, it was mine, and I'll accept the blame."

"Very well."

CHAPTER 20

WE SENT TORCH, PENG-LOK, AND NIANZU BACK UP THE STAIRS TO SPREAD out and guard the passageway to the crypt; they needed to give us as early a warning as possible if anyone were to approach. Wolf and Deshi were tasked with hauling the battered Archbishop farther from us and standing guard over him.

We asked Gavin to watch for any unusual "intangible" changes within the crypt.

"Please observe everything you can," Krithannia said. "Tell me what you see, and I'll do the same."

"Of course," he said. "Though I'll not get too close to this ritual. Neither will the spirits."

I made a face. *More than one. Fantastic.*

I could tell that the Hellhound bodies were down here somewhere, albeit out of my sight. I also remembered Vo'traj's body had been gone from the balcony when we arrived, presumably brought down among the rest of the ancient and not-so-ancient dead. The smell hadn't grown too bad yet; the bodies were fresh.

Scents of blood and battle. Nothing strange.

Still bizarre to be dressing down as I was. My surviving spiders rested atop the nearest sarcophagus where I could see them. Off came my cloak, my belt, my boots, my leather armor, and my bracers.

"I'll not tell you how much to remove," Krithannia had said shortly before this. "But know that close contact with Jael is necessary. The three of you must touch in whatever way is most comfortable between you."

I'd frowned. "Is it like warming someone exposed to the cold?"

The Naulor lifted her brows. "What do you mean?"

"I mean would bare skin help more than trying through clothes?"

The Guild Mistress had glanced to the side, seeming to ponder this. "Well… Yes. Simply put, yes, it would help."

So now, here I was, considering stripping naked in a Manalari tomb with cracked and shattered bones spread out all around us. Or rather, I considered at least going topless, because Mourn had removed his cloak and harness. He wore no boots, no gloves, no shirt anyway, so all he was wearing for my Sister was pants, the coverage of his legs easily made up for in the length of a bare, slithering tail.

We'd removed Jael's boots, and the key had worked smoothly on the bright metal manacles. She was free of those damned things, though the rest of her things were gone, too. She wore only a torn shirt and damaged pair of leathers.

I'd stopped in my consideration and Mourn noticed.

"Sirana?"

"Hm," I grunted, crossing my arms to take the bottom of my shirt and pull it over my head. I tossed it on top of my things.

He blinked but took that moment to admire me. While the Humans were giving us respectful distance to do this thing, they shifted in surprise.

"Um, help me remove her shirt," I said in our native tongue, wanting some privacy in this public moment. *"We can be chest-to-chest-to-chest, at least."* I paused. *"Unless it would help even more to go all the way? Strip naked?"*

Mourn surprised me by chuckling as we carefully removed Jael's shirt. *"I may be too comfortable with you like that."*

"Ah. It would be bad for the ritual to get an erection?"

292

"I never said that." He straightened up, folding my Sister's shirt neatly and setting it near our cloaks. *"I will have one regardless. Only a matter of whether you find it too distracting or uncomfortable if nothing lies between us."*

Implying that it wouldn't be so for him.

My eyebrows lifted at that mental image. *"Hm. And if we... used it in the mending? That's even more contact, isn't it?"*

Mourn gave me a wry look at which I couldn't help chuckling. It had felt good, saying that to see his reaction, but then I shrugged awkwardly. *"I'm jesting. This is enough skin for the ritual."*

"Is it?"

Now it was my turn to blink.

Mourn tilted his head, inquiring. *"No pressure but know that I would not refuse."*

"You wouldn't?"

"No. I see an offer to maintain your end of the Bargain here and now, while assisting your Sister at the same time. After our time on the boat, I also see it as the quickest way for us to begin the song to heal her."

"The song?"

"You have heard it. Our auras working together to mend hers. We can do this without sex, I assure you, but it will take longer to get there because we have less practice."

Less practice just listening to each other, he meant, and far more with our focus on him seating himself deeply between my legs. Heat spread through my face and chest as I read his expression and his tail.

They each said the same thing. He was *not* jesting.

"Um. What about her pants?"

"We can leave them on."

I glanced down. The ridge in his pants suggested the necessity of filling my cunt in an old Human crypt with several "observers" nearby didn't bother him. I saw the advantage in gifting his Hoard while we could. He'd used an impressive array of magic for my benefit and kept his Word. We'd saved Jael before the Humans killed her.

"This would be the... fastest way to heal her?" I reiterated for the sake

of the sudden, discomfiting arousal in my leathers.

"For you and me? Yes. For another set of Elves attempting to heal a different aura? Perhaps not."

Well, pleasant to hear him acknowledge himself as sufficiently Elven for this task.

"Alright," I agreed, tugging loose the leather ties on both hips and refusing to look behind me at the group farther down. *"Please take off your pants. I accept your lead. Show us what to do."*

Mourn pushed his bottoms down to his thighs, freeing a lengthening phallus while pulling his tail free in one smooth draw. He stepped out of them, picked them up, and folded them before laying them with his cloak near my guardians.

By that point, I was naked and wearing only my "jewelry:" a gold ring, a blue pendant, and now a Dragon pearl earring. We'd moved the backpacks and laid the two blankets flat atop each other before resting my open-eyed Sister there.

"You must be in the middle," he said, giving his swelling prick an absent-minded pull. *"We can try on our sides first. Hold her facing you while I tuck in behind you."*

An insistent smile climbed on my face. *"Ooo. Our tits smashed and me pierced by cock from behind? Yeah, we've done that. My Sisters and I."*

The Dragon son showed me fang, and his own cock bobbed once with interest. *"Good. She will be less confused when she awakens."*

When she awakens. *Yes, please.*

I laid down first, centered on the blanket, while Mourn helped to position Jael close and on her side until I could pull her to me. For a moment, it felt as if we prepared for Reverie on my pallet in the Cloister.

Then Mourn stepped over us and settled down behind me, his entire front cradling my back and his unusual member wedged firmly in the cleft of my buttocks and thighs. He neither smelled nor felt anything like Jaunda or Gaelan, but I assisted him when he lifted my knee and placed that atop Jael's covered hip, opening my thighs to give him access.

He began by pleasantly pushing his erection lengthwise along the outside of my slit, massaging my netherlips, my clit, and his own turgid flesh at once.

"*Nice, but I'm…not quite wet enough,*" I murmured.

"*Do not worry. I will wait. Focus on her.*"

On her. *Yes.*

Even if Jael wasn't truly with me yet, I kissed her lips while I had the chance. I wrapped my arms around her, encouraging her limp arm to rest atop my shoulder. I held tighter, focusing on how soft and cool her tits felt against mine as Mourn moved gently against me. Her skin needed a scrub, and her hair a deeper lather, but I inhaled her scent anyway. It was different somehow, but close enough. I counted myself lucky to even be here to recognize that it had changed.

That *she* had changed.

And so had I.

Curling up my arm, I lightly brushed her face, her jaw, and her ear with my fingers. I noticed the latter was bleeding.

Her ear had a deep bite mark. Quite fresh.

That rutting Pyte.

Mourn drew my focus when he spread one buttock with his hand and settled his glans as if about to penetrate. I gasped. He held still as my sex clenched in reflex, moistening the pointed head so he could slip in deeper.

~*Oh, Goddess…*~

Yes. Perfect.

I hadn't even *thought* to make the mindlink; the connection had slipped into place as easily as his prick. Now that it was there, it was easy to maintain.

Keep listening, he said. *Be patient.*

Listen. *Yes.*

I'd done that before, too.

Abruptly, I only listened to *myself,* moaning as Mourn withdrew only to push in deeper before I caught myself and bit my lip. I kept quiet with difficulty as he eased in, giving me more length and *plenty* of girth. My clit stiffened up and tingled as he stretched me, eventually squeezing in that lower ridge to disappear between my netherlips. His firm flesh scraped along the spot that made me want to cum.

~*Oh…!*~

Yes, Kiabil, he murmured, holding still and pressed as deep as he could comfortably go.

He withheld his first, full thrust until his tail could slide around my thigh propped up on my Sister's hip, wrapping twice around it. Then the tip of that tail languidly flicked and teased the tiny, aching nub between my legs.

"Ah!" I cried aloud before biting my lip as feet shuffled somewhere beyond the sarcophagi. ~*Are you trying to make me cum right now?*~

Mourn chuckled in my mind. *Are you that close already?*

~*I…I don't—maybe?*~

He teased my clit again, his prick withdrawing not even the length of half a finger before rocking in, resettling deeper in my hungry sheath.

~*Ohhhh…*~

I shivered, my cunt squeezing him as my arms held Jael tighter. Mourn hummed, caressing my skin with his palm, and paused to wait. In the following quiet, an answering hum stirred inside my ears, within my mind. Myself. My aura, as I was today.

My eyes widened. *Shit.* I *was* that close!

~*Morixxyleth—!*~

He shuddered. *Oh… Kiabil.*

~*I'm gonna—!*~

Yes.

The tip of his tail rubbed me firmly as he fell into three, long thrusts as if he couldn't resist another sample.

Sampling was all it took.

Clinging to Jael, I squeezed my eyes shut, a mewl escaping my throat as I climaxed in the crypt, and the saphgar lit up the darkness between stone caskets. Then I was floating, coasting down. My lower belly felt tight and full, swamped with an endless warmth.

And a familiar "song" finally reached my ears from wherever it had been hiding.

Perfect, Mourn whispered, and reached across my shoulder to cradle Jael's neck in his broad, strong hand.

Something cacophonic entered the song when he did this, and a tiny spike of fear surged in my gut.

Shhh, he soothed. *You're safe. I have us.*

Us.

A deep part of me liked that. *Very much.*

His cock hard and deep inside me, Mourn unwrapped his tail only long enough to shift my leg so that he could recoil it around both my Sister and me, tying us together. The Dragon's son started mating me then, taking the leverage to thrust in long, even strokes.

Little by little, the song shifted to become harmonic and less grating on my ears. Before my eyes, Jael's brow drew down, her face formed a pout of concentration. Her lids had slipped down of their own accord, half-closed. Her lips parted, and she moaned softly with pleasure.

Not pain.

A surge of joy swept through my chest to hear it.

~*That was real! She's closer!*~

In heightened response, Mourn fucked me faster, holding us tighter with his arm and tail. His aura seemed to crackle as the song grew louder.

He was getting close, too.

Jael's arm slipped from my shoulder, jostled by Mourn's growing enthusiasm, and she reflexively grappled for me again, snuggling closer and pressing her mouth to the damp skin at my neck.

~*Jael... you're awake...*~

Her eyes had finally closed, all troubles gone from her face when she lifted her head and tilted her chin up.

Offering her mouth.

I leaned forward and took it, sliding my hand up her spine only to discover Mourn's hand already there.

Oh, right.

I covered his hand with mine and deepened the kiss with Jael. Pure elation followed when she kissed back, for she was not mindlessly mimicking. Her tongue engaged mine, and her teeth nipped my upper lip as she liked to do, fingers massaging my bare shoulder as she drank in further kisses. She grunted, her hand struggling to loosen the ties of her leathers.

~*Jael...*~ I grinned. ~*Do you need to cum?*~

She bared her teeth in a playful snarl and opened her eyes. Focusing on me. In the blue light of the pendant, her eyes remained the brightest copper I'd ever seen.

I slipped my hand back from Mourn's to move it down, in between me and my Sister to finish what her restrained fingers had started. With her leathers pushed most of the way over her ass, Jael sucked in a breath and muttered unintelligibly when my hand slid down along her fur patch to her crotch.

Between my legs, Mourn's cock had slowed its pace as my bodyguard paid attention to what we were doing. For the moment, I didn't question why Jael did not seem to know he was there.

Gradually, I worked my hand between her legs, my two middle fingers gliding in welcome between her netherlips, lightly exploring the outside of her hole. She was wet enough. With her mound resting in my palm, I pressed the heel of my hand in circles against her clit as my digits penetrated deeper. She moaned like I did earlier. We kissed, and I heard her eager impatience in my mind.

Ah, fucking stalk-holers, harder! Faster!

Mourn recognized the futility in matching the pace Jael liked as I lifted the heel of my hand off her bud so she could be properly fucked with my fingers. My legs remained apart for his leisured strokes as he watched us, his tongue flashing in my periphery to taste our scents. I felt the swollen base of his prick tempting me with more.

So easy to forget where we were.

Jael didn't even try to be quiet leading up to her peak; neither Mourn nor I dared interrupt her as the strength of the song careened around us. Her breath accelerated, her voice climbing higher with each gasp closer to the edge, until she stopped altogether and started trembling. The heel of my hand returned to push against her clit, and the gentle mashing released it all and set her free.

"Oh-h-h, *g-god-d—!*" she cried with the greatest of relief.

~*Yes, Jael!*~

Sssargt, ohhh…

But for the lack of well-earned physical signs, I could have imagined I'd orgasmed again. Instead, as I lay between them, my song seemed helplessly awash in both of theirs. As Jael's slit flexed and her thighs clenched tight on my hand, Mourn's tail tightened around our thighs. The Dragonchild took my hair in his teeth, his soaked and rigid pole spilling yet another load of cream into my willing and well-worked sex.

The only sensation I didn't feel between them was the knot, and for that reason alone, Mourn withdrew first. In body and mind, gently and with caution, my bodyguard moved off the blanket and offered us space while Jael panted to catch her breath. He stood up in silence, the song fading peacefully, and my swimming head slowly settled.

Everything about holding Jael in her afterglow seemed… normal. *Please be back.*

"*Mmm,*" she murmured in contentment. "*Thanks. That felt good.*"

"*Understatement,*" I chuckled, watching her resting face, and holding her relaxed body close to me.

Admittedly, I was reluctant to let her draw away, to let reality flood this moment too quickly. I didn't know where to begin once it did. Fortunately, Mourn and the others gave us some time for that same thought to tap Jael's shoulder one too many times. In time, she lifted her head, looking confused as her eyes noted the long, stone fixtures on either side of us and the random broken bones not far in either direction.

"*Where are we?*" she asked first.

"*Safe for now,*" I murmured. "*We're in a Human burial room beneath the Temple.*"

"Burial?"

I couldn't think of a Davrin equivalent. "*Where they keep bones of their dead.*"

She made a face. "*Okay…*"

"*Well. Many prefer not to come here, I think. It reminds them how soon they will die.*"

Jael frowned, shaking her head as if to toss aside some distracting chain of thought. *"Wait. We're beneath the Temple of Manalar?"*

"Yes."

"Then how are you here?" A hint of the last day's horrors showed in her eyes. *"How did you find me?"*

"I found help," I said, maintaining that skin-to-skin contact which seemed reassuring for us both. *"Or I wouldn't have been able to find you."*

"You found 'help?' " she repeated skeptically.

"Yeah. Help." I swallowed, brushing my fingers across white hair stuck to her temple. *"Like you and Shyntre found Jaunda to help find me before it was too late."*

That was enough to put it in perspective for her quickly. Her eyes dropped and trailed over me while she considered this, and I didn't know whether her unusually thoughtful calm was from delayed shock, from something she'd learned from the experience itself, or an influence from Mourn after mending and "anchoring" her aura.

Regardless, I couldn't help but notice all the cuts and scrapes covering her skin before we'd started were gone. Even the bite mark on her ear had vanished, leaving behind only a touch of crusted blood.

Healed in more than one way.

"Who was willing to help you?" she asked.

"Good question," I said, my nerves rising. *"Do you think you can stand up and meet them while I get dressed?"*

"Yeah. You... we should."

My Sister and I were careful getting to our feet. We also didn't have a lot of water to waste, but one barely-damp cloth for each of us to wipe down would have to do. Mourn had stepped farther away to do the same, dressed in his usual by the time Jael and I were to the point of being covered.

I left the dimly glowing pendant out as a light source, looking around, and only then did Mourn signal the others to head our way. Jael jerked her attention toward the noise, overtaken by fear and confusion as she took in my bodyguard's appearance.

Mourn signed, *No harm to you. We are protectors.*

My younger Sister blinked to understand the motion of his hands so easily. Then Gavin, Krithannia, Deshi, and Wolf—dragging a gagged and groaning Archbishop Keros by his ankle—came close enough to make out their details. The Deathwalker withdrew a familiar, glowing knucklebone to replace the fading blue light of Shyntre's pendant. If any of them had been amused or discomfited by what had happened between us on the crypt floor, they weren't showing it.

"*Fucking Goddess,*" Jael muttered as she stared at Mourn first, for he stood in the best light.

The Dragonblood smirked, showing in his expression that he'd understood her, and I touched my shoulder to hers as he began the introduction in Trade.

"We are all from the city of Augran. Sirana found a group of taskers-for-hire. She hired us to find and recover you." He smiled wider. "So, here we are."

Such simplicity could not be stripped down further, I thought, but Jael grappled with this, attempting to reconcile a diversity of forms and faces. I wasn't sure she'd ever been exposed to this many before. I certainly hadn't been before seeing the city for myself.

"*I-I don't understand,*" she said finally, frustration tightening her throat.

"Can you speak Trade?" Mourn asked.

"Uh…" Jael looked at me, eyes widening briefly in a panic.

"Can you?" I asked. "Have you practiced?"

She shook her head, her eyes shimmering a moment. "B-bad. I not practice."

Oh.

"How well do you understand Trade?" the half-blood followed up, drawing her attention back.

Jael swallowed. "Better?"

"You understand more than you can speak."

She nodded. "Manalari none also."

"Understood." He bowed his head. "Call me Shadow. I am Sirana's bodyguard."

The cait did a double-take and looked at me to confirm.

"Yes, he is my bodyguard."

*"And what **is** he, exactly?"* she asked bluntly in our native tongue.

I grinned. *"Why? Does he look familiar?"*

"I'm not sure," she said with caution. *"But he's not a Sathoet."*

"My mother was Davrin," he said in his Vuthra'tern accent, startling her.

Still, I was glad he gave that to her freely.

Jael squinted sidelong at him. *"Was?"*

Mourn kept his face stoic. *"It's more difficult to birth a Dragon's son than a demon's. So I was told."*

My Sister stared at him as even her native thoughts suffered trouble crossing her tongue. Perhaps her second look at his scale patches made more sense.

"He's from a second Davrin city hiding from our Valsharess," I murmured to her, hoping I sounded reassuring, *"but he ran away from the Deepearth centuries ago. He found me on the Surface, working with a less-helpful group of mercenaries he was tracking to kill anyway."* I shrugged. *"He proved to be better and knew how to reach the taskers in Augran, so we made a deal."*

Jael needed time to absorb that. *"Alright,"* she replied, sounding skeptical. *"Why does he have those gold eyes?"*

"What do you mean 'why?' He was born with them."

"I have my sire's eyes," Mourn added.

"Your sire?" Jael repeated as a troubled look crossed her face.

I frowned. *"Have you seen them before now? Back home, perhaps?"*

Had she seen the portrait in the Sanctuary, too?

Jael shook her head. *"No, not back home."*

Oh.

She looked around the crypt again, recognizing it after all the destruction. *"Here. I saw them here. When we found the shield that I was sent for."*

Mourn hissed something that sounded Draconic. *"Did he speak to you?"*

Pure panic flashed across her face, and she shook her head. *"No. I,* uh—" She pointed at Keros on the ground. *"What are you going to do with this Drider egg?"*

Mourn frowned at her but opted not to push it as he looked at the rest of our crew. It was only as he shared a look of concern with Krithannia that Jael received her next jolt.

"You!" she said in Trade. "You are...?"

"Krithannia," said the Guild Mistress, granting her a bow. "I am of the Naulor Queendom."

Jael's mouth dropped. "Naulor? Are they...?"

"All pale like me?" The elder smiled with peaceful amusement. "We are."

"You've been through this already," Jael muttered to me.

I chuckled. *"Yeah. I'm sorry. It's only where we are that we can't take more time with this."*

"And you don't expect them to stab us in the back?"

"No, I don't. I've been living well for weeks with their guidance, and we found you. That's all I wanted."

She grunted, accepting that much for now, before looking at the three Humans. Wolf's coloring was probably the most familiar to her as she appraised him quickly but peered longer at Deshi while each man offered his name. She stared in a way to suggest the Yungian was far more appealing to her than Gavin.

The Deathwalker noticed her look because he'd been waiting for it and grunted, shaking his head. "If your sister is well enough, Sirana, may we discuss something urgent pertaining to this tomb?"

"*Uhh*-of course," I said, glancing up at the balcony to make sure it was empty. "What urgency, Gavin?"

He withdrew the thurible made of white gold from where it had hung on his belt. "Keros woke while you were in ritual. He recognized this, claiming ownership as he'd intended to come back to get it after they found the shield."

Mourn straightened up. "Does Keros know what it does?"

"He does not," the Deathwalker replied, "but he said the crowd shouted about the shield and the thurible, demanding Isboern have the former and he have the latter."

My bodyguard frowned in confusion. "That is not true."

"Isn't it?"

"They never said both. Just the shield." Mourn glanced at me. "Sirana and I were there. This censer was never mentioned in any of Reprisal's reports, either."

Wolf nodded. "Confirming. Thought it was a strange claim."

Mourn stepped over to Keros, kneeling and slapping the man's face alert before pulling the cloth gag out of his mouth. He made a demand in Manalari, scaring the greying redhead into a brief exchange before the Archbishop's face flushed and contorted with hatred. I grimaced as the elder man started shouting.

Fool bastard.

The Dragonblood punched him in the face, returning the cleric to unconsciousness. A surprised laugh escaped Jael's mouth before she covered it. I smirked in satisfaction on her behalf.

"Keros heard about the thurible through a locked door," Mourn grumbled, his tail lashing as his posture changed to high alert. "Someone he thought he recognized told him about it."

"What do you mean," I asked, "someone he 'thought' he recognized?"

"Remember Mathias helping to stoke the crowd?" he asked in return.

I quieted, glancing at Krithannia and Wolf, who seemed concerned. "The sorcerer?"

"Huh? A wizard?" Jael asked, baffled by my sudden apprehension.

"He could be here now," Mourn agreed. "In the Temple."

Gavin seemed satisfied with this explanation. "It's reasonable that the Deathless might know about both relics in this crypt, and more of the history here before the Ma'ab arrival."

"Then we can't stay here," replied my bodyguard. "It's not as secure as we thought."

"Where else can we go?" Krithannia asked.

That was a good question, but we had Keros to deal with first before we could decide collectively on an answer.

Chapter 21

"First question, Deathwalker," Mourn asked.

"Yes?"

"What became of the Ma'ab bodies?"

"*Oh, yes, that,*" Krithannia murmured, putting a gloved hand to her mouth as if the answer surprised even her.

At the same time, Deshi shifted his weight and looked elsewhere like someone trying to keep a straight face while Wolf cocked an eyebrow at him. I started smiling again, and Jael tossed me a sidelong glance.

Gavin held the thurible by the chain at the top, allowing the bright, compact vessel to swing gently. I didn't realize he was offering half of his answer until he opened his mouth.

"Well," he began, slow and deliberate. "I discovered one use for this relic. No doubt there are others, as the success of my experiment relied on adapting a method I already use. The result was enhanced."

The half-blood listened patiently. "What did you do?"

"The Vis of the Hellhounds lingered within the crypt. Unlike Vo'traj, they would not speak to me and were willing to be consumed by their masters. So, as a test..." Gavin held up the thurible. "This can be used as a temporary soul trap."

Mourn pointed. "So, the Vis of the Hellhounds are in there?"

"Correct. Not fixed in their present state, but at least they won't degrade and potentially foul an area should they become lost on their way to Ennikar."

"Huh." My bodyguard lifted his chin and sniffed the air. "And where are the bodies?"

"That's the other interesting discovery," Krithannia said, folding her hands formally in front of her.

I was surprised to see Gavin smile a bit. "Beyond interesting. Potentially quite useful before the Ma'ab army breaches the wall."

"Oh?" Mourn asked, quite interested.

"Indeed. Let me show you."

Mourn motioned for Wolf and Deshi to stay with Keros and Krithannia, though invited me to come.

★Jael, too, if she wishes.★

My Sister read his hands, pursed her lips, and opted to stay at my side even as she muttered, *"Wager I'll regret this."*

I grinned at her. *"I've learned to enjoy how seriously Gavin demonstrates his craft. On this, he never lies."*

"Is that so?" She squinted. *"And what 'craft?' "*

"He's a mage and scholar on Human death."

Jael kicked a femur out of the way. *"Hmph. He must like it here."*

By then, Gavin had brought us where Mourn had fought and killed the four large men with spiked chains. The space wasn't empty; it was littered with bodies but nothing fresh. I looked around the sarcophagi and wall burials before I realized that the dried-up corpses on the floor *were* the Ma'ab Hellhounds.

"How did you do this?" Mourn asked as Jael emitted a moan of disgust.

"I removed every mote of the Vitas the bodies possessed," Gavin explained, "and drew all of it into the thurible."

"And this mummified them?"

"Not my intention. I wanted to test the enhanced concentration the relic grants me. The speed expelled the life water in a short enough time that it preserved the body to some extent."

"And how long did this take?"

"While I focused, a few minutes." Gavin shrugged. "The process can also be passive, as it continued drawing the last mote of Vitas from the other bodies in the crypt while you were gone."

The Dragonchild had the same expression I did. "And why would you do this?"

"To prevent another death mage from doing what Vo'traj did," Gavin replied serenely. "These bones will not stand up a second time."

Mourn allowed several moments to pass, his tail weaving to each side a few times as he considered something of interest to him. "So, if the Ma'ab cross the wall, you have a means to deny them raising the dead on both sides to use against the Manalari."

"Correct."

"You can also draw in the Vis for safekeeping, denying the death mages of the Far North the souls of Manalar's fallen, and even their own."

"Also, correct." Gavin hadn't blinked in a long while. "I admit I'm impressed how quickly you saw the potential."

"Oh, this is a fantastic strategy and one that levels the field." The Dragonchild paused. "What is the limit of drawing and containing souls?"

"Distance is a factor in drawing it," Gavin began, "although any future testing while trying to remain hidden will stifle my ability to know the potential full range of the effect. It creates a 'current.' The closer the soul to the thurible, the more certain the pull. I can increase this current, but the effect becomes more easily traced back to the source."

Jael stared at him with incredulity and then my smiling face as Mourn responded.

"Understood. That's good to know. What about limits of containment?"

A low sigh escaped the Deathwalker as he considered the artifact hanging from his belt. "Its capacity is hard to judge due to fluctuations between individual souls, but if I were to gauge roughly...?"

"That is all I can ask, scholar."

"The enchantment is potent for being so old. I believe it should handle the dead and dying from both armies save for the few unknown outliers. For example, I'm unlikely to draw the Deathless should his body fall."

Mourn dipped his chin. "Noted."

"Also know, this is only for temporary containment. By no means is this a long-term method. In fact, if nothing else is done, there appear to be inbuilt mechanisms to let the Vis and Vitas drain out and prevent such a permanent concentration of souls, unlike... other artifacts."

Gavin didn't look toward me, but I had no doubt which other artifact he might refer to. Thus far, I hadn't needed to draw Soul Drinker, yet I could imagine the jealous shriek of the demon to realize Gavin was collecting more Vis and Vitas while being *passive*, of all states, only to let it escape over time.

"Hm," Mourn began, "you mentioned it being old. If the Deathless may have enough knowledge of what came before to mention it to Keros, do you think the shield and the thurible were used together in past battles?"

Gavin frowned. "Not in battle. The challenges brought by the Ma'ab Ascended are unique to *this* age. Although it is extremely clear from studying this crypt that my Lady was once revered here, so the thurible may have been used in the rites of the dead in any season, during peace or conflict. I could imagine the comfort this may bring to soldiers and defenders of the mount, knowing that their clerics could guide and safeguard their souls after they fall, and they would not be lost in the Grey."

"Interesting."

Indeed, it was. If the Grey Maiden had once held worship in this Temple alongside Musanlo, there could have been other Deathwalkers once. That would have been before Mourn's time on the Surface; before the Ma'ab arrived from the Nexus; and before the Bishops consolidated the power of *Pisc'sagrad*. Gavin seemed to be following an old path forgotten by his short-lived race, but I wondered about any other being who might remember those times.

Like the Valsharess. She sent Jael here to get involved…

Did my Queen know what a Deathwalker was?

"I wonder," Mourn considered, "if some of that balance could be returned after this sacred spring is free."

I cleared my throat. "That sounds suspiciously like we're going to stay for the entire war."

My bodyguard shook his head. "That was not the plan. But if this can be set passively, that would aid the defenders more than they can know following severance of *Pisc'sagrad* from the Bishops."

Jael grimaced and rubbed her head like it ached, and I was instantly aware that she was not only out of the loop on the intricate plans we'd gone over in Augran, but she may not even understand all the words to make any sense out of them.

In addition, she was a new mage without any training, possessing the clothes on her back. Not even a dagger. Anyone who spotted her would want to kill her after what happened above, especially after their Archbishop disappeared.

This vulnerability struck me like a blow.

"Is there a…" I began, looking at Mourn, "um, a way that Jael and I can leave now? Go back to the gate and wait for you in Kerut? We… I-I didn't know we'd find her so far ahead of the Ma'ab arrival, and if you aren't going for the pool until then…?"

The Dragon's son frowned. "Hm. I see your point. We may need to adjust plans, but first," he smiled at my Sister, "let us deal with the 'Drider egg.' I believe our Deathwalker has given us a perfect opportunity to make certain he's never found."

ONCE WE'D RECONVENED, MOURN DIDN'T TAKE LONG FOR THE OTHERS IN the crypt to understand and agree with his plan for Keros.

"If I can get Sirana and Jael out of here, and if Keros's husk stays where none are likely to look for him, or recognize him if they do, then as far as anyone knows, the Archbishop fled the city in its dire hour of need."

"If there's no body," Krithannia said, "then in the minds of the people, he could be alive but an exile in disgrace."

"But as there *will* be a body," Wolf growled, "we'll make sure he never turns up to cause people strife again."

"*Ki-hua*," Deshi said in agreement.

From enchanted bracers, Mourn produced the Archbishop's silver blade he'd taken from the white altar room. "We shall get it done. Deathwalker, be ready with the thurible."

Gavin peered at the blade in Mourn's hand. "Hm. Curious. Where did you find that?"

"*That's what the white-beard wearing black robes used on me,*" Jael snarled.

She not only startled me, but her tone tugged on my guilt at missing the rage on her face until she had to say something.

"*I don't know what it did,*" she added, "*but I've never felt such... strange and terrifying pain.*"

"What did she say?" Gavin asked me.

"Uh," I pointed. "The Inquisitor used that on her. It sounds like that's when he damaged her aura, causing the tear you saw."

"Ah. Interesting." He looked at Mourn. "May I see it?"

The Dragonchild held it out handle first, and Gavin hooked his relic to his belt before accepting the weapon like it might be a living thing. His fingers never touched the blade itself, and after a time, he removed a cloth to wrap around the handle, as if brushing the silver pommel or the hilt was unwelcomed.

We waited while he inspected it then closed his eyes, hissing something in the strange tongue. The crypt was cool regardless, being underground, but more than one of us shivered as if a chilled wind swept around us. The time this was taking caused several of us to keep checking the balcony, despite not hearing word from Torch of anyone coming.

Finally, Gavin moved. Wordless, he took those few steps to stand beside the unconscious Archbishop. Leaning over, he drew a small cut with the tip of the blade on the man's cheek and straightened back up, observing the spot of red blood he'd taken. Some time when I hadn't been looking, his irises had disappeared.

"This manipulates the life aura," Gavin said. "It would easily control a victim's sense of well-being, for better or worse, in the hands of a knowledgeable mage. If the Inquisitor used it on Jael, and she was as you brought her here, I imagine it was an uneducated misuse of its intended purpose."

My Sister crossed her arms and sneered at that, glaring at one of the stone coffins as if it annoyed her.

"Can you use it on *him?*" Wolf asked, nodding to the beaten and bound cleric on the floor.

"Obviously," Gavin replied, inspecting the blood.

"No, I mean, can you do something more than stab him?"

"We have much to discuss before something happens," Krithannia countered before the Deathwalker answered Wolf's question.

"I could use it to attune Jacob's shard further to the Bishops themselves and refine the targets for *Pisc'sagrad's* surge even more."

Each of us paused, absorbing that to various degrees.

"How long would that take?" Mourn asked.

Gavin peered at him with solid black eyes; they possessed an odd shine like an insect. "Not nearly as long as it took to form the shard in the first place."

"Then do it as swiftly as you can. When you're finished, show me what you can do with the thurible when you focus."

With no hesitation or concern, Gavin got to work. We watched from a slight distance, Deshi closer than the rest of us, as the Deathwalker knelt beside the Archbishop and withdrew Jacob's shard, weighing both it and the blade in each hand. Then Gavin pressed both sharp ends into the hollow of the man's sweaty throat, where it slowly filled with red blood as the death mage chanted in the dead tongue.

The crypt grew colder, and I had the repeated sense that someone was standing behind me. I looked more than once, but no one was there. My back itched until Gavin finished his spell, after which the Archbishop appeared pale and ill.

Gavin's thin lips had stopped moving as he gently wrapped the pneuma flint shard and tucked it away on his body. He remained mute as he counted the Archbishop's ribs and felt with his fingers for a specific place to insert the bloodied point of the blade.

"Hm," Mourn grunted. By his tail, he seemed approving.

Still, the gaunt scholar turned his head to peer at us while hunched over the body. In the pale blue light, it was an unsettling sight.

"The heart will stop first," Gavin said, as if feeling the need to explain. "There will not be much blood."

"Agreed," Mourn said, stepping closer on the other side of Keros. "And good choice. May I?"

Gavin moved his hand which had counted the ribs and held the blade in place with two fingers on the leather-wrapped handle. The mercenary clasped the pommel and handle in his large hand and pushed down in one hard stroke, burying the blade to the hilt. Keros's bound body jerked as far as it could, breath rattling briefly, and then lay still.

The Deathwalker brought out his relic. "Leave the blade for now and stand back."

Mourn took his advice and rejoined us, and we got to see firsthand with the Archbishop what had happened to Vo'traj and her Hellhounds. While I could not see Vis, Vitas, or even any kind of aura if I wasn't mindlinked with another mage, I had the sense of motion, of something flowing like wind or water from the body to the thurible. It was the strangest feeling.

Then, as Gavin stood up and stepped back, all his focus on the artifact and its task as he left the silver dagger in place, we watched the body begin to desiccate. The skin wrinkled like berries under the sun, his eyelids, nose, and lips shriveling and skin stretching over his face to become more grotesque than Gavin's. The body cavity collapsed steadily like someone relieving their bladder, and I was exceedingly glad the vestments and boots covered him.

Within a few minutes, exactly as my ally claimed, the body of Archbishop Keros appeared like it had been left to dry under the Sun for an untold time, though the air around us smelled odd and more humid.

Gross.

"Impressive," Mourn said.

"Glad he's never standing up again," Jael grumbled. *"Even as a puppet."*

Mourn glanced at her, understanding as I did that she had at least grasped some of what Gavin was talking about.

"Indeed," the Dragonblood agreed. "Everyone wait here while I hide a few things."

Mourn made the silver dagger vanish into his bracers then lifted the Archbishop's body onto his shoulder, climbing the crypt wall concerningly high before stuffing the corpse into one of the recently emptied vaults. There, my bodyguard sliced and ripped off the distinctive garments, setting them on fire with a Word, and allowing the ashes to float all over the crypt floor.

Now unencumbered, Mourn dropped down to collect the Ma'ab chains first, making those disappear before shoving each Hellhound corpse into a random wall space of his own. Finally, the Dragonblood placed Vo'traj's husk into the sarcophagus where Gavin had found the thurible before pushing the stone slab closed. He left the other tomb, where the Manalari had found the shield, open and exactly as they had left it.

Krithannia chuckled as her long-time partner rejoined us, breathing deeply. "Good work."

Smirking, Mourn ducked his head in a bow. "Let us leave the crypt and head farther down to discuss what we do next."

DOUSING OUR LIGHT AND ADJUSTING IN THE QUIET, OUR TEAM CLIMBED THE wide stairway out of the crypt, joining Nianzu first where he'd been guarding the secret door leading back out. Peng-lok stood in the dark farther down, crouched in the rubble of the unsealed hallway and covering the narrow stairwell leading up. The third Yungian brother sensed us and recognized the sign to regroup.

We paused with Nianzu and Peng-lok as Krithannia called Torch through the pearl. He'd posted his watch farther up the stairs and closer to the hall leading to the dungeon.

Shuiblith, Mourn thought, reaching to work on opening the hidden door while his tail encouraged us to give him space.

A moment later we could all read the Naulor's and Wolf's face.

What's happening? Jael signed to me.

~Mourn?~

Armored men coming down the stairs. They turned our way instead of going to the dungeon and are moving fast.

I hand-signed this for Jael as I heard it, hating the look of dread that crossed her face.

Torch is ahead of them. He'll be here soon. Mourn pushed the door open and motioned us through. *Hurry.*

Wolf and Peng-lok entered first to clear the narrow, uneven stairs to the barren chamber below as Krithannia and Gavin followed them with Deshi and Nianzu behind. I motioned for Jael to follow them, which she reluctantly did only when I took a step toward the same exit. There were enough of us that Torch swept around the corner into view before there was quite enough room for him and Mourn on the stairs behind us.

All that while, the clattering metal armor and heavy bootsteps got louder while a light source stretched closer. Mourn spun to slide the door closed, his tail thwacking Torch, who leaned into me to give him more space.

Then I heard the man in front shout out.

"Agirda!"

Fuck.

"Perfavi, guardos! Alyadis eternis, agirda!"

Everyone who understood Manalari turned their heads with a mix of strange expressions I couldn't read. More importantly, they paused on the steps.

Mourn hadn't given up his momentum, however. The door was almost closed before halting suddenly with a thunk, as if someone had placed a brick on the floor to prop it open a hand-width. I saw nothing keeping it open, even as my Dark Sight flipped to see all colors.

"Isboern," Jael whispered.

Was it?

Mourn cursed, and a falcon screeched over top of him. We all flinched in the fading dark.

"Tamuril," Krithannia murmured, then her mind's voice spilled over into the link. *Shadow, don't! Please let them in!*

There are four Templars with the Captain, and they make enough noise to draw the whole Temple on us!

Let all of them in, let them come down here. Seal and ward the door. We'll talk. We must.

Torch, Jael, and I had to get off the stairs quickly to make room for that many men in full armor. Mourn was in the unenviable position of being the only one able to let them pass and secure the way behind us, so he couldn't keep much focus on me.

~I've got my spiders and the dagger. I'll use them if they come at us.~

Stay alert.

~Yes.~

I could hear the Dragonchild hissing to the Captain once the man caught up with the door. They were in brief but tense negotiations as the Manalari quieted down, and the Guildsmen were both casting and preparing their own spells while Jael and I could only be ready for hand-to-hand.

"What did he say that made you all pause?" I whispered to Gavin, who grunted before delivering the translation in his typical monotone.

"Wait. Please, guardians, eternal allies, wait."

I kept watch on Mourn's tension through his tail and was slow to absorb that. "Eternal allies?"

"The odd part," Gavin agreed.

"He know," Jael growled, her arms folded as she had no weapons or equipment and absolutely nothing to do with her hands. "He know what… we are. *Davrin*."

So, she knew, too. She'd probably spoken with him, but what

information had they exchanged? Was I even ready to meet another psion when my Sister didn't know what I was now?

Ready or not...

Mourn came to an agreement with the Captain and slid the door open. I deduced the details when he produced one of the Ma'ab dark stained chains he'd taken off the Hellhounds. With visible discomfort, each Templar took hold of the spiked chain in both hands before he would turn sideways to enter the door, squeezing past Mourn and clopping down to make room for his brother-in-arms.

Each of them had a soft yellow light source attached to his belt, and this lit up the chamber where we huddled, making us squint as we backed up for more space. None of the Templars released the chain as a young Human with a falcon on his shoulder entered next, clasping his hands close to his chest rather than touch the chain.

The youth matched the Guild's description of Tamuril's disguise.

I wonder how they found out.

Finally, Willven Isboern entered, holding the chain nearest to Mourn's grip without complaint and stepping with care past my bodyguard. He was the only one with a golden shield on his back.

Tamuril and the Manalari remained crowded on the steps, none moving or interfering when the Dragonblood closed the door fully this time and cast more than one ward to secure it. Finally, Mourn turned and motioned for them to descend to the floor while he held the chain.

The thought crossed my mind that Mourn could send a lightning bolt through each man if one proved a threat, but also why Tamuril wasn't holding the chain. Krithannia would be horrified. Still, interesting that no one, not even Mourn, considered this one female a threat at any level.

They must feel confident with stone beneath their feet. Meeting her with soil and tree roots beneath mine wasn't so harmless.

I noticed Jael scowling at the Druid and her falcon, but when the Captain turned his head to glance at her, his smile seeming apologetic, Jael stepped closer to me, our shoulders touching. My spiders moved in my hair, though they mostly felt curious.

"We don't have much time," Captain Isboern began in Trade, his enunciation clear and without a Manalari accent like mine.

He hadn't let go of the Hellhound chain and neither had Mourn or the Templars as they stood in a line facing us and the Guildsmen. Somehow, he seemed to speak to all of us without focusing on one.

"First, thank you for coming and rescuing your sister. The Templars will not stop you or try to take her back to the Bishops. We would rather she leaves free, for her service and the great risk she had to take to help rediscover an important symbol for Manalar."

"No service!" she barked. "Not to you!"

The Captain bowed his head. "I understand the circumstances had nothing to do with Humans, Red Sister. We thank you all the same."

In frustration, Jael bit her inner cheek and looked away.

"Second, I wanted to ask if you would take the falcon boy with you. Get him safe and far from here."

So, even his men didn't know...

The Druid didn't appear surprised at this; indeed, her boy's face looked pleading as they met eyes. It wasn't difficult to see the psionic exchange as they talked in private. Isboern never appeared angry, his eyes concerned and sky blue like mine, and eventually she acquiesced.

"Of course, we will, Captain," Krithannia answered, her face un-readable as a morose Human boy stepped cautiously around the line of chain to stand closer to her.

Then the Guild Mistress exchanged gazes with Mourn, and they had a similar exchange as Tamuril and her psion before Krithannia looked back to him. "Is this the only reason you tried so hard to confront us when you could have let us go?"

The four Templars had been looking over each of us, even the Yungians, with their caution plain on their faces. Gavin in particular worried them, and one defender with a red and gold beard asked his Captain something.

Isboern acknowledged him with a nod but answered Krithannia's question. "No, this isn't the only reason, my lady. We would know, having found you within the mount, do you act in any way on behalf of the Ma'ab Empire against the people of Manalar?"

"You wouldn't be able to stop us if we were," Mourn stated.

"Perhaps, but that is not what I asked, legend."

My bodyguard narrowed his eyes. "Why do you call me 'legend?' "

"The old wanderer," Isboern replied without hesitation, "who visits our woods back home has spoken of you. A legend who has passed like a shadow through those same mountains for centuries."

Though subtle, the Yungians responded positively to this claim, like they would agree, while Mourn smirked, gripping the Hellhound chain in one hand. He gave it a shake, testing the Manalari's hold. No Templar dropped it.

"This chain," the Dragon's son said, "belonged to a Ma'ab infiltrator team we tracked on the east side this morning. I killed them so they could not bring word of *him* back to their masters." Mourn tilted his head at our Deathwalker while maintaining his gaze with the Captain. "The Empire's recruitment methods are even harsher than the Witch Hunters. No, Captain. We do *not* act in any way on behalf of the Ma'ab."

If I had to guess, Isboern tried but couldn't read the half-blood's mind while staring at him any more than I could while genitally tied to him.

In the end, Isboern needed to take what Mourn said on its face, so he rephrased his focus with quiet calm. "Do you act against the people of Manalar, even if only by your own motive?"

Mourn showed his fangs. "Only specific people of Manalar."

The Templars shifted their weight. They and the Captain seemed to have taken this largest male to be the leader, which was interesting, but then again, Isboern also knew about some old tale from Mourn's early days on the Surface.

Regardless, the Guild Mistress didn't seem to mind that they asked her no questions, for the Guildsmen more easily communicated with her while guarding as Mourn drew the most attention. The other three teams would be fully apprised of the goings-on and the outcome of this encounter. For this, each of us was calm and ready.

Each of us except Jael.

Gently, I squeezed her wrist above her closed fist and signed, ★You will leave here with us. Promise.★

She nodded slightly.

"May I ask," the Captain continued with Mourn, "who are these specific people of Manalar you act against?"

"You may ask, but what would you give to know, Captain?"

Isboern's blond eyebrows lowered. "Do we trade, legend?"

"Such 'legends' are known for this, and we were on our way out when you stopped us."

"Then what would you accept? We have a treasury. You could take your pick among the pieces."

"Interesting offer."

Jael was becoming tenser watching these negotiations, and I wasn't sure why beyond a general fear of being captured again.

"What is it?" I whispered in her ear.

She leaned in when I offered mine. *"He sounds like the voice in the crypt. When we found the shield."*

I frowned.

"Is it him?" she asked. *"The gold eyes."*

I recalled Mourn's question which she'd dodged earlier.

"So," I began, *"the presence spoke to you?"*

Her face answered the question.

"What did he say?"

My Sister shook her head. *"That a bargain was fulfilled, and I was the first unfortunate one. I don't know what he meant. But he talked like this."*

That was concerning.

"I will decline the treasury for now," Mourn said to the blond man with his shiny helm and shield. "What I would rather ask is an equally honest answer for a question of my own."

"Such as?"

"With the reports of the Ma'ab in sight from the Crest Tower—"

Isboern frowned. "How did you know that?"

"What does it matter? I agree we haven't much time. I ask you, with everything you see now, after these years since you came from that forest... what do you hope to accomplish for the people of Manalar?" Mourn tilted his head, playful and inscrutable. "Captain Willven Isboern, Defender of the Wall."

In the time Isboern paused before giving his answer, I could reflect and see what Jael meant. This wasn't Mourn's habitual behavior but seemed like a performance. Krithannia watched it all with grace as reports no doubt flew between her and the men from Augran. If Mourn intended to distract or hold another's attention, perhaps he acted like the other golden-eyed figure who'd spoken to Jael?

The 'presence' who should be asleep.

"What do I hope to accomplish?" Isboern began as he shared a look with his men. Their expressions held something in common with Tamuril, who let silent tears drip from her cheeks as she gently stroked her falcon's feathers. All of them were grounded and grim.

"And you'll tell me," Isboern said firmly, "who at Manalar you act against."

"Yes," Mourn replied. "A balanced trade."

But if the mercenary answered honestly, how that might *unbalance* things pertaining to Gavin's quest?

I hope they know what they are doing.

"In God's truth," the Captain began, "I hope to find some way to help as many non-combatants escape before the siege as possible."

The Dragonblood shifted his weight, tilting his head the other direction. "We're on the eve of this siege. It is late to start evacuations now."

"Our Archbishop was supremely confident it would not be necessary," Isboern replied. "He has overridden every source of counsel asking for this leniency, and he even denied safe passage to traders and citizens from other cities. Now, he has vanished. We do not know where, but the High Inquisitor has agreed to help me turn the enforcement around with the Witch Hunters. The Bishops may yet listen to reason."

I wasn't the only one to look skeptical at that last statement, but the Godblood straightened his back and shared his blue gaze between Mourn, Krithannia, and…me.

"We want to get people *out*," he insisted, his eyes brightening with passion. "We could start with those who were never meant to be stuck here and families willing to leave. The Templari, myself, and our forces at the walls are willing to give them what time as we can and extract a heavy cost for the Ma'ab taking *Pisc'sagrad*." The Godblood stared at the Dragon's son. "*This* is what I hope to accomplish, legend, after everything which has happened since I left home. It has come to this."

The chamber quieted through a handful of heartbeats before Mourn looked at Krithannia. I thought of Talov's part in our plans, about sending a larger team of Dwarven mages to manage the gate behind the mountain.

"If the Clans are gonna be down there an' usin' the gate, there's a good chance we're gonna hafta disable or destroy it as we leave. So, fer one last trip, send those fleeing our way, especially women an' kids willing tah leave. If they make it, the Dwarves will take 'em with."

I wondered if the Clans had arrived yet.

"Why are you so certain of defeat, Captain?" Mourn asked. "That seems poor for morale."

"It is, yes, and I'd have not spoken such fatalism at any time but in a bargain such as ours." The Captain's face firmed with resolve. "But we know, legend. We know. As a city, we are not unified, and all it took was *one* Elven captive to break a partnership of decades between the two highest positions in power. I'm not blind, nor am I deaf. Jael told us that her Queen saw a vision. That the city will fall."

The Godblood swallowed. "I believe her warning as I believe my senses and judgments. Unfortunately, they align toward the same end. We've run out of time to reconcile on the Mount. All I want is to get people out before the Ma'ab find them in their homes. Can you help us?"

He'd asked a different question at the end, but if Krithannia answered with the truth I saw in her eyes, we'd provide the answer to his question posed to the Dragon son.

None of us were here to act against the people whom the Godblood wanted most to protect.

Some of us had come prepared to help.

Chapter 22

Gavin spoke first.

"What if I came to assure the Ma'ab did *not* take control of *Pisc'sa-grad*?"

The Manalari fixed their tense focus on him, absorbing that his native accent was just like theirs.

"*Qen'el?*" the red-blond warrior murmured to the others. "*Qi'el?*"

Gavin looked at him and answered directly. "*Estuv Gavin. Sone ut menaxiro.*"

Isboern lifted one hand from the chain to motion to his men and murmured something which sounded reassuring. He soon replaced that hand so Mourn would see it, even as half of us knew the Captain didn't need his hands if he wished to attack us. It was a gesture of plain negotiations, nothing more.

The Captain cleared his throat and bowed his chin to greet the Deathwalker. "Gavin the messenger. I hear you. Where did you come from, and what brought you here?"

"I was born and raised in Paxia, as you were not," he said brusquely. "My father was Manalari. My mother was Ma'ab. I follow the gods of neither of them but, before my early death, had discovered another who's been forgotten. Whose form and heraldry of crows you saw in the crypt where the shield was buried, I believe."

The men of Mount Sonai were quite easy to read. Most looked afraid.

"We did see her sign, yes," the Godblood answered forthrightly. "Who is she, messenger?"

"She is the Grey Maiden," Gavin recited, "the Grave Mother, or the Maiden of Shrouds. In the time of the Bishops isolating and keeping influence of *Pisc'sagrad* for themselves, her purpose to Manalar has been repressed but not destroyed."

"I see. And why have you returned in the name of the Grey Maiden?"

The Deathwalker's ghastly face peered at him without blinking. "Because the Ma'ab would be as destructive to every mageborn in these lands as the Bishops, but for far longer of an age. My purpose is to interfere with your expected 'fatalism,' not to prevent the fall but to discourage the Ma'ab from making the same mistake and allowing all future mageborn of Paxia and beyond to seek their potential regardless of worship."

The Godblood considered this even as his men looked resistant. The psion could take another "eternal ally" at face value, whether or not he detected any thoughts clearer than whispers.

"We act against the Bishops and Witch Hunters of Manalar," Mourn said then, fulfilling his trade with Draconic thoroughness. "We do not act against the city's people. In thanks for protecting your Elven captive as long as you did, we need not act against you. Lastly, to be doubly clear, we do *not* act on behalf of the Empire."

Isboern bowed his head in gratitude. "Thank you for your true words, guardian."

The hybrid seemed appeased by this, and the Guild Mistress chose then to lift her voice.

"We can also help you further, Captain," Krithannia said, "in what you hope to accomplish. We know the way out through this mountain, unseen by an army camped to the west."

"You do," Isboern repeated, relief clear in his voice. "There is a way?"

"Yes. But we can only help if you and your most trusted men may work with us. Can you? And *will* you?"

Isboern's eyes landed briefly on Tamuril in disguise, and he smiled. "Yes. I know I can and keep my vows."

"*Et ous'vo presheni isbisrae, Capitan,*" countered a Templar with a dark brown beard, daring a look at Mourn.

"*Verit, verit,*" Isboern responded. "But we are the defenders of the city first. Reflect on that day swearing in, and the one revisited last year."

They sounded as one reciting a passage in rhythmic tempo.

Gavin listened with interest, his mouth downturned. "You swear to protect and keep the peace *between* the Holy Order and the city?"

"Strange wording," Mourn agreed.

"It is," the Captain said. "At first, we did not understand why the Archbishop required a renewal of our oath. Once we repeated after him, and noticed our duties change, especially mine, then I understood." His shoulders lifted. "We were to let the Temple run itself and prevent the masses from organizing outside of it. Our adjusted focus."

"Keros push *Capitan* back to the wall where he join first!" said one Templar in thickly accented Trade, sounding insulting. "His close officers no further guard within sanctum. Call upon less, stand outside long."

"Keros jealous of the people's love," grumbled another. "As favor of God's light shifts away."

"Now he locked away *from* people," the red blonde sneered. "*Cosharde* pushed *Vi Inqisitir* from window for *lu'daeva!*"

Jael puffed up with indignance when the Templar pointed at her. "I know nothing you say!"

"*Calm,*" I pleaded in Davrin, clutching her shoulder. "*If you know nothing, say nothing. They will not take you again.*"

It was too late for the discussion not to focus on her, however, for the Templars did ask their leader a question. Isboern had to address it whether he'd intended to bring it up or not.

"It is...quite clear," the Captain began, "that Jael escaped Archbishop Keros and rejoined you somehow, and you were on your way out of the mountain when we caught you, correct?"

"Correct," Krithannia responded, smiling.

"We are looking for Archbishop Keros. The entire Temple is. Do you know what happened to him?"

Wolf looked at Deshi and shrugged in one of the most convincing displays of bored apathy I'd witnessed. In response, the Yungian sighed and waited on the rest of us while his brothers frowned in contemplation of the question.

Meanwhile, Mourn shook his head. "We do not, Captain. Jael was frightened when Keros attempted to murder the Inquisitor. The three had been awake all night in interrogation, and she told us Keros was acting erratic before pushing Kegyek through the window and when he dragged her through secret passages where the other Bishops wouldn't see her. When she heard our message that we were in the crypt, she'd regained enough of her magic to escape him and ran."

For my part, I imagined it had gone down exactly that way.

For Isboern's part, he didn't believe us but listened respectfully and bowed his head when Mourn finished. "I see. Very well. Then, we should not keep those who were just leaving, and we must report on our own unsuccessful search." He peered at each of us. "Who intended to stay to see Gavin's purpose done?"

Clever man. Most certainly not a fool.

"We were sorting that out when you caught us," Mourn replied with complete truth and a smile. "Though plans on behalf of the city are in flux."

Isboern smiled back. "Indeed, they are. We'll say nothing of this meeting." He placed a solemn fist over his heart, and each Templar released the Ma'ab chain to do the same.

"You can let go now," the Dragonblood said with clear humor, drawing it rattling back to him as they were more than glad to do so.

I heard several subtle gasps and one "*Nomilu sancji*" as he made it disappear in his bracers.

The Captain breathed out, recovering first. "Will the ancients who wish to help come to the garden on the south side at sunset to discuss plans for evacuation? I swear for our part, all caution and protection within my power will be taken to guard your secrecy and freedom."

Krithannia nodded. "Thank you. We will."

"We must confirm what logistics we can before then," Mourn added. "Think about what we told you, Captain, and the secrets you and your men must keep. If you believed the vision of Jael's Queen as much as your own eyes, then know many others watch, and they have not yet brought hands out from behind their backs."

Isboern frowned. "Who do you mean?"

"Jael was your proof," answered the Dragonchild, "that other ancients are aware of the precarious hold the Bishops have on a place far older than Humans have existed. You cannot save either them or their hoarded prestige tied to those sacred waters, Godblood. They have drawn their own end for centuries, and that end is now. You and your men will share their fate if you try to interfere. Do you understand?"

The psion didn't blink. "I understand, legend."

"Good. Do not forget what you hope to accomplish, Godblood. Focus on your duty to the city's people so that its fall will *not* be their end. Succeed, and your Sun will rise again."

AT KRITHANNIA'S SIGNAL, WE MOVED FARTHER INTO THE DARK AS MOURN let the Templars back out and secured the door behind them. Tamuril followed only reluctantly, her sad boy's face fading to a sad Naulor's face once Willven Isboern was out of sight. Had he been maintaining her illusion somehow? How could that be?

By all appearances, the Guildsmen had been expecting the change, and the Yungian brothers offered the Druid a bow of respect. Peering at her hands and clothing, Tamuril offered them a weak smile before glancing at her sister.

Jael, however, had *not* been prepared as she stared with an open-mouthed indignance at the taller blonde and her bird. I grimaced as Mourn turned around to come down the stairs.

Come on, he said through the pearl. *We need to cover some distance and find a secure place to talk.*

The message was passed around, but it was clear that Krithannia, Tamuril, Gavin, Jael, and myself all had the most to say. We were only keeping the peace until then. We confirmed Tamuril could see in the dark when needed, though this was an uncomfortable reminder of her fateful foray into the underground only to encounter Jaunda. Especially for how often she and Pilla looked at me and Jael.

All concern, suspicion, and wariness.

I nudged Jael's elbow before signing near my middle. *Did the pale one do you harm?*

Her bird exposed my hiding place, she replied, gritting her teeth. *I was captured because of that 'fal-con boy' and know it was a pale Elf who did it!*

Hoo bua…

Who did she expose you to?

Jael tossed her chin back the way we came. *Isboern and his Templars. He…* She hesitated. *He said the 'god warriors' were coming. The torturers. And that it didn't have to be 'hard.'*

Isboern meant to find you first, I answered.

I don't even know how the Humans knew to compete for me!

I swallowed. *I'm sorry. I think that was me.*

Jael started, her hands trembling without response.

I am sorry, I repeated. *I encountered Tamuril first, in the forest where I was headed. She is afraid of Davrin because she's seen us before.*

What? How?

Jaunda's team… the Lead had gone to the Surface before you were recruited.

My Sister frowned, nodding slowly.

*Jaunda tortured the pale Elf when they crossed paths. This was in the same tunnelswhere you and I trained to be in the Sun. She told me she did it so the pale one wouldn't come back and she might warn others away, but… then I found Tamuril later in the mountains.★

Jael narrowed copper eyes. ★And from knowing this, somehow you *told* her about my mission?★

★Not in… I mean…★ I was trying to remember what I had been thinking at the time. ★The pale one knew about the coming war, and I was trying to discover what *she* knew, so I might…★

★Might what?★

★Might come after you. And…help. She assumed another 'dark one' was sent to kill Isboern and ran away before I could discover anything at all. I had to use other sources of knowledge to track you.★

Because my compulsion wouldn't let me leave Kurn and what he'd known about Vesram; the geas had stopped me when I'd been tempted to follow Tamuril to Manalar.

I needed to look for male half-bloods instead.

Would it have been better if I had gone with the Druid? Would it only have been more dangerous because we wouldn't have had Mourn and the Guild on our side? Or would Krithannia have introduced us to Mourn in the end? Perhaps I wouldn't have had to swallow the failure of finding Gaelan, but the warp rot might be spreading if she did not find the resources to stop it.

I didn't know if anything would have been better. *Just different.*

Jael had formed fists of her hands and stopped signing to me, so I leaned my hands into her view.

★Did Tamuril do harm *after* you were captured?★ I asked.

She wrinkled her nose and motioned brusquely. ★No. He… *she* cleaned and spied for her blond man. She hardly got near me.★

I felt some relief before she added, ★So you knew you'd compromised me and came to fix it.★

Inside, I groaned. ★I never knew any of your mission beyond the direction Rausery implied it to be. I didn't even know the city. I stumbled into that, piecing it together talking to others about events while looking for you and Gaelan. I *never* knew about the shield being your real focus until I saw a man falling from the tower where we found you!★

Jael paused before repeating, *Me *and* Gaelan? What did you find out about her?*

I shook my head. *I lost her trail in a corrupted forest. If she was sent to deal with that, then it was an impossible task. I needed both the death mage and the Dragon son you see here to help return the balance.*

Jael scowled. *Wait, you're saying you did her mission *for* her?*

I don't know, I never found her. Maybe? Because it was a problem before us that we'd be foolish to ignore.

'Us?' she mimicked as her face pinched. *You mean like ignoring the problem of the Ma'ab taking the pool in this war? Since when are those our problems? If a forest is cleansed and the Human has his relic, what should *we* care? *We* need to leave while we can!*

I felt the bitter slant of her hands and had no reply. Jael watched for a response, saw only my uncertainty, and turned her attention forward with a scowl, either ignoring me or going through too many things in her mind.

I was in the latter state.

Perhaps we *should* run while we can. That was the deal I'd asked for pending the fortune of finding her like this. I wasn't here to influence the outcome; the others were. Yet I knew so much more of the history, the centuries leading to this day, and Gavin wouldn't leave. Neither would the Guild, which included Mourn.

Wouldn't helping to assure their success be better for me and Jael in the broad view? Or would it lessen our chances of returning to the Ley Tower and going home? Would it only get us killed sooner? Could Jael and I leave for the Tower without Gavin and take on Sarilis by ourselves?

Foolish. He helped you navigate even the basic death magic at that place. And you made a Bargain with the To'vah-krav, Sirana, and he spoke about extending it. You need that, you can't just leave…

I had a geas and a mission to complete while Jael didn't seem to realize how she'd changed now that I was certain she was free of hers. Or perhaps she knew but wasn't acknowledging it. She'd had no affinity facing Keros and Kegyek alone, but…

Now she did, presumably.

Her aura.

Yet another hand I'd had in the pot, interfering, in altering her path while knowing nothing of what lay ahead for her. I only knew where I'd been; I knew who would track us no matter where we ran, and how vulnerable we were on the Surface. That would only get worse if I couldn't get enough to eat, and even if I never went hungry, eventually…

Something has to change.

And Jael knew none of that, either.

Goddess…

A few curving and uneven stairs down, Krithannia and Mourn selected a narrow, single-file crack in the wall that I'd missed coming up. Although the rough-walled room seemed like storage space too small for a meeting, the Dragonchild soon forced open another stone door into a larger space with better structure.

Immediately stepping through, most of us heard and smelled the water spring. Our collective thirst arose as Mourn secured the door behind us and the Guild Mistress assisted with the wards on the way in.

"We're free to speak," Krithannia said aloud.

"May we have light as well?" Tamuril murmured.

"Of course." Krithannia took care of that herself, placing an active, yellow glowstone high in a chink on the wall, illuminating most of the room without getting in our eyes. "Please, everyone, drink your fill and replenish your skins."

"There's another way out if anyone approaches from this direction," my bodyguard added while we moved to the spring. "And we'll receive plenty of warning, though I don't believe we were followed."

Still, at least a few minds above knew we were down here, and no telling when or whether the Ma'ab might follow the path where Vo'traj had disappeared. We could not be too cautious or dare let down our guard.

While we drank, everyone took the moment to eat something from their rations. Mourn finally remembered to pass the three cakes he'd taken from upstairs to Jael. She blinked at him, sniffing the dense, nutty bread. Her appetite awakened when I offered to taste test it; she pulled it out of my reach on impulse.

"I had one from their stores," I said. "Safe, pretty good, a bit dry."

"I eat," she grumbled, hunching over her fare to nibble on it, glancing at Mourn. "Thank."

Not only did Jael eat all three cakes, but I don't think she dropped a crumb. Watching her made me even more aware of my hollow middle now that we were out of danger.

I want to eat everything I have, I confessed to Mourn through the pearl on my ear. *And bug Gavin for the extra bites he's not going to eat.*

My bodyguard restrained his smile, though not much. *Go ahead and eat it all. I was thinking we could collect more from the gate.*

Have the Dwarven teams arrived, then?

They have. But let us move onto the same map together to save time.

I doubled the rations I was planning to eat, though I tried to go slow as I listened to our leaders.

"Alright," Krithannia began, her poise and practice with public speaking clear as a sunny sky. "For the sake of those not privy to as much, this is where we stand on the Mount. First and foremost, the Ma'ab army has been spotted. It's early afternoon outside, and our estimates place the main body leaving the Raguruos Mountains by sunset and begin encampment on the western fields into the night."

The Guildsmen waited somberly while Tamuril displayed enough dread at the news for all of us.

"There may be skirmishes and traps depending on what defenses the Manalari put in place ahead of time," the dark-haired Naulor continued. "However, our spies say there is nothing which will stop the Ma'ab host from setting themselves up about a league from the city's outer wall. Anyone who leaves the mountain from any direction should be exceedingly cautious of being ensnared by danger meant for the Ma'ab."

Jael was frowning with a touch of impatience but listened intently, picking up what information she could. Gavin's face was oddly similar but lacking the edge of fidget from my Sister; his comprehension would be near perfect.

"Our teams are doing well, undiscovered thus far. Their non-combative disguises and our communications have allowed them to get a complete view of the city at present, which we shall use in our negotiations with the Templars. Team One has withdrawn from the Temple for now, as the Witch Hunters have been directed to search the outer roads for the Archbishop and 'his witch' before the Ma'ab get too close. It is too dangerous for Reprisal to stay in the one place filled with trained mages."

More nodding.

"Team Two has been trailing Mathias Briar since Sirana spotted him, but he's not yet led them anywhere to meet Brom Troshin. He has not yet used a disguise and is mostly attempting to avoid being conscripted. They're working on an opportunity to corner and question him, though I've asked them to hold back if they can, given we suspect Brom might be masked as one of the clergy."

Tamuril either twisted nervously at her fingers or stroked Pilla's wings but spoke at this point. "Who is Brom? How could he not be recognized as one who doesn't belong?"

Mourn smirked wryly but waited for his Guild partner to answer.

"Good question, Tamuril. I will explain. You and Jael must know."

With graceful hands and soft, lilting words, Krithannia cast a quick illusion suspended in the air. It was a reasonably accurate depiction of Brom as the innkeeper I'd first met.

"Brom Troshin is a sorcerer from a town recently burned by Witch Hunters," she explained. "The fire occurred because they tried to capture Sirana, though she escaped, but they succeeded in capturing and killing Gavin. Among other things, Brom attempted to prevent Sirana from unwittingly completing Gavin's ritual where he could reclaim his body after death. At the same time, he made plans to enslave Sirana and keep her with him against her will. He may attempt to capture any Elf he encounters, as he has a long history with us."

Jael's eyes widened and she stared at me. I pursed my lips and signed confirmation.

"We believe he's come to Manalar not only to find Sirana but to reclaim a dagger she stole from him."

Wolf looked where my belt would be if my cloak weren't covering the view; he and I met eyes.

He remembers.

"Brom is a haunted individual with multiple faces," the Naulor told us, but especially Tamuril, "and inordinately dangerous, for he is older than he may appear. The Ma'ab call him 'the Deathless', and he is one of the ancients watching who could interfere with our preferred outcome of this conflict. Once he reveals himself, the three best able to confront him are Shadow, Sirana, and Gavin. All others should put space between you and Brom immediately."

"He may also use the name Cris-ri-phon," I said. "It's his oldest."

"Strange sound," Jael remarked.

My eyes slid to one side. "It's from the Red Desert. Zauyrian language."

She shrugged. "Don't care. Will move fast."

That was a relief.

She grinned. "And stab in back if he has you."

I made a face and motioned at Mourn. "I hired a bodyguard for this because I knew Brom was a problem. If this sorcerer appears, Sister, *you* stay back. Let my guard do his work."

Jael glanced at Mourn, bright copper irises looking him up and down. "Fine. He better guard good."

She agreed too easily.

"To continue," Krithannia said. "Clan Baradum is on the Manalar side of their jump gate, preparing it for defense and repeated use. We must work out *exactly* what we can offer Willven Isboern regarding the evacuation of Manalari citizens. We want realism and honesty working with the Captain, nothing else will suffice in how little time we have. The more people leaving, the more likely they shall be noticed, and the gate could fall under attack by either side."

Finally, Krithannia looked at Gavin. "At the same time, we must make certain the Bishops' control of *Pisc'sagrad* is severed. If the Captain is willing to let this happen to save his people, and if we can assure him that we can block the Ma'ab's claim, then we may get to choose the timing."

The Deathwalker considered. "I was willing to disrupt it at any opportunity, but this plan would have a greater and unfavored effect if the Ma'ab were allowed to camp outside the walls first."

"Agreed. So that means we must try for late tonight or the next morning, depending on what happens with the Godblood this evening."

"So we have time to return to the gate," Mourn said, "speak with the Clans, and return to the south wall where Reprisal first entered."

"Correct." Krithannia met his eyes. "It's only a matter of who goes."

"Aren't we all?" Tamuril asked, her pale face becoming paler when her sister shook her head.

"One of us *must* meet Isboern, we cannot risk being kept off the mountain and miss it. Better to never leave it."

"Agreed," Gavin said. "I'm not inclined to go, and I have no physical needs forcing me to."

Nodding, Wolf spoke up. "My teams are finding food and drink enough in the city, plus places to rest out of the Sun. We'll stay in Manalar and report every change."

He looked at Torch, who bowed and confirmed, "Yes. All of us stay."

"With Gavin and Reprisal, I feel safe," Krithannia said. "I volunteer to stay to be sure we meet the Captain. I will take no risks to compromise it."

"Very well," Mourn said. "I'll escort Tamuril to the gate so she may leave before the battle starts."

The Druid looked horrified. "What?"

"Jael as well?" Wolf asked, seeming to expect our recovered prisoner to jump from the sinking ship at the first opportunity.

My Sister glowered at him. "Only if Sirana goes."

Hoo bua...

"We'll work it out," Mourn said. "We'll return to the gate and learn what Krithannia needs to know for tonight. Easier with a small group."

"Thank you." Everything about the Naulor was sincere as she turned to take her sister's hands. "Your Captain asked us to lead you to safety and we have a way out. You are safe with Shadow. Please, go with him. He is also protecting the Red Sisters."

Jael snorted softly, and Tamuril grimaced to say, "They need it?"

"Yes, they do."

My Sister added a guffaw, earning a look of annoyed suspicion from the falcon. Meanwhile, I wasn't sure what made Tamuril cease her protests, but something crossed green eyes on which she gave some thought. Finally, her throat flashing on a deep swallow, the blonde Naulor looked at her soft brown boots and agreed to go.

"Thank you, sister," Krithannia said, "for everything you've done to this point. Be safe, and I shall see you when this is resolved."

Tamuril breathed out. "When do we leave?"

"As soon as possible," Mourn said. "The more time to plan and scout, the better."

"A-alright."

During that exchange, Gavin and I met eyes. He tilted his head in question, and I shrugged in answer. I didn't know if I was coming back or not.

"I haven't forgotten Sarilis and the Ley," I said. "Or Vesram."

The first ally I'd met on the Surface nodded. Apparently, this was good enough for him.

Chapter 23

Mourn had to lead the way, so after we left the secure room with the water spring, he remained up front. Tamuril stayed behind him, with me behind her. Or rather, I walked as the buffer between the two females who weren't fully trusting of me right now but more wary of each other.

I regretted that I couldn't see more than the side of Mourn's face when we turned a corner. For his part, he displayed his back to Jael—really, to all three of us—without a tremor of concern. His tail acted as a long sensor maintaining his space to respond to threats. If Jael or Tamuril did something unexpected, they'd be surprised how effective that limb was when Mourn's instincts took control of the situation.

I'd sure been once, lying flat on a *dorji-ka* floor unable to breathe.

No one spoke, signed, or made eye contact for the first half hour, and the awkward tension did not ease, nor did the constant, simmering squints from Pilla on her Druid's shoulder. I resigned myself to a long trek back down to the canyon despite it being all downhill and tried to focus on potential hazards in this deep labyrinth.

Sirana?

I smiled slightly, concentrating on this welcome feeling.

~Yes, Mourn?~

I was watching your hands with Jael earlier.

~I figured you would. For all I know, Wolf and the Yungians could partly read it, too.~

Perhaps. It was clear you were arguing. I wanted to say you did well by her, no matter how it came to be. Given her cooperation now, I suggest she needs time to weigh her priorities, but you have not lost her yet.

I accepted that balm. ~I tried to help her.~

You succeeded. That is truth, no matter what happens next. I've rarely met one so persistent in their goal.

I smirked. ~Except you?~

He turned his head until I could see one gold eye, the corners creased in a smile. Our mindlink fell quiet but comfortable. Whatever went on in the heads of my Sister and Tamuril, I could travel while feeling calmer inside.

~Am I correct in guessing you will not leave Manalar until Gavin and Krithannia have succeeded at the pool?~

His tail waved at me. *Correct.*

~Would Jael and I be safe going through the gate and waiting for you at Kerut?~

The hovering appendage slowed, and I heard a mental sigh.

I have been thinking about it, he said. *On one hand, after seeing Vesram with Vo'traj and Jael with Keros, perhaps it would be smarter to get as many Elves off the field as possible. Perhaps sending you to Kerut before the Deathless shows himself will reduce the risk significantly.*

~Mm-hm. I feel that concern. But, on the other hand?~

"On the other hand, we know a mass of unknown Humans will be using the Dwarven gate. In the chaos and confusion we must expect, the Clans cannot vet with certainty that all these people are harmless, or that one may not be Mathias or the Deathless himself. Without myself, Krithannia, or Gavin to read auras while Jael and you are alone more than three days' ride away, this reeks of over-confidence to say nothing will go wrong. It is impossible for me to ignore.*

~Yeah. I agree.~

Mourn paused to check the next set of crumbling stairs before he closed his thoughts. *There is no simple choice here. There never is in war.*

Should I fail in our Bargain by sending you through that gate without me, there are consequences for that. Yet, the consequence is the same or worse if I go with you and Krithannia loses her life or freedom, or if the sacred pool either never leaves Manalari control or the Ma'ab Ascended take ownership of it for the next age.

My mouth felt tight. ~*So, it's possible I'm 'safer' near you in the middle of a battle over a surging magical pool than I would be anywhere else at this time and place.*~

I heard him exhale, long and slow. *That is the most balanced place I see for you and me, yes. Granted, it's not perfectly balanced.*

~*And my Sister's 'most balanced' place?*~

His shoulders seemed to tense. *We must consider the effects of Gavin's success, which may be felt as far as the Great Lake. After the Deathwalker's warnings, imagine her alone or even with only you, as a newly born, just-healed mage anchored by the To'vah but untrained in its power.*

My eyes widened in the dark as I remembered the extra talisman Gavin had given me for her. ~*Oh, fuck...*~

Yes. She would be safer with me, with both of us, though I'm aware of the arrogance she could interpret in the claim. She may not understand why or choose to believe us even if she does. That is her decision along with its consequence.

The Dragonblood let me walk in silence to think about this. I appreciated how it cut through some of the fog in my worries and fears. Even walking away from Gavin and the Guild this moment, I wanted to go back this evening, especially if Mourn was going regardless.

Jael had said she wouldn't go through the gate if I didn't, so that tilted her decision our way if she'd been truthful in her remark to Wolf.

That left Tamuril. Would she go through the gate and start walking back West to her forest? She could. She'd somehow covered that distance faster than Jael despite starting far behind, and she lived in the wilderness by choice, her magic attuned to it. The City of the Sun had probably caused her as much distress over the days Jael was in captivity as the underground when she'd gone searching for that mushroom.

The Druid may be the only one better off leaving before the Ma'ab arrived tonight.

THE TRIP BACK TOOK US TWO HOURS TO WIND THROUGH THE MAZE AND JOG through the canyon under Mourn's camouflage magic. Although our greatest concern was whether enemies lay in wait near the narrow crevice leading to the cliffside, my bodyguard was confident that his alarms lay undisturbed before we would set foot into daylight.

No scent of the Abyss, either.

That was a relief.

Nonetheless, eyes seemed to watch these eastern hills. No one had to tell another to be careful and step lightly.

Not many, Mourn observed, noting a few places on the north side of the canyon but none on the south. *But the Ma'ab are here.*

And the Guild atop Mount Sonai would know this as well.

My stomach had grown hollow and aching despite emptying my food stores and waterskin. My appetite had been mercifully numb, starting with discovering Vesram and the Ma'ab in the crypt and remaining suppressed through saving Jael.

But now, my body reminded me of this lack.

Not as severe as when Soul Drinker starved me, at least.

Regardless, my limbs felt weak, and I wasn't looking forward to climbing back up that mountain with enough time to reach the garden by sunset.

I hope Mourn's correct that the Dwarves brought extra food…

"Wait here," Mourn whispered to us after we'd crouched beneath a yellow stone overhang streaked with white quartz. "Let me check security."

He received three nods and slipped out without wasting time. Now that I could catch my breath and Jael was holding still, I reached into my pouch holding three of Gavin's bone talismans. I pulled out one, supposing it didn't matter which, and showed it to Jael.

She cocked an eyebrow, and her hand moved. *Runes?*

Not a reflexive refusal. *That's good.*

When Gavin does what he must do, I replied with my other hand, *no matter where you are, you will feel it. A magic surge shall cover all of Paxia, affecting all Elves and mages.* I lifted the knucklebone. *This will absorb some of the impact and leave you less dazed.*

Jael peered at the bone and then me. *Do you have one?*

Without hesitating, I dug out one of the two to show her. *Yes. Please, take this one. I meant to give it to you as soon as we found you. I don't want this to catch you unaware.*

Pursing her lips, my Sister accepted the bone, and I watched her tuck it behind her stocking partway down her boot. She truly had no tools, not even a pouch. I wondered what else the Dwarves might have brought with them.

I asked, *Do you know where your armor and equipment lay?*

Jael shook her head, eyes on the ground, but I nudged her so she'd look back at me.

Maybe Isboern could tell us tonight.

Her white brows drew down. *Us?*

I sighed through my nose. *Maybe he will tell my allies.*

Jael let that sit between us as she looked over at the Druid, who was inspecting her own ink-inscribed piece of bone. I didn't know when Krithannia had passed that to her, but I was glad she remembered earlier than me.

"This feels cold," Tamuril whispered under her breath.

"Really?" I murmured, closing the bone in my hand. "Not to me."

The Druid glanced at me uncomfortably. "So, he is the one who…"

She fell silent, listening to the wind rustling the sturdy hills around us, and did not speak when Mourn returned to lead us safely to the Dwarven cave.

THE CLANS HAD A SCOUT AND DEFENSE SETUP LIKE WE'D HAD IN THE CRYPT, to give them early warning and methods of slowing hostile entry while sealing off their valuable escape route.

The Dwarves might not wish to get involved in every Human conflict on the Surface, given how frequent they were, but I'd not forgotten that the Clans crafted in trade some of the armor and weapons the Humans used against each other. The Clans also made their own gear for defensive situations such as this, and the quality was leagues better than what the Tragar could craft for themselves down below.

I counted another thirty Dwarves in pockets along the passageway, actively expanding and hollowing out the rock to make more room for standing bodies. Though I hadn't heard chisel, hammer, or cart until we'd been allowed past the well-armed guards, they were in the process of filling up an internal dead-end with loose dirt and rocks. They all wore masks over their noses and mouths, with beards tightly braided and sometimes coiled out of the way.

All the miners wore lighter armor which allowed them to work, and each kept a small axe and dagger on them, but the guards were armed, armored, and apparently trained to fight with much heavier equipment. They appeared broad and capable enough, even being outnumbered, they might plug the tunnel and stop an invading Ma'ab team in their tracks.

I noted with interest the presence of female Dwarves among both the guard and mining crafters. Almost half in each group and with the appropriate tools, though this took closer looks for the absence of beards or heavier curves around the bust and hips to tell young males from females.

Once we entered the gate room, I was also convinced the Clans had sent enough mages to handle an influx of Manalari refugees. With slightly more females in this group, these Dwarves were dressed similarly to the miners, with lighter armor and smaller weapons, but also wore more jewelry and carried a suspicious number of pouches on their belts. The dust being kicked up by the workers somehow never reached this space; it remained easy to breathe.

A male blackbeard turned to greet us with a large, white smile. His features felt familiar to me, mostly his peridot green eyes.

"Ah, Shadow! There ye be with…" Those colorful eyes grew bigger. "Whoo! Three ov 'em? An' none are Krithannia. Stonbird's shit!"

"Hello, Rodge," Mourn said with a chuckle. "This is Tamuril, Sirana, and Jael. We're here for food and rest, and to discuss the Clans' capabilities over the next day."

The armored gate mage bowed at his stocky waist, which gave me the impression he was about to roll over like a boulder. "Heard o' Sirana an' Tamuril, fer sure!" His eyes twinkled like Talov's. "Jael is new, but happy tah see proof o' yer success."

My Sister wasn't comfortable to hear this, especially as he couldn't quite pronounce her name correctly. The suspicious scowl remained fixed on her face when Mourn looked to us.

"This is Rodge Baradum, Talov's grandson."

"Aha," I said, nodding. "I wondered if they shared blood."

Rodge chuckled. "It's the eyes, ain't it? Sure don' have the beard."

"Why would you? You're not old enough to be grey."

"Aye, I mean when he was in his prime," said the Dwarf who seemed to be in his prime as well. "GrandDa Talov was all crimson fire-hair like my sister, Ragura."

"Aye, Rodge?" one of the mages called from where she worked with the gate.

"Well! Since ya sharpened yer ears this mornin'," he said, sounding to be jesting, "will ya grab that food crate an' step over here a sec?"

The female "fire hair" offered no qualm to lifting a square box from atop another and walking over to join us. Ragura was beardless and also had blue eyes, but in a lighter shade from me, Willven, or Keros. More like Wolf's eyes.

So many blue eyes up here…

"Greetings," she said. "Hungry?"

"Yes," Mourn said first.

She set the box down and removed the well-fitting top. "Help yerself."

Jael and I crowded Mourn to look inside, though my nose informed me of the hard sausage, cheese, and dry breads present before my eyes parsed out the bounty in front of them. After some inspection, I also found easy travel bags containing nuts and dried fruits.

"You're hungry," Mourn said. "Take what you need."

Although both Rodge and Ragura agreed, Jael waited until I grabbed something first, taking a bite of hard cheese and nodding. Then she and I kept collecting items, one after another, glancing at each other with probably the same thought: eat as much as we could and stash what we could carry for later. However, Jael collected her food as though forgetting she had no pack or belt to carry it.

"Gimme yer skins," Ragura said. "I'll refill 'em from the barrel."

Mourn and I handed over ours, though my Sister and the Druid stared at her.

"Heh," the redhead smirked. "I'll grab two more."

"Do you have a spare satchel for Jael's food?" I asked.

"I'll look," the Dwarf replied, walking away while we chose a place against the wall to sit out of the way.

In the meantime, Tamuril chose mostly the nuts and dried fruit in much more modest amounts. It was interesting to watch her chew some of the hard strips of meat to moisten them before feeding them to her falcon. That was an unpleasant thought at first, but I remembered that was how most birds fed their young.

No sense giving the ever-complaining falcon a stomachache.

Ragura brought water for Tamuril and Jael and handed over a wide waist pouch which the latter could wrap twice around her middle. It was more than enough to stash what my sister didn't eat now, though we were in the middle of discovering that limit. At least her being ravenous after imprisonment made my appetite seem less unusual.

Mourn ate more slowly as he spoke with the Dwarven siblings about the resources available, and the reason for asking. Green and blue eyes opened wide as they learned of the Manalari Captain's willingness to work with them.

"Well, shit," Rodge muttered, sharing an intense look with Ragura as he stroked his beard in thought. "This changes things."

"But not a lot," she countered. "We planned fer refugees. Just gotta ramp 'em up."

"Aye. Could be comin' in waves all through th' night an' morning. We're gonna need more gems prepped, an' camps set up on th' other side, too."

"Aye. Let's send some messages, get what Shadow an' Cloud need."

"Thank you," Mourn said. "We have about an hour before we leave."

"Should be enough time."

"Very well. We'll wait."

Only an hour to rest and explain. Damn.

"Before 'we' leave?" Jael leaned to whisper, almost a hiss.

Or to explain before resting.

I'd made my decision on the way down, but where to start?

"May I ask you something?" I murmured in our native tongue.

Her bright eyes were wary as ever. *"What?"*

"How did you hold your ground for a night and a morning against two elder Human mages?"

She swallowed, keeping her mouth shut.

"I know they hurt you, and intended to beat you into submission, but… until that silver blade came into play, am I correct that they never kept their hands on you for long?"

I heard her teeth grind. *"I made them regret it every time Keros touched me."*

"I believe you." I looked over her rough clothing. *"You are changed. Everyone who is a mage has told me that you are like them but untrained."*

She flinched. *"Not possible. There are no mages in my House."*

"It shouldn't be possible, but it is. You fulfilled your mission, didn't you? Was your magic somehow…given by this success?"

My Sister shook her head emphatically. *"No. No! That's not what happened. The Valshiaress did not give this to me!"*

"Shh, alright. I was guessing, but I'm wrong. Then…you mentioned a presence with golden eyes like my bodyguard?"

Jael glared at me. *"He knows something about that. I can tell."*

"Well, he hasn't told me anything yet, though if I had to guess, it was an older Dragon awakened by what was going on in the crypt. Do you think that could be it?"

Her lips parted to speak but snapped shut. Her eyes had begun to shimmer, and I saw the shame in them but didn't understand why it was there.

I moved to face her with my back to the room, blocking the casual Dwarven looks our way. Tamuril and Pilla tensed even as they remained near us. Mourn had given us space but I imagined he listened in. I risked taking Jael's hands, squeezing them. My Sister didn't draw away or push me off, though her shoulders hunched up.

"What caused the eyes to appear?" I asked. *"What happened immediately before you heard that voice?"*

Her throat must've hurt when she swallowed. *"I didn't succeed in my mission, Sirana. I failed. Isboern had the shield in his hands, and I could feel the geas lifting. But then he gave it to the Archbishop, and I... I tried to stop them, but...it was stupid. Just...kicking out as my House always does, only to get beaten worse for it. My insides felt like they were going to burst."*

My hands were covered by gloves, and hers weren't. I was glad I didn't experience any of this in a memory; I could imagine too well from the warnings of my own bindings. Still, I looked at her eyes because I wanted to know.

"How did you survive it, Jael?"

Jael glanced at the Druid even though Tamuril didn't know our words. Her expression warred with anger, fear, confusion, and a clear desire to cry despite the added humiliation that would bring. She tried a few times to whisper an answer as she focused on our hands held together.

"Her 'god-blood' healed me," she muttered. *"He was...in my head the whole time, staying with me while it felt like hanging off the edge of a Drider pit, and I couldn't see the bottom. He shouted to be heard, reaching for me, to pull me back up and...wrap me in light. When he did, the threads around me, these invisible, sharp things... well, they snapped."*

I stared. This psion had saved my Sister from dying of failure? He had *healed* her. Had he freed her from the geas as well?

Where had a Human like this come from?

"The Valsharess said…" Jael hesitated but, enviously, no pain came to stop her. She licked her lips before trying again. *"The Valsharess said the 'Dragon's shield' placed in this specific Human's hands was the only way to keep the Deepearth closed."*

I frowned. *"What? Closed?"*

Jael shrugged with a grimace. *"I don't know what She meant. It didn't matter if She was right or just ranting over a bad Reverie."*

"No, I suppose not." I rubbed the backs of her hands with thumbs. *"Alright. So, you saw the Dragon shield and the Dragon eyes. The god-blood broke the spell and healed your body, but you have got a mage's aura, Jael. You do. That's why Keros and Kegyek turned on each other. They couldn't break you."*

She'd turned her head to one side, eyes on the ground, but her cheek was wet when she looked back. *"It hurt. A lot. More when they dragged me onto the altar."* She scoffed. *"No surprises there. They're just like home."*

I winced. *"How do you feel now?"*

She shrugged. *"Still kinda numb, but… Better? I don't know why."* I spotted a hint of a smirk. *"Unless waking up horny and kissing you was what I was missing."*

I took that chance to smile. *"I missed you, too. And I'm glad you're alive to be angry with me."*

Jael's hands squeezed mine hard, like a reflex before she pulled them free, crossing her arms. My knees complained of the hard rock anyway, so I shifted back to sit beside her, as close as she'd allow. She leaned her shoulder into me, and I shifted closer.

"I'm not angry," she muttered. *"Just… feel like I'm far behind you."*

I weighed if now was a good time to mention the psionics. I had a better comparison in Captain Isboern than either the Tragar or Ornilleth.

"You're not gonna jump out of this, are you?" she said.

One corner of my mouth tightened. *"I thought about it. But… I made both enemies and allies to find you—"*

348

Jael arched her eyebrow. *"Such that you always need bodyguards now? You're that well known on the Surface?"*

"To the right and wrong Surfacers, yeah." I grimaced. *"I'm sorry, but it's true. And I'm... not done yet. I can't leave."*

That was the closest I could say while being truthful enough about past events too complex to go into yet. Jael seemed to accept this, if only because the pain of her own release was so fresh. She drew in a deep breath and let it out, her mood sullen as she turned my words over in her head.

"And something else?" I offered.

She grunted. *"What?"*

"I asked Shadow about your new aura. He can see it. He said if you decided to stay with us, he could teach you mage things you need to know."

Her eyes rolled up toward the ceiling. *"Oh, he could?"*

"He's near the age of Elder D'Shea. He's experienced and willing. Why not?"

My Sister blinked in surprise to hear that, sneaking another look at the Dragonblood presently talking with the Dwarven siblings at the gate. The rest of the room buzzed with more conversation since the news shared at our arrival had spread.

"He's that old?" she whispered. *"He doesn't look it."*

I grinned. *"He's young for a Dragon's son. He might beat the Valsharess in age, given the chance."*

Jael's mouth opened, but she closed it. *"Hm. And he's a good fighter, too?"*

"He has learned skill with any weapon we use and more which we don't. He uses magic to win fights, too, but he can change his shape and appearance, so he does not always have to fight. Again, this is how I found you."

"And you trust him?"

"After the last month working with him, yes. Like I would trust Jaunda and you. I've made deals or agreements with many Surfacers getting this far. The Dragonblood and the death mage are the only two who did not change their minds or ask too much in helping me."

Jael smirked playfully. *"You must have something they want."*

I shrugged. *"I learned what motivated them, they learned the same about me. We discovered it had more to do with sharing knowledge and weighing our influence on events than a simple trade."*

Slowly, my Sister shook her head, though a wider smile came with it. *"You sound like D'Shea."*

I answered her smile but honestly didn't know how to respond.

"So, you, the Dragonblood, and those others need to influence things here," she said. *"Was finding me a side payment to you for helping them build their 'knowledge and influence?'"*

I winced. *"Well... Yes. I suppose that's right."*

"Hmph. Well, thanks for not pretending otherwise. Though I'm confused where they think you'd make a difference on the Surface. What are you supposed to do?"

Feeling a flush of heat, I rubbed my head and scratched my scalp, grunting with my mouth sealed. Shrugging, I gave her a pleading look.

"Oh," Jael grimaced. *"Sorry. Yeah, that was stupid to ask after what I just described..."*

I breathed out, thinking we were getting somewhere when, abruptly, she climbed to her feet and announced, *"I need to piss."*

Surprised, I leaned to give her space. *"Want me to go with you?"*

"I need to figure out where to go first." She offered a strained smile. *"But no... I need to step out and think."*

I tensed. *"Please, don't go alone."*

She made a face. *"What do you mean? Grab a Dwarf?"*

"I can escort you," Mourn offered, as Rodge signed something to him and moved off with his sister. *"If you're willing to wait here, Sirana?"*

I sighed, at once relieved and confused. *"Yes. I might need to go next."*

Mourn motioned with his arm, signing directions Jael would understand. She frowned but shrugged and headed toward the passageway.

"I'll be back," she said. *"Promise."*

I only believed that because my bodyguard was going with her.

We're making progress.

"I did not expect you to care so much," Tamuril spoke to my right. "You try hard to convince her. She is foolish if she does not believe you."

Her Trade had grown smoother since last time. Both of ours had.

"Do you know what we were saying?" I asked.

The Druid shook her head, her eyes sad as she petted the banded feathers on her well-fed falcon. "No. But your arrival speaks more than pretty words. If you are blessed with time to share those pretty words, she should believe you... As she refused to believe Willven, despite all he did for her and how much patience he showed. I do not understand why she made all this so difficult."

That sounded about right, unfortunately. I shrugged. "She has... mind scars, some formed young, some from our training. I recognize them. Anger and distrust have kept her alive. I do not think she knows how to rest from it yet."

Tamuril gave me an odd look. "And... you do?"

"I've learned." Nervously, I rubbed at a pain in my head. "I've been angry like her, assuming only lies from family and elders. But all of it... broke me before you and I met."

The blonde Elf appeared hurt by this. "What? Broke you?"

"I've been mending," I hurried to add. "Learning how to ...rest from anger. There is too much up here to see, to always act like Jael in her cell. It makes me tired, so I must learn an easier way."

The Naulor watched me with something close to astonishment before she smiled slightly. "Too much? So much is all I know. But perhaps you are right. It cannot *all* be illusion and threat, and the easier path *is* the honest one. Although, if you and your sister came from a place where you must always look for lies, then...of course, she would not recognize a man like Willven."

A man like...

"The way you say his name," I began with a grin. "Such appreciation. Is he your lover?"

Pilla made a noise threatening to become a louder screech, but I ignored that to watch Tamuril's face flush becomingly pink. The Druid earnestly shook her head.

"No!" she insisted, green eyes flicking around for others listening.

"No, he is not..."

But you want him to be.

I closed my lips over that reply and looked around. Fortunately, the gate mages were busy planning for the news we'd brought.

"Though, I..." the Druid began, "I can see that...um..."

I lifted my brows. "See what?"

"Y-you and the Dragon son are such...companions."

The blonde's face flushed the hottest I'd seen while it dawned on me that she could probably read auras as well as Krithannia.

Shit.

"I am...surprised he has accepted you, in light of your..." Tamuril unfolded her fingers in the vague direction of my middle. "Um, condition."

Quickly, I drew up my knees to hide any aura visible in my womb. "What? Of course he has! That was part of the deal."

"Deal?" The pink-cheeked blonde blinked with even greater surprise. "Has he...uhm, agreed, then?"

I shook my head at her vaguery. "There's much we've agreed on. That's the *essence* of a deal, Druid."

"Oh!" Her face brightened, nearing a smile. "Then he shall be your...um, what was your word? Sire?"

Sire? What in the web is she...?

I dropped my voice and leaned closer despite the falcon's clapping beak. "The 'sire' is already chosen. Long before we met. You know that."

"N-no, I meant," the Druid tried again, "will he adopt the role of father? Y-you can't raise a child up here alone, and at least he shares your blood. He is not a bad choice."

Oh my goddess.

Now *my* face flushed. The Naulor assumed I wasn't going back home *and* that Mourn would continue protecting me through the birth? Even afterward?!

Him? A governor bathing an infant in the nursery?

That was insane.

Pilla opened her wings the moment I intended to close in so we could whisper. I stopped and lowered my voice.

"Please be quiet," I hissed, keeping one eye on that aggressive wing while staying out of reach. "Don't tell Jael until I can. In fact, better not to speak of it at all. Brom tried to capture me for this 'condition.' I do not need more Human hunters overhearing this."

Tamuril was flustered, drawing her bird closer. "I-I am sorry. Of course, Sirana, you are right. Sorry…"

Mourn and Jael returned from outside before our nerves had settled. Although more distracted than I wished to be, I could read a reasonable calm between the two, and it was easy to spot the used belt around her waist securing two long daggers at her hips. They were of Elven make but large for what we were used to.

Clearly, they had spoken and came to an agreement satisfactory enough for my Sister to plop down next to me and fold her arms with a sigh.

"Staying with you," she stated. "I will do all not to be captured again."

"She's agreed to listen to us both," Mourn said. "If we give her warning or command, she will heed us."

My sister pointed at him. "*Only* if you teach me things."

The To'vah-krav nodded. "I shall. As we have agreed, Jael Aurenthietti."

My Sister gave him a smart nod and dug out her waterskin for a drink.

That was fast.

I exhaled and smiled at them. "I am glad to hear this. And I see the new weapons?"

"Mine," Mourn said. "She's borrowing them. We can also get a cloak and leather torso piece from the Dwarves."

Tamuril straightened up from her slouch. "Wait, you are *not* leaving through the gate with me?" She looked at Mourn and Jael. "*None* of you?"

The Dragonchild shook his head. "I know Captain Isboern asked you to leave the battlefield, as did your sister. You may do so and return to the wilderness. You will have to wait until the first time the gate is used to transfer in more supplies and defenses, but this takes you three days' ride to the north of Manalar. You'll have to cross the Big Ker River and be wary of Witch Hunters, but you should recognize the Midway mountains before reaching the prairie."

He paused as she stared fearfully at him, eyes like huge green leaves.

"Or," Mourn added, "you could wait with the Dwarves at the rendezvous point. Perhaps you can help with the refugees from Manalar coming through. Krithannia will be coming back this way, and myself with Sirana and Jael if possible."

"What about Willven?"

The half-blood looked confused. "The Guild is not making decisions for the Templars on when to retreat."

"W-wait," she stuttered, "so you three are heading back to plan with him tonight? After all we did to help Jael get free, she's going *back in?*"

"We must see through this change. We trade safe passage for his people for this chance, and Jael is safer with Sirana and me."

Tamuril opened her mouth to look at me in pure disbelief, but snapped it closed when she looked at the Dragonblood, blood rushing into her neck. The conflict on the Naulor Druid's face suggested a thousand fears passing behind her eyes. The display reminded me of our last moments arguing outside the Ley Tower before she ran away in a panic.

"I-I don't know if I can leave yet," she squeaked, tears ready to spill from her eyes. "If you don't know how Willven will be getting out."

Jael and I exchanged a glance. Goddess, the reality that Isboern might not make it out hadn't even occurred to her.

She never asked, and he never said.

"Would you like to wait here in this room with the Dwarves?" Mourn offered. "You could help with refugees on this side and jump with Krithannia when she returns here, and she would tell you what she knows of the Captain."

For the first time today, Tamuril appeared like she was looking for a trick. "Stay here? But weren't you told to make certain I left?"

"No," he replied, mildly insulted. "I'm not your keeper, Tamuril. I'm not one of your fathers here to push you out the gate whether you're ready or not."

She flinched and looked away from his face.

"I *do* think," he continued, "that Captain Isboern sent you with us because he might not be able to protect you once the fighting starts, and this distraction on his part could get him and his men killed. I recommend considering whether you wish to see war up close when you do not have to, and whether any actions you take might cause the deaths of others, particularly those you care for most."

The Naulor chewed her lip as Pilla squawked protectively and chirped in an attempt to comfort. I wondered what the Druid had been thinking about on the way down the mountain, if not this? I had no idea, but she'd certainly presumed some interesting things about the Bargain between Mourn and me, so the assumptions about Isboern's plans could have been anything.

"I will stay here with the Dwarves," the Druid murmured, eyes on the ground. "P-please tell Willven I hope to see him again and will pray for him. And tell Krithannia, I love her and hope she succeeds."

Mourn bowed his head in Yungian style. "I will tell them. Do what you can to help here but, above all, you stay safe. Agreed?"

Tamuril muttered something vaguely affirmative but did not look up again, even when it was time for us to leave.

CHAPTER 24

MOURN LED US SAFELY THROUGH THE CANYON, UNSEEN BENEATH THE EYES OF the Ma'ab scouts in the hills. Jael was reasonably quiet despite the leather armor and gloves not fitting her well. Her borrowed cloak had also needed to be hemmed quickly, the hood with plenty of room to cover her head.

We'd see if any of this distraction caused her to trip or get caught on something, though it was better than nothing.

We turned toward the south side, and we started climbing, seeking that empty rock quarry with a passage that would take us underneath the wall. It was an incredible weak point, so short and direct compared to the labyrinth I'd crawled through twice.

~How is this open after the last two days?~ I asked. ~Does no one living in Manalar know about it?~

Captain Isboern knows about it, he answered.

~He does?!~

And he is keeping it open. When Jael was taken with the shield, he withdrew most guards away from that wall. The Captain told Tamuril to pass on the details to the Guild.

~Tamuril told the Guild? When?~

While we were sailing on the boat. Krithannia didn't receive that message from our plant until Reprisal walked the streets. Nonetheless, knowing the Captain made it extremely easy for us to get inside without anyone dying aided the decision to meet him tonight. ★

~Hm. I take it he didn't know about the under-mountain pathway the Ma'ab found to sneak in?~

★*No. None of them did except me. Unfortunately, I think Vesram was near enough at the same time to recognize my bending the light. The Sathoet likely pointed his mistress there while I checked the south entry point. Then Vo'traj found that spirit to guide them to the crypt.* ★ He sighed. ★*I smelled the demonblood then, but too faintly. I wasn't certain what kind of Abyssal influence it was, whether living or an object the Ma'ab carried.* ★

Like Soul Drinker, he didn't say.

The dagger was a demonic object I was as reluctant to use as Mourn had been reluctant to mention the living presence. If I never drew it from its sheath while on this mountain, then Gavin's mission was going exceedingly well.

I'd take that, should it come to be.

★*I believe the Captain keeps the rock quarry open for citizens to escape,* ★ Mourn continued. ★*Either Keros forgot about it and Isboern never mentioned it, or Keros told him to seal it and he chose not to.* ★

I arched my brow. ~He'd disobey his superiors that blatantly?~

★*Isboern told us his duty: defending the wall and the city's people from the Bishops. To keep peace. He's a flexible problem solver who didn't grow up here, bringing new thoughts to the commoners that challenge the Bishops' version of the world. At the same time, desperation has been escalating for weeks, especially when the Witch Hunters started conscripting and preventing Augran traders from leaving.* ★

I wrinkled my nose. ~What's the point of that?~

★*An exercise in raw power. I assume forcing others to do what they'd rather not sounds familiar to a Red Sister?* ★

~Hmph.~

He smiled at my expression, and Jael blinked as she glanced between us. ★*But Reprisal has heard talk that those non-natives intent on sabotage or causing trouble to retaliate against the Bishops have been allowed to escape, probably through the mansion cellar controlled by the Templars.*

~Ah. Keeping peace.~

Indeed. More than one way to do it. Isboern has even looked the other way for a few wealthy families who have disappeared, but it has been too volatile to organize anything larger for the poorer citizens who cannot fight, until now.

~Why he's so willing to talk to us.~

We can trust him as an honest negotiator. As a psion, he's also capable of knowing who to rely on and can sense when someone has changed their mind about him. This meeting has the lowest chance of betrayal of any I've attended in four hundred years, so Krithannia and I will do our part to keep the peace.

A clandestine meeting of high risk with low chance of betrayal.

This was a new one for me as well.

~And I'll do mine.~

We were in the quarry tunnels themselves when Jael nudged me, frowning as she signed, *Have you two been talking this entire time?*

I grimaced and took hold of my earlobe with the pearl attached. *Yes, I'm sorry. It's a magic item, like a message pellet but reusable. There weren't enough for everyone on this mission.*

She squinted as Mourn paused, reading our exchange.

We'll share anything critical, I signed. *You will know. It's been some reflection on our strategy so far, now that we made it this far.*

Strategy talk? she answered with a smirk. *Fine. I can wait. I just wanted to know why you were making faces at him. He's a lot harder to read than you are.*

My mouth twisted, choosing not to mention how much I enjoyed watching his tail. *Noted, Sister. I'll practice to be less telling.*

Jael shrugged as if she didn't care.

The freshly scratched quarry tunnels led to another, hidden passage much older, with worn stairs leading down rather sharply before rising back up. An underground stream flowed at the lowest point where the rain and spring water collected, no doubt joining the healthy flow of water running down the canyon. Crossing it was a Dwarven-built bridge still standing after centuries.

When the way levelled out and Mourn took three successive corners before pushing open a segment of stone, I realized we'd walked straight into an underground cellar. The space was large with stores enough to feed...

~*A mansion?*~

Indeed. One of the noble families who fled first since their land connects to this passage. The Templars are using the space above as a makeshift armory and barracks to protect the escape route.

~*Couldn't those who have left tell the Ma'ab about it? Especially those resenting the Bishops and Hunters?*~

Absolutely, they could. But, one problem at a time.

I felt something familiar shift in our link then.

Morixxyleth!

Krithannia. We're in the cellar—

Hold there a moment. I'm so glad I caught you!

Mourn's tail coiled. *Do we **not** head to the garden?*

Correct. A group of novitiates are gathered there, and the Captain has needed to place more of his men on the wall to keep an eye on them. The Temple search for Keros has begun to question the Inquisitor.

Mourn arched his scaly brow in obvious comment. *The man Keros pushed out the window is under suspicion after His Holiness's disappearance with a black witch?*

None of the Bishops saw that. With their highest Temple enforcer siding with the Wall Captain to control the Witch Hunters, of course they suspect insurrection.

Indeed. This could also be the sorcerer's nudging.

Agreed, though it does seem odd if he's come for Sirana.

True, but in line if he told Keros about the thurible.

She sighed. *Yes. Can you meet us at the old library in the Bestirs Quarter? We just arrived and are expecting Captain Isboern soon. There's a connecting passage, I believe?*

I remember. Through the sewer. We'll shed the stench before entering.

I grimaced at Jael, warning her. *Prepare to hold your breath.*

Fortunately, we were not expected to somehow squeeze through the "shit pipes" where the city's filth left the wealthy quarters and washed down the slopes. Mourn found a crawl space which took us first to another maze below the city, this one laying outside the Temple walls. They were dusty and stale but relatively clean.

How long had the Tundar Dwarves lived here to build all these?

From there, we needed to enter the widest drain located directly beneath the city's "Temple street" to reach the segmented passages on the other side, and that space collected much of the refuse from the Temple and all those living closest to it.

At least we're not downstream from the Butchers' Market, Mourn remarked as we all pinched our noses. He ducked his head to avoid brushing horns and hair along the filthy ceiling.

~*Where's that?*~

Other side. Northwest quadrant where the messy work gets done. The wind tends to take the smell away from those higher on the mountain.

~*Unsurprising. Pretty sure it would be like that in Sivaraus if we had wind.*~

Also in the caste system of Ennikar, from what I've seen and heard.

~*And Augran?*~

It's more patchwork as close villages grew together over time. I've seen filthy areas be cleaned and rejuvenated when the Tundar and Yungar put their heads together. Taiding is like a cleaner version of this but with less ability to change without some strong explosions and a lot of falling rock.

~*Heh. Interesting.*~

Finally, we escaped the sewer and moved into another series of underground spaces much like the first. The thorough lack of debris suggested whoever had once lived here had enough time to move everything out. Then it seemed to be just…closed up and forgotten.

We entered the old library in the same way we'd left the mansion: through a tight squeeze of stone and dead air connecting a random hall in the maze to the library's cellar wall. To speak of patchworks, that was what Manalar belowground had become. Only a wandering Dragonchild keeping tabs on a version of the city he had helped to create would care to memorize this all over hundreds of years.

A good thing for us.

Mourn climbed the creaking cellar stairs at the same time we heard footsteps above the floorboards coming toward us, followed by the sound of a bar being slid away. My bodyguard's tail signaled all was well, and my eyes soon confirmed this after we'd climbed up into the tiny kitchen to greet Krithannia and Torch without speaking.

Next, they led us across the hall toward a large room of shelves filled with books. Before we reached it, I glanced up, spotting Wolf and more of Reprisal atop the first flight of stairs. They relaxed and signed welcome before melting back out of sight.

Gavin was there as I walked into the room, a tall, lanky figure in dark grey robes perusing to his great contentment. He barely acknowledged me as his pupils flickered and most of his attention lay elsewhere. I let him be, greeting Deshi and his two brothers who kept watch for shadows at the two small, opaque windows on the ground floor, each of us listening for boots outside.

The daylight faded as we had arrived at sunset. Now that we stood above ground, the city noise outside seemed too quiet for its size.

Jael nudged me to sign, *If the god-blood isn't here yet, how did the pale one know the garden was no good?*

Mourn read that and responded. *A reasonable concern, Jael. Reprisal noticed the sudden increase of the guard on the south wall and a Templar walking the perimeter alone where he could be seen. Wolf recognized him as one who held the Ma'ab chain beneath the Temple and approached with caution. The Templar tossed him a bloodstone and kept going. Krithannia received the details of the message in Isboern's voice.*

Watching our hands, Krithannia pulled out a dark green gemstone streaked with red, signing, *True.*

Huh. So Humans can use that method when necessary.

No doubt a damning confession if a Bishop had gotten hold of that and heard the Captain's words, it also proved his sincerity and the trust he placed in the men closest to him in passing word to the right pair of pointed ears. It wasn't like that stone could repeat the words once shared, not like a written note failing to be destroyed.

We spread out to keep watch, with Mourn, Jael, and me near the front door. The Yungians guarded the two ground level windows which were open a crack for fresh air and to better hear outside. Half of Wolf's team guarded the barred cellar door while he and the rest claimed any windows on the second floor.

We had nothing to do but wait and dared not light the room after sunset passed and darkness fell. I heard Gavin's sigh as he learned that Dark Sight wasn't too good for reading and finally put the last book away.

Isboern was late, and we quickly grew tense about that.

~*That is a question,*~ I thought, sneaking food despite my nerves. ~*Is he going to march here in full armor surrounded by Templars?*~

That was the thought for the garden, Mourn replied with chagrin. *They would have cause to be near that wall. Less so in visiting a library off limits for decades.*

~*Off limits?*~

I am surprised they have not destroyed it before. Few alive can read all it contains, and one of them is being held upstairs taking a restful nap.

I smirked to learn only one Human lived here alone. ~*What does it contain?*~

Written history, life and war stories, and legends in varied languages. Dwarven texts on construction, planning, and design.

~*Anything about the Grey Maiden or Elves?*~

Krithannia and I collected what little there was about Elves, for that had more value to us. We left the texts about death reverence here on the chance it would be rediscovered. We couldn't leave too many holes on the shelves.

I frowned. ~*Where do you think Isboern got the idea to suggest meeting here if he didn't have an easy way to justify his presence?*~

I have a suspicion, and Krithannia agrees. If I'm right, but something turned bad for Isboern, we'll leave here and head for the Temple pool tonight. We couldn't wait any longer in that case."

~Hm. What's your suspicion?~

Not what, but who. High Inquisitor Kegyek would be one of the few with access to this door, and Isboern just saved his life.

I grimaced and looked at Jael, who went rigid against the wall.

★What?★ she demanded. ★What's that look?★

★Well… What would you do if the man in black showed up here as part of negotiations?★

She narrowed her eyes, grinding her teeth, then shrugged it off to lean back against the wall. ★I'd watch him, but heed you or Shadow about what happens to him. As I agreed.★

Mourn smiled a little, and I exhaled with soft relief and a nod.

Soon after that semi-pleasant surprise, we heard footsteps and someone opening the gate outside then leaving it open. Everyone climbed to their feet and put hands on their weapons. We waited as Mourn slipped behind the door, listening as someone stepped quietly up the stone steps.

The Dragonchild flicked out his tongue thrice, signing and sending through the pearls simultaneously: *High Inquisitor. Alone.*

Shit.

No one interfered as the white-haired man unlocked the door and opened it wide enough to let himself in. He carried a lantern, soft orange light filling the entry hall as he closed the door swiftly behind him.

Kegyek froze, staring at Mourn's chest before looking up, his pale face becoming ghostly as dark eyes widened with terror. The half-blood snatched the lantern before the man could drop it and closed his other dark hand around his throat. Any noise he meant to make did not escape.

I heard Jael snicker.

"*Ondi'el Isboern?*" Mourn asked, granting the man enough air to answer.

"*Chegiado,*" the man whispered, gasping out further details in Manalar's rolling tongue as Gavin appeared in the doorway of the library to listen.

"He's coming," Mourn translated aloud for Jael and me, as the only two unable to understand him. "Isboern asked him to unlock the gate and the door and tell whoever he found here that he'd be here within the hour."

"Do we believe him?" Gavin asked.

"Not completely, but he did arrive alone. No one else stands on these grounds at present."

So, we'd discover the truth of the Inquisitor's message, one way or another.

"Interesting to see the Temple keeps one death mage to this day," Gavin said, startling the whitebeard. "You're not as old as you appear, despite having been pushed from a tower this afternoon."

"Wh-what do you speak, creature?" Kegyek rasped, catching his feet as Mourn released him, visibly rattled as he looked between my unique allies with mounting concern.

While Krithannia, Jael, and I stayed out of his direct sight, Deshi poked his head out of the door frame, peering at the Inquisitor with intense eyes as if warning him not to try anything. Kegyek gasped softly to see yet another foreign face.

"What deal with devils has the Capitan made?" he demanded.

"I'll point out a devil to you if I see one, Inquisitor," Mourn rumbled. "Let's knock that stubborn untruth aside to save time. We're neither devils nor demons."

Although Kegyek was successful in tearing his eyes from Gavin and Deshi back to Mourn, his crush of expression didn't have the space left on his face to show much comprehension. "Untruth...? Then what are you?"

"Different kinds of mages, of other races which share the world with yours. We're nothing stranger than that if you care to look deeper."

The man recoiled. "You *cannot* be just...mages."

"We are. I believe you even failed to get a 'demoness' confession out of the last mage you tortured without understanding."

Jael took the cue and leaned out from behind Mourn then, glaring at

Kegyek in an odd echo to Deshi and Gavin as I listened to the Manalari's racing heartbeat.

"Nomilu sancji," he whispered, clasping his sunburst pendant. "Where is Emil Keros?"

"He run," Jael said, tilting her head toward our bodyguard. "Keros run and piss when he see *this*. Will *you* run, too?"

She grinned like it was a dare and she'd love to give chase. Kegyek trembled and chose not to move.

Instead, he asked Mourn, "What will you do with Capitan Isboern?"

"Why do you want to know?" came the reply.

"Does he walk into a trap?"

"Again, why do you want to know?"

"We… need him," the Inquisitor said. "The city cannot fight the Ma'ab without him. The Bishops cannot do this alone."

"Ah. I'm glad to hear you realize this."

"Took you long enough," Wolf said upstairs, making the man jump to glimpse the additional manpower.

The Dragon son glanced toward Reprisal with a chuckle. "What will we do with the Captain? We will bargain with him, as agreed. This assumes no one interferes and he truly sent you to tell us he'd be late."

"It's true!" Kegyek insisted. "But a bargain? For what?"

"That is for him to discuss."

"For his soul?"

Several men guffawed, giving the Inquisitor an even better guess how many eyes were watching him.

"No," Mourn answered, drawing out the word. "Again, we are mages, not devils, and we do not buy souls. The Godblood is interested in saving the soul of his city, however, despite the corruption in that of its leaders."

Many of us wanted to laugh as the impulse to argue erupted clear on Kegyek's face, but he looked at Gavin as if remembering the remark about being pushed from a tower. As if remembering the fall itself.

The Deathwalker took it as an invitation, moving one step out into the main entrance with us. "I heard you were the one who uncovered the knowledge of where the sun shield was buried."

The Inquisitor gnashed his teeth, revealing his disgust. "How could you know, horrid Ma'ab traitor?"

"She told me."

The man's face drained of blood; all expression wiped by fear. "She?"

"The archivist who remains here. Unlike you, I am not from the Far North. She recognizes my heritage."

Kegyek reacted like his gut had been struck by a fist. "H-heritage? Where else *but* the Far North could one like *you* come from?"

Gavin straightened up and did something unusual, reaching to stretch the neck of his robe down to expose his pale, bony shoulder. He turned toward the Inquisitor enough to show us the sunburst scar branded into his skin. Deshi, getting the closest look, was aghast.

"My father was Archimandrite Petris Alazar at the Chirtu Monastery," my ally said like a confession as he pulled his robe up to cover the brand and faced us. "Perhaps you recall the name, Inquisitor?"

I studied the man. If I'd been reading a surprised Noble at Court, I'd have wagered he most certainly did.

"Archimandrite Alazar was poisoned," said the older man. "Some years ago. Most of the monastery was. Those who survived left. W-we closed it down."

"Good. It was a foul place haunted by resentful spirits."

"But Alazar never had a son," Kegyek stated, dismissing that remark. "Monks choose to abstain from bearing families."

The Deathwalker shrugged. "I witnessed quite early how few kept their vow of celibacy. I was proof regardless the Archimandrite succumbed to earthly appetites, as often as he beat me to keep quiet about it. I only wished I'd found where they buried the Ma'ab 'witch' who gave birth to me, because they certainly wouldn't have burned her in proper ritual. Unfortunately, I don't know where he hid her. Even questioning his ghost did not reveal this to me. False piety had the Archimandrite babbling convoluted innocence."

"I do not understand," Kegyek whispered. "What did he say? Why did he keep her long enough to make you…"

Something darkened the room, and the Inquisitor stopped talking as Gavin narrowed inhuman eyes. Then my ally lifted his shoulders as if to reject the unseen weight.

"She was a vulnerable runaway, perhaps?" Gavin suggested. "No one around to see them. Nowhere in Paxia she could work or eat without abuse. Astonishing as it seems, not every Ma'ab wishes to stay at Ennikar to be used and consumed. The most determined among the poor might leave if they have little to defend otherwise. Captain Isboern recognizes this because it's the same here. We come to negotiate for the common blood he wishes to free from a death trap."

Yet another column of the Manalari's temple seemed to topple over before Kegyek's eyes. Although it should have been simple to deny all these possibilities, I suspected that the black-robed man was aware of how the Archbishop mutilated young women like Lurili Derfoli behind closed doors. Just as well that he'd suffered by his Archbishop when they'd failed to break Jael.

Kegyek swallowed nervously, seeming to look from Gavin's tall frame to somewhere over his shoulder. Struggling for words at first, he forced out, "If you knew about the shield, do you also know about another artifact?"

"I do. A thurible, correct?"

"Um. Yes."

"We were working on this when you arrived, Inquisitor," Gavin said. "I imagine you saw the carvings of the shrouded woman with crows down in the crypt."

A muscle flexed in Kegyek's jaw. "And if I did?"

"The shield that Isboern carries represents Musanlo. The thurible represents the Grey Maiden, from long before the Ma'ab arrived. They are both part of the heritage of Mount Sonai. If you can accept this new knowledge, perhaps you can assist by unlocking the upper chambers of this library."

"Assist…?" The Inquisitor gasped. "Where is Chaplain Vorbines?"

"He's fine!" Wolf called down. "He's sleeping comfortably in his little bedroom up here."

Most of us had smiles on our faces as the Archbishop's former interrogator peered around us. His battered mind must be desperate to stitch together possibilities which had never fit in his life's tapestry before. I thought it impressive that Kegyek hadn't sunk onto the floor in a stupor to stare at the wall.

"Will you unlock the upper chambers, Inquisitor?" Mourn asked directly. "There may be something regarding the shield which will help Isboern as well."

"Um," Kegyek said, reaching into his pocket where he held his keys to this place. "I, uh…wait, as well?" He looked at Gavin with a shudder. "You were in the crypt… Did you *find* the thurible?"

The Deathwalker folded his arms. "We did."

The man blinked. "May I see it?"

"No."

"What do you mean to do with it?" He sounded angry.

"I shall bear it here against the Ma'ab, in the name of my Lady, Nyx, also known as the Grey Maiden, the Grave Mother, the guide for the dead. She whose form you've seen, Inquisitor, and whose anchored spirits remain on this sacred mountain to guide the living who can see them regardless of their worship."

Again, Kegyek lifted his eyes to look over Gavin's shoulder at nothing visible. I'd never seen someone quake so while ignoring so many warm bodies with weapons.

"V-very well," he said, catching his breath. "I will unlock the doors."

Mourn and Jael moved out of his way, though the Inquisitor hesitated until the Deathwalker moved to climb the stairs. Kegyek missed Krithannia and me in the shadows as he slipped by Mourn with head turned away, his eyes fixed on something we couldn't see.

Suddenly, the whitebeard pressed his back to the wall at the base of the stairwell before continuing, leaving a suspiciously wide gap between him and Gavin on the way up.

Idly, I wondered if the topic of Gavin's eyes and strange black teeth and fingernails might be broached where I couldn't hear. I imagined how Kegyek might react to learning that, even knowing the Witch Hunters always made things worse for common people, that they really had chased after the wrong monk's son this time.

Gavin intended to make it cost all the Bishops everything they clung to. I smirked.

Once the two death mages had gone from my sight, their steps making the ceiling creak, Mourn's tail finally signaled a change outside. I listened, hearing horses loping along cobblestone not close but not too far away. Once that had stopped and all was quiet for a time, I waited for the fall of boots on armored men next.

Instead, I heard the psion's voice, one of the clearest and most soothing experiences of my life. The darker thoughts from before washed away.

~*Legend, Elves, and Guildsmen, can you hear me? Are you here in the archives?*~

I replied without effort. ~*We are here, Godblood. We are waiting for you.*~

The mindlink refocused with purpose, narrowing its net around me, and strengthened even further with clarity. Somehow, all in one moment, I knew what he knew.

Willven had the same four men with him as when we'd spoken down below, no one else. They'd masked their auras after dismounting and leaving their horses where they were unlikely to be found. Their footsteps were muffled by magic; both the shine and clink of their armor were muted.

No minds but theirs sneaked through the green toward the forbidden building. Most alive in the city never knew what was in it.

This was the first time these five would see the inside of the library.

~*We come in peace,*~ Isboern said. ~*I pray you can and will help. I've brought Jael's belongings with me. They are undamaged.*~

~*Oh! Thank you. The door is unlocked. Kegyek is here and unharmed, if a little frightened. We are ready to act through the night.*~

The Captain tasted my honesty as I could taste his.

Remembering the others, I forced my heavy tongue to work between my lips. "Five men, here to negotiate safe passage for those who want to leave. No one else. We're safe. No betrayal."

We know, Krithannia said softly through her pearl. *We can feel it.*

Well done, Mourn added.

I wasn't looking, but I could feel his grin.

Broad enough to show fang.

CHAPTER 25

THE TEMPLARS AND THEIR CAPTAIN WERE SMILING AND HOPEFUL BUT NONETHE-less seemed pressured for time. It wasn't hard to guess why.

"Forgive me, but may we skip the formalities?" Isboern began, holding out a bundle wrapped in a familiar black cloak.

"Of course," Krithannia answered, accepting this on Jael's behalf. "Speak."

The Captain glanced at me, bowing his chin. "May we negotiate the details through a mind connection? I didn't know until now we had the option, but it's much faster and clearer than language. The more of the night we conserve, the more lives we save."

"Are you willing?" Mourn asked me directly.

"Willing for what, exactly?" I asked.

"Tell me if I miss something, Captain," my bodyguard said, "but I understand the mind connection would require you and Sirana to convey the 'non-language' details between our two groups, evaluating resources, goals, motives, and roles at once to decide the tactics and strategy."

"Correct," the Captain replied. "What might take two hours will take minutes."

That sounded good.

Jael poked me. "Why you?"

She was concerned, waving away her bundle as Krithannia set it in the corner for later. I froze with my words stuck in my throat. Isboern's face pinched slightly as he noted the exchange, then enlightenment entered his rich blue eyes.

"Ah," he began, "is this ability of yours a new gift, like Jael's?"

The Captain wanted honesty between us now, not later.

"New gift?" Jael asked, looking between Mourn and me.

Hoo bua...

~*I sense your fear,*~ Isboern said, caressing my mind softer than a message pellet. ~*It's the same as hers. And I can see the connections between you, Jael, and the Legend son. They're not yet fully linked, but they will be. You cannot avoid it, so you must tell her if you will fight together. If you do not, your risk and losses have no words.*~

Fuck.

Barely a second had passed as I shrugged and turned to my Sister, speaking in Davrin. *"Um, so it should be impossible that you're a mage now, right? But you have a lot to learn because you can't...avoid it?"*

She frowned, cocking an eyebrow. She said nothing.

"I've been struggling with similar change since before I met you. The Elders didn't want me to tell anyone because the Prime would kill me."

I paused when both her eyebrows lifted high together. She waited for more. I hated that tears crept into my vision as I prepared to speak it.

"I fought the same clan of Tragar as you did during your trial, but it... went bad. Really bad. Something during that fight changed how my mind and aura works. Gavin and Mourn can both see it. They've known and still, um...work with me."

Jael stared at me, glanced at the blond Captain, and back. *"Oh. You're... psionic now? Like him?"*

"Like him?" I thought she meant Kain at first until I followed her eyes. *"Oh, like Isboern?"*

"Yeah."

Well. That was the more flattering comparison.

"But not as strong. I need to learn things."

Jael swirled her finger in the air to indicate our group. *"Starting with this? A mind plan?"*

"Well...yes. It would help."

"That's no shit." One corner of her lips drew up as tension eased.

I remembered to breathe then, looking between my bodyguard, the Guild Mistress, and Isboern. "Ah, yes. I am willing."

The Captain placed his armored fist over his heart. "Thank you."

"Who needs to be present?" Mourn asked him.

"Ideally, all decision-makers you have in this building."

"Does Gavin count?" Jael asked.

"I'm not sure," I said. "He's upstairs with the Inquisitor looking up books."

This remark seemed surreal to the Templars, who all looked like we'd lightly slapped their faces with a glove.

"Well, this is more about the refugees than the Bishops," Krithannia said. "But we should ask him."

"For its worth," Isboern said, "I will not include the High Inquisitor in this, just the men you see here. You are correct, elder, this is about the common people, not anything going on in the Temple."

We touched base with our teams, but in the end, Gavin chose not to join us once he understood what it entailed; he remained upstairs where he would find more of what truly interested him. Similarly, Jael understood and was anxious but also not wishing to fall farther behind in these swift-flowing events.

"The experience will help your training," Mourn said in Davrin. *"You will get caught up more quickly, and you will know Sirana better, which is good for both of you."*

Jael firmed up her jaw. *"Sounds good. I'll do this."*

Wolf, Crow, and Torch joined us when we climbed back down into the cellar, leaving seven Guildsmen on the main floor to stand guard.

"We won't be long," Krithannia promised them.

With proper warning, Isboern summoned brighter light downstairs for him and his men; even then, the rest of us squinted and rubbed our eyes.

"Have you learned anything about the shield?" Krithannia asked aloud. "Gavin said the legend around it suggests the magic varies from bearer to bearer."

"Ah, no, I have not," the psion said with chagrin. "There hasn't been much time, but I will gladly hear all that you know in our meeting."

"It isn't much," said the Guild Mistress, "but I'll bring it forward. How do we start?"

Willven Isboern began removing one glove, and the Templars flanking him did the same. I looked down at my boots and chuckled, wondering why I was surprised.

"We'll be holding hands?" Wolf asked.

"In a chain or circle?" Krithannia added.

Isboern shook his head. "No. That's…better for some spells, I understand, but in this case, we must all reach in with one hand to create a center point."

He and his Templars demonstrated first. With arms outstretched and shoulders touching, they stacked their hands upon each other.

Crow shared a grin with Wolf. "I've seen this. A huddle?"

"Correct," Isboern answered with welcoming confidence. "Will you join us to plan, our legends and allies of Augran?"

It was a tight fit adding three more men, three Elves, and one large hybrid, but soon enough, all our hands created a towering "center point" and a strange sensation of flowing contact. My hand happened to be in between Jael's and Mourn's, with his below and hers on top; I wasn't complaining.

The psion reached out to me. ~*When you are ready, Sirana, look in my eyes. I will guide, you will anchor.*~

I hoped I would figure out in time what that meant.

The Godblood of Manalar smiled when I looked up. ~*Trust and you shall.*~

WILLVEN'S ENTOURAGE SHARED THE NAMES THEIR FRIENDS CALLED THEM.

Robi, Imran, Erik, and Sohl.

Over the last five years, these four Templars had grown closest to Capitan Isboern's vision for their city. They believed in their capacity to change and draw back from punitive living and become less like their worst enemies.

They had experienced the "god view" with their blessed leader already, and they looked forward to bearing witness from an even higher view.

★Because Sirana will anchor us, Godblood?★

~She already is, my brothers of hope. We can feel the years behind her will and that of her sister-in-battle, yes?~

★Yes. Older than our grandfathers, yet they are not old women. Their years are young ones, like ours but passing slower.★

~Indeed, do not forget. See their extraordinary elders above us, and also see the defenders who believe in the same capacity for change.~

★Like us.★

★Those men are like us.★

~Much like us. Go on. Reach out. Don't be afraid.~

I sensed from the Templars that this beginning differed from the "god view" of previous huddles, when Willven had acted as both the anchor and the guide. He could not explore the "farther" knowledge without losing time, direction, and clarity with those minds not yet ready to cross the plane.

~Whatever that means...~

~When you are ready, Sirana, you'll cross the plane.~

In this moment, however, Willven bestowed his gratitude as he extended our mental bond, slowly at first, gathering and stretching our wills to reach our current potential. A minimum of two mind mages could weave one shared moment between many individuals, tightening many threads of thought into one still-point in the center of the continuous, natural storm of overlapping and conflicting thoughts.

This entwining of our minds wasn't invasive or forceful. The boundaries between our shared knowledge and our senses of self did not blur and mix as it had when I'd lacked both an anchor and guide.

Like our hands piled atop each other, our minds aligned in an intuitive order based on interconnection. One psion, me, grounded the plaited strands of thought to our bodies, while the second, more powerful mind mage reached out to the edge of our thoughts.

Willven Isboern rose above the noise of the minds' storm; we held together as one long thread of knowledge. He brought us with him into peace and calm, into certainty of bearing the will to understand what we'd created.

Our varied languages did not impede introductions as we offered our preferred names of the Guild and its allies.

Wolf, Crow, Torch, Shadow, Cloud, Sirana, and Jael.

~Greetings.~

Willven, Robi, Imran, Erik, and Sohl.

We knew we bore different purposes; we knew and accepted that we had other desires and goals in why we were here, but we agreed on one thing. Everyone was willing to help women, children, and others who could not fight to find the Dwarven gate.

A magic gate taking them closer to Augran.

We did not know this was here.

We could not have used it if we had.

~Yes. We need your help. What is the best way to work together?~

There are three ways out, Shadow shared.

The first passage was known: the shorter southside quarry through which the Guild had come and the Templars kept guarded. This was easiest to reach but had the longest run over open ground to the safety of the cave.

Second, the longer labyrinth beneath the Temple leading to the base of the mountain. This was difficult to reach while the Bishops kept the public out. But, once through the maze and standing outside, it had the shortest run to the safety of the cave.

Third, the northern passages through the system of cisterns and stairs, leading under the wall and directly into the hills known to be watched by Ma'ab scouts. Undesirable to attract such attention from both their enemies and those staying to defend the wall.

Nonetheless, Shadow said, *when circumstances change, know that this pathway is here. It is probably the easiest for the wounded to navigate. As of early this morning, the passageway within the hills remained hidden and unused recently.*

~We must watch that vulnerability. For anyone leaving tonight, the south wall is both safest and most accessible, even though it is farthest.~

What about the Ma'ab watching in the hills? Wolf asked.

Willven's response did not feel celebratory. ~I do not have the man-power with proper training, so will ask for strategic Guild assassinations, either voluntary or paid, to delay the discovery of the Dwarven gate as long as possible. Whatever I can provide you to compensate for the efforts on our behalf, please ask.~

A blitz of an exchange passed between Wolf and Crow, too fast to read but their thought circled back soon enough to rejoin the pool of thought.

Our teams who've come first can keep that simple for you, Captain. Templar and civilian kills are forbidden; we will only run or incapacitate to evade capture in the case of mistaken identity. Ma'ab kills are necessary to meet objectives.

I sensed a round of nods from the Templars.

Witch Hunter kills, however, Wolf continued, *are voluntary and encouraged, as we've trained as long as you have to break the back of their organi-zation given the chance. We believe this is our chance. Do not set obstacles in our way, and our actions will benefit your people.*

We felt the dissonance and conflict from the Templars at this bargain. Erik's thought was strongest and became clear first: *There are a hundred and twenty strong men in that 'organization,' and some can use magic. We may need them to fight.*

But will they? Wolf challenged. *Or will they stay in the Temple comfortably guarding the Bishops? When things turn for the worse outside where the army is fighting, will 'God's warriors' look for the first opportunity to escape and meet up with their brothers along the Big Ker? Do they have **any** accountable duty, as you do, in protecting the wall and the city itself?*

~No, they do not.~ Willven's answer broke the truth to his men. ~Their duty is to each other and to enforce the Bishops' laws. Justice does not matter to them, for they do not serve the people and do not want to. No one is worthy enough. Those below them are always a source of thievery, violence, and those corrupted by witchery. No matter the circumstances, nearly all have been found guilty once they are accused. Only self-exile or strong connections save them.~

The sorrow and disappointment were palatable.

~We've all heard the stories of what happens in the countryside, and we all know they are little more than intimidators and bludgeons within the city walls. They make our duty harder, having to ask for trust and cooperation with our city. They see us as competition for influence and seek only to appear more powerful than the Templars at any cost and interpretation of the law.~

We recognized the proof in their experiences.

Then I propose, Wolf bargained, *the Templars do not step in to protect Witch Hunters and, in return, the Guild will take care of Ma'ab who threaten the way to the jump gate. Any Witch Hunters who **stay** with you at the wall are the safest they'll ever be from us.*

I heard Willven exhale. ~Understood. We will not protect the Witch Hunters from their Reprisal, especially near the Temple or otherwise far from the wall.~

The terrible joy within the smiling Guildsmen mirrored that of their targets when they found a new witch. They knew this and had for a long time. *Do not regret, Captain. We are the monsters they created.*

~I know. And I am sorry for that.~

~Gavin will be joining you,~ I remarked. ~Made not just by Witch Hunters but by the Temple men themselves.~

A volatile mixture of laughter and satisfaction surrounded us when I revived the fresh encounter in my mind between our Deathwalker and the High Inquisitor.

~Ah. So that's what happened before we arrived,~ Willven mused.

Indeed, and Sirana is right, thought Cloud. *Without Bictrius's attack at Troshin Bend, the Deathwalker would not be here now. He is the greatest threat to the Bishops, though they do not know it.*

~Hm. *Consequences coming back around…~*

And like Reprisal ready to break the Dyos Guerrimos, the Deathwalker is ready to reveal what the Bishops have kept secret about the Temple pool. ★

Indeed, and even the Inquisitor knows it's coming, ★ Torch observed. *He's afraid of Gavin speaking to the ghost in the library.* ★

As the Bishops are afraid of the people talking with the Godblood, ★ agreed Imran. *Afraid the less tutored will learn what lies outside the walls and question the mage right to rule.* ★

And more, question their exclusive right to Pisc'sagrad, ★ Robi added.

Shadow breathed in, drawing our focus. *Our visions are compatible, at least. Please show us what happened after the Inquisitor was pushed from the tower. Where do the Bishops stand?* ★

We heard first of the arguments and bickering amid the hectic and floundering search for Emil Keros. No one here had witnessed it, but the only official solution to emerge and be passed to the Captain and Inquisitor was attempting to prepare the collective defense spells without the Archbishop.

~Which they've never done. They are afraid.~

I'm surprised one isn't jostling to replace him, ★ Jael remarked, *and hoping he's never found.* ★

She makes a good point, ★ Shadow said. *What about Cognate Horus? Is he absent or presently involved?* ★

Willven's mind sharpened as he followed the meaning of the question. ~Cognate Horus…?~

We received a memory of a man with hazel-green eyes and deeply tanned skin, he was about a decade younger than Keros, blond with silver hairs his temples.

~I've received my last two missives from him, so he's acting leadership in Keros's absence.~

Have you been near him in the last day? ★

~I have not.~

If you see him, test if he's wearing a mask. The real Horus may be dead. ★

What? ★

How could anyone infiltrate the Bishops?! ★

Within the Temple, no less!

What does the Guild know?

Sensing the answer first, Willven gazed at me, the anchor near the ground, and I grimaced inside.

~I am sorry. On the same night the Witch Hunters murdered Gavin, I awakened a much older soul within Brom Troshin. The sorcerer was wearing a mask, but I knocked it off. And he knew we were headed to Manalar.~

Sirana also saw one of his agents on the Temple grounds, Shadow said, offering us an image of the skin hunter I'd traveled with. *Mathias Briar has followed Sirana twice on behalf of Brom Troshin. He was among the people who witnessed you save Inquisitor Kegyek, but he fled before you received the shield.*

The Templars' thoughts had sobered a lot.

~One of the ancients you warned was watching,~ Willven said.

Correct, Captain.

~How many more?~

I wait for sure tells.

~Very well, but I am not sure if I can get into the Temple tonight to confirm if Horus is himself or not.~

That wasn't the deal, Captain. Let the Bishops hide in their palace while you prepare your people to move under the wall tonight. The Guild will guard their path and deal with the Ma'ab. If the Temple is compromised by someone other than the Ma'ab, it will make no difference until the Northern army makes its first move, which is likely to be infiltration.

The Godblood refocused at once. ~Understood.~

Tell us what your reports say about the Ma'ab host approaching the walls and setting up their camps.

~Ah yes, why we can't stay long.~

We collected the string of concerning but unsurprising updates over the early evening. Of course, the Manalari were outnumbered three men for every five of those massive males from the Far North. Mount Sonai's mages were all male and specialized in defending the city while the fighters knew its best tactics using the land.

And the Ma'ab's magical capability?

Their Ma'ab mages are well-hidden at the moment.

Most of them will be female of small stature, Cloud stated. *From a distance, they may look like a girl child, but they are grown women and dangerous mages.*

I felt and recognized the source of dismay from the Templars.

Our men will hesitate, Imran thought.

Your enemies are counting on that, Shadow replied. *The women present in their camps will be well-trained death mages and act nothing like Manalari women. You mustn't treat them the same way. Any female Ma'ab should be priority targets even above their Hellhounds. Watch long enough, and you'll see the men take lethal attacks to protect them. They tend to cluster around one woman and act as bodyguards, though, due to competitiveness, Ma'ab women don't tend to cluster around each other.*

The Templars accepted this odd information which I could've mistaken for Davrin in overhearing it, if not for the size of the males.

~Then, before I forget, ancient one,~ Willven turned to the Naulor, ~what do you know about the shield buried beneath the Temple?~

She smiled. *Do not fear it bending or breaking. It will not. The shield can protect those behind it against any evocative magic. Stand in natural light if you can. It responds to the sun and the moons the most. Listen to it, learn its name. As I've heard the tales, the enchantment appears to respond differently to each bearer. I would consider asking for what you need, though I cannot tell you what will happen. That is all I know.*

~I hear you, ancient. Thank you. Now, let's go over the numbers of what the Dwarves told you they could do...~

The exchange of plans and information continued. I experienced a strange flow of imagery trickling "down" to collect somewhere beneath my feet only for all of it to rise again as a clear, collective memory. This view of my world was stronger than any I'd ever perceived alone, riddled with nuance and intersecting detail.

Wow...

The column was awe-inspiring, embracing every facet and color I could imagine, turning on its own like the passing of each day to light up vivid patterns, knowledge, and faces as I reflected upon them.

This represented only the first night of the assault. Perhaps something would happen that cut the column of hopes short. Regardless, we'd saved hours creating something precious and lacked the worry of being misunderstood or sabotaged. Beautiful, in its way.

When we were done, Willven came back down, joining me as another anchor and the thread of minds unraveled like the motion of a soft breeze.

When we awoke, we were alone.

Wolf rubbed the dark brown hair on his face, amazed when he turned toward the cellar door at the top of the stairs. "Hey, how long has it been?"

"A few minutes," another Guildsman answered. "Why? Do you need something before you start?"

A wave of smiles broke in that cellar.

"No, we're done."

"What? You are?!"

"Indeed," Krithannia said.

"Let's get on with the rest of our night," Willven invited with an admittedly charming smile.

Once we'd collected on the main floor again, our gaunt death mage walked into view at the stairs on the second floor, his long, black hair falling in front of his eyes.

He showed Mourn and Krithannia a pouch that clacked with many pieces inside. "Do you need this?"

"We'll take it," the Dragonblood accepted, prepared to catch it once the Deathwalker lobbed it down to him, a good aim as Mourn snatched it.

"Are we leaving?"

"Not yet. Continue with your search."

My dour scholar didn't have to be told twice.

Once Gavin had gone from view again, Mourn turned and offered the bag to Isboern.

"What is this?" asked the Captain as he accepted it, weighing it in his palm without trying to open it.

"After tonight," Mourn answered, "*Pisc'sagrad* will be the most contested and volatile location on the mountain. Should the Bishops or any mage disrupt the pool, there's a strong chance of a surge that could take anyone with affinity to magic off their feet and unable to cast for a time."

Willven frowned, looking at his trusted men, who shrugged. "Would the Bishops know this?"

"Possibly not, since the last time the Bishops needed to invoke the power of *Pisc'sagrad* under pressure was when Keros was a young man. Without him, the chances of an uncontrolled surge are even higher. We came prepared and had twenty extra charms for allies. I regret that this is not enough for all your Templars, Captain, but if you trust us in this, you are welcome to pass them to whom you choose. One per mage should be enough to swiftly recover in the event of a pool surge. The rest should recover but may take longer. Non-mages will not be much affected and do not need charms."

The Manalari men's eyes were all wide.

"Thank you," Isboern said, closing his hand around the pouch. "We accept."

"Start gathering your first refugees as quietly as you can. The Guild will meet you at the Treynora mansion to show the way, and more are arriving soon to clear the Ma'ab out of the hills. If you need us, any Guildsman will be able to pass the signal to us."

"Thank you." Willven smiled at me. "And if you and I are in range, may I call to you as I did before?"

"Yes," I replied. "If I hear you, I'll pass the messages."

The Captain breathed out with the first suggestion he felt any nerves at all. "Let us go, then. And may we all be here to greet the sun at dawn."

Gavin remained upstairs with Kegyek when the Templars left. The night outside had barely changed, and the Inquisitor sounded to be opening a third door, explaining something about another story across the way. Our clandestine meeting had taken barely long enough for the Manalari men's steeds to catch their breath.

Feeling somewhat in awe of what had happened, I studied Jael's face when she plucked my sleeve. My Sister had understood all that I had.

"I can't believe how deep you got into this before I even got here," she muttered wryly.

"Heh. Wondering when or how we're going to leave?"

Jael's copper gaze flicked to Mourn and back. *"Not anymore. And, fuck, maybe the Valsharess already knows how this will end, but if She doesn't …?"*

I waited, inviting her to continue with my eyebrows, and she grinned.

"Wouldn't it be fun to show up in Sivaraus when they all thought we were dead?" She smirked. *"We'd report on what went down here like we knew what we were doing."*

I chuckled with her on the surface, nodding to acknowledge her willingness not only to see this through with me, but to return to the Western mountains.

She still wants to go home.

I stopped myself before my hand covered my gut. The thought of going back wasn't quite as entertaining when I knew I was the only one our Seer Queen *expected* to return. I was the one, She said, who *had* to return.

Retrieving more of my stash from the Dwarves while we waited, I almost…*almost* wished I knew what She might have seen for my baby on this mission. One way or the other, I could stop wondering if it was worth all the eating. As far as I knew, the Queen believed the sire was Shyntre. What had She said about him?

"He has not exposed his Vis to a cait in centuries…"

His Vis. How could She know this? Why had She spoken like a death mage about D'Shea's son?

"He has not sparked a new gift for Us in even longer. He has been spiteful."

How long since that last "gift," I wondered? Could Vesram the Sathoet remember anything about the Queen and Shyntre? He'd known Wilsira and Kerse; he was glad they were dead. He knew Lelinahdara, too, and claimed she had "turned" on his mother.

She was why they'd been sent to the Surface.

Vesram's mother might have been even less prepared for this world than I was to vanish near the Ley Tower. Her Sathoet would be enslaved long enough to have met Gavin's mother before she conceived him. What was more, only with Vesram's help would Ada run away to meet Archimandrite Alazar.

To bear Gavin. Only to die.

Decades later, I wondered if the Valsharess still held Visions about our missing blood. Had they been clear enough to compel me to search for this half-blood son in order to bring me to the Ley Tower and meet Ada's son? To imagine that the Valsharess *had* Seen all these connecting threads was, somehow, frightening to me.

If a Davrin Queen could parse a pattern out of the crush of changes on the Surface but only follow certain ends through pain and compulsion...

No wonder we quietly wondered if She was going mad.

Chapter 26

At first, Jael ignored her armor and equipment in the corner by the doorway, to the point I had forgotten about it until the nervous Inquisitor was called to lock the gate and front door. Once he had climbed reluctantly back upstairs, my Sister finally collected the bundle wrapped in her cloak and inspected the pieces, cautious and curious as she went over what was left.

Eventually, she traded out everything except the long daggers Mourn had loaned her. The Dwarven armor and cloak were tucked into a small closet, as no one opted to carry the extra weight, but Jael offered him back his borrowed belt along with her original daggers attached. The Dragonblood accepted, intending to keep them for her and trade back later.

Telling that she prefers his blades to those she brought from Sivaraus.

After that, Mourn spent some time with my Sister, following up on their Bargain while I hovered, watching their hands. They didn't say a lot, mostly staring at each other's eyes, sometimes with bare hands lightly touching and placed flat on their thighs. I understood enough to know she dedicated this time to learning when her aura hummed a "pitch" which was, for her, most open to magical possibilities. Although she wanted to learn how to attack, Mourn only taught her breathing.

When you're exhausted and about to fall, he signed, *this will keep you running.*

Meanwhile, the pieces of the war shifted around well into the night, as most of us remained in the library locked by the nervous Inquisitor. Bit-by-bit, we heard of the changes in the city through the pearls while Gavin remained upstairs.

The Witch Hunters have been pulled back to the Temple to stand guard through the night. The Temple mages haven't found Keros and the Bishops are concerned the grounds will be penetrated.

Several of us smirked.

We received other news not long after that.

The first evacuation has started. Most are non-native conscripts 'abandoning' their post after the Witch Hunters were called back to the Temple. Most are able to move fast without help.

The next pause was brief.

Confirming the arrival and dispersal of both assassination and escort teams from Augran. They brought a shitload of gear and supplies with them.

Excellent sign, Mourn replied. *We didn't feel the magic up here.*

Did Tamuril and Pilla leave? Krithannia asked.

No, Cloud, they're still there. Several tried to convince your sister to jump.

Did she say why she will not?

No, she did not.

The Naulor sighed.

Not much later, we heard of a skirmish on the north side.

An unsuccessful attempt to access the cisterns. The Ma'ab were sighted outside before getting under the wall. Lots of fire, five confirmed kills. Part of the regular fighters.

Mourn shook his head. *Diversion.*

That's what we're watching for. We've got Manalari men inside the northern passage and eyes on the outside. It's secure.

Do not relax. Either that is a prelude to action, or they've already done it. What happens in the Temple?

*A lot of activity among the novitiates, they're keeping the lights burning. We think they're making potions amid the other work. The Bishops are keeping to their chambers. *Witch Hunters are patrolling the halls, but the sanctum doors are sealed. We don't know if anyone is inside.*

Noted.

None of us who'd been in the huddle seemed tired or in need of sleep afterward, and I wasn't the only one to notice as Deshi and a few others yawned before midnight. More than four hours past sunset, and we felt rested as if we hadn't been running up and down the mountain through the previous day.

Isboern's doing, Mourn said to me as the rest of Reprisal napped while they could. *He was subtle about it, but I was the only one he couldn't figure out where the 'switch' was before I evaded him.*

~Evaded?~

His mouth turned wry. *Sleep works similarly in the younger races, regardless of length. He did no harm and certainly helped. But no one should attempt to influence how the To'vah rest.*

I smiled. ~Am I correct that you haven't 'rested' in that sense of falling unconscious since I met you?~

Hm. Correct.

~Should I be concerned?~

He lifted one broad shoulder, his eyes catching the moonlight filtering through the glass. *Not yet.*

Meanwhile, we heard the news that an easy twenty Ma'ab scouts had fallen to sleep rather suddenly in the eastern hills, unlikely to awaken until well after dawn. During that time, the first escapees had entered the cave and crouched behind the Dwarves, waiting for the next group before the mages offered the first jump to Kerut.

The Templars let the second group into the southern passage an hour ago. It's mostly women and children, so they're moving slower. No blood spilled so far, aside from a scraped shin or gouged hand while climbing by lantern.

Good news, Krithannia acknowledged, having given the order herself not to kill the Ma'ab scouts but to put them to sleep. *We expect certain commanders will be able to tell if their scouts are dead after some passage of time. We might as well delay finding out how long that is.*

While refugees tried to leave through the night, the goal was to avoid killing Ma'ab watchers, to keep everything breathing but quiet. Fortunately, the powders and darts had worked quickly and as expected after their potency had been scaled up for the enemy size.

~*What about Vo'traj?*~ I'd asked, and a rare grimace crossed Mourn's face.

Assuming she told them where she was going, they're going to miss her sooner than we'd like because of Vesram's escape. We've got eyes on the labyrinth entrance and just inside of it. We will wait and respond to what comes.

The first gate jump happened around an hour past midnight and was successful. I listened as Reprisal reported sixty conscripts and thirty Manalari women, each carrying one child, had passed through, while replenishments for the Guild and new gems for the Dwarves came in.

They have enough gems for five jumps, but at this rate, we only have time for two total before dawn.

That's still over two hundred people.

Yeah, but out of the thousand who want to go. It's going to be harder to hide the movement in the daytime, even with the clouds coming in. Crowds are starting to fill the streets too close to the Temple. The Crest watchtower is going to see them first.

Isboern is taking care of that, Mourn said. *Like the south wall, there should be no obstruction from the Crest.*

The Focus who mentioned the clouds rolling in was right. Long before dawn, overcast covered the moons, unexpectedly helping with the too-clear lines of movement. We received further reports of two more fleeing groups larger than the first making it into the canyon.

Sentries kept watch to the south and west in case Ma'ab scouts were sent near the quarry while continued distractions erupted at the northwest wall. This time, the Ma'ab were making trouble farther down the slope from where they'd attempted to break into the cisterns.

What are they doing now? Wolf asked Bear.

Flinging corpses over the wall, which are unfortunately standing back up even with broken bones. It's terrifying the Manalari but they've been chopping them to bits quickly and setting them ablaze.

That explained some of the false light we'd detected across the city, to where some had thought dawn had arrived from the wrong direction.

What are they using to fling the corpses? Mourn asked curiously.

Onager. One of thirteen built on the way. Lots of lumber in the Raguruos.

Heh. One of the Templars set it on fire after archers hit it with something volatile. Got a nice bonfire going.

One down. Twelve to go.

I was enjoying the mental images of these updates a little too much when Mourn reached to tap my knee and motioned to the stairs. I looked, seeing Gavin stepping down voluntarily. He carried no scrolls or bound works, but he did carry the thurible swinging from its chain. It looked cleaner.

Mourn and I got to our feet, and Krithannia joined us quickly from the far side of the shelves on the main floor.

"Where is Kegyek?" she asked.

"Upstairs with the archivist," Gavin replied. "He is weighing leaving. There is not much he can do at the wall or the Temple."

Mourn shrugged. "If the Templars will let him pass. He doesn't have much time to decide."

"What have *you* decided?" I asked the Deathwalker, for he was pondering something quite deeply.

His icy pupils slid up toward the stairs, suggesting he wouldn't say while the other death mage could be listening. Krithannia lightly touched his shoulder, shivered, but managed to receive a magical answer. Gavin remained wary of joining me psionically when not necessary, and I couldn't blame him given how I'd heard the voice of his Grey Maiden recently.

After the shard enters the pool and following the surge, Krithannia explained, *he is confident the thurible will allow him to reach his Lady and receive her boon for completing the task. He's decided what that boon will be.*

Yes? Mourn asked, his tail showing high interest.

The Naulor smiled. *To balance the loss of the Bishops for the city's defense, he will ask for neutral guardians to defend Pisc'sagrad until the battle is decided. The Manalari can then focus on the wall and their adversaries.*

Interesting, the Dragonchild replied. *That does sound like Nyx holds preference to deny the Ascended possession of Pisc'sagrad.*

Krithannia exchanged something with Gavin, who frowned in amusing balance to the pale Elf's smile. *He says, of course she does. The Grey Maiden was once worshipped here and would be again. She will not, however, decide mortal battles by her own power. The Bishops are the primary magical defense of the city, but if they are lost early in the battle through the actions of Nyx's messenger, then this is what she can offer that same messenger to rebalance the battle itself.*

Mourn considered this and dipped his head deeply. *Very well. We can accept this.*

Gavin straightened up and lifted his chin. His tendency to slouch caused me to forget how tall he really was.

He says we should go to the Temple now, Krithannia continued. *The Bishops will be gathering at first light to prepare their best defenses. Should the Deathless be among them, it's better if he does not perform the Archbishop's role. He could usurp the ritual, then we do not know if the shard will work, and we do not know if he will or will not act to benefit the Ma'ab.*

Agreed, Mourn responded. *So, we are ready to sever the connection, even without a first act of defense from the Temple against the Ma'ab?*

If the Deathless is present, Krithannia passed on, *this is necessary. If he is not, perhaps—*

She and Mourn jumped when a new report broke in.

Pack of five Hellhounds spotted on the inside of the wall, moving fast! North side heading east toward the Temple.

Mourn's pupils thinned as he growled, *Best assume at least ten got in. They'll split up on the streets. Tell Isboern to stay at the wall. We'll take the Temple.*

I cocked a brow. ~'Take' the Temple? As in take control?~

He smirked. *We are. As we have been planning to do since Yong-wen, Sirana.*

True, but I hadn't expected this moment to feel so different from the previous one. ~Is the rest of Reprisal coming?~

Yes. All of them.

Because the Temple was where the Witch Hunters were.

Along with the Bishops, possibly the Deathless, soon the Hellhounds, then the Guild. And us.

I glanced at Jael, whose face conveyed her awareness that something interesting had just happened. Her eyes sparkled with excitement.

Finally, time to move.

Reprisal forcibly removed both the former Inquisitor and the suddenly awakened Chaplain Vorbines from the library, taking their keys.

"Last chance, old men," Wolf said, pointing toward the wealthy district. "Run that way. Don't stop. And don't look back."

The Guildsman locked the gate and the door on the rattled and befuddled pair, handing the keys to Krithannia when he met the rest of us down in the cellar. A bit of magic helped to slide bars in place on each side of the door covering the entrance into the earthen space. Without another spoken word, we ducked into the dead space between the library and the underground passages, moving from there to the sewer.

This time, we didn't cross that smelly tunnel but ran uphill for some distance, trying not to slip on unrecognizable blobs or step in the trickling puddles. At last, Mourn found another slimy door, pulling it open with a metal hook that appeared in his hand, called from his bracer. He entered first to guide us into yet another segment of the city.

⋆This will take us back to the dungeon beneath the Temple,⋆ he said. *⋆From there, I know how to reach the sanctum.⋆*

Meanwhile, our two teams on the streets reported they were near the Temple grounds.

⋆We'll keep watch outside and avoid Hellhounds and Witch Hunters until you catch up to us,⋆ Bear confirmed.

My heart grew audible in my ears.

Time to take the Temple.

And possibly confront Cris-ri-phon again.

I'D SPENT ENOUGH TIME WITH REPRISAL IN AUGRAN TO UNDERSTAND THE layout of the Temple, if not the ins and outs of accessing the between-wall passages like Mourn. Once we'd reached the dead-end behind the dungeon where we'd exit the empty, underground city, we paused for the final time.

First, we refreshed the basic design of the Temple for Jael and the Yungians especially, drawing out the ideal route we would take if all went well to the sanctum, plus two alternates and points to spread out if it didn't.

There were thirteen of us which made for a long line of feet in narrow passages. Nonetheless, we were prepared to split into three groups at a moment's notice. Most importantly, when we *did* break up, we talked as though we stood together anywhere in or under the Temple, visible or not.

The Dragon pearls truly had made the difference in avoiding trouble until we were ready to look for it.

Bear and Hawk, Krithannia said. *We're in position to enter the prison. Enter the Temple now. Dispel all wards you can, and we'll do the same. Keep us apprised of Hellhounds and Witch Hunters.*

Avoid the former as long as you can, do not engage, Mourn added as a reminder, *but kill the latter at any opportunity.*

Um... Hawk began.

Everyone with a pearl tensed.

Something set off a ward on the north side, he said. *The Witch Hunters are alerted, and the clerics are getting up. Crisis speed.*

Same here, Bear said. *West side, second story. It isn't us.*

Mourn motioned for our group to move faster, worrying less about silence though taking time to dispel wards rather than create further alarm upstairs. We listened to Hawk speak.

The Hunters are splitting their forces at the northeast corner and—Oh, fuck.

What is it? Krithannia demanded.

A Hellhound smashed a chamber door. The man inside is screaming.

Same here on the second floor, Bear added. *They're targeting the largest *doors.* *

*How many in sight?** Mourn asked.

Three, Hawk said.

Thr—No, four, Bear replied.

Watch for ten or fifteen, Mourn said. **They attack in fives. Stay ahead of them and watch for flanking.**

Check. Next steps?

Get into the sanctum as soon as they open it. All the mages will gather there. Prepare to shield yourself above all else but start cutting down the Witch Hunters however possible. We're heading straight in and will attempt to reach Pisc'sagrad.

Skimming past the cells and up the central stairs, we reached the main hall underground which would lead either to the crypt or the Temple. This time, we took the hall stairs leading up.

Mourn signed for me and Jael to stay behind him, with Gavin and Krithannia behind us, and the Yungians watching our backs. Wolf, Crow, and their Focus team split to the right as soon as our boots hit the first blue carpet on the main floor, heading toward the sanctum but also to back up their brothers in the hallways.

We turned left where the embellishments grew more frequent, passing metal-framed paintings and detailed wall sculptures which were mostly a blur of color to me: blue, gold, and silver, some red, orange and purple. *All with the Sun motif, of course.*

Meanwhile, the cracking wood and bending metal, the bellowing and screaming men, and the clashing swords grew louder.

"There's about to be a crush of Hunters, Bishops, Hellhounds, and Guildsmen in one place," Mourn said aloud. "Gavin, Sirana, Jael, stay with me or Krithannia for shielding or you could be hit by anything. We'll try to get Gavin close to the pool. Torch's team will clear more space as needed."

"*Hui-sha,*" the Yungian confirmed.

"Could we drop the shard from the third-floor balcony?" suggested the Guild Mistress.

"Not if any single Bishop is behind the chancel barrier. We could look down at them, but the shard will bounce off the sanctuary spell. Climbing the stairs might take too long, or we could be stopped or boxed in. Getting back down to help others would require rappelling down the walls."

"So we'll be in the center of everything."

"Better to draw the Deathless into the sanctum if he's not there already," Mourn said. "Or draw the Bishops and the Hellhounds, and keep Reprisal focused on the Witch Hunters."

"If the pigs don't run," Jael muttered in Davrin, and I smirked.

"I'm ready," Gavin said, drawing only the air needed to speak.

Krithannia's breath was somewhat heavier. "Very well. I'll focus most on shielding behind and to the sides, Mourn must handle the front so he can attack. Sirana, Jael, watch for anything getting around or through when I must recast."

"Understoo—"

I choked on the word when a grinning, black-streaked Ma'ab loped out into our path from the next intersection.

"Stop!" Mourn commanded, planting his feet to mark our point.

My spiders trilled as Jael and I dropped forward into a crouch behind him, braced to roll sideways should the others barrel into us.

The Hellhound's massive right arm swung a dimly glowing chain lined with thorns of black metal. Unnatural strength hauled the weapon around then toward us with little momentum lost from raking plastered walls and the fixed art upon them. Mourn lifted both arms, his bracers touching, though no weapon appeared in his hands when the rumbling bass of two male casters overlapped in my ears.

"Huj-khal!"

"Los'oedot!"

The spiked chain struck like a spinning arrow, yet my bodyguard caught it like a serpent by its head. Turning once in place, the Dragonblood wrapped the weapon around his bracers, his tail slapping my shoulder as his legs bunched, squatting low with claws digging into the carpet.

My pearl fell silent when the two males pulled back, the chain taut as they sought control in this second test of strength. Their lips formed a snarl, mouths beginning to move in other spells.

My aim was clear.

I drew Soul Drinker free of its sheath, the motion trailing a sound like a hollow breath in my mind.

Hhhhh....

The spine-tickling moment vanished like a wisp when I spoke a command word from memory, calling upon the surety of Callitro's ring, and drew back my arm. I flung it as hard as I could at the Hellhound's chest. The relic wheeled over itself before the black point struck beneath his sternum.

The Ma'ab fell mute, and Mourn unexpectedly won the contest of strength, ripping the thorny chain from large, calloused hands and down the forearm. Justly surprised, the Dragonchild had to catch his balance before he could haul the bloodied weapon to him and make it vanish.

As the Far North's warrior stared down at the red runes glowing on the weapon in his chest, I saw no pain on his face. By the time the glow stopped, his dark eyes had emptied of all presence. The giant of a man began to lean before his knees buckled, then he collapsed.

Mourn grabbed my arm to carry me forward and off the floor, urging me to regain my feet. *Retrieve it before someone touches it!*

I hurried to follow through, my eyes taking in the stark difference between this creature and the pretender Kurn. His scalp was pale and hairless with blue veins visible in places, his ears broad and round, his nose hawkish, and his eyes black as the Deepearth. He hadn't even the stubble of a beard but was long past his boyhood.

Like Vo'traj's fighters in the crypt, this one had tattoos covering much of his rough face and thick throat. The markings continued across his shoulders and arms, disappearing beneath his clothes. Unlike those in the crypt, he was older by a decade or more, his pale skin scarred, stained, and worn to such an extent that the unbroken lines of ink struck me as unnatural.

His clothing and armor were dark and minimal but seemed too thin to turn even a regular dagger. The only purpose seemed to help his stealth by blending easily and covering expanses of white skin. Around him, red drops of blood and bits of flesh and torn clothing which didn't belong to him scattered the carpet. He'd trailed it with his chain from wherever he'd last been.

With a steadying thought to my little guardians, I reclaimed my weapon from his chest. Soul Drinker released the corpse with uncanny ease and not a whisper of complaint. Still, my breath seemed too quick.

Sirana? Say something.

~I'm fine, Mourn. No voice or vision. No gatekeeper.~

But I *had* just used Callitro's enchantment on the first threat I saw. *Damn.*

At least it worked.

Mourn spoke to everyone then. "Two crucial things. First, do not expect another Hellhound to go down that easily. Sirana used a unique weapon. Second, *nobody* touches that weapon but Sirana. The blade has accepted her as the wielder, no one else. It will *kill* you. If an enemy tries to grab it, do not stop them. Understood?"

The entire group stared at him, then me, but signed affirmative. Jael looked as shocked and aggravated as a buzzing insect trapped in a glass pot.

"*What else haven't you told me?*" she whispered in Davrin.

I'm pregnant…?

My tongue balked to say that here, even in our native tongue.

"*I'm sorry.*" I wiped the blood off on his coarse pants and sheathed the dagger. "*It's been so much—*"

"Not now," Mourn said, having moved to peer around the corner from which the Hellhound had come, tasting the many scents in the air. "They've opened the sanctum. The way's clear, but we need to get in before they try to seal it. Yungians, with me."

Torch, Peng-lok, and Nianzu hustled forward, the Focus ordering Deshi to stay with Gavin and the rest of the "spirits." Noise above us filtered down, desperate and aggressive, while the pounding of feet and urgent calls seemed to be converging at the center of the Temple ahead.

As we ran closer, I realized the shouts and harsh tones coming from that large chamber were all Manalari, yet the echoes suggested the doors were open.

Easy to assume something had gone exceptionally wrong for them.

We made two sharp turns at a full run, moving into dimmer hallways but following the voices and sounds of conflict. The fact that the pearl chatter had ceased since we hit the main level didn't strike me until Mourn's feet tore into the carpet.

The Dragonblood accelerated, pulling ahead of us in a blink, and without slowing, he slammed his shoulder into the left side of a bronzed double-door at the end of the hall. Opened a crack already, Mourn's weight threw the door wide, knocking back a Witch Hunter on the left as one of Hawk's team cheered on the right side. The Guildsmen called to us in welcome as the Yungians rushed in with us right behind.

Not luck that Mourn hit the Witch Hunter but not Hawk.

The Guild's Shadow had arranged that entrance through the pearls, but I wasn't hearing them now. I wondered why.

A curved sword appeared in Mourn's hand as he stepped into the sanctum, and he swung to decapitate the Witch Hunter on the floor in one stroke, barely pausing before he focused on the chamber ahead. We left the doors damaged and ajar, following his slithering tail to the right and away from most of the noise to the left.

Briskly, we moved along the outer wall made of reddish stone, underneath what must be the second floor lined with smokeless torches, our boots muffled by red and gold carpet. One after another, Jael, the Yungians, Krithannia drew weapons; even Gavin readied his spade to be prepared for close conflict, though none came upon us yet.

I considered drawing my Sisterhood dagger, which was longer than Soul Drinker, but knew we headed toward more Hellhounds. I didn't need to be switching sheaths when instants mattered in the fight, though the relic was best not brandished naked without a focused target. I could clip an ally or, worse, my own Sister.

For now, I kept my hands free, my eyes and ears keen, and my two remaining spiders at the ready.

Mourn held back the pace for Gavin's sake as his gear rattled the most. Our group was partially protected by the unlit walkway opposite the current fighting, located beneath a second story supported by columns. While my pearl was quiet and hauling our backsides took all my breath, I didn't speak. Instead I took in more details from the chaos within the echoing chamber.

I'd seen the Guild's drawings of this place; on parchment, I had an idea what to expect. Yet, with three massive chandeliers hanging from heavy chains from the ceiling and countless smokeless torches lining the walls above our heads lighting up most areas at night, the sanctum of the Manalari Temple was resplendent.

An immense structure too dizzying to see all at once, and far longer than it was wide, this place of worship had a ceiling so high it could house colonies of bats *and* birds, and each keep their own territory. The space below was generous enough for many times the number of worshippers it did now.

I counted three sets of wide stone stairs, one on each wall except for the front pointing East. Each stairwell had a shining golden rail dividing it in two and led to a second floor of mostly open space. The upper floor appeared little more than a massive balcony, lacking any doors but lining three-quarters of the chamber with standing space behind further support columns and a continuous, waist-high balustrade.

Across from us, a disordered spread of clerics in blue and silver vestments scrambled among younger monks in brown and grey robes. They seemed to be moving with reluctance from the main floor and up both sides of the golden rail marking the north-wall stairs while being pushed and shoved by their God's warriors shouting orders at them.

Many Witch Hunters had fallen upon the ground floor, and those standing were harried by the Guildsmen. I didn't understand at first why all those clerics fluttered and ducked around their roil of manic enforcers, even when they had the space to cast.

Then I realized *all* of Reprisal used either offensive spells to inflict wounds and confusion or defensive spells to cover those casting. By comparison, only three in ten Witch Hunters proved capable of returning the same to their opponents. The *Dyos Guerrimos* wore metal armor and swung plenty of sharp weapons at Reprisal, but few had shields to cover the ranking warriors who could perform magic.

The Hand, the Focus, the Flame, and the Aether of Reprisal had taken swift advantage of the situation and granted God's Warriors no quarter. The Guild's coordinated and merciless demonstration as darkly dressed infiltrators might as well be part of the Ma'ab forces, and petrified Bishops and novitiates alike obeyed their protectors' desperate yells whether it was a good idea or not.

Meanwhile, Reprisal's collective focus held to cutting down the Bishops' enforcers, leaving them and their novitiates spattered in blood, tripping over corpses if they attempted to flee for the ground floor. About forty Temple clerics and sixty Witch Hunters were still standing.

But where are the Hellhounds?

I looked behind me to see the massive, scarred men with bald heads and tattoos spread out on the main floor nearer to the west-wall stairs. There were seven of them, bouncing on their feet, their skin damp with sweat, black-stained grins on their faces as they waited on some signal to explode into action. Their spiked chains were wrapped around one arm and held with the other, ready to twirl and throw like a noose.

Yet they held their actions.

The Hellhounds were just laughing, letting the Guildsmen do what they would. By their positions alone, they'd made it impossible for anyone to run their gauntlet unscathed should they try for an exit.

As a taunt, they'd left all the doors open.

As if in response, three monks who'd been pacing that second-floor balcony broke from their protection.

The novitiates ran full tilt, arms pumping as they tried to reach the south-side stairs while skipping the west-side stairs. The closest of the Hellhounds swung his chain twice over his head and, in a blinding strike, loosed it to catch one of the Manalari, dragging him screaming down the west steps as the other two kept going with apologetic calls over their shoulders.

Fuck.

I wondered when the Guild and the Hellhounds had made that non-hostility agreement and how long it would last, but at least I had a hint why Mourn wasn't passing Reprisal's "pearl chatter" through for me to hear.

Booming voices and unsettling shrieks rushed through the main floor as Mourn ducked behind the south-side staircase, followed by the sound of a body landing on a group of men. We gathered behind him, crouching in unclaimed shadows when the two survivors flew down the steps in front of us.

I expected them to flee for any exit available, but they did not. They ran toward the East end of the sanctum.

"Afinis Horus! Sanctui!" they cried. *"Concetus sanctui!"*

"Ven entri," an older man replied, his placid voice incongruous with the desperation of the rest of the Manalari.

What the—?

Mourn hissed through his teeth, sounding annoyed but saying nothing as he watched the young men fleeing to the eastern end of the sanctum. Jael and I waited tensely, each of us attempting to peek out. From here, I had an exceptional view of the chancel barrier, that extraordinary and ornate wall sectioning off the sacred pool from the rest of the sanctum.

The chancel barrier reached the height of three men and was anchored just below the second level balcony on the north and south sides. Wrought of pure iron and painted in pale yellow and orange, the design presented a multitude of the Sun and its rays reaching out in every direction. While impossible even to squeeze a hand through, the barrier nonetheless allowed worshippers on the outside to see light and movement around the pool itself.

As for why Mourn's tail grumbled, I saw the man who looked like Cognate Horus standing within the archway leading through the chancel barrier. He'd opened the only gate available and motioned to the two desperate novitiates, letting them through and closing the gate at once.

As the Witch Hunters continued to fall, Reprisal continued to fight and slay with the strength of their fierce hatred. As more monks attempted to get past the Hellhounds, all of them failed after hesitating in fear. As the Bishops watched and cringed, clutching their golden pendants, they could only seem to yell toward the chancel barrier.

The dispersal of the Manalari felt like a slow and grinding inevitability.

"Hm," Gavin grunted.

"What?" I whispered, leaning close to hear him underneath the cacophony.

"The Bishops trapped on the stairs are demanding Cognate Horus do something to help them," the death mage muttered. "He's the only Bishop standing inside the chancel barrier, watching to see who joins him."

"That is not Horus," Mourn growled.

"Indeed," Gavin replied.

Even without the pearls, we knew why we crouched out of sight behind these stairs, undecided on our next action while the Guild Mistress weighed something heavy.

"The sorcerer could attempt to dispatch our teams once the Witch Hunters are broken," she said in concern.

"The Hellhounds will do the same," Mourn said. "They wait to keep the Bishops fenced in, and we do not know if Brom is allied with them as well."

"We have means to distract and engage the Deathless," Gavin said, somehow *not* looking at me. "We could find out before the Witch Hunters are all culled."

"Risky," Deshi said, yet seemed prepared to help. "Our backs to the Hellhounds to face the sorcerer?"

Krithannia pointed up. "There's the third floor. We'd have to hurry."

Once I'd focused that far up, I saw she was right. The third floor was segmented with smaller balconies, and it was not clear how to reach them. I glimpsed the tops of doors closer together, suggesting rooms and access quite different from the second floor, which seemed to exist only to give more eyes a view of the main floor before leading them all back to the main exits.

"Very well," Mourn agreed, motioning to us. "Let's get up there."

"I'll stay down here," Gavin said.

We froze in place, staring at him a moment until we blinked.

"I can't reach *Pisc'sagrad* from up there," he explained, annoyed. "You said it yourself, the sanctuary spell."

"True," Mourn acknowledged.

"Then we stay," Torch whispered to Krithannia, indicating him and his three brothers, Deshi nodding in earnest agreement.

"Um," the Naulor hesitated. "Then perhaps I should not leave."

"*Hrm*," Mourn grunted with a nod. "Very well. You stay hidden down here. I will take Sirana and Jael. We will get the sorcerer to look up at us, not our Guildsmen, and not the Deathwalker. We can also help defend and attack from above."

This plan seemed to work for all of us, even if I still felt queasy.

403

Chapter 27

My bodyguard stood up from his crouch and signed toward his chest and abdomen. *Stash your pack and hop on. As we practiced on the rooftops.*

Jael squinted at me while my face heated.

Then he signed to her, *Sheath your weapon and jump on my back.*

He's going to carry both of us?

We're not taking the stairs? I signed.

No. Too many locked doors and blind corners slowing us down. We'll be scaling the wall and shielded.

Okay, then.

I dropped my pack and waterskin, stuffing them into the deepest shadows, moving without further delay to "hop" into that familiar position. Mourn adjusted me with his hands on my ass and back, and my crotch responded, tingling as I pressed against him.

Truly? Now?

Ridiculous.

Next, Jael took hold of the back part of his harness near his shoulders and sprang up. Her chin hooked over one side, and her legs came around wide over mine, her heel striking me in the hip. I grimaced but didn't complain.

Cozy.

"What is this?" my Sister whispered tensely, grinding her hips against him.

"My spines," he answered with an odd tone of voice.

"Huh?"

"They lie flat," he added. *"Most of the time."*

By the way Jael's eyes widened, I imagined he'd flexed, giving her a demonstration beneath his cloak.

*"Try **not** to spear my holes, To'vah."*

"Why I designed the harness this way, novice. Sometimes it can't be helped."

"Hurry," Krithannia whispered, concerned as she peeked out at the fast-changing battle. "The Hellhounds are playing 'fish' with the clerics using their chains."

Jael and I made faces. We'd seen their first successful catches.

Although Horus-Brom had moved behind the chancel barrier to obstruct our view from the ground, Mourn spoke his Words which would allow us to see the sorcerer from above. I sensed the hum of his aura as the muscles beneath his scales hardened further; as he drew in a rich, measured breath, I grew further aroused despite my self-chastisement.

Jael sucked in a startled breath, and my eyes flew to meet her gaze.

~*Jael? Are you well?*~

She blinked in surprise, quivering slightly, but I saw no pain.

Uhhh...good? she thought, pursing her lips, her brow drawing down in concentration. *Can you hear me?*

Her face was so cute.

~*Yes, I can.*~

Weird.

Hold tight, Mourn instructed.

We did, each feeling his power in more than one way as the Dragonchild burst into action.

Beginning with a running leap out from beneath the stairs, Mourn caught the ledge of the balcony and pulled us up to the second floor first.

Bracing himself, he sprang with both legs over the short wall, forcing a grunt out of Jael as he sprinted down the empty pathway toward the chancel barrier. As we approached that boundary, he accelerated even more despite two clinging Davrin weighing him down.

Hang on!

The distance between the second and third floors was greater than between the first and second. Mourn wasn't aiming for the lowest ledge over his head this time, but for the fast-approaching wall which would stop a curious congregation before they could see much over the chancel barrier.

~Whoa, bua...!!~

My body tightened down as the warm, individual lights from the torches and chandeliers spun and blurred around me. Jael squeaked as the half-blood hauled us both up using the space between the end wall and its nearest support column.

When he neared the top, he flung out a grappling hook from his bracer, attached it to the easternmost balcony on the third floor, and pulled us up with breathtaking speed. I closed my eyes, fighting the force and vertigo threatening to dislodge me from my bodyguard's torso, gripping the handholds on his harness until my hands ached.

The heat of his effort poured out of him as he dropped behind the balcony wall on his knees, steadying me with one arm as he put the other to catch himself from falling over. He panted hard enough to make me regret leaving my waterskin down under the stairs.

Jael let go of him abruptly, grunting as she fell off with a thump.

"Oof! Ow, fuck... Stupid chair."

I started chuckling with extreme relief as Mourn gently unpeeled my shaking limbs and set me on the rug. The arched ceiling above me was well lit, but one chandelier was quite close. If it were to fall, all that metal and crystal would land right in front of the chancel barrier archway.

"Stay low," Mourn whispered after two deep draws to catch his breath.

Rolling onto my knees, I curled low on his left, joined by my Sister as she crawled on her belly. We watched him prepare a defensive spell before poking his horned head over the side and looking down.

I fixed my eyes on something behind his head: the curved, multi-colored glass window facing the outside. In no way reachable from the ground by the average Human, its height measured from the second level floor to the third level ceiling. The sky outside was dark, so the precise design of frame lines and colored glass was difficult to see past the chandelier.

Nonetheless, dawn would be hard to miss in this Temple.

I waited to hear Cris-ri-phon's voice, either shouting a challenge or an insult, or laughing in delight that we'd shown ourselves at last. Only the continued sounds of chains and fighting, of injured and dying men filled the sanctum.

My nose caught more than that as a strange, cool breeze passed by, smelling like rain. I looked at Jael to speak, but she'd already noticed, and we stared at the ceiling above the East end cradling the sacred pool.

Or rather, the lack of one.

This divine space was open to the sky, as the East wall—bare but for that large window—continued up well past the chandeliers. I couldn't see the outside from where we were, but I could sense it. The Sun would shine on *Pisc'sagrad* not only upon a clear dawn but also at the highest point of midday when its light was strongest. It was certainly one of the highest points seen on the outside.

Huh.

Uh-oh...

I blinked. ~Mourn? What is it?~

Look. He is not focused upward.

Could the sorcerer have missed the bulky black streak scrambling up the column wall? Was he not expecting us, despite my worry?

I crawled to peer cautiously over and down from the short wall. Jael mimicked me, and Mourn did not suggest she stay down.

Far below, a pool of water lay centered within the alcove formed by the East-end wall. It was encircled with a fence made of golden-tipped spears. The height of this fence was too tall and smooth for a heavy man to scale without risking impalement, assuming they were mundane enough to touch.

The water was unbelievably clear, its surface moving gently, peacefully, despite the rage of men in the sanctum. The depth extended far beyond my body length, though the angle would not let me see the bottom. I studied the circular hole in the earth bordered with smooth, white marble and beyond it. Large, creamed-colored tiles covered the entire floor behind the chancel barrier, but those around the perimeter of the golden-spear gate had been carved with strong, blue runes. There were no other altars or artifacts I could see.

Only the two young men whom Horus had allowed in were present behind the painted iron wall. It seemed they had been earnestly praying on their knees where the north wall met the barrier, but as I watched, the monks' arms fell lax at their sides, their mouths gaping open, their eyes unfocused upon the south side.

~Oh, no.~

We watched as Horus forced one monk to stand, drawing him by the arm closer to the golden-spear gate. The older man's expression was intense and quietly menacing; unfortunately, it was also familiar.

~He's going to spill the boy's blood in the pool,~ I said. ~What would that do?~

I do not know, Mourn replied, *but the only object we should want in Pisc'sagrad is Gavin's soul shard.*

~Do I seize his attention?~

Wait…

Mourn's tail coiled as we pushed our luck, observing Horus lift the young man's left hand before drawing a ceremonial dagger from his belt and cutting his palm deeply enough that red easily sprang into view.

Rather than thrust the blood source between the golden spears as I expected, Horus used the young man's finger to redraw some of the blue runes, connecting some lines and crossing others while leaving the rest alone.

The shapes changed from blue to purple to red and back to purple, *Pisc'sagrad* began to ripple and shimmer, and my ears started to tingle.

~*Mourn?*~

⋆*Quick. Can you see anything in the water? Show me through our link.*⋆

Why would I see something he couldn't?

Swallowing, I dared to focus on the glitter of refracted light, attempting to see anything underneath. A vague blob coalesced, a shadow of swirling water. The longer I focused, the more it oddly reminded me of Mourn's shadow drake, Graul, curled up on the red chaise next to me in Yong-wen.

~*No, that's absurd, I don't know where that came from.*~

⋆*It is not absurd. Keep looking, psion. Show me what* he *wants to see.*⋆

What he wants...?

What Cris-ri-phon wants. Was that the reflection I saw within *Pisc'sagrad*?

I exhaled, not having blinked as the vision grew clearer, the shades shifting from dark shadows of the earth to become clear lines of red and white tinged with the faintest yellow. I thought I could make out large wings like Kerse had grown, and a long, curling tail like Mourn's.

Or like Graul when he shifted in his sleep.

High upon the mountain, the Temple started to shake. I gripped the solid banister, my heart lodging in my throat as I saw cracks appear, fretting that the stone beneath my feet was about to crumble.

The shaking stopped. The cracks vanished.

My heart still pounded.

~*Shit. What was that?*~

⋆*Not anything we want,*⋆ Mourn's mind whispered as we watched Horus smile.

Gingerly, standing upon flawless tiles, the mage touched the golden gate. Finding it harmless, he then dragged the insensible youth closer, lifting his dagger toward the vulnerable throat.

Mourn's claws scratched the banister as he stood up.

"Deathless, drop the blade!"

Horus jerked back, fumbling the dagger. His illusion flickered on his face as he finally looked up.

I rose next to my bodyguard. "Cris-ri-phon! What in the Abyss are you doing?!"

Standing over the young Manalari, the robed Bishop reformed before our eyes into the muscular Zauyrian General from Troshin Bend, with silver-grey hair, dark, leathery skin, and eyes like brittle slate.

Jael tried to stand up beside me, but Mourn's tail wrapped around her waist and jerked her onto her backside behind him.

Hey!

Stay out of sight for now, Red Sister.

I hadn't realized we were linked.

"Sirana." The Zauyrian spoke it softly like a threat, pausing before he surprised me with a clear answer. "What am I doing? What everyone else is trying to do. Free *Pisc'sagrad*."

"Not that way, sorcerer," Mourn said. "Do *not* awaken the Sargt."

"Why not, Dragon son?" the General chuckled. "We were known to each other long before you were born. It's always been a sure way to revive the flow of Io'sulta after a period of stagnation. Am I not correct?"

"We have another way."

The ancient man snarled. "You'll *not* use that degenerate death mage's black vials to foul this spring."

"We can't," I replied. "We used those to deal with the warp rot *you* ignored, innkeeper."

Cris-ri-phon scowled at me, yet for a second looked relieved. A laugh escaped him. "Well! Whatever you would do, *Vloszia Dalna*, I hope it doesn't involve sinking that dagger at your belt."

"That would be worse than the vials," Mourn said.

"We're agreed," said the sorcerer more lightly, crossing his arms and glancing out toward the screams and clatter beyond the barrier. "Are all the Bishops dead yet? Do the Guildsmen cull them next, or is that left for the Hellhounds at their leisure?"

The way he asked set me on edge, especially as the monk's blood continued to drain from his hand and leak into the grooves of the runes, changing their color despite his throat remaining intact. The crimson-winged sleeper remained visible in the shimmering water.

~Mourn. Is that…?~

★The Red Dragon. He Sleeps near here.★

~And if he Awakens?~

★Gavin's shard will no longer work, and everyone near Manalar's walls will die when the Sargt arrives.★

I shuddered. *~Is it too late?~*

★No. But we need to save some Bishops.★

~You're jesting.~

★If all the Bishops die, we will be hard-pressed to stop the Deathless from doing what he planned.★

Mourn must have been conveying the crucial details through his pearls, for the tenor of the battle abruptly shifted. The Hellhounds roared at the top of their lungs, shocked and swiftly turning berserk as Reprisal shielded the Bishops of Manalar from the raking and tearing of their favorite weapons.

~What do we—?~

A familiar, desperate call reached through all the confusion.

~Sirana! Answer if you hear me!~

I gasped. "Isboern."

"What?" Mourn began. Then, "Wait."

He pulled me down from the sorcerer's view, staring into my eyes.

~Sirana! Can you hear me?~

~Yes, I hear you. We are in the Temple.~

★Godblood,★ Mourn added, gently threading himself into the link. *★We need your help.★*

~How? What is happening there?~ he demanded. *~With or without Keros, the Bishops should have erected the basic defenses before dawn!~*

★They're being kept from the inner sanctuary by a sorcerer and Hellhounds who broke in. Can any of the Templars assist?★

I hadn't yet witnessed the Captain display a habit of cursing, but he came close.

~For God's sake, why didn't anyone tell me? There's only so much we can do to defend the wall if the Bishops never begin their work at all!~

★Can any of the Templari assist,★ Mourn repeated, *★in getting the Bishops*

inside the sanctuary?

~We can! We're right outside!~

The Godblood proved true to his word, as the largest, west-facing doors burst inward like an invisible giant had stepped through, startling a fair number of combatants to pause and look toward the clear sound of armored men approaching.

The closest Hellhound struck out with his chain into the hall before a single man appeared. The spiked weapon stopped, trembling like a paralyzed snake before flopping loudly onto the floor without returning to its bewildered master.

The Hellhound started dragging it manually, backing up from the approaching defenders, only to be struck by an unseen fist hard enough for his spine to collide with a nearby column. His own chain moved against him, wrapping twice around his chest and the stone behind him, twisting around itself and trapping his arms.

A Guildsman—it looked like Tak—took swift advantage before the Ma'ab could attempt to snap the chain. Leaping up with arm raised, the man from Augran stabbed the bound brutalizer deeply through the eye.

The other Ma'ab screamed in shrill threats at this and the first sight of the leading Captain through the door. Simultaneously, the surviving Bishops and novitiates cried out for help, pointing and shouting to be heard.

I heard Isboern's mental sigh.

His Templars drew their swords, which started to glow with white light, and moved in to engage the Hellhounds threatening their clerics.

Move back, Mourn said, touching my shoulder and drawing me and Jael back behind the gilded chairs.

Breaking the lock with a sharp twist, the Dragonblood urged us to slip out through the narrow door and into a dark, cool, and quiet hallway.

I'm joining the fight downstairs, he said. *The sooner the Hellhounds are down and the sooner the Deathless is out of the sanctuary, the sooner Gavin gets his chance.*

~Agreed,~ I said. ~I'll help draw him out if I can.~

Well, perhaps you—

We're joining the fight, Jael interrupted, glaring at him. *Oh, teacher who is taking his sweet time.*

I nearly laughed out loud. ~He's known for that.~

Mourn cocked a brow ridge.

~And I'm not putting three Temple floors between us,~ I added, calling out my spiders where he could see them, ~my patient guardian.~

I heard another mental sigh.

Very well. Let's find another balcony to drop off of.

~And hurry.~

As we rappelled down, three on one line I privately hoped wouldn't break, most of the original sounds and location of the battle inside the Temple remained, with one exception. The presence of the Templars added flashes of white light mostly lacking in noise, so these weren't thunderstones or summoned lightning strikes. Their swords half-blinded me as often as their opponents.

Many thanks for the reinforcements, Cloud, Wolf said through the pearls, sounding distracted and trying to ignore pain. *But a lot of us need to retreat. We can't take these guys up close, and our shield spells are breaking more often. They're wearing us down to trap us along a wall.*

Agreed, Krithannia answered. *Disengage at your next opportunity. Captain Isboern will protect the Bishops.*

Understood. Thank you.

When the Guildsmen began to spread out one or two at a time, I saw how many of them were bleeding, holding brutal wounds, and limping to a better position to escape the second floor and vanish by magic or the first accessible exit. Fortunately, the Templars proved much better protected with equal coordination to Reprisal, and I suspected why.

No doubt Isboern's men could hear each other think.

The results were tactics both impressive and flexible, with enough mage-warriors to block the Hellhounds' ranged offenses one moment then bend and shift as one to hold a line or disallow the tattooed giants' mobility trying to reach the clerics directly. That first Hellhound to be tied by his own spiked chain to one of the columns before he was dispatched was not the last.

Ten of these city defenders with their Captain were worth more than the sixty Witch Hunters who'd once been on their feet.

The only concerns I could sort out on my way down with Mourn were that five more Hellhounds had appeared from *somewhere* and, unless their corpse was bound to a column, the remaining man-beasts had far too few wounds for how often they were being hit with practically no armor. These Ma'ab infiltrators could suck up a demoralizing amount of magical endurance.

It must be the tattoos.

Meanwhile, all living clerics moved East at Isboern's orders. I saw no remaining *Dyos Guerrimos.*

Shadow! Sirana! Krithannia called.

Landing now, he replied, dropping us a little too hard; this time, Jael and I *both* fell off with a grunt. *Behind the stairs.*

My Sister and I rolled up and moved low to rejoin our allies while Mourn reclaimed his grappling hook. I felt an odd sensation, as if we'd passed through a barrier, recognizing it next as a magical boundary; a shield or an illusion obscuring us.

No wonder they hadn't been attacked yet.

Gavin's face struck me first upon entering the shelter, not for any startlement or fright on my part, but because I'd never seen such intense concentration, authentic concern, nor his eyes filled with such anticipation before.

Our Deathwalker has been suppressing his aura, the Naulor explained. *This grows harder to do. He says the Vis and Vitas from the accumulating bodies come to the thurible, drawing power to him whether we are ready to reveal ourselves or not.*

Suddenly, Gavin's ice blue pupils flicked to me and Mourn. His thin lips were extremely tight, but they moved. "I want to test something. I will have to reveal myself to do it."

"Test what?" I whispered back.

"While the current is ongoing," he said, "I may be able to command the corpses to stand up without needing to be close enough to use my blood. They could help obstruct the Hellhounds and escort the Bishops to the chancel barrier. When I want them to lie down, I merely draw the final mote to me, and the bodies cannot be raised by other death mages during this war."

The Yungians whispered among themselves, making spirit-knowledge motions with their hands. Deshi withdrew his matte black, Nyx-blessed blade and murmured something which sounded like a prayer.

Mourn exchanged a mere glance with the Naulor before agreeing. "Do it. We'll guard you and confront the Deathless first if he grows weary of watching."

Krithannia said to me, "We'll tell the Guild. You tell Isboern so he can warn his Templars."

I hoped the young Godblood with an impossible weight on his back would have a segment of his attention available for me. Our Deathwalker could wait no longer.

His pack tucked away, Gavin grasped his spade from Troshin Bend and the thurible from the crypt in his white, long-fingered hands. Standing up, he walked calmly out from behind the steps. Deshi followed him while the other three Yungians remained with Krithannia.

"Shit," Mourn whispered, signing to me, ★Take off one glove.★

Uh...

I pulled off the left one, and my bodyguard seized my hand before we left the shelter with Jael. We strode into the broad center of the Temple where three Hellhounds tried to gang up on the Captain; his men gave them no mercy each time they did.

This had to be now, before the Deathless decided to join us.

~Isboern!~ I called, the psionic call tight enough to make my spiders chime with bewilderment.

He seemed to have been waiting for me.

~Sirana. I'm listening.~

415

I paused as I tried to think how to describe what was about to happen.

~*Show me instead,*~ he encouraged. ~*No words.*~

That part was shockingly easy, flowing like a river as many more thoughts and memories slipped free than I meant to think about in the middle of this bloody chaos. I held no sense that the other psion had pulled them from me unwillingly; more like I'd spilled the pitcher of water containing the hidden jewels on the floor.

~*Oh...*~ he thought, plainly horrified. ~*Oh, no.*~

Isboern had known Gavin's purpose before. Within a second, he understood what would happen to the Immersed of the Mount when Gavin threw Jacob's shard, now anointed by the Archbishop's blood, into *Pisc'sagrad*. The Captain also knew about the Deathless controlling access to the pool, his presence for at least two days in the Temple, and the two young monks under his spell.

The psion grasped from my memory the vague essence of Cris-ri-phon's unnatural existence and the Zauyrian's Desert link to the Elves. Isboern recognized through my eyes the haunted and ancient General behind the Deathless mask, and felt pain on my behalf, understanding the circumstances under which I'd last seen this man.

Lastly, Isboern understood the catastrophe Morixxyleth had narrowly helped to avoid. ~*The Red Dragon Awakening from beneath us...*~

The Captain recalled that the Guild helped both him and Gavin, and that they had every intention to destroy the Witch Hunters and the Bishops. The Deathwalker and Reprisal would eradicate them from the Mount as their price.

~*Holy light above us,*~ the Captain prayed, sorrow and regret spilling into our link. ~*Is there no better way than this?*~

Shit.

~*The Ma'ab are here to destroy the Bishops and enslave the common folk, dead or alive!*~ I said. ~*Gavin didn't lie to you when he asked for a way to break the Bishops' power yet prevent the Ascended from claiming Pisc'sagrad. He knows both sides of his blood seek it only to abuse it.*~

~*I know, I...believe him. He does not want it for his Lady. She does not seek it.~*

★You also believed Jael that the city would fall, Captain,★ Mourn joined us, squeezing my hand tight, *★and you told me your only purpose was to get people out. Would you rather the Ascended take Manalar if Gavin does not follow through? Or if the Red Awakens? I guarantee you, this legend is not as cautious of small creatures beneath his feet as the Wanderer you've heard about out West.★*

The Captain's sudden horror and denial lessened, replaced by resolve. *~No, I would not want that.~* The psion's powerful will steeled to collide with three Ma'ab chains trying to trap him at once. *~If the city falls but somehow avoids a scorched earth and poisoned roots, we will rebuild... This has happened many times.~*

Only a few steps ahead of me, Gavin lifted the white gold artifact like a lantern while facing the largest cluster of bodies on the north stairs. Though I could see no change at first, the barest wisps of white appeared within the pale blue aura of the thurible itself, seeming to be sucked into the holes as if something inside were breathing in slowly.

In response, the first bodies of the fallen monks, Bishops, and *Dyos Guerrimos* began to stand up. Bearing every wound to be gained in battle, they faced the Deathwalker first before turning their heads jerkily toward the Ma'ab. Then, one after another, the dead turned their feet and walked.

The clerics of the Temple noticed first and erupted in panic.

"*Isboern!*"

"*Capitan, Capitan!*"

"*Herex gi lo'guerrimos maldize!*"

At least Isboern's men didn't act surprised when a shuffling mass of previously killed Witch Hunters began to file in between them and the Hellhounds.

"*Alitij, alitij!*" barked four of the Templars in annoyance, pushing the surviving men with armored shoulders and shields with more force toward the chancel barrier.

At last, once the standing corpses had filled all available space between the combatants, even proving too deep for one Hellhound to take a running leap over, the Bishops had their chance to run for the main floor.

Sirana.

Belatedly, I realized Mourn wasn't holding my hand. He'd stepped away to my right as Jael stood on my left. My bodyguard was blocking my view of the chancel archway, but the fact that he had both his long sliders out and ready told me who must be standing there.

Oh, fuck.

Would the Zauyrian continue to block the Bishops from entering the sanctuary?

"Well. This is interesting. Now I'm curious, Sirana. What happens if I let them in?"

The sorcerer's voice, though unraised, carried like a fingertip running along the edge of my ear. I suppressed a shudder, turning to look over my shoulder when a body moved into my periphery.

I wasn't required to respond, it seemed. The Deathless voluntarily stepped out of the archway, into the public part of the chamber, and took a few steps south in front of the barrier. He'd left the gate open.

Uh-oh.

Mourn wasn't the only one forced to turn his back to the Hellhounds crowded by the scrambling dead. *Closer to Gavin. Backs to each other.*

We sidled that way, even Jael, and we turned our backs once we felt the chill of the Deathwalker's aura, acting as a small, surrounded squad in the middle of the sanctum. Deshi stood guard with his Death Spirit and looked bewildered; nonetheless, he recognized the formation and fit himself into it to help watch our backs.

Cris-ri-phon tilted his head with amusement, tapping fingers to his lips as he studied us intently. He might look the same as back at the inn, but his expression was no longer familiar to me, nor was his body language.

"So you rescued the '*daeva*,'" he said, his calm, overbearing voice clashing with everything around us. "I was tempted to do it myself, you know, when I saw her being dragged through the Temple. But…then I recalled that Davrin cunts these days don't *want* to be rescued. I wager she's House D'Shauranti."

Jael sneered and muttered, *"You lose, cock mold."*

The sorcerer acted like he might have heard her; he shrugged before glancing at Mourn. "And now I know what was creeping about the inn the night of the fire. Rather insightful. I wonder how long you've been around to meddle in man's affairs."

"Not as long as you have," Mourn replied.

~*He's not acting like before,*~ I thought.

You described a clash between an innkeeping sorcerer and a Desert General-Consort to a Queen, Mourn replied. *Soul Drinker probably destroyed the innkeeper but the General remains. We have no idea how many other lives he has to draw on.*

So what? Jael said. *An unfamiliar venomous spider is venomous, right? Don't get bitten.*

That's good advice, novice, he returned. *I hope you take it.*

Indeed, that was the best tactic now that I knew the Zauyrian was dangerous.

But once you're in the web, the bite is hard to avoid.

The Deathless took a few more steps away from the archway as the Manalari clerics sprinted straight for it. The Templars were guarding their backs from the Hellhounds, who were busy tearing apart Witch Hunter bodies to make them stay down for the second time.

~*Do you need assistance?*~ Isboern asked, touching me gently.

He's too dangerous to provoke, Mourn answered. *Better to take down the Hellhounds if you can.*

~*Acknowledged, understood.*~

Watching this but not seeming to hear the conversation, Cris-ri-phon started laughing, shaking his head. He did not attack us, and he did nothing to prevent the surviving six Bishops and their ten novitiates from rushing through the iron gate and slamming it shut behind them. None of them looked at him, as if they couldn't see him.

"There," the ancient sorcerer said from across the way, the blood of the young monk staining his hands. "The flock is safe and sound with their enemies outside the gates. So, Sirana, what has the Deathwalker told you happens next?"

"You should know," I said without shouting; he heard me fine. "Mathias told you what happened in the shed with Thetri Jacob, correct?"

"Oh, that." His tone was neither impressed nor disgusted. "Are you sure he understands what his inscrutable prophetess is asking? I would be concerned. A Deathwalker should *never* be able to spin pneuma flint into being as he did unless they're in the Nexus."

Gavin spoke then. "An existence I held for quite some time, you recall, with interest enough in rituals and study."

"And I've been there, too." Cris showed a hint of revulsion. "A wretched existence, such a malleable and bitter taste."

"Why a world eater always comes home," the death mage replied. Jael jerked as if startled.

~Danger?~

*He... he said 'world eater.' **That's** the world eater?*

What do you know, Jael? Mourn asked, pacing in front of us and turning his swords, to give Cris-ri-phon something to look at. It worked.

*The Valsharess... said a 'deathless' one was coming to Manalar, and if Isboern didn't have the golden shield when the 'world eater' arrives..."

~Then what?~

She didn't reply, but I recognized that regal, terrifying voice in her memory.

"...then you will kill the mortal man and then kill yourself for failing, Aurenthin."

"Hmm," Cris-ri-phon hummed, lifting his stubbled chin, and focused on the Templars next, who'd gone on the offensive with the remaining Hellhounds. "Still five left. You should have beaten them by now. I take it this brave young man leading them has no idea how to use that shield? Unlike *you*, Gavin, doing quite well with that thurible. You might as well have Sirana wade in to begin stabbing them if the 'Capitan' doesn't step up."

"Perhaps you could *assist* them instead," Mourn said, tail flicking in irritation.

The sorcerer fixed his eyes on him. "Oh, so could you, To'vah-krav. You'd make short work of them."

"That's not why I'm here."

"Heh! Me, neither." Cris-ri-phon glanced at me. "But if I were to help you against the Ma'ab... What might you offer me? I'm sure you have a few valuable suggestions that would persuade me."

~No fucking deal,~ I thought before we could feel the slightest doubt.

My stony silence was filled by the desperate chanting of clerics. The Deathless looked down at his boots, his arms crossed as he chuckled. He glanced through the chancel barrier as a crackling hum began behind it then turned to me.

"Of course," he said, "you won't like the consequences if you won't make an offer. I'll get what I want either way."

The drone behind the screen grew louder, and my skin prickled listening to his too-familiar threat.

I am here, Mourn said. *Be calm. He will not stay much longer.*

~How do you know?~

His aura is repelled by the Bishops' ritual. He creates excuses to leave on his terms.

Was he?

"Think about it, Sirana," Cris-ri-phon said with an oily smile that didn't belong to the Desert General I'd met before. "I shall give you a chance to return what you've stolen *and* get something for it. It's the most I can do after letting Kurn have his way with you." He smiled as I flinched. "Oh, but I know you're tough, Red Sister. And you like it rough. Until later."

Abyss damn him.

At least Mourn had been correct about his leaving. The Deathless vanished before my eyes as the white light intensified from behind the chancel barrier, piercing through the painted iron and into my eyes.

He is gone, the Dragonblood assured me.

~Not just invisible?~

Not just invisible. He cannot withstand Pisc'sagrad's focus.

I was shaking as I rubbed my eyes. Jael touched me with concern but kept her thoughts to herself. I had to look away from the brightness, checking on Gavin's response to such a spell.

He concentrated hard on rushing the Hellhounds with the corpses of both the Witch Hunters and their brethren. I heard familiar, reassuring laughter and voices from the Guildsmen watching nearby. My Deathwalker displayed no discomfort, but his skin changed from white to black far more quickly than if he'd stood in broad daylight.

I was concerned about a wisp with a disturbing scent. I couldn't tell if it had come to the thurible or had drifted off him.

~Is it dawn?~ I asked.

Almost. Mourn stepped behind us, tapping my Sister and me with his tail. *Come. Let us aid Isboern and clear the Hounds from the Temple. Jael, I can teach you something useful.*

Finally, she grumbled.

Finally, indeed.

I took a deep breath, my fingers wrapped around the grip of Soul Drinker. We'd kill Hellhounds first, regain Isboern's help next.

And toss in Gavin's soul shard, somehow.

CHAPTER 28

MY WOMB FELT SCORCHING HOT AS I STOOD SO CLOSE TO GAVIN WORKING his death magic. Mourn seemed to notice. Cris-ri-phon hadn't called it out but I was waiting for Jael to say something since she was a mage now, too.

"Sirana, stay to defend Gavin," the Dragonblood rumbled, stepping toward the West end with Jael, each with two blades drawn. "Gavin, draw back the corpses gradually as we move in. Use them to guard yourself, Sirana, and Deshi."

"Very well," the Deathwalker rasped.

Use Soul Drinker on anything that surprises you, Mourn added to me through the pearl.

~Of course.~

Yet the spike of apprehension when my Sister and my bodyguard stepped away unnerved me as much as the Deathless had. The Temple was becoming *too* bright from the ritual at the East end, and it was impossible to make out if anyone was standing on the third floor ready to ambush us. The two fears intertwined as I anticipated him taking this opportunity to reappear and demand his "offer."

At the same time, I wasn't eager to wade into melee with Ma'ab Hellhounds solely to stay close to Mourn. All it would take was one hard kick to my middle or one of those chains tearing into my gut… I supposed there was reasonable cause for keeping pregnant Davrin out of battle, whether in the Deepearth or the ancient Desert. The distraction was real and a potential danger to those around me.

Yet all this hadn't exactly been my choice, and the alternatives were even worse.

"We with you, Janshi," Deshi whispered as we stood back-to-back with Gavin, surrounded by those the Guild and Templars had already killed. "Master Shi says a wise warrior does not break their role to begin counting the dead laid out by his blade."

The Yungian held up his own clean, blessed weapon, not having marked even one enemy's soul for Nyx as the young mage refused to leave Gavin's defense or his own learning to use it.

I smiled weakly, raising the red-runed relic, thankful it no longer screamed at me to feed it. We were certainly willing to take anything that got close, though. The dagger could work with me and my spiders instead of against us.

Assuming the crystal doesn't crack.

I jumped when a boom erupted among the cluster of living men.

"Whoa!!" Jael cried loudly among them, her voice tinged with a familiar battle glee.

~Mourn?!~

We are well, Kiabil.

A burst tossed a Hellhound out of the morass, splattering red and gore against the pale staircase. His skin looked flayed.

Brutal! Look how scared they are!

That was not planned, novice.

Could have fooled me! What happened?

There was a pause as if Mourn blocked someone and took another swing. *We may have caused one of those tattoos to grow unstable.*

Oo! So, like crushing a magic gem?

Maybe.

Let's try again! Gimme your tail!

My eyebrows raised as Mourn gently closed the connection.

What the fuck is going on in there?

My imagination didn't get far before I sniffed, wrinkling my nose. "Um. Are you alright, Gavin?"

"Yes," he said as the empty-eyed bodies in possession of both legs tightened their circle around us. "Probably the corpses you smell."

I suppressed a shudder, my heart racing. "Uh, no. It's burnt."

Gavin paused, lifting both arms and letting his sleeves roll back, comparing between the one holding the thurible and the one holding the shovel. The latter looked darker and drier, some of the creases in his skin starting to turn grey like ash, while the arm holding Nyx's artifact remained lighter with fewer creases.

From behind the iron screen, the Bishops chanted.

"Nomilu sancji!"

My ally lowered his arms as one of his risen Hellhounds collapsed.

"We do not have much time," he said.

I had to believe him. The chanting behind the barrier was growing louder. And louder.

A disquieting pressure building up…

Until—

"Shahalah ignomini!" cried five Bishops in unison. *"Thrin-chalah ignoforus!"*

Whatever we might've anticipated, I did not expect them to shatter the glass of the Temple's massive window right above them. The young monks covered their heads with their arms, but the six Bishops didn't care if they were cut by the glass as ecstatic faces kept looking up.

"Nomilu sancji!"

High through that eastern wall, I could see the Sun rising. Enough of the clouds had cleared for this earliest daylight to strike the sacred waters directly, its aurora washing over its most devout clerics.

Their power swelled within the chamber at an alarming rate.

"Nomilu sancji!"

Shit.

~Mourn!~

Almost done.

Jael's mean-spirited giggle slipped through our link. I was tempted to stand on my tiptoes to look over the dead Witch Hunters' heads, but I stayed flat and focused. My headache only increased with the light anyway.

~Hurry! Gavin can't withstand the Bishops' aura, either. He's burning up!~

How fast?

~Like a smoldering campfire but worsening. The thurible seems to be slowing it down but the corpses are slipping out of his control.~

How do you feel?

My vision speckled with drifting spots. ~Fine, I guess? My gut has a hot coal in it.~

An immediate uproar among the fighters followed as the skirmish escalated, the noise rising to the ceiling to drown out prayer at the other end. Jael released a Red Sister battle yell, having the most fun of any now that she was free of her captivity.

And apparently finding delight in being a mage.

Weapons and chains clashed, armor and shields blocked blunt force blows, and bodies hit the floor. Underneath all that, I heard blades spinning and an encouraging humming song that came with them.

I kept waiting for this to finish.

Hurry.

In front of me, another two of Gavin's corpses leaned back, losing their balance, and knocking against others on their way down. This time, it came with the barest complaint of pain from my Deathwalker. I couldn't recall the last time I'd heard that sound, and this chilled me as much as his aura.

"Gavin?"

~Sirana!~ Isboern reached out, his touch matching the focus of boots running toward us. ~The Bishops haven't erected the city's defenses! They're purifying the Temple, starting with the risen dead! They're trying to destroy the Deathwalker!~

I gritted my teeth, feeling the Captain's distress at this realization while the proof of Gavin's draining power toppled around us with wet, fleshy smacks.

Well, what did we *expect* when we gave them the opening? That they'd defend the city after we'd stopped Cris-ri-phon from waking the Red Dragon?

~*Gavin needs to get out!*~ the Captain continued. ~*The west door is open, and we've cleared the way. He'll be safe outside.*~

"Gavin, they're trying to destroy you. You need to—"

"No."

The Deathwalker halted my message as the last of the dead bodies fell.

"I'll not... have another chance."

He spoke with care, as if his tongue wasn't fully reliable. His face was fully black and drying in the intense light, his cheeks sunken. I could barely make out his black eyes within tight, desiccated eyelids.

"Deshi," he whispered.

"Sho'shien?" the young man acknowledged, at once perplexed and distressed looking at him.

"Ssstay here."

Gavin turned toward the East end, taking one long stride over a Witch Hunter corpse.

"But the gate is locked!" I cried.

"I..." He flinched as more smoke rose from within his grey robes. "Mm... presssume the Guild will sssolve that shhhortly."

My ally continued toward the chancel barrier without looking back. I squinted after him, hoping the glow I spotted beneath his robe was a trick of the light and not him being incinerated from the inside.

★Sirana!★

I jumped.

~*Wh... Krithannia?*~

★Is Gavin intending to drop the shard now?★

~*Yes, now or never,*~ I confirmed. ~*But he can't open the gate.*~

Jael and the Templars joined us then, sweating and panting and all with bloodied blades. The armored men encircled me, Jael, and Deshi, shoving the bodies farther with their boots. Isboern stayed nearby, positioned between his men and the chancel barrier, while Mourn streaked past us, catching up with and overtaking Gavin.

The Dragonchild's sliders hummed as he positioned himself before the archway with plenty of space to spin and swing. His voice rumbled to a crescendo of his own to counter the Bishops.

"NIF'KOUS-SHAK!"

Mourn swept his blades down and before him, cutting the air an instant before pure force ripped the wrought iron in two, shearing and bending the once-luxurious art into a contorted mess with a gap in the middle.

"Penidos di'struja!" one of the Templars cried in genuine horror.

Several reacted in similar shock to watch their sanctum being torn apart.

"Capitan!"

"Qen'el kitash?!"

The Templars questioned the side they'd chosen, and Jael and I were in the center of them.

Uh-oh.

"Fe'ni vu citiedel, Templari!" Isboern shouted, lifting his golden shield, reminding them of its presence while pointing toward Gavin's smoldering form. *"Fo'no le vanida cregos!"*

I couldn't tell if the pain would erupt into anger.

~*Should we run for it?*~

No, be calm, Krithannia answered. *The Godblood reminds them of the Archbishop's vanity which got them here, and that their oath is to the city, not to any one Bishop in the Temple. They'll listen.*

Meanwhile, Mourn spoke while spinning his blades, sweeping one arm to his left and then the other to the right. The left half of the chancel barrier shrieked to the side, followed by the other to the right to create enough space for Mourn and his weapons, and certainly for Gavin, who was beginning to leave black, sooty foot marks with each step toward the pool.

I cringed along with the Templars at the violent noise and destruction, but the warriors held themselves in check to their leader.

The monks who were not part of the ritual, however, weren't going to let them just walk in. The novitiates rushed to block the compromised space with their bodies, faces flushed with rage and railing curses upon their enemy. Yet, this was one of the most foolish parts of the fight I'd witnessed thus far, for they were *not* calm or united.

The Temple-bound youths pushed at each other and wailed like a panicked flock of birds, casting in a baffling staccato. In their short spate on the offense, they did not find a single effective spell to use against the Dragon son before he cut them down without even crossing the line they'd drawn.

Only six Bishops were left, held fast in a collective trance with their ritual going strong.

Steadily, Gavin approached the torn barrier, securing the thurible to his belt before withdrawing the black soul shard for what we hoped would be the final time. Its aura bore a rainbow of colors which even I could see, strengthening with its proximity to the sacred waters.

The bright spot on his smoking back grew intense enough for me to recognize its shape: the sunburst brand given by his Archimandrite father.

Mourn stepped forward, prepared to defend the Deathwalker's approach and entry into the sanctuary. He cast one more "break" spell, and four of the golden-tipped spears snapped in half. The metal debris should have fallen into *Pisc'sagrad*, but a strange bubble pushed back against the broken spears landing in it. The nearest Bishop shuddered and stumbled back from the water, temporarily weakening the mages' bond.

The rest held fast on their feet, using whatever defenses they had around themselves with arms raised to the dawn. The nameless one leading them nearly lost his concentration when he glimpsed the two inhuman creatures approaching.

"Uganta tenlous!" the blonde Bishop cried. *"Nomilu sancji-masicfiq!"*

Gavin entered the archway and Mourn stepped onto the cream tiles of the altar room. Suddenly, the sanctuary lit up with flares spreading along the floor like oil atop water, surrounding the Bishops and the pool. My bodyguard roared with pain within the ball of light, as if the Sun itself had fallen upon Miurag and landed in this Temple.

~*Morixxyleth?!*~

Getting out!

I could do nothing to help them, but Isboern sprinted forward as Mourn hooked his broad arm around Gavin's ribs and hauled him backwards off the platform and outside the wrecked barrier. The Death-walker's spade went flying, bouncing and scraping along the Temple floor. Mourn curled up, his reaching hand reminding me that he never wore boots.

Shit. His feet...

The Bishops took this moment of weakness. A tight arrow of light flashed from the inner circle, striking Gavin in the chest. He jerked uncontrollably before falling limp.

~*No!*~

A second burning ray burst out and would have hit Mourn but smashed into the Godblood's shield as he crouched in front of them. The force of it nearly toppled the Captain off his feet.

Jael released the breath she'd been holding. I tried to do the same.

The attacks from within the sanctuary stopped, but the burning light remained. Inside, the chanting continued, and Gavin's body lay unmoving and continued to deteriorate.

~*I'm sorry, I don't know,*~ Isboern said, seeming to want me to hear his answer to a question I couldn't hear. ~*That spell is protection for Pisc'sagrad. Only Musanlo's clerics can walk upon it or even fly over it. No, I'm sorry, even I cannot go there.*~

"*Shit,*" whispered my Sister as if she could hear us. "*What are we going to do?*"

"A moment," I muttered, my jaw locked as I sheathed Soul Drinker and pulled out my pendant to grasp it in my bare hand. *Breathe.*

~*Gavin?*~

I knew he didn't like it, but if he wasn't gone, he *had* to hear me!

~*Gavin!*~

His empty black, skeletal hand twitched; his other had never dropped the shard and only clenched tighter.

~*Gavin! Get up! I see your brand shining through your robe. Use it. Focus!*~

Something latched onto my will, like a hand reaching out of the water to grab my boot.

I heard him.

Help... Focus.

~*Yes. See it?*~

I stared at Gavin's sunburst brand as Mourn and Isboern helped him back to his feet. The mark glowed visibly under his robe, centered high between his shoulder blades. Gavin could see it through my eyes and when he recognized it, the color changed from glowing white to ice blue. His body was emaciated, but his magic grew resilient against the onslaught.

~*Join the other priests across the barrier,*~ I encouraged. ~*They're waiting for you, and you've known it all your life. This is your last chance.*~

Our Deathwalker's skin fell as ash, and most of his hair was gone. My headache grew worse, but I held the mindlink and any willpower he was willing to share to bear it. He pulled his fallen hood up and over to shield his face, turning toward the light once again.

Isboern held out his palm to Mourn, pleading for him to stay back as Gavin walked fearlessly into the ruined archway and back onto the glowing floor, vanishing through the wall of light.

I could no longer see him, but I could *feel* the space and uncertain balance as he staggered at the slam of power while blindly navigating the bodies of the monks within the sanctuary.

Moving sightless never frightened a Davrin; it was easier to keep our balance, and Gavin noticed.

Help. Focus.

I offered him insight on how to do it, how it should feel.

~*Like this. Carefully. Quietly.*~

The remaining Bishops, locked in their magical trance, did not realize Gavin was there, nor did they seem to care how their fallen cooked and sizzled upon the floor. Maybe with all those mage-priests missing from their circle, the ritual welcomed another priest with the same scarring.

The Deathwalker set one smoking foot in front of the other. He knew his flesh had wasted away, but like in the Nexus, believed the cost to be worth it.

Outside, The Sun's power swelled as the chants continued. No searing beams shot out while Isboern and his shield covered Mourn, who paced the barrier of light, searching for a weak spot. The Dragon son's tongue flicking out, and whatever he smelled caused the spines to strain against his harness.

Sirana?

~He's in there,~ I confirmed. ~Still walking.~

"Capitan!" the Templari shouted around us. "Capitan!"

The Dragonblood and Isboern rejoined us only after confirming there was no way in. As they approached, the defenders begged for answers in their native tongue. The Godblood answered them in Trade.

"The Grey Maiden's messenger can walk upon the hallowed light of *Pisc'sagrad*," Isboern said softly, shading his eyes. "My Templari, not even *I* can do this. I shall take this as the change we've been praying for. Do not fear that it is here."

"Better hope he makes it," Jael muttered in Davrin. "You only have one of him, right?"

I wanted to smile, but it felt heavy as I did not get the sense Gavin cared if he returned to us. Maybe he and his Lady had planned for this, or maybe we had underestimated Musanlo's own servants.

Another wave of magic caught us unaware; it weakened our knees and made our heads throb. Heat shimmered in waves, rising toward the jagged aperture of the Eastern window, and as I looked up, the Sun shone full in the sky beyond.

It certainly made the headaches worse.

"Your God broke his word."

I jumped to hear Gavin's low voice fill the chamber. It was him but didn't sound *exactly* like him.

"His faithful have corrupted his teachings."

I sensed the grey mage step onto the tiles with the blue runes, joining the circle in ritual as a black figure with the sunburst shining blue on his back, facing six others bearing the same mark in gold.

"The Godblood heralded your time of judgment."

His voice turned hoarse and grating.

"You were warned. You chose to ignore its approach."

He sounded like the emissary of a Greylord while the mortals wheezed around him.

"N-nomuli sancji...nus posibili..."

"Musanlo abandunos..."

"Silien, Ocu!"

"Suis cosa! Miran'o selgi!"

The light within the Temple wavered beneath the Sun. I could only hope the Bishops of Manalar had nothing left to throw at us when Gavin lifted his black, skeletal arm.

"Be judged by the purity of your chosen champions. They are the seeds of your destruction."

I felt the moment when Gavin finally let go of the black shard, the weight lifted from him in allowing it to drop into *Pisc'sagrad*. Unlike the broken poles Mourn had snapped off, no bubble arose to prevent the sharp flint from breaking the surface of the water.

I wondered if anyone heard the tiny *"plop"* it made besides me and Gavin.

At once, the light upon the floor faded. Through Gavin's shrunken vision, I saw the water was no longer clear but looked like someone had spilled a jug of wizard's ink into it. The darkness spread out from Jacob's soul, anointed by the red blood Keros had spilled.

The Bishops screamed, their faces contorted in anguish and fear as their sacred power turned against them.

★All Guild, take cover!★ Mourn ordered through the pearls.

~*Templari, brace yourselves!*~

Fuck.

I turned to run for the stairs, but my bodyguard seized me first. Having the practice, I clutched to his front as he sprinted back to Krithannia with Jael and Deshi chasing us with impressive speed. We ducked down into place, wordlessly welcomed by our companions and the other Guild who'd found us.

"Suppress your auras all you can!" Mourn barked, holding my belly tight against him and wrapping his tail around Jael's waist and making her yelp.

What about Gavin…?

I didn't have the chance to look for him as all the magic left the smokeless torches, and all three chandeliers went dark at once. I heard the Bishops screaming, beseeching their god, but something much, much lower rose up to drown them all out.

The Temple itself trembled and Mourn pressed me low as when he'd shielded Gavin and me from the warp rot unraveling. Drawing down on my aura, withdrawing into my own mind until all I heard were my spiders pealing, I expected the floor beneath my body to crumble, or to be buried by a collapsing staircase.

Whether what ultimately struck me was a mountain of stone or the newly unrestrained power of the Ley, I wouldn't know unless I regained consciousness.

Even then, everything will have changed.

CHAPTER 29

WARM, SHUDDERING BREATH DREW ME TO THE SURFACE. I WASN'T ALONE. My left hand felt cold, touching a hot surface, hard and dry.

His ribs expanded in another breath, pushing patches of scales against my hand, and I opened my eyes to look into his. It was dark enough that I couldn't see the gold color. I inhaled, and the air tasted strange crossing my tongue, like watery flakes of dust.

I didn't know where we were, but a sense of urgency returned to sweep in and chill the rest of me.

~*We need to get up.*~

Agreed. Silently, if you can.

~*Jael?*~

Ugh... here...but not so loud, hai? My head...

As Mourn drew back, I discovered why my right hand *wasn't* cold: because it was squished between my Sister's thighs. At some point, Mourn had pulled Jael under the shelter of his body with me, mashing us together during the surge. I smiled despite the disquieting atmosphere, withdrawing my hand with a mental sigh as more came back to me.

~*Krithannia?*~

Oh! Uhm. Here.

~*And Torch? Deshi and his brothers?*~

435

We are awake, Janshi.

Hia-yo...We feel strange...

Whewf. You are not the only ones.

I blinked, looking around us beneath the stairs to see a familiar, blue-eyed man. ~Wolf?~

Yeah. He winced, holding his side. *Needed a place to hide from some stone-hided Ma'ab after helping goddamned Bishops to live longer...*

But they should be dead now, Hand, right? thought the Guildsman right beside him.

Wolf shook his head. *I dunno, Tak. Where is everyone? Sound off.*

As Reprisal counted their remaining heads, I heard them all but looked bewildered at Mourn, who tasted the air to his satisfaction.

~Are you doing this?~

He peeked out from behind the stairs into the sanctum at large. *Doing what?*

~Letting me hear all the pearls.~

He shook his horned head once. *Not this time. You initiated contact. Let me know if you need help closing the links. It can be a lot of distracting chatter if you aren't used to it.*

~Um...~

Less distracting, more overwhelming. I covered my ears first as if that would help when I understood that not all of Reprisal had made it after retreating from the Hellhounds. Two had bled out, and something worse had happened when Gavin fulfilled his quest.

I don't know what happened, Wolf! a man wept such that I didn't recognize who it was. *The surge must've burned him out! He's barely breathing and just stares at me!*

How could that be? Gavin had said it shouldn't outright cripple any mages except for those attuned to Pisc'sagrad. Perhaps the Guildsman had lost his protective charm during the fight, and he was more vulnerable to the surge than he knew?

I checked the charms in my pouch. They'd turned to dust.

Breathe, Hawk, steady. You're with us, and we're not out of danger yet.

Can you move him—? Mourn asked.

He didn't finish his thought, but the alarm I read in his tail had me lunging for the stairs to look out from the other side.

Cris-ri-phon.

Standing over Gavin's body.

Leaning down to study the thurible.

Shit!

Reprisal, Mourn growled through the pearls. **Shadow brothers. Practice your spells. Light as many of the sanctum torches as you can and realign yourself with the Ley. Quickly.**

Some of the men groaned trying to move and lay eyes on an extinguished torch. I shook my head at the overlapping thoughts.

Quiet them, Sirana. Like this.

It was Krithannia allowing me to feel it, offering me the insight to "turn down" the noise from the message pearls I'd somehow invited myself into.

Mourn had focused on my Sister, taking hold of her wrists directly to stand behind her, and wrapping his tail around her ankle as if to ground them both.

He's helping to realign her new aura quickly, Krithannia said. **It's swirling too much for a neophyte to do herself.**

Yes. I would rather he do that for her rather than leave her to drown. Thank goddess we hadn't discovered her gone and "burned out," too.

My attention snapped back to Gavin and the Deathless when the latter jolted upright, looking above him while clusters of torches sputtered to life. Something else spooked the sorcerer beyond this, for he turned toward the North wall, leaving the long, black skeleton behind him. Meanwhile, sparks and magic continued to skip like a flat stone tossed upon water, returning visible light to the sanctum.

Now it's working… one of the Guildsmen said.

Yeah, I'm getting the hang of this.

The most startling change was the chancel barrier. The high, dense wall of tangled iron had been pushed forward until most of it was flat upon the stone. Blocks of the stone floor where it had landed were cracked or bashed into gravel, and I spied pulpy parts of flesh and bone mashed into the spaces between the metal like roots through a cooking mesh.

Ugh.

The inner sanctuary lay exposed with a few other fortunate bodies more like Gavin's: tossed back from the pool but collapsing mostly whole, if unmistakably dead with skulls broken or spines snapped to allow the corpses to lie in grotesque positions which made me shudder.

Underneath these strewn bodies, the tiles no longer glowed, not even the circle of scorched, blood-stained runes. All had been sprayed by liquid yet appeared to be dry now, only a blackish tint left behind.

Pisc'sagrad churned like it boiled in a pot above a fire, but there was no visible heat source. The grey-white vapor which flowed out was not a billowing rise of steam but a low and heavy mist which creeped out, gradually filling the chamber with an eerie chill. I looked outside the broken window above and spotted grey clouds obscuring the morning, overcast thick enough to trigger my Dark Sight beneath the stairs.

Isboern appeared from behind the opposite staircase as the torchlight returned by the collective efforts of Guild and Templari testing their spellcasting. His shield glimmered from the wild flares and guttering flames which spread to light the chandeliers. I had the sense that this was what had caused Cris-ri-phon to turn around and ignore Gavin and the thurible.

Perhaps the two leaders of men had been talking in silence.

"What do you want, ancient one?" the Captain asked forthrightly, his face suggesting he was in no mood for politics or pleasantries.

The Zauyrian sorcerer lifted empty hands in a gesture of peace which meant nothing among mages, and the Captain raised his shield.

"I'm here to help you, *Capitan*," Cris-ri-phon said, smiling with the innkeeper's charm. "I was like you once, a leader of many men, all of whom depended on me. I know what you carry with great weight and pride. *Mitneh'thran* can help save your city. You've heard this, and it is true."

Mourn sighed with aggravation, rubbing my Sister's hands as if they were sore, then motioned with his head to come out with him.

Putting on my missing glove, I hurried to flank him with Jael. My spiders crawled out to be visible on my shoulders and remind Cris they were not trapped in a sorcerer's ball this time. I would persuade the guileful dung log to move away from Gavin's body.

Cris-ri-phon twisted his head when he heard us, unconcerned what Isboern might do when he looked away. He sighed with similar exasperation upon recognizing Mourn, his steel-grey eyes tracing quickly over my Sister and me. I was certain he noted my spiders.

With another sigh, the Zauyrian turned his back to the pool, moving so that he could see all of us on either side. He left enough space for me to get close to Gavin without standing next to the Sorcerer-General who'd tried to enslave me.

A first step in the right direction, at least.

"If you wish to bargain with the Captain, Deathless," Mourn said, stepping forward until he was in between Gavin's corpse and Cris-ri-phon. "I will stand as witness and advisor."

"I know your blood can't help but lust after such opportunities, To'vah-krav," the sorcerer replied, glancing with suspicion as I knelt down near the thurible. "Do you *really* think the Godblood has the time to play with you?"

Isboern cleared his throat loudly. "The wall is quiet following the shock, but it won't be for long. The legend and I have bargained, sorcerer. I am satisfied and commend his conduct. What do you offer to aid this crisis?"

Nothing we can count on.

I pursed my lips shut, stubbornly keeping down all the same confusion and grief trying to force its way out to look down at Gavin's body this way. Somewhat like the dream in the mist we'd shared on the boat, most of his bones showed through patches of charred flesh. His tall skeleton was solid black, though his body was neither picked clean nor burned bare.

Thanks to the Deathwalker's leather armor, enough charred skin remained upon his torso to retain awful-smelling organs and connective tissues within his rib cage. His Nexus-blessed blood seeped out as black sludge, still wet.

Dangerous to touch, he said. Perhaps Cris sensed it.

I inspected the artifact, sure that the Deathless would rather I not. White mist flowed into the crow-shaped holes in thick threads while remaining cool to the touch. The top ring had been looped to Gavin's frayed belt, but the moment I touched the charred leather, it crumbled.

The bottom ring clanked against the stone, and everyone paused in their debate to look at me.

"Apologies," I muttered, using a scrap of his robe to wrap the thurible holding chain a couple times around Gavin's fleshless hand. "Continue talking."

"What are you doing?" the Deathless asked.

"The thurible is drawing in Vis and Vitas," I said, certain he could see it so there was no point in lying. "It's healing him. We wait long enough, he will stand up again." My eyes flicked up with a smile. "Like last time in your shed."

He huffed a wry laugh. "Do you *have* that much time?"

"Do Deathwalkers 'heal' like men?" Isboern asked, sounding curious but skeptical.

"Not this one, he's not a man," Cris-ri-phon replied, rubbing his jaw. "Hm. But this took most of a day last time. If this isn't fast enough, I know how to use the thurible to keep the dead down for good." He smiled warmly at the wall's defender. "The Ma'ab will not be able to use your own against you. Between you and me, the shield, and the thurible, Manalar may stand a chance without your Bishops."

"Sounds good," Isboern responded with caution. "And what would you want in return, ancient?"

"To begin, I want the soul dagger in Sirana's possession." The sorcerer fixed his eyes on the Human man, ignoring me when I glared at him. "She stole it from me."

The look on the Captain's face suggested he remembered why I'd stolen it in the first place. Why I'd *stabbed* him with it.

"Isboern can't bargain for something not in his power to give," Mourn stated plainly.

"Ah, but he can *persuade* her to return it."

"I will not," Isboern said simply. "Ask for something else."

"Oh? Why not?"

"I do not have the ability to persuade her of something she is not willing to do."

Cris-ri-phon changed his posture; his voice dripped with skepticism. "I very much doubt that, *Godblood*."

The Captain's stony face reddened as if he was insulted. "I will be leaving the Temple soon to defend the wall, ancient. Ask for something else or stay to bargain with the legend instead."

Aggravating as it was to listen to them speak about me as if I wasn't in the Temple, the distraction worked in our favor as I confirmed that Gavin's body was gradually restoring itself. I imagined Mourn was telling Jael frequently to stay quiet, because her body language conveyed even more annoyance with these males.

Captain Isboern proved difficult to manipulate, however, and could shield his thoughts while keeping the Zauyrian focused on the shield. Meanwhile, I wondered what connection, if any, Gavin might retain with *Pisc'sagrad*, and if he could reach out to his mistress at this dire time?

I did not enjoy the possibility of Cris-ri-phon recalling *Pisc'sagrad* was free of the Bishops and more malleable to the sorcerer than it had been in a long time.

The Zauyrian pinched the bridge of his nose. "*Capitan*. Take heed of the consequences of your ignorance about powers you do not understand."

"I *want* to defend my city," Isboern said. "If I may use this ancient symbol of Manalar, and you use the thurible, isn't that enough? Surely, you'd be honored as a leader among the people."

Ohhh, don't say that…

Cris-ri-phon grunted a bitter laugh. "Perhaps if you hadn't gotten involved with Elves to the point you will defend them in the stupidity of obeying their own Queens."

A mistake the Sorcerer-General had made as well if we were making harsh judgments.

Jael grumbled something beneath her breath but worked for distraction and engagement over provocation. She'd said, "*queens*" in Davrin, though, and I felt another chill.

Shit. He knew about Tamuril? Or did he mean Krithannia?

The negotiation continued in this manner as I realized the sorcerer was truly stuck on Soul Drinker and began to doubt that he cared to recapture me. Maybe only the dagger would suffice, but he hadn't reached the point of challenging Mourn to take it by force.

The Deathless could always leave and wait for another opportunity. He could ambush us at the Ley Tower, or might be more interested in following me back home.

What... ambush at the Tower...?

I froze, staring at the skeletal face with ears, lips, and eyelids gone, glossy black teeth exposed, and void-black eyes shriveled.

~...Gavin? Is it you?~

Yes...

I saw in my mind the day we had first met and made our bargain against Sarilis. Our interactions flashed by again, yet it was from his view.

It was unnervingly detailed.

I swallowed, swiftly tutoring my face toward placidity. ~*How will you beseech your Lady for guardians? We need them.*~

His eye sockets slowly filled with blood, draining out as that vast, nebulous space in which we spoke swelled with more and more whispers, whirling around like an active breeze.

I...already have, he said.

Oh, Goddess.

~*And? What was her decision?*~

Dip the thurible into Pisc'sagrad. Trail the water back to me. She will answer then.

I hesitated. ~*The charms are dust. Will this harm my baby?*~

No. You are... Lewensbluen.

Even in thought, I did not recognize the concept. Like something growing and dying at once?

~I am what?~

You are the deliverer. Pisc'sagrad would not harm you. Neither shall my Lady. Dip it until it fills, lift it, and trail the water back to me.

~Uh…understood. Um. Be right back.~

I withdrew from the deep, whispering space, suppressing the shiver up my spine as I hurried to unwrap the chain from his unmoving hand. Without pausing to explain, I stood up and hurried onto the platform and toward the water.

"Sirana!" Cris-ri-phon barked. "Stop what you are doing!"

Pissing in your mouth, world eater.

Mourn stood with arms crossed, golden eyes fixed on the sorcerer, as Jael hissed; she also did not draw her swords. As baffling as that restraint was, Cris-ri-phon only had to turn toward me to run nose-first into an invisible shield.

By then, the thurible had filled with water.

"Let her be," Isboern said. "She acts on behalf of her ally and on behalf of this city."

The Deathless didn't respond as I brought the dripping incense burner off the platform, splattering liquid toward Gavin's corpse. The water behaved no differently from any well or stream I'd drawn from in my life.

I stopped once I reached my ally, letting the thurible sprinkle water onto his feet. He twitched.

My heart pounding, I dared to glance at Cris-ri-phon, shocked to see that he appeared…

Worried.

Worried about what the Deathwalker had told us would happen once the Bishops were gone.

Because he still doesn't know.

Even Gavin hadn't known it all.

We are about to find out.

CHAPTER 30

THE BRIGHT CHANDELIERS AND LINES OF TORCHES DIMMED AS THE GREY MIST rose up from the floor, expanding to fill the Temple of the Sun. *Pisc'sa-grad* had become calm, but the water rose until it overflowed the boundaries of the marble. Clear water spread quickly across the damaged floor, avoiding the remains of the iron barrier, and following the pathway I'd created with the thurible.

I dropped the thurible and backed up from the water's edge, assisted further as both Mourn and Jael reached for my arms to pull me along. We retreated toward the stairs, ready to climb them if the water didn't stop, and I wasn't the only one.

Cris-ri-phon moved so quickly toward the opposite stairs that his aura became visible to me for an instant, trailing jagged wisps of color before coalescing tightly near his skin once he stopped.

Looking back, I watched water pooling around Gavin's body but slowing down as it moved beyond, bending unnaturally to the North and away from us. The extension was either following the Deathless, or...

Isboern?

He was the only one who hadn't moved. The Godblood stared at the puddle on the floor approaching him. He took a step forward to meet it.

~*Uh, is that a good idea?*~

~*I'm not afraid, Sirana.*~ Willven placed one foot in the puddle before slowly taking to one knee and resting the bottom rim of the golden shield in the water. ~*The wise Elf suggested that I must ask for what I need.*~

~*Must ask for...? But she was talking about the light!*~

~*And that is what we must be for others in the dark, mustn't we?*~

Mourn could read the panic on my face; he shook his head and squeezed my shoulder. Apparently, we would only watch.

The ten Templari came out from beneath the Northern stairs, giving Cris-ri-phon a wide berth as they formed a circle between him and their Captain, all facing outward for the best view of the Temple in the mists. Several made a familiar motion of respect or devotion across their eyes and chest, murmuring their words to join a brief, simple prayer shared by their Godblood in the sacred waters.

There could be no confusion about his intent.

~*Musanlo, the oppression of the Immersed is relinquished at last. I kneel humbly to accept the protection offered for these ancient waters, to avoid usurpation until the new stewards of the Mount are decided.*~

~*I welcome the messenger of the Grey Maiden and beseech her favor. May her guidance return to the Mount of the Sacred Waters at the dawn of war, for all mortals facing their deaths today. We are in desperate need.*~

When muted light appeared in the air above *Pisc'sagrad*, Mourn gently pushed me behind him as he stepped to shield me. It was thin at first, as if a dagger had cut through cloth pulled taut, but then widened, and an incorporeal passageway resembling grey dust extended away from us. Its depth was a trick to the eye, passing beyond the wall of the Temple without breaking it.

I blinked, and four figures stood in that ethereal doorway, close enough to step out. Their feet landed in silence upon the pool's edge and into the water spilled upon the broken tiles.

Captain Isboern straightened up to acknowledge the arrivals with a local salute. They returned it with one of their own.

"*Oh my goddess,*" Jael whispered, peeking out farther from behind the half-blood than I was. *"What...the fuck...are they?"*

Whatever I might have expected to see in "neutral" guardians summoned from the Nexus, three of them were impossible to match as anything from this world.

The largest one towered above the other three, appearing male and possessing a Ma'ab fighting body, though his hands and bare feet had extremely thick digits with sturdy fingernails. He wore no armor at all, however, and carried nothing but a caddy of scrolls with a book buckled at his side. The Nexus male's skin was thick and greenish grey, his ears short but pointed, and his eyes jade green in texture as much as color. He inhaled slowly through a prominent, cavernous nose attached to a heavy-boned and hairy face, with red hair faded but covering most of his head.

Behind him hid a smaller creature huddling in a cloak and clutching something beneath it. The legs drew most of my focus: dark, thin, segmented, and glossy. No soft flesh or muscle like the male in front, but instead reminded me of any number of insects I'd seen on the Surface.

Cris-ri-phon leaned to get a better look, but the scroll-bearer and a smaller, armored one shifted to block his view when the creature chittered in alarm. The wide brute smiled, showing a lone tusk jutting up from his lower lip; he bowed his head with respect.

The sorcerer narrowed his eyes in suspicion. "Do I know you?"

The scholar said nothing as a much smaller woman stepped forward, her face covered by her helm.

"We know you, Cris," she said with a hoarse whisper which nonetheless projected quite well within the misty Temple.

Her body was the most Human I could recognize, yet she was dressed and well-equipped like a soldier. The helm, gauntlets, visible weapons, and armor were not made of metal, however. They appeared wrought from something once living but painted with white, grey, and deep blue abstract markings. A thread of gold hinted at a rising Sun.

The Sorcerer-General didn't believe her and resented the assumed familiarity.

None of this seemed to matter to the fourth and final guardian, who was the first to follow the water out from the sanctuary beyond the fallen chancel barrier. Gavin's body was her focus and destination, which became apparent at the same time she drew close enough for me to see all the macabre details of her form.

At first, I believed she wore a close-fitting uniform like Jael and me, made of strange black and grey leather yet showing more skin in unusual places. The clothing was stitched together not in standard order but artistically pinned to her body with sutures piercing her flesh.

As she came to stand beside our mending Deathwalker, I could see this woman was tiny, smaller than Amelda, yet with the familiar Ma'ab coloring. Her black hair was smooth and cut short, with a swath from one temple to her nape shorn away to show the fine black-needle piercings forming a rune as part of her scalp.

Her eyes were hardly visible, void-like as when Gavin worked his magic, until I noticed a glint in the one socket.

Oh...

A sculpted piece of obsidian or tempered flint fit in her left socket as an eye replacement.

"Oh..." Jael hushed. *"Gross..."*

Needles and barbs had been inserted under the guardian's white skin, bloodless and barely swollen around the puncture wounds. They were linked with jeweler's chains in ways which suggested additional sigils. Other sutures simply held and cupped various parts of her female form, such as the bottom half becoming an open-fronted skirt, its hems attached across her thighs down to her knees before flowing free to touch the floor.

All this, and she appeared to feel no pain.

Or if she was, it wasn't enough to make her stop smiling down at Gavin, her lips further warped by pins and piercings, showing grey, smooth teeth.

The Templars were extremely nervous as this female approached them, yet the Deathless peered at her as if he might truly recognize *this* one as opposed to the other two, who hadn't taken their gaze from him.

Isboern glanced at me as if to gauge whether intervention was necessary, but all I could do was shake my head. *~He called them.~*

~He did. And I opened the door.~

The Captain remained nearby in the middle of a puddle as this morbid little woman stretched the integrity of her attire to kneel next to Gavin's glistening corpse.

"*I hope this isn't worse,*" my Sister muttered.

~Me, too...~

The mist swirled and cleared before rushing back in as she heaved him up by his skeletal neck and gaunt shoulders, showing no concern for the black, bloody mess swiftly staining her ornate gown. With a strength and determination that belied her appearance, the distorted woman cradled him against her breast and began singing softly enough that I couldn't hear the words.

"*What is she doing?*" Jael whispered.

"*I don't know,*" I said.

"*I might.*" Mourn tapped my Sister's shoulder. "*Tell me. Compared to the other three, how similar is her aura to Gavin's?*"

Jael scowled as she squinted at them, paying less attention to the oddly intimate caressing and rocking than I was. "*Uh...very?*"

"*Very. Rare to mirror so, but when they do, it's always close blood. Twins. Siblings.*"

"*Mother and child?*" I guessed.

"*Or sire and child. Yes.*"

I hadn't spent a moment considering this before the small woman reached into Gavin's leaking torso, the act setting my spine rigid, my tongue ready to protest as I expected her to rip out his heart. Then I realized she wasn't pulling but... squeezing.

His hand flexed, and one of his legs kicked.

Several Templars jumped, and the strange woman laughed, sounding oddly joyful as she reached to tear a larger hole in her gown, which also tore open a section of skin high on her breast. Wrapping her gory arm fully around him again, she held him close like a suckling infant.

My stomach waffled between sickness at the sight and astonishment at an extraordinary possibility.

"Ada?" I whispered aloud.

She looked up suddenly, her obsidian eye glowing the same ice blue as Gavin's. She peered straight at me. I clutched Mourn's harness but resisted hiding since I'd been caught. She smiled and mouthed something I couldn't read.

Gavin started coughing, and Ada reluctantly pulled him away from her breast, allowing him to roll over on his front and brace himself on his elbows. She replaced her pins and barbs, her breast smeared black and red, while his emaciated body began to swell with new, wet muscle before our eyes, as if the black bones were in a hurry to cover themselves.

After our Deathwalker regained enough strength to rise to all fours, he began growing skin. Real skin, and white like hers, but without a single mark, scar, or brand I recalled from his old flesh.

Renewed.

As Gavin's hair, nails, and eyes returned, Jael groaned and hid to put her head down, breathing deeply against nausea. I was somehow feeling better and wondered at my resilience after enough time around the death mage.

At least it didn't smell bad.

"H-how…w-who…?" rasped my revived ally, using a throat not quite ready for speech as he pushed himself to his feet. The filthiest scraps of his ravaged leather jerkin barely clung to him, which matched his mother's style more than not.

Gavin fell silent, staring down at the pale, smiling woman covered in his black blood and none the worse for it. Ada was much shorter than him, barely coming up to his chest, but she reached up the rest of the way to touch his gaunt cheek with her sticky fingertips.

"Worth every lash," she whispered.

Gavin was at a loss, not a twitch or quiver in his body as he studied the piercings covering hers. He did not jerk back from her touch as I thought he might, but he appeared blank in how to respond to praise like this.

More than praise.

I saw a mother's pride in her expression which she did not hide.

The former monk faced someone unequivocally content that he had been born, a sentiment which had probably never been directed at him before.

Had all leading to this moment been a test or a reward? If so, for who, Gavin? Or for Ada?

"Votary," said the other small Greylands woman in armor.

When Ada turned to acknowledge her, the soldier motioned for the least-Human looking among them to come forward. The insectal child hid behind the greenish grey male, and not much larger than Ada in size. As they obeyed their leader, the concealing cloak parted to show four arms bearing a pack close to their chest, and the creature lowered their hood.

"*Whoa,*" whispered the Guildsmen behind us.

I could only describe a giant wasp with a sentient but alien face, dark hair crowning their head with active, quivering antennae sprouting up. They were bipedal but seemed to mimic our more familiar sentient's shape.

"Oh, yes," said Gavin's mother. "We brought you clothes, Herald."

Herald?

The insectal courier scuttled forward on strong, hind legs, offering Gavin the bundle with all four arms. He accepted, staring after the creature as they returned to the pool. After a beat, my twice-risen death mage unfolded a new grey robe, pouch-loaded belt, and boots.

"Votary," the soldier said again, motioning Ada back as Gavin dressed. "We need you here."

With a quiet, regretful hum, Ada offered a pleasant, if grotesque, bow first to Captain Isboern and then to Gavin before returning through the watery path between the iron. She took her place with the others, forming four points around the sacred pool while the portal above stayed open.

"You are emissaries of the Grey Maiden, then?" Isboern asked. "Here to guard *Pisc'sagrad* as requested by her Herald Gavin?"

At first, I thought that was obvious, then I realized they'd never said.

"We are, Godblood. Each of us once called this world our home." The soldier offered a salute but glanced at Cris-ri-phon, whose expression had grown with anger. "We shall help level the battlefield by lifting this burden from you in the place of your Bishops. But we may not leave the Temple or influence the outcome."

"That is all we may ask." Isboern saluted back. "Thank you."

Then the Captain turned to Gavin stamping his foot into his new boot. As the Deathwalker adjusted his belt and picked up the thurible, I spotted the awkward moment closing in, about which there'd been no discussion.

"Will you stay, Deathwalker?" the blond man asked with a genuine edge of desperation, "And help to assure the dead lie down in peace when they fall in battle?"

"Of course," Gavin replied.

I jolted with shock.

Of course...? *Of course?!*

Shit!

~*If Gavin stays, what are we going to do?*~ I asked. ~*Jump through the gate and wait for him?*~

Mourn didn't reply at first, his tail coiled slowly behind him. He was staring at Cris-ri-phon. *That answer may depend more on the Deathless, Sirana. It might be better to help Isboern and Gavin and to deal with him now, rather than escape or let him vanish only to reach the Ley Tower ahead of you. Or follow you home.*

I gritted my teeth. ~*Deal with him how?*~

He's vulnerable to Soul Drinker. He's unsettled by these Nexus guardians who claim to know him. He tried to threaten and bargain but failed in both. He has yet to attack, but he won't leave.

~*What does he want?*~

I believe he just wants Soul Drinker, but he will cause unimaginable harm if he obtains it. I also do not believe it would spare you retaliation.

Retaliation, such as claiming a body to bring his Queen back; one with which she may delight in delivering a new child for them soon.

Oh, Goddess.

Don't panic.

"Hey, Gavin?" I called, and he turned. "Who are these guardians? What are their names?"

The large, tusked male smiled and spoke at last. "Oskar."

Oskar.

Where had I heard that name?

"Once," he added, "I was a Deathwalker in V'Gedra."

Stunned, I couldn't react but the Deathless growled, "Impossible! Oskar was Human!"

The bulky neck leaned in a nod. "Yes, I was. I saved your daughter from the assassins. Despite everything, she always loved her father. To the end."

That looked like a strike to the face.

"A-and you?" Cris-ri-phon demanded of the armored woman. "Who do you claim to be?"

Mourn touched my back. *Be ready.*

The soldier removed her helm, watching him peacefully, and the Deathless swallowed.

Her hair was as black as Ada's and cut short, but her skin was ashen-brown, similar to the Zauyrian sorcerer. Her face was marked with artistic, ritual scars stained with charcoal, her eyes crystal blue with black encroaching from the sides.

My confused rut with Brom at the inn returned to my mind's eye, along with the dreams of a young mage coupling with a royal Davrin beneath the Desert waterfall.

He knew this one, too.

"Houda," Cris-ri-phon croaked.

The Deathwalker from the Zauyrian Realms who had taken care of him when he was ill as a boy. The woman who'd been teaching him death magic before he met the Davrin Qu'eesan Innathi.

The one who'd first watched him turn his back on resigning to a mortal death, to quest for the sake of an Elf.

"*Why are you here?!*" he roared. "To stand there and gloat, to see how nothing's changed? To mock me for failing?"

Houda looked saddened. "Nothing will change while Serenity remains, Cris. I've chosen to bear witness. There is no mockery in this."

Isboern stepped closer to Gavin, motioning his Templars to join him. They obeyed, seeming less repulsed by the Deathwalker than they'd been a moment ago.

"You've fought for Mount Sonai before," Houda said. "You have returned. Why not make the choice again?"

"As if it will be different after the fighting and wailing is finished?" he sneered, shaking with emotion. "They're *all* the same. Every battle... all of them! I *wanted* to stay out of this!" His steely eyes darted hatefully at me. "But I couldn't. Always... always cruel, manipulative Elves pulling the threads..."

"He's deranged," Jael muttered.

I grunted in agreement. A fact, unfortunately, for which I could not deny a probable cause. The Queen had been pulling our threads, too, and who knew if we'd ever get free of them?

At all this, Isboern was beginning to look overwhelmed.

~I... I need to go,~ he pleaded. ~I must check on the wall. The evacuations are ongoing...~

Go, Mourn answered. *This is beyond your service, Captain. Go to your people.*

~And the jump gate?~ he asked, suddenly afraid. ~Is it...?~

It's still up. The Guild and the Clans hold to their word. Go.

Isboern saluted, side-stepping away from the raging immortal to approach Gavin as he reclaimed the shovel from the floor. My ally looked at me and used his spade to bid us farewell.

Well, shit.

Gavin hurried toward the Western exit with the Captain and his Templari. Behind them, Ada smiled gruesomely while the insect child observed in silence as the two Deathwalkers of ancient V'Gedra faced Cris-ri-phon's verbal onslaught as further memory seemed to unfold before his eyes.

Much of what passed the Deathless's lips had seized events and accusations of which I had no knowledge and little understanding but gave me a sense of what happened when a Human General served a Queendom for centuries only to lose everything.

How did that even happen? Why couldn't he die? Or did he, but kept coming back from the Nexus? Was that a "world-eater," as Gavin had said, that will always "come home?"

Most importantly, how do we deal with him now?

"How dare you! My daughter is dead! All of them, *killed* by their envious, venomous aunt! They are lost!"

"They are not lost," Houda replied with ethereal calm. "The Grey Lady knows. You need only to find them."

Cris was sweating, shaking from grief and fury. Once again, he looked at me, then at the dagger at my belt. "I found her. *She* was lost, too, but I *found* her. After so long, I *know* where she is, and I'll have her *back*."

"Do not follow that path, Cris," Houda said. "After so long, let her go. Let all the River children go. *Your* children need you more. They are here. They *remain*, Cris. I promise you this truth spoken by the Grave Mother herself. They need a guide. They have been waiting for one out there, in your home."

Tears spilled from the grey-haired sorcerer's eyes as he shuddered, fearful of believing her, more so of denying it. I would have said that he was near the edge of breaking his convictions. He was almost convinced, nearly persuaded to change his course, and follow his old teacher's advice.

But he had to walk away and leave me as the dagger's wielder.

To look for another purpose.

"I..." He gasped for breath, turning from the platform. "I-I...Yes... My daughter. I will find—"

The sorcerer's entire body stiffened, and he clutched his head as he bellowed in agony at the chandeliers. In the mist-filled and quiet Temple, the blow to our senses was numbing.

"Cris!" Houda called, taking one step forward as the Dragonblood finally called his sliders into his hands and moved toward the main floor.

Morrixxyleth! Krithannia cried. *There's another presence here!*

What presence? he barked. *Who?*

I don't know but be wary!

Gooseflesh broke out all over me listening to them. The Stormseeker was more terrified than she had been by *anything* else thus far.

Seemingly unaware of anything or anyone, the Deathless pulled the firebird ring from his finger and spun back toward *Pisc'sagrad*, rushing for the slowly drying water mixed with Gavin's and Ada's blood. Clutching the ring in one hand, he drew a mundane dagger and savagely slashed his own arm as he ran.

"No!" Mourn spun his blades above his head. "Get down!"

Jael and I hit the stairs the same moment Cris-ri-phon hit the pool of Nexus blood, adding his own crimson flow to the mix. Once again, the casters' voices overlapped in a thunderous crash of willpower above my head.

"Xr zymy mag'qrh, ush'abalok!"

"Jikmada thrae'terenj!"

"Cris, stop!!"

An icy green bolt of lightning scorched the stains upon the floor, following it back to *Pisc'sagrad* as we gaped in horror.

Mourn's spell blasted the sorcerer the next instant, throwing his body back against the farthest column with force enough that I could hear bones snap.

It was too late. Although I expected *Pisc'sagrad* to turn that frosty green color or erupt or boil over again, the bolt instead skipped along the surface of the water and struck straight up at the Nexus passageway itself, absorbing into it and causing a blinding flash.

Augh!

Desperately, I rubbed my eyes, trying to see as voices of alarm began to rise within the Temple. Something else crackled after the rumble of both spells passed. Blinking through the blur, I feared what I saw might be real.

Further cracks had appeared above the Nexus portal, crawling like tree limbs up into the open tower leading outside. The cracks thickened, poured in grey and blue mists like a waterfall as they widened the rift between one place of existence and ours.

"Ohhh, *fuck*...!" Jael squeaked, higher pitched than I'd heard in years.

The torches struggled to stay lit, and our field of vision closed in as the mist became impenetrable.

All that, and my bodyguard was gone.

Heart surging in my chest, I scanned the mists of the Temple for any sign of swift movements within. I spotted the swirls which might indicate his sliders, but then noticed several more like it, and then *more*.

A rush of these murky shapes rose in synchrony to the third floor above us before, all at once, ice blue eyes opened, peering out and down at us. Several opened their mouths and smiled, their sharp teeth and maws glowing just like their eyes.

There were scores of them lining the Temple balcony.

Oh, we are so dead.

Jael and I hustled to get off the stairs and hide with Krithannia and the Guild. The Naulor patted us when we got close, her face flushed and her eyes wide with fear. Noticing everyone who'd dropped their pack had reclaimed it, I grabbed mine and pressed it into Jael's hands while I took Gavin's.

Mourn roared deep within the mist, and I jumped, weighing the wisdom of calling out. *Bah. You don't have to.*

~Mourn!~

Sirana! Where are you?

~Under the stairs! Jael, too.~

Good! Stay there. I'm coming.

~Careful! A lot of glowing eyes with teeth!~

I see them. I...think they're more guardians from Nyx.

~Why do you think?~

Mourn appeared then, slipping around and underneath the stairs. I smelled blood before looking into his metallic eyes. His pupils were wickedly thin.

Because they only watched the Deathless and me exchange blows.

Who won? Jael asked.

The half-blood jerked his head in a negative. *Undecided. He fled through a portal, and I'm damn sure he didn't summon it.*

Fuck.

~That other 'presence' that wouldn't let him leave?~

Mourn's tail lashed. *Likely.*

~What now?~

"Defenders of Manalar!" Houda called. "Please show yourselves! Time is short to guide you!"

The Dragonblood exhaled, meeting the eyes of everyone beneath the stairs. *I guess we find out.*

As we cautiously left shelter, I felt the Guild's call through the pearls.

All of Reprisal, Mourn said. *If you're willing and able to continue the larger battle, please join us at the sacred pool.*

If you are not, Krithannia followed, *retreat from the city immediately. Help and encourage others to do the same. And be well.*

CHAPTER 31

KRITHANNIA CHANTED SOMETHING LYRICAL, RAISING HER HANDS AND SWEEP-ing them to one side. A large section of the heavy mist followed, briefly opening a pathway toward the sacred platform and its guardians.

When the obscuring fog began to close in again, Peng-lok cast something similar but less effective, followed by Nianzu, and then Deshi. Wolf and Tak each took their turn, the former limping slightly. None were quite as strong as the Naulor's attempt, but they mentioned getting used to how their magic worked after the surge.

At least the effects were cumulative and cleared a space where we could see the splintering extensions high above Nyx's portal, the color gradients overlapping and shifting from grey to blue to green. The broken window drew out some of the mist but only because more continued to billow up into the Eastern tower open to the sky.

"Do not fear the shadows up high, defenders!" Houda called. "They serve our Lady as well. Hurry!"

After hearing this, members of Reprisal rushed down the length of the sanctum to catch up.

Draw Soul Drinker, Mourn said as the other pearls briefly went dead in my ears. *Stay in front of me.*

I frowned. ~In front?~

Yes. Jael will stay behind and right.

~You want them to see it?~

I do.

His tail bumped into my Sister's leg like he wasn't used to anyone hovering there, or he was more nervous than any could tell.

I want to see their response, and I have a suspicion that blade will be especially intimidating to any other Nexus creature which jumps out.

~Because...?~

Wait.

He was right; Houda and Oskar recognized it at once.

"Ah. So you *did* claim it, Davrin," said the leading Deathwalker, not delighted but not wasting time. "That blade will stop or destroy any Nexus denizen not intelligent enough to be repelled by it. The soul dagger will also lead your hand to the weakest point on their form if you let it. Those around you will be protected from any incorporeal sycophants attempting to cling to you. Do you understand?"

"Yes." As much as I could before some practical examples.

"And you," Houda pointed at Deshi. "What is that at your belt?"

The Yungian jumped but did not hesitate to draw his prized long dagger, laying it across his palms and lifting to where they could see it. "The... Herald blessed it in the name of his Lady, honored ancestor."

Houda and Ada exchanged a quick glance before the former said, "Excellent. Are you willing to distract your adversary away from your brothers, so they may take advantage?"

Deshi looked at Torch, Peng-lok, and Nianzu, all of whom murmured something in Yungian to him. It sounded reassuring, and the young death mage dipped his chin. "I am, ancestor."

Houda smiled warmly. "Then allow Ada to add her blood to the point of your blade."

Deshi came forward to meet the macabre visage of Sho'shien's mother, and Ada stepped to the edge of the platform to meet him. Raising one arm with grace, she firmly pressed her finger to the tip until the skin broke. She gasped as the crimson bead appeared.

"What denizens come?" Krithannia asked, sensing the urgency as a deep thrum arose within the Temple.

"We do not know exactly," Houda answered.

"The Deathless called upon the Devourer," Oskar said, his deep voice rumbling. "This Lord has many servants."

Ada chuckled. "Among those servants used to be the Ma'ab. Before those you call the Ascended revolted."

Shock rolled over our group, but Tak blurted it out first. "Wait, you mean we're gonna meet things with a grudge against the Ma'ab because they got away from their master from the land of the dead?!"

"Correct," Houda confirmed. "But make no mistake. They will take any souls they can claim, Ma'ab or other. All in their path are fair game."

"He *is* the Devourer," Ada reminded us with a smirk.

"Could the Ma'ab recognize them," Mourn asked, "and understand that personal threat against them?"

"Some of their leaders might," replied the large, scholarly male. "It depends on what the Ascended told them about their origins. All the same, know that once they step onto this world, they can be cut down the same as any creature born upon it and their incorporeal defenses will not work. These rifts which the Deathless created will close naturally in time, and all invaders will lose strength as this happens. If they do not retreat to the Nexus before the rift closes, they are stuck here and will only weaken further."

"They can be hunted down," Ada added with a viscerally disturbing smile. "Especially by your Herald."

During a pause, most of us were distracted by the odd, persistent buzzing on the far side *Pisc'sagrad*. The insect child crouched down and appeared to be working some sort of industrious magic around the perimeter.

"She is building a unique shelter over your sacred site," Houda explained. "It will mask the waters from invaders and will absorb smaller surges from the rift so as not to disturb the natural Ley too much."

"Magical mud, I like to call it," Oskar smiled, showing tusks.

"Yes," Krithannia breathed. "That would be good, if… she can do that for us."

"She can. She's quite skilled."

The creature's large, glossy eyes flicked toward him as if she recognized the pride in his tone as much as I'd seen it on his face.

"If you have time to draw back and spread the warnings," Houda began, "I recommend leaving the Temple. Do not be trapped here when they arrive. We shall protect this place." She drew our attention up to the scores of burning blue eyes watching. "We are sworn."

"Yes, we'll go," Krithannia said. "We'll try to get as many Manalari out of their pathway as possible."

Houda saluted, her face set to a careful neutral. She did not wish us victory over the Ma'ab, perhaps because she couldn't. She and Nyx's other chosen guardians had been generous to tell us much about what the city was about to face, for none of us had managed to stop Crisri-phon before it was too late.

"Let's move," Mourn said, guiding me so I held my naked blade on the right-hand fringe of our group. "We must find Captain Isboern and the Templars. We may be able to turn the brunt of this against the Ma'ab."

"The latest report, he was headed to the south wall."

Where the biggest crowd of Humans would be.

At least we could explain all this to a psion in seconds instead of minutes.

We ran through the mist, clearing a visible path with gusts of air to the main exit where Isboern had gone. I saw little of the color and decoration from the first time in but recognized crossing the wide hallway where we'd met the first Hellhound. After taking a short flight of stairs down into a smaller chamber, we found the stairs leading back up to massive double doors which normally were hard to miss.

Jael grumped, *They closed it.*

I would have in their place, Mourn replied, prepared with the proper Words to test first a push and then a pull before we reached it.

The doors opened inward, and a sliver of blurry light spread over the floor like a spill as thick mist escaped the Temple. We paused to listen for ambush outside.

Instead, we heard many feet running toward us.

"Abries! Abries, grei ti'Dyos!"

Krithannia gasped. "Citizens."

Shit.

Terrified Manalari commoners shouted prayers, approaching the first stairs leading up from the courtyard. Mourn was tempted to close the door again, I could tell, but then where would we go next?

Suddenly, four creatures appeared in the doorway before us, streaking in so fast I wondered if I'd been staring too long at the public.

They were long, gaunt figures which seemed to lack feet, their forms blacker than the night sky, mimicking the random scatter of stars with blue points shining within their torso. They wore white, expressionless masks, hiding their faces as black, shadowy tendrils draped like ropes of hair. Their legs were covered by a red garment wrapped around waists too slender to be healthy for the living, each with a sword attached, which remained sheathed.

With hands empty, they lifted spindly arms together, creating a deep and hollow sound like wailing wind. An oppressive wave of fear rushed out of the Temple and among the people. The screaming shredded my ears as the citizens scattered back into the courtyard.

The next moment, the four sentries turned and parted for us, motioning outside. Those glowing, blue eyes behind the masks gave us a hint who they were.

"Well," Mourn muttered to his Guild partner, "at least they didn't rush inside."

Indeed, this was the worst possible time for the Temple to fill up with people.

We exited as mist flooded the courtyard, leaving the doors open when Nyx's sentries obstructed us from closing them. Entering the flat stone way as one group, we ignored the panicked and huddling Humans but also made sure we moved too quickly for them to become a threat to us.

The front gates were wide open as we approached; at the same time horsemen approached at a gallop.

"Sirana, check if it's Isboern," Mourn ordered aloud for the sake of our larger force.

Okay, then.

I "opened up" my mind as I had at the library, though not as carefully, for the general fear of the Humans crowded me. I was shut in by a loud and angry fence while trying to be heard above the noise.

~Isboern?~

~Sirana!~

"It's him."

"Oh, good," Krithannia breathed with relief.

~Sirana, do you know what's happening to the city? The Ma'ab aren't doing this!~

Uh-oh. *~The Ma'ab aren't doing what?~*

~Look around you! Gavin says the presence of the Nexus is growing stronger!~

~Well, that's true…~

Nor was it simply overcast or rain clouds above us obscuring the Sun this morning. Turning around for the first time, I could not miss the ominous, grey vapor escaping from the East tower where *Pisc'sagrad* would be open to the sky, nor the streams falling from every crack or gap in the construction of the building itself. Now, the mist was filling the streets, rising up, and cloaking anything beyond Mount Sonai from our vision.

As if we were isolated from the rest of the Surface.

~What happened after I left?~ Isboern asked.

~We don't have much time. Is Gavin with you?~

~He is. Why?~

~There is hope to turn this against the Ma'ab. We'll explain.~

~Alright,~ he thought, probably gritting his teeth. *~We'll be there soon.~*

Sound seemed muted as he withdrew, and beyond the horses, I heard no other animals. No birds or insects, no dogs or cats. Only wailing in the distance and crying in the courtyard, and the itching dread of something worse inbound behind us.

Or maybe they wouldn't come through. Maybe they missed their chance?

The look that had been on Houda's face made me push that wish aside. If the Deathwalkers of ancient V'Gedra were anything like Gavin, they did not lie about their craft and purpose on Miurag.

The Devourer was coming.

We left the courtyard far behind to meet the mounted Templars several streets down. Manalari commoners were running toward the Temple, slowly filling up the courtyard.

~Why are they doing that?~ I asked as the distance closed fast.

~They've refused to evacuate,~ Isboern answered. *~But the Ma'ab threaten the northern wall most, so they believe they will be safe in the Temple.~*

~They are not! That's the worst place they can be!~

His presence in my mind intensified. *~How? What happened?~*

Our groups were close, but the young Human needed something *now*.

~Houda nearly convinced the Deathless to leave without a fight! Something we couldn't see stopped him and compelled the sorcerer to disrupt the Grey Maiden's portal. He vanished but it's letting in more creatures who are not so neutral! Houda told us how we can best confront them, and Gavin will be able to help.~

~Oh, God...~

The Manalari defender had guided me to a wider marketplace where they could dismount farther from Mourn, and we could all fit in a "huddle." Gavin was with them, and I did a quick count.

Eighteen of Reprisal had been willing and able to keep going; between them, the Yungians, and our team we totaled twenty-seven with special training, magic, or unique roles.

Captain Isboern had brought twenty-five of his own, including the four trusted officers: Robi, Imran, Erik, and Sohl. We wouldn't be able to do the huddle exactly like in the library, but grasping the backs of the neck of the man in front would help the psionic pull.

Gavin must be part of it, which didn't thrill him, but he was first to kneel and place his hand out so it would be on the bottom, his palm facing the ground. He looked at me, and I pulled off my glove to add my bare hand atop his.

We built our impossibly fast communication web up and out from the center, and while it felt more fragile with so many inexperienced minds added, those of Reprisal and the Templari who'd been with us before supported those most startled by the bonds forming. No one outright rejected us or panicked enough to cause a collapse. Every fighter here was both frightened and determined to face what was coming.

Of this, we had no doubt.

The "legend teams" filled Gavin and the Templari in on the extraordinary events within the Temple after they'd left. We told them what Houda had conveyed about our weapons and the new adversaries soon to show themselves. Isboern returned the favor.

~The Ma'ab haven't breached the wall in large numbers, but we are losing our own to lucky arrows and the onager tactics. There are a few packs of Hellhounds that got in and are causing terror in the streets. They've been trying to reach a gate to weaken it but thus far have been chased off with oil and fire spells. Every time they're delayed, they kill whomever they find, taking no prisoners.~

Of course not. Their death mage officers would need the bodies later.

~The south wall remains the evacuation point,~ he continued, ~vulnerable but as yet undiscovered. Another two hundred citizens have left the city and hurry toward the gate. Tamuril is there as well. Ma'ab scouts have begun falling to Guild blades——~

What? Krithannia snagged a thought before it moved past. *What of Tamuril?*

Isboern refocused. ~The forest Druid left the Dwarves in the cave and followed the trail of people back to the south wall. She's been helping the Templari with scouting through her falcon's eyes and is growing vine-ropes to lash trees and shrubs together to create a railing for the people to use. Our refugees have been able to climb down the mountain faster and with fewer injuries or accidental deaths.~

Fewer?

The Templari shared a poignant moment of regret.

~We've been rushing them, and the fog makes it harder. Our people are frightened, all of them burdened by possessions and some are lame or elderly. Yes, some have fallen, either breaking limbs or finding their deaths trying to escape. Tamuril is easing this burden and saving their lives. I would like her to continue for as long as she can.~

Her eyes troubled, Krithannia offered a mental nod to continue.

Are more citizens running for the south wall? Mourn asked. *Now that the fighting has begun?*

~Not as many as we'd hoped, though they know the direction if they change their mind. We can no longer spare escorts.~ The Captain's brilliant blue eyes flicked to the Guild Mistress. ~And we know the Dwarves have only enough gems to take so many.~

We'll help all who show up, Captain, Krithannia repeated. *Until we must seal the gate to protect those who went through. The Clans have been prepared to keep it open longer each time as larger groups have arrived. The first ones were the tests.*

The city's defender bowed his head. ~Our... deepest gratitude, elder.~

We returned to the detailed report of the known equipment and tactics used so far: Hellhound infiltrators killing and starting fires anywhere in the city; the onagers flinging walking corpses over the wall, along with thunderstones, offal, feces, and mounds of rot covered in mushrooms which caused people's faces to swell and to choke on spores.

Where are they focused on overcoming the wall? Mourn asked.

~Northern cisterns and western front gate. The quarry and steep cliffs make the south and east sides too difficult for their undead units and positioning their contraptions.~

Have you seen any skin kites or Strigor in the skies or upon roofs or steeples? Gavin asked abruptly.

Through the psionic link, the Deathwalker showed us exactly what to look for. The first was a temporary magical "flapper" made of skin through which a death mage could spy from the air. In contrast, a Strigor was a living creature, sometimes called a blood drake but didn't resemble any drake I'd ever seen. Its beak shaped to suck blood, the flying creature had eleven limbs: two sets of wings, three pairs of grasping claws, and a prehensile tail. They were cunning hunters about the size of an eagle and could be trained for retrievals.

~No, Herald, we've not seen them yet.~

The mist helps in this, for it arrived at dawn when the skin kites might've been useful. The Strigor might see at night but would not be of use in either sun or heavy mist such as this.

~Very well. We will keep an eye out.~

What about the Crest watchtower? Mourn said.

~Clear of threat and assigned four men for now, but they can't see anything.~ Isboern paused. ~Is there nothing more we can do to prepare for the Nexus?~

I felt amusement from Gavin. *We can attempt to empty the courtyard of vulnerable souls while the Shaegoth prevent them from entering. We can bear witness to the first denizens coming through and attempt to respond. That is about all.*

Guild, Templari, and legend alike agreed. We prepared to end the mindlink.

Oh, wait, Gavin stopped us a moment longer. *Does anyone have silver weapons?*

~Silver?~

These are especially damaging to those with Nexus blood.

Many eyebrows raised but none of us questioned how he knew this.

I have five silver daggers I can share, Mourn said.

We do, replied multiple Templars. *But they're small daggers.*

Good, Gavin replied. *Test them for any creature that gets too close. I believe you'll be satisfied with the result.*

~Excellent. Thank you, Herald. Anything else?~

Not until something comes through.

~Alright. Let's do it.~

The bonds unraveled gently, freeing our minds back to their private thoughts. That the horses were blowing to catch their breaths suggested mere seconds had passed. One of them burred and reared up as the rider caught its reins, releasing a louder whinny of alarm and giving away our presence.

Out of the mist stepped a limping woman, and several men drew swords before any of us realized she was also transparent.

Any of us besides Gavin.

"Interesting," he said. "You can see her? All of you?"

Unnerved men nodded their heads, and Gavin looked at me and Jael.

"Yep," my Sister said, and I answered with a nod.

"Have any of you seen any ghosts before the huddle?" Gavin asked, drawing his thurible up from his belt by its chain and moving toward her.

"We didn't...?"

"Uhhh..."

"No. No, I don't think we did..."

The woman raised her arms, the lines of her form undefined around the edges. She walked as if trying to remember how.

"*Ushirra*," she whispered, her posture supplicating, her face grief-stricken.

"*Reesgret*," Gavin answered, beckoning to her.

The Deathwalker's irises became bluer for a moment as the spirit relaxed, and her face turned to pure joy before her form... *dissolved*. She became part of the mist and flowed gently into the thurible. I heard an array of whispers, motions, and prayers in three different languages around me.

"What did she want, Sho'shien?" Deshi asked.

"A guide," Gavin replied. "I've already collected several lost souls here, but none of you were able to see them before—"

From the direction of the Temple came a *thwump* sound, like a mountain top had burst far away. A crackle of blue and green light swept through the streets, causing the hanging vapor to sparkle as a low rumble and ground tremor followed close behind.

Briefly, more bodies appeared outlined in the mist, walking toward us from all sides.

"*Pyhua!*" Peng-lok jumped as the Templari mounted their skittish horses.

"Calm," Gavin said, raising the thurible and concentrating to extend his reach. "These are all native spirits. They will not harm you."

As he'd described in the crypt, I could see the "current" he created to draw the spirits closer. All of them went without a struggle, only confusion seemed to slow their dissolution. With Isboern and the Templari mounted, their Captain waited until the Human spirits were gone from view.

"We must return to the courtyard and do what we can."

"Indeed," Gavin agreed.

"Sirana on my right," Mourn said. "Gavin on my left. Templari in front, the Guild behind me. Everyone, try to stay within three horse lengths of either the Deathwalker or the Davrin as we approach the courtyard."

No one asked why he gave that advice; we'd all been there at the huddle. Whether with two legs or four at our disposal, we sprinted back toward the jewel of the city. Before we crossed the final street to enter the front gate, however, I spotted the second invasion starting.

Broad, winged creatures flew out of the East tower, their grey skin matching the color of the mist to disappear behind the thick cover. I counted five of them before the high courtyard wall obscured their exit point as we split up to pause on either side of the gate.

~*Did you see those?*~ I asked Mourn and Willven.

~*Yes, I did.*~

Large enough for a rider, the Dragonchild confirmed.

I leaned out from the wall. ~*Gavin? Have a guess what those were?*~

Those are Roh'ghast.

~*What?*~

Screaming terrors.

~*They scream?*~

They can. They're sky hunters.

~*That's not helping.*~

Oh? I thought it was.

~Allow us to enter the courtyard first,~ Isboern said. ~See if we can get the people to leave without resistance.~

The Guild confirmed as we spread the word fast.

"Mina xete de Manalar!" called the Captain of the Templari, riding out front and pacing with his horse as the Templari took their formation. "Mina xete!"

"Capitan!" a woman cried, followed by several men.

"Capitan!"

"Meeri que'il fixeron!"

They wailed in grief, perhaps explaining why they'd been waiting for him. I peeked around the corner to see them pointing at the open door of the Temple. I could not see the unsettling eyes and maws of the Shaegoth but felt their lingering dread.

"No! Mina xete," Isboern repeated, projecting powerfully through the fog. "Il Sanctro itus perigras. Che mandi, machitrus la'muri sul!"

Forceful, Gavin commented. *He's commanding them to the south wall.*

One of them tried to obey at once, but a bearded man grabbed their arm to keep them in place. The man then attempted to bargain with the Defender of the Wall, crossing his wrists and pulling his arms to the sides with his head jerking a firm negative.

So much for no resistance.

I frowned, peering at the one who'd tried to leave. ~Why is that one wearing a blanket over their head? They can't see.~

A Noble woman, Mourn answered. *It's not a blanket but a gown. Her veil allows her to see out. I'll admit her peripheral vision is poor.*

How can she run in that billowy garb? Jael asked as she looked over my shoulder. *Or climb down a mountain? It'll get caught on everything!*

Hiding her from the eyes of others seems more important to the man beside her. Even now.

What? And she has nothing to say on such stupidity?

They weren't planning to climb down a mountain today.

Mourn sounded tired evading Jael's question, focusing instead on summoning five silver daggers from his bracers. He passed them to Jael, Krithannia, Torch, Peng-lok, and Nianzu. "Your blade is better than silver, Deshi."

The young death mage grinned.

Suddenly, a louder *thwump* struck somewhere within the Temple, and the same crackle of blue and green rushed out through the open front doors to set the mist alight with glittering droplets. As we realized these same effects had preceded the Roh'ghast flying into the air, the sense of dread increased.

"*Templari!*" Isboern cried with renewed urgency, drawing his sword at last and lifting it up in the air. "*Esculta mi'xete ao sul! Mina xete! Machitrus! Ahra!*"

The mounted men attempted to herd this stubborn part of their populace planted outside a building which was no longer secure. Most who acted indignant with this treatment weren't wearing blankets.

A Guildsman asked, *Should we help them?*

No, Mourn answered. *Be prepared to cover them if something comes out that door. Gain distance from the gate if they manage to move people out.*

Unfortunately, the Templari could not accomplish this in the spare moments we had before the next new arrival stepped outside.

~*Look!*~ I cried. ~*At the door!*~

If there wasn't space at the gate, every Guildsman scrambled up to see over the wall. None of the Templari responded, however. *Shit.*

~*Isboern! The Temple door!*~

Immediately, the Captain and his men forewent their herding of citizens and turned horses around to line up and stand between the people and whatever had just stepped out.

At first glance, it was primitive, a tall figure, grey-skinned like the flyers but standing on two thick-footed limbs. It gripped a blunt, inelegant weapon, both arms extending most of the way to its knees. Sharp teeth were on clear display for the Nexus creature lacked lips of any visible sort.

The thing had no eyes, but if it had, they'd have been enormous. The long, bestial face appeared as though that tough grey skin had been stretched smooth over the sockets to permanently blind it. Long, frayed grey hair grew down a blackened back, and in this hair lay the only bit of color. Streaks of muted red and yellow had been bound into a queue with the rest of its grey mane.

"Malok," Gavin said. "A known race in the Nexus, but these are wearing the colors of the Devourer."

I passed that along. "Keep talking. I'm telling them."

"That's a blood runner, so we may expect more of them working in packs, with a harvester for each pack. The runners' weapons and tactics are meant to shatter bodies so the harvester can efficiently capture Vis and Vitas, which is more likely to flee the body in the trauma."

As if to demonstrate, the Malok lifted the large, blunt weapon, giving us a better look at what it intended to use. Not a club or mace but as if two flat, wooden swords had been bound together by tendon, with many long pieces of sharpened, black flint jutting out from the center. Crude, heavy, and double-edged, capable of crushing heads and limbs while the cutting edges would tear out chunks of flesh. Anyone sane would make it their goal *not* to be struck by such a thing.

The Malok barked something unintelligible but eager over its shoulder.

Uh-oh.

"It's showing its 'pack' the way out, isn't it?" Jael growled.

That was exactly what it was doing.

Five more Malok appeared, and we confirmed none of them possessed any metal. Even the partial armor—meant to protect shins, forearms, groin, and the shoulder on the side bearing the weapon—was made of bone, leather, and that molded, hard plate like Houda the Deathwalker wore. This had been reworked less, so the raw shape was easier to identify. Like the carapace of a giant insect.

Six long jaws and muzzles lifted into the air, chests expanding, and the creatures pointed keen noses toward Isboern, whose horse was on the verge of realizing this obvious reason to panic.

"Shit!" I cursed. "How do they know to target the Godblood?"

Gavin shrugged. "His aura is the brightest in the courtyard."

"Not for long," Mourn replied, somehow without boasting.

Join the Templari! Krithannia ordered through the pearls. *Gavin, stay near Isboern.*

Of course.

Those without a silver or enchanted weapon, Mourn said, *work with someone who has one!*

~And Jael and me?~ I asked.

Stay with me. I'll figure out how these soul hunters work, and you pass the details on. Jael, move with me, remember to breathe, and use the shock boost you did before if you have a chance to strike.

Yesss! Jael crowed.

Our burst of activity into the courtyard roused the citizens out of their petrified stupor, but unfortunately, we scared them *away* from the main gate as they fled screaming to the far corners.

Well, at least they were out of the way.

Between the new howls, barks, and whistles building inside the Temple and Mourn skimming past in the periphery of the horses, the Templari finally dismounted as their mounts grew too unruly to control.

Most men grabbed what they would and slapped their horse once they got them pointed back toward the front gate, although a couple panicked and galloped to either end of the courtyard. The men let them go to get in formations called by Isboern and Krithannia to best blend their disparate mages together in collective defense.

Meanwhile, the first Malok tilted its head as the three of us approached; after clicking in its throat to those behind it, the hunter stalked forward, sniffing the air as it closed the distance.

Stop here. Watch the other five.

Jael and I stood farther out at Mourn's flanks while he strode a few paces in front. I had Soul Drinker ready, and Jael had her silver dagger and longer blade comfortably in her hands. She breathed in deliberate, audible draws, holding them before exhaling. I gave it a try, too, but wasn't sure it did the same for me as it might for a new mage like her.

Mourn's sliders were out but locked as the two fighters slowed and sized each other up out of range of the other's weapons. The Malok stood a full head taller than the Dragonblood with a longer reach, truly a giant above other bipedal races of our lands.

The To'vah-krav took the first swing with no obvious spell active, a near miss but probably on purpose. The Malok eagerly returned the gesture, sweeping that crippling weapon with great power but less speed. In quick reflex, Mourn blocked it with a slider, but the sword-club was heavy and had to be deflected rather than stopped. Mourn spun the slider free, simultaneously calling a subtle orange flow. Heat waves trailed his weapon in the mist as he successfully feinted and struck the Malok's unprotected shoulder.

The Greylands hunter growled with irritation. The blow should have gone deeper, but the grey skin proved extremely thick and tough. At least it bled, although…it was black.

"Uh-oh," Jael muttered, braced for a fight when the posturing was done.

I reached out to Krithannia. ~*Ask Gavin what the black blood means.*~

It indicates a native Nexus race. Probably not poisonous.

I jumped at hearing his voice directly. ~Oh. Um. Probably?~

Yes. The harvester will be the magical one. Be wary of that blood. Regardless, it's a sign the fighter should be sensitive to silver.

~Very well. If you say so.~

Have him try it.

On it, Mourn answered, startling me.

I still wasn't used to this.

The Dragonblood engaged his opponent to draw the Malok farther from its observing pack then rolled to come up behind. He managed an excellent piercing move up beneath the ribcage with his heated slider which should have ruptured a kidney. However, the Malok did not behave like a living body receiving such a wound.

Roaring angrily, Mourn's opponent spun around as if it had been poked in the ass, nearly yanking the slider from his grasp. He managed to keep his weapon and gained distance when the Malok spoke to him in a penetratingly harsh whisper.

"*Awshuu'cur frrekinok.*"

~*Wait. Gavin, they can speak?!*~

"*They speak the dead tongue, yes,*" he confirmed. *I imagine the howls and such are for quick communication.*

~*What did it say?*~

It thanked him for showing them where to strike. Apparently its vital organs are not in the same places as ours.~

Oh, damn.

Not to be left wanting about this new threat, Mourn attacked again, speeding up and dancing more to put the slower Malok on guard. The creature's chitinous armor chimed strangely as the single slider struck the organic plating several times before Mourn was finally close enough to attempt a strike with a silver blade called into his hand at the last moment.

The Malok screeched in shock, recoiling from the much smaller weapon with a deeper stab in his right pectoral. It retreated to the pack, where together they watched as the skin blistered and sizzled, turning black around the edges of the wound and spreading out.

The Malok pack inhaled deeply, grey bristles on their black dorsal stripes rising straight up; together, they shrieked. Two smaller Malok exited the Temple then, each carrying a bone-and-flint object shaped like a lantern mixed with a thurible.

Soul traps, Gavin said. *Die in sight of one and you'll find out who these Malok call their master.*

That statement made all the men extremely nervous.

They weren't alone. *Marvelous.*

These "harvesters" also carried two catchpoles, weapons of control which I *did* recognize. Each had been crafted to include spikes intended to dig into the throat or legs of the captive. The injured blood runner hissed something to them in the dead tongue, brandishing its teeth with menace. The harvesters listened and pointed their muzzles toward us, noses twitching.

Not a good sign.

Retreat back to us! Krithannia called.

"*Damn,*" Jael griped but moved as fast as I did to regroup with

Mourn.

From what they're saying, Gavin said while we lined up in front of Krithannia, Gavin, and Isboern, *they don't recognize your essences.*

~Meaning what, Herald?~ Isboern asked.

Meaning they've never hunted Elves or Dragons in the Greylands. They don't know how to collect these souls, or even if they can. Although I'm sure they'd simply want you out of the way to get to the Humans.

~I take it they hunt Human souls in the Greylands?~

Indeed, some of their favorite eidolons. Though they would not run into many capable of offensive spells drawn straight from the Ley of a living world, so I imagine they'll have much more trouble taking any of you.

Behind me, I *felt* every one of the Guild and the Templari grin.

A second pack of blood runners arrived to join their harvesters before all these Malok began jogging toward us, building up speed as if to overrun our defense.

Watching them come, the Dragonblood's chest expanded as he took a deep breath and thought, *Let's take them all out of the battle.*

Then Mourn exhaled, growling in his Sire's tongue.

"Ixen bakmadahhh....!"

A vaporous, orange fire left the half-blood's mouth to blend unnaturally with the mist, creating a burning wall too close for the Malok to avoid. The orange vapor stuck to them as they came through it, passing some pain but not nearly enough.

They smelled terrible.

~Templari, allies,~ the Captain commanded, ~knock them back through, as hard as you can!~

Isboern demonstrated first, psionically shoving two of them into the hanging fire a second time to collide with their packmates and share the sticky burn. The howling and anger increased as I discovered then that not only could Isboern do this, but so could Mourn, Krithannia, a handful of the Guild and half the Templari. The Malok packs went down from the successive blows; some smoldered when Torch cast a fireball in the center of them.

"Whoa!" Jael cried from the hot burst coming a bit too close.

Instead of being irritated with him, however, she tossed me a wry smirk as our adversaries shrieked and our allies cheered.

Feelin' useless here. I can't get close enough to use the magic blade.

I smiled back. ~Pfeh. You **want** catchpoles to stop well before dagger distance.~

Oh well. At least they're getting up.

~That's not a good thing, Sister.~

She wasn't wrong, though. Had we destroyed *any* of them?

Unfortunately not, and the least scorched of them sprang up to bellow at us with mouth wide open. Bulling forward, the Malok aimed for Deshi on my left, who stood on the edge of our defense and had lifted his twice-blessed weapon toward it. The hunter sped up as if killing this one Yungian from our group would be enough.

"Are you willing to distract your adversary away from your brothers...?"

Proof that he was.

I reacted before Deshi's brothers could recast in his defense, sprinting in front of three mages to reach the Guildsman first. I never got close enough to stab the Malok with Soul Drinker. I didn't have the chance.

The Nexus hunter turned its head toward me, nostrils flaring wide, and slammed its huge feet down upon the cobblestone in a desperate bid to stop. With rune dagger aimed and my arm outstretched, I swiped at the beast from the Greylands as it scrambled back, escaping me with a terrified howl.

I was speechless, and Deshi's eyes were the widest I'd ever seen in a Human.

Abyss be damned.

It worked.

Thwump...!

...crackle...

Oh, no.

A sudden swell of wailing wind rose behind the excited howls and running feet filling the antechamber in the Temple. The Shaegoth were nowhere to be seen.

That is the main host, Gavin said, giving away genuine concern for the first time. *And a Slaugh swarm is inbound. We must weather it.*

I didn't know what a "Slaugh" was, but through Isboern and his wordless inquiry, we found the closest answer in the Yungians, who were terrified.

Hungry ghosts.

The brothers had ancient stories from Yung-An about winter-starved cannibals whose feral spirits lingered to feed upon their living descendants.

That's essentially right, Gavin confirmed.

In a circle! Mourn ordered. *The Captain and Elves in center. Templari surround them, Guildsman integrate. Gavin and Deshi outside with me, facing the Temple!*

A flood of excited Malok warriors exited the front door with ground tremors beneath our feet; most of them pounded straight for the open streets of Manalar. In addition to the huge cutting club, they carried familiar weapons we knew from battle or hunting: barbed spears, harpoons, clubs, hooked nets, stout crossbows, and bolts made of bone.

This wasn't our immediate concern, however. The two packs were convinced to leave us alone for now, joining the host and dissuading most who slowed to consider sampling our selection of souls for themselves. To those foolish enough to discount the warning, Krithannia had another trick in her pouch which served as a warning.

Bright light, she warned.

We closed our eyes before she cast a spell; it surrounded her body as if she stood in full daylight and reflected part of it. The Malok hissed, howled, and shrieked with as much distaste as most Davrin might have for the Sun, which seemed odd for creatures without eyes.

Finally, the blood runners and harvesters passed us by. All told, at least fifty of these giant pack hunters left the courtyard of the Temple and vanished into the mist.

~We must warn my men at the wall what comes behind them!~ Isboern cried.

Agreed, that was most urgent.

Unfortunately, the hungry, wailing wind entered the courtyard, sweeping in to lunge upon everyone in it.

Before we could warn anyone at all about the Malok, we had to weather the foulest wind on Miurag.

CHAPTER 32

AFTER THE LEADING FORCE STRUCK US ALL IN THE COURTYARD, NO ONE WAS left on their feet, some barely on their knees, whether they were Templar, Guild, legend, or noble.

Even in the center of the most powerful mages and minds defending Manalar, those piercing shrieks twisting through an intense burst of dry, cold wind deafened me, coursing down my spine as uncontrollable shivering overtook my body. I collapsed to curl into a ball, protecting my head with my arms until someone grabbed my hand.

I gripped back.

The will was wordless, and so was the shelter.

For what seemed an eternity, swarms of hungry, desperate hands pawed at us. Layers upon layers of hands with fingers like needles covered us like smothering blankets before someone finally whipped it off and tossed it away, taking all those little, tiny claws with it.

"S-Sirana?" Jael whispered.

A plea in need of an answer.

I felt for her, cupped her face with my hands, and kissed her, drinking in the real scent and taste. She reciprocated, and the air warmed around us as the jagged noise in our heads lost its edge. The courtyard quieted until we could hear our own heartbeats.

At last, we could breathe. We had our answer.

~*We're alive.*~

She exhaled in relief, and slowly we straightened up and opened our eyes in a fog seeming brighter. Without a scratch on my skin, my body was sore and aching. We were not alone, as Krithannia, Isboern, and the fighting men around us attempted to do the same.

The first sight which made sense to me beyond a mass of us crouching on the stone was Mourn and Gavin pulling out five men from our cluster: Torch, Crow, another Guildsman, and two Templars. As Mourn removed the helms from the Manalari, Gavin kneeled beside Torch first, hanging the thurible above his chest. The Deathwalker's void-black eyes possessed a subtle, pale blue sheen over the surface as he spoke the dead tongue above the Yungian.

"G-Groa?" Krithannia asked with concern as his brothers spoke with distress in their native tongue.

The pearl-bearer of our team spasmed, his spine bowing as a frighteningly clear and horrific spectral face stretched and contorted as it was pulled from his chest and into the thurible. Then Torch collapsed, his face breaking out in a sweat, gasping desperately for breath.

The other four had stopped breathing, I realized then, and Gavin turned around to hover the Manalari relic above Crow next, discomfitingly drawing a second possessive spirit out of his body.

One of the Templari moaned and Mourn produced a catchpole of his own—one without spikes—to pin the man to the ground by his neck should he try to sit up.

"Captain?" the Dragonblood asked. "Would you please attempt to mend those exorcised? We have enough time to save them all."

"Of course," the psion said, exhaling and climbing to his feet to join the lineup.

Overall, this took less time than for all of us to gather our bearings, as Gavin purged one unwelcome spirit after another while Mourn stood guard over those growing restless. After them, Isboern removed his gauntlet and placed a bare hand upon the damp brow of each man, speaking a prayer over them which swiftly cleared their mind and brought them back to us.

"Stand as soon as you can," Mourn said to them while glancing at Krithannia, Jael, and me.

I signed, *We are well.*

He signed confirmation and said to the rest, "Keep watch for anyone walking the mist. Do not stray."

"But I have to piss," muttered Tak under his breath.

"Go ahead," Wolf said with a smirk. "I'll cover your back if you cover mine."

I was surprised by how many of the others decided this was a good moment and started making similar deals. Some of the Templari were even desperate enough to overcome there being females nearby as long as their battle-mate turned toward us and gave them partial cover.

Jael giggled softly, blatantly watching them. As I listened to the draining spatters, I only felt thirsty and reached for a waterskin before I recalled that I had Gavin's pack. I reached for Jael instead to drink, reflecting to make sure.

Nope. I didn't have to piss.

Shuffling noises at the north end of the courtyard drew my attention.

"Don...donti ekavo?" a woman's voice called out. She sounded on the verge of weeping. *"Ekavis Fiernal?"*

The Captain had revived his second Templar and helped the man to his feet. Turning that way, Isboern projected his voice, soothing and calm.

"Neh-vis Fiernal, signala. Eco ese."

We couldn't see her but heard her gasp and turn toward us.

"Capitan?"

"Sic, signala, soun Capitan Isboern. Nomilu sancji, seug ami voze."

By the fall of her footsteps, she was hesitant. Perhaps she worried about being tricked by a devil pretending to be Isboern. By the time we could finally see her through the mist, weaving between sculpted plants, I believed I recognized the same hidden noblewoman weighed down by heavy, pale blue cloth.

Isboern beckoned her closer, reassuring, promising help.

"Gavin," I asked. "Is she 'clear?' "

He glanced at her with disinterest. "She is."

"How did she survive?"

He shrugged. "It's possible to weather a swarm by one's natural constitution. Not wholly unthinkable that one such individual would be among the nobles, though I admit some surprise…"

Gavin's voice drifted off, and he paused, narrowing his eyes beyond her when the woman tripped over something behind a low shrub. She looked down and began weeping, muttering *"Fiernal"* over and over in a variety of phrases. She bunched up her garb in clutching hands and started moving faster.

"Oh, dear," he said.

"What is it?"

The veiled Manalari emitted a short scream after coming around another hedge, yanking her foot away. She stumbled, fell, and was suddenly crawling on all fours as fast as she could.

"Algi asirame!" she yelled. *"Asirame!"*

"Wait, somebody grabbed her?!" Wolf exclaimed.

"Indeed," Gavin said, preparing his thurible and spade together. "There are scores of rising dead in this courtyard."

I heard something I fully recognized by now: hollow, trapped air escaping lungs as a body shifted long past its moment of death. More such hisses and rattles arrived in quick succession around us in the mist.

"Scores?" demanded the Templar Imran. "Where did they come from?"

"From all the other nobles who *didn't* survive the swarm."

Krithannia exhaled. "Defensive positions, everyone."

A dark-haired man with a full black beard shambled into view, twitching in fits before lunging for the shrouded female. He caught hold of her sleeve, and she screamed in terror, taking hold of the fabric and trying to wrench it free. Imran sprinted forward without an order and lopped the hungry dead's hand off at the wrist to free the noblewoman, pushing him away with a hard blow to the chest.

"Take the head," Gavin ordered.

Imran hesitated as the corpse fell then started getting up while the woman huddled at his back.

"Can he be saved?" Isboern asked.

"No," said the Deathwalker. "He is consumed."

The Godblood exhaled. *"Curteze il'torbaz, Templari. Deix reposire."*

Imran obeyed then, shielding the noblewoman with his armored body as he cut two-handed across the neck, decapitating the attacker. It collapsed instantly, and Gavin lifted the thurible higher as he stepped forward, drawing an obvious presence from the headless body from across the way.

Moans and ominous stirrings around us grew louder as Imran took the woman's arm and hauled her to our group where she continued gibbering and distracting the men.

Jael tightened the corners of her mouth as she glanced at me, and I shrugged.

"Best tactics?" Mourn asked Gavin as we tightened up our formation.

"Destroy the heads and limbs," he replied, "so no Slaugh can use the corpse to feed on the living. Not now or later."

"But you can draw the demons *out*, Deathwalker," protested Erik. "We saw you! We do not have to destroy our people!"

Isboern shook his head. "I'm sorry, Erik. He is correct."

"But, sir—"

"These are not demons," the grey mage replied, turning his mouth to be heard but keeping an eye on the bodies drawing in all around us. "I reached our teams in time to prevent this fate, and your Godblood healed the damage to the mind. The window of opportunity to repeat this method has closed."

"I'll stop the majority," Mourn said, stepping back and calling forth his sliders. "The rest of you, protect the survivor and don't be ambushed. Behead any who get through me or come from behind. Gavin will trap these 'hungry ghosts' so they cannot fly out and take another body elsewhere."

"Huixia!" confirmed the Yungian brothers, as the four most willing

to quell the restless dead as quickly as possible, without hesitation.

The Deathwalker nodded, the Guild signed affirmative, and the Captain said, resigned, "Understood. We're ready, legend."

Our groups shifted defensive formations as Mourn went out farther to meet the hungering nobility. Jael and I positioned ourselves around Krithannia to protect her, and my Sister looked twice at me.

"*Why are you smiling?*" she asked.

"*You're in for a vision,*" I replied. "*Using two weapons with four blades to cut down throngs of mindless cannibals bearing down on us was the first thing I hired him for.*"

"*Really. Where?*"

"*Warp rot forest.*"

Her white teeth stood out in her dark face. "*I hope he leaves some for us.*"

After withstanding the initial distress of the swarm's invasion, I quickly realized the worst had passed for a force such as ours. The threat of numbers, as bodies or as an incorporeal wind, made them dangerous and surely deadly to anyone alone or without defense. Against a Deathwalker and a Dragonchild with a trained force of mages backing them, it was only a matter of time before we'd clear the courtyard of another of the Devourer's influences.

At first, Mourn did not need to use the magic he'd once called to deal with the threats of chaos farther North. He had the equipment, reach, speed, and intelligence over the shrieking mob of consumed and possessed Humans. They seemed to always lunge for the nearest target without being able to judge the likelihood of success.

For that reason alone, Mourn kept on the move and frequently placed himself at the nearest point to any clusters who showed themselves. So many heads dropping and bouncing off from bodies dressed in finery proved to be something most of the Templari would not watch if they were not being directly attacked.

When two clusters flanked us, a few smaller and veiled hungry dead made it through Mourn. Gavin was the next closest; he tucked the thurible on his belt while it sucked in the ghosts, preparing his spade for a swing.

When the Deathwalker had still been a red-blooded man, he'd used this same tool in his defense against the Witch Hunters in Troshin Bend. He'd only clipped the other man back then, though it opened the throat and sent blood spurting.

This time, Gavin took the heads of the approaching Manalari in one clean stroke, sending one flying upward to hang a while before plopping on the ground like a bruised melon. By then, the stubborn phantasm lost hold of its shell and vanished shrieking into the relic.

Jael's wide eyes blinked at me. *"Has he gotten stronger?"*

"Hm. Maybe."

The Yungians and Reprisal dove in to take the rising numbers getting through the Dragonblood's moving perimeter, beheading them as soon as Gavin wrenched the possessing spirit out. The Templari did their best to shield the one sobbing woman with them from such gruesome sights while attacking any that came within reach, helping to make sure they would not stand up again.

My Sister growled under her breath with impatience.

"What are you waiting for?" I asked curiously.

"You," she said, glancing at my red-runed blade. *"Beasts five times your size run away from that. We could get out there and bring more corpses down."*

"Can **you** *chop off heads in one blow after another?"*

She grimaced, copper eyes glancing down at her relatively tiny weapons, and sighed. *"I prepared for targets with working vitals."*

"Patience, Red Sister," Isboern said with brooding humor. "I'm sure your time to kill comes soon."

At long last, all the others finished up, collecting more than seventy additional bodies in front of the Temple, none of them suitable for the Slaugh to use. Most everyone who'd been chopping or bashing heads gasped for breath.

"Well…" Wolf panted. "At least none of the bodies in the Temple came out, too."

"But could they?" Tak asked, worried.

"Many from the Nexus know the Slaugh as a nuisance," Gavin said, "and would have taken care of them. But there will be more in the city. I can draw them to me to clear the streets relatively quickly but would need defense while I concentrate."

"Shouldn't be a problem," said the Hand.

"No, wait," Isboern said. "Either the Malok, the swarm that bypassed us, or *both* could have headed either for our walls' inner defenses or the evacuation point with those flyers giving away their presence."

The expressions spread as one: pure denial. *No.*

"Hold on," Krithannia said, breathing in and closing her eyes. "We'll get an update for you."

"Please, elder. We need to know where to go next."

Subtly, Mourn dragged me into this. I tried not to react to the intensity while catching on quickly that there had been Guild updates before now.

Yes, Cloud, all movement to the gate has stopped. Those fucking flyers have been hovering. They're landing somewhere on the cliffs near the Crest tower, screaming at the refugees to make them freeze up. We've had to stay low to the ground or in between buildings. They don't seem willing to land in tight spaces.

We're sitting ducks for whatever else came through after those pulses in the Temple! interjected another Guild Hand.

Has anyone become violent or catatonic? Krithannia asked.

No...

Not yet, someone else added. *Why?*

Hungry ghosts make the streets near the Temple dangerous. The Death-walker says they are drawn first to anything living and then to usable corpses to attack the living. If anyone seems to be struggling with their mind, cast a healing spell to purge the ghost if you can reach them fast enough. If not, decapitate them.

I heard an array of cursing affirmatives.

Good. Next. Have you seen any large, grey, eyeless giants roving in hunting packs?

Oh, fuck, now we have to worry about those?!

Krithannia sounded relieved. *We'll do our best to keep them away from you. Tell Tamuril to start building screens blocking the alleys that a Human could* *slip underneath but would ensnare a bear.* *

*Confirmed. *

*Keep everyone quiet and hidden until you receive word to move. *

My attention returned with the Naulor as Wolf asked Gavin a question.

"Is there any way the Grey Maiden can close it sooner to stop more things coming through after we leave here?"

"She recommends leaving it open," Gavin replied, "so they may return the way they came."

"So, that's a no. But won't there be more pulses coming behind us?"

Gavin paused, the blue glow in his irises flickering for a moment. "The rift has stopped growing, so that was likely the last wave."

"How sure are you of that?" Krithannia asked, interested, not doubtful.

He shifted his eyes and peered at her. "I am certain enough to suggest we start clearing the streets and release the Defender of the Wall to act as such."

"Thank you, Deathwalker," Isboern said, his blue eyes intense. "Our men have held the line all morning, but they need morale and direction, especially with imminent danger at their backs. Krithannia, I take it there is no emergency at the evacuation point?"

"You are correct, Captain."

"Then will one of your teams escort *Signala* Verina to the south wall and then rejoin us?"

Verina? Huh. Not bad.

Easier to pronounce than "Halete."

The Guild Mistress considered his request before, looking at my bodyguard. "Shadow, will you escort *Signala* Verina and scout for anything to be done about those Roh'ghast?"

Isboern blinked with surprise. "The Roh'ghast?"

"They are on the eastern cliffs," she said, "and have forced our evacuations to stop."

"Oh. I see."

Mourn smirked but bowed his head to accept. "Very well. We will meet you farther west toward the central city after *Signala* Verina is safe at the south wall."

"Wait," a Templar interjected, his accent thick. "You say no man of Templari or Reprisal goes with her?"

Krithannia acknowledged him. "That is correct, *Tentente*."

"She will be safe with us," Mourn replied. "We will get her to the wall and see if we can restart the evacuation. We will not be long."

Isboern had to touch the woman's head and press his brow to her, speaking in hushed, soothing tones to get this idea through in a way she could understand it. She stank of pure fear as she wept.

Jael's mouth had twisted to one side again, her expression suggesting this was the lowest duty she could have hoped for.

"I will let you take out your frustration on the first shambler we meet," Mourn said to her in Davrin.

That brightened her mood.

THE GUILD HELPED THE TEMPLARI LOCATE AND GATHER WHAT HORSES HAD survived the swarm when we entered the eerily quiet streets. We passed the corpses of two mounts first, and I overheard Gavin say the incorporeal hungry ghosts had latched onto the horses, killing them rather swiftly.

"Why didn't they stand up afterward?" Tak asked. "Like the nobles in the courtyard."

"The Slaugh were once Human eidolons," Gavin answered. "Now too degraded to solve a puzzle like puppeting horses to feed on flesh. They consumed the Vitas and left."

I supposed that was better than ghosts which could overtake any corpse at all, even birds or cats. *A pity Nightmare isn't here. They couldn't take her.*

Maybe she'd eat *them.*

Jael took point with eyes and ears open in the mist for anything approaching us. I walked beside the sole survivor from the courtyard and Mourn walked behind us, which absolutely kept the *Signala* moving. We were still far from the south wall when she was gasping for breath and threatening to stumble. We heard a whimper of pain.

"Sirana, slow a moment."

I took Verina's arm and pulled us to a halt; Jael glanced behind at us.

"Let me see her shoes."

I frowned but agreed it was better I do it than him. She shrieked in alarm as I hooked one arm tight to keep both of hers down, lifting the hem of her garb enough to peer over the generous swell of her breasts to her feet.

She wore decorative sandals like a Consort.

"She's not getting down a mountain in those," Jael commented.

Mourn sighed. *"We should have grabbed something from the bodies."*

My Sister grinned. *"Maybe we'll get another chance."*

"You have a morbid way of looking up, young Sister."

Jael shrugged, nonplussed. *"Hard to avoid learning it when your House is always at the bottom. It's the only way to look up."*

She had a point, but I refrained from commenting as Mourn lifted the terrified, enveloped woman in his arms the same way he had me after the warp rot when I couldn't stand. I had been in much worse shape so enjoyed some amusement at how quickly she passed out.

"Let us run," he said.

Indeed, why not take advantage of the relative quiet?

Stretching my legs felt good, as did Jael getting her chance to slice at three walking dead coming toward us when we crossed an intersection.

"Hey, look," she said, pointing with her borrowed blade. *"Boots! Smaller, even."*

"Go for them," Mourn replied. *"Sirana, use Soul Drinker to keep the Slaugh from escaping to another host."*

Jael and I sprinted to meet them, sliding into a shockingly familiar state as I sensed her battle-joy while watching her back. With two longer blades, she disabled the bodies more easily by slicing off limbs rather than heads, giving me quick and easy lunges with Soul Drinker to suck the spirit out.

During this brief purge, I lost any fear of these Nexus obstructions, recalling only the empty creepiness in their eyes. *Nuisance*, Gavin had called them, suggesting even the Malok would help us be rid of the hungry ghosts rather than let them eat the same souls the raiders had come for.

"Got the boots!" Jael crowed, jogging back with her leather trophies from her last kill, while I'd had the afterthought to grab the stockings.

Mourn set Verina on the ground, confirming that her abundant curves hadn't been my imagination. *"Quickly, let us exchange them and move on."*

"Why are we doing this again?" Jael whispered to me as we tried to speed up this awkward process of handling the Human's feet.

I shrugged. *"Because she's not dead?"*

"That's another question. Why isn't she?"

"Have you not seen her mage potential, novice?" Mourn replied.

"Well…"

She squinted at Verina.

"You mean like Dandan?" I asked.

Jael stopped squinting. *"Who is 'dan-dan?' "*

Mourn chuckled. *"Later. Sadly, Verina's awakening was much harsher."*

We arrived deeper in the wealthy district under an hour after the courtyard, where we confirmed Tamuril had received Krithannia's message. The first two alleys we passed had been blocked with familiar, thorny vines. We were expected, however, and Mourn guided us down a wider street where the Guildsmen popped up from behind wagon barricades, ready to take the Manalari noble off our hands.

By then, Verina was awake and breaking in her used boots, seeming dazed. She asked no questions where they came from and allowed herself to be led where her arm was pulled until, at last, she encountered another Templar who moved her into one of the tight-packed shelters awaiting the moment to climb down.

We'd never seen her face, but I would recognize her scent and her voice. This *signala* made me wonder how Auslan would react in a refugee situation and had to ditch his sandals.

The next thought struck like a thunderbolt.

Goddess… Where was he now? Still in solitary? He'd said in my dream that it was "better than it was" but offered no specifics. Assuming that had truly been him in the present and not me wishing it was.

Shit. Not now, Sirana.

Mourn was conversing with the Guildsmen and the few Templari who were stationed here; they discussed the Roh'ghast and their riders upon the cliffs behind Mount Sonai. The men assigned to the Crest had managed to annoy one rider enough to detach and harry them instead, but then they'd been locked in the watchtower until the Nexus raider simply flew off to harass someone else.

"There are eight more of them," said the man in charge. "They've tried snatching a few people who were caught on the mountain, but the druid's vine-rails covered them even if part of her work was wrecked."

"Hm," Mourn considered, looking up at the mist. "The flyers are mostly watching and inhibiting our movement, but no Malok were summoned here."

"What do you mean?" asked one focused Human while his trench-mate kept looking at Jael and me.

Mourn glanced back in the general direction of the Temple. "A detour to a trapped and dense pocket of souls would have been easy if the main host had known where the Roh'ghast had gone."

"A lovely thought, Shadow."

"One we best prepare for if the Manalari lose the north or west wall. But for now, I take it the raiders do not have long-distance communication besides the Roh'ghast screams, to which the Malok have not yet paid attention."

The Guildsman sighed. "Understood. What about the creatures themselves? We can't see them, and we haven't wanted to give away our presence with multiple fire spells or accidentally blast debris onto those hiding on the trail itself."

"What about wind?"

The man grimaced. "We'd just make it windy and maybe remove

our own cover from the Malok. We've no one mage with such focused power."

I coughed.

"But we must resume the evacuation," Mourn said.

"We're agreed, Shadow. Any ideas how?"

Jael poked the To'vah-krav's arm. He glanced at her, then held his gaze on her. She blinked innocently.

"What?" she asked. *"I was going to say, you're the most 'focused' mage in the city right now, correct?"*

His tail swiped at the fog, and he rumbled, *"We need a spell with an area of effect compressed to target eight giant flyers with riders on cliffs, below which any debris would fall upon the people in hiding. In addition, the duration must be short enough that it doesn't clear all the mist from the evacuation point and draw immediate focus."*

"Yeah?"

He was staring at her. Then at me.

~*What?*~

She's never stood in the role of a mage's conduit, has she?

~*Um, no. But I have. I could try to guide?*~

He grunted, lifted his jaw to narrow his eyes at a rooftop, and said to the Guildsman, "Pass the word to shelter in place but be ready to move at any moment."

"Oh?" The Guild Hand finally focused on my Sister and me as much as the quiet one at his shoulder. "Perhaps you three can make an opening?"

"Indeed," Mourn agreed, showing a bit of fang. "Perhaps we can."

WE SCOUTED AROUND LONG ENOUGH TO HEAR ONE MORE SCREECH BEFORE Mourn chose his rooftop to climb to, summoning a grappling hook for all three of us to move up two levels with a flatter roof than some. It had been a while for me.

Mourn's feet had just left the ground when Tamuril hurried around the corner.

"There you are!" she gasped. "Wait! What will you do about those creatures?"

"Why must you know?" he asked, dropping back to the ground.

"Pilla is out there. Do I call her back?"

Mourn's eyes widened. "Yes. Yes, do that."

Pain entered her eyes at the realization he'd missed that.

Oops.

"Good work creating the handholds down the mountain," he said, tugging the grappling hook which he'd already checked for security. "Please signal us when Pilla is secure so we can clear the way for the refugees to keep using them."

For my sanity, I could not read the Druid's flustered response to that. Surprise, pleasure, discomfort, and something darker all smeared together on her face.

"Th-they need mending," she said.

Mourn nodded and started climbing.

"May I come up with you?"

Jael made a face. "Can you climb?"

She stiffened. "Y-yes."

"We need to concentrate," Mourn said.

"I-I will observe." She glanced at me. "I'll not interfere."

He sighed. "Very well. Climb quickly, everyone. The reports I am hearing about the walls are not encouraging. We must take care of this and move to help."

"Is Willven alright?" Tamuril blurted in obvious worry.

"For now. So is Krithannia."

They shared a look as the Naulor blushed deeper, then the Dragonblood climbed up with Jael hopping on behind him. I made a motion to her.

"No, um, thank you," she replied. "You, first."

Odd exchange.

We didn't have time to talk, however, and having the Naulor behind

494

on the rope motivated me to scale as quickly and smoothly as I could, despite how long it had been since I needed to. Mourn helped each of us over the final edge, for which I was grateful, and where we discovered a flat, open-air balcony deliberately built and facing East. The rest of the roof behind us was slanted with overlaying red-stone tiles.

Tamuril tried to refuse Mourn's hand at the top, but I had the feeling he wasn't going to risk having to explain to Krithannia why her sister fell off a rooftop. He took her arm firmly, brought her to safety, and that screeching falcon dived in out of the mist as if complaining that he had touched her.

"*Trenili*, Pilla, *trenili!*" cried her blonde handler, lifting her leather-bound arm so the circling threat could land.

Once the falcon was perched and satisfied that the Dragonchild hadn't mishandled her Druid, Tamuril offered us a weak smile and moved away from us to find a place to sit with her bird.

Apparently, she really meant observing, for she said nothing more as Mourn chose his place to stand and signed for me to stand in front of him, and Jael in front of me.

~*Know any reason why she wants to watch?*~

★*That's what an observer does,*★ he replied, closing his hands around my waist while his tail slid past to wrap around Jael's.

"*Whoa.*" She looked down and back at us as I placed my hands on her shoulders and massaged them.

"*Can you feel something?*" Mourn asked. "*Like in the Temple?*"

"*Yeah...*"

"*Good. Kneel down in case one of you grows dizzy.*"

After doing so, Jael twisted her neck more to focus on me. "*So, you used to do this 'conduit' method with Elder D'Shea to... enhance spells?*"

I squeezed her. "*Healing.*"

"*Healing who?*"

"*Reishel. After the Prime revisited her trials. Because of the mind thing.*"

"Oh." She turned back around.

★*Reishel?*★ Mourn asked, like her name was familiar.

I swallowed. ~*Struck down by Ornilleth. We thought she was well,* but… *she was taken by the mind flayers in the end. We… when we were on the boat…?~*

Ah. I remember. I am sorry.

~Mm.~ I kept my hands on Jael's solid shoulders, reassured that at least she had made it. ~*What do you mean about Tamuril being an observer?~*

Commanded by her Queen, rather like you. Sooner or later, she will return home. She will tell them what she observed.

My stomach chilled. ~*And that doesn't threaten you?~*

He moved his hands from my waist up to my shoulders, where he massaged them in turn. It felt good. His To'vah aura grew stronger as we spoke.

It might be more interesting if it did feel threatening, but the chances of the Naulor Elves acting on what Tamuril tells them while it bears relevancy are non-existent.

~*Whew. Strong certainty. How do you know this?~*

Because I have seen in my Dreams and heard from elders that the Naulor have remained as hidden as the Davrin for millennia. The oldest stories suggest signs of true interest to engage with the outside world would have male Naulor emerging. There've been none in the time I've known Krithannia. Only her and one frightened edain who acts like she serves a punishment, not a purpose.

I could believe that, based on what little I knew about her.

Jael gasped. "Uh, what are you two doing?"

I started to grin as she leaned into me. "*Does it feel good?*"

"Heh! Yeah…weirdly so."

"*I think it's supposed to.*"

"It can, and now that you've opened, Red Sister," Mourn said to Jael like a reminder, "*I shall need to draw on your aura's strength to heighten the precision of this spell. I will not take so much that you pass out.*"

"I know," she replied, trembling under my hands. "Do it."

"Di hansa," he said, not a direct reply but the first words to create a current, somewhat like Gavin and his thurible, flowing through my Sister and me and back around from Mourn.

"Di hansa svorl."

True air flowed around us then, as the magical current we shared translated readily to something physical. My spiders nestled farther up my scalp into my braid as gusts and puffs of air buffeted us before continuing on to join the rising spin.

Mourn spoke his Sire's words, for the inaudible vibrations they caused could only be Draconic. He added variations which crafted an air funnel closing in tight around us, yet I did not have to close my eyes against debris nor were the mists widely disturbed.

"Riliwir..."

Gradually, he chanted and built up his spell.

"Riliwir svorl..."

Jael's spine straightened, her shoulders drew back, and she tilted her head back until she leaned it against me. Her gaze drifted as if she saw more than wind whirling above us.

"Wow..." she whispered, leaning slightly.

I dropped my hands from her shoulders to wrap arms around her waist instead, sensing the wordless approval for grounding her as Mourn slowly released my shoulders with no lost connection.

He lifted his arms to the obscured sky.

"Riliwir svorl di hansa!"

And his will became manifest.

The air funnel launched up from us straight as an arrow, cutting through the clouds with unnaturally little disturbance. It vanished from sight for a few heartbeats and dropped down at an angle, aiming for the spot where we'd last heard a Roh'ghast scream.

The funnel had grown while out of my sight but reappeared and expanded with breathtaking speed. Barely a blink on my part before I heard the roar of a blast of air striking the fog-banked cliffs of Mount Sonai, powerful enough to muffle the surprised and distressed calls of multiple Greylands flyers.

I didn't know if he slammed them all; I didn't even know how many of the nine known beasts had been clustered in that spot. I could only see part of the south side of the mountain laid bare and the air spinning back on itself like a reverse wave of water.

At least five massive, struggling grey bodies had been forcibly detached from the cliffs. I only caught a glimpse of them tumbling through the air and out of sight down into the canyon. The shrieks had been torn to pieces enough to be faint, and the mist within the city walls swirled faster for a while but did not reveal the shelters of huddling people at the south wall.

Mourn's tail was lashing back and forth, more aggressively than I'd ever seen. I glanced up and back, spotting his eyes shifting from some darker color back to gold. He chuckled.

All the Roh'ghast are gone from the cliffs, he said while the magic was running hot, and Jael writhed in my arms. *Seven were struck down and have fallen upon the rocks. Let the Guild take care of them. One flyer sensed the blast before it arrived and escaped. Two will be somewhere over the city and may give away our location but are unlikely to return to that spot. Resume the evacuation immediately.*

The voices that came through the pearls sounded elated.

Yes, sir!

Getting on it!

"Jael?" I asked, as I helped her stand.

Her body was unusually warm, yet she wasn't sweating, somewhat as Mourn tended to be when using magic. She turned her head and bit the tip of my nose. I blinked and smirked. Or when warm from cumming.

~Are you alright?~

"Dunno...big rush."

She weaved slightly, putting a hand to her brow. She mumbled something like, "Fuckin' Priestesses," though I wasn't sure from all the pearl noise.

Then Krithannia broke through loud and clear.

Morixxyleth, we need help!

Mourn removed his cloak and began rearranging his harness, preparing to change shape. *Coming now. Update us.*

Gavin's taken care of the Slaugh. We're focused on the Malok, who took out the Manalari defense at the northwest point to let the Ma'ab enter the city. The two have been slaughtering each other as Isboern ordered a fighting retreat to slow any advance toward the Temple and the south wall. ⋆

⋆*That didn't take long.* ⋆

⋆*Gavin says the Malok smelled the huge number of Ma'ab close by, and we've discovered ways of discouraging the packs from deviating on that path. Unfortunately, the Manalari are being pinched and must abandon the wall. The fighting is moving into the streets.* ⋆

Jael's and Tamuril's eyes grew huge as Mourn shifted into his runner's form while I listened. He turned to show his left flank and swung his head toward us.

"Packs with Tamurrril," he growled, tongue rolling. "Get on."

I dropped Gavin's pack and brought it to the silently observing Naulor, who accepted not knowing who it belonged to. Jael dropped my pack near her feet, and together we moved close enough so I could pick up his cloak and fold it into a saddle blanket.

"Get on," I repeated. "It's fun and fast."

"Right," she breathed, shaking her head to collect her wits before choosing her handholds and swinging a leg over.

I got on behind her, settling in close along her back and feeling far too relaxed and comfortable considering where we were headed.

"Keep grapple," the four-legged Mourn said to the Druid. "Make more barrierrrs, then get out."

Staring with leaf-green eyes, she nodded. "I-I will."

With a trotting turn and a deceptively gentle leap to climb onto the red roof tiles, Mourn looked around for his next leap, either to move across rooftops like in Augran or jump back down and take the streets.

"Ohhh, Goddess," Jael muttered, clinging tight, her thighs squeezing our mount and hardening against mine.

No matter which way we went, getting there would be another rush.

CHAPTER 33

CAPTAIN ISBOERN'S ORDERS HAD TRAVELED SUCH THAT MOST DEFENDERS HAD left the south wall to barricade the wealthy district where refugees gathered. A few remained as sentries, but the heavy mist meant approaching non-Human and non-living opponents would be too close before they were seen to do much good.

Mourn avoided these last scouts to lessen their alarm as he sorted out his roof-jumper path through the southwestern district. Jael and I were getting the hang of the landings when a wide gap and high, interior wall separated this segment of Manalar from the rest down the long, gradual mountain slope.

The hybrid used two balconies to get us close enough to the ground, dropping with a talon-clicking thud onto the cobblestone, then took off to the north and swerving through the first blockade set up at a market gate. We couldn't help but alarm these men by leaping over their heads, but the Dragonblood continued without slowing and none were fast enough to attack us in error.

I'd lost track of what time of day it was; the grey sky and enveloping mist made my sense of time irrelevant on the Surface. Nonetheless, the scents had taken time to change. The miscellany of fragrance, the plants, animals, and Human activities during the summer heat were oddly muted upon this established mountain, fast fading away. In their place arrived the scents of old, sterile dust like in the crypt, the unmistakable tangs of red blood and metal, the rank fumes of guts, vomit, and feces, and the sour sweat of fear.

We're almost there, Mourn spoke through the pearls as we passed more barricades. We were leaving the cleaner areas of Manalar for the "slum." *What do you need most?*

Light spells, she replied, sounding distracted. *The Malok recoil from them.*

Mostly defense?

Yes! Gavin is invaluable in usurping corpses the Ma'ab have ensnared, and his blood and spells are intimidating the Malok, who harry him because he's snatching our dead away from them.

He's in direct competition with the harvesters.

Yes, it's mostly them he's been throwing his blood at.

That mental image made me chuckle.

And the Templars?

Isboern and the Templars are creating light to keep the Greylands raiders fenced in and targeting Ma'ab along the wall instead of the Guild or the Manalari farther inward, but these giants are tougher than the Hellhounds and show no sign of leaving. The silver we have keeps them away but hasn't killed one yet. We'd have to get too close.

What about Mitneh'thran?

The Captain uses the shield as a focus which seems to enhance his spells, and it's easy to see as a rally point.

Mourn galloped for several strides as he pondered then thought, *Banishing the mist might force the Malok to retreat back to the rift.*

Krithannia didn't reply.

It would also grant the Godblood the sunlight needed to better oppose the Ma'ab.

I perked up, wondering what her hesitation meant.

Mourn spoke again. *I tested the cloud layer with the Roh'ghast. It's unnaturally thin for how dark the city is but made of water. I could open pockets to the Sun, but you, Stormseeker, can push it up and spread it out to clear the entire *sky.*

I might have heard the Naulor's heart had we been standing together in person.

I... I would need time, she said, cautiously optimistic.

We will defend you and give you that time.

I've been shielding many allies. I won't be able to continue.

We'll adapt tactics. If this succeeds, the balance shifts in our favor at once.

We passed over more and more barriers on our way in: crates, overturned carts, pools of stinking, oily liquid ready to be set ablaze. The noise grew as the familiar cries of rage and agony blended with foreign roars, barks, and whistles as heavy feet pounded the broken street. Smoke from other fires obscured our vision further and choked the air. I glimpsed broken barriers down the side-streets, past which the enemy groups had advanced.

We were in the thick of it now.

Sirana, Mourn said. *Try to keep as many of us linked while still using Soul Drinker.*

I had no idea where Isboern or Gavin were and could not "reach out" to find them in this roiling madness. I began the link with Jael.

~Hey—~

There you are! Who do we stab first?

Alright, then.

Mourn answered. *Target the three Malok threatening Gavin, Krithannia, and the Yungians. I'll run behind them and you two cut the backs of their legs with your daggers.*

~Understood.~

Yee!

Mourn launched out of a narrow alley to skim the rough line of Malok blood runners swinging brutal strikes on Krithannia's shields as Gavin and the Guild gradually backed up. Jael and I struck out together, gouging any grey flesh we could reach regardless of aim. The startled bellows preceded three abrupt swipes with those deadly flint chip swords but Mourn wrenched us out of the way.

Hang on!

Watch out!

A moment later, the Malok fell to their knees, shocking the battleground and anyone who could see it.

Heading back!

Mourn sprung onto a corner wall, using it to reverse direction and launch back at them. I was thankful everything spinning was grey regardless.

Sirana! Finish them!

Jael kept guard with her silver blade out, and our mount slowed beside each crippled raider long enough for me to achieve one deep stab in their torso with the soul blade. The third one quivered in a last, desperate attempt to stop me, possibly pleading or hissing denial in the dead tongue before I killed that one, too.

Good! Dismount and defend Krithannia while I change.

Jael and I hopped off in front of the Naulor as Mourn padded another few steps to Gavin and Deshi to begin shifting his form. The sounds of fighting rose in other streets, but in this city square, everyone who'd witnessed the three Malok drop paused to gape.

Krithannia took advantage, pointing back up the slopes. "Malok! Return to the rift. Go back where you came from or be consumed!"

Gavin translated for her, adding something of his own, and I noticed how the Deathwalker's form had changed. Disturbing, black, glossy spikes had ripped through his new robes at his shoulders and back, catching on his forearms. His black fingernails had grown into formidable defensive claws. Despite this, he kept his spade, the edges of which were spattered with gore. I could see his aura in the mist, like swirling ashes and blue embers.

The blood runners considered this new warning, but after a moment with the harvesters scouring the tasty options around them, the Malok opened their throats and communicated their choice with their packmates in other streets.

They don't sound ready to break, Jael thought.

~No.~

Fine with me.

503

The Godblood reached out to me then. Jael, Mourn, and Krithannia could hear him at once.

~Sirana! The Ma'ab have withdrawn from this quarter and build defenses outside the wall against the Malok. The west gate is ours but under pressure from other Ma'ab units. What next?~

~Uhm, if we protect Krithannia long enough, she may be able to reveal the Sun. That might drive the Malok back to the rift.~

But she will not be able to shield anyone, Mourn said, *not even herself.*

The leaps of thoughts and possible outcomes which followed only made sense to the leader of men, and every Templar and Manalari soldier shifted their stances to put their backs toward her as if he'd silently passed the word.

Several men spoke Manalari prayers and made a circle and two intersecting lines over the sunburst symbol on his chest. They *wanted* their Sun to return, even by way of a foreign, pale Elf.

~Please, elder legend,~ the Captain said. ~Try. We'll hold the line.~

I'll do all I'm able, she promised.

By now, the Dragonblood had finished changing, rethreading his arms through his harness to secure it, and tossed his cloak aside. The Deathwalker escorted the Naulor to the sturdiest wall to keep at her back when Krithannia gave her pearl to Gavin, then kneeled with her fingers delicately touching the ground. She closed her eyes.

I felt her gently withdraw from the mind links as the yelps down the street grew louder. Gavin stepped forward, looking less Human than ever, and word was spreading. The Guildsmen and Templari were quickly shuffling defensive duties, and the Naulor had a giant target painted on her face, one more urgent to claim than before.

Many tall creatures with tremendous reach were coming at once to face off with my little dagger, and I could feel Mourn's heart speed up as he assessed the threat. The first twinge of intimidation hooked into my heart, and a chill began to spread.

~Sirana,~ Isboern began.

Lead your men, Captain. Mourn stepped up to me. *The Guild's fastest and best defense will also be our smallest.*

"Uh—" I began.

He leaned to kiss me on the mouth as he so rarely did anyone. His firm, oddly textured lips barely protected me from sharp teeth as he sucked lightly on my much softer lips. A branding tongue flicked hot and tangy against mine, dexterous enough to enter my mouth with or without my opening wider.

Our night in Yong-wen.

Isboern withdrew, polite and immediate, and the pearls closed off other distractions as Mourn held my focus. His free hand grabbed hold of my crotch as he let his aura flare, and the pleasurable shock was enough to sweep aside any lingering fear.

Kiabil. Open for me a little more.

Immediately aroused, my heart racing, I felt his magic soaking me like a storm.

Ohhh, what the fuck? Jael asked.

She recognized it, too, and welcomed its potent flavor and strength.

Link us, he commanded.

Weren't we already?

Yes. Deeper.

He grabbed hold of Jael, too, but not with his hand; a constricting tail wrapped around her thigh as his other hand summoned one slider. She squealed, tugging at his tail as if it sent the same shock through her.

But then she stopped trying to get loose.

Link us, Sirana, and we will know how to fight this battle as a squad.

~...like Vian...?~

Yes! Jael echoed.

Agreement. *Willingness* to link like his family in Vuthra'tern. The Rin'oveaus who could defeat Ornilleth by working together.

Come on, let's fight, Sirana! my Sister crowed.

My sapphire seared my skin beneath my armor when the To'vah-krav tightened his aura around us further. The sound Jael made caused me to wish she was naked.

Do it now, Vloszia Dalna. Trust our Bargain, and embrace us.

At first, I struggled to find the direction he meant in the disorienting flood of emotion and magic hurled at me from the two of them. Mourn kept hold on my crotch, and I may have groaned as his rippling power shined all around me in a tapestry of black diamond, evening purple, and the purest wind blended with the sunset.

Another pulse, and my limited perception had struck a boundary, trying to push past it. A storm didn't cover what I felt now; I was being swept away downstream, toward an inevitable fall, working as hard as I could to stay afloat.

I could not contain it, control it; I could not even comprehend it anymore. I knew not how long I fought to breathe before I let go and slipped underneath the surface.

Hoping I wouldn't drown.

IN THE DARK, WE FOUND EACH OTHER. IN THE DARK, WE MERGED, IF HAPHAZ-ardly. All three minds were afraid on some level, but at least one of us had done something like this before.

For once in our lives, we were not alone. We were three, not one, and we knew this, but we each knew the next move that we would take to help others, and we made it together. Our skills and our speed we shared willingly, and we borrowed the experience and training necessary, as if our own bodies remembered the work that we'd put them through.

More than seven hundred years combined into one focus, lessons learned far underneath and far above. Decades and centuries of training, so many missions, repeated combat and continuous practice. Teaching others. Learning those calm strategies. Succumbing to hot rage when strength was needed. Building endurance and familiar motions which would become reflex.

We were ready to fight as someone much older and larger than ourselves.

The Outsiders tore down the barriers on the streets, kicking mounds of meat out of their way, and crushing the bones and wet flesh beneath broad feet as they flanked from three directions.

"Surround your Mistress," we rumbled.

Our Guild was too well trained to question.

The Deathwalker's aura hid much of the Naulor's ethereal scent from the Malok noses as she communed with her elders, as she prayed for their assistance. We were prepared to give the battle priestess time. The enemy would not reach her; they would not reach our men or the strongest heart and soul of Manalar. We would watch them fall under living fire and shadow, suffering bite after bite of pure silver if necessary.

The Godblood and his city's men slowed the charge on the right with blinding bursts of light, only a sample of what would happen if we cleared the sky. The Deathwalker and the Guild faced the left flank, surprising them with the last of one mage's precious, silver dust as others shot crossbow bolts and threw daggers painted with Gavin's blood.

We took the center, moving forward, and the pack of Outsiders before us slowed to scent us, pulling in the uniqueness of our essence through the wet folds of their nasal cavities and along their tongues. We understood they did not know what we were, even less so now that we had blended.

We lifted our weapons.

"Have a taste," we said.

The eldest kept his long-reach weapons high, blocking them and drawing their attention while the two young "boot daggers" lunged in low and stabbed deep into the closest body. The blood runner roared a cry unlike any of this world, and we watched the grey skin around the wounds blacken quickly, cracking and drying to become a much wider opening.

Black blood spilled out only to turn into grey sand before it hit the street, the large body collapsing after the cursed dagger had finished drinking. Other Malok hesitated, backing up into their harvesters. They might have run if the catchpoles had not speared into them from behind accompanied with two short barks.

We did not need the same whistles and calls to communicate; we did not even need the same words we'd had before to be ready.

Three attacked at once, shrieking and moving with admirable unity. They tried to break us apart, grunting and signaling in haunted sounds. The next closest five prepared to move on each strange, dark-skinned attacker once this happened.

"More space!" we warned the Guild as the Malok pressed forward, pushing everyone back along the western street.

Our allies made the room quickly, and the blades of our eldest began to spin and sing, taking their full reach to create a moving blade trap. We were ready when the next blood runner charged, willing to take the hit, to try to knock the sliders down and open the way for who followed.

Branding-hot metal sliced deeply, scoring the tough hide, and flaying one arm open to its pale grey bone. Its sacrifice failed as the other two flanking the slider trap could not evade the agony-inducing daggers of our younger minds.

They backed away.

We did not give them respite.

The youngest part of us crossed her borrowed blades before her, magic swelling on her tongue as she spoke To'vah for the first time.

"*Kayo pabixen-sheh!*"

Her pronunciation was perfect, but the Words left her mouth sore as she pulled blades of differing lengths apart with great force. A circle of power slid down the metal where the edges met, gaining momentum toward whomever was directly in front of her.

A familiar orange ball manifested but soon turned white as it slid down and off the blades, striking and splattering over the adversaries set to charge us. Fire the color of shimmering pearls stuck to them like honey, burning upon thick, grey hide. This forced a break in their charge as it ate its way down toward the muscle underneath. It was too bright to look at.

The eldest of us followed with the same spell a heartbeat later, doubling those affected by white-hot burns. We smelled roasted meat and burning decay. We forced them back as they began to break, our eldest recovering a pattern of dance with blades that sent trills of magic and sound through the city.

The Malok roared at us in fury.

*"These souls are **not** yours!"* we roared back, our anger exceeding theirs. *"Leave our world at once! Get out!"*

Twin sliders blocked those foolish enough to attack, and daggers continued to cut them. The cursed one drained grey skin of their stale essence too quickly for them to fight while the bright, reactive silver caused too much pain for them to prevent it.

We decapitated one with our long double-blades in two strikes, the head hanging by a thread of skin as the corpse fell. Proof for the others these Outsiders could be stopped without silver or an ancient relic, but it required massive damage.

In the next breath, we lost an ally to a crossbow bolt with a rope of flesh attached, puncturing through the chest where the body could be pulled forward to disappear into the pack of Malok.

The only salve to the sting was the Deathwalker with his thurible, who was so much faster to claim the soul than the harvesters' more primitive soul traps. Their screeches of frustrated denial were songs to our ears.

The Herald of Nyx infuriated the Greylands hunters, but they were also afraid of him. We understood why; we knew the purpose of his bones erupting from beneath his flesh and clothes. This contest lied not between the Nexus lanterns and one ancient censer found in a crypt. Gavin *himself* had become the soul trap with a much stronger draw and influence over the fallen of this battle.

The Deathwalker commanded our lost ally's body still skewered on the Malok's bolt, raising the Guildsman's arm to stab his killers with a silver dagger. They disrupted the pack long enough to give us room.

We attacked again.

The Outsiders gave up on their first target, withdrawing from the Deathwalker and the pale priestess's defenders. One vocal signal turned all remaining Malok to the Godblood, the shining soul who was shielding nearly every other Human soul as they worked to obstruct the Malok, even if they could not kill.

We followed the shrinking horde, the elder's tail wrapped around the youngest's hot and potent body. The center mind linking us together crouched her body down, anchoring us, and showing us where to strike as we released a greater effect of this spell than ever before.

"Jikmada thrae'terenj!"

A score of towering bodies were thrown off balance, stumbling sideways into each other or losing their feet entirely as they flew northward to crash into the nearest buildings. Their wretched and blood-stained equipment scattered across the cobblestones, but they would not stay down.

Then a fresh breeze swept away the musty scent of the crypt. Behind it came the familiar scent of the Big Ker River hidden from us all morning. We blinked as our eyes began to ache; our skin noticed when the air grew warmer. We could see our close, blended shadows as the grey clouds thinned.

At last, the fog began to burn off.

"Nomilu sancji!" Isboern cried, swiftly echoed in a roar of boosted spirits.

"She did it! She did it!"

"Nomilu sancji!"

"The sun returns!"

"Louve Dyos!"

By the angle of the Sun, it was midday, and as powerful as the light could be in beating down from above upon the Greylands creatures. The Malok bellowed, their skin darkening somewhat like Gavin's, but most importantly they behaved as if they were…

Blind.

They couldn't find their prey under the Sun, so they turned their muzzles toward the Temple. These Outsiders could still sense the direction where their homeland lay, if little else.

"Get out!" we shouted. "Return through the rift or we will destroy every one of you and take back the Ma'ab souls you've earned!"

The Deathwalker repeated this demand on our behalf.

This time, the Malok listened.

The remaining packs broke into a collective run toward the Temple, including others we hadn't faced abandoning their hunting ground. They'd lost about half of their numbers. Their urgent yelping, barking, and whistling faded up the mountain.

~*We will make certain they leave through the rift,*~ we thought.

~*Wait!*~ Isboern said, having levitated his body up to a damaged roof to join one of his scouts. ~*The Ma'ab are coming to clean up.*~

~*The Guild is weakened and your men need a rest, Captain.*~

~*Agreed, but they come all the same. We need to withdraw to the next line, though it will leave the west gate vulnerable.*~

Krithannia returned to the discussion through her Dragon pearl. *Not yet, you don't, Captain. We've given you back the sun. Use it.*

~*You're in perfect position,*~ we agreed. ~*You have Mitneh'thran. Ask for what you need.*~

We felt the ground trembling as the Malok ran back up the slope; we felt the Godblood return into his own mind as he kneeled to commune with his god and the gifts of light from his world.

Above us, the once-muting clouds had lost their grip, but two massive flyers marred the blue sky. Dark wings outspread, they dove for the Captain and his scout upon the roof.

"Roh'ghast!" Gavin shouted.

~*Godblood, above you!*~ we called.

The fighters on the ground took cover, and Isboern's helmed head lifted skyward, his body turning as if to block grasping claws with the shield. Inevitably, he would be knocked clear off the edge and fall to the street.

We prepared to catch him when a burst of pure light erupted from the surface of the artifact, enveloping one Roh'ghast and rider in a scorching beam of daylight and clipping the other on its wing. We paused.

The burns and smoking flesh were visible even to us, and as the one which suffered a direct hit plummeted out of the sky, the other limped through the air in the direction of the Temple. We weren't sure if it would make it.

Then the Ma'ab shouted as they drew nearer, spotting their adversaries.

"No!" Isboern shouted. *"Vou crishar tet min cuidi!"*

From about the height where the Roh'ghast had been struck, something shining appeared in that blue sky, extending swiftly out as an iridescent barrier. We recognized the smaller shield spell, but this effect was *massive.*

The Godblood formed magical protection sectioning out the entire part of the wall which had been lost thus far, extending even beyond it to cut Ma'ab units apart. The enemies entering the city ran noses-first into it and would be confused and angry for a while.

~I will hold the line as long as you need,~ Isboern said to us. *~Make sure the Malok leave. We'll face one problem at a time.~*

~We will, and shall return as soon as possible.~

~May God's merciful eye remain upon us.~

CHAPTER 34

WE SPRINTED AFTER THE MALOK PACKS, OUR ENDURANCE ENHANCED BY shared magic. We witnessed how many bodies lay in their wake from the first time the Malok ran through, how much destruction they'd indulged in on their raid. Once, the packs' trail leading back to the Temple veered away from the way they'd come in. We discovered a group of Humans who had strayed too close. The Malok had smelled them and taken them as final trophies. The blood was fresh.

As we neared the Temple, stark pain lanced through our middle, followed by a distressing weakness in our limbs. One of us was about to collapse.

~*Wait! Wait, slow... stop... I can't...*~

Mind bonds began to unravel, the threads slipping free with a fluid glide before they could fray or snap altogether. Auras sang inward around me but as separate, concentrated notes instead of simultaneous harmony.

Mourn caught me when I would have fallen, gripping my wrist to keep Soul Drinker far from him. I was shaking, my head feeling ready to crack beneath the bright light. The air felt so hot.

"I am sorry," he said, panting as he set me on the ground and helped me sheath the relic. We moved beneath some shade, into a doorway free of corpses, and Mourn retrieved a vial from his harness. "Here, drink this."

I accepted, cracking the seal, and quaffing the bitter but recognizable healing potion which eased the stress and thirst of the last hour. I was ravenous, however, and nothing would care for that but food.

What had happened weeks ago in the warp rot forest seized me. The bound gatekeeper of Soul Drinker had shared a false strength with me for so long I forgot to eat and drink. I'd fallen ill the moment that strength was withdrawn. The demon had tried to purge my baby, and my spiders would have been next. The voracious, bottomless thing wanted me alone.

I reached for the nuts and fruit on my belt.

"Yes, eat," my bodyguard agreed when he realized what I needed. "We'll take time to rest."

My spiders inspected me after what must have been a truly strange shift in my mind's voice while I chewed quickly but tried not to fill my cheeks with each handful. Meanwhile, Mourn checked on my Sister. Jael had slumped down on an abandoned bench.

"Are you alright, Red Sister?" he asked.

She was still panting, having sheathed her blades. Answering with a nod, she spoke in Davrin. *"I don't... I can't do that... sword-fire thing again... can I? I don't remember how..."*

"Correct," he said. *"That was Sirana sharing body knowledge I could give you with a thought. Such as the Ornilleth and Tragar can do."*

"Damn," she whispered, seeming stunned as she looked at the signs of the Malok passage. *"But... you could teach me things like that? The singing blade and the sticky fire?"*

He sounded cautious. *"With time, perhaps. You did what was necessary but took me more than a century to learn. Take it as motivation to apply yourself once we finish here."*

Jael made a face like they were at Court and the bua had teased her all night before escaping into his room alone. I could see where she sat but also recognized the irreplaceability of Mourn's experience with controlling dangerous spells like this in a street fight.

My Sister looked at me, seeming to notice I'd downed the first pouch we'd obtained from the Dwarves and would finish a second before we left. She opted to take a handful herself from her own belt, chewing thoroughly but without much apparent appetite.

"Here," Mourn offered, adjusting his harness as he prepared for his runner's form. "I will carry you the rest of the way."

"She'll be fine," Jael said in my defense, looking from him to me. "You can run, right?"

"We must catch up," he countered. "My four legs are faster than our six without endurance spells."

Jael couldn't argue, and neither did I. After he'd changed, I mounted up first and she got on behind me. Mourn launched into a sprint toward the Temple, granting me respite and, unfortunately, time alone in my mind.

Gavin, Brom, Krithannia, and everyone else who'd hung around me long enough noticed these sudden moments of weakness and my urgent need to eat as much as I could in one sitting. *Including her.*

Should I tell her now? I was surprised she did not appear to have gleaned it from our surreal, mind-and-body bond just now, nor did she seem to recognize a new aura low in my gut.

No, I decided. The battle wasn't over, and we hadn't escaped yet. Maybe something would still go wrong, and my body would purge the drain on its resources to save itself with or without D'Shea's potion.

Pursing my lips, I sighed through my nose and held on tight as Mourn weaved through the streets, discovering where the Manalari had retreated before the Malok arrived to break down their barricades in the quieter part of the city. We found no additional bodies, so I wondered about their advance notice.

Or maybe the men were smart enough to run upon seeing such a stampede.

Mourn slowed before cautiously entering the Sun-drenched courtyard strewn with bright red body parts drawing flies and crows. His muscles were tense, ready to run in case of an ambush, but none of us sensed imminent danger as he slid behind a hedge for us to dismount so he could shift.

Meanwhile, I looked at the Temple. The front doors were not only open but could not be closed any time soon. The damage from two sweeps of Malok rushing through had been too much to leave them functional. The shadowy, masked spindles with swords were absent for the moment.

"Come on," Mourn whispered as he reclaimed his birth form. From the smell of him, I had to think he grew tired from the constant shifting. "I can scent the trail. The Malok went inside but let us check on the rift while we're here."

The three of us entered the Temple with caution. The first lobby was dirty and disheveled, the artwork destroyed, though signs of true violence seemed limited to blood droplets fallen from weapons.

I looked upward and tapped Mourn's shoulder. ~*What's that?*~

My head did not hurt as much when he responded.

Wow. That is… a depiction of the Grey Maiden.

Part of the high wall had crumbled and fallen during the pulses and shakes from the rift opening, revealing that it was only a patch covering up a large and intricate engraving of an eyeless woman wearing tattered shrouds. This was one of the few things intact, for the Malok couldn't reach it even with their height.

We peeked both ways before crossing the first, broad hallway, finding similar destruction and a few more bodies with bloody handprints on the smooth stone walls. All the fog was gone, however, and while the torches had not been relit, more natural daylight filtered through the dimmer interior from the Temple windows.

The west doors of the central sanctum had been broken off their hinges and laid flat on the floor, and a stronger mix of odors flowed into the short hallway leading from the main one. The many bodies of Hellhounds, Witch Hunters, and clergy which hadn't stood up and spilled out into the courtyard had indeed been bashed and crushed to further mulch by the passing of the Greylands raiders.

The torches and chandeliers remained unlit, and some small amount of mist remained here. Sunlight streamed through the eastern window and skylight, causing the altar and sacred spring revealed behind the chancel barrier to glow. The floor was dry from the earlier flood from *Pisc'sagrad*, and the chancel barrier remained two lumps of twisted iron upon the shattered floor.

The green rift splintering off from Nyx's ice blue portal remained but was much smaller than it had been when we had run from here. A flow of Greylands mist spilled in as if to protect the beings who remained behind but was unable to overcome the power of the Sun to fill the Temple again.

Appropriately, more plaster had cracked and broken off from the strong disturbances, and in addition to the Sun and mountain sculptures were more of crows, winds, and…women like the one I'd seen in the street, begging Gavin to guide her.

I looked up at the third floor. All the Shaegoth appeared to have left, but then Mourn tensed up next to us. I heard a sound suggesting his dorsal spines had tried to rise, stretching against his harness.

~*Uh-oh. What?*~

The altar. Count them.

I blinked against the glare, squinting at the blurry mix of fog and Sun. Oskar, Houda, and Ada were easier to make out as they remained in their equidistant places. I spotted the wasp child crouching protectively over the waters then recognized Cris-ri-phon standing farther to the left and watching *Pisc'sagrad*.

~*Oh, no. He's back.*~

Yes, but that counts five.

I searched for any other shapes I could make out, fixing on one which wavered in and out of focus, standing, hovering above the wasp child with its arm lifted above the water.

~*Is it bleeding?*~

Probably.

~*So, six. Any others?*~

No, but that sixth is plenty.

As if hearing us, the figure turned to the west, lifting that same arm to beckon. A male voice projected our way without shouting, smooth, calm, and reassuring.

"Ah, come in. Be mindful of where you step."

I swallowed. He'd spoken in Davrin, and it was a similar, older accent to Cris-ri-phon.

"Jael," Mourn murmured.

"Hm?"

"Stay close to us. No matter what. My aura can help protect you."

"Uhm. Sure. Will do."

Following Mourn's lead, we came down the steps into the main floor of the sanctum, stepping over and around the worst puddles and piles of gore while keeping our eyes on those surrounding the sacred spring.

None of Nyx's guardians seemed *too* agitated except for the insect girl. Houda had drawn her sword but balanced its point on the floor as she kept her eyes and chin down. Oskar kept his body between his ruffled charge and the new arrival but kept a stoic face. Ada boldly watched him as if mostly curious.

Only after we'd walked half the distance did the form solidify more, and I gasped. He was a...

A brown Elf.

Like those I'd seen riding in the red sands of Auslan's dreams!

"Keep going," Mourn murmured. *"Mind your thoughts."*

This proved extremely difficult when the new arrival focused on me. My breath hitched, and my stomach clenched and began to turn.

The strange Elf was bronze-skinned and naked from the waist up, his legs covered by a long, brown wrap somewhat like a Consort. Long, auburn hair reached his lower back, and his ears, while not as long as a Naulor's, were upswept like a Davrin's. His eyes were the most striking shades of blue and green I'd ever seen, as if the lushest grass, the clearest sky, and the sparkle of the Great Lake lit by the Sun all vied to exist within the same impossibly perfect gemstone.

"How grand to see you are well after all this," he said with a warm smile which captivated me.

My limbs sought to melt inside my skin; my bodyguard took hold of my arm to keep me upright and on our path.

~*I know him!*~ I cried through our link. ~*I know him from some-where!*~

"Shhh," Mourn hushed me.

"*No, no,*" the brown Elf said. "*Let her speak her mind.*"

"*Not unless you introduce yourself properly,*" the To'vah-krav growled.

The beautiful blend of a Naulor and a Davrin smirked, tossing me a look as if to question if I'd let the half-blood call the shots on my behalf. I swallowed, feeling the prick to my pride even as I jumped when Jael ducked behind Mourn's broad body.

"*Shit… shit…!*" she hissed, pressing close to his back in a way I'd never seen her do to anyone.

"*What are you doing to her?*" I asked the strange Elf.

"*Nothing malevolent,*" he replied with ease. "*Her aura is not yet set… How strange. But she merely seeks the strongest pull to what's familiar. Natural, for her heritage.*"

The visitor's eyes narrowed on me as if in silent remark on what was natural for Davrin. He glanced at the black dagger on my belt. Mourn moved to make sure our arms touched. This helped to ground me.

"*Where do you believe you know me?*" the stranger asked curiously.

His manner of speaking and his presence were so familiar. Why couldn't I…?

Something prompted me to look at Cris-ri-phon, who kept his back to the north wing of the altar, far from *Pisc'sagrad* like he was a less worthy novitiate. His grey eyes gazed into emptiness as though he were in a trance. Distant voices from a long-ago exchange returned from when I'd lain ill in Mourn's cave after cleansing the warp rot. A dream about entering a prison in the Red Desert, only to discover that the golden-eyed bua was missing.

"*Leave, now. This grave is under my protection.*"

"*The Sorcerer-General needs something here, law keeper. We shall not be long.*"

"*Time matters not. I do not keep law if I bend it for you, deal broker.*"

"*Trade, then. What do you want?*"

"*Nothing. You shall not defile and rob from the grave of your kin, by your*" *own hand or that of a puppet."*

"Obstinate fool! I am not defiling. We brought a Deathwalker to perform the correct rites..."

My attention shifted to the hulk who claimed to be Oskar. This was not the gaunt, Zauyrian body of the death mage who'd stood beside Cris-ri-phon back then. Had this Deathwalker been there, nonetheless?

"I believe you were..." I said in the Trade tongue. "The merchant in the Red Desert."

The brown Elf tilted his head, silky, auburn locks falling over his right shoulder. "Oh?"

I licked my lips, glancing at Oskar. "Called Toushek. The deal broker."

The male Deathwalker absolutely recognized this name and even looked surprised as he gave the mysterious Elf another look. At the same time, Cris lifted his eyes and focused on us.

The brown Elf noticed this and chuckled. "Fascinating. I see you are not above rooting deep for memories which do not belong to you."

"Do not pretend you do not do the same," Mourn said.

Aquatic eyes darted to him. "I never did, Dragon son, and it's been a pleasure to witness our races regain interest in the preciousness of our world." Toushek looked at the sorcerer. "Isn't that right, General? Do you remember what this spring was called the last time you fought for its freedom? Remember when one could stand here and view the entire sky and land out to the river?"

The Deathless was sweating, gasping for breath as far too many thoughts whirled behind his eyes. He swallowed and winced in pain, then answered, "Na... Nalari."

"Indeed. Nalari." Toushek turned around and smiled, his canines seeming too pointed. "Nalari. Nalamar. Manari. Manalar..." The cooing of names was gently spoken like a night song meant to relax. "There shall be many more names, I'm sure, with how quick and un-reliable Human memory becomes. But *their* names do not matter, do they, Dragon son? No more than a bird chirping in a breeze."

Mourn narrowed his eyes with suspicion but said nothing.

Letting this go, Toushek peered directly at Soul Drinker on my belt, and I could not tell what emotion touched his beautiful face. It could have been... joy, relief, desire, *or* anger.

"You were not gifted that relic, were you, granddaughter?" he asked.

I glanced at the Deathless and shook my head before finding my tongue. "No."

Toushek smiled with mischievous delight. "You stole it."

His ethereal whisper overflowed within my ears, making me shudder.

"Yet you earned the role of wielder," he continued, the smile fading. "Not the other way around. I am impressed. But you must know, your solution is temporary." The rush of dread was overwhelming as the warm smile returned. "I could take this burden from you, granddaughter. You would never have to listen to the Black Heart again."

"Uhm—"

"For no cost, 'merchant?'"

Toushek narrowed his eyes at yet another interruption from my bodyguard. "What sort of exchange has only one direction of change, Dragon son? There *must* be a cost. You know this."

"Do not bargain with him," Mourn advised me.

The brown Elf sighed deeply. "She is old enough to speak for herself, To'vah-krav."

"And you have still not introduced yourself. She does not know the true face with whom you would have her negotiate. This is not balanced."

"Balance is an approximated target always in motion, to be sought by those brave enough to seek it." The bronze Elf smirked. "But very well. You say no bargain, keep the dagger and all its consequences. Regardless, I gift *all* of you with this."

He pointed up at the rift with one smooth, toned arm. We looked and blinked.

"The rifts are... vanishing," I said.

"I healed the wound," Toushek agreed with a brief bow at the waist.

"Only the neutral guardians remain. And now, I must go."

In between Cris-ri-phon and Oskar and beyond the deal broker's graceful hand, a doorway of deep blue light opened. The brown Elf moved to step through it without another word but then paused, looking over his shoulder with a scathing look at Houda.

"Your Cris is gone," he said. "Your time is dead. For all our sakes, do not reveal what does not belong to you again."

The ancient Elf left through the door, after which it winked out of existence with a puff of icy wind.

The Deathless blinked, caught himself before he collapsed, and clutched his head with a groan. When he looked back up, he ignored Houda as if she weren't there and focused straight on me.

"Innathi... I could... *hear* her." His face contorted with hatred as the color in his face returned. He drew a longsword. "Give her back to me... All of you."

Mourn moved in front of me as I pulled Jael back a few steps. She could finally take a full breath to speak.

"Who the fuck was that?"

"Um—"

"Sirana!" Cris-ri-phon roared, boots stomping off the platform toward us. "I said give. Her. *Back!*"

"Run outside," Mourn said, summoning his twin blades as we backed up and using them to scatter the first bolt of magic the sorcerer tossed at us from his open hand.

"But—"

"I will cover your back and lead him out of the Temple. If we do not, he will destroy it."

~*What will—?*~

I have called for back-up. We must deal with him now. We have no choice.

~*Hoo bua...*~

Jael and I ran for the courtyard while Mourn engaged the man I'd met as an innkeeper governing his own town. Now, this creature of cobbled memory wasn't even of his own will from how it appeared to me.

An Elf who remembered the Desert Queendom had some leash upon the Deathless, one who was far more than a "merchant."

He must be a ruler, too.

At least as old as the Valsharess.

How much had changed in only a few months. I only hoped my ignorance wasn't about to explode in my face.

"What in the fuck just happened?!" JAEL DEMANDED AS WE SPRINTED OUT OF the Temple side-by-side.

"A reminder why we built Sivaraus, I think," I huffed.

She made a noise between a growl and a groan. *"What are we going to do? How do we kill that sire-fucker?"*

We ducked behind the still-flowing fountain with body parts floating in it. Her question whirled in my mind. What else could we do against him?

"I-I don't know," I stuttered. *"I stabbed him with the rune blade last time. It didn't kill him, only slowed him down, yet it stopped everything else I've so much as cut. My spiders would go after him again, but he'd kill them this time. I... don't have anything else except Mourn."*

"More than I ever had," she said, grinding her teeth as we peeked toward the noise nearing the Temple doors. *"So, I guess we keep moving and try not to get hit?"*

"A start. I will use what I have if he gets close. Mourn said he's called for back-up."

"From who?"

"I don't know. Gavin?"

I could hope. From the start, the innkeeper Brom hadn't been comfortable with the Deathwalker's observations. What about now that he was a "herald"?

I recognized Mourn's roar as he backed his way outside of the Temple and Cris's throaty laugh as they exchanged red and gold blasts focused by their swords. At first, I feared my bodyguard was being overwhelmed, but his feet were steady, and his tail moved with familiar, controlled balance. The roar must have been a challenge or distraction, and the Deathless responded.

"*A half-blood in House D'Shauranti, now?*" Cris-ri-phon snarled in Davrin, coming down the steps. "*And one trained in blade song… How long has it been?*"

The Zauyrian sounded confused and angry but Mourn said nothing as they maneuvered around the courtyard.

"*You… you are doomed, like my Queen's children, yet you… you have those cursed gold eyes.*" The Zauyrian gripped his sword so hard it trembled in one hand. "*That **cursed** bua… Stop your pleading! Be gone from me and my family!*"

All the rings on the sorcerer's fingers crackled with energy as he lifted his hand toward the Dragonblood. Cris cut the air with a crimson blast which smashed against a shimmering, golden shield in front of my bodyguard. Vibrations coursed through the ground beneath me.

"*Are **you** why Ishuna left V'Gedra for all those months?*"

Again, the Dragonblood did not respond, holding his focus on defense and testing his opponent with methodical attacks.

"*Was my Queen's sister held captive and forced to bear you for your sire? Is **that** why she wouldn't tell us what happened?*"

Any plants not trampled by the invaders were soon singed or burning from magical flares. Mourn remained silent as he guided the fight around the courtyard. Their auras burned so strongly that even I could sense them without a mindlink.

"*Do I know, at last, where that bua came from?*" Cris-ri-phon growled. "*Is **that** why Xala could never even speak of it?!*"

Xala?

Like, *Captain* Xala?

The Deathless cast something which made Mourn dive toward the fountain, his spinning blades speeding up.

Get down! my bodyguard ordered.

I grabbed Jael and flattened us against the masonry an instant before an explosion struck the ground in front of us. The fountain cracked like a hammer splitting stone with a chisel, and cold water spilled out to soak us. I gasped as my spiders shrilled with alarm, though my hood was up to catch them.

Sirana!

~Unhurt. Moving back.~

It's a dead end. Run toward the street. I'll cover you.

I glanced up, squinting through the glare of magic and daylight. Both opponents were climbing back to their feet as the boom dissipated but Mourn would be up first.

"Run," I whispered, signaling the direction.

Jael nodded and scrambled up with me. Cris began laughing as he spotted us, staggering to his feet. He stood too close for comfort, for I could see the whites of his eyes had turned blood-red.

"Sirana!" he shouted, his hand crackling. "Stop!"

My breath was the only part of me to obey him during the instant my back was exposed. Mourn filled the space with blades crossed and lifted, deflecting the sorcerer's power where edges intersected and returning it in a punishing blow. Still, the Deathless returned to his feet.

"How far?" Jael huffed.

"Not far."

We hid behind the first standing wall we could find, and Cris started bellowing when he failed a second time to advance out of the courtyard. Mourn was no longer in defensive retreat.

"Have you come to drag the Red Sister's find back to your Queen-Mother, Mazdel?" the Zauyrian shouted.

I trembled to hear that name while awake.

"Now that she has Innathi's ultimate punishment to help her maintain control? Surely you'll be rewarded, though never with freedom."

We weathered another flashing, ground-shaking blast, squeezing our eyes shut against it.

"I wonder why Ishuna needs it. Is the Seer losing their respect so soon?"

I heard Mourn respond but only to combine the To'vah Words with his sword-casting. A blurt of pain followed by an air-clearing wind seemed to have set Cris-ri-phon back on his heels. I peeked around the corner.

Even from here, I could see the sorcerer's wide, reddened eyes when he was suddenly on the defensive. At the same time, Mourn appeared much like the mercenary fighting against the denizens of the warped forest, crossing magical heat and the force of air with the perfect edge of his metal sliders.

With Cris-ri-phon and Mourn locked in combat within the courtyard, my ears picked up galloping hooves down the street behind us. The horse stopped one crossway down from where I crouched, but I recognized Krithannia jumping off the back of the horse and Isboern dismounting after her.

"What the fuck is he doing here?!" Jael whispered. *"Who's holding the wall?"*

A worthy concern but, unfortunately, not among our most immediate.

My first concern was the ragged shape which had seemed tethered behind the horse but then settled upon the ground. The creature was bipedal and vaguely man-shaped yet enveloped by an ashen cloud swirling with embers like glittering ice, punctuated by black, obsidian spurs. Then I saw his eyes, the spade, and the artifact of white gold swinging from his belt.

~Gavin?~

Yes?

No recoil or hesitation. Fuck me with a mage staff.

~How many antlers are you going to grow?~

He felt vaguely amused. *Enough to neutralize all the dead necessary.*

~Including the Deathless?~

He paused. *We're about to find out.*

Uh-oh.

Krithannia and Isboern ran up to Jael and me while Gavin walked past us to join Mourn and Cris, standing at the gate to the courtyard.

Willven placed his hand on my shoulder. ~We're here, legend. We will protect them while you fight for us.~

I sensed the wordless affirmative as Mourn rumbled something aloud, intensely focused on managing another assault of mage's fire. He attempted to turn this larger, less-focused blaze back to its source, but part of it divided away from the rest and blew out a section of the wall.

The following wash of residual magic made me and Jael nauseous. What the...?

Move back gradually, Mourn growled. *Not too fast so he doesn't get past us, but don't stay too close. He will follow Soul Drinker out into the city.*

Confirmed.

The Guild Mistress leaned partway out of cover, standing on her tiptoes as if to see above Gavin and Mourn's heads. Her concern was clear.

*You are right, Morixxyleth. It is no illusion. He is unravelling, and it accelerates. I promise we'll do everything to shelter them, but you and Gavin **must** stop him.*

I know.

I could not make out the shouts behind the next series of explosions as pieces of the courtyard wall burst outward, causing whole sections to collapse.

"What happens?!" Jael asked in Trade as Isboern hustled us several buildings down.

By then, I'd gleaned the real fears from the Naulor's thoughts. Isboern understood, too; this was why he was here to help keep Mourn's part of our Bargain despite the Ma'ab laying destruction upon his walls.

"The sorcerer's aura is damaged beyond any ability to stabilize it," Krithannia explained. "That wound looks weeks, if not months, old."

Shit.

Jael shook her head, her shoulders lifting. "Meaning?"

"Meaning the sorcerer is becoming warp rot," I said.

My Sister jerked her eyes to me. "What?"

"Like what killed Gaelan." I gritted my teeth. "The world-eater probably caused what she was sent to stop."

"Correct, Sirana," Krithannia said, a shimmer of tears in her eyes. "If the Deathless falls apart here, immense upheaval shall engulf all

Paxia. The entire mountain could become a center of chaos larger than you saw before."

The building nearest to the Temple wall took another blast which collapsed one wall forming the corner Jael and I had first hidden behind. We took that moment to move back one more alley, but I could not stop from looking out the way we came.

Through the blowing dust, Mourn and Gavin spread out to take advantage of more space. The hybrid stepped up his attacks and the aggression behind them now that he didn't have to protect me simultaneously, and the Deathwalker held his spiny black arm out toward the sorcerer, his spade glowing with a subtle aura.

Although I could imagine Gavin's expression as he concentrated to draw any vulnerable Vis toward him, I could not tell if it was working without the Greylands mist filling the city.

"Accursed queen agents!" the Deathless howled so loudly even we could hear him. "Release us! Let...us...*be!!*"

The Deathless broke the Deathwalker's focus with a silent impact, making him stagger, his nose bleeding black. The sorcerer lunged for Gavin with the flaming sword pointed forward but Mourn deflected the blade and struck back.

He moved more like a true snake than I realized was possible.

The Dragon son opened his mouth and lifted his long, lavender tongue, two strong streams of fluid jetting out. They splashed Cris in the eyes, and he jerked and cried out, stumbling as his bejeweled hand reached up to his face.

Mourn followed up by champing his mouth into the meat between the neck and shoulder, and the deathless body spasmed. The half-blood's bite left only two neat puncture wounds in our adversary's flesh. He hadn't intended to rip out a chunk of flesh.

Wait. Are Deepearth Dragons venomous...?

Cris-ri-phon's limbs soon shook as the toxin spread with his furiously pounding heart and Mourn used one locked slider to slice across his left bicep, much deeper than any hit prior. The innkeeper's scream was oddly satisfying to me as the Dragonblood forced him to back up far away from Gavin, who wiped dark fluid with the back of his black-skinned hand.

The ash-and-ember aura around the Deathwalker regained strength but, unfortunately, the Zauyrian's fury had summoned a shell Mourn could not break in his next attack. Both auras had recovered at the same speed.

The Deathless also refused to fall from the venom attack, remaining on his feet long enough to purge it. Much of his strategy shifted to shield himself from further damage as the three remained in tight conflict for far too long without giving ground. At one point, they sent a wave of energy which struck like a fist, making me see double.

I forced down nausea as Krithannia tightened her hands on my shoulders, apologizing softly. Soon I felt better.

"Gavin needs to speak to Mourn," she said to me.

Swallowing at the hard lump which had come with the urge to puke, I nodded, breathing in. ~*Gavin? Talk to us.*~

*★This bog of Vis will **not** come apart,★* he thought as if he'd waited hours to speak. *★No matter how I attempt to separate them, they act like that chancel barrier guarding Pisc'sagrad. A multitude of complex anchors prevent it from being dragged out of the body.★*

★Alright,★ Mourn replied. *★What can you do, Deathwalker?★*

★I can drain the Vitas keeping him alive.★

★Focus all you have on that. I shall make the body unpleasant for the Vis to stay without Vitas.★

His blades hummed with song, and his voice rumbled louder than before as Mourn cast three consecutive spells, each erupting from the intense, visible corona of churning magic leaping off his blades. I dared hope it would take all Cris's concentration to respond; perhaps he could not counter them all.

First, a white-hot whip of energy lashed out, entangling the sorcerer's flaming sword and jerking it briefly to the side as the second effect manifested. In the time it took to blink, a golden hook then caught Brom behind the knee, halting any slack given as a flame-orange arrow pierced whatever protection the sorcerer had at his chest.

"Augh!" Cris cried, his eyes bulging as the bolt penetrated, leaving no outward wound but certainly wreaking havoc on the inside. He nearly fell even as he succeeded in dispersing the hook and whip.

Gavin drew on the unnatural life aura of the Deathless, using it to manifest a tight ball of pure, blue magic, which he sent barreling at the same point Mourn's arrow had hit, knocking the Zauyrian down without visible damage.

"Thrae, ternesj!" Mourn called out, spinning one slider, and throwing a deluge of energy from it. His spell lifted the sorcerer before, once again, hurling him into the nearest wall.

Whatever remaining stubborn quality had saved Cris's neck and spine from breaking against the stone didn't save the stone from the sorcerer's impact. The base of the wall cracked, and bricks fell upon him one after another. The Deathless truly seemed annoyed by this as he bellowed once and stood up, leaving his extinguished sword on the ground.

"Is this your best?!" the Deathless challenged them, the smile broken into a snarl on one side of his mouth. "You try to drain the Great Lake with a spoon—?"

~Duck.~

A blast of golden light bright enough to blind us struck Cris-ri-phon as Mourn and Gavin ducked down and to one side. Something shifted in my mind until I could see through the Godblood's eyes, reassuring me it wasn't an ambush from somewhere else.

~I'm sorry,~ thought a desperate man. *~This...eternal tormenter keeps us here while all my people struggle for their lives!~*

Continue! Mourn replied, preparing another action. **Be ready to shield your bodies and minds. Krithannia will anchor your auras.**

Captain Isboern guarded us in front and used *Mitneh'thran* in a straight shot down the street. Intensely focused daylight burned flesh and laid pressure upon our enemy's aura to such an extent that Gavin needed both the thurible and all his pneuma flint bones to keep up with collecting the Vitas through the wounds.

Cris started laughing, a sound which made me sick.

He'd slithered into the link. He could hear us.

I pity you, Willven Isboern, he jeered. *You've always loved them, haven't you? Since you first saw the 'forest spirit' long spoken of by your clan. So beautiful, that sun-haired druid bathing naked in the lake. It was the same with me, from the first day I saw her underneath the waterfall.*

~Get out,~ the Captain demanded.

*Oh, but we can't. You're **entangled**, the same as me, and **we** cannot get out. Just another mortal fool who does not yet know he walks the same path I did. After all they've shown you, can you watch her remain a flower in full bloom while you wither, growing old and weak? Will you turn your back on them, **Godblood**? Will you give up, and die once you've lost your mind to the decay of time?*

The psion shuddered, his willpower dampening as Krithannia wrapped us in her layers of chants.

Stop him now! the Naulor cried with no less than five voices. *Please!*

Mourn brought down his blades from above his head, unleashing a concussive burst which broke the body to pieces as Gavin wrung the living aura out of each one. The backlash of memories struck me, scouring like a sandstorm as Willven braced his body and shield in front to take the brunt of the physical backlash.

Still, the past all came through, and I screamed my throat raw.

Sirana!

Kiabil!

An inky black shape tore through the whirlwind of centuries, dipping and weaving through time to find me where I reached up for help. Cooling shadows blocked the harsh lightstorm, wrapping around me, shielding my essence, and sinking us beneath the roaring chaos. I took a breath and found a quiet center.

Something made me look up.

The sky appeared impossibly distant, broken in a peculiar, ordered way. The lines reminded me of candle-lit quartz.

~Yes!~ called the Godblood within the storm. ~There! Help the last of him to cross the plane!~

I wasn't the only one who heard him. I existed in the relative calm below, anchoring all those prepared to hurl the inextricable core of the Deathless elsewhere. I knew not where.

Only that it wouldn't be here.

Each of them helped. *Gavin, Willven, Krithannia, Morixxyleth…*

Even Jael.

I witnessed a spinning, gossamer ball of impossible life and light pitched so far and fast… that it crossed the plane.

The sandstorm dissipated and vanished.

I could return to my memories, my own time and place, knowing the dire harm to our world would cease as it had been before.

Only for a time.

CHAPTER 35

THE DAY BURNED BRIGHT, AND MOST OF US RETREATED TO ANY SHADE AVAIL-able to appraise our wounds and pass around what few healing or vitality vials were left. Mourn and Gavin each bore gouges, abrasions, and bruises, and at first glance, the latter looked worse off as none of the Dragonblood's scale patches had been penetrated. My bodyguard consumed two vials, one which escaped destruction on his harness, and the other from Krithannia, while the Deathwalker raised his hand against any personal assistance for him.

"I need no intervention."

Indeed, Gavin's long, hooked nose had stopped bleeding and his Sun-blackened skin closed simultaneously at several points while I watched, wolfing down the last of my food from my belt.

I was trying not to choke without enough moisture in my mouth because, unfortunately, no one had any water. I was tempted to suck some of the lingering fountain's dampness from my cloak, but Jael stopped me.

"*That thing was bloody and oily and gross,*" she said hoarsely. "*I don't get how you can eat right now anyway.*"

My stomach cramped as if to agree with her, while Mourn, Gavin, and Krithannia minded their business. Willven looked at me with concern, though, his brilliant blue eyes glancing down to my gut like he understood why this urgent appetite had arisen.

Fuck.

~Don't say anything,~ I warned him, my next mouthful of nuts fighting against the hard spot forming in my throat. *~It may not survive the stress anyway.~*

The Captain swallowed, and suddenly, the food passed more easily down my throat. *~As you wish. I... am sorry you must be here risking such loss at all.~*

~Pfeh. Not your doing, Captain, and I doubt I'm the only one today.~

"So, what's happening now?" I asked aloud, making the man blink. "What happened at the wall?"

Isboern's eyes filled with tears as he measured his breath with care. "Lost. Shortly after I left. Houda and Ada told Gavin about a threat which would render this entire battle meaningless. Then the legend called for aid against it." He looked pained. "My Templari *asked* me to go. They're leading our army to slow the advance through the city toward the south wall, but they lose ground as the streets are culled of any hiding out."

"How many citizens remain at the evacuation point?" Mourn asked, his tail waving, slow and tight. His wounds were healing though crusts of blood remained.

Isboern paused, his eyes losing focus as he stared into the sky's reflection in *Mitneh'thran*. "One-fifty or two hundred who must make it down the mountain."

"Over seven hundred women, children, and grand-folk have made it through the gate, Captain," Krithannia reported to ease his pain. "The next jump will move another hundred, plus all the walking wounded who retreated when the rift opened. The Dwarves are preparing for two more big jumps where nothing comes through, everything moves one way, including them, the Guild, and every Manalari fighter able to come with us."

"Right," Willven whispered, taking a deep breath in his resolve. "So the... Ma'ab Ascended may be the new stewards of *Pisc'sagrad*."

"Not for certain, Captain," Mourn said. "Taking the city is different from holding it."

Isboern frowned. "I don't...understand."

"No reason that you would, but something has changed."

The Dragonblood looked to Gavin, who was scowling as usual, the handle of his spade propped upon the cobblestones.

"When we were called," the Deathwalker began, "I learned from Houda that my Lady's guardians aren't leaving *Pisc'sagrad* in the event of your retreat, Captain Isboern. Not unless you concede to the Ascended and surrender the city to them."

"Never," the Godblood replied, baring teeth. "They must kill all of us first."

Gavin seemed to take note. "The threats of the Malok and the Deathless all but guaranteed the Manalari loss in this first battle. My Lady agreed that her guardians would stay until the war was decided if the rift could be sealed and the Deathless prevented from escaping into the Nexus."

"She agreed with whom?" Mourn asked suspiciously.

The Deathwalker looked at him. "A figure I believe you saw. She only referred to him as the deal broker."

Well. We'd paid that part of the deal without realizing it.

"Some 'gift,' " I commented.

Mourn acknowledged me with a rumble of irritation, too worn to summon a larger response against the Elven ruler. "So. *Pisc'sagrad* is protected from the Ascended until the Ma'ab achieve a more decisive win *not* involving two problems the deal broker brought upon us in the first place."

The Deathwalker dipped his chin. "As I understand it, yes."

We looked at Isboern, who appeared as if he'd been slapped upside the face. "Wait. There is... no time limit for the protection of *Pisc'sagrad?*"

"There is a limit," Gavin replied. "Your lifetime. The Grey Maiden doesn't count days as meaningful in a deal like this but prefers to count lifetimes."

"Then we could come back," Willven whispered. "As long as we live."

"As long as *you* live," the death mage reiterated. "You are the last Human soul of the Mount engaged in this conflict who gave of yourself to *Pisc'sagrad*. The rest have transitioned."

The Godblood quivered, his eyes dropping to the shield. "We need not fight to the last man. The more lives we save now, the greater chance of a second battle later…"

"Weighed against how many Ma'ab are culled before you leave," Mourn commented.

"Will you help me, elders?"

Krithannia answered gently, "We chose to help you years ago, Captain."

"And we stand right here," Mourn added.

I listened to the man's heartbeat, strong but fast as light returned to his eyes.

"My Templari and I need assistance holding back the advance," he said, "so that more soldiers can retreat. We must also cut down as many of the Ma'ab as possible on our way out."

Mourn looked at the rest of us, gauging our willingness. Nothing had changed from the last several hours. "Agreed."

"And one more request, elders?"

My bodyguard exchanged a glance with the Guild Mistress. "Yes?"

"If my lifetime determines how long we have to route the Ma'ab from Mount Sonai," Isboern said, "then I'll take no reckless risks to cut that time short. As this is my truth, may I work with your psion to expand my reach to my people from a distance, to reassure and strengthen everyone who needs guidance?"

'Your' psion? I swallowed the nerves which surged up, glancing around.

No one *disagreed* with Isboern, and he paused long enough for an immediate refusal from any of us. He didn't get one as Mourn's metallic eyes narrowed with deeper thought.

"*Hm*," my bodyguard began. "I have promised Sirana protection."

"I swear my oath to you both," the Captain urged, "Sirana will be safe and protected with me, and we shall warn you in time before we can be overwhelmed. This way, you may challenge the strongest the Ma'ab can throw at us, and in doing so, protect us all."

Jael bit her lip and glanced up at him. Her eyes brightened at the suggestion.

Mourn glanced at me, and I nodded. "I am willing."

The Captain was a good read of others, apparently. This would place me and my Sister one-on-one with the proper tutors who could teach us the most.

"Very well," said the Dragonblood. "Agreed. Find your horse, Captain. Let us return to battle."

"May it be the final for today," Isboern said, "but not the last for the Manalari to win back our home."

MOURN CARRIED JAEL AND I ON FOUR LEGS, RUNNING AHEAD OF THE OTHERS. Not only did he gain distance from their terrified mount but also scouted out the safest path for the Godblood to rejoin the fight.

I need you to stay linked with me and the Guild through the pearls, he said, *no matter how many others Isboern reaches out to. Do you think you can manage this?*

~Yes,~ I replied. ~We've joined a couple times between the Guild and the Templari.~

This will be more chaotic with the Manalari outnumbering our mages in simultaneous conflicts. There shall be many currents pushing you toward various foci, threatening to drown you, but I believe you can handle it.

My face warmed. ~Understood. I'll learn what I can from Isboern, I won't be a passive conduit for him to use.~

That is all I can ask.

Will it be the same for Jael?

*I will do what I can, Kiabil. There will be times I must either override a *novice mistake or join our auras to greater effect, but such actions will be to keep her alive.* ⋆

~Then that is all I can ask of you.~

Krithannia, Gavin, and the Captain weren't too far behind us, and Mourn made it possible for them to avoid any unexpected obstacles.

The hybrid leaped and climbed atop a three-story mansion with balconies. The position was good; the house rested atop a small, natural cliff within the city walls, revealing more streets not yet overrun by the approaching fight.

Mourn dropped beneath some shade from the Sun. *Wait here for Isboern. We'll need Gavin with us at the battlefront.* ⋆

I dismounted, kissing Jael before she shifted forward on his back. ~And Krithannia?~

⋆*She will retreat to the evacuation point with Tamuril and assist to keep order there.* ⋆

Sounded good to me.

I watched them jump off the balcony to a lower roof, seeking faster acceleration upon the streets. At the same time, Isboern rode toward me at a full gallop with Krithannia on the back. I wasn't sure where Gavin was but worried about his vulnerability the least at this point.

There would be many other death mages aware of the Manalari ally who could neutralize one of their most significant threats as the bodies piled up. Death mages had tricks to use against other death mages, no doubt, but I imagined the Ascended had not prepared to deal with one who had been revived by a long-dead runaway while lying in a puddle formed from the sacred waters of Manalar.

Isboern approached the balcony upon which I stood and slowed his horse to a stop, dismounting as Krithannia leaned back to make room. The Naulor shifted forward into his saddle and took the reins from him, turning and urging the blowing beast onto the closest south-pointing road.

Here we go.

From the street underneath, the Godblood began lifting himself up in the air, slow and steady, as I'd seen him do once before when the sky had been cleared. Levitation spells weren't unknown to me, but...

~Are you using psionics?~

The Captain's eyes were half-closed in concentration, but he smiled as he landed with care beside me and out of direct daylight.

~I am. I can also lift both of us back down if necessary, and if either of us fall from here, I can catch us so the landing won't kill.~

I smirked. *~Like you caught the Inquisitor?~*

Willven blinked. *~Ah...you saw that?~*

I snickered, nodding. *~Excellent powerplay. I enjoyed that moment. Kegyek deliberately broke with Keros in his gratitude to you.~*

The Captain grimaced. *~I honestly wasn't thinking about that. I saw a man falling, and I could do something to save him. It didn't matter who he was.~*

~So you would have saved Keros, if the fight had turned the other way?~

Isboern looked out above the rooftops and down the slope of his city. Many fires burned, black smoke rising toward the mountain crest. *~Yes. I would have.~*

~Hmm.~

I watched him remove his left gauntlet and bare his rosy, pale hand, reaching out to me.

~Will you, please? We shall not go as deeply as you did with your bonds against the Malok, but what I do may feel like flying at times.~

With my face warming, I tugged off my right glove one finger at a time. *~I need to keep the Guild informed of what's happening.~*

~Agreed. Your pearl-holders should know what the Templari and my officers are doing. It's the only way to save the most we can for another fight.~

Right.

~Pull up your hood. Begin to breathe.~

I chuckled as I did so. *~Haven't I been breathing?~*

~Heh, you count coup. What I mean is, make it the only goal you have. Close your eyes if you need to.~

Alright.

The intensity of the day lessened further as I shut my eyes and breathed deeply. I felt my belly swell out with more air as I concentrated on this, oddly aware of the rest of my insides nudging against the hard ball of muscle deep in my gut. Warm and painless.

Stepping out into Sunlight, our linked minds reached out to the many. When Willven said his first tasks might feel like flying, that was as accurate as any description could be for one who never had.

We became lighter than air.

THE DAY-SHIELD REAPPEARED IN THE MIDDLE OF *Rua Po'sol*, PAST THE CENTER of the city, and rose well above the tallest steeple. Cutting off three-quarters of the Ma'ab host from their frontline, we stopped the advance along the rooftops as well. Several Ma'ab leaders recognized immediately what had happened and spun around, wildly looking for the blond man leading their foes as they shouted curses at him.

Sir!! Robic cried, elated the moment we touched him. **You've returned!**

Tell us! Imran added.

Tell us what is next! Sohl agreed.

~ *Pisc'sagrad is safe and shall be guarded by the Grey Maiden for years if necessary. This is our boon for destroying the threat to life on this mount. Next, we work with the Guild to kill as many Ma'ab as possible on our way out.*~

On our way...?

Do we retreat?

We're leaving?

~*Yes. Everyone leaves for the final jump through the gate. All who survive will receive the chance to return. The war is not over if we escape now. But, if we all stay here and die, then it* **is** *over. The Ascended claim Pisc'sagrad, and no one ever comes home.*~

Countless faces of sweat-and-blood-stained men appeared in our mind's eye as the news swept through the eighty surviving Templari first and then spread out to the officers who'd been at the wall all day. From there, our message and our hope flew through the exhausted, terrified hearts of those who'd spoken their prayers and goodbyes while facing the walking corpses of their own kin.

Even if the Manalari people didn't understand all the names or reasons, they recognized the thoughts. They understood the feelings.

~We're leaving, my Manalari. If we live and save ourselves and our families, we may return. Musanlo and the Grey Maiden have promised us. All is not lost, unless we stay.~

Like the nobility at the Temple...?

~Exactly. There is only one chance left to escape and fight again. That day shall happen beneath the same Sun, but when we are unified and not bickering amongst ourselves.~

I knew it. The Bishops lost us this battle from the start!

~Perhaps, or it was the many small things which led to this moment. This does not matter. The Manalari getting out alive is our only concern. The Guild of Augran and Clans of Taiding have given us this option, and the Bishops have already paid their price. I beg you, do not throw away your God-given chance to see another sunrise.~

As our thoughts flew among them, the Manalari recognized the flanking pressure had been lifted thanks to the golden shield. The orders came through as the army prepared to hit back harder while slowly giving ground.

The soldiers' lines tightened up, pulling in from the fringe as hit-and-run outliers rushed in and off the rooftops to dive behind barriers and attack from there. The Templari lined up in front of the barriers, casting at the massive brutes of the Far North to knock them back or down as closer teams finished them off.

In the time Gavin had been gone, however, the frightening and well-defended "girl-child" death mages had collected more of the fallen, not only on both sides, but from among the hiding citizens discovered and killed in that time. Many of the opponents were our own mutilated dead.

The Dragonblood and his apprentice appeared on the battlefield to join them, startling some of the Manalari who hadn't witnessed their alliance yet.

~Ancient allies!~ we called. ~They will help us defend the line!~

The men were convinced when a black-skinned warrior larger than their adversaries lobbed several additional fire and thunder spells among those Ma'ab whose backs were up against the massive day-shield. The explosions tossed them forward onto their sword and shield mates, pushing down empty-eyed corpses and creating clusters for the blade-spinner to cut down.

The Dragonblood's small Red Sister guarded his back in just the right spot to avoid the blades while he severed heads and limbs. Their auras merged, sharing strength, endurance, and battle joy amid the North's disordered defense.

Behind them, the Herald of Nyx strode forward, numerous black, crystalline horns and spikes jutting from his body. He'd arrived to make certain both their enemies' and our lost people's bodies gave up the fight for good. When the Deathwalker raised up the thurible where it could be seen, he seemed surprised when many of the Manalari began to cheer and praise Musanlo for his mercy.

~Thank you, Gavin,~ we added sincerely to the chorus.

The Deathwalker waved his shovel vaguely, as if a fly had buzzed around him, and focused on the task at hand. Soon, the risen dead had turned upon the Ma'ab, and the living line broke into disarray with one small female trampled.

Good work, Captain, Sirana, the Dragonblood responded. *Begin the first retreat to shore up the south wall. We'll put all these down, then you move the shield to a different street to section off more targets. We start again. Keep doing this as long as it works but expect them to change direction sharply a few times or send more forces to flank from the north.*

~Confirmed. We'll cut off multiple streets if necessary.~

Don't push yourself too hard.

~We won't.~

The injured and depleted Manalari soldiers were given their orders to pull back from the multi-block battle and join the evacuees. An equal number of ready fighters accompanied them with new missions to set up additional blockades facing the streets running north and south.

~If you hear or witness Ma'ab forces entering the Temple, do not, I repeat,

do not *approach, attack, or attempt to stop them. They cannot claim Pisc'sagrad, and we can rebuild the Temple. Your focus is on the living people. Help us get your brothers out alive.~*

These orders unsettled many less-informed minds, but they prayed for forgiveness and were ready and willing to follow them. We left them to reconcile while we shifted our day-shield, blocking in another group of enemy forces to face the shadow legend without back-up. The Ma'ab railed against the "cheating," searching for the Godblood among them.

They will know where he is soon.

We listened as Gavin began to speak.

I see a score of skin kites surveilling the grounds. If you must stand in sunlight to do what you're doing, then they will see you eventually.

Yes. We had to stand beneath the Sun to defend the people. and we could not focus on an illusion; maintaining the shield and speaking among our Templari took too much effort.

~*Damn.*~

I'm coming, Krithannia began.

No, Mourn protested. *Stay with Tamuril. Make sure you both get out.*

~*Agreed. We'll draw back when the time comes. We expect the shield to grow smaller around us as the Ma'ab continue to press in.*~

Estimated, how many are left?

~*The men on the Crest say we are outnumbered two-to-one. As we draw back, this pressure will worsen.*~

What are they still doing there? the Guild Mistress said. *Please tell them to join the evacuation. They're running out of time not to be trapped up there.*

~*Understood, elder. It is done.*~

The battle played out much as Mourn and Krithannia had strategized. We were only able to cut off two lines from the host and cull them before we encountered row upon row of revived undead, most of them Manalari corpses, all with the sole focus of obstructing anything which grew close. We couldn't find the female mages who must have sent them in, but all the large, living Ma'ab males were sprinting uphill toward the Temple, trying to get around the shimmering wall.

We moved the grand protection to frustrate and confuse them as if they roamed an invisible maze until the Dragonchild, Red Sister, and Templars could catch up, but we also began to witness the limits of our use of *Mitneh'thran*.

Much as we all wished, the relic could not expand effective protection indefinitely, and if it grew too tall or long, one insistent, mundane fighter with a war hammer could disrupt it enough to pass through.

The Deathwalker made quick work of the fresh, shambling corpses and older, rotting skeletons, laying them all down to rest before turning east to join the rest of our defenders.

Where are the Ma'ab death mages? he asked. *Hardly any contested will over the dead that time.*

~We haven't seen but the one trampled so far.~

They aren't among the forces here, Mourn confirmed. *What's happening to the north?*

Krithannia spoke. *The Guild reports mundane whistles and explosions being set off after the Manalari withdrew from the cistern passageways, but fewer of the magical ones. I think they're beneath the city, passing under the wall.*

It is only a matter of time before they confirm the numbers in the canyon and regroup to cut through the blackwood, Mourn growled. *Godblood, pull the rest of your army back south. Leave only the Templari and us in the streets. Send the rest of them down to help defend the canyon path to the gate.*

~Only if you withdraw far enough that we can shield the streets from mountain to wall.~

It'll show them exactly where and how tightly grouped we are.

~Not too fast, then, but they shall figure that out regardless.~

My spiders chimed urgently for my attention, and I blinked, returning my focus outward. A disgusting piece of flapping skin hovered out of arm's reach just off the balcony.

"Ah, shit."

~Huh? Sirana, what...? Oh.~

What is it?

~*The skin kites,*~ I thought separately. ~*They located the source of the day-shield.*~

~*My men coming down from the Crest confirmed,*~ Isboern added, ~*there are Ma'ab 'witches' and Hellhounds entering the Temple. The Ma'ab secondary forces are in the northeast quadrant but heading straight to the southeast.*~

Mourn exhaled. *Alright. Show us how much space we have to work with while boxed in at the edge of a mountain, Godblood.*

~*I will. Retreat with the Templari back to where you left Sirana. We'll begin there.*~

Chapter 36

Mourn reclaimed his quadruped form to carry Jael as his well-armed rider, and the Godblood spread the order through his Templari and lieutenants before the distant, insufficient day-shield was to come down.

~All defenders fall back to the barricades near Late Light Way. A new shield will be risen to protect the last of you as we all leave the city for the jump gate.~

Meanwhile, Isboern upheld his golden shield, concentrating to maintain his moving obstruction while his shrinking army disengaged and retreated to the final rendezvous point. Our experience thus far had been balanced, like we were each raising one side of a reflective plank to aim where the light needed to go. Isboern's will had endured long enough that I finally noticed an ache in my head and an echoing tiredness which the Godblood had kept masked until now.

There is enough gap, Captain, Mourn reported, **and your men are moving fast. Choose your place for your last stand. We shall be there soon.**

Reluctantly, the shield holding most Ma'ab forces at the center of the city vanished, and a distant roar of aggression and victory arose above the floundering city of Manalar. I sensed the barest anger as the skin kite fluttering before us crumbled and dropped to the street, as if an unseen hand had reached out to crush it in its fist.

~Whoa. I want to learn how to do that.~

The Captain's bemused smile reminded me of Deshi the last time I'd complimented him. *~It's easier to push or lift something than to crush it, and there are limits.~*

Another familiar trill ran up my neck, and I looked up, shading my eyes with my hood. ~Hm. *Like crushing all those at once?~*

Isboern followed my focus to the twenty other fluttering spies spreading out high above the wealthy district and sighed. ~Yes. *Our focus is needed elsewhere.~*

I knew the Human Captain didn't want me to climb down. Since we lacked a secure rope, I wouldn't insist on free-handing it but instead looked for another sun-drenched balcony we might be able to use.

~*Maybe run the rooftops and 'lift' us across the streets?~*

Isboern considered it although, in his armor, he wasn't nearly as nimble as Mourn to traipse across slanted tiles.

~*Maybe a bad idea. Could you lift us down——?~*

Oh my fuck!! my Sister broke into my head the instant it seemed Mourn was about to talk. Her thoughts were a vortex of condensed terror and utter elation. *What did you just do?!*

She wasn't asking me.

Well done, her tutor responded. *But could you grip something less soft?*

~Jael?~ I asked. ~*Are you alright?~*

Y-yeah!

~*What in the Abyss happened?~*

He jumped off a wall in one alleyway and appeared in another much closer! she crowed. *We skipped five streets like a jump circle and are only three away from you!*

~Wow. *How did you do that?~*

Shadow jumping, Mourn growled a reply. *I have never tried it with a passenger other than Graul.*

Who's Graul? she asked.

An old friend. But it worked with you, so that is fortunate.

Should we try it again?

Yes, I think so.

I felt their anticipation before our link winked out of existence for a partial breath. Down below, Mourn prowled out from behind a deeply shaded overhang in the center of an alley and came out into the Sun directly beneath us.

~Amazing, legend,~ Isboern responded, his hand tightening on mine. ~How useful that would be with the skin kites watching our every move.~

Mourn paused, looking up with glinting eyes. *Captain… do you realize Mitneh'thran is a Draconic name?*

~Uh… No, not until now.~

Would you like an approximate translation?

~Yes, legend, I would.~

Roughly, it means 'light-leaper.' I know it is possible to leap using light as I jump using shadow. We can take Sirana to the Treynora mansion to wait for you, and you might ask for one more boon. If it works, you move freely and avoid sitting as a Ma'ab target, no matter how many skin kites they have.

For the moment, Isboern's weariness lifted.

~Yes. I accept. Thank you.~

I was more capable climbing down the decorative wall than Willven had been wanting to test, but with the climbing vines, lanterns, odd statues, thick sills, and rough stonework, there were more handholds than many a cliff in the Deepearth.

Not only that, but the psion and the Dragonchild were both watching carefully in case I slipped. I didn't want either of them wasting more effort due to that, nor did I think too much on how to get down. I moved how I was trained.

Jael kissed me when I was about to mount up behind her. She was sweaty and her heart pounded; she seemed to be enjoying the chaos. At least we were learning a lot about what we'd become.

I will not shadow jump with you on board, Mourn said, building speed through the streets using four feet. *It has never been easy with anyone besides Graul, and Jael is not sick or unconscious—*

~It's fine,~ I interjected, understanding his true meaning about the risk. ~I'd rather not if it's a straight shot. Heh, I just ate.~

Mourn took us to the Treynora mansion, which I learned then was the place with the evacuation tunnels to the quarry. About two hundred people waited on the grounds to get inside from the street, all of them men at this point.

The huddling women and children were gone, as were the white-beards and those clutching a walking cane. Some Guildsmen remained with the Manalari officers to help organize and direct the constant flow of people, but there were fewer of them than before.

Everyone was trying to leave the city as fast as possible.

~*How are we getting out?*~ I asked, because I hadn't received any sense or concern from Jael about that.

Mourn's deep breath expanded his ribcage and moved our thighs apart. *With Isboern. Any way possible. He must live, or the pool's protection disappears.*

~*Yeah, I was thinking that, too.*~

That why we left him alone just now? Jael asked wryly.

There's a reason we're standing in sunlight, novice.

What do you mean?

A mental tug caught my attention, and it wasn't my spiders although the odd sensation could be described as one balancing on a single thread of silk connected to me from somewhere much higher.

Suddenly, the Godblood appeared next to us, looking stunned. Jael yelped in surprise but Mourn remained firm on his feet, long tail waving behind him.

"I-It worked," the man whispered, staring at his shield. His heart was pounding.

Mourn showed his fangs. *Well done, Captain. How do you feel?*

He blinked blue eyes, turning inward. ~*Good. No harm done.*~

Try it again. Mourn indicated the high flat roof where he'd summoned the air burst against the Roh'ghast hidden in the fog. *Up there. Sirana can join you and help defend you.*

~*Right.*~

Isboern closed his eyes, pulled the shield closer to his chest…

And vanished.

When we looked up at the lounge on the next block, the armored man was there, lifting his arm high and waving.

Mourn's tail moved with excitement. *Fantastic.*

~My men are ducking under the Druid's barriers,~ Willven said, ~and Gavin is with them. I must raise the shield. Sirana's help would be invaluable.~

Mourn looked at me as I dismounted. *Stay with Isboern, do not leave him unless I tell you.*

~Check. Stay ahead of the cutting edge.~

Mourn turned with Jael and sprinted off to rejoin the battle while I ran toward the psion. I learned what it felt like to be lifted by one's will, nothing like that which required ropes, wheels, or levers. More like being swaddled in a thin, tight blanket, unable to move while a gentle parent recovered you from a deep hole: fast, at first, then slowing as you reached the top.

A little frightening. One had to trust him not to drop you.

Isboern gently set me down, though his attention seemed drawn outside the south wall, where he could see people rushing to leave the quarry and begin the climb down to the canyon.

~What is it?~ I asked.

He swallowed and shook his head, bringing his attention back to face the opposite direction, where the Ma'ab were closing in. After a moment, even in the daylight, I spotted what he'd been looking at.

Pilla flew above the cliffs, focused on the climbing Humans. The falcon frequently attacked the skin kites, snatching them up with her talons and tearing them to pieces mid-air before dropping them. Clever. I wondered if Krithannia had given her sister that order.

~Tamuril told us the handholds needed mending after the Roh'ghast,~ I said. ~That's probably what she's doing.~

A strong, emotional tremor passed between us as Willven took a deep breath. He exhaled slowly through his lips.

~Right. Let's bring the day-shield back and give them time to run.~

THE GODBLOOD'S NEW SHIELD ENCOMPASSED ABOUT THREE HUNDRED REmaining men, stretching in a curve from the south wall to the eastern cliff beside the Temple. Exerting more pressure on himself, the psion also formed a dome to protect against skin kites flying in close among their forces and against launch attacks of thunder and fire.

Though smaller in scope, it was even more effective than before. The Ma'ab had no recourse but to rampage through the streets looking for any weak point, to break a wall or a building to funnel through, or any way to scrabble underneath.

This would take them time and reinforcements.

In his effort not to accidentally trap one of his own people on the wrong side of the barrier, Isboern sliced off a small portion of the invading army from the rest, placing them on the inside of the shield to be culled.

Gavin, Mourn, and Jael were ready.

With the Templari holding their position as the final line of defense, the To'vah-krav leaped through shadows to surprise the slim line of Ma'ab soldiers, less bothered by the undead as Gavin focused on them. Using Mourn's finer weapons, Jael cut thick hamstrings or pierced them deeply with results implying a poisoned blade.

Gavin removed the chance of these new corpses being reused before he started systematically collapsing the few other undead inside the shield. Only then did he become aware of a tiny woman screeching at him from the back of a restless war horse.

There's a maknuut tied to the back of this mount, he said, moving back far enough to curl his hands and strike with another blue ball as he had with the Deathless.

The attack hit the large male rider in the chest, causing him to scream in agony and send the horse spinning around. The Ma'ab pitched to the side and fell off, his boot caught in the stirrup. The small, pale woman could not move forward or reach the reins as horse reared and panicked.

~Why is she bound?~ Isboern asked.

So she neither falls off nor deserts the battlefield.

I felt Isboern's revulsion as my bodyguard streaked by the panicking horse, slashing the man's throat open with his claws before leaping up so Jael could strike the mage, neatly removing her head. Mourn rebounded off a wall and disappeared in shadow, leaving the horse to drag a bound, headless body and a heavy fallen soldier to the nearest shelter.

~*Wow. Well done.*~

Best tactic if we see that again, the Dragonblood said. *Keep an eye out for cavalry carrying their mage women.*

Word passed, and once Gavin had claimed the *maknuut's* essence in a whirl of ashes and blue embers, he seized control of the undead pressing their faces against the shield to look for their mistress.

Turn around. Attack anything living.

They obeyed their new master. The small massacre inside the shield did not last long, and the larger disruption grew outside of it.

Meanwhile, injured Manalari natives received their chance to fall back from the barricades toward Treynora mansion. About forty Templari remained as the last fighter-mages regrouping, regaining their breath as they prepared should the shield come down. For now, it continued to hold. The only active fighters remaining on behalf of the city were the shadow-jumping assassins and the Deathwalker in an ever-expanding contest of wills over the fate of the dead.

The Ma'ab were growing furious.

~*How... many?*~ Isboern asked, the thought intense and clipped.

Krithannia answered, forthright and steady. *Four hundred passed through the gate since you called the retreat. We have one jump left. Three hundred soldiers are navigating the slopes with half your Templari guarding them while the Guild and the Clans defend against more undead spilling into the canyon from the north. So, the Ma'ab leaders know we're here.*

Send Deshi to assist, Gavin said, attempting to taunt another *maknuut* back-saddle rider closer to the shield with his mere presence. *His blade will keep the dead down as well.*

Thank you. We will. Tamuril also tells me Pilla spotted smaller forces following the outside wall from the west end coming south. They'll reach the quarry in less than an hour but too late to block the retreat.

Unless we stayed here too long.

~*Speak if the canyon is at great risk,*~ Isboern said as I reflected on how numb we felt.

Yes, Captain.

Watch the Ma'ab who entered the Temple, and what they do next, Mourn added, pausing somewhere out of sight. *That will inform our next move.*

Unfortunately, this was our largest blind spot. The men from the Crest had reached the canyon, and from where we stood, we could not get a clear view of the Temple and "higher" streets. The skin kites were beginning to swarm Pilla any time she approached, until she had to retreat behind Mount Sonai.

All I can tell you, Gavin answered, *is that the guardians are still there, and my Lady keeps her bargain.*

Mourn and Jael soon had to pause from their hit-and-run tactic, both from exhaustion and a few close calls where one of them received a glancing blow.

They worked out our targets, he panted. *We took out four maknuut and twelve officers.*

~*They do appear disorganized—*~ Mentally, I squinted. ~*Wait.*~

What?

~*Small females clinging to the backs of Hellhounds, coming from the direction of the Temple.*~

How many do you see?

~*Fifteen Hellhounds. Five of them carry mages.*~

Twenty Hellhounds entered the Temple earlier, Krithannia said. *And at least ten mages. They could have died in the Temple, but we must assume they've split to return north and are headed for the canyon.*

They're sending most Hellhounds this way? Jael asked, proving she was listening.

Yes. The Godblood and the Deathwalker are both here.

Not to mention the rest of us oddities.

~*But with more death mages headed to threaten the gate and capture more bodies...*~

You've never fought against Taiding Dwarves defending their secrets, Captain, Krithannia said with confidence. *They will show them no mercy.*

~*Very well,*~ Willven said. ~*But I can hold the day-shield, leap through light, or attack with the power of the sun one at a time. It is thanks to Sirana that I can speak to you like this. Elders, what is our best focus now?*~

Can you move down the mountain and maintain the shield? Mourn asked.

~No,~ he admitted. ~*The more attacks upon it, the more strain... like trying to hold a tree above your head.*~

I could agree with that. My mouth had twisted into an odd shape as I remained woven into part of that concentration.

Very well. So you choose the time to drop the shield, and everyone must be prepared when you do. You light-leap down with Sirana as far as you can into the canyon and make for the gate. We'll follow after.

~*And when the shield itself falls?*~

I watched the Hellhounds running through the streets, dodging in and out of sight, during a brief pause.

Did I witness a similar 'attack with the sun' spell among your Templari against the Malok? Krithannia asked. *Light with heat enough to burn?*

~You did.~

And if all forty of them unleashed at once when you drop the shield...?

~A good idea. I...we will have to...speak to them. Like a huddle.~

Make ready, Captain. We'll be prepared to hit as hard as we can, one last time, and run.

Gradually, Willven weaved one Templari after another into our mindlink, releasing the Guild links for now.

How will we outrun Hellhounds down a mountain?

~Our allies and I will draw them away. You go first.~

We can't leave you unprotected, Capitan!

~Musanlo has blessed me so that I may protect you. So you may return to challenge the loss of our city. No matter how fast you run, I shall catch up.~

The warriors were reluctant but acknowledged the necessity only because the Godblood withheld the detail that his lifetime alone determined their chance to reclaim *Pisc'sagrad*. I kept my figurative mouth shut, for he wasn't wrong about the speed with which we could meet them at the gate.

~Then we're agreed. When I give the word, we release as powerful of a spell as we can summon together, and then you run for the canyon gate. Do not stop except to kill an enemy in your path.~

Forty men with shields in position. They began to chant and to pray as the skin kites threw themselves against the dome. When Mourn touched me through his pearl, I split my attention and looked outward, witnessing the Hellhounds reach the rear of their forces and slow for an update with their officers trapped at the shield.

The whole time, small females' feet never touched the ground.

~They will not lead from the front,~ I informed Mourn.

★Confirmed.★

My closest allies had retreated behind the line of Templari, out of harm's way. The closest Ma'ab knew something was about to happen and tried to get their leaders' attention.

~NOW.~

I felt the tremendous pressure lift from Willven's shoulders as the shield came down. With the speed of thought, we were suddenly there, standing next to them, protected behind *Mitneh'thran* as a singular power and voice swelled to fill the streets.

"QUO HAUXA LUZTI!"

I ducked behind Isboern, hood down and clutching my eyes with both hands as the largest collective blast of mages I'd ever heard of exploded. The roar of power unleashed filled my ears and muted the alarm and agony cut short as further stone and brick cracked and crumbled, walls collapsing with a massive dust cloud atop the Ma'ab army. I had the suspicious feeling the Dragonchild had added something on top of it all.

~RUN FOR THE CANYON.~

The Templari obeyed to a man, turning for the trampled, empty grounds of Treynora, leaving their Capitan to his allies of legend. Gavin was occupied drawing in all the souls he could, as quickly as he could, while Mourn and Jael launched into another targeted assassination flurry inside that giant dust cloud. Up front, we only saw piles of bodies on the ground, but Mourn and Jael had done *something* vicious which set the Hellhounds to howling.

Shadow!! Krithannia called. *Forces at the south wall split off and scaled the wall ahead of the quarry! They're inside and encountering Tamuril's barriers!*

Damn. Get out while you can. Deathwalker, retreat to Treynora manor.

Gavin had started moving before our thoughts even finished. Perhaps he'd received a more personal command of his own.

If we don't stop them, Krithannia said, *they're close enough to follow us and the Templari through the tunnel before we reach the quarry!*

Meanwhile, what was left of the Ma'ab army to the north was getting to their feet, kicked and harried by Hellhounds rattling their chains in a growing fury.

Godblood, Mourn ordered, *use the shield to get Gavin, Sirana, and Krithannia into the canyon and stay there with them. We'll help give your Templari time to reach backup on the slope.*

~Agreed.~

In a blink, Isboern withdrew us from the Ma'ab, where he and I stood within the Treynora grounds, welcomed briefly in sign by Penglok and Nianzu. Torch and Deshi were gone.

Gavin was running toward us in long strides, though we did not find the Guild Mistress until Torch silently pointed to her. Krithannia was hauling her blonde sister by the arm and away from frantically growing, spiny vines. Even once the Druid's focus had left them, the vines overtook the soil inside the wall at breathtaking speed.

"Tamuril!" Willven cried in dismay. "Why are you still here?!"

Her green eyes were huge, looking at him. "I-I'm sorry! I've been trying to slow them down and help us see!"

"You *have* been helping," Krithannia assured with strained patience, "but I thought you were outside mending the handholds."

"I finished! And you weren't coming out! Why must you be *last?!*"

Gavin sighed. "I will block the entrance."

The Druid's bug-eyed attention swung to the Deathwalker with enhanced horror as he set down his spade and drew his black-stained dagger, tugging up his sleeve to cut his arm deeply in between the spines.

As the thick, black fluid flowed and he flung it out upon the grounds, my ally's voice became gravely and eerie. *"Remove the Elves from the path of the Ma'ab, Godblood, unless you want to witness what happens then."*

Gavin began his sibilant chants, turning his back to us and facing the open gate and the incoming Hellhounds. A barbed, ethereal wall of black vapors arose from his blood, mimicking the impassible thickets grown by the blonde Naulor. He blocked the gate first before next sending his spell creeping along the property wall.

"How many can you light-leap at once?" Krithannia asked.

This was the first time I saw panic in Willven's eyes. He answered, "Only one other. I'm… sorry, I—"

The Guild Mistress pushed the Druid closer to him. "Take her first. Do not argue."

I had never witnessed Tamuril blush fiercer than when the Captain wrapped his arm around her waist, pulling her behind the shield with him. The Druid's eyes filled with tears as she bit her lip as we stared at them, for it took Willven a distressing number of moments to garner the concentration to make that first leap.

Finally, they vanished in broad daylight. I could only hope they landed safely on the other side of Mount Sonai.

What's happening? Mourn demanded. *Sirana. Krithannia. Are you at the manor or the canyon?*

Shit.

~The manor. Willven can only take one at a time. Tamuril was first. Gavin is casting something to slow the Hellhounds' approach.~

The half-blood dropped silent as he kept his opinion to himself.

A few seconds later, Mourn and Jael jumped out of an eastern shadow and loped over near me. My Sister leaped off, and my bodyguard shifted back to his birth form, righting his harness before summoning his sliders. He did not pause before claiming more room to spin his weapons, making them hum within moments. He aimed a fast-building spell toward the side of the manor which contained the escape tunnel.

~Wait, what—?~

Too late to run this way.

His pearl-link seemed to shut down as he spoke. *"Airem wer cos!"*

I didn't see any specific color or form, but the next thing I knew, the foundation of the manor cracked, and the upper stories of half the dwelling collapsed and filled the cellar, closing off that escape route but also preventing anyone from following.

I looked around. "And how are we getting out?"

Willven and his shield reappeared, and I smiled.

"Oh, goo—"

The Captain collapsed with a loud clang of armor, relinquishing the golden shield.

...fuck.

"Isboern!" Krithannia cried, diving to check his vitals with Penglok offering a vial.

Mourn turned around, as surprised as I'd ever seen him. He shared a look with me and Jael before drawing me into further updates through the pearls.

Yes, Shadow, the Druid is here. She won't go inside without her falcon. We're waiting on her.

The north canyon crawls with Ma'ab and their leashed dead! Torch said. *Too much for one death blade.*

But we have plenty o' axes! answered one of the Dwarves. *An' that new death-boy ain't done yet!*

They're gonna have to seal the gate soon, said someone so tired I barely recognized him; I thought it was Wolf. *Whoever's not here is getting left behind.*

I see the Templari! someone called excitedly. *They made it out of the quarry and are at the top vines!*

"The Captain is alright," the Stormseeker whispered aloud, her hands trembling as she patted Willven's cheek. "He... pushed too far."

We exhaled.

"He should not have come back," Mourn murmured.

"He misjudged his limits trying to hold out and help us."

The Dragonblood didn't reply, and Krithannia looked up worriedly as the Ma'ab began surrounding the manor grounds. Those who tried to climb the plants found themselves ensnared and punctured by burning thorns the same as I once had. Those who tested Gavin's less tangible version soon found their strength sapped away and more black tendrils reaching out for the next living body.

The Hellhounds paced outside, watching what happened to those first falling into our defenses as they pondered their next tactic. Fortunately, we were well out of range of their spiked chains.

I hope.

Mourn's tail lashed with agitation as he gripped his weapons, his pupils thin as he considered our options. I had no suggestions so remained quiet, and Jael followed my lead.

"Stay here," he said, moving out about half the distance between us and the border of our defenses.

Slamming the points of his blades into the ground, the Dragonblood cut a circle into the ground, murmuring what I assumed to be the spell for a defense border such as the one he'd made in the warp rot forest. This included Gavin, barely, who remained focused on his own continuously expanding spell.

I fretted about our position, being surrounded by death mages and Hellhounds and needing to cut them down one at a time. Not only were these enemies not mindless, malfunctioning bodies with a singular focus, but they could delay us so long that the Dwarves would have to leave us behind.

Even if we lasted long enough to escape this dead-end, I didn't know how we'd get off the mountain with such dogged pursuit. Did Mourn mean to fight long enough to delay things until Willven woke to use the shield?

As if Mourn hasn't been fighting for hours on end.

A roll of fear alongside choking thirst and hunger pangs gripped my body. I blinked against a wash of darkness and light-headedness, fervently trying not to end up like Isboern.

As if we all haven't been crawling over this mountain for two straight days.

Mourn confirmed something with Gavin, who nodded, before approaching Krithannia. "Can you shield us for a time? Follow the line I have drawn."

"Of course."

The Naulor left the unconscious Godblood in Yungian care as she knelt nearby, closing her eyes, and beginning to cast.

Jael and I waited expectantly.

"Jael, will you—?"

"Yes! Yes, whatever magic you need, I'll give it. Do what you have to."

Finally, Mourn looked to me. "I need time so we can claw our way out of this. Will you defend me and Isboern? Do not leave. Kill all enemies."

I drew the red rune blade. "Yes. I won't leave."

"Alright."

My bodyguard surprised me when he sent away his sliders, leaving his hands empty. Drawing Jael by her waist using his tail, he kneeled between the Godblood and the Guild Mistress, placing his hands gently on the soiled, hard-trodden earth. Lowering his horned head, he began to speak.

"Myvish velva… dask treskri… opsola di wer bekiw…"

I didn't know how long this would take, but every moment felt like repeated missed chances to escape as the Ma'ab surrounded us. Bulky, lightly armored foot soldiers sacrificed themselves with blood and lifeforce to create a flesh-bridge and encourage others to attempt to cross the barriers.

Among them, I spotted five more of the screaming *maknuut* trying to dismantle Gavin's barrier. Not all small females but taller, lanky males like him, all mutilated long before they'd reached Manalar, missing pieces of their faces or limbs. They cut themselves further right now, bleeding red, screaming, and chanting as they attempted to muster the strength to pass through his wiry strings of black barbs.

Gavin wasn't intimidated. He might've been the only one.

Other small women, the cleaner ones with whole faces and both ears, stood barely visible in the back. They were dressed like Vo'Traj in uniform and hairstyle, bearing similar expressions of hatred and contempt as they conferred with each other about how to handle this challenge.

They would wait for enough "slum" bodies to wear us down before doing the first thing in this fight. Meanwhile, the constant wailing and foreign taunts made me shudder with every shrill crescendo.

A Hellhound seemed to disobey his orders to wait and watch, however. The tattooed warrior approached and pitched a thunderstone into the manor grounds.

Krithannia's shield was tall and strong enough to take the strike without breaking, but the agony of light and thunder threatened to dismantle the mage's concentration. Mourn's rumbling To'vah grew louder, and Gavin responded to the attack by summoning a cold, blue fog to cover us, pushing it out beyond the walls.

The Ma'ab nobles protested no longer being able to watch the progress, but then all sound grew muffled. When the next thunderstones came arching over the walls, they flashed less brightly and the thunderstrike sounded much farther away.

I could breathe again.

"*Myvish velva... dask treskri... opsola di wer bekiw...*"

Looking behind me, I saw Mourn's claws had sunk farther into the earth, his tail wrapped around my new Sister-mage. Jael's eyes were closed; she looked to be in a restful trance. His eyes opened, however, as he lifted his chin toward the crest of the mountain, his throat working in ways impossible for me to mimic.

His eyes.

They were no longer gold but reflecting a star-filled, dusky sky which hadn't appeared yet.

"*Myvish velva... opsola di wer bekiw...dask treskri...*"

The Ma'ab had torn themselves apart to get through Tamuril's thickets. Bodies had fallen as Gavin's death barbs drained them of their vitality, though some corpses were reclaimed by the noble Ma'ab and pushed forward yet again to help the others get through.

Finally, they spilled into the grounds, running up to Mourn's line drawn in the ground. Pounding on Krithannia's shield directly with every tool at their disposal, even bare fists, they attacked with intense focus to make it shatter. By the expression on Krithannia's face, that would work eventually.

Thank goddess they were muffled, even though their faces would haunt my Reverie. How could Gavin stay so near the boundary, pick up his spade, and stare at them like that? Perhaps he knew that he would draw the worst of their ire regardless.

Adjusting my grip on the dagger, I glanced at Isboern, wondering if he'd grown paler. Had we passed the point where the Manalari could win this war?

~Are you dying, Godblood? Have the Ma'ab won Pisc'sagrad already?~

His eyelids fluttered. He grunted a complaint, maybe a protest.

~I'll take that as a negative.~

The ground shook under me, a rumble following like a sudden flood of water down from the crest. In a panic, I looked up, but could see nothing immediate.

Morixxyleth...

Who said that?

A flare of purple and gold sprouted where the Dragonblood had cut into the ground, crackling and sizzling at the boot tips of our enemies as it circled like a fire catching hold of an accelerant. Magic filled the circle simultaneously, like sand rushing in to fill a hole.

For only a moment, I feared I would drown.

Air popped in my ears.

Mount Sonai vanished from view.

CHAPTER 37

I LANDED WITH A SPLASH, GASPING AT THE COLD WHICH RUSHED IN AROUND me. My smallest guardians chimed in alarm, on the verge of being washed away, and I shoved my hands against the first solid object to keep my head above the surface. Pain lanced through my right hand, two of my fingers going numb as I fumbled my dagger in the rushing stream.

No!

Reaching forward through the current, I scraped the hard pommel with my fingertips and scrambled in the riverbed, dragging my sodden cloak behind me. A running boot slammed into the water, splashing me as I pressed the black dagger down on the smooth stones, regrasping the handle. I was too close to the water to risk my spiders.

I lifted the relic, water streaming from the tip as I prepared to strike.

"Whoa, hold up!" cried one of Reprisal as he leaped back. "We're good, Sirana! Ally!"

I couldn't remember his name, but he had a crossbow ready and scanned around us for immediate threats. The cacophony of battle rushed in upon me then, and my periphery recognized that I was in the middle of hundreds of men and Dwarves down in the eastern canyon. The long shadow of Mount Sonai stretched toward us as the afternoon wore on.

Mourn had gotten us off the mountain.

I forced myself to my feet, searching desperately for Mourn and Jael, Gavin, and Isboern...

What the fuck happened?

I wasn't the only one reclaiming my feet after a disorienting drop from several feet above solid earth. Behind me, Jael was on all fours, coughing like she'd inhaled a lot of water, while Mourn and Krithannia were trying to keep Willven's head above the surface. Peng-lok and Nianzu nervously guarded the golden shield.

Behind them, I saw a linear stretch of about forty men wearing the armor of the Templari, staggering and reaching for their shields as a sudden attack of arrows rained down from the canyon side to target those of us in the stream. Ducking lower into the water with the Guildsman, I avoided a hit in that first volley by luck but heard several men cry out, including Peng-lok and Nianzu.

Shit.

"Jael!" I shouted.

"F-fine!" she called.

She didn't sound fine; she sounded about to pass out.

Gavin climbed out onto the bank lined with smooth stones, gripping his spade despite everything. His torn robe dripped both clear water and diluted, dark blood as he approached the northern side of the canyon. He'd taken one arrow in the shoulder, but this failed to stop him from beginning, once again, to withdraw the core power fueling the Ma'ab's inflated numbers.

"*Yitu Sho'shien!*" Deshi crowed, followed by Torch.

"*Ayoo*, Deathwalker!"

"Look! The Templari! They made it!"

"How the fuck? Weren't they way up there—?"

"Yeah, fuckers appeared outta fuckin' thin air!"

Two Dwarven voices boomed one after the other.

"*GUILD! TAH THE CAVE!*"

"*Clans! Shield wall along the stream!*"

Erik, Robi, Imran, and Sohn rushed forward to help carry their Captain and the shield, while others came forward to help those injured by the arrow volley. Meanwhile, dust kicked up as Dwarves lined up along the water, two deep and forming two rows of interlocking shields in front of the targets in the water.

"Behind us! Behind us! Follow th' line tah the cave!"

Briefly fighting upstream, I grabbed Jael's arm with my spare hand and pulled her toward our arriving cover. The drenched, stumbling gaggle of fighters hustled out of the water to obey, ducking behind the stout, armored Dwarves as a second volley of arrows plinked and thudded around us. Someone else cried out.

"Eyes ahead!" Mourn called aloud. "Move! Don't stop!"

I wasn't sure if he spoke to me or to everyone. Our mindlink had severed and I heard nothing more from him. By the frayed ends of all our senses, neither of us could reach out. Regardless, those few words were my entire plan.

Most withdrawing Guildsmen and Manalari fighters sprinted past us on two good feet if they had them. The Templari, however, wouldn't break from each other or from their Captain. More than we'd wished were injured, and we were easily the slowest group. Regardless, Gavin, Mourn, and Krithannia refused to leave the Templari behind after they'd passed Peng-lok and Nianzu to Deshi and Torch.

The Guild's leaders acted on the critical goal of getting Willven out alive, and they remained our best bet to escape. I stuck close to them while my Sister hadn't the strength to dissent, kept Soul Drinker out, and attempted to sort out the chaos of threats. By attrition of encumbrance, Jael and I ended up leading the way to the cave.

New, spine-rattling battle calls flooded the hills on the north side as a rush of Dwarves charged the Ma'ab army, each wielding two heavy axes, wearing helmets, but surprisingly little armor compared to their shield brothers. The sheer, brazen insanity of their arrival as they began splitting Ma'ab bodies with single strokes set the forward push back on its heels for a moment. We used the opening to make tracks as our group trailed blood behind the Clan's body-wall.

"Gavin!" Mourn called. "Retreat! To the cave, *now!*"

At first, I wasn't sure if the Deathwalker was going to respond; he seemed determined to take every Ma'ab soul with him. Then something made him turn around, and he wasn't looking at Mourn.

I followed his gaze to the south side of the canyon.

Across the stream, barely visible within the dry-bark trees, was a team of five Hellhounds watching us.

Ohhh no...

The bald one in the front was the largest Human I'd ever seen, a head taller than the other Ma'ab soldiers, to whom I only stood chest high. The tattooed warrior was visibly older, his posture conveying without question he was their leader.

His placid expression didn't so much as flicker. His dark eyes stared through us. Through *me*.

"Don't stop!" Mourn roared.

Gavin had indeed retreated, joining us on the other side of the defending Dwarves who gradually shifted to close around us like a bubble.

The Hellhounds could have attacked us, but the leader made no motion at all. He stood like stone, turning his head only slightly when the Deathwalker moved deliberately to block my sight of him.

"Divigna," my death mage muttered. "Kurn's father."

Comforting.

Surrounded by Dwarves and shields as tall as they were, the Templari and we squeezed inside the well-defended entrances to the cave. Finally, we were out of the Sun, and I struggled to sheath Soul Drinker before I made a mistake in tight quarters.

"Berserkers, fall back!" the Dwarven shield leader called outside. "Fall back!"

No one was given the chance to slow or stop. The passageway was packed full of bodies, stuffy and churning with dust, urgent voices in a slew of languages reverberating off the walls. An elbow rammed into my side as I stepped on someone's foot, and though Jael growled and stumbled after someone shoved her, she didn't have the space to fall.

Soon, Mourn and Gavin moved in to act as buffers, while Isboern was carried by his officers behind us. Like a burrowing worm with infinite legs, we pushed through the tunnel, coughing and choking, until we reached the gate room. It was packed, the shimmering runes and wavering, translucent stone visible above the many helms.

"Keep walking!"

"Walk through!"

"Hup, hup! *Move!*"

Our turn for the gate arrived before Jael had much chance to doubt anything. I grabbed her arm and pulled as Mourn took both our shoulders and pushed.

Like those vanished instants between my standing on churned-up evacuation grounds and dropping into the canyon stream, I lost several more to stepping between Manalar and what I hoped were the Kerut Mounds.

Though we arrived with no further disruption beyond a stomach drop, weak knees, and more hands and shoulders pushing behind us, I didn't recognize a thing.

"Hurry, hurry…"

"This way."

"Bring 'im here."

If it wasn't Tamuril with Pilla and the same Dwarven siblings I'd met before who'd hooked us to follow them down a random, underground passage, I might have hesitated like Gavin.

"C'mon!" Ragura urged us, her red curls bouncing. "Lotta kin comin' behind ya! Gotta give 'em room tah seal the gate."

We'd lost track of Deshi and the injured Yungians, and those Templari limping and bleeding were siphoned off into other hallways with rooms hopefully set up to receive them. The rest were directed into a crowded common room as Isboern's four officers dragged him and his artifact with us awkwardly through the torch-lit hallways.

Jael would have fallen several times if I hadn't been holding her up. None of us had either breath or words to speak before Rodge picked one door from many, unlocking it after knocking a rapid and specific rhythm. Without resistance, we followed them where the air was cleaner and cooler than it had been in a long while.

Inside were several pallets along the wall, and the Templari officers followed Tamuril's direction to lay Isboern down and begin removing his armor to check him for hidden injuries. Meanwhile, I noticed the small band of Dwarves present as if waiting for us. One of them had been sitting in a stout and sturdy seat but braced against the arms to push himself to his wide feet.

"*Talov...*" Mourn uttered, gathering me and Jael closer to Krithannia and Gavin.

The subtle, panicked plea in his voice sent chills down my back, and I finally got a good look at his face as the tips of his ears lost color.

Oh, Goddess.

"Kid? Can ye hear me——?"

The Dragonchild weaved on his feet, his tail dropping onto the floor like a wet sack before the rest of him followed.

"Aww, shit! Catch 'im!"

Rodge, Ragura, and two other young beards flanking Talov surged in as Jael and I pushed Krithannia out of the way. They managed to clasp enough of Mourn to slow his collapse, placing him without further injury on the bare stone ground.

Next to me, Jael was shaking and sank to her knees, struggling to stay awake. *"W-what... the fuck happened?"*

The greybeard and Guild Mistress knew, and I had a hunch.

His light, intangible presence in my mind had vanished, replaced with utter silence. For weeks I'd never caught Mourn so much as dozing. He'd told me not to worry, but it seemed my bodyguard had pushed himself too far to fulfill our Bargain.

We made it out. Now he must rest.

"Well," Talov began awkwardly. "Really happy ya made it, bruises an' all. Best be ready tah settle in, though. Yer gonna be here fer a while."

CHAPTER 38

THE LAST TIME JAUNDA HAD REPORTED TO THE PALACE, THE VALSHARESS HAD given her a ring to wear.

"This will assure you search deeper, Lead."

She had frivolously hoped she might be taken off this mission once confirming the Ornilleth conclave obstructed the ancient path her Queen had shared with her.

The Red Sister found no such release.

Instead, she got this gold-and-emerald ring to warn her when mind flayers were nearby.

"You are learning the wilderness, so find another path."

Not an exaggeration. Jaunda had left Sivaraus five times now, becoming familiar with veins and tunnel branches below Sivaraus that were normally only a concern for the Deep Traders. She had returned after four of those solo explorations.

Well. Mostly solo.

The last one had really felt like she was being watched, and that feeling hadn't faded on this new trek.

Ostensibly, Jaunda had a mission; there was an end-goal in this directionless wandering.

Does She really have no idea where one Dragon might hole up to sleep?

Assuming he even existed. The Lead was beginning to doubt.

These repeated, exhaustive, fruitless searches felt mostly punitive at this point. The Valsharess probably could have given her more to go on if there was something the Davrin Queen really needed to be found, but She chose not to because the Lead had helped kill a Sathoet gone insane without Her permission.

Yeah, well… Kerse needed to be put down. Finally.

A pity the others might be dead somewhere on the Surface by now. *I miss my Sisters.*

During a longer rest, curled up in a defensible hole with enough muck to mask her heat and scent, Jaunda saw their familiar faces in Reverie: Gaelan, Sirana, and Jael. Her regret for where they'd been sent brought back memories of her last trip up to the Surface with Elder Rausery's blessing.

I wanted to see if I could find that tower she mentioned.

Maybe whoever lived there knew something about Irrwaer and Vesram going missing. Maybe Rausery knew and couldn't say, like so many things down here, but it wasn't against the rules if Jaunda found out for herself. Maybe the Elder had overlooked something twenty turns ago.

In a bad stroke of luck, Jaunda and her Sisters didn't have enough time to get acclimated for a multi-day trek farther West before trouble showed up at their threshold.

The pale Elf and those Humans finding our camp and our stuff.

Fucking none of those Human Surfacers spoke words which made any sense to Jaunda. It wasn't as if she couldn't make *some* of the trade talk, and it had sounded kind of like that? But…

Bah.

Maybe the Red Sisters had been a little afraid, but they also knew what needed to be done.

The blonde Elf *could* have known about Irrwaer and her son, if only they shared words. The Humans saw something alien and terrifying, but the pale Elf had at least recognized a Davrin when she saw one. For some reason, it made the willowy one tempting when she refused to talk. Among creatures of the dark, Jaunda knew when she'd been seen; only actions counted then.

In Reverie within the deepest tunnels, the Lead dreamed of clutching blonde hair in her fist, of her teeth nipping rose-tipped ears in the underground wilderness. Gradually, the Elf underneath her shifted colors, her hair becoming loose, white locks, and her skin a dusky black with purplish netherhole wrapped around her cock. The once-pink ear was darker and not as long but very warm. The Lead ran her tongue along its lavender edge as the two of them hid in a Sanctuary supply closet.

Neither Elf had particularly *wanted* Jaunda's Feldeu up their ass the first time, but with Irrwaer, there had been cooperative follow-ups.

'Training,' she'd called it.

Until that moment later upon the altar, when Irrwaer had *asked* for Jaunda's help. How the acolyte had turned her rear end up, presenting so prettily, waiting for the next lash to warm up her skin.

Before I warmed up her slit for that demonic sire.

Oohh… Very nice. Yes.

Jaunda's gut woke her, and she lifted her gloved hand to focus on any warning of Ornilleth. The ring was cool and quiet.

But that hadn't been *her* thought. *Or* her mind's own voice.

Who's there?

Silently, the Red Sister leaned to peek out of her hole, studying every contour of darkness. Just the usual creepers and crawlers.

Until something yellow flickered farther down the way.

Shit.

What was it? Fire?

Jaunda waited patiently, hoping the glimmer would return. When it did, she had the sense it had winked at her then vanished. Eyes?

She frowned. *Sure fucking hope not.*

The creature would be a lot taller than her if she'd just seen a pair of yellow eyes, and worse if they were demonic. But… Why would they be? Weren't Sathoet all kept in Sivaraus?

Well. Most of them. One of them got out, for better or worse.

The shine appeared one more time, blinking before disappearing again. Jaunda's heart threatened to become audible.

Not yellow. *Gold.*

The Red Sister felt for her pouch, checking for the large, wrapped coins in their pouch that she'd been hauling around this entire time.

Still there.

Jaunda exited her temporary nest to continue her search, not quite sure at which point she'd awakened from Reverie. Maybe it didn't matter.

Maybe the trail was finally getting warm.

The battle is over, but the war is not won. Battle-weary and on the edge of collapse, we retreat to a Dwarven redoubt, hoping to heal and begin to reconcile the massive disruption in Paxia.

Meanwhile, something strange stirs in the Deepearth. After spans of fruitless searching, Lead Jaunda meets an ancient force the Davrin have not seen for centuries.

Awake in the Dark: Sister Seekers Book 9 Coming Soon! at https://smarturl.it/ReadSisterSeekers

Thank you for reading about Sirana and her journey on Miurag! Help others to find the dark epic fantasy they want and leave a review for Book 8 here. at https://smarturl.it/ss8BFM

The Sister Seekers Prequel is now available for free!

A century ago, one Priestess left for the Surface. She vanished. This is her story.

"What if…" Irrwaer began.

Jaunda leaned closer. "If?"

At least she wanted to play.

"What if Juliran authorized me to make a trade with you? An act for an act?"

The Corpora huffed through her nose, conveying all her skepticism for deals with the Sanctuary in one breath. Irrwaer was certain that sentiment should be returned in full, but she must work with what her Priestess had given her.

*Prove useful to a Red Sister, and you **will** see her again.*

That could be a warning or a promise.

Irrwaer is an acolyte serving in the Sanctuary, the religious seat in the underground city of Sivaraus. She's troubled no one, bedded no one, and seeks no higher service. She wants to be left alone.

Nowhere is safe in the Queen's web once the Priestesses know her name. To discover more of her betters is to risk tripping into their tangled threads, trapped as another's meal or amusement.

The subtlest path is to spin her own web before joining the larger with as few tremors as possible. The only place to spin unseen is between threads where Priestesses prefer not to walk.

As Irrwaer works among meek males, rowdy Red Sisters, and the sinister sons of demons, the acolyte must ask a troubling question:

In a matriarchy where power passes through daughters, why are the Priestesses only competing for sons?

In *Sons to Keep*, Etaski introduces the political sphere of Sivaraus through the eyes of the least ambitious.

These events occur one hundred years before the birth of the protagonist Sirana in *No Demons But Us*, yet their effects still ripple out from the center of a tightly woven tapestry.

Read *Sons to Keep: a Sister Seekers Prequel* FREE when you join Etaski's newsletter. Subscribe here! at https://etaski.com/about/

Would you love to learn more about Sirana's world? Do you enjoy maps, timelines, and extra details about the people, places, and objects in the story?

Be sure to visit Etaski's series lore at World Anvil! at https://mi-urag.etaski.com

Follow Etaski on Amazon for new release updates and don't miss Book 9: *Awake in the Dark!* at https://smarturl.it/etaskiamazon

Sister Seekers is a dark epic fantasy series with an ever-broadening scope. It is perfect for fans who enjoy character-driven plots, challenging themes, elements of erotic horror, and immersive worldbuilding.

Sexuality and inner conflict play into the story with intrigue, action, and fantastical magic. The series begins underground with an isolated race of Dark Elves whose intricate webs catapult the reader to places a Red Sister can only imagine in her dreams.

ACKNOWLEDGMENTS

Lo! We made it to the end of my summer marathon! Innumerable thanks my friends and beta readers always trying to keep up with the walls of text landing in their inbox:

Eris Adderly, Ile Depak, Axelotl, Leonard, Dark Pulse, Necrosis-Bob, & Pastor of Muppets.

Love and gratitude to my Hubs, for believing in me and making this possible for us.

Special appreciation to Doc Kangey, working behind the scenes to improve my tools and options. Check out our hard work and lore yet to come at Etaski.com & Miurag.Etaski.com.

Finally, to my top patrons who support all my efforts and make new things possible!

Sir Cumference, Baelus, Jesse C., Does, John K., Julie S., Paul B., Carla H., Briana R., Josanna, RainbowNight, Lesley PLAY, Kalculys-zero, NotSoWeird, Zenor , Kelly D., Lady Dia Meter, Raymond T., Lexanii, Zeroharas, Johnathon Matlock, Chris R., Daolord, and Roy Meyer, and in loving memory, Stacy Meyer.

ABOUT THE AUTHOR

Etaski has entertained herself with fantasy stories since the first day she sat on a school bus looking out the window. When hand-written letters were disappearing, she scribbled no less than five pages to be worth the postage. Her early stories were written by hand, and she had a writer's callus and three embarrassing novels before graduating high school.

She studied science, archaeology, history, and theater. Frank discussions of sexuality or death were rare growing up, so she wrote fantasies, theories, and observations within stories for deeper contemplation or just to be entertained.

History speaks little on sexuality, yet biology demonstrates how it sways basic choices. Drama reveals our strongest bonds but may fade to black at its most intimate. In the Sister Seekers, the sex and the story are inseparable, and their discoveries will change the journey of Miurag without cutting away.

Etaski's Website: etaski.com
Etaski on Patreon: www.patreon.com/etaski
Etaski's World Anvil: miurag.etaski.com
Sister Seekers on Amazon: smarturl.it/readsisterseekers
Etaski on GoodReads: www.goodreads.com/etaski
Etaski on BookBub: www.bookbub.com/authors/a-s-etaski
Etaski on Facebook: www.facebook.com/asetaski
Etaski on Twitter: www.twitter.com/asetaski